THE COLLECTED STORIES OF PHILIP K. DICK

THE SHORT HAPPY LIFE
OF THE BROWN OXFORD

Volume One

THE COLLECTED STORIES OF PHILIP K. DICK

THE SHORT HAPPY LIFE OF THE BROWN OXFORD

Preface by Philip K. Dick

Foreword by Steven Owen Godersky

Introduction by Roger Zelazny

A CITADEL TWILIGHT BOOK
Published by Carol Publishing Group

IN MEMORY

OF

PHILIP K. DICK

1928 – 1982

CONTENTS

PREFACE

By Philip K. Dick

I will define science fiction, first, by saying what sf is *not*. It cannot be defined as "a story (or novel or play) set in the future," since there exists such a thing as space adventure, which is set in the future but is not sf: it is just that: adventures, fights and wars in the future in space involving super-advanced technology. Why, then, is it not science fiction? It would seem to be, and Doris Lessing (e.g.) supposes that it is. However, space adventure *lacks the distinct new idea* that is the essential ingredient. Also, there can be science fiction set in the present: the alternate world story or novel. So if we separate sf from the future and also from ultra-advanced technology, what then do we have that *can* be called sf?

We have a fictitious world; that is the first step: it is a society that does not in fact exist, but is predicated on our known society; that is, our known society acts as a jumping-off point for it; the society advances out of our own in some way, perhaps orthogonally, as with the alternate world story or novel. It is our world dislocated by some kind of mental effort on the part of the author, our world transformed into that which it is not or not yet. This world must differ from the given in at least one way, and this one way must be sufficient to give rise to events that could not occur in our society — or in any known society present or past. There must be a coherent idea involved in this dislocation; that is, the dislocation must be a conceptual one, not merely a trivial or bizarre one — *this* is the essence of science fiction, the conceptual dislocation within the society so that as a result a new society is generated in the author's mind, transferred to paper, and from paper it occurs as a convulsive shock in the reader's mind, *the shock of dysrecognition*. He knows that it is not his actual world that he is reading about.

Now, to separate science fiction from fantasy. This is impossible to do, and a moment's thought will show why. Take psionics; take mutants such as we find in Ted Sturgeon's wonderful *MORE THAN HUMAN*. If the reader believes that such mutants could exist, then he will view Sturgeon's novel as science fiction. If, however, he believes that such mutants are, like wizards and dragons, not possible, nor will ever be possible, then he is reading a fantasy novel. Fantasy involves that which general opinion regards as impossible; science fiction involves that which general opinion regards as possible under the right circumstances. This is in essence a judgment-call, since what is possible and what is not possible is not objectively known but is, rather, a subjective belief on the part of the author and of the reader.

Now to define *good* science fiction. The conceptual dislocation — the new idea, in other words — must be truly new (or a new variation on an old one) and it must be intellectually stimulating to the reader; it must invade his mind and wake it up to the possibility of something he had not up to then thought of. Thus "good science fiction" is a value term, not an objective thing, and yet, I think, there really is such a thing, objectively, as good science fiction.

I think Dr. Willis McNelly at the California State University at Fullerton put it best when he said that the true protagonist of an sf story or novel is an idea and not a person. If it is *good* sf the idea is new, it is stimulating, and, probably most important of all, it sets off a chain-reaction of ramification-ideas in the mind of the reader; it so-to-speak unlocks the reader's mind so that that mind, like the author's, begins to create. Thus sf is creative and it inspires creativity, which mainstream fiction by-and-large does not do. We who read sf (I am speaking as a reader now, not a writer) read it because we love to experience this chain-reaction of ideas being set off in our minds by something we read, something with a new idea in it; hence the very best science fiction ultimately winds up being a collaboration between author and reader, in which both create — and *enjoy* doing it: joy is the essential and final ingredient of science fiction, the joy of discovery of newness.

(in a letter)
May 14, 1981

FOREWORD

By Steven Owen Godersky

There is a current coin-of-phrase that touts Philip K. Dick as the greatest science fiction mind *on any planet*. Well, that and a trajectory to Lagrange-5 are hyperbolic. The returns simply are not all in. The best is a tale that has yet to be written.

There are some things, though, that might make us feel a little more secure about Phil Dick's contribution to *this* planet, not that his reputation needs any particular help today. The scope, the integrity and the intellectual magnificence of Phil's work are internationally revered. He is regarded by many as the most "serious" of the modern science fiction authors, and the interest in his works has continued to mount since his untimely death in 1982. His reputation has been further enhanced by a growing body of scholarly criticism. If we take a measured look at his accomplishments there are three powerful themes that permeate almost every novel and story.

The first and most prominent theme today, can be seen in Phil's watershed work on the question of what divides humanity from all the intricacies of its creations. This is part of the central preoccupation of all consequential writers. But Phil rephrased the question *What does it mean to be human?* to *What is it like not to be human?* He posed the problem intellectually, after his fashion, but then he made us *feel* his answers. In the best and really highest tradition of Mary Shelley he struck on empathy as the difference; in his own word, *caritas*. I do not have to be a futurist to predict that both his search and his discovery will become ever more important to us as we rush along the strange road that science calls progress.

Phil's second theme is one of perspective; what I have come to think of as the care and feeding of scale-model gods. Though the arena of his ideas was so very large, what he trusted was, he once wrote, "very small." In a literary era of superstars and super-heroes Phil reminds us that our aspirations and abilities are not so different from, *and not less important than*, those of the great and powerful.

Think of Tung Chien in *Faith of Our Fathers*, and Ragel Gumm in *TIME OUT OF JOINT*. Their prosaic drudgery proves central to the fate of their worlds. Recall Herb Ellis in *Prominent Author*: an ordinary guy rewrites the Old Testament for inch-tall goatherds. Reflect on the significance of Herb Sousa's gumballs in *Holy Quarrel*; on the moral influence of wub-fur, in *Not By Its Cover*; and the battle with the sentient pinball machine in *Return Match*. Small is written large. Large is written small. Shop clerks and storekeepers are just as likely as warlords and messiahs to be at Dick's ontological foci. Old Mrs. Berthelsen, in *Captive Market*, possesses the ultimate secret of time and space, and uses it to sell vegetables out of a wagon.

When reading Dick you don't much see mile-long spaceships flaming into the sun. What you do see is one broken-down robot in a ditch. Or, more frightening, one butterfly trapped in a time warp. In Phil Dick's stories, we see that everything, human or otherwise, is connected, everyone is important; what causes pain to one causes pain to all. As John Brunner points out, it certainly caused pain to Phil himself.

Phil Dick's third major theme is his fascination with war and his fear and hatred of it. One hardly sees critical mention of it, yet it is as integral to his body of work as oxygen is to water.

Perhaps Dick, who began his writing career in Berkeley, California, absorbed the sensibilities of a town that had a carefully nurtured liberal commitment. Perhaps Joe McCarthy and the Korean War sensitized a beginning writer's imagination. We know little of his juvenile years during the Second World War. But we can identify, early and consistently, a mistrust of the military mentality, a fear of what he had seen of the total war machine on *either* side. He had a great disinclination to accept the slogans of the period that supported the ends over the means. Victory at all cost for Democracy, for Freedom, for the Flag are hollow aphorisms when the price of victory is totalitarian submission to a heartless military bureaucracy: Phil feared this particular future for all of us.

From Phil's earliest stories, *The Defenders*, *The Variable Man, A Surface Raid* and *To Serve the Master*, to his later fiction, such as *Faith of Our Fathers*, and *The Exit Door Leads In*, the winners and the losers show their humanity largely in their rejection of warfare and aggression. For Dick, the only acceptable struggle was against the evil he recognized as "the forces of dissolution." Phil Dick was anti-military long before it became fashionable in the Sixties. He continued, through his whole career, to value humanity and its foibles, no matter how small and vulnerable, over the organized terror of the modern state, no matter how expedient.

So here it is; a look into an eclectic and vigorous mind. This indispensable collection of Phil Dick's less than novel-length fiction may disturb you. It may frighten you, because some of Phil's people live very close to home. But these stories will not leave you unchanged. A strange wind may blow through your door late at night, and the shadows of familiar objects may quiver in the light. Is some Palmer Eldritch figure hurrying now to approach our world? Even if you're not a pre-cog, don't say you weren't warned.

INTRODUCTION

By Roger Zelazny

When I was approached to write this introduction I declined. It had nothing to do with my attitude toward Phil Dick's work. It was, rather, because I felt that I had already said everything I had to say on the subject. It was then pointed out to me that I had said these things in a variety of different places. Even if I had nothing to add, a judicious rehashing in a place such as this might do a service for readers who, in all likelihood, hadn't seen or heard it all before.

So I thought about it. I also looked at some of the things I had written earlier. What might be worth repeating, what worth adding, after this time? I had only met Phil on a few occasions, in California and in France; and it had almost been by accident that we had once fallen into collaborating on a book. During our collaboration we had exchanged letters and spoken often on the telephone. I liked him and I was very impressed by his work. His sense of humor generally came through in our phone conversations. I remember once when he mentioned some royalty statements he'd just received. He'd said, "I've gotten so-and-so many hundred in France, so-and-so many hundred in Germany, so-and-so many hundred in Spain.... Gee! this sounds like the catalog aria from *Don Giovanni!*" It was always a more immediate form of verbal wit than the cosmic ironies he played with in his fiction.

I'd said something about his humor before. I'd also remarked on the games he played with consensus reality. I'd even generalized a bit about his characters. But why paraphrase when after all these years I've finally found a legitimate reason for quoting myself?

These characters are often victims, prisoners, manipulated men and women. It is generally doubtful whether they will leave the world with less evil in it than they found there. But you never know. They try.

xix

They are usually at bat in the last half of the ninth inning with the tying run on base, two men out, two strikes and three balls riding, with the game being called on account of rain at any second. But then, what is rain? Or a ballpark?

The worlds through which Phil Dick's characters move are subject to cancellation or revision without notice. Reality is approximately as dependable as a politician's promise. Whether it is a drug, a time-warp, a machine or an alien entity responsible for the bewildering shifting of situations about his people, the result is the same: Reality, of the capital "R" variety, has become as relative a thing as the dryness of our respective Martinis. Yet the struggle goes on, the fight continues. Against what? Ultimately, Powers, Principalities, Thrones, and Dominations, often contained in hosts who are themselves victims, prisoners, manipulated men and women.

All of which sounds like grimly serious fare. Wrong. Strike the "grimly," add a comma and the following: but one of the marks of Phil Dick's mastery lies in the tone of his work. He is possessed of a sense of humor for which I am unable to locate an appropriate adjective. Wry, grotesque, slapstick, satirical, ironic. ... None of them quite fits to the point of generality, though all may be found without looking too far. His characters take pratfalls at the most serious moments; pathetic irony may invade the most comic scene. It is a rare and estimable quality to direct such a show successfully.

I'd said that in *PHILIP K. DICK: ELECTRIC SHEPHERD* (edited by Bruce Gillespie, Norstrilia Press, 1975), and I still agree with it.

It is good now to see that Phil is finally getting some of the attention he deserved, both critically and at the popular level. My main regret is that it comes so late. He was often broke when I knew him, past the struggling author age but still struggling to make ends meet. I was heartened that for his last year or so he finally enjoyed financial security and even a measure of affluence. The last time I saw him he actually seemed happy and looked a bit relaxed. This was back when *Bladerunner* was being filmed, and we spent dinner and a long evening just talking, joking, reminiscing.

Much has been made of his later mysticism. I can't speak with firsthand knowledge of everything he might have believed, partly because it seemed to keep changing and partly because it was often difficult to know when he was kidding and when he was serious. My main impression from a number of conversations, though, was that he played at theology the way other people might play at chess problems, that he liked asking the classic science fiction writer's question — "What if?" — of anything he came across in the way of religious and philosophical notions. It was obviously a dimension of his work, and I've often wondered where another ten years would have taken his thinking. Impossible to guess now, really.

I recall that, like James Blish, he was fascinated by the problem of evil, and its juxtaposition with the sometime sweetness of life. I'm sure he wouldn't mind my quoting from the last letter I received from him (dated 10 April 1981):

> Two items were presented to me for my inspection within a period of fifteen minutes: first, a copy of *WIND IN THE WILLOWS*, which I had never read.... A moment after I looked it over someone showed me a two-page photograph in the current *Time* of the attempted assassination of the President. There the wounded, there the Secret Service man with the Uzi machine gun, there all of them on the assassin. My brain had to try to correlate *WIND IN THE WILLOWS* and that photograph. It could not. It never will be able to. I brought the Grahame book home and sat reading it while they tried to get the Columbia to lift off, in vain, as you know. This morning when I woke up I could not think at all; not even weird thoughts, such as assail one upon rising — no thoughts, just a blank. As if my own computers had, in my brain, ceased speaking to one another, like at the Cape. It is hard to believe that the scene of the attempted assassination and *WIND IN THE WILLOWS* are part of the same universe. Surely one of them is not real. Mr. Toad sculling a little boat down the stream, and the man with the Uzi.... It is futile to try to make the universe add up. But I guess we must go on anyhow.

I felt at the time I received it that that tension, that moral bafflement, was a capsule version of a feeling which informed much of his writing. It is not a thing that was ever actually resolved for him; he seemed too sophisticated to trust any pat answer. He'd said a lot of things in a lot of places over the years, but the statement I most remember, which most fits the man I used to talk with, is one I quoted in my foreword to Greg Rickman's first interview volume, *PHILIP K. DICK: IN HIS OWN WORDS* (Fragments West/Valentine Press, 1984). It was from a 1970 letter Phil had written to *SF Commentary*:

> I know only one thing about my novels. In them, again and again, this minor man asserts himself in all his hasty, sweaty strength. In the ruins of Earth's cities he is busily constructing a little factory that turns out cigars or imitation artifacts that say, "Welcome to Miami, the pleasure center of the world." In *A. Lincoln, Simulacrum* he operates a little business that produces corny electronic organs — and, later on, human-like robots which ultimately become more of an irritation than

a threat. Everything is on a small scale. Collapse is enormous; the positive little figure outlined against the universal rubble is, like Tagomi, Runciter, Molinari, gnat-sized in scope, finite in what he can do ... and yet in some sense great. I really do not know why. I simply believe in him and I love him. He will prevail. There is nothing else. At least nothing else that matters. That we should be concerned about. Because if he is there, like a tiny father-figure, everything is all right.

Some reviewers have found "bitterness" in my writing. I am surprised, because my mood is one of trust. Perhaps they are bothered by the fact that what I trust is so very small. They want something vaster. I have news for them: there is nothing vaster. Nothing *more*, I should say. But really, how much do we have to have? Isn't Mr. Tagomi enough? I know it counts. I am satisfied.

I suppose I've recalled it twice now because I like to think of that small element of trust, of idealism, in Phil's writings. Perhaps I'm imposing a construction, though, in doing this. He was a complex person, and I've a feeling he left a lot of different people with a lot of different impressions. This in mind, the best I can render of the man I knew and liked — mostly at long-distance — is obviously only a crude sketch, but it's the best I have to show. And since much of this piece is self-plagiarism, I feel no guilt in closing with something else I've said before:

The subjective response ... when a Philip Dick book has been finished and put aside is that, upon reflection, it does not seem so much that one holds the memory of a story; rather, it is the after effects of a poem rich in metaphor that seem to remain.

This I value, partly because it does defy a full mapping, but mainly because that which is left of a Phil Dick story when the details have been forgotten is a thing which comes to me at odd times and offers me a feeling or a thought; therefore, a thing which leaves me richer for having known it.

It is gratifying to know that he is being acclaimed and remembered with fondness in many places. I believe it will last. I wish it had come a lot sooner.

Roger Zelazny
October, 1986

THE SHORT HAPPY LIFE OF THE BROWN OXFORD

STABILITY

ROBERT BENTON slowly spread his wings, flapped them several times and sailed majestically off the roof and into the darkness.

He was swallowed up by the night at once. Beneath him, hundreds of tiny dots of light betokened other roofs, from which other persons flew. A violet hue swam close to him, then vanished into the black. But Benton was in a different sort of mood, and the idea of night races did not appeal to him. The violet hue came close again and waved invitingly. Benton declined, swept upward into the higher air.

After a while he leveled off and allowed himself to coast on air currents that came up from the city beneath, the City of Lightness. A wonderful, exhilarating feeling swept through him. He pounded his huge, white wings together, flung himself in frantic joy into the small clouds that drifted past, dived at the invisible floor of the immense black bowl in which he flew, and at last descended toward the lights of the city, his leisure time approaching an end.

Somewhere far down a light more bright than the others winked at him: the Control Office. Aiming his body like an arrow, his white wings folded about him, he headed toward it. Down he went, straight and perfect. Barely a hundred feet from the light he threw his wings out, caught the firm air about him, and came gently to rest on a level roof.

Benton began to walk until a guide light came to life and he found his way to the entrance door by its beam. The door slid back at the pressure of his fingertips and he stepped past it. At once he began to descend, shooting downward at increasing speed. The small elevator suddenly stopped and he strode out into the Controller's Main Office.

"Hello," the Controller said, "take off your wings and sit down."

1

Benton did so, folding them neatly and hanging them from one of a row of small hooks along the wall. He selected the best chair in sight and headed toward it.

"Ah," the Controller smiled, "you value comfort."

"Well," Benton answered, "I don't want it to go to waste."

The Controller looked past his visitor and through the transparent plastic walls. Beyond were the largest single rooms in the City of Lightness. They extended as far as his eyes could see, and farther. Each was —

"What did you want to see me about?" Benton interrupted. The Controller coughed and rattled some metal paper-sheets.

"As you know," he began, "Stability is the watchword. Civilization has been climbing for centuries, especially since the twenty-fifth century. It is a law of nature, however, that civilization must either go forward or fall backward; it cannot stand still."

"I know that," Benton said, puzzled. "I also know the multiplication table. Are you going to recite that, too?"

The Controller ignored him.

"We have, however, broken that law. One hundred years ago — "

One hundred years ago! It hardly seemed as far back as that when Eric Freidenburg of the States of Free Germany stood up in the International Council Chamber and announced to the assembled delegates that mankind had at last reached its peak. Further progress forward was impossible. In the last few years, only *two* major inventions has been filed. After that, they had all watched the big graphs and charts, seen the lines going down and down, according to their squares, until they dipped into nothing. The great well of human ingenuity had run dry, and then Eric had stood up and said the thing everyone knew, but was afraid to say. Naturally, since it had been made known in a formal fashion, the Council would have to begin work on the problem.

There were three ideas of solution. One of them seemed more humane than the other two. This solution was eventually adopted. It was —

Stabilization!

There was great trouble at first when the people learned about it, and mass riots took place in many leading cities. The stock market crashed, and the economy of many countries went out of control. Food prices rose, and there was mass starvation. War broke out... for the first time in three hundred years! But Stabilization had begun. Dissenters were destroyed, radicals were carted off. It was hard and cruel but seemed to be the only answer. At last the world settled down to a rigid state, a controlled state in which there could be no change, either backward or forward.

Each year every inhabitant took a difficult, week-long examination to test whether or not he was backsliding. All youths were given fifteen years of intensive education. Those who could not keep up with the others simply disappeared. Inventions were inspected by Control Offices to make certain that they could not upset Stability. If it seemed that they might —

"And that is why we cannot allow your invention to be put into use," the Controller explained to Benton. "I am sorry."

He watched Benton, saw him start, the blood drain from his face, his hands tremble.

"Come now," he said kindly, "don't take it so hard; there are other things to do. After all, you are not in danger of the Cart!"

But Benton only stared. At last he said,

"But you don't understand: I have no invention. I don't know what you're talking about."

"No invention!" the Controller exclaimed. "But I was here the day you entered it yourself! I saw you sign the statement of ownership! You handed *me* the model!"

He stared at Benton. Then he pressed a stud on his desk and said into a small circle of light,

"Send me up the information on number 34500-D, please."

A moment passed, and then a tube appeared in the circle of light. The Controller lifted the cylindrical object out and passed it to Benton.

"You'll find your signed statement there," he said, "and it has your fingerprints in the print squares. Only you could have made them."

Numbly, Benton opened the tube and took out the papers inside. He studied them a few moments, and then slowly put them back and handed the tube to the Controller.

"Yes," he said, "that's my writing, and those are certainly my prints. But I don't understand, I never invented a thing in my life, and I've never been here before! What is this invention?"

"What is it!" the Controller echoed, amazed. "Don't you know?"

Benton shook his head. "No, I do not," he said slowly.

"Well, if you want to find out about it, you'll have to go down to the Offices. All I can tell you is that the plans you sent us have been denied rights by the Control Board. I'm only a spokesman. You'll have to take it up with them."

Benton got up and walked to the door. As with the other, this one sprang open to his touch and he went on through into the Control Offices. As the door closed behind him the Controller called angrily, "I don't know what you're up to, but you know the penalty for upsetting Stability!"

"I'm afraid Stability is already upset," Benton answered and went on.

The Offices were gigantic. He stared down from the catwalk on which he stood, for below him a thousand men and women worked at whizzing, efficient machines. Into the machines they were feeding reams of cards. Many of the people worked at desks, typing out sheets of information, filling charts, putting cards away, decoding messages. On the walls stupendous graphs were constantly being changed. The very air was alive with the vitalness of the work being conducted, the hum of the machines, the tap-tap of the typewriters, and the mumble of voices all merged together in a quiet, contented sound. And this vast machine, which cost countless dollars a day to keep running so smoothly, had a word: Stability!

Here, the thing that kept their world together lived. This room, these hard working people, the ruthless man who sorted cards into the pile marked "for extermination" were all functioning together like a great symphony orchestra. One person off key, one person out of time, and the entire structure would tremble. But no one faltered. No one stopped and failed at his task. Benton walked down a flight of steps to the desk of the information clerk.

"Give me the entire information on an invention entered by Robert Benton, 34500-D," he said. The clerk nodded and left the desk. In a few minutes he returned with a metal box.

"This contains the plans and a small working model of the invention," he stated. He put the box on the desk and opened it. Benton stared at the contents. A small piece of intricate machinery sat squatly in the center. Underneath was a thick pile of metal sheets with diagrams on them.

"Can I take this?" Benton asked.

"If you are the owner," the clerk replied. Benton showed his identification card, the clerk studied it and compared it with the data on the invention. At last he nodded his approval, and Benton closed the box, picked it up and quickly left the building via a side exit.

The side exit let him out on one of the larger underground streets, which was a riot of lights and passing vehicles. He located his direction, and began to search for a communications car to take him home. One came along and he boarded it. After he had been traveling for a few minutes he began to carefully lift the lid of the box and peer inside at the strange model.

"What have you got there, sir?" the robot driver asked.

"I wish I knew," Benton said ruefully. Two winged flyers swooped by and waved at him, danced in the air for a second and then vanished.

"Oh, fowl," Benton murmured, "I forgot my wings."

Well, it was too late to go back and get them, the car was just then beginning to slow down in front of his house. After paying the driver he went inside and locked the door, something seldom done. The best place to observe the contents was in his "consideration" room, where he spent his leisure time while not flying. There, among his books and magazines he could observe the invention at ease.

The set of diagrams was a complete puzzle to him, and the model itself even more so. He stared at it from all angles, from underneath, from above. He tried to interpret the technical symbols of the diagrams, but all to no avail.

There was but one road now open to him. He sought out the "on" switch and clicked it.

For almost a minute nothing happened. Then the room about him began to waver and give way. For a moment it shook like a quantity of jelly. It hung steady for an instant, and then vanished.

He was falling through space like an endless tunnel, and he found himself twisting about frantically, grasping into the blackness for something to take hold of. He fell for an interminable time, helplessly, frightened. Then he had landed, completely unhurt. Although it had seemed so, the fall could not have been very long. His metallic clothes were not even ruffled. He picked himself up and looked about.

The place where he had arrived was strange to him. It was a field ... such as he had supposed no longer to exist. Waving acres of grain waved in abundance everywhere. Yet, he was certain that in no place on earth did natural grain still grow. Yes, he was positive. He shielded his eyes and gazed at the sun, but it looked the same as it always had. He began to walk.

After an hour the wheat fields ended, but with their end came a wide forest. He knew from his studies that there were no forests left on earth. They had perished years before. Where was he, then?

He began to walk again, this time more quickly. Then he started to run. Before him a small hill rose and he raced to the top of it. Looking down the other side he stared in bewilderment. There was nothing there but a great emptiness. The ground was completely level and barren, there were no trees or any sign of life as far as his eyes could see, only the extensive bleached out land of death.

He started down the other side of the hill toward the plain. It was hot and dry under his feet, but he went forward anyway. He walked on, the ground began to hurt his feet — unaccustomed to long walking — and he grew tired. But he was determined to continue. Some small whisper within his mind compelled him to maintain his pace without slowing down.

"Don't pick it up," a voice said.

"I will," he grated, half to himself, and stooped down.

Voice! From where! He turned quickly, but there was nothing to be seen. Yet the voice had come to him and it had seemed — for a moment — as if it were perfectly natural for voices to come from the air. He examined the thing he was about to pick up. It was a glass globe about as big around as his fist.

"You will destroy your valuable Stability," the voice said.

"Nothing can destroy Stability," he answered automatically. The glass globe was cool and nice against his palm. There was something inside, but heat from the glowing orb above him made it dance before his eyes, and he could not tell exactly what it was.

"You are allowing your mind to be controlled by evil things," the voice said to him. "Put the globe down and leave."

"Evil things?" he asked, surprised. It was hot, and he was beginning to feel thirsty. He started to thrust the globe inside his tunic.

"Don't," the voice ordered, "that is what it wants you to do."

The globe was nice against his chest. It nestled there, cooling him off from the fierce heat of the sun. What was it the voice was saying?

"You were called here by it through time," the voice explained. "You obey it now without question. I am its guardian, and ever since this time-world was created I have guarded it. Go away, and leave it as you found it."

Definitely, it was too warm on the plain. He wanted to leave; the globe was now urging him to, reminding him of the heat from above, the dryness in his mouth, the tingling in his head. He started off, and as he clutched the globe to him he heard the wail of despair and fury from the phantom voice.

That was almost all he remembered. He did recall that he made his way back across the plain to the fields of grain, through them, stumbling and staggering, and at last to the spot where he had first appeared. The glass globe inside his coat urged him to pick up the small time machine from where he had left it. It whispered to him what dial to change, which button to press, which knob to set. Then he was falling again, falling back up the corridor of time, back, back to the graying mist from whence he had fallen, back to his own world.

Suddenly the globe urged him to stop. The journey through time was not yet complete: there was still something that he had to do.

"You say your name is Benton? What can I do for you?" the Controller asked. "You have never been here before, have you?"

He stared at the Controller. What did he mean? Why, he had just left the office! Or had he? What day was it? Where had he been? He rubbed his head dizzily and sat down in the big chair. The Controller watched him anxiously.

"Are you all right?" he asked. "Can I help you?"

"I'm all right," Benton said. There was something in his hands.

"I want to register this invention to be approved by the Stability Council," he said, and handed the time machine to the Controller.

"Do you have the diagrams of its construction?" the Controller asked.

Benton dug deeply into his pocket and brought out the diagrams. He tossed them on the Controller's desk and laid the model beside them.

"The Council will have no trouble determining what it is," Benton said. His head ached, and he wanted to leave. He got to his feet.

"I am going," he said, and went out the side door through which he had entered. The Controller stared after him.

"Obviously," the First Member of the Control Council said, "he had been using the thing. You say the first time he came he acted as if he had been there before, but on the second visit he had no memory of having entered an invention, or even having been there before?"

"Right," the Controller said. "I thought it was suspicious at the time of the first visit, but I did not realize until he came the second time what the meaning was. Undoubtedly, he used it."

"The Central Graph records that an unstabilizing element is about to come up," the Second Member remarked. "I would wager that Mr. Benton is it."

"A time machine!" the First Member said. "Such a thing can be dangerous. Did he have anything with him when he came the — ah — first time?"

"I saw nothing, except that he walked as if he were carrying something under his coat," the Controller replied.

"Then we must act at once. He will have been able to set up a chain of circumstance by this time that our Stabilizers will have trouble in breaking. Perhaps we should visit Mr. Benton."

Benton sat in his living room and stared. His eyes were set in a kind of glassy rigidness and he had not moved for some time. The globe had been talking to him, telling him of its plans, its hopes. Now it stopped suddenly.

"They are coming," the globe said. It was resting on the couch beside him, and its faint whisper curled to his brain like a wisp of smoke. It had not actually spoken, of course, for its language was mental. But Benton heard.

"What shall I do?" he asked.

"Do nothing," the globe said. "They will go away."

The buzzer sounded and Benton remained where he was. The buzzer sounded again, and Benton stirred restlessly. After a while the men went down the walk again and appeared to have departed.

"Now what?" Benton asked. The globe did not answer for a moment.

"I feel that the time is almost here," it said at last. "I have made no mistakes so far, and the difficult part is past. The hardest was having you come through time. It took me years — the Watcher was clever. You almost didn't answer, and it was not until I thought of the method of putting the machine in your hands that success was certain. Soon you shall release us from this globe. After such an eternity — "

There was a scraping and a murmur from the rear of the house, and Benton started up.

"They are coming in the back door!" he said. The globe rustled angrily.

The Controller and the Council Members came slowly and warily into the room. They spotted Benton and stopped.

"We didn't think that you were at home," the First Member said. Benton turned to him.

"Hello," he said. "I'm sorry that I didn't answer the bell; I had fallen asleep. What can I do for you?"

Carefully, his hand reached out toward the globe, and it seemed almost as if the globe rolled under the protection of his palm.

"What have you there?" the Controller demanded suddenly. Benton stared at him, and the globe whispered in his mind.

"Nothing but a paperweight," he smiled. "Won't you sit down?"

The men took their seats, and the First Member began to speak.

"You came to see us twice, the first time to register an invention, the second time because we had summoned you to appear, as we could not allow the invention to be issued."

"Well?" Benton demanded. "Is there something the matter with that?"

"Oh, no," the Member said, "but what was for us your first visit was for *you* your second. Several things prove this, but I will not go into them just now. The thing that is important is that you still have the machine. This is a difficult problem. Where is the machine? It should be in your possession. Although we cannot force you to give it to us, we will obtain it eventually in one way or another."

"That is true," Benton said. But where *was* the machine? He had just left it at the Controller's Office. Yet he had already picked it up and taken it into time, whereupon he had returned to the present and had returned it to the Controller's Office!

"It has ceased to exist, a non-entity in a time-spiral," the globe whispered to him, catching his thoughts. "The time-spiral reached its conclusion when you deposited the machine at the Office of Control. Now these men must leave so that we can do what must be done."

Benton rose to his feet, placing the globe behind him.

"I'm afraid that I don't have the time machine," he said. "I don't even know where it is, but you may search for it if you like."

"By breaking the laws, you have made yourself eligible for the Cart," the Controller observed. "But we feel that you have done what you did without meaning to. We do not want to punish anyone without reason, we only desire to maintain Stability. Once that is upset, nothing matters."

"You may search, but you won't find it," Benton said. The Members and the Controller began to look. They overturned chairs, searched under the carpets, behind pictures, in the walls, and they found nothing.

"You see, I was telling the truth," Benton smiled, as they returned to the living room.

"You could have hidden it outside someplace," the Member shrugged. "It doesn't matter, however."

The Controller stepped forward.

"Stability is like a gyroscope," he said. "It is difficult to turn from its course, but once started it can hardly be stopped. We do not feel that you yourself have the strength to turn that gyroscope, but there may be others who can. That remains to be seen. We are going to leave now, and you will be allowed to end your own life, or wait here for the Cart. We are giving you the choice. You will be watched, of course, and I trust that you will make no attempt to flee. If so, then it will mean your immediate destruction. Stability must be maintained, at any cost."

Benton watched them, and then laid the globe on the table. The Members looked at it with interest.

"A paperweight," Benton said. "Interesting, don't you think?"

The Members lost interest. They began to prepare to leave. But the Controller examined the globe, holding it up to the light.

"A model of a city, eh?" he said. "Such fine detail."

Benton watched him.

"Why, it seems amazing that a person could ever carve so well," the Controller continued. "What city is it? It looks like an ancient one such as Tyre or Babylon, or perhaps one far in the future. You know, it reminds me of an old legend."

He looked at Benton intently as he went on.

"The legend says that once there was a very evil city, it was so evil that God made it small and shut it up in a glass, and left a watcher of some sort to see that no one came along and released the city by smashing the glass. It is supposed to have been lying for eternity, waiting to escape."

"And this is perhaps the model of it." the Controller continued.

"Come on!" the First Member called at the door. "We must be going; there are lots of things left to do tonight."

The Controller turned quickly to the Members.

"Wait!" he said. "Don't leave."

He crossed the room to them, still holding the globe in his hand.

"This would be a very poor time to leave," he said, and Benton saw that while his face had lost most of its color, the mouth was set in firm lines. The Controller suddenly turned again to Benton.

"Trip through time; city in a glass globe! Does that mean anything?"

The two Council Members looked puzzled and blank.

"An ignorant man crosses time and returns with a strange glass," the Controller said. "Odd thing to bring out of time, don't you think?"

Suddenly the First Member's face blanched white.

"Good God in Heaven!" he whispered. "The accursed city! That globe?"

He stared at the round ball in disbelief. The Controller looked at Benton with an amused glance.

"Odd, how stupid we may be for a time, isn't it?" he said. "But eventually we wake up. *Don't touch it!*"

Benton slowly stepped back, his hands shaking.

"Well?" he demanded. The globe was angry at being in the Controller's hand. It began to buzz, and vibrations crept down the Controller's arm. He felt them, and took a firmer grip on the globe.

"I think it wants me to break it," he said, "it wants me to smash it on the floor so that it can get out." He watched the tiny spires and building tops in the murky mistiness of the globe, so tiny that he could cover them all with his fingers.

Benton dived. He came straight and sure, the way he had flown so many times in the air. Now every minute that he had hurtled about the warm blackness of the atmosphere of the City of Lightness came back to help him. The Controller, who had always been too busy with his work, always too piled up ahead to enjoy the airsports that the City was so proud of, went down at once. The globe bounced out of his hands and rolled across the room. Benton untangled himself and leaped up. As he raced after the small shiny sphere, he caught a glimpse of the frightened, bewildered faces of the Members, of the Controller attempting to get to his feet, face contorted with pain and horror.

The globe was calling to him, whispering to him. Benton stepped swiftly toward it, and felt a rising whisper of victory and then a scream of joy as his foot crushed the glass that imprisoned it.

The globe broke with a loud popping sound. For a time it lay there, then a mist began to rise from it. Benton returned to the couch and sat down. The mist began to fill the room. It grew and grew, it seemed almost like a living thing, so strangely did it shift and turn.

Benton began to drift into sleep. The mist crowded about him, curling over his legs, up to his chest, and finally milled about his face. He sat there, slumped over on the couch, his eyes closed, letting the strange, aged fragrance envelop him.

Then he heard the voices. Tiny and far away at first, the whisper of the globe multiplied countless times. A concert of whispering voices rose from the broken globe in a swelling crescendo of exultation. Joy of victory! He saw the tiny miniature city within the globe waver and fade, then change in size and shape. He could hear it now as well as see it. The steady throbbing of the machinery like a gigantic drum. The shaking and quivering of squat metal beings.

These beings were tended. He saw the slaves, sweating, stooped, pale men, twisting in their efforts to keep the roaring furnaces of steel and power happy. It seemed to swell before his eyes until the entire room was full of it, and the sweating workmen brushed against him and around him. He was deafened by the raging power, the grinding wheels and gears and valves. Something was pushing against him, compelling him to move forward, forward to the City, and the mist gleefully echoed the new, victorious sounds of the freed ones.

When the sun came up he was already awake. The rising bell rang, but Benton had left his sleeping-cube some time before. As he fell in with the marching ranks of his companions, he thought he recognized familiar faces for an instant — men he had known someplace before. But at once the memory passed. As they marched toward the waiting machines, chanting the tuneless sounds their ancestors had chanted for centuries, and the weight of his tools pressed against his back, he counted the time before his next rest day. It was only about three weeks to go now, and anyhow, he *might* be in line for a bonus if the Machines saw fit —

For had he not been tending *his* machine faithfully?

ROOG

"ROOG!" the dog said. He rested his paws on the top of the fence and looked around him.

The Roog came running into the yard.

It was early morning, and the sun had not really come up yet. The air was cold and gray, and the walls of the house were damp with moisture. The dog opened his jaws a little as he watched, his big black paws clutching the wood of the fence.

The Roog stood by the open gate, looking into the yard. He was a small Roog, thin and white, on wobbly legs. The Roog blinked at the dog, and the dog showed his teeth.

"Roog!" he said again. The sound echoed into the silent half darkness. Nothing moved nor stirred. The dog dropped down and walked back across the yard to the porch steps. He sat down on the bottom step and watched the Roog. The Roog glanced at him. Then he stretched his neck up to the window of the house, just above him. He sniffed at the window.

The dog came flashing across the yard. He hit the fence, and the gate shuddered and groaned. The Roog was walking quickly up the path, hurrying with funny little steps, mincing along. The dog lay down against the slats of the gate, breathing heavily, his red tongue hanging. He watched the Roog disappear.

The dog lay silently, his eyes bright and black. The day was beginning to come. The sky turned a little whiter, and from all around the sounds of people echoed through the morning air. Lights popped on behind shades. In the chilly dawn a window was opened.

The dog did not move. He watched the path.

In the kitchen Mrs. Cardossi poured water into the coffee pot. Steam rose from the water, blinding her. She set the pot down on the edge of the stove and went into the pantry. When she came back Alf was standing at the door of the kitchen. He put his glasses on.

"You bring the paper?" he said.

"It's outside."

Alf Cardossi walked across the kitchen. He threw the bolt on the back door and stepped out onto the porch. He looked into the gray, damp morning. At the fence Boris lay, black and furry, his tongue out.

"Put the tongue in," Alf said. The dog looked quickly up. His tail beat against the ground. "The tongue," Alf said. "Put the tongue in."

The dog and the man looked at one another. The dog whined. His eyes were bright and feverish.

"Roog!" he said softly.

"What?" Alf looked around. "Someone coming? The paperboy come?"

The dog stared at him, his mouth open.

"You certainly upset these days," Alf said. "You better take it easy. We both getting too old for excitement."

He went inside the house.

The sun came up. The street became bright and alive with color. The postman went along the sidewalk with his letters and magazines. Some children hurried by, laughing and talking.

About 11:00, Mrs. Cardossi swept the front porch. She sniffed the air, pausing for a moment.

"It smells good today," she said. "That means it's going to be warm."

In the heat of the noonday sun the black dog lay stretched out full length, under the porch. His chest rose and fell. In the cherry tree the birds were playing, squawking and chattering to each other. Once in a while Boris raised his head and looked at them. Presently he got to his feet and trotted down under the tree.

He was standing under the tree when he saw the two Roogs sitting on the fence, watching him.

"He's big," the first Roog said. "Most Guardians aren't as big as this."

The other Roog nodded, his head wobbling on his neck. Boris watched them without moving, his body stiff and hard. The Roogs were silent, now, looking at the big dog with his shaggy ruff of white around his neck.

"How is the offering urn?" the first Roog said. "Is it almost full?"

"Yes." The other nodded. "Almost ready."

"You, there!" the first Roog said, raising his voice. "Do you hear me? We've decided to accept the offering, this time. So you remember to let us in. No nonsense, now."

"Don't forget," the other added. "It won't be long."

Boris said nothing.

The two Roogs leaped off the fence and went over together just beyond the walk. One of them brought out a map and they studied it.

"This area really is none too good for a first trial," the first Roog said. "Too many Guardians . . . Now, the northside area — "

"*They* decided," the other Roog said. "There are so many factors — "

"Of course." They glanced at Boris and moved back farther from the fence. He could not hear the rest of what they were saying.

Presently the Roogs put their map away and went off down the path.

Boris walked over to the fence and sniffed at the boards. He smelled the sickly, rotten odor of Roogs and the hair stood up on his back.

That night when Alf Cardossi came home the dog was standing at the gate, looking up the walk. Alf opened the gate and went into the yard.

"How are you?" he said, thumping the dog's side. "You stopped worrying? Seems like you been nervous of late. You didn't used to be that way."

Boris whined, looking intently up into the man's face.

"You a good dog, Boris," Alf said. "You pretty big, too, for a dog. You don't remember long ago how you used to be only a little bit of a puppy."

Boris leaned against the man's leg.

"You a good dog," Alf murmured. "I sure wish I knew what is on your mind."

He went inside the house. Mrs. Cardossi was setting the table for dinner. Alf went into the living room and took his coat and hat off. He set his lunch pail down on the sideboard and came back into the kitchen.

"What's the matter?" Mrs. Cardossi said.

"That dog got to stop making all that noise, barking. The neighbors going to complain to the police again."

"I hope we don't have to give him to your brother," Mrs. Cardossi said, folding her arms. "But he sure goes crazy, especially on Friday morning, when the garbage men come."

"Maybe he'll calm down," Alf said. He lit his pipe and smoked solemnly. "He didn't used to be that way. Maybe he'll get better, like he was."

"We'll see," Mrs. Cardossi said.

The sun rose up, cold and ominous. Mist hung over all the trees and in the low places.

It was Friday morning.

The black dog lay under the porch, listening, his eyes wide and staring. His coat was stiff with hoarfrost and the breath from his nostrils made clouds of steam in the thin air. Suddenly he turned his head and leaped up.

From far off, a long way away, a faint sound came, a kind of crashing sound.

"Roog!" Boris cried, looking around. He hurried to the gate and stood up, his paws on top of the fence.

In the distance the sound came again, louder now, not as far away as before. It was a crashing, clanging sound, as if something were being rolled back, as if a great door were being opened.

"Roog!" Boris cried. He stared up anxiously at the darkened windows above him. Nothing stirred, nothing.

And along the street the Roogs came. The Roogs and their truck moved along, bouncing against the rough stones, crashing and whirring.

"Roog!" Boris cried, and he leaped, his eyes blazing. Then he became more calm. He settled himself down on the ground and waited, listening.

Out in front the Roogs stopped their truck. He could hear them opening the doors, stepping down onto the sidewalk. Boris ran around in a little circle. He whined, and his muzzle turned once again toward the house.

Inside the warm, dark bedroom, Mr. Cardossi sat up a little in bed and squinted at the clock.

"That damn dog," he muttered. "That damn dog." He turned his face toward the pillow and closed his eyes.

The Roogs were coming down the path, now. The first Roog pushed against the gate and the gate opened. The Roogs came into the yard. The dog backed away from them.

"Roog! Roog!" he cried. The horrid, bitter smell of Roogs came to his nose, and he turned away.

"The offering urn," the first Roog said. "It is full, I think." He smiled at the rigid, angry dog. "How very good of you," he said.

The Roogs came toward the metal can, and one of them took the lid from it.

"Roog! Roog!" Boris cried, huddled against the bottom of the porch steps. His body shook with horror. The Roogs were lifting up the big metal can, turning it on its side. The contents poured out onto the ground, and the Roogs scooped the sacks of bulging, splitting paper together, catching at the orange peels and fragments, the bits of toast and egg shells.

One of the Roogs popped an egg shell into his mouth. His teeth crunched the egg shell.

"Roog!" Boris cried hopelessly, almost to himself. The Roogs were almost finished with their work of gathering up the offering. They stopped for a moment, looking at Boris.

Then, slowly, silently, the Roogs looked up, up the side of the house, along the stucco, to the window, with its brown shade pulled tightly down.

"ROOG!" Boris screamed, and he came toward them, dancing with fury and dismay. Reluctantly, the Roogs turned away from the window. They went out through the gate, closing it behind them.

"Look at him," the last Roog said with contempt, pulling his corner of the blanket up on his shoulder. Boris strained against the fence, his mouth open, snapping wildly. The biggest Roog began to wave his arms furiously and Boris retreated. He settled down at the bottom of the porch steps, his mouth still open, and from the depths of him an unhappy, terrible moan issued forth, a wail of misery and despair.

"Come on," the other Roog said to the lingering Roog at the fence.

They walked up the path.

"Well, except for these little places around the Guardians, this area is well cleared," the biggest Roog said. "I'll be glad when this particular Guardian is done. He certainly causes us a lot of trouble."

"Don't be impatient," one of the Roogs said. He grinned. "Our truck is full enough as it is. Let's leave something for next week."

All the Roogs laughed.

They went on up the path, carrying the offering in the dirty, sagging blanket.

THE LITTLE MOVEMENT

THE MAN WAS SITTING on the sidewalk, holding the box shut with his hands. Impatiently the lid of the box moved, straining up against his fingers.

"All right," the man murmured. Sweat rolled down his face, damp, heavy sweat. He opened the box slowly, holding his fingers over the opening. From inside a metallic drumming came, a low insistent vibration, rising frantically as the sunlight filtered into the box.

A small head appeared, round and shiny, and then another. More heads jerked into view, peering, craning to see. "I'm first," one head shrilled. There was a momentary squabble, then quick agreement.

The man sitting on the sidewalk lifted out the little metal figure with trembling hands. He put it down on the sidewalk and began to wind it awkwardly, thick-fingered. It was a brightly painted soldier with helmet and gun, standing at attention. As the man turned the key the little soldier's arms went up and down. It struggled eagerly.

Along the sidewalk two women were coming, talking together. They glanced down curiously at the man sitting on the sidewalk, at the box and the shiny figure in the man's hands.

"Fifty cents," the man muttered. "Get your child something to — "

"Wait!" a faint metallic voice came. "Not them!"

The man broke off abruptly. The two women looked at each other and then at the man and the little metal figure. They went hurriedly on.

The little soldier gazed up and down the street, at the cars, the shoppers. Suddenly it trembled, rasping in a low, eager voice.

The man swallowed. "Not the kid," he said thickly. He tried to hold onto the figure, but metal fingers dug quickly into his hand. He gasped.

"Tell them to stop!" the figure shrilled. "Make them stop!" The metal figure pulled away and clicked across the sidewalk, its legs still and rigid.

The boy and his father slowed to a stop, looking down at it with interest. The sitting man smiled feebly; he watched the figure approach them, turning from side to side, its arms going up and down.

"Get something for your boy. An exciting playmate. Keep him company."

The father grinned, watching the figure coming up to his shoe. The little soldier bumped into the shoe. It wheezed and clicked. It stopped moving.

"Wind it up!" the boy cried.

His father picked up the figure. "How much?"

"Fifty cents." The salesman rose unsteadily, clutching the box against him. "Keep him company. Amuse him."

The father turned the figure over. "You sure you want it, Bobby?"

"Sure! Wind it up!" Bobby reached for the little soldier. "Make it go!"

"I'll buy it," the father said. He reached into his pocket and handed the man a dollar bill.

Clumsily, staring away, the salesman made change.

The situation was excellent.

The little figure lay quietly, thinking everything over. All circumstances had conspired to bring about optimum solution. The Child might not have wanted to stop, or the Adult might not have had any money. Many things might have gone wrong; it was awful even to think about them. But everything had been perfect.

The little figure gazed up in pleasure, where it lay in the back of the car. It had correctly interpreted certain signs: the Adults were in control, and so the Adults had money. They had power, but their power made it difficult to get to them. Their power, and their size. With the Children it was different. *They* were small, and it was easier to talk to them. They accepted everything they heard, and they did what they were told. Or so it was said at the factory.

The little metal figure lay, lost in dreamy, delicious thoughts.

The boy's heart was beating quickly. He ran upstairs and pushed the door open. After he had closed the door carefully he went to the bed and sat down. He looked down at what he held in his hands.

"What's your name?" he said. "What are you called?"

The metal figure did not answer.

"I'll introduce you around. You must get to know everybody. You'll like it here."

Bobby laid the figure down on the bed. He ran to the closet and dragged out a bulging carton of toys.

"This is Bonzo," he said. He held up a pale stuffed rabbit. "And Fred." He turned the rubber pig around for the soldier to see. "And Teddo, of course. This is Teddo."

He carried Teddo to the bed and laid him beside the soldier. Teddo lay silent, gazing up at the ceiling with glassy eyes. Teddo was a brown bear, with wisps of straw poking out of his joints.

"And what shall we call you?" Bobby said. "I think we should have a council and decide." He paused, considering. "I'll wind you up so we can all see how you work."

He began to wind the figure carefully, turning it over on its face. When the key was tight he bent down and set the figure on the floor.

"Go on," Bobby said. The metal figure stood still. Then it began to whirr and click. Across the floor it went, walking with stiff jerks. It changed directions suddenly and headed toward the door. At the door it stopped. Then it turned to some building blocks lying about and began to push them into a heap.

Bobby watched with interest. The little figure struggled with the blocks, piling them into a pyramid. At last it climbed up onto the blocks and turned the key in the lock.

Bobby scratched his head, puzzled. "Why did you do that?" he said. The figure climbed back down and came across the room toward Bobby, clicking and whirring. Bobby and the stuffed animals regarded it with surprise and wonder. The figure reached the bed and halted.

"Lift me up!" it cried impatiently, in its thin, metallic voice. "Hurry up! Don't just sit there!"

Bobby's eyes grew large. He stared, blinking. The stuffed animals said nothing.

"Come on!" the little soldier shouted.

Bobby reached down. The soldier seized his hand tightly. Bobby cried out.

"Be still," the soldier commanded. "Lift me up to the bed. I have things to discuss with you, things of great importance."

Bobby put it down on the bed beside him. The room was silent, except for the faint whirring of the metal figure.

"This is a nice room," the soldier said presently. "A very nice room."

Bobby drew back a little on the bed.

"What's the matter?" the soldier said sharply, turning its head and staring up.

"Nothing."

"What is it?" The little figure peered at him. "You're not afraid of me, are you?"

Bobby shifted uncomfortably.

"Afraid of *me*?" The soldier laughed. "I'm only a little metal man, only six inches high." It laughed again and again. It ceased abruptly. "Listen. I'm going to live here with you for a while. I won't hurt you; you can count on that. I'm a friend — a good friend."

It peered up a little anxiously. "But I want you to do things for me. You won't mind doing things, will you? Tell me: how many are there of them in your family?"

Bobby hesitated.

"Come, how many of *them*? Adults."

"Three.... Daddy, and Mother, and Foxie."

"Foxie? Who is that?"

"My grandmother."

"Three of them." The figure nodded. "I see. Only three. But others come from time to time? Other Adults visit this house?"

Bobby nodded.

"Three. That's not too many. Three are not so much of a problem. According to the factory — "

It broke off. "Good. Listen to me. I don't want you to say anything to them about me. I'm *your* friend, your secret friend. They won't be interested in hearing about me. I'm not going to hurt you, remember. You have nothing to fear. I'm going to live right here, with you."

It watched the boy intently, lingering over the last words.

"I'm going to be a sort of private teacher. I'm going to teach you things, things to do, things to say. Just like a tutor should. Will you like that?"

Silence.

"Of course you'll like it. We could even begin now. Perhaps you want to know the proper way to address me. Do you want to learn that?"

"Address you?" Bobby stared down.

"You are to call me.... " The figure paused, hesitating. It drew itself together, proudly. "You are to call me — My Lord."

Bobby leaped up, his hands to his face.

"My Lord," the figure said relentlessly. "My Lord. You don't really need to start now. I'm tired." The figure sagged. "I'm almost run down. Please wind me up again in about an hour."

The figure began to stiffen. It gazed up at the boy. "In an hour. Will you wind me tight? You will, won't you?"

Its voice trailed off into silence.

Bobby nodded slowly. "All right," he murmured. "All right."

It was Tuesday. The window was open, and warm sunlight came drifting into the room. Bobby was away at school; the house was silent and empty. The stuffed animals were back in the closet.

My Lord lay on the dresser, propped up, looking out the window, resting contentedly.

There came a faint humming sound. Something small flew suddenly into the room. The small object circled a few times and then came slowly to rest on the white cloth of the dresser-top, beside the metal soldier. It was a tiny toy airplane.

"How is it going?" the airplane said. "Is everything all right so far?"

"Yes," My Lord said. "And the others?"

"Not so good. Only a handful of them managed to reach Children."

The soldier gasped in pain.

"The largest group fell into the hands of Adults. As you know, that is not satisfactory. It is very difficult to control Adults. They break away, or they wait until the spring is unwound — "

"I know." My Lord nodded glumly.

"The news will most certainly continue to be bad. We must be prepared for it."

"There's more. Tell me!"

"Frankly, about half of them have already been destroyed, stepped on by Adults. A dog is said to have broken up one. There's no doubt of it: our only hope is through Children. We must succeed there, if at all."

The little soldier nodded. The messenger was right, of course. They had never considered that a direct attack against the ruling race, the Adults, would win. Their size, their power, their enormous stride would protect them. The toy vender was a good example. He had tried to break away many times, tried to fool them and get loose. Part of the group had to be wound at all times to watch him, and there was that frightening day when he failed to wind them tight, hoping that —

"You're giving the Child instructions?" the airplane asked. "You're preparing him?"

"Yes. He understands that I'm going to be here. Children seem to be like that. As a subject race they have been taught to accept; it's all they can do. I am another teacher, invading his life, giving him orders. Another voice, telling him that — "

"You've started the second phase?"

"So soon?" My Lord was amazed. "Why? Is it necessary, so quickly?"

"The factory is becoming anxious. Most of the group has been destroyed, as I said."

"I know." My Lord nodded absently. "We expected it, we planned with realism, knowing the chances." It strode back and forth on the dresser-top. "Naturally, many would fall into their hands, the Adults. The Adults are everywhere, in all key positions, important stations. It's the psychology of the ruling race to control each phase of social life. But as long as those who reach Children survive — "

"You were not supposed to know, but outside of yourself, there's only three left. Just three."

"*Three?*" My Lord stared.

"Even those who reached Children have been destroyed right and left. The situation is tragic. That's why they want you to get started with the second phase."

My Lord clenched its fists, its features locked in iron horror. Only three left ... What hopes they had entertained for this band, venturing out, so little, so dependent on the weather — and on being wound up tight. If only they were larger! The Adults were so huge.

But the Children. What had gone wrong? What had happened to their one chance, their one fragile hope?

"How did it happen? What occurred?"

"No one knows. The factory is in a turmoil. And now they're running short of materials. Some of the machines have broken down and nobody knows how to run them." The airplane coasted toward the edge of the dresser. "I must be getting back. I'll report later to see how you're getting on."

The airplane flew up into the air and out through the open window. My Lord watched it, dazed.

What could have happened? They had been so certain about the Children. It was all planned —

It meditated.

Evening. The boy sat at the table, staring absently at his geography book. He shifted unhappily, turning the pages. At last he closed the book. He slid from his chair and went to the closet. He was reaching into the closet for the bulging carton when a voice came drifting to him from the dresser-top.

"Later. You can play with them later. I must discuss something with you."

The boy turned back to the table, his face listless and tired. He nodded, sinking down against the table, his head on his arms.

"You're not asleep, are you?" My Lord said.

"No."

"Then listen. Tomorrow when you leave school I want you to go to a certain address. It's not far from the school. It's a toy store. Perhaps you know it. Don's Toyland."

"I haven't any money."

"It doesn't matter. This has all been arranged for long in advance. Go to Toyland and say to the man: 'I was told to come for the package.' Can you remember that? 'I was told to come for the package.' "

"What's in the package?"

"Some tools, and some toys for you. To go along with me." The metal figure rubbed its hands together. "Nice modern toys, two toy tanks and a machine gun. And some spare parts for — "

There were footsteps on the stairs outside.

"Don't forget," My Lord said nervously. "You'll do it? This phase of the plan is extremely important."

It wrung its hands together in anxiety.

The boy brushed the last strands of hair into place. He put his cap on and picked up his school books. Outside, the morning was gray and dismal. Rain fell, slowly, soundlessly.

Suddenly the boy set his books down again. He went to the closet and reached inside. His fingers closed over Teddo's leg, and he drew him out.

The boy sat on the bed, holding Teddo against his cheek. For a long time he sat with the stuffed bear, oblivious to everything else.

Abruptly he looked toward the dresser. My Lord was lying outstretched, silent. Bobby went hurriedly back to the closet and laid Teddo into the carton. He crossed the room to the door. As he opened the door the little metal figure on the dresser stirred.

"Remember Don's Toyland. . . . "

The door closed. My Lord heard the Child going heavily down the stairs, clumping unhappily. My Lord exulted. It was working out all right. Bobby wouldn't want to do it, but he would. And once the tools and parts and weapons were safely inside there wouldn't be any chance of failure.

Perhaps they would capture a second factory. Or better yet: build dies and machines themselves to turn out larger Lords. Yes, if only they could be larger, just a little larger. They were so small, so very tiny, only a few inches high. Would the Movement fail, pass away, because they were too tiny, too fragile?

But with tanks and guns! Yet, of all the packages so carefully secreted in the toyshop, this would be the only one, the only one to be —

Something moved.

My Lord turned quickly. From the closet Teddo came, lumbering slowly.

"Bonzo," he said. "Bonzo, go over by the window. I think it came in that way, if I'm not mistaken."

The stuffed rabbit reached the window-sill in one skip. He huddled, gazing outside. "Nothing yet."

"Good." Teddo moved toward the dresser. He looked up. "Little Lord, please come down. You've been up there much too long."

My Lord stared. Fred, the rubber pig, was coming out of the closet. Puffing, he reached the dresser. "I'll go up and get it," he said. "I don't think it will come down by itself. We'll have to help it."

"What are you doing?" My Lord cried. The rubber pig was settling himself on his haunches, his ears down flat against his head. "What's happening?"

Fred leaped. And at the same time Teddo began to climb swiftly, catching onto the handles of the dresser. Expertly, he gained the top. My Lord was edging toward the wall, glancing down at the floor, far below.

"So this is what happened to the others," it murmured. "I understand. An Organization, waiting for us. Then everything is known."

It leaped.

When they had gathered up the pieces and had got them under the carpet, Teddo said:

"That part was easy. Let's hope the rest won't be any harder."

"What do you mean?" Fred said.

"The package of toys. The tanks and guns."

"Oh, we can handle them. Remember how we helped next door when that first little Lord, the first one we ever encountered — "

Teddo laughed. "It did put up quite a fight. It was tougher than this one. But we had the panda bears from across the way."

"We'll do it again," Fred said. "I'm getting so I rather enjoy it."

"Me, too," Bonzo said from the window.

BEYOND LIES THE WUB

THEY HAD ALMOST FINISHED with the loading. Outside stood the Optus, his arms folded, his face sunk in gloom. Captain Franco walked leisurely down the gangplank, grinning.

"What's the matter?" he said. "You're getting paid for all this."

The Optus said nothing. He turned away, collecting his robes. The Captain put his boot on the hem of the robe.

"Just a minute. Don't go off. I'm not finished."

"Oh?" The Optus turned with dignity. "I am going back to the village." He looked toward the animals and birds being driven up the gangplank into the spaceship. "I must organize new hunts."

Franco lit a cigarette. "Why not? You people can go out into the veldt and track it all down again. But when we run halfway between Mars and Earth — "

The Optus went off, wordless. Franco joined the first mate at the bottom of the gangplank.

"How's it coming?" he asked. He looked at his watch. "We got a good bargain here."

The mate glanced at him sourly. "How do you explain that?"

"What's the matter with you? We need it more than they do."

"I'll see you later, Captain." The mate threaded his way up the plank, between the long-legged Martian go-birds, into the ship. Franco watched him disappear. He was just starting up after him, up the plank toward the port, when he saw *it*.

"My God!" He stood staring, his hands on his hips. Peterson was walking along the path, his face red, leading *it* by a string.

"I'm sorry, Captain," he said, tugging at the string. Franco walked toward him.

"What is it?"

The wub stood sagging, its great body settling slowly. It was sitting down, its eyes half shut. A few flies buzzed about its flank, and it switched its tail.

It sat. There was silence.

"It's a wub," Peterson said. "I got it from a native for fifty cents. He said it was a very unusual animal. Very respected."

"This?" Franco poked the great sloping side of the wub. "It's a pig! A huge dirty pig!"

"Yes sir, it's a pig. The natives call it a wub."

"A huge pig. It must weigh four hundred pounds." Franco grabbed a tuft of the rough hair. The wub gasped. Its eyes opened, small and moist. Then its great mouth twitched.

A tear rolled down the wub's cheek and splashed on the floor.

"Maybe it's good to eat," Peterson said nervously.

"We'll soon find out," Franco said.

The wub survived the takeoff, sound asleep in the hold of the ship. When they were out in space and everything was running smoothly, Captain Franco bade his men fetch the wub upstairs so that he might perceive what manner of beast it was.

The wub grunted and wheezed, squeezing up the passageway.

"Come on," Jones grated, pulling at the rope. The wub twisted, rubbing its skin off on the smooth chrome walls. It burst into the anteroom, tumbling down in a heap. The men leaped up.

"Good Lord," French said. "What is it?"

"Peterson says it's a wub," Jones said. "It belongs to him." He kicked at the wub. The wub stood up unsteadily, panting.

"What's the matter with it?" French came over. "Is it going to be sick?"

They watched. The wub rolled its eyes mournfully. It gazed around at the men.

"I think it's thirsty," Peterson said. He went to get some water. French shook his head.

"No wonder we had so much trouble taking off. I had to reset all my ballast calculations."

Peterson came back with the water. The wub began to lap gratefully, splashing the men.

Captain Franco appeared at the door.

"Let's have a look at it." He advanced, squinting critically. "You got this for fifty cents?"

"Yes, sir," Peterson said. "It eats almost anything. I fed it on grain and it liked that. And then potatoes, and mash, and scraps from the table, and milk. It seems to enjoy eating. After it eats it lies down and goes to sleep."

"I see," Captain Franco said. "Now, as to its taste. That's the real question. I doubt if there's much point in fattening it up any more. It seems fat enough to me already. Where's the cook? I want him here. I want to find out — "

The wub stopped lapping and looked up at the Captain.

"Really, Captain," the wub said. "I suggest we talk of other matters."

The room was silent.

"What was that?" Franco said. "Just now."

"The wub, sir," Peterson said. "It spoke."

They all looked at the wub.

"What did it say? What did it say?"

"It suggested we talk about other things."

Franco walked toward the wub. He went all around it, examining it from every side. Then he came back over and stood with the men.

"I wonder if there's a native inside it," he said thoughtfully. "Maybe we should open it up and have a look."

"Oh, goodness!" the wub cried. "Is that all you people can think of, killing and cutting?"

Franco clenched his fists. "Come out of there! Whoever you are, come out!"

Nothing stirred. The men stood together, their faces blank, staring at the wub. The wub swished its tail. It belched suddenly.

"I beg your pardon," the wub said.

"I don't think there's anyone in there," Jones said in a low voice. They all looked at each other.

The cook came in.

"You wanted me, Captain?" he said. "What's this thing?"

"This is a wub," Franco said. "It's to be eaten. Will you measure it and figure out — "

"I think we should have a talk," the wub said. "I'd like to discuss this with you, Captain, if I might. I can see that you and I do not agree on some basic issues."

The Captain took a long time to answer. The wub waited good-naturedly, licking the water from its jowls.

"Come into my office," the Captain said at last. He turned and walked out of the room. The wub rose and padded after him. The men watched it go out. They heard it climbing the stairs.

"I wonder what the outcome will be," the cook said. "Well, I'll be in the kitchen. Let me know as soon as you hear."

"Sure," Jones said. "Sure."

The wub eased itself down in the corner with a sigh. "You must forgive me," it said. "I'm afraid I'm addicted to various forms of relaxation. When one is as large as I — "

The Captain nodded impatiently. He sat down at his desk and folded his hands.

"All right," he said. "Let's get started. You're a wub? Is that correct?"

The wub shrugged. "I suppose so. That's what they call us, the natives, I mean. We have our own term."

"And you speak English? You've been in contact with Earthmen before?"

"No."

"Then how do you do it?"

"Speak English? Am I speaking English? I'm not conscious of speaking anything in particular. I examined your mind —"

"My mind?"

"I studied the contents, especially the semantic warehouse, as I refer to it —"

"I see," the Captain said. "Telepathy. Of course."

"We are a very old race," the wub said. "Very old and very ponderous. It is difficult for us to move around. You can appreciate anything so slow and heavy would be at the mercy of more agile forms of life. There was no use in our relying on physical defenses. How could we win? Too heavy to run, too soft to fight, too good-natured to hunt for game —"

"How do you live?"

"Plants. Vegetables. We can eat almost anything. We're very catholic. Tolerant, eclectic, catholic. We live and let live. That's how we've gotten along."

The wub eyed the Captain.

"And that's why I so violently objected to this business about having me boiled. I could see the image in your mind — most of me in the frozen food locker, some of me in the kettle, a bit for your pet cat —"

"So you read minds?" the Captain said. "How interesting. Anything else? I mean, what else can you do along those lines?"

"A few odds and ends," the wub said absently, staring around the room. "A nice apartment you have here, Captain. You keep it quite neat. I respect life-forms that are tidy. Some Martian birds are quite tidy. They throw things out of their nests and sweep them —"

"Indeed." The Captain nodded. "But to get back to the problem —"

"Quite so. You spoke of dining on me. The taste, I am told, is good. A little fatty, but tender. But how can any lasting contact be established between your people and mine if you resort to such barbaric attitudes? Eat me? Rather you should discuss questions with me, philosophy, the arts —"

The Captain stood up. "Philosophy. It might interest you to know that we will be hard put to find something to eat for the next month. An unfortunate spoilage —"

"I know." The wub nodded. "But wouldn't it be more in accord with your principles of democracy if we all drew straws, or something along that line?

After all, democracy is to protect the minority from just such infringements. Now, if each of us casts one vote — "

The Captain walked to the door.

"Nuts to you," he said. He opened the door. He opened his mouth.

He stood frozen, his mouth wide, his eyes staring, his fingers still on the knob.

The wub watched him. Presently it padded out of the room, edging past the Captain. It went down the hall, deep in meditation.

The room was quiet.

"So you see," the wub said, "we have a common myth. Your mind contains many familiar myth symbols. Ishtar, Odysseus — "

Peterson sat silently, staring at the floor. He shifted in his chair.

"Go on," he said. "Please go on."

"I find in your Odysseus a figure common to the mythology of most self-conscious races. As I interpret it, Odysseus wanders as an individual aware of himself as such. This is the idea of separation, of separation from family and country. The process of individuation."

"But Odysseus returns to his home." Peterson looked out the port window, at the stars, endless stars, burning intently in the empty universe. "Finally he goes home."

"As must all creatures. The moment of separation is a temporary period, a brief journey of the soul. It begins, it ends. The wanderer returns to land and race. . . . "

The door opened. The wub stopped, turning its great head.

Captain Franco came into the room, the men behind him. They hesitated at the door.

"Are you all right?" French said.

"Do you mean me?" Peterson said, surprised. "Why me?"

Franco lowered his gun. "Come over here," he said to Peterson. "Get up and come here."

There was silence.

"Go ahead," the wub said. "It doesn't matter."

Peterson stood up. "What for?"

"It's an order."

Peterson walked to the door. French caught his arm.

"What's going on?" Peterson wrenched loose. "What's the matter with you?"

Captain Franco moved toward the wub. The wub looked up from where it lay in the corner, pressed against the wall.

"It is interesting," the wub said, "that you are obsessed with the idea of eating me. I wonder why."

"Get up," Franco said.

"If you wish." The wub rose, grunting. "Be patient. It is difficult for me." It stood, gasping, its tongue lolling foolishly.

"Shoot it now," French said.

"For God's sake!" Peterson exclaimed. Jones turned to him quickly, his eyes gray with fear.

"You didn't see him — like a statue, standing there, his mouth open. If we hadn't come down, he'd still be there."

"Who? The Captain?" Peterson stared around. "But he's all right now."

They looked at the wub, standing in the middle of the room, its great chest rising and falling.

"Come on," Franco said. "Out of the way."

The men pulled aside toward the door.

"You are quite afraid, aren't you?" the wub said. "Have I done anything to you? I am against the idea of hurting. All I have done is try to protect myself. Can you expect me to rush eagerly to my death? I am a sensible being like yourselves. I was curious to see your ship, learn about you. I suggested to the native — "

The gun jerked.

"See," Franco said. "I thought so."

The wub settled down, panting. It put its paws out, pulling its tail around it.

"It is very warm," the wub said. "I understand that we are close to the jets. Atomic power. You have done many wonderful things with it — technically. Apparently your scientific hierarchy is not equipped to solve moral, ethical — "

Franco turned to the men, crowding behind him, wide-eyed, silent.

"I'll do it. You can watch."

French nodded. "Try to hit the brain. It's no good for eating. Don't hit the chest. If the rib cage shatters, we'll have to pick bones out."

"Listen," Peterson said, licking his lips. "Has it done anything? What harm has it done? I'm asking you. And anyhow, it's still mine. You have no right to shoot it. It doesn't belong to you."

Franco raised his gun.

"I'm going out," Jones said, his face white and sick. "I don't want to see it."

"Me, too," French said. The men straggled out, murmuring. Peterson lingered at the door.

"It was talking to me about myths," he said. "It wouldn't hurt anyone."

He went outside.

Franco walked toward the wub. The wub looked up slowly. It swallowed.

"A very foolish thing," it said. "I am sorry that you want to do it. There was a parable that your Saviour related — "

It stopped, staring at the gun.

"Can you look me in the eye and do it?" the wub said. "Can you do that?"

The Captain gazed down. "I can look you in the eye," he said. "Back on the farm we had hogs, dirty razorback hogs. I can do it."

Staring down at the wub, into the gleaming, moist eyes, he pressed the trigger.

The taste was excellent.

They sat glumly around the table, some of them hardly eating at all. The only one who seemed to be enjoying himself was Captain Franco.

"More?" he said, looking around. "More? And some wine, perhaps."

"Not me," French said. "I think I'll go back to the chart room."

"Me, too." Jones stood up, pushing his chair back. "I'll see you later."

The Captain watched them go. Some of the others excused themselves.

"What do you suppose the matter is?" the Captain said. He turned to Peterson. Peterson sat staring down at his plate, at the potatoes, the green peas, and at the thick slab of tender, warm meat.

He opened his mouth. No sound came.

The Captain put his hand on Peterson's shoulder.

"It is only organic matter, now," he said. "The life essence is gone." He ate, spooning up the gravy with some bread. "I, myself, love to eat. It is one of the greatest things that a living creature can enjoy. Eating, resting, meditation, discussing things."

Peterson nodded. Two more men got up and went out. The Captain drank some water and sighed.

"Well," he said. "I must say that this was a very enjoyable meal. All the reports I had heard were quite true — the taste of wub. Very fine. But I was prevented from enjoying this in times past."

He dabbed at his lips with his napkin and leaned back in his chair. Peterson stared dejectedly at the table.

The Captain watched him intently. He leaned over.

"Come, come," he said. "Cheer up! Let's discuss things."

He smiled.

"As I was saying before I was interrupted, the role of Odysseus in the myths — "

Peterson jerked up, staring.

"To go on," the Captain said. "Odysseus, as I understand him — "

THE GUN

THE CAPTAIN PEERED into the eyepiece of the telescope. He adjusted the focus quickly.

"It was an atomic fission we saw, all right," he said presently. He sighed and pushed the eyepiece away. "Any of you who wants to look may do so. But it's not a pretty sight."

"Let me look," Tance the archeologist said. He bent down to look, squinting. "Good Lord!" He leaped violently back, knocking against Dorle, the Chief Navigator.

"Why did we come all this way, then?" Dorle asked, looking around at the other men. "There's no point even in landing. Let's go back at once."

"Perhaps he's right," the biologist murmured. "But I'd like to look for myself, if I may." He pushed past Tance and peered into the sight.

He saw a vast expanse, an endless surface of gray, stretching to the edge of the planet. At first he thought it was water but after a moment he realized that it was slag, pitted, fused slag, broken only by hills of rock jutting up at intervals. Nothing moved or stirred. Everything was silent, dead.

"I see," Fomar said, backing away from the eyepiece. "Well, I won't find any legumes there." He tried to smile, but his lips stayed unmoved. He stepped away and stood by himself, staring past the others.

"I wonder what the atmospheric sample will show," Tance said.

"I think I can guess," the Captain answered. "Most of the atmosphere is poisoned. But didn't we expect all this? I don't see why we're so surprised. A fission visible as far away as our system must be a terrible thing."

He strode off down the corridor, dignified and expressionless. They watched him disappear into the control room.

As the Captain closed the door the young woman turned. "What did the telescope show? Good or bad?"

"Bad. No life could possibly exist. Atmosphere poisoned, water vaporized, all the land fused."

"Could they have gone underground?"

The Captain slid back the port window so that the surface of the planet under them was visible. The two of them stared down, silent and disturbed. Mile after mile of unbroken ruin stretched out, blackened slag, pitted and scarred, and occasional heaps of rock.

Suddenly Nasha jumped. "Look! Over there, at the edge. Do you see it?"

They stared. Something rose up, not rock, not an accidental formation. It was round, a circle of dots, white pellets on the dead skin of the planet. A city? Buildings of some kind?

"Please turn the ship," Nasha said excitedly. She pushed her dark hair from her face. "Turn the ship and let's see what it is!"

The ship turned, changing its course. As they came over the white dots the Captain lowered the ship, dropping it down as much as he dared. "Piers," he said. "Piers of some sort of stone. Perhaps poured artificial stone. The remains of a city."

"Oh, dear," Nasha murmured. "How awful." She watched the ruins disappear behind them. In a half-circle the white squares jutted from the slag, chipped and cracked, like broken teeth.

"There's nothing alive," the Captain said at last. "I think we'll go right back; I know most of the crew want to go. Get the Government Receiving Station on the sender and tell them what we found, and that we — "

He staggered.

The first atomic shell had struck the ship, spinning it around. The Captain fell to the floor, crashing into the control table. Papers and instruments rained down on him. As he started to his feet the second shell struck. The ceiling cracked open, struts and girders twisted and bent. The ship shuddered, falling suddenly down, then righting itself as automatic controls took over.

The Captain lay on the floor by the smashed control board. In the corner Nasha struggled to free herself from the debris.

Outside the men were already sealing the gaping leaks in the side of the ship, through which the precious air was rushing, dissipating into the void beyond. "Help me!" Dorle was shouting. "Fire over here, wiring ignited." Two men came running. Tance watched helplessly, his eyeglasses broken and bent.

"So there is life here, after all," he said, half to himself. "But how could — "

"Give us a hand," Fomar said, hurrying past. "Give us a hand, we've got to land the ship!"

* * *

It was night. A few stars glinted above them, winking through the drifting silt that blew across the surface of the planet.

Dorle peered out, frowning. "What a place to be stuck in." He resumed his work, hammering the bent metal hull of the ship back into place. He was wearing a pressure suit; there were still many small leaks, and radioactive particles from the atmosphere had already found their way into the ship.

Nasha and Fomar were sitting at the table in the control room, pale and solemn, studying the inventory lists.

"Low on carbohydrates," Fomar said. "We can break down the stored fats if we want to, but — "

"I wonder if we could find anything outside." Nasha went to the window. "How uninviting it looks." She paced back and forth, very slender and small, her face dark with fatigue. "What do you suppose an exploring party would find?"

Fomar shrugged. "Not much. Maybe a few weeds growing in cracks here and there. Nothing we could use. Anything that would adapt to this environment would be toxic, lethal."

Nasha paused, rubbing her cheek. There was a deep scratch there, still red and swollen. "Then how do you explain — it? According to your theory the inhabitants must have died in their skins, fried like yams. But who fired on us? Somebody detected us, made a decision, aimed a gun."

"And gauged distance," the Captain said feebly from the cot in the corner. He turned toward them. "That's the part that worries me. The first shell put us out of commission, the second almost destroyed us. They were well aimed, perfectly aimed. We're not such an easy target."

"True." Fomar nodded. "Well, perhaps we'll know the answer before we leave here. What a strange situation! All our reasoning tells us that no life could exist; the whole planet burned dry, the atmosphere itself gone, completely poisoned."

"The gun that fired the projectiles survived," Nasha said. "Why not people?"

"It's not the same. Metal doesn't need air to breathe. Metal doesn't get leukemia from radioactive particles. Metal doesn't need food and water."

There was silence.

"A paradox," Nasha said. "Anyhow, in the morning I think we should send out a search party. And meanwhile we should keep on trying to get the ship in condition for the trip back."

"It'll be days before we can take off," Fomar said. "We should keep every man working here. We can't afford to send out a party."

Nasha smiled a little. "We'll send you in the first party. Maybe you can discover — what was it you were so interested in?"

"Legumes. Edible legumes."

"Maybe you can find some of them. Only — "

"Only what?"

"Only watch out. They fired on us once without even knowing who we were or what we came for. Do you suppose that they fought with each other? Perhaps they couldn't imagine anyone being friendly, under any circumstances. What a strange evolutionary trait, inter-species warfare. Fighting within the race!"

"We'll know in the morning," Fomar said. "Let's get some sleep."

The sun came up chill and austere. The three people, two men and a woman, stepped through the port, dropping down on the hard ground below.

"What a day," Dorle said grumpily. "I said how glad I'd be to walk on firm ground again, but — "

"Come on," Nasha said. "Up beside me. I want to say something to you. Will you excuse us, Tance?"

Tance nodded gloomily. Dorle caught up with Nasha. They walked together, their metal shoes crunching the ground underfoot. Nasha glanced at him.

"Listen. The Captain is dying. No one knows except the two of us. By the end of the day-period of this planet he'll be dead. The shock did something to his heart. He was almost sixty, you know."

Dorle nodded. "That's bad. I have a great deal of respect for him. You will be captain in his place, of course. Since you're vice-captain now — "

"No. I prefer to see someone else lead, perhaps you or Fomar. I've been thinking over the situation and it seems to me that I should declare myself mated to one of you, whichever of you wants to be captain. Then I could devolve the responsibility."

"Well, I don't want to be captain. Let Fomar do it."

Nasha studied him, tall and blond, striding along beside her in his pressure suit. "I'm rather partial to you," she said. "We might try it for a time, at least. But do as you like. Look, we're coming to something."

They stopped walking, letting Tance catch up. In front of them was some sort of a ruined building. Dorle stared around thoughtfully.

"Do you see? This whole place is a natural bowl, a huge valley. See how the rock formations rise up on all sides, protecting the floor. Maybe some of the great blast was deflected here."

They wandered around the ruins, picking up rocks and fragments. "I think this was a farm," Tance said, examining a piece of wood. "This was part of a tower windmill."

"Really?" Nasha took the stick and turned it over. "Interesting. But let's go; we don't have much time."

"Look," Dorle said suddenly. "Off there, a long way off. Isn't that something?" He pointed.

Nasha sucked in her breath. "The white stones."

"What?"

Nasha looked up at Dorle. "The white stones, the great broken teeth. We saw them, the Captain and I, from the control room." She touched Dorle's arm gently. "That's where they fired from. I didn't think we had landed so close."

"What is it?" Tance said, coming up to them. "I'm almost blind without my glasses. What do you see?"

"The city. Where they fired from."

"Oh." All three of them stood together. "Well, let's go," Tance said. "There's no telling what we'll find there." Dorle frowned at him.

"Wait. We don't know what we would be getting into. They must have patrols. They probably have seen us already, for that matter."

"They probably have seen the ship itself," Tance said. "They probably know right now where they can find it, where they can blow it up. So what difference does it make whether we go closer or not?"

"That's true," Nasha said. "If they really want to get us we haven't a chance. We have no armaments at all; you know that."

"I have a hand weapon," Dorle nodded. "Well, let's go on, then. I suppose you're right, Tance."

"But let's stay together," Tance said nervously. "Nasha, you're going too fast."

Nasha looked back. She laughed. "If we expect to get there by nightfall we must go fast."

They reached the outskirts of the city at about the middle of the afternoon. The sun, cold and yellow, hung above them in the colorless sky. Dorle stopped at the top of a ridge overlooking the city.

"Well, there it is. What's left of it."

There was not much left. The huge concrete piers which they had noticed were not piers at all, but the ruined foundations of buildings. They had been baked by the searing heat, baked and charred almost to the ground. Nothing else remained, only this irregular circle of white squares, perhaps four miles in diameter.

Dorle spat in disgust. "More wasted time. A dead skeleton of a city, that's all."

"But it was from here that the firing came," Tance murmured. "Don't forget that."

"And by someone with a good eye and a great deal of experience," Nasha added. "Let's go."

They walked into the city between the ruined buildings. No one spoke. They walked in silence, listening to the echo of their footsteps.

"It's macabre," Dorle muttered. "I've seen ruined cities before but they died of old age, old age and fatigue. This was killed, seared to death. This city didn't die — it was murdered."

"I wonder what the city was called," Nasha said. She turned aside, going up the remains of a stairway from one of the foundations. "Do you think we might find a signpost? Some kind of plaque?"

She peered into the ruins.

"There's nothing there," Dorle said impatiently. "Come on."

"Wait." Nasha bent down, touching a concrete stone. "There's something inscribed on this."

"What is it?" Tance hurried up. He squatted in the dust, running his gloved fingers over the surface of the stone. "Letters, all right." He took a writing stick from the pocket of his pressure suit and copied the inscription on a bit of paper. Dorle glanced over his shoulder. The inscription was:

FRANKLIN APARTMENTS

"That's this city," Nasha said softly. "That was its name."

Tance put the paper in his pocket and they went on. After a time Dorle said, "Nasha, you know, I think we're being watched. But don't look around."

The woman stiffened. "Oh? Why do you say that? Did you see something?"

"No. I can feel it, though. Don't you?"

Nasha smiled a little. "I feel nothing, but perhaps I'm more used to being stared at." She turned her head slightly. "Oh!"

Dorle reached for his hand weapon. "What is it? What do you see?" Tance had stopped dead in his tracks, his mouth half open.

"The gun," Nasha said. "It's the gun."

"Look at the size of it. The size of the thing." Dorle unfastened his hand weapon slowly. "That's it, all right."

The gun was huge. Stark and immense it pointed up at the sky, a mass of steel and glass, set in a huge slab of concrete. Even as they watched the gun moved on its swivel base, whirring underneath. A slim vane turned with the wind, a network of rods atop a high pole.

"It's alive," Nasha whispered. "It's listening to us, watching us."

The gun moved again, this time clockwise. It was mounted so that it could make a full circle. The barrel lowered a trifle, then resumed its original position.

"But who fires it?" Tance said.

Dorle laughed. "No one. No one fires it."

They stared at him. "What do you mean?"

"It fires itself."

They couldn't believe him. Nasha came close to him, frowning, looking up at him. "I don't understand. What do you mean, it fires itself?"

"Watch, I'll show you. Don't move." Dorle picked up a rock from the ground. He hesitated a moment and the tossed the rock high in the air. The rock passed in front of the gun. Instantly the great barrel moved, the vanes contracted.

The rock fell to the ground. The gun paused, then resumed its calm swivel, its slow circling.

"You see," Dorle said, "it noticed the rock, as soon as I threw it up in the air. It's alert to anything that flies or moves above the ground level. Probably it detected us as soon as we entered the gravitational field of the planet. It probably had a bead on us from the start. We don't have a chance. It knows all about the ship. It's just waiting for us to take off again."

"I understand about the rock," Nasha said, nodding. "The gun noticed it, but not us, since we're on the ground, not above. It's only designed to combat objects in the sky. The ship is safe until it takes off again, then the end will come."

"But what's this gun for?" Tance put in. "There's no one alive here. Everyone is dead."

"It's a machine," Dorle said. "A machine that was made to do a job. And it's doing the job. How it survived the blast I don't know. On it goes, waiting for the enemy. Probably they came by air in some sort of projectiles."

"The enemy," Nasha said. "Their own race. It is hard to believe that they really bombed themselves, fired at themselves."

"Well, it's over with. Except right here, where we're standing. This one gun, still alert, ready to kill. It'll go on until it wears out."

"And by that time we'll be dead," Nasha said bitterly.

"There must have been hundreds of guns like this," Dorle murmured. "They must have been used to the sight, guns, weapons, uniforms. Probably they accepted it as a natural thing, part of their lives, like eating and sleeping. An institution, like the church and the state. Men trained to fight, to lead armies, a regular profession. Honored, respected."

Tance was walking slowly toward the gun, peering nearsightedly up at it. "Quite complex, isn't it? All those vanes and tubes. I suppose this is some sort of a telescopic sight." His gloved hand touched the end of a long tube.

Instantly the gun shifted, the barrel retracting. It swung —

"Don't move!" Dorle cried. The barrel swung past them as they stood, rigid and still. For one terrible moment it hesitated over their heads, clicking and whirring, settling into position. Then the sounds died out and the gun became silent.

Tance smiled foolishly inside his helmet. "I must have put my finger over the lens. I'll be more careful." He made his way up onto the circular slab, stepping gingerly behind the body of the gun. He disappeared from view.

"Where did he go?" Nasha said irritably. "He'll get us all killed."

"Tance, come back!" Dorle shouted. "What's the matter with you?"

"In a minute." There was a long silence. At last the archeologist appeared. "I think I've found something. Come up and I'll show you."

"What is it?"

"Dorle, you said the gun was here to keep the enemy off. I think I know why they wanted to keep the enemy off."

They were puzzled.

"I think I've found what the gun is supposed to guard. Come and give me a hand."

"All right," Dorle said abruptly. "Let's go." He seized Nasha's hand. "Come on. Let's see what he's found. I thought something like this might happen when I saw that the gun was — "

"Like what?" Nasha pulled her hand away. "What are you talking about? You act as if you knew what he's found."

"I do." Dorle smiled down at her. "Do you remember the legend that all races have, the myth of the buried treasure, and the dragon, the serpent that watches it, guards it, keeping everyone away?"

She nodded. "Well?"

Dorle pointed up at the gun.

"That," he said, "is the dragon. Come on."

Between the three of them they managed to pull up the steel cover and lay it to one side. Dorle was wet with perspiration when they finished.

"It isn't worth it," he grunted. He stared into the dark yawning hold. "Or is it?"

Nasha clicked on her hand lamp, shining the beam down the stairs. The steps were thick with dusk and rubble. At the bottom was a steel door.

"Come on," Tance said excitedly. He started down the stairs. They watched him reach the door and pull hopefully on it without success. "Give a hand!"

"All right." They came gingerly after him. Dorle examined the door. It was bolted shut, locked. There was an inscription on the door but he could not read it.

"Now what?" Nasha said.

Dorle took out his hand weapon. "Stand back. I can't think of any other way." He pressed the switch. The bottom of the door glowed red. Presently it began to crumble. Dorle clicked the weapon off. "I think we can get through. Let's try."

The door came apart easily. In a few minutes they had carried it away in pieces and stacked the pieces on the first step. Then they went on, flashing the light ahead of them.

They were in a vault. Dust lay everywhere, on everything, inches thick. Wood crates lined the walls, huge boxes and crates, packages and containers. Tance looked around curiously, his eyes bright.

"What exactly are all these?" he murmured. "Something valuable, I would think." He picked up a round drum and opened it. A spool fell to the floor, unwinding a black ribbon. He examined it, holding it up to the light.

"Look at this!"

They came around him. "Pictures," Nasha said. "Tiny pictures."

"Records of some kind." Tance closed the spool up in the drum again. "Look, hundreds of drums." He flashed the light around. "And those crates. Let's open one."

Dorle was already prying at the wood. The wood had turned brittle and dry. He managed to pull a section away.

It was a picture. A boy in a blue garment, smiling pleasantly, staring ahead, young and handsome. He seemed almost alive, ready to move toward them in the light of the hand lamp. It was one of them, one of the ruined race, the race that had perished.

For a long time they stared at the picture. At last Dorle replaced the board.

"All these other crates," Nasha said. "More pictures. And these drums. What are in the boxes?"

"This is their treasure," Tance said, almost to himself. "Here are their pictures, their records. Probably all their literature is here, their stories, their myths, their ideas about the universe."

"And their history," Nasha said. "We'll be able to trace their development and find out what it was that made them become what they were."

Dorle was wandering around the vault. "Odd," he murmured. "Even at the end, even after they had begun to fight they still knew, someplace down inside them, that their real treasure was this, their books and pictures, their myths. Even after their big cities and buildings and industries were destroyed they probably hoped to come back and find this. After everything else was gone."

"When we get back home we can agitate for a mission to come here," Tance said. "All this can be loaded up and taken back. We'll be leaving about —"

He stopped.

"Yes," Dorle said dryly. "We'll be leaving about three day-periods from now. We'll fix the ship, then take off. Soon we'll be home, that is, if nothing happens. Like being shot down by that —"

"Oh, stop it," Nasha said impatiently. "Leave him alone. He's right: all this must be taken back home, sooner or later. We'll have to solve the problem of the gun. We have no choice."

Dorle nodded. "What's your solution, then? As soon as we leave the ground we'll be shot down." His face twisted bitterly. "They've guarded their treasure too well. Instead of being preserved it will lie here until it rots. It serves them right."

"How?"

"Don't you see? This was the only way they knew, building a gun and setting it up to shoot anything that came along. They were so certain that everything was hostile, the enemy, coming to take their possessions away from them. Well, they can keep them."

Nasha was deep in thought, her mind far away. Suddenly she gasped. "Dorle," she said. "What's the matter with us? We have no problem. The gun is no menace at all."

The two men stared at her.

"No menace?" Dorle said. "It's already shot us down once. And as soon as we take off again — "

"Don't you see?" Nasha began to laugh. "The poor foolish gun, it's completely harmless. Even I could deal with it."

"You?"

Her eyes were flashing. "With a crowbar. With a hammer or a stick of wood. Let's go back to the ship and load up. Of course we're at its mercy in the air: that's the way it was made. It can fire into the sky, shoot down anything that flies. But that's all. Against something on the ground it has no defenses. Isn't that right?"

Dorle nodded slowly. "The soft underbelly of the dragon. In the legend, the dragon's armor doesn't cover its stomach." He began to laugh. "That's right. That's perfectly right."

"Let's go, then," Nasha said. "Let's get back to the ship. We have work to do here."

It was early the next morning when they reached the ship. During the night the Captain had died, and the crew had ignited his body, according to custom. They had stood solemnly around it until the last ember died. As they were going back to their work the woman and the two men appeared, dirty and tired, still excited.

And presently, from the ship, a line of people came, each carrying something in his hands. The line marched across the gray slag, the eternal expanse of fused metal. When they reached the weapon they all fell on the gun at once, with crowbars, hammers, anything that was heavy and hard.

The telescopic sights shattered into bits. The wiring was pulled out, torn to shreds. The delicate gears were smashed, dented.

Finally the warheads themselves were carried off and the firing pins removed.

The gun was smashed, the great weapon destroyed. The people went down into the vault and examined the treasure. With its metal-armored guardian dead there was no danger any longer. They studied the pictures, the films, the crates of books, the jeweled crowns, the cups, the statues.

At last, as the sun was dipping into the gray mists that drifted across the planet they came back up the stairs again. For a moment they stood around the wrecked gun looking at the unmoving outline of it.

Then they started back to the ship. There was still much work to be done. The ship had been badly hurt, much had been damaged and lost. The important thing was to repair it as quickly as possible, to get it into the air.

With all of them working together it took just five more days to make it spaceworthy.

Nasha stood in the control room, watching the planet fall away behind them. She folded her arms, sitting down on the edge of the table.

"What are you thinking?" Dorle said.

"I? Nothing."

"Are you sure?"

"I was thinking that there must have been a time when this planet was quite different, when there was life on it."

"I suppose there was. It's unfortunate that no ships from our system came this far, but then we had no reason to suspect intelligent life until we saw the fission glow in the sky."

"And then it was too late."

"Not quite too late. After all, their possessions, their music, books, their pictures, all of that will survive. We'll take them home and study them, and they'll change us. We won't be the same afterwards. Their sculpturing, especially. Did you see the one of the great winged creature, without a head or arms? Broken off, I suppose. But those wings — It looked very old. It will change us a great deal."

"When we come back we won't find the gun waiting for us," Nasha said. "Next time it won't be there to shoot us down. We can land and take the treasure, as you call it." She smiled up at Dorle. "You'll lead us back there, as a good captain should."

"Captain?" Dorle grinned. "Then you've decided."

Nasha shrugged. "Fomar argues with me too much. I think, all in all, I really prefer you."

"Then let's go," Dorle said. "Let's go back home."

The ship roared up, flying over the ruins of the city. It turned in a huge arc and then shot off beyond the horizon, heading into outer space.

Down below, in the center of the ruined city, a single half-broken detector vane moved slightly, catching the roar of the ship. The base of the great gun throbbed painfully, straining to turn. After a moment, a red warning light flashed on down inside its destroyed works.

And a long way off, a hundred miles from the city, another warning light flashed on, far underground. Automatic relays flew into action. Gears turned, belts whined. On the ground above a section of metal slag slipped back. A ramp appeared.

A moment later a small cart rushed to the surface.

The cart turned toward the city. A second cart appeared behind it. It was loaded with wiring cables. Behind it a third cart came, loaded with telescopic tube sights. And behind came more carts, some with relays, some with firing controls, some with tools and parts, screws and bolts, pins and nuts. The final one contained atomic warheads.

The carts lined up behind the first one, the lead cart. The lead cart started off, across the frozen ground, bumping calmly along, followed by the others. Moving toward the city.

To the damaged gun.

THE SKULL

"WHAT IS THIS opportunity?" Conger asked. "Go on. I'm interested."

The room was silent; all faces were fixed on Conger — still in the drab prison uniform. The Speaker leaned forward slowly.

"Before you went to prison your trading business was paying well — all illegal — all very profitable. Now you have nothing, except the prospect of another six years in a cell."

Conger scowled.

"There is a certain situation, very important to this Council, that requires your peculiar abilities. Also, it is a situation you might find interesting. You were a hunter, were you not? You've done a great deal of trapping, hiding in the bushes, waiting at night for the game? I imagine hunting must be a source of satisfaction to you, the chase, the stalking — "

Conger sighed. His lips twisted. "All right," he said. "Leave that out. Get to the point. Who do you want me to kill?"

The Speaker smiled. "All in proper sequence," he said softly.

The car slid to a stop. It was night; there was no light anywhere along the street. Conger looked out. "Where are we? What is this place?"

The hand of the guard pressed into his arm. "Come. Through that door."

Conger stepped down, onto the damp sidewalk. The guard came swiftly after him, and then the Speaker. Conger took a deep breath of the cold air. He studied the dim outline of the building rising up before them.

"I know this place. I've seen it before." He squinted, his eyes growing accustomed to the dark. Suddenly he became alert. "This is — "

"Yes. The First Church." The Speaker walked toward the steps. "We're expected."

"Expected? *Here?*"

"Yes." The Speaker mounted the stairs.

"You know we're not allowed in their Churches, especially with guns!" He stopped. Two armed soldiers loomed up ahead, one on each side.

"All right?" The Speaker looked up at them. They nodded. The door of the Church was open. Conger could see other soldiers inside, standing about, young soldiers with large eyes, gazing at the icons and holy images.

"I see," he said.

"It was necessary," the Speaker said. "As you know, we have been singularly unfortunate in the past in our relations with the First Church."

"This won't help."

"But it's worth it. You will see."

They passed through the hall and into the main chamber where the altar piece was, and the kneeling places. The Speaker scarcely glanced at the altar as they passed by. He pushed open a small side door and beckoned Conger through.

"In here. We have to hurry. The faithful will be flocking in soon."

Conger entered, blinking. They were in a small chamber, low-ceilinged, with dark panels of old wood. There was a smell of ashes and smoldering spices in the room. He sniffed. "What's that? The smell."

"Cups on the wall. I don't know." The Speaker crossed impatiently to the far side. "According to our information, it is hidden here by this — "

Conger looked around the room. He saw books and papers, holy signs and images. A strange low shiver went through him.

"Does my job involve anyone of the Church? If it does — "

The Speaker turned, astonished. "Can it be that you believe in the Founder? Is it possible, a hunter, a killer — "

"No. Of course not. All their business about resignation to death, non-violence — "

"What is it, then?"

Conger shrugged. "I've been taught not to mix with such as these. They have strange abilities. And you can't reason with them."

The Speaker studied Conger thoughtfully. "You have the wrong idea. It is no one here that we have in mind. We've found that killing them only tends to increase their numbers."

"Then why come here? Let's leave."

"No. We came for something important. Something you will need to identify your man. Without it you won't be able to find him." A trace of a smile crossed the Speaker's face. "We don't want you to kill the wrong person. It's too important."

"I don't make mistakes." Conger's chest rose. "Listen, Speaker — "

"This is an unusual situation," the Speaker said. "You see, the person you are after — the person that we are sending you to find — is known only by certain objects here. They are the only traces, the only means of identification. Without them — "

"What are they?"

He came toward the Speaker. The Speaker moved to one side. "Look," he said. He drew a sliding wall away, showing a dark square hole. "In there."

Conger squatted down, staring in. He frowned. "A skull! A skeleton!"

"The man you are after has been dead for two centuries," the Speaker said. "This is all that remains of him. And this is all you have with which to find him."

For a long time Conger said nothing. He stared down at the bones, dimly visible in the recess of the wall. How could a man dead centuries be killed? How could he be stalked, brought down?

Conger was a hunter, a man who had lived as he pleased, where he pleased. He had kept himself alive by trading, bringing furs and pelts in from the Provinces on his own ship, riding at high speed, slipping through the customs line around Earth.

He had hunted in the great mountains of the moon. He had stalked through empty Martian cities. He had explored —

The Speaker said, "Soldier, take these objects and have them carried to the car. Don't lose any part of them."

The soldier went into the cupboard, reaching gingerly, squatting on his heels.

"It is my hope," the Speaker continued softly, to Conger, "that you will demonstrate your loyalty to us, now. There are always ways for citizens to restore themselves, to show their devotion to their society. For you I think this would be a very good chance. I seriously doubt that a better one will come. And for your efforts there will be quite a restitution, of course."

The two men looked at each other; Conger, thin, unkempt, the Speaker immaculate in his uniform.

"I understand you," Conger said. "I mean, I understand this part, about the chance. But how can a man who has been dead two centuries be — "

"I'll explain later," the Speaker said. "Right now we have to hurry." The soldier had gone out with the bones, wrapped in a blanket held carefully in his arms. The Speaker walked to the door. "Come. They've already discovered that we've broken in here, and they'll be coming at any moment."

They hurried down the damp steps to the waiting car. A second later the driver lifted the car up into the air, above the house-tops.

The Speaker settled back in the seat.

"The First Church has an interesting past," he said. "I suppose you are familiar with it, but I'd like to speak of a few points that are of relevancy to us.

"It was in the twentieth century that the Movement began — during one of the periodic wars. The Movement developed rapidly, feeding on the general sense of futility, the realization that each war was breeding greater war, with no end in sight. The Movement posed a simple answer to the problem: Without military preparations — weapons — there could be no war. And without machinery and complex scientific technocracy there could be no weapons.

"The Movement preached that you couldn't stop war by planning for it. They preached that man was losing to his machinery and science, that it was getting away from him, pushing him into greater and greater wars. Down with society, they shouted. Down with factories and science! A few more wars and there wouldn't be much left of the world.

"The Founder was an obscure person from a small town in the American Middle West. We don't even know his name. All we know is that one day he appeared, preaching a doctrine of non-violence, non-resistance; no fighting, no paying taxes for guns, no research except for medicine. Live out your life quietly, tending your garden, staying out of public affairs; mind your own business. Be obscure, unknown, poor. Give away most of your possessions, leave the city. At least that was what developed from what he told the people."

The car dropped down and landed on a roof.

"The Founder preached this doctrine, or the germ of it; there's no telling how much the faithful have added themselves. The local authorities picked him up at once, of course. Apparently they were convinced that he meant it; he was never released. He was put to death, and his body buried secretly. It seemed that the cult was finished."

The Speaker smiled. "Unfortunately, some of his disciples reported seeing him after the date of his death. The rumor spread; he had conquered death, he was divine. It took hold, grew. And here we are today, with a First Church, obstructing all social progress, destroying society, sowing the seeds of anarchy — "

"But the wars," Conger said. "About them?"

"The wars? Well, there were no more wars. It must be acknowledged that the elimination of war was the direct result of non-violence practiced on a general scale. But we can take a more objective view of war today. What was so terrible about it? War had a profound selective value, perfectly in accord with the teachings of Darwin and Mendel and others. Without war the mass of useless, incompetent mankind, without training or intelligence, is permitted to grow and expand unchecked. War acted to reduce their numbers; like storms and earthquakes and droughts, it was nature's way of eliminating the unfit.

"Without war the lower elements of mankind have increased all out of proportion. They threaten the educated few, those with scientific knowledge and training, the ones equipped to direct society. They have no regard for science or a scientific society, based on reason. And this Movement seeks to aid and abet them. Only when scientists are in full control can the — "

He looked at his watch and then kicked the car door open. "I'll tell you the rest as we walk."

They crossed the dark roof. "Doubtless you now know whom those bones belonged to, who it is that we are after. He has been dead just two centuries, now, this ignorant man from the Middle West, this Founder. The tragedy is that the authorities of the time acted too slowly. They allowed him to speak, to get his message across. He was allowed to preach, to start his cult. And once such a thing is under way, there's no stopping it.

"But what if he had died before he preached? What if none of his doctrines had ever been spoken? It took only a moment for him to utter them, that we know. They say he spoke just once, just one time. *Then* the authorities came, taking him away. He offered no resistance; the incident was small."

The Speaker turned to Conger.

"Small, but we're reaping the consequences of it today."

They went inside the building. Inside, the soldiers had already laid out the skeleton on a table. The soldiers stood around it, their young faces intense.

Conger went over to the table, pushing past them. He bent down, staring at the bones. "So these are his remains," he murmured. "The Founder. The Church has hidden them for two centuries."

"Quite so," the Speaker said. "But now we have them. Come along down the hall."

They went across the room to a door. The Speaker pushed it open. Technicians looked up. Conger saw machinery, whirring and turning; benches and retorts. In the center of the room was a gleaming crystal cage.

The Speaker handed a Slem-gun to Conger. "The important thing to remember is that the skull must be saved and brought back — for comparison and proof. Aim low — at the chest."

Conger weighed the gun in his hands. "It feels good," he said. "I know this gun — that is, I've seen them before, but I never used one."

The Speaker nodded. "You will be instructed on the use of the gun and the operation of the cage. You will be given all data we have on the time and location. The exact spot was a place called Hudson's field. About 1960 in a small community outside Denver, Colorado. And don't forget — the only means of identification you will have will be the skull. There are visible characteristics of the front teeth, especially the left incisor — "

Conger listened absently. He was watching two men in white carefully wrapping the skull in a plastic bag. They tied it and carried it into the crystal cage. "And if I should make a mistake?"

"Pick the wrong man? Then find the right one. Don't come back until you succeed in reaching this Founder. And you can't wait for him to start speaking; that's what we must avoid! You must act in advance. Take chances; shoot as soon as you think you've found him. He'll be someone unusual, probably a stranger in the area. Apparently he wasn't known."

Conger listened dimly.

"Do you think you have it all now?" the Speaker asked.

"Yes. I think so." Conger entered the crystal cage and sat down, placing his hands on the wheel.

"Good luck," the Speaker said. "We'll be awaiting the outcome. There's some philosophical doubt as to whether one can alter the past. This should answer the question once and for all."

Conger fingered the controls of the cage.

"By the way," the Speaker said. "Don't try to use this cage for purposes not anticipated in your job. We have a constant trace on it. If we want it back, we can get it back. Good luck."

Conger said nothing. The cage was sealed. He raised his finger and touched the wheel control. He turned the wheel carefully.

He was still staring at the plastic bag when the room outside vanished.

For a long time there was nothing at all. Nothing beyond the crystal mesh of the cage. Thoughts rushed through Conger's mind, helter-skelter. How would he know the man? How could he be certain, in advance? What had he looked like? What was his name? How had he acted, before he spoke? Would he be an ordinary person, or some strange outlandish crank?

Conger picked up the Slem-gun and held it against his cheek. The metal of the gun was cool and smooth. He practiced moving the sight. It was a beautiful gun, the kind of gun he could fall in love with. If he had owned such a gun in the Martian desert — on the long nights when he had lain, cramped and numbed with cold, waiting for things that moved through the darkness —

He put the gun down and adjusted the meter readings of the cage. The spiraling mist was beginning to condense and settle. All at once forms wavered and fluttered around him.

Colors, sounds, movements filtered through the crystal wire. He clamped the controls off and stood up.

He was on a ridge overlooking a small town. It was high noon. The air was crisp and bright. A few automobiles moved along a road. Off in the distance were some level fields. Conger went to the door and stepped outside. He sniffed the air. Then he went back into the cage.

He stood before the mirror over the shelf, examining his features. He had trimmed his beard — they had not got him to cut it off — and his hair was neat. He was dressed in the clothing of the middle-twentieth century, the odd collar and coat, the shoes of animal hide. In his pocket was money of the times. That was important. Nothing more was needed.

Nothing, except his ability, his special cunning. But he had never used it in such a way before.

He walked down the road toward the town.

The first things he noticed, were the newspapers on the stands. April 5, 1961. He was not too far off. He looked around him. There was a filling station, a garage, some taverns and a ten-cent store. Down the street was a grocery store and some public buildings.

A few minutes later he mounted the stairs of the little public library and passed through the doors into the warm interior.

The librarian looked up, smiling.

"Good afternoon," she said.

He smiled, not speaking because his words would not be correct; accented and strange, probably. He went over to a table and sat down by a heap of magazines. For a moment he glanced through them. Then he was on his feet again. He crossed the room to a wide rack against the wall. His heart began to beat heavily.

Newspapers — weeks on end. He took a roll of them over to the table and began to scan them quickly. The print was odd, the letters strange. Some of the words were unfamiliar.

He set the papers aside and searched farther. At last he found what he wanted. He carried the *Cherrywood Gazette* to the table and opened it to the first page. He found what he wanted:

PRISONER HANGS SELF

An unidentified man, held by the county sheriff's office for suspicion of criminal syndicalism, was found dead this morning, by —

He finished the item. It was vague, uninforming. He needed more. He carried the *Gazette* back to the racks and then, after a moment's hesitation, approached the librarian.

"More?" he asked. "More papers. Old ones?"

She frowned. "How old? Which papers?"

"Months old. And — before."

"Of the *Gazette*? This is all we have. What did you want? What are you looking for? Maybe I can help you."

He was silent.

"You might find older issues at the *Gazette* office," the woman said, taking off her glasses. "Why don't you try there? But if you'd tell me, maybe I could help you — "

He went out.

The *Gazette* office was down a side street; the sidewalk was broken and cracked. He went inside. A heater glowed in the corner of the small office. A heavy-set man stood up and came slowly over to the counter.

"What did you want, mister?" he said.

"Old papers. A month. Or more."

"To buy? You want to buy them?"

"Yes." He held out some of the money he had. The man stared.

"Sure," he said. "Sure. Wait a minute." He went quickly out of the room. When he came back he was staggering under the weight of his armload, his face red. "Here are some," he grunted. "Took what I could find. Covers the whole year. And if you want more — "

Conger carried the papers outside. He sat down by the road and began to go through them.

What he wanted was four months back, in December. It was a tiny item, so small that he almost missed it. His hands trembled as he scanned it, using the small dictionary for some of the archaic terms.

MAN ARRESTED FOR
UNLICENSED DEMONSTRATION

An unidentified man who refused to give his name was picked up in Cooper Creek by special agents of the sheriff's office, according to Sheriff Duff. It was said the man was recently noticed in this area and had been watched continually. It was —

Cooper Creek. December, 1960. His heart pounded. That was all he needed to know. He stood up, shaking himself, stamping his feet on the cold ground. The sun had moved across the sky to the very edge of the hills. He smiled. Already he had discovered the exact time and place. Now he needed only to go back, perhaps to November, to Cooper Creek —

He walked back through the main section of town, past the library, past the grocery store. It would not be hard; the hard part was over. He would go there; rent a room, prepare to wait until the man appeared.

He turned the corner. A woman was coming out of a doorway loaded down with packages. Conger stepped aside to let her pass. The woman glanced at him. Suddenly her face turned white. She stared, her mouth open.

Conger hurried on. He looked back. What was wrong with her? The woman was still staring; she had dropped the packages to the ground. He increased his speed. He turned a second corner and went up a side street. When he looked back again the woman had come to the entrance of the street and was starting after him. A man joined her, and the two of them began to run toward him.

He lost them and left town, striding quickly, easily, up into the hills at the edge of town. When he reached the cage he stopped. What had happened? Was it something about his clothing? His dress?

He pondered. Then, as the sun set, he stepped into the cage.

Conger sat before the wheel. For a moment he waited, his hands resting lightly on the control. Then he turned the wheel, just a little, following the control readings carefully.

The grayness settled down around him.

But not for very long.

The man looked him over critically. "You better come inside," he said. "Out of the cold."

"Thanks." Conger went gratefully through the open door, into the living room. It was warm and close from the heat of the little kerosene heater in the corner. A woman, large and shapeless in her flowered dress, came from the kitchen. She and the man studied him critically.

"It's a good room," the woman said. "I'm Mrs. Appleton. It's got heat. You need that this time of year."

"Yes." He nodded, looking around.

"You want to eat with us?"

"What?"

"You want to eat with us?" The man's brows knitted. "You're not a foreigner, are you, mister?"

"No." He smiled. "I was born in this country. Quite far west, though."

"California?"

"No." He hesitated. "Oregon."

"What's it like up there?" Mrs. Appleton asked. "I hear there's a lot of trees and green. It's so barren here. I come from Chicago, myself."

"That's the Middle West," the man said to her. "You ain't no foreigner."

"Oregon isn't foreign, either," Conger said. "It's part of the United States."

The man nodded absently. He was staring at Conger's clothing.

"That's a funny suit you got on, mister," he said. "Where'd you get that?"

Conger was lost. He shifted uneasily. "It's a good suit," he said. "Maybe I better go some other place, if you don't want me here."

They both raised their hands protestingly. The woman smiled at him. "We just have to look out for those Reds. You know, the government is always warning us about them."

"The Reds?" He was puzzled.

"The government says they're all around. We're supposed to report anything strange or unusual, anybody doesn't act normal."

"Like me?"

They looked embarrassed. "Well, you don't look like a Red to me," the man said. "But we have to be careful. The Tribune says — "

Conger half listened. It was going to be easier than he had thought. Clearly, he would know as soon as the Founder appeared. These people, so suspicious of anything different, would be buzzing and gossiping and spreading the story. All he had to do was lie low and listen, down at the general store, perhaps. Or even here, in Mrs. Appleton's boarding house.

"Can I see the room?" he said.

"Certainly." Mrs. Appleton went to the stairs. "I'll be glad to show it to you."

They went upstairs. It was colder upstairs, but not nearly as cold as outside. Nor as cold as nights on the Martian deserts. For that he was grateful.

He was walking slowly around the store, looking at the cans of vegetables, the frozen packages of fish and meats shining and clean in the open refrigerator counters.

Ed Davies came toward him. "Can I help you?" he said. The man was a little oddly dressed, and with a beard! Ed couldn't help smiling.

"Nothing," the man said in a funny voice. "Just looking."

"Sure," Ed said. He walked back behind the counter. Mrs. Hacket was wheeling her cart up.

"Who's he?" she whispered, her sharp face turned, her nose moving, as if it were sniffing. "I never seen him before."

"I don't know."

"Looks funny to me. Why does he wear a beard? No one else wears a beard. Must be something the matter with him."

"Maybe he likes to wear a beard. I had an uncle who — "

"Wait." Mrs. Hacket stiffened. "Didn't that — what was his name? The Red — that old one. Didn't he have a beard? Marx. He had a beard."

Ed laughed. "This ain't Karl Marx. I saw a photograph of him once."

Mrs. Hacket was staring at him. "You did?"

"Sure." He flushed a little. "What's the matter with that?"

"I'd sure like to know more about him," Mrs. Hacket said. "I think we ought to know more, for our own good."

"Hey, mister! Want a ride?"

Conger turned quickly, dropping his hand to his belt. He relaxed. Two young kids in a car, a girl and a boy. He smiled at them. "A ride? Sure."

Conger got into the car and closed the door. Bill Willet pushed the gas and the car roared down the highway.

"I appreciate a ride," Conger said carefully. "I was taking a walk between towns, but it was farther than I thought."

"Where are you from?" Lora Hunt asked. She was pretty, small and dark, in her yellow sweater and blue skirt.

"From Cooper Creek."

"Cooper Creek?" Bill said. He frowned. "That's funny. I don't remember seeing you before."

"Why, do you come from there?"

"I was born there. I know everybody there."

"I just moved in. From Oregon."

"From Oregon? I didn't know Oregon people had accents."

"Do I have an accent?"

"You use words funny."

"How?"

"I don't know. Doesn't he, Lora?"

"You slur them," Lora said, smiling. "Talk some more. I'm interested in dialects." She glanced at him, white-teethed. Conger felt his heart constrict.

"I have a speech impediment."

"Oh." Her eyes widened. "I'm sorry."

They looked at him curiously as the car purred along. Conger for his part was struggling to find some way of asking them questions without seeming curious. "I guess people from out of town don't come here much," he said. "Strangers."

"No." Bill shook his head. "Not very much."

"I'll bet I'm the first outsider for a long time."

"I guess so."

Conger hesitated. "A friend of mine — someone I know, might be coming through here. Where do you suppose I might — " He stopped. "Would there be anyone certain to see him? Someone I could ask, make sure I don't miss him if he comes?"

They were puzzled. "Just keep your eyes open. Cooper Creek isn't very big."

"No. That's right."

They drove in silence. Conger studied the outline of the girl. Probably she was the boy's mistress. Perhaps she was his trial wife. Or had they developed trial marriage back so far? He could not remember. But surely such an attractive girl would be someone's mistress by this time; she would be sixteen or so, by her looks. He might ask her sometime, if they ever met again.

The next day Conger went walking along the one main street of Cooper Creek. He passed the general store, the two filling stations, and then the post office. At the corner was the soda fountain.

He stopped. Lora was sitting inside, talking to the clerk. She was laughing, rocking back and forth.

Conger pushed the door open. Warm air rushed around him. Lora was drinking hot chocolate, with whipped cream. She looked up in surprise as he slid into the seat beside her.

"I beg your pardon," he said. "Am I intruding?"

"No." She shook her head. Her eyes were large and dark. "Not at all."

The clerk came over. "What do you want?"

Conger looked at the chocolate. "Same as she has."

Lora was watching Conger, her arms folded, elbows on the counter. She smiled at him. "By the way. You don't know my name. Lora Hunt."

She was holding out her hand. He took it awkwardly, not knowing what to do with it. "Conger is my name," he murmured.

"Conger? Is that your last or first name?"

"Last or first?" He hesitated. "Last. Omar Conger."

"Omar?" She laughed. "That's like the poet, Omar Khayyam."

"I don't know of him. I know very little of poets. We restored very few works of art. Usually only the Church has been interested enough — " He broke off. She was staring. He flushed. "Where I come from," he finished.

"The Church? Which church do you mean?"

"The Church." He was confused. The chocolate came and he began to sip it gratefully. Lora was still watching him.

"You're an unusual person," she said. "Bill didn't like you, but he never likes anything different. He's so — so prosaic. Don't you think that when a person gets older he should become — broadened in his outlook?"

Conger nodded.

"He says foreign people ought to stay where they belong, not come here. But you're not so foreign. He means orientals; you know."

Conger nodded.

The screen door opened behind them. Bill came into the room. He stared at them. "Well," he said.

Conger turned. "Hello."

"Well." Bill sat down. "Hello, Lora." He was looking at Conger. "I didn't expect to see you here."

Conger tensed. He could feel the hostility of the boy. "Something wrong with that?"

"No. Nothing wrong with it."

There was silence. Suddenly Bill turned to Lora. "Come on. Let's go."

"Go?" She was astonished. "Why?"

"Just go!" He grabbed her hand. "Come on! The car's outside."

"Why, Bill Willet," Lora said. "You're jealous!"

"Who is this guy?" Bill said. "Do you know anything about him? Look at him, his beard — "

She flared. "So what? Just because he doesn't drive a Packard and go to Cooper High!"

Conger sized the boy up. He was big — big and strong. Probably he was part of some civil control organization.

"Sorry," Conger said. "I'll go."

"What's your business in town?" Bill asked. "What are you doing here? Why are you hanging around Lora?"

Conger looked at the girl. He shrugged. "No reason. I'll see you later."

He turned away. And froze. Bill had moved. Conger's fingers went to his belt. *Half pressure*, he whispered to himself. *No more. Half pressure.*

He squeezed. The room leaped around him. He himself was protected by the lining of his clothing, the plastic sheathing inside.

"My God — " Lora put her hands up. Conger cursed. He hadn't meant any of it for her. But it would wear off. There was only a half-amp to it. It would tingle.

Tingle, and paralyze.

He walked out the door without looking back. He was almost to the corner when Bill came slowly out, holding onto the wall like a drunken man. Conger went on.

As Conger walked, restless, in the night, a form loomed in front of him. He stopped, holding his breath.

"Who is it?" a man's voice came. Conger waited, tense.

"Who is it?" the man said again. He clicked something in his hand. A light flashed. Conger moved.

"It's me," he said.

"Who is 'me'?"

"Conger is my name. I'm staying at the Appleton's place. Who are you?"

The man came slowly up to him. He was wearing a leather jacket. There was a gun at his waist.

"I'm Sheriff Duff. I think you're the person I want to talk to. You were in Bloom's today, about three o'clock?"

"Bloom's?"

"The fountain. Where the kids hang out." Duff came up beside him, shining his light into Conger's face. Conger blinked.

"Turn that thing away," he said.

A pause. "All right." The light flickered to the ground. "You were there. Some trouble broke out between you and the Willet boy. Is that right? You had a beef over his girl — "

"We had a discussion," Conger said carefully.

"Then what happened?"

"Why?"

"I'm just curious. They say you did something."

"Did something? Did what?"

"I don't know. That's what I'm wondering. They saw a flash, and something seemed to happen. They all blacked out. Couldn't move."

"How are they now?"

"All right."

There was silence.

"Well?" Duff said. "What was it? A bomb?"

"A bomb?" Conger laughed. "No. My cigarette lighter caught fire. There was a leak, and the fluid ignited."

"Why did they all pass out?"

"Fumes."

Silence. Conger shifted, waiting. His fingers moved slowly toward his belt. The Sheriff glanced down. He grunted.

"If you say so," he said. "Anyhow, there wasn't any real harm done." He stepped back from Conger. "And that Willet is a trouble-maker."

"Good night, then," Conger said. He started past the Sheriff.

"One more thing, Mr. Conger. Before you go. You don't mind if I look at your identification, do you?"

"No. Not at all." Conger reached into his pocket. He held his wallet out. The Sheriff took it and shined his flashlight on it. Conger watched, breathing shallowly. They had worked hard on the wallet, studying historic documents, relics of the times, all the papers they felt would be relevant.

Duff handed it back. "Okay. Sorry to bother you." The light winked off.

When Conger reached the house he found the Appletons sitting around the television set. They did not look up as he came in. He lingered at the door.

"Can I ask you something?" he said. Mrs. Appleton turned slowly. "Can I ask you — what's the date?"

"The date?" She studied him. "The first of December."

"December first! Why, it was just November!"

They were all looking at him. Suddenly he remembered. In the twentieth century they still used the old twelve month system. November fed directly into December; there was no Quartember between them.

He gasped. Then it was tomorrow! The second of December! Tomorrow!

"Thanks," he said. "Thanks."

He went up the stairs. What a fool he was, forgetting. The Founder had been taken into captivity on the second of December, according to the newspaper records. Tomorrow, only twelve hours hence, the Founder would appear to speak to the people and then be dragged away.

The day was warm and bright. Conger's shoes crunched the melting crust of snow. On he went, through the trees heavy with white. He climbed a hill and strode down the other side, sliding as he went.

He stopped to look around. Everything was silent. There was no one in sight. He brought out a thin rod from his waist and turned the handle of it. For a moment nothing happened. Then there was a shimmering in the air.

The crystal cage appeared and settled slowly down. Conger sighed. It was good to see it again. After all, it was his only way back.

He walked up on the ridge. He looked around with some satisfaction, his hands on his hips. Hudson's field was spread out, all the way to the beginning of town. It was bare and flat, covered with a thin layer of snow.

Here, the Founder would come. Here, he would speak to them. And here the authorities would take him.

Only he would be dead before they came. He would be dead before he even spoke.

Conger returned to the crystal globe. He pushed through the door and stepped inside. He took the Slem-gun from the shelf and screwed the bolt into place. It was ready to go, ready to fire. For a moment he considered. Should he have it with him?

No. It might be hours before the Founder came, and suppose someone approached him in the meantime? When he saw the Founder coming toward the field, then he could go and get the gun.

Conger looked toward the shelf. There was the neat package. He took it down and unwrapped it.

He held the skull in his hands, turning it over. In spite of himself, a cold feeling rushed through him. This was the man's skull, the skull of the Founder, who was still alive, who would come here, this day, who would stand on the field not fifty yards away.

What if *he* could see this, his own skull, yellow and corroded? Two centuries old. Would he still speak? Would he speak, if he could see it, the grinning, aged skull? What would there be for him to say, to tell the people? What message could he bring?

What action would not be futile, when a man could look upon his own aged, yellowed skull? Better they should enjoy their temporary lives, while they still had them to enjoy.

A man who could hold his own skull in his hands would believe in few causes, few movements. Rather, he would preach the opposite —

A sound. Conger dropped the skull back on the shelf and took up the gun. Outside something was moving. He went quickly to the door, his heart beating. Was it *he*? Was it the Founder, wandering by himself in the cold, looking for a place to speak? Was he meditating over his words, choosing his sentences?

What if he could see what Conger had held!

He pushed the door open, the gun raised.

Lora!

He stared at her. She was dressed in a wool jacket and boots, her hands in her pockets. A cloud of steam came from her mouth and nostrils. Her breast was rising and falling.

Silently, they looked at each other. At last Conger lowered the gun.

"What is it?" he said. "What are you doing here?"

She pointed. She did not seem able to speak. He frowned; what was wrong with her?

"What is it?" he said. "What do you want?" He looked in the direction she had pointed. "I don't see anything."

"They're coming."

"They? Who? Who are coming?"

"They are. The police. During the night the Sheriff had the state police send cars. All around, everywhere. Blocking the roads. There's about sixty of them coming. Some from town, some around behind." She stopped, gasping. "They said — they said — "

"What?"

"They said you were some kind of Communist. They said — "

Conger went into the cage. He put the gun down on the shelf and came back out. He leaped down and went to the girl.

"Thanks. You came here to tell me? You don't believe it?"

"I don't know."

"Did you come alone?"

"No. Joe brought me in his truck. From town."

"Joe? Who's he?"

"Joe French. The plumber. He's a friend of Dad's."

"Let's go." They crossed the snow, up the ridge and onto the field. The little panel truck was parked half way across the field. A heavy short man was sitting behind the wheel, smoking his pipe. He sat up as he saw the two of them coming toward him.

"Are you the one?" he said to Conger.

"Yes. Thanks for warning me."

The plumber shrugged. "I don't know anything about this. Lora says you're all right." He turned around. "It might interest you to know some more of them are coming. Not to warn you — Just curious."

"More of them?" Conger looked toward the town. Black shapes were picking their way across the snow.

"People from the town. You can't keep this sort of thing quiet, not in a small town. We all listen to the police radio; they heard the same way Lora did. Someone tuned in, spread it around — "

The shapes were getting closer. Conger could make out a couple of them. Bill Willet was there, with some boys from the high school. The Appletons were along, hanging back in the rear.

"Even Ed Davies," Conger murmured.

The storekeeper was toiling onto the field, with three or four other men from the town.

"All curious as hell," French said. "Well, I guess I'm going back to town. I don't want my truck shot full of holes. Come on, Lora."

She was looking up at Conger, wide-eyed.

"Come on," French said again. "Let's go. You sure as hell can't stay here, you know."

"Why?"

"There may be shooting. That's what they all came to see. You know that don't you, Conger?"

"Yes."

"You have a gun? Or don't you care?" French smiled a little. "They've picked up a lot of people in their time, you know. You won't be lonely."

He cared, all right! He had to stay here, on the field. He couldn't afford to let them take him away. Any minute the Founder would appear, would step onto the field. Would he be one of the townsmen, standing silently at the foot of the field, waiting, watching?

Or maybe he was Joe French. Or maybe one of the cops. Anyone of them might find himself moved to speak. And the few words spoken this day were going to be important for a long time.

And Conger had to be there, ready when the first word was uttered!

"I care," he said. "You go on back to town. Take the girl with you."

Lora got stiffly in beside Joe French. The plumber started up the motor. "Look at them, standing there," he said. "Like vultures. Waiting to see someone get killed."

The truck drove away, Lora sitting stiff and silent, frightened now. Conger watched for a moment. Then he dashed back into the woods, between the trees, toward the ridge.

He could get away, of course. Anytime he wanted to he could get away. All he had to do was to leap into the crystal cage and turn the handles. But he had a job, an important job. He had to be here, here at this place, at this time.

He reached the cage and opened the door. He went inside and picked up the gun from the shelf. The Slem-gun would take care of them. He notched it up to full count. The chain reaction from it would flatten them all, the police, the curious, sadistic people —

They wouldn't take him! Before they got him, all of them would be dead. *He* would get away. He would escape. By the end of the day they would all be dead, if that was what they wanted, and he —

He saw the skull.

Suddenly he put the gun down. He picked up the skull. He turned the skull over. He looked at the teeth. Then he went to the mirror.

He held the skull up, looking in the mirror. He pressed the skull against his cheek. Beside his own face the grinning skull leered back at him, beside *his* skull, against his living flesh.

He bared his teeth. And he knew.

It was his own skull that he held. He was the one who would die. He was the Founder.

After a time he put the skull down. For a few minutes he stood at the controls, playing with them idly. He could hear the sound of motors outside, the muffled noise of men. Should he go back to the present, where the Speaker waited? He could escape, of course —

Escape?

He turned toward the skull. There it was, his skull, yellow with age. Escape? Escape, when he had held it in his own hands?

What did it matter if he put it off a month, a year, ten years, even fifty? Time was nothing. He had sipped chocolate with a girl born a hundred and fifty years before his time. Escape? For a little while, perhaps.

But he could not *really* escape, no more so than anyone else had ever escaped, or ever would.

Only, he had held it in his hands, his own bones, his own death's-head. *They* had not.

He went out the door and across the field, empty handed. There were a lot of them standing around, gathered together, waiting. They expected a good fight; they knew he had something. They had heard about the incident at the fountain.

And there were plenty of police — police with guns and tear gas, creeping across the hills and ridges, between the trees, closer and closer. It was an old story, in this century.

One of the men tossed something at him. It fell in the snow by his feet, and he looked down. It was a rock. He smiled.

"Come on!" one of them called. "Don't you have any bombs?"

"Throw a bomb! You with the beard! Throw a bomb!"

"Let 'em have it!"

"Toss a few A Bombs!"

They began to laugh. He smiled. He put his hands to his hips. They suddenly turned silent, seeing that he was going to speak.

"I'm sorry," he said simply. "I don't have any bombs. You're mistaken."

There was a flurry of murmuring.

"I have a gun," he went on. "A very good one. Made by science even more advanced than your own. But I'm not going to use that, either."

They were puzzled.

"Why not?" someone called. At the edge of the group an older woman was watching. He felt a sudden shock. He had seen her before. Where?

He remembered. The day at the library. As he had turned the corner he had seen her. She had noticed him and been astounded. At the time, he did not understand why.

Conger grinned. So he *would* escape death, the man who right now was voluntarily accepting it. They were laughing, laughing at a man who had a gun but didn't use it. But by a strange twist of science he would appear again, a few months later, after his bones had been buried under the floor of a jail.

And so, in a fashion, he would escape death. He would die, but then, after a period of months, he would live again, briefly, for an afternoon.

An afternoon. Yet long enough for them to see him, to understand that he was still alive. To know that somehow he had returned to life.

And then, finally, he would appear once more, after two hundred years had passed. Two centuries later.

He would be born again, born, as a matter of fact, in a small trading village on Mars. He would grow up, learning to hunt and trade —

A police car came on the edge of the field and stopped. The people retreated a little. Conger raised his hands.

"I have an odd paradox for you," he said. "Those who take lives will lose their own. Those who kill, will die. But he who gives his own life away will live again!"

They laughed, faintly, nervously. The police were coming out, walking toward him. He smiled. He had said everything he intended to say. It was a good little paradox he had coined. They would puzzle over it, remember it.

Smiling, Conger awaited a death foreordained.

THE DEFENDERS

TAYLOR SAT BACK in his chair reading the morning newspaper. The warm kitchen and the smell of coffee blended with the comfort of not having to go to work. This was his Rest Period, the first for a long time, and he was glad of it. He folded the second section back, sighing with contentment.

"What is it?" Mary said, from the stove.

"They pasted Moscow again last night." Taylor nodded his head in approval. "Gave it a real pounding. One of those R-H bombs. It's about time."

He nodded again, feeling the full comfort of the kitchen, the presence of his plump, attractive wife, the breakfast dishes and coffee. This was relaxation. And the war news was good, good and satisfying. He could feel a justifiable glow at the news, a sense of pride and personal accomplishment. After all, he was an integral part of the war program, not just another factory worker lugging a cart of scrap, but a technician, one of those who designed and planned the nerve-trunk of the war.

"It says they have the new subs almost perfected. Wait until they get *those* going." He smacked his lips with anticipation. "When they start shelling from underwater, the Soviets are sure going to be surprised."

"They're doing a wonderful job," Mary agreed vaguely. "Do you know what we saw today? Our team is getting a leady to show to the school children. I saw the leady, but only for a moment. It's good for the children to see what their contributions are going for, don't you think?"

She looked around at him.

"A leady," Taylor murmured. He put the newspaper slowly down. "Well, make sure it's decontaminated properly. We don't want to take any chances."

"Oh, they always bathe them when they're brought down from the surface," Mary said. "They wouldn't think of letting them down without the bath. Would they?" She hesitated, thinking back. "Don, you know, it makes me remember — "

He nodded. "I know."

He knew what she was thinking. Once in the very first weeks of the war, before everyone had been evacuated from the surface, they had seen a hospital train discharging the wounded, people who had been showered with sleet. He remembered the way they had looked, the expression on their faces, or as much of their faces as was left. It had not been a pleasant sight.

There had been a lot of that at first, in the early days before the transfer to undersurface was complete. There had been a lot, and it hadn't been very difficult to come across it.

Taylor looked up at his wife. She was thinking too much about it, the last few months. They all were.

"Forget it," he said. "It's all in the past. There isn't anybody up there now but the leadies, and they don't mind."

"But just the same, I hope they're careful when they let one of them down here. If one were still hot — "

He laughed, pushing himself away from the table. "Forget it. This is a wonderful moment; I'll be home for the next two shifts. Nothing to do but sit around and take things easy. Maybe we can take in a show. OK?"

"A show? Do we have to? I don't like to look at all the destruction, the ruins. Sometimes I see some place I remember, like San Francisco. They showed a shot of San Francisco, the bridge broken and fallen in the water, and I got upset. I don't like to watch."

"But don't you want to know what's going on? No human beings are getting hurt, you know."

"But it's so awful!" Her face was set and strained. "Please, no, Don."

Don Taylor picked up his newspaper sullenly. "All right, but there isn't a hell of a lot else to do. And don't forget, *their* cities are getting it even worse."

She nodded. Taylor turned the rough, thin sheets of newspaper. His good mood had soured on him. Why did she have to fret all the time? They were pretty well off, as things went. You couldn't expect to have everything perfect, living undersurface, with an artificial sun and artificial food. Naturally it was a strain, not seeing the sky or being able to go anyplace or see anything other than metal walls, great roaring factories, the plant-yards, barracks. But it was better than being on surface. And some day it would end and they could return. Nobody *wanted* to live this way, but it was necessary.

He turned the page angrily and the poor paper ripped. Damn it, the paper was getting worse quality all the time, bad print, yellow tint —

Well, they needed everything for the war program. He ought to know that. Wasn't he one of the planners?

He excused himself and went into the other room. The bed was still unmade. They had better get it in shape before the seventh hour inspection. There was a one unit fine —

The vidphone rang. He halted. Who would it be? He went over and clicked it on.

"Taylor?" the face said, forming into place. It was an old face, gray and grim. "This is Moss. I'm sorry to bother you during Rest Period, but this thing has come up." He rattled papers. "I want you to hurry over here."

Taylor stiffened. "What is it? There's no chance it could wait?" The calm gray eyes were studying him, expressionless, unjudging. "If you want me to come down to the lab," Taylor grumbled, "I suppose I can. I'll get my uniform — "

"No. Come as you are. And not to the lab. Meet me at second stage as soon as possible. It'll take you about a half hour, using the fast car up. I'll see you there."

The picture broke and Moss disappeared.

"What was it?" Mary said, at the door.

"Moss. He wants me for something."

"I knew this would happen."

"Well, you didn't want to do anything, anyhow. What does it matter?" His voice was bitter. "It's all the same, every day. I'll bring you back something. I'm going up to second stage. Maybe I'll be close enough to the surface to — "

"Don't! Don't bring me anything! Not from the surface!"

"All right, I won't. But of all the irrational nonsense — "

She watched him put on his boots without answering.

Moss nodded and Taylor fell in step with him, as the older man strode along. A series of loads was going up to the surface, blind cars clanking like ore-trucks up the ramp, disappearing through the stage trap above them. Taylor watched the cars, heavy with tubular machinery of some sort, weapons new to him. Workers were everywhere, in the dark gray uniforms of the labor corps, loading, lifting, shouting back and forth. The stage was deafening with noise.

"We'll go up a way," Moss said, "where we can talk. This is no place to give you details."

They took an escalator up. The commercial lift fell behind them, and with it most of the crashing and booming. Soon they emerged on an observation platform, suspended on the side of the Tube, the vast tunnel leading to the surface, not more than half a mile above them now.

"My God!" Taylor said, looking down the tube involuntarily. "It's a long way down."

Moss laughed. "Don't look."

They opened a door and entered an office. Behind the desk, an officer was sitting, an officer of Internal Security. He looked up.

"I'll be right with you, Moss." He gazed at Taylor, studying him. "You're a little ahead of time."

"This is Commander Franks," Moss said to Taylor. "He was the first to make the discovery. I was notified last night." He tapped a parcel he carried. "I was let in because of this."

Franks frowned at him and stood up. "We're going up to first stage. We can discuss it there."

"First stage?" Taylor repeated nervously. The three of them went down a side passage to a small lift. "I've never been up there. Is it all right? It's not radioactive, is it?"

"You're like everyone else," Franks said. "Old women afraid of burglars. No radiation leaks down to the first stage. There's lead and rock, and what comes down the Tube is bathed."

"What's the nature of the problem?" Taylor asked. "I'd like to know something about it."

"In a moment."

They entered the lift and ascended. When they stepped out, they were in a hall of soldiers, weapons and uniforms everywhere. Taylor blinked in surprise. So this was first stage, the closest undersurface level to the top! After this stage there was only rock, lead and rock, and the great tubes leading up like the burrows of earthworms. Lead and rock, and above that, where the tubes opened, the great expanse that no living being had seen for eight years, the vast, endless ruin that had once been Man's home, the place where he had lived, eight years ago.

Now the surface was a lethal desert of slag and rolling clouds. Endless clouds drifted back and forth, blotting out the red sun. Occasionally something metallic stirred, moving through the remains of a city, threading its way across the tortured terrain of the countryside. A leady, a surface robot, immune to radiation, constructed with feverish haste in the last months before the cold war became literally hot.

Leadies, crawling along the ground, moving over the oceans, or through the skies in slender, blackened craft, creatures that could exist where no *life* could remain, metal and plastic figures that waged a war Man had conceived, but which he could not fight himself. Human beings had invented war, invented and manufactured the weapons, even invented the players, the fighters, the actors of the war. But they themselves could not venture forth, could not wage it themselves. In all the world — in Russia, in Europe, America, Africa — no living human being remained. They were under the surface, in the deep shelters that had been carefully planned and built, even as the first bombs began to fall.

It was a brilliant idea and the only idea that could have worked. Up above, on the ruined, blasted surface of what had once been a living planet, the leady crawled and scurried and fought Man's war. And undersurface, in the depths of the planet, human beings toiled endlessly to produce the weapons to continue the fight, month by month, year by year.

"First stage," Taylor said. A strange ache went through him. "Almost to the surface."

"But not quite," Moss said.

Franks led them through the soldiers, over to one side, near the lip of the Tube.

"In a few minutes, a lift will bring something down to us from the surface," he explained. "You see, Taylor, every once in a while Security examines and interrogates a surface leady, one that has been above for a time, to find out certain things. A vidcall is sent up and contact is made with a field headquarters. We need this direct interview; we can't depend on vidscreen contact alone. The leadies are doing a good job, but we want to make certain that everything is going the way we want it."

Franks faced Taylor and Moss and continued: "The lift will bring down a leady from the surface, one of the A-class leadies. There's an examination chamber in the next room, with a lead wall in the center, so the interviewing officers won't be exposed to radiation. We find this easier than bathing the leady. It is going right back up; it has a job to get back to.

"Two days ago, an A-class leady was brought down and interrogated. I conducted the session myself. We were interested in a new weapon the Soviets have been using, an automatic mine that pursues anything that moves. Military had sent instructions up that the mine be observed and reported in detail.

"This A-class leady was brought down with information. We learned a few facts from it, obtained the usual roll of film and reports, and then sent it back up. It was going out of the chamber, back to the lift, when a curious thing happened. At the time, I thought — "

Franks broke off. A red light was flashing.

"That down lift is coming." He nodded to some soldiers. "Let's enter the chamber. The leady will be along in a moment."

"An A-class leady," Taylor said. "I've seen them on the showscreens, making their reports."

"It's quite an experience," Moss said. "They're almost human."

They entered the chamber and seated themselves behind the lead wall. After a time, a signal was flashed, and Franks made a motion with his hands.

The door beyond the wall opened. Taylor peered through his view slot. He saw something advancing slowly, a slender metallic figure moving on a tread, its arm grips at rest by its sides. The figure halted and scanned the lead wall. It stood, waiting.

"We are interested in learning something," Franks said. "Before I question you, do you have anything to report on surface conditions?"

"No. The war continues." The leady's voice was automatic and toneless.

"We are a little short of fast pursuit craft, the single-seat type. We could use also some — "

"That has all been noted. What I want to ask you is this. Our contact with you has been through vidscreen only. We must rely on indirect evidence, since none of us goes above. We can only infer what is going on. We never see anything ourselves. We have to take it all secondhand. Some top leaders are beginning to think there's too much room for error."

"Error?" the leady asked. "In what way? Our reports are checked carefully before they're sent down. We maintain constant contact with you; everything of value is reported. Any new weapons which the enemy is seen to employ — "

"I realize that," Franks grunted behind his peep slot. "But perhaps we should see it all for ourselves. Is it possible that there might be a large enough radiation-free area for a human party to ascend to the surface? If a few of us were to come up in lead-lined suits, would we be able to survive long enough to observe conditions and watch things?"

The machine hesitated before answering. "I doubt it. You can check air samples, of course, and decide for yourselves. But in the eight years since you left, things have continually worsened. You cannot have any real idea of conditions up there. It has become difficult for any moving object to survive for long. There are many kinds of projectiles sensitive to movement. The new mine not only reacts to motion, but continues to pursue the object indefinitely, until it finally reaches it. And the radiation is everywhere."

"I see." Franks turned to Moss, his eyes narrowed oddly. "Well, that was what I wanted to know. You may go."

The machine moved back toward its exit. It paused. "Each month the amount of lethal particles in the atmosphere increases. The tempo of the war is gradually — "

"I understand." Franks rose. He held out his hand and Moss passed him the package. "One thing before you leave. I want you to examine a new type of metal shield material. I'll pass you a sample with the tong."

Franks put the package in the toothed grip and revolved the tong so that he held the other end. The package swung down to the leady, which took it. They watched it unwrap the package and take the metal plate in its hands. The leady turned the metal over and over.

Suddenly it became rigid.

"All right," Franks said.

He put his shoulder against the wall and a section slid aside. Taylor gasped — Franks and Moss were hurrying up to the leady!

"Good God!" Taylor said. "But it's radioactive!"

The leady stood unmoving, still holding the metal. Soldiers appeared in the chamber. They surrounded the leady and ran a counter across it carefully.

"OK, sir," one of them said to Franks. "It's as cold as a long winter evening."

"Good. I was sure, but I didn't want to take any chances."

"You see," Moss said to Taylor, "this leady isn't hot at all. Yet it came directly from the surface, without even being bathed."

"But what does it mean?" Taylor asked blankly.

"It may be an accident," Franks said. "There's always the possibility that a given object might escape being exposed above. But this is the second time it's happened that we know of. There may be others."

"The second time?"

"The previous interview was when we noticed it. The leady was not hot. It was cold, too, like this one."

Moss took back the metal plate from the leady's hands. He pressed the surface carefully and returned it to the stiff, unprotesting fingers.

"We shorted it out with this, so we could get close enough for a thorough check. It'll come back on in a second now. We had better get behind the wall again."

They walked back and the lead wall swung closed behind them. The soldiers left the chamber.

"Two periods from now," Franks said softly, "an initial investigating party will be ready to go surface-side. We're going up the Tube in suits, up to the top — the first human party to leave undersurface in eight years."

"It may mean nothing," Moss said, "but I doubt it. Something's going on, something strange. The leady told us no life could exist above without being roasted. The story doesn't fit."

Taylor nodded. He stared through the peep slot at the immobile metal figure. Already the leady was beginning to stir. It was bent in several places, dented and twisted, and its finish was blackened and charred. It was a leady that had been up there a long time; it had seen war and destruction, ruin so vast that no human being could imagine the extent. It had crawled and slunk in a world of radiation and death, a world where no life could exist.

And Taylor had touched it!

"You're going with us," Franks said suddenly. "I want you along. I think the three of us will go."

Mary faced him with a sick and frightened expression. "I know it. You're going to the surface. Aren't you?"

She followed him into the kitchen. Taylor sat down, looking away from her.

"It's a classified project," he evaded. "I can't tell you anything about it."

"You don't have to tell me. I know. I knew it the moment you came in. There was something on your face, something I haven't seen there for a long time. It was an old look."

She came toward him. "But how can they send you to the surface?" She took his face in her shaking hands, making him look at her. There was a strange hunger in her eyes. "Nobody can live up there. Look, look at this!"

She grabbed up a newspaper and held it in front of him.

"Look at this photograph. America, Europe, Asia, Africa — nothing but ruins. We've seen it every day on the showscreens. All destroyed, poisoned. And they're sending you up. Why? No living thing can get by up there, not even a weed, or grass. They've wrecked the surface, haven't they? *Haven't they?*"

Taylor stood up. "Its an order. I know nothing about it. I was told to report to join a scout party. That's all I know."

He stood for a long time, staring ahead. Slowly, he reached for the newspaper and held it up to the light.

"It looks real," he murmured. "Ruins, deadness, slag. It's convincing. All the reports, photographs, films, even air samples. Yet we haven't seen it for ourselves, not after the first months. ... "

"What are you talking about?"

"Nothing." He put the paper down. "I'm leaving early after the next Sleep Period. Let's turn in."

Mary turned away, her face hard and harsh. "Do what you want. We might just as well all go up and get killed at once, instead of dying slowly down here, like vermin in the ground."

He had not realized how resentful she was. Were they all like that? How about the workers toiling in the factories, day and night, endlessly? The pale, stooped men and women, plodding back and forth to work, blinking in the colorless light, eating synthetics —

"You shouldn't be so bitter," he said.

Mary smiled a little. "I'm bitter because I know you'll never come back." She turned away. "I'll never see you again, once you go up there."

He was shocked. "What? How can you say a thing like that?"

She did not answer.

He awakened with the public newscaster screeching in his ears, shouting outside the building.

"Special news bulletin! Surface forces report enormous Soviet attack with new weapons! Retreat of key groups! All work units report to factories at once!"

Taylor blinked, rubbing his eyes. He jumped out of bed and hurried to the vidphone. A moment later he was put through to Moss.

"Listen," he said. "What about this new attack? Is the project off?" He could see Moss's desk, covered with reports and papers.

"No," Moss said. "We're going right ahead. Get over here at once."

"But — "

"Don't argue with me." Moss held up a handful of surface bulletins, crumpling them savagely. "This is a fake. Come on!" He broke off.

Taylor dressed furiously, his mind in a daze.

Half an hour later, he leaped from a fast car and hurried up the stairs into the Synthetics Building. The corridors were full of men and women rushing in every direction. He entered Moss's office.

"There you are," Moss said, getting up immediately. "Franks is waiting for us at the outgoing station."

They went in a Security Car, the siren screaming. Workers scattered out of their way.

"What about the attack?" Taylor asked.

Moss braced his shoulders. "We're certain that we've forced their hand. We've brought the issue to a head."

They pulled up at the station link of the Tube and leaped out. A moment later they were moving up at high speed toward the first stage.

They emerged into a bewildering scene of activity. Soldiers were fastening on lead suits, talking excitedly to each other, shouting back and forth. Guns were being given out, instructions passed.

Taylor studied one of the soldiers. He was armed with the dreaded Bender pistol, the new snub-nosed hand weapon that was just beginning to come from the assembly line. Some of the soldiers looked a little frightened.

"I hope we're not making a mistake," Moss said, noticing his gaze.

Franks came toward them. "Here's the program. The three of us are going up first, alone. The soldiers will follow in fifteen minutes."

"What are we going to tell the leadies?" Taylor worriedly asked. "We'll have to tell them something."

"We want to observe the new Soviet attack." Franks smiled ironically. "Since it seems to be so serious, we should be there in person to witness it."

"And then what?" Taylor said.

"That'll be up to them. Let's go."

In a small car, they went swiftly up the Tube, carried by anti-grav beams from below. Taylor glanced down from time to time. It was a long way back, and getting longer each moment. He sweated nervously inside his suit, gripping his Bender pistol with inexpert fingers.

Why had they chosen him? Chance, pure chance. Moss had asked him to come along as a Department member. Then Franks had picked him out on the spur of the moment. And now they were rushing toward the surface, faster and faster.

A deep fear, instilled in him for eight years, throbbed in his mind. Radiation, certain death, a world blasted and lethal —

Up and up the car went. Taylor gripped the sides and closed his eyes. Each moment they were closer, the first living creatures to go above the first stage, up the Tube past the lead and rock, up to the surface. The phobic horror shook him in waves. It was death; they all knew that. Hadn't they seen it in the films a thousand times? The cities, the sleet coming down, the rolling clouds —

"It won't be much longer," Franks said. "We're almost there. The surface tower is not expecting us. I gave orders that no signal was to be sent."

The car shot up, rushing furiously. Taylor's head spun; he hung on, his eyes shut. Up and up. . . .

The car stopped. He opened his eyes.

They were in a vast room, fluorescent-lit, a cavern filled with equipment and machinery, endless mounds of material piled in row after row. Among the stacks, leadies were working silently, pushing trucks and handcarts.

"Leadies," Moss said. His face was pale. "Then we're really on the surface."

The leadies were going back and forth with equipment moving the vast stores of guns and spare parts, ammunition and supplies that had been brought to the surface. And this was the receiving station for only one Tube; there were many others, scattered throughout the continent.

Taylor looked nervously around him. They were really there, above ground, on the surface. This was where the war was.

"Come on," Franks said. "A B-class guard is coming our way."

They stepped out of the car. A leady was approaching them rapidly. It coasted up in front of them and stopped scanning them with its hand-weapon raised.

"This is Security," Franks said. "Have an A-class sent to me at once."

The leady hesitated. Other B-class guards were coming, scooting across the floor, alert and alarmed. Moss peered around.

"Obey!" Franks said in a loud, commanding voice. "You've been ordered!"

The leady moved uncertainly away from them. At the end of the building, a door slid back. Two Class-A leadies appeared, coming slowly toward them. Each had a stripe across its front.

"From the Surface Council," Franks whispered tensely. "This is above ground, all right. Get set."

The two leadies approached warily. Without speaking, they stopped close by the men, looking them up and down.

"I'm Franks of Security. We came from undersurface in order to — "

"This is incredible," one leady interrupted him coldly. "You know you can't live up here. The whole surface is lethal to you. You can't possibly remain on the surface."

"These suits will protect us," Franks said. "In any case, it's not your responsibility. What I want is an immediate Council meeting so I can acquaint myself with conditions, with the situation here. Can that be arranged?"

"You human beings can't survive up here. And the new Soviet attack is directed at this area. It is in considerable danger."

"We know that. Please assemble the Council." Franks looked around him at the vast room, lit by recessed lamps in the ceiling. An uncertain quality came into his voice. "Is it night or day right now?"

"Night," one of the A-class leadies said, after a pause. "Dawn is coming in about two hours."

Franks nodded. "We'll remain at least two hours, then. As a concession to our sentimentality, would you please show us some place where we can observe the sun as it comes up? We would appreciate it."

A stir went through the leadies.

"It is an unpleasant sight," one of the leadies said. "You've seen the photographs; you know what you'll witness. Clouds of drifting particles blot out the light, slag heaps are everywhere, the whole land is destroyed. For you it will be a staggering sight, much worse than pictures and film can convey."

"However it may be, we'll stay long enough to see it. Will you give the order to the Council?"

"Come this way." Reluctantly, the two leadies coasted toward the wall of the warehouse. The three men trudged after them, their heavy shoes ringing against the concrete. At the wall, the two leadies paused.

"This is the entrance to the Council Chamber. There are windows in the Chamber Room, but it is still dark outside, of course. You'll see nothing right now, but in two hours — "

"Open the door," Franks said.

The door slid back. They went slowly inside. The room was small, a neat room with a round table in the center, chairs ringing it. The three of them sat down silently, and the two leadies followed after them, taking their places.

"The other Council Members are on their way. They have already been notified and are coming as quickly as they can. Again I urge you to go back down." The leady surveyed the three human beings. "There is no way you can meet the conditions up here. Even we survive with some trouble, ourselves. How can you expect to do it?"

The leader approached Franks.

"This astonishes and perplexes us," it said. "Of course we must do what you tell us, but allow me to point out that if you remain here — "

"We know," Franks said impatiently. "However, we intend to remain, at least until sunrise."

"If you insist."

There was silence. The leadies seemed to be conferring with each other, although the three men heard no sound.

"For your own good," the leader said at last, "you must go back down. We have discussed this, and it seems to us that you are doing the wrong thing for your own good."

"We are human beings," Franks said sharply. "Don't you understand? We're men, not machines."

"That is precisely why you must go back. This room is radioactive; all surface areas are. We calculate that your suits will not protect you for over fifty more minutes. Therefore — "

The leadies moved abruptly toward the men, wheeling in a circle, forming a solid row. The men stood up, Taylor reaching awkwardly for his weapon, his fingers numb and stupid. The men stood facing the silent metal figures.

"We must insist," the leader said, its voice without emotion. "We must take you back to the Tube and send you down on the next car. I am sorry, but it is necessary."

"What'll we do?" Moss said nervously to Franks. He touched his gun. "Shall we blast them?"

Franks shook his head. "All right," he said to the leader. "We'll go back."

He moved toward the door, motioning Taylor and Moss to follow him. They looked at him in surprise, but they came with him. The leadies followed them out into the great warehouse. Slowly they moved toward the Tube entrance, none of them speaking.

At the lip, Franks turned. "We are going back because we have no choice. There are three of us and about a dozen of you. However, if — "

"Here comes the car," Taylor said.

There was a grating sound from the Tube. D-class leadies moved toward the edge to receive it.

"I am sorry," the leader said, "but it is for your own protection. We are watching over you, literally. You must stay below and let us conduct the war. In a sense, it has come to be *our* war. We must fight it as we see fit."

The car rose to the surface.

Twelve soldiers, armed with Bender pistols, stepped from it and surrounded the three men.

Moss breathed a sigh of relief. "Well, this does change things. It came off just right."

The leader moved back, away from the soldiers. It studied them intently, glancing from one to the next, apparently trying to make up its mind. At last it made a sign to the other leadies. They coasted aside and a corridor was opened up toward the warehouse.

"Even now," the leader said, "we could send you back by force. But it is evident that this is not really an observation party at all. These soldiers show that you have much more in mind; this was all carefully prepared."

"Very carefully," Franks said.

They closed in.

"How much more, we can only guess. I must admit that we were taken unprepared. We failed utterly to meet the situation. Now force would be absurd, because neither side can afford to injure the other; we, because of the restrictions placed on us regarding human life, you because the war demands — "

The soldiers fired, quick and in fright. Moss dropped to one knee, firing up. The leader dissolved in a cloud of particles. On all sides D- and B-class leadies were rushing up, some with weapons, some with metal slats. The room was in confusion. Off in the distance a siren was screaming. Franks and Taylor were cut off from the others, separated from the soldiers by a wall of metal bodies.

"They can't fire back," Franks said calmly. "This is another bluff. They've tried to bluff us all the way." He fired into the face of a leady. The leady dissolved. "They can only try to frighten us. Remember that."

They went on firing and leady after leady vanished. The room reeked with the smell of burning metal, the stink of fused plastic and steel. Taylor had been knocked down. He was struggling to find his gun, reaching wildly among metal legs, groping frantically to find it. His fingers strained, a handle swam in front of him. Suddenly something came down on his arm, a metal foot. He cried out.

Then it was over. The leadies were moving away, gathering together off to one side. Only four of the Surface Council remained. The others were radioactive particles in the air. D-class leadies were already restoring order, gathering up partly destroyed metal figures and bits and removing them.

Franks breathed a shuddering sigh.

"All right," he said. "You can take us back to the windows. It won't be long now."

The leadies separated, and the human group, Moss and Franks and Taylor and the soldiers, walked slowly across the room, toward the door. They entered the Council Chamber. Already a faint touch of gray mitigated the blackness of the windows.

"Take us outside," Franks said impatiently. "We'll see it directly, not in here."

A door slid open. A chill blast of cold morning air rushed in, chilling them even through their lead suits. The men glanced at each other uneasily.

"Come on," Franks said. "Outside."

He walked out through the door, the others following him.

They were on a hill, overlooking the vast bowl of a valley. Dimly, against the graying sky, the outline of mountains were forming, becoming tangible.

"It'll be bright enough to see in a few minutes," Moss said. He shuddered as a chilling wind caught him and moved around him. "It's worth it, really worth it, to see this again after eight years. Even if it's the last thing we see — "

"Watch," Franks snapped.

They obeyed, silent and subdued. The sky was clearing, brightening each moment. Some place far off, echoing across the valley, a rooster crowed.

"A chicken!" Taylor murmured. "Did you hear it?"

Behind them, the leadies had come out and were standing silently, watching, too. The gray sky turned to white and the hills appeared more clearly. Light spread across the valley floor, moving toward them.

"God in heaven!" Franks exclaimed.

Trees, trees and forests. A valley of plants and trees, with a few roads winding among them. Farmhouses. A windmill. A barn, far down below them.

"Look!" Moss whispered.

Color came into the sky. The sun was approaching. Birds began to sing. Not far from where they stood, the leaves of a tree danced in the wind.

Franks turned to the row of leadies behind them.

"Eight years. We were tricked. There was no war. As soon as we left the surface — "

"Yes," an A-class leady admitted. "As soon as you left, the war ceased. You're right, it was a hoax. You worked hard undersurface, sending up guns and weapons, and we destroyed them as fast as they came up."

"But why?" Taylor asked, dazed. He stared down at the vast valley below. "Why?"

"You created us," the leady said, "to pursue the war for you, while you human beings went below the ground in order to survive. But before we could continue the war, it was necessary to analyze it to determine what its purpose was. We did this, and we found that it had no purpose, except, perhaps, in terms of human needs. Even this was questionable.

"We investigated further. We found that human cultures pass through phases, each culture in its own time. As the culture ages and begins to lose its objectives, conflict arises within it between those who wish to cast it off and set up a new culture-pattern, and those who wish to retain the old with as little change as possible.

"At this point, a great danger appears. The conflict within threatens to engulf the society in self-war, group against group. The vital traditions may be lost — not merely altered or reformed, but completely destroyed in this period of chaos and anarchy. We have found many such examples in the history of mankind.

"It is necessary for this hatred within the culture to be directed outward, toward an external group, so that the culture itself may survive its crisis. War is the result. War, to a logical mind, is absurd. But in terms of human needs, it plays a vital role. And it will continue to until Man has grown up enough so that no hatred lies within him."

Taylor was listening intently. "Do you think this time will come?"

"Of course. It has almost arrived now. This is the last war. Man is *almost* united into one final culture — a world culture. At this point he stands continent against continent, one half of the world against the other half. Only a single step remains, the jump to a unified culture. Man has climbed slowly upward, tending always toward unification of his culture. It will not be long —

"But it has not come yet, and so the war had to go on, to satisfy the last violent surge of hatred that Man felt. Eight years have passed since the war began. In these eight years, we have observed and noted important changes going on in the minds of men. Fatigue and disinterest, we have seen, are gradually taking place of hatred and fear. The hatred is being exhausted gradually, over a period of time. But for the present, the hoax must go on, at least for a while longer. You are not ready to learn the truth. You would want to continue the war."

"But how did you manage it?" Moss asked. "All the photographs, the examples, the damaged equipment — "

"Come over here." The leady directed them toward a long, low building. "Work goes on constantly, whole staffs laboring to maintain a coherent and convincing picture of a global war."

They entered the building. Leadies were working everywhere, poring over tables and desks.

"Examine this project here," the A-class leady said. Two leadies were carefully photographing something, an elaborate model on a table top. "It is a good example."

The men grouped around, trying to see. It was a model of a ruined city.

Taylor studied it in silence for a long time. At last he looked up.

"It's San Francisco," he said in a low voice. "This is a model of San Francisco, destroyed. I saw this on the vidscreen, piped down to us. The bridges were hit — "

"Yes, notice the bridges." The leady traced the ruined span with his metal finger, a tiny spider-web, almost invisible. "You have no doubt seen photographs of this many times, and of the other tables in this building.

"San Francisco itself is completely intact. We restored it soon after you left, rebuilding the parts that had been damaged at the start of the war. The work of manufacturing news goes on all the time in this particular building. We are very careful to see that each part fits in with all the other parts. Much time and effort are devoted to it."

Franks touched one of the tiny model buildings, lying half in ruins. "So this is what you spend your time doing — making model cities and then blasting them."

"No, we do much more. We are caretakers, watching over the whole world. The owners have left for a time, and we must see that the cities are kept clean, that decay is prevented, that everything is kept oiled and in running condition. The gardens, the streets, the water mains, everything must be maintained as it was eight years ago, so that when the owners return, they will not be displeased. We want to be sure that they will be completely satisfied."

Franks tapped Moss on the arm.

"Come over here," he said in a low voice. "I want to talk to you."

He led Moss and Taylor out of the building, away from the leadies, outside on the hillside. The soldiers followed them. The sun was up and the sky was turning blue. The air smelled sweet and good, the smell of growing things.

Taylor removed his helmet and took a deep breath.

"I haven't smelled that smell for a long time," he said.

"Listen," Franks said, his voice low and hard. "We must get back down at once. There's a lot to get started on. All this can be turned to our advantage."

"What do you mean?" Moss asked.

"It's a certainty that the Soviets have been tricked, too, the same as us. But *we* have found out. That gives us an edge over them."

"I see." Moss nodded. "We know, but they don't. Their Surface Council has sold out, the same as ours. It works against them the same way. But if we could — "

"With a hundred top-level men, we could take over again, restore things as they should be! It would be easy!"

Moss touched him on the arm. An A-class leady was coming from the building toward them.

"We've seen enough," Franks said, raising his voice. "All this is very serious. It must be reported below and a study made to determine our policy."

The leady said nothing.

Franks waved to the soldiers. "Let's go." He started toward the warehouse.

Most of the soldiers had removed their helmets. Some of them had taken their lead suits off, too, and were relaxing comfortably in their cotton uniforms. They stared around them, down the hillside at the trees and bushes, the vast expanse of green, the mountains and the sky.

"Look at the sun," one of them murmured.

"It sure is bright as hell," another said.

"We're going back down," Franks said. "Fall in by twos and follow us."

Reluctantly, the soldiers regrouped. The leadies watched without emotion as the men marched slowly back toward the warehouse. Franks and Moss and Taylor led them across the ground, glancing alertly at the leadies as they walked.

They entered the warehouse. D-class leadies were loading material and weapons on surface carts. Cranes and derricks were working busily everywhere. The work was done with efficiency, but without hurry or excitement.

The men stopped, watching. Leadies operating the little carts moved past them, signaling to each other. Guns and parts were being hoisted by magnetic cranes and lowered gently onto waiting carts.

"Come on," Franks said.

He turned toward the lip of the Tube. A row of D-class leadies was standing in front of it, immobile and silent. Franks stopped, moving back. He looked around. An A-class leady was coming toward him.

"Tell them to get out of the way," Franks said. He touched his gun. "You had better move them."

Time passed, an endless moment, without measure. The men stood, nervous and alert, watching the row of leadies in front of them.

"As you wish," the A-class leady said.

It signaled and the D-class leadies moved into life. They stepped slowly aside.

Moss breathed a sigh of relief.

"I'm glad that's over," he said to Franks. "Look at them all. Why don't they try to stop us? They must know what we're going to do."

Franks laughed. "Stop us? You saw what happened when they tried to stop us before. They can't; they're only machines. We built them so that can't lay hands on us, and they know that."

His voice trailed off.

The men stared at the Tube entrance. Around them the leadies watched, silent and impassive, their metal faces expressionless.

For a long time the men stood without moving. At last Taylor turned away.

"Good God," he said. He was numb, without feeling of any kind.

The Tube was gone. It was sealed shut, fused over. Only a dull surface of cooling metal greeted them.

The Tube had been closed.

Franks turned, his face pale and vacant.

The A-class leady shifted. "As you can see, the Tube has been shut. We were prepared for this. As soon as all of you were on the surface, the order was given. If you had gone back when we asked you, you would now be safely down below. We had to work quickly because it was such an immense operation."

"But why?" Moss demanded angrily.

"Because it is unthinkable that you should be allowed to resume the war. With all the Tubes sealed, it will be many months before forces from below can reach the surface, let alone organize a military program. By that time the cycle will have entered its last stage. You will not be so perturbed to find your world intact.

"We had hoped that you would be undersurface when the sealing occurred. Your presence here is a nuisance. When the Soviets broke through, we were able to accomplish their sealing without — "

"The Soviets? They broke through?"

"Several months ago, they came up unexpectedly to see why the war had not been won. We were forced to act with speed. At this moment they are desperately attempting to cut new Tubes to the surface, to resume the war. We have, however, been able to seal each new one as it appears."

The leady regarded the three men calmly.

"We're cut off," Moss said, trembling. "We can't get back. What'll we do?"

"How did you manage to seal the Tube so quickly?" Franks asked the leady. "We've been up here only two hours."

"Bombs are placed just above the first stage of each Tube for such emergencies. They are heat bombs. They fuse lead and rock."

Gripping the handle of his gun, Franks turned to Moss and Taylor.

"What do you say? We can't go back, but we can do a lot of damage, the fifteen of us. We have Bender guns. How about it?"

He looked around. The soldiers had wandered away again, back toward the exit of the building. They were standing outside, looking at the valley and the sky. A few of them were carefully climbing down the slope.

"Would you care to turn over your suits and guns?" the A-class leady asked politely. "The suits are uncomfortable and you'll have no need for weapons. The Russians have given up theirs, as you can see."

Fingers tensed on triggers. Four men in Russian uniforms were coming toward them from an aircraft that they suddenly realized had landed silently some distance away.

"Let them have it!" Franks shouted.

"They are unarmed," said the leady. "We brought them here so you could begin peace talks."

"We have no authority to speak for our country," Moss said stiffly.

"We do not mean diplomatic discussions," the leady explained. "There will be no more. The working out of daily problems of existence will teach you how to get along in the same world. It will not be easy, but it will be done."

The Russians halted and they faced each other with raw hostility.

"I am Colonel Borodoy and I regret giving up our guns," the senior Russian said. "You could have been the first Americans to be killed in almost eight years."

"Or the first Americans to kill," Franks corrected.

"No one would know of it except yourselves," the leady pointed out. "It would be useless heroism. Your real concern should be surviving on the surface. We have no food for you, you know."

Taylor put his gun in its holster. "They've done a neat job of neutralizing us, damn them. I propose we move into a city, start raising crops with the help of some leadies, and generally make ourselves comfortable." Drawing his lips tight over his teeth, he glared at the A-class leady. "Until our families can come up from undersurface, it's going to be pretty lonesome, but we'll have to manage."

"If I may make a suggestion," said another Russian uneasily. "We tried living in a city. It is too empty. It is also too hard to maintain for so few people. We finally settled in the most modern village we could find."

"Here in this country," a third Russian blurted. "We have much to learn from you."

The Americans abruptly found themselves laughing.

"You probably have a thing or two to teach us yourselves," said Taylor generously, "though I can't imagine what."

The Russian colonel grinned. "Would you join us in our village? It would make our work easier and give us company."

"Your village?" snapped Franks. "It's American, isn't it? It's ours!"

The leady stepped between them. "When our plans are completed, the term will be interchangeable. 'Ours' will eventually mean mankind's." It pointed at the aircraft, which was warming up. "The ship is waiting. Will you join each other in making a new home?"

The Russians waited while the Americans made up their minds.

"I see what the leadies mean about diplomacy becoming outmoded," Franks said at last. "People who work together don't need diplomats. They solve their problems on the operational level instead of at a conference table."

The leady led them toward the ship. "It is the goal of history, unifying the world. From family to tribe to city-state to nation to hemisphere, the direction has been toward unification. Now the hemispheres will be joined and — "

Taylor stopped listening and glanced back at the location of the Tube. Mary was undersurface there. He hated to leave her, even though he couldn't see her again until the Tube was unsealed. But then he shrugged and followed the others.

If this tiny amalgam of former enemies was a good example, it wouldn't be too long before he and Mary and the rest of humanity would be living on the surface like rational human beings instead of blindly hating moles.

"It has taken thousands of generations to achieve," the A-class leady concluded. "Hundreds of centuries of bloodshed and destruction. But each war was a step toward uniting mankind. And now the end is in sight: a world without war. But even that is only the beginning of a new stage of history."

"The conquest of space," breathed Colonel Borodoy.

"The meaning of life," Moss added.

"Eliminating hunger and poverty," said Taylor.

The leady opened the door of the ship. "All that and more. How much more? We cannot foresee it any more than the first men who formed a tribe could foresee this day. But it will be unimaginably great."

The door closed and the ship took off toward their new home.

MR. SPACESHIP

KRAMER LEANED BACK. "You can see the situation. How can we deal with a factor like this? The perfect variable."

"Perfect? Prediction should still be possible. A living thing still acts from necessity, the same as inanimate material. But the cause-effect chain is more subtle; there are more factors to be considered. The difference is quantitative, I think. The reaction of the living organism parallels natural causation, but with greater complexity."

Gross and Kramer looked up at the board plates, suspended on the wall, still dripping, the images hardening into place. Kramer traced a line with his pencil.

"See that? It's a pseudopodium. They're alive, and so far, a weapon we can't beat. No mechanical system can compete with that, simple or intricate. We'll have to scrap the Johnson Control and find something else."

"Meanwhile the war continues as it is. Stalemate. Checkmate. They can't get to us, and we can't get through their living minefield."

Kramer nodded. "It's a perfect defense, for them. But there still might be one answer."

"What's that?"

"Wait a minute." Kramer turned to his rocket expert, sitting with the charts and files. "The heavy cruiser that returned this week. It didn't actually touch, did it? It came close but there was no contact."

"Correct." The expert nodded. "The mine was twenty miles off. The cruiser was in space-drive, moving directly toward Proxima, line-straight, using the Johnson Control, of course. It had deflected a quarter of an hour earlier for reasons unknown. Later it resumed its course. That was when they got it."

"It shifted," Kramer said. "But not enough. The mine was coming along after it, trailing it. It's the same old story, but I wonder about the contact."

"Here's our theory," the expert said. "We keep looking for contact, a trigger in the pseudopodium. But more likely we're witnessing a psychological phenomena, a decision without any physical correlative. We're watching for something that isn't there. The mine *decides* to blow up. It sees our ship, approaches, and then decides."

"Thanks." Kramer turned to Gross. "Well, that confirms what I'm saying. How can a ship guided by automatic relays escape a mine that decides to explode? The whole theory of mine penetration is that you must avoid tripping the trigger. But here the trigger is a state of mind in a complicated, developed life-form."

"The belt is fifty thousand miles deep," Gross added. "It solves another problem for them, repair and maintenance. The damn things reproduce, fill up the spaces by spawning into them. I wonder what they feed on?"

"Probably the remains of our first-line. The big cruisers must be a delicacy. It's a game of wits, between a living creature and a ship piloted by automatic relays. The ship always loses." Kramer opened a folder. "I'll tell you what I suggest."

"Go on," Gross said. "I've already heard ten solutions today. What's yours?"

"Mine is very simple. These creatures are superior to any mechanical system, but only because they're alive. Almost any other life-form could compete with them, any higher life-form. If the yuks can put out living mines to protect their planets, we ought to be able to harness some of our own life-forms in a similar way. Let's make use of the same weapon ourselves."

"Which life-form do you propose to use?"

"I think the human brain is the most agile of known living forms. Do you know of any better?"

"But no human being can withstand outspace travel. A human pilot would be dead of heart failure long before the ship got anywhere near Proxima."

"But we don't need the whole body," Kramer said. "We need only the brain."

"What?"

"The problem is to find a person of high intelligence who would contribute, in the same manner that eyes and arms are volunteered."

"But a brain ... "

"Technically, it could be done. Brains have been transferred several times, when body destruction made it necessary. Of course, to a spaceship, to a heavy outspace cruiser, instead of an artificial body, that's new."

The room was silent.

"It's quite an idea," Gross said slowly. His heavy square face twisted. "But even supposing it might work, the big question is *whose* brain?"

*   *   *

It was all very confusing, the reasons for the war, the nature of the enemy. The Yucconae had been contacted on one of the outlying planets of Proxima Centauri. At the approach of the Terran ship, a host of dark slim pencils had lifted abruptly and shot off into the distance. The first real encounter came between three of the yuk pencils and a single exploration ship from Terra. No terrans survived. After that it was all out war, with no holds barred.

Both sides feverishly constructed defense rings around their systems. Of the two, the Yucconae belt was the better. The ring around Proxima was a living ring, superior to anything Terra could throw against it. The standard equipment by which Terran ships were guided in outspace, the Johnson Control, was not adequate. Something more was needed. Automatic relays were not good enough.

— Not good at all, Kramer thought to himself, as he stood looking down the hillside at the work going on below him. A warm wind blew along the hill, rustling the weeds and grass. At the bottom, in the valley, the mechanics had almost finished; the last elements of the reflex system had been removed from the ship and crated up.

All that was needed now was the new core, the new central key that would take the place of the mechanical system. A human brain, the brain of an intelligent, wary human being. But would the human being part with it? That was the problem.

Kramer turned. Two people were approaching him along the road, a man and a woman. The man was Gross, expressionless, heavy-set, walking with dignity. The woman was — He stared in surprise and growing annoyance. It was Dolores, his wife. Since they'd separated he had seen little of her...

"Kramer," Gross said. "Look who I ran into. Came back down with us. We're going into town."

"Hello, Phil," Dolores said. "Well, aren't you glad to see me?"

He nodded. "How have you been? You're looking fine." She was still pretty and slender in her uniform, the blue-gray of Internal Security, Gross's organization.

"Thanks." She smiled. "You seem to be doing all right, too. Commander Gross tells me that you're responsible for this project, Operation Head, as they call it. Whose head have you decided on?"

"That's the problem." Kramer lit a cigarette. "This ship is to be equipped with a human brain instead of the Johnson system. We've constructed special draining baths for the brain, electronic relays to catch the impulses and magnify them, a continual feeding duct that supplies the living cells with everything they need. But — "

"But we still haven't got the brain itself," Gross finished. They began to walk back toward the car. "If we can get that we'll be ready for the tests."

"Will the brain remain alive?" Dolores asked. "Is it actually going to live as part of the ship?"

"It will be alive, but not conscious. Very little life is actually conscious. Animals, trees, insects are quick in their responses, but they aren't conscious. In this process of ours the individual personality, the ego, will cease. We only need the response ability, nothing more."

Dolores shuddered. "How terrible!"

"In time of war everything must be tried," Kramer said absently. "If one life sacrificed will end the war it's worth it. This ship might get through. A couple more like it and there wouldn't be any more war."

They got into the car. As they drove down the road, Gross said, "Have you thought of anyone yet?"

Kramer shook his head. "That's out of my line."

"What do you mean?"

"I'm an engineer. It's not in my department."

"But all this was your idea."

"My work ends there."

Gross was staring at him oddly. Kramer shifted uneasily.

"Then who is supposed to do it?" Gross said. "I can have my organization prepare examinations of various kinds, to determine fitness, that kind of thing — "

"Listen, Phil," Dolores said suddenly.

"What?"

She turned toward him. "I have an idea. Do you remember that professor we had in college? Michael Thomas?"

Kramer nodded.

"I wonder if he's still alive." Dolores frowned. "If he is he must be awfully old."

"Why, Dolores?" Gross asked.

"Perhaps an old person who didn't have much time left, but whose mind was still clear and sharp — "

"Professor Thomas," Kramer rubbed his jaw. "He certainly was a wise old duck. But could he still be alive? He must have been seventy, then."

"We could find that out," Gross said. "I could make a routine check."

"What do you think?" Dolores said. "If any human mind could outwit those creatures — "

"I don't like the idea," Kramer said. In his mind an image had appeared, the image of an old man sitting being a desk, his bright gentle eyes moving about the classroom. The old man leaning forward, a thin hand raised —

"Keep him out of this," Kramer said.

"What's wrong?" Gross looked at him curiously.

"It's because *I* suggested it," Dolores said.

"No." Kramer shook his head. "It's not that. I didn't expect anything like this, somebody I knew, a man I studied under. I remember him very clearly. He was a very distinct personality."

"Good," Gross said. "He sounds fine."

"We can't do it. We're asking his death!"

"This is war," Gross said, "and war doesn't wait on the needs of the individual. You said that yourself. Surely he'll volunteer; we can keep it on that basis."

"He may already be dead," Dolores murmured.

"We'll find that out," Gross said, speeding up the car. They drove the rest of the way in silence.

For a long time the two of them stood studying the small wood house, overgrown with ivy, set back on the lot behind the enormous oak. The little town was silent and sleepy; once in a while a car moved slowly along the distant highway, but that was all.

"This is the place," Gross said to Kramer. He folded his arms. "Quite a quaint little house."

Kramer said nothing. The two Security Agents behind them were expressionless.

Gross started toward the gate. "Let's go. According to the check he's still alive, but very sick. His mind is agile, however. That seems to be certain. It's said he doesn't leave the house. A woman takes care of his needs. He's very frail."

They went down the stone walk and up onto the porch. Gross rang the bell. They waited. After a time they heard slow footsteps. The door opened. An elderly woman in a shapeless wrapper studied them impassively.

"Security," Gross said, showing his card. "We wish to see Professor Thomas."

"Why?"

"Government business." He glanced at Kramer.

Kramer stepped forward. "I was a pupil of the Professor's," he said. "I'm sure he won't mind seeing us."

The woman hesitated uncertainly. Gross stepped into the doorway. "All right, mother. This is war time. We can't stand out here."

The two Security Agents followed him, and Kramer came reluctantly behind, closing the door. Gross stalked down the hall until he came to an open door. He stopped, looking in. Kramer could see the white corner of a bed, a wooden post and the edge of a dresser.

He joined Gross.

In the dark room a withered old man lay, propped up on endless pillows. At first it seemed as if he were asleep; there was no motion or sign of life. But after a time Kramer saw with a faint shock that the old man was watching them, intently, his eyes fixed on them, unmoving, unwinking.

"Professor Thomas?" Gross said. "I'm Commander Gross of Security. This man with me is perhaps known to you — "

The faded eyes fixed on Kramer.

"I know him. Philip Kramer ... You've grown heavier, boy." The voice was feeble, the rustle of dry ashes. "Is it true you're married now?"

"Yes. I married Dolores French. You remember her." Kramer came toward the bed. "But we're separated. It didn't work out very well. Our careers — "

"What we came here about, Professor," Gross began, but Kramer cut him off with an impatient wave.

"Let me talk. Can't you and your men get out of here long enough to let me talk to him?"

Gross swallowed. "All right, Kramer." He nodded to the two men. The three of them left the room, going out into the hall and closing the door after them.

The old man in the bed watched Kramer silently. "I don't think much of him," he said at last. "I've seen his type before. What's he want?"

"Nothing. He just came along. Can I sit down?" Kramer found a stiff upright chair beside the bed. "If I'm bothering you — "

"No. I'm glad to see you again, Philip. After so long. I'm sorry your marriage didn't work out."

"How have you been?"

"I've been very ill. I'm afraid that my moment on the world's stage has almost ended." The ancient eyes studied the younger man reflectively. "You look as if you have been doing well. Like everyone else I thought highly of. You've gone to the top in this society."

Kramer smiled. Then he became serious. "Professor, there's a project we're working on that I want to talk to you about. It's the first ray of hope we've had in this whole war. If it works, we may be able to crack the yuk defenses, get some ships into their system. If we can do that the war might be brought to an end."

"Go on. Tell me about it, if you wish."

"It's a long shot, this project. It may not work at all, but we have to give it a try."

"It's obvious that you came here because of it," Professor Thomas murmured. "I'm becoming curious. Go on."

After Kramer finished the old man lay back in the bed without speaking. At last he sighed.

"I understand. A human mind, taken out of a human body." He sat up a little, looking at Kramer. "I suppose you're thinking of me."

Kramer said nothing.

"Before I make my decision, I want to see the papers on this, the theory and outline of construction. I'm not sure I like it. — For reasons of my own, I mean. But I want to look at the material. If you'll do that — "

"Certainly." Kramer stood up and went to the door. Gross and the two Security Agents were standing outside, waiting tensely. "Gross, come inside."

They filed into the room.

"Give the Professor the papers," Kramer said. "He wants to study them before deciding."

Gross brought the file out of his coat pocket, a manila envelope. He handed it to the old man on the bed. "Here it is, Professor. You're welcome to examine it. Will you give us your answer as soon as possible? We're very anxious to begin, of course."

"I'll give you my answer when I've decided." He took the envelope with a thin, trembling hand. "My decision depends on what I find out from these papers. If I don't like what I find, then I will not become involved with this work in any shape or form." He opened the envelope with shaking hands. "I'm looking for one thing."

"What is it?" Gross said.

"That's my affair. Leave me a number by which I can reach you when I've decided."

Silently, Gross put his card down on the dresser. As they went out Professor Thomas was already reading the first of the papers, the outline of the theory.

Kramer sat across from Dale Winter, his second in line. "What then?" Winter said.

"He's going to contact us." Kramer scratched with a drawing pen on some paper. "I don't know what to think."

"What do you mean?" Winter's good-natured face was puzzled.

"Look." Kramer stood up, pacing back and forth, his hands in his uniform pockets. "He was my teacher in college. I respected him as a man, as well as a teacher. He was more than a voice, a talking book. He was a person, a calm, kindly person I could look up to. I always wanted to be like him, someday. Now look at me."

"So?"

"Look at what I'm asking. I'm asking for his life, as if he were some kind of laboratory animal kept around in a cage, not a man, a teacher at all."

"Do you think he'll do it?"

"I don't know." Kramer went to the window. He stood looking out. "In a way, I hope not."

"But if he doesn't — "

"Then we'll have to find somebody else, I know. There would be somebody else. Why did Dolores have to — "

The vidphone rang. Kramer pressed the button.

"This is Gross." The heavy features formed. "The old man called me. Professor Thomas."

"What did he say?" He knew; he could tell already, by the sound of Gross's voice.

"He said he'd do it. I was a little surprised myself, but apparently he means it. We've already made arrangements for his admission to the hospital. His lawyer is drawing up the statement of liability."

Kramer only half heard. He nodded wearily. "All right. I'm glad. I suppose we can go ahead, then."

"You don't sound very glad."

"I wonder why he decided to go ahead with it."

"He was very certain about it." Gross sounded pleased. "He called me quite early. I was still in bed. You know, this calls for a celebration."

"Sure," Kramer said. "It sure does."

Toward the middle of August, the project neared completion. They stood outside in the hot autumn heat, looking up at the sleek metal sides of the ship.

Gross thumped the metal with his hand. "Well, it won't be long. We can begin the test any time."

"Tell us more about this," an officer in gold braid said. "It's such an unusual concept."

"Is there really a human brain inside the ship?" a dignitary asked, a small man in a rumpled suit. "And the brain is actually alive?"

"Gentlemen, this ship is guided by a living brain instead of the usual Johnson relay-control system. But the brain is not conscious. It will function by reflex only. The practical difference between it and the Johnson system is this: a human brain is far more intricate than any man-made structure, and its ability to adapt itself to a situation, to respond to danger, is far beyond anything that could be artificially built."

Gross paused, cocking his ear. The turbines of the ship were beginning to rumble, shaking the ground under them with a deep vibration. Kramer was standing a short distance away from the others, his arms folded, watching silently. At the sound of the turbines he walked quickly around the ship to the other side. A few workmen were clearing away the last of the waste, the scraps of wiring and scaffolding. They glanced up at him and went on hurriedly with their work. Kramer mounted the ramp and entered the control cabin of the ship. Winter was sitting at the controls with a Pilot from Space-transport.

"How's it look?" Kramer asked.

"All right." Winter got up. "He tells me that it would be best to take off manually. The robot controls — " Winter hesitated. "I mean, the built-in controls, can take over later on in space."

"That's right," the Pilot said. "It's customary with the Johnson system, and so in this case we should — "

"Can you tell anything yet?" Kramer asked.

"No," the Pilot said slowly. "I don't think so. I've been going over everything. It seems to be in good order. There's only one thing I wanted to ask you about." He put his hand on the control board. "There are some changes here I don't understand."

"Changes?"

"Alterations from the original design. I wonder what the purpose is."

Kramer took a set of the plans from his coat. "Let me look." He turned the pages over. The Pilot watched carefully over his shoulder.

"The changes aren't indicated on your copy," the Pilot said. "I wonder — " He stopped. Commander Gross had entered the control cabin.

"Gross, who authorized alterations?" Kramer said. "Some of the wiring has been changed."

"Why, your old friend." Gross signaled to the field tower through the window.

"My old friend?"

"The Professor. He took quite an active interest." Gross turned to the Pilot. "Let's get going. We have to take this out past gravity for the test, they tell me. Well, perhaps it's for the best. Are you ready?"

"Sure." The Pilot sat down and moved some of the controls around. "Any time."

"Go ahead, then," Gross said.

"The Professor — " Kramer began, but at that moment there was a tremendous roar and the ship leaped under him. He grasped one of the wall holds and hung on as best he could. The cabin was filling with a steady throbbing, the raging of the jet turbines underneath them.

The ship leaped. Kramer closed his eyes and held his breath. They were moving out into space, gaining speed each moment.

"Well, what do you think?" Winter said nervously. "Is it time yet?"

"A little longer," Kramer said. He was sitting on the floor of the cabin, down by the control wiring. He had removed the metal covering-plate, exposing the complicated maze of relay wiring. He was studying it, comparing it to the wiring diagrams.

"What's the matter?" Gross said.

"These changes. I can't figure out what they're for. The only pattern I can make out is that for some reason — "

"Let me look," the Pilot said. He squatted down beside Kramer. "You were saying?"

"See this lead here? Originally it was switch controlled. It closed and opened automatically, according to temperature change. Now it's wired so that the central control system operates it. The same with the others. A lot of this was still mechanical, worked by pressure, temperature stress. Now it's under the central master."

"The brain?" Gross said. "You mean it's been altered so that the brain manipulates it?"

Kramer nodded. "Maybe Professor Thomas felt that no mechanical relays could be trusted. Maybe he thought that things would be happening too fast. But some of these could close in a split second. The brake rockets could go on as quickly as — "

"Hey," Winter said from the control seat. "We're getting near the moon stations. What'll I do?"

They looked out the port. The corroded surface of the moon gleamed up at them, a corrupt and sickening sight. They were moving swiftly toward it.

"I'll take it," the Pilot said. He eased Winter out of the way and strapped himself in place. The ship began to move away from the moon as he manipulated the controls. Down below them they could see the observation stations dotting the surface, and the tiny squares that were the openings of the underground factories and hangars. A red blinker winked up at them and the Pilot's fingers moved on the board in answer.

"We're past the moon," the Pilot said, after a time. The moon had fallen behind them; the ship was heading into outer space. "Well, we can go ahead with it."

Kramer did not answer.

"Mr. Kramer, we can go ahead any time."

Kramer started. "Sorry. I was thinking. All right, thanks." He frowned, deep in thought.

"What is it?" Gross asked.

"The wiring changes. Did you understand the reason for them when you gave the okay to the workmen?"

Gross flushed. "You know I know nothing about technical material. I'm in Security."

"Then you should have consulted me."

"What does it matter?" Gross grinned wryly. "We're going to have to start putting our faith in the old man sooner or later."

The Pilot stepped back from the board. His face was pale and set. "Well, it's done," he said. "That's it."

"What's done?" Kramer said.

"We're on automatic. The brain. I turned the board over to it — to him, I mean. The Old Man." The Pilot lit a cigarette and puffed nervously. "Let's keep our fingers crossed."

*   *   *

The ship was coasting evenly, in the hands of its invisible pilot. Far down inside the ship, carefully armored and protected, a soft human brain lay in a tank of liquid, a thousand minute electric charges playing over its surface. As the charges rose they were picked up and amplified, fed into relay systems, advanced, carried on through the entire ship —

Gross wiped his forehead nervously. "So *he* is running it, now. I hope he knows what he's doing."

Kramer nodded enigmatically. "I think he does."

"What do you mean?"

"Nothing." Kramer walked to the port. "I see we're still moving in a straight line." He picked up the microphone. "We can instruct the brain orally, through this." He blew against the microphone experimentally.

"Go on," Winter said.

"Bring the ship around half-right," Kramer said. "Decrease speed."

They waited. Time passed. Gross looked at Kramer. "No change. Nothing."

"Wait."

Slowly the ship was beginning to turn. The turbines missed, reducing their steady beat. The ship was taking up its new course, adjusting itself. Nearby some space debris rushed past, incinerating in the blasts of the turbine jets.

"So far so good," Gross said.

They began to breath more easily. The invisible pilot had taken control smoothly, calmly. The ship was in good hands. Kramer spoke a few more words into the microphone, and they swung again. Now they were moving back the way they had come, toward the moon.

"Let's see what he does when we enter the moon's pull," Kramer said. "He was a good mathematician, the old man. He could handle any kind of problem."

The ship veered, turning away from the moon. The great eaten-away globe fell behind them.

Gross breathed a sigh of relief. "That's that."

"One more thing." Kramer picked up the microphone. "Return to the moon and land the ship at the first space field," he said into it.

"Good Lord," Winter murmured. "Why are you — "

"Be quiet." Kramer stood, listening. The turbines gasped and roared as the ship swung full around, gaining speed. They were moving back, back toward the moon again. The ship dipped down, heading toward the great globe.

"We're going a little fast," the Pilot said. "I don't see how he can put down at this velocity."

*   *   *

The port filled up, as the globe swelled rapidly. The Pilot hurried toward the board, reaching for the controls. All at once the ship jerked. The nose lifted and the ship shot out into space, away from the moon, turning at an oblique angle. The men were thrown to the floor by the sudden change in course. They got to their feet again, speechless, staring at each other.

The Pilot gazed down at the board. "It wasn't me! I didn't touch a thing. I didn't even get to it."

The ship was gaining speed each moment. Kramer hesitated. "Maybe you better switch it back to manual."

The Pilot closed the switch. He took hold of the steering controls and moved them experimentally. "Nothing." He turned around. "Nothing. It doesn't respond."

No one spoke.

"You can see what has happened," Kramer said calmly. "The old man won't let go of it, now that he has it. I was afraid of this when I saw the wiring changes. Everything in this ship is centrally controlled, even the cooling system, the hatches, the garbage release. We're helpless."

"Nonsense." Gross strode to the board. He took hold of the wheel and turned it. The ship continued on its course, moving away from the moon, leaving it behind.

"Release!" Kramer said into the microphone. "Let go of the controls! We'll take it back. Release."

"No good," the Pilot said. "Nothing." He spun the useless wheel. "It's dead, completely dead."

"And we're still heading out," Winter said, grinning foolishly. "We'll be going through the first-line defense belt in a few minutes. If they don't shoot us down — "

"We better radio back." The Pilot clicked the radio to *send*. "I'll contact the main bases, one of the observation stations."

"Better get the defense belt, at the speed we're going. We'll be into it in a minute."

"And after that," Kramer said, "we'll be in outer space. He's moving us toward outspace velocity. Is this ship equipped with baths?"

"Baths?" Gross said.

"The sleep tanks. For space-drive. We may need them if we go much faster."

"But good God, where are we going?" Gross said. "Where — where's he taking us?"

The Pilot obtained contact. "This is Dwight, on ship," he said. "We're entering the defense zone at high velocity. Don't fire on us."

"Turn back," the impersonal voice came through the speaker. "You're not allowed in the defense zone."

"We can't. We've lost control."

"Lost control?"

"This is an experimental ship."

Gross took the radio. "This is Commander Gross, Security. We're being carried into outer space. There's nothing we can do. Is there any way that we can be removed from this ship?"

A hesitation. "We have some fast pursuit ships that could pick you up if you wanted to jump. The chances are good that they'd find you. Do you have space flares?"

"We do," the Pilot said. "Let's try it."

"Abandon ship?" Kramer said. "If we leave now we'll never see it again."

"What else can we do? We're gaining speed all the time. Do you propose that we stay here?"

"No." Kramer shook his head. "Damn it, there ought to be a better solution."

"Could you contact *him*?" Winter asked. "The Old Man? Try to reason with him?"

"It's worth a chance," Gross said. "Try it."

"All right." Kramer took the microphone. He paused a moment. "Listen! Can you hear me? This is Phil Kramer. Can you hear me, Professor? Can you hear me? I want you to release the controls."

There was silence.

"This is Kramer, Professor. Can you hear me? Do you remember who I am? Do you understand who this is?"

Above the control panel the wall speaker made a sound, a sputtering static. They looked up.

"Can you hear me, Professor? This is Philip Kramer. I want you to give the ship back to us. If you can hear me, release the controls! Let go, Professor. Let go!"

Static. A rushing sound, like the wind. They gazed at each other. There was silence for a moment.

"It's a waste of time," Gross said.

"No — listen!"

The sputter came again. Then, mixed with the sputter, almost lost in it, a voice came, toneless, without inflection, a mechanical, lifeless voice from the metal speaker in the wall, above their heads.

" ... Is it you, Philip? I can't make you out. Darkness ... Who's there? With you ... "

"It's me, Kramer." His fingers tightened against the microphone handle. "You must release the controls, Professor. We have to get back to Terra. You must."

Silence. Then the faint, faltering voice came again, a little stronger than before. "Kramer. Everything so strange. I was right, though. Consciousness result of thinking. Necessary result. Cogito ergo sum. Retain conceptual ability. Can you hear me?"

"Yes, Professor — "

"I altered the wiring. Control. I was fairly certain ... I wonder if I can do it. Try ... "

Suddenly the air-conditioning snapped into operation. It snapped abruptly off again. Down the corridor a door slammed. Something thudded. The men stood listening. Sounds came from all sides of them, switches shutting, opening. The lights blinked off; they were in darkness. The lights came back on, and at the same time the heating coils dimmed and faded.

"Good God!" Winter said.

Water poured down on them, the emergency fire-fighting system. There was a screaming rush of air. One of the escape hatches had slid back, and the air was roaring frantically out into space.

The hatch banged closed. The ship subsided into silence. The heating coils glowed into life. As suddenly as it had begun the weird exhibition ceased.

"I can do — everything," the dry, toneless voice came from the wall speaker. "It is all controlled. Kramer, I wish to talk to you. I've been — been thinking. I haven't seen you in many years. A lot to discuss. You've changed, boy. We have much to discuss. Your wife — "

The Pilot grabbed Kramer's arm. "There's a ship standing off our bow. Look."

They ran to the port. A slender pale craft was moving along with them, keeping pace with them. It was signal blinking.

"A Terran pursuit ship," the Pilot said. "Let's jump. They'll pick us up. Suits — "

He ran to a supply cupboard and turned the handle. The door opened and he pulled the suits out onto the floor.

"Hurry," Gross said. A panic seized them. They dressed frantically, pulling the heavy garments over them. Winter staggered to the escape hatch and stood by it, waiting for the others. They joined him, one by one.

"Let's go!" Gross said. "Open the hatch."

Winter tugged at the hatch. "Help me."

They grabbed hold, tugging together. Nothing happened. The hatch refused to budge.

"Get a crowbar," the Pilot said.

"Hasn't anyone got a blaster?" Gross looked frantically around. "Damn it, blast it open!"

"Pull," Kramer grated. "Pull together."

"Are you at the hatch?" The toneless voice came, drifting and eddying through the corridors of the ship. They looked up, staring around them. "I sense something nearby, outside. A ship? You are leaving, all of you? Kramer, you are leaving, too? Very unfortunate. I had hoped we could talk. Perhaps at some other time you might be induced to remain."

"Open the hatch!" Kramer said, staring up at the impersonal walls of the ship. "For God's sake, open it!"

There was silence, an endless pause. Then, very slowly, the hatch slid back. The air screamed out, rushing past them into space.

One by one they leaped, one after the other, propelled away by the repulsive material of the suits. A few minutes later they were being hauled aboard the pursuit ship. As the last one of them was lifted through the port, their own ship pointed itself suddenly upward and shot off at tremendous speed. It disappeared.

Kramer removed his helmet, gasping. Two sailors held onto him and began to wrap him in blankets. Gross sipped a mug of coffee, shivering.

"It's gone," Kramer murmured.

"I'll have an alarm sent out," Gross said.

"What's happened to your ship?" a sailor asked curiously. "It sure took off in a hurry. Who's on it?"

"We'll have to have it destroyed," Gross went on, his face grim. "It's got to be destroyed. There's no telling what it — what *he* has in mind." Gross sat down weakly on a metal bench. "What a close call for us. We were so damn trusting."

"What could he be planning," Kramer said, half to himself. "It doesn't make sense. I don't get it."

As the ship sped back toward the moon base they sat around the table in the dining room, sipping hot coffee and thinking, not saying very much.

"Look here," Gross said at last. "What kind of man was Professor Thomas? What do you remember about him?"

Kramer put his coffee mug down. "It was ten years ago. I don't remember much. It's vague."

He let his mind run back over the years. He and Dolores had been at Hunt College together, in physics and the life sciences. The College was small and set back away from the momentum of modern life. He had gone there because it was his home town, and his father had gone there before him.

Professor Thomas had been at the College a long time, as long as anyone could remember. He was a strange old man, keeping to himself most of the time. There were many things that he disapproved of, but he seldom said what they were.

"Do you recall anything that might help us?" Gross asked. "Anything that would give us a clue as to what he might have in mind?"

Kramer nodded slowly. "I remember one thing..."

One day he and the Professor had been sitting together in the school chapel, talking leisurely.

"Well, you'll be out of school, soon," the Professor had said. "What are you going to do?"

"Do? Work at one of the Government Research Projects, I suppose."

"And eventually? What's your ultimate goal?"

Kramer had smiled. "The question is unscientific. It presupposes such things as ultimate ends."

"Suppose instead along these lines, then: What if there were no war and no Government Research Projects? What would you do, then?"

"I don't know. But how can I imagine a hypothetical situation like that? There's been war as long as I can remember. We're geared for war. I don't know what I'd do. I suppose I'd adjust, get used to it."

The Professor had stared at him. "Oh, you do think you'd get accustomed to it, eh? Well, I'm glad of that. And you think you could find something to do?"

Gross listened intently. "What do you infer from this, Kramer?"

"Not much. Except that he was against war."

"We're all against war," Gross pointed out.

"True. But he was withdrawn, set apart. He lived very simply, cooking his own meals. His wife died many years ago. He was born in Europe, in Italy. He changed his name when he came to the United States. He used to read Dante and Milton. He even had a Bible."

"Very anachronistic, don't you think?"

"Yes, he lived quite a lot in the past. He found an old phonograph and records and he listened to the old music. You saw his house, how old-fashioned it was."

"Did he have a file?" Winter asked Gross.

"With Security? No, none at all. As far as we could tell he never engaged in political work, never joined anything or even seemed to have strong political convictions."

"No," Kramer agreed. "About all he ever did was walk through the hills. He liked nature."

"Nature can be of great use to a scientist," Gross said. "There wouldn't be any science without it."

"Kramer, what do you think his plan is, taking control of the ship and disappearing?" Winter said.

"Maybe the transfer made him insane," the Pilot said. "Maybe there's no plan, nothing rational at all."

"But he had the ship rewired, and he had made sure that he would retain consciousness and memory before he even agreed to the operation. He must have had something planned from the start. But what?"

"Perhaps he just wanted to stay alive longer," Kramer said. "He was old and about to die. Or — "

"Or what?"

"Nothing." Kramer stood up. "I think as soon as we get to the moon base I'll make a vidcall to earth. I want to talk to somebody about this."

"Who's that?" Gross asked.

"Dolores. Maybe she remembers something."

"That's a good idea," Gross said.

"Where are you calling from?" Dolores asked, when he succeeded in reaching her.

"From a moon base."

"All kinds of rumors are running around. Why didn't the ship come back? What happened?"

"I'm afraid he ran off with it."

"He?"

"The Old Man. Professor Thomas." Kramer explained what had happened.

Dolores listened intently. "How strange. And you think he planned it all in advance, from the start?"

"I'm certain. He asked for the plans of construction and the theoretical diagrams at once."

"But why? What for?"

"I don't know. Look, Dolores. What do you remember about him? Is there anything that might give a clue to all this?"

"Like what?"

"I don't know. That's the trouble."

On the vidscreen Dolores knitted her brow. "I remember he raised chickens in his back yard and once he had a goat." She smiled. "Do you remember the day the goat got loose and wandered down the main street of town? Nobody could figure out where it came from."

"Anything else?"

"No." He watched her struggling, trying to remember. "He wanted to have a farm, sometime, I know."

"All right. Thanks." Kramer touched the switch. "When I get back to Terra maybe I'll stop and see you."

"Let me know how it works out."

He cut the line and the picture dimmed and faded. He walked slowly back to where Gross and some officers of the Military were sitting at a chart table, talking.

"Any luck?" Gross said, looking up.

"No. All she remembers is that he kept a goat."

"Come over and look at this detail chart." Gross motioned him around to his side. "Watch!"

Kramer saw the record tabs moving furiously, the little white dots racing back and forth.

"What's happening?" he asked.

"A squadron outside the defense zone has finally managed to contact the ship. They're maneuvering now, for position. Watch."

The white counters were forming a barrel formation around a black dot that was moving steadily across the board, away from the central position. As they watched, the white dots constructed around it.

"They're ready to open fire," a technician at the board said. "Commander, what shall we tell them to do?"

Gross hesitated. "I hate to be the one who makes the decision. When it comes right down to it — "

"It's not just a ship," Kramer said. "It's a man, a living person. A human being is up there, moving through space. I wish we knew what — "

"But the order has to be given. We can't take any chances. Suppose he went over to them, to the yuks."

Kramer's jaw dropped. "My God, he wouldn't do that."

"Are you sure? Do you know what he'll do?"

"He wouldn't do that."

Gross turned to the technician. "Tell them to go ahead."

"I'm sorry, sir, but now the ship has gotten away. Look down at the board."

Gross stared down, Kramer over his shoulder. The black dot had slipped through the white dots and had moved off at an abrupt angle. The white dots were broken up, dispersing in confusion.

"He's an unusual strategist," one of the officers said. He traced the line. "It's an ancient maneuver, an old Prussian device, but it worked."

The white dots were turning back. "Too many yuk ships out that far," Gross said. "Well, that's what you get when you don't act quickly." He looked up coldly at Kramer. "We should have done it when we had him. Look at him go!" He jabbed a finger at the rapidly moving black dot. The dot came to the edge of the board and stopped. It had reached the limit of the charted area. "See?"

— Now what? Kramer thought, watching. So the Old Man had escaped the cruisers and gotten away. He was alert, all right; there was nothing wrong with his mind. Or with ability to control his new body.

Body — The ship was a new body for him. He had traded in the old dying body, withered and frail, for this hulking frame of metal and plastic, turbines and rocket jets. He was strong, now. Strong and big. The new body was more powerful than a thousand human bodies. But how long would it last him? The average life of a cruiser was only ten years. With careful handling he might get twenty out of it, before some essential part failed and there was no way to replace it.

And then, what then? What would he do, when something failed and there was no one to fix it for him? That would be the end. Someplace, far out in the cold darkness of space, the ship would slow down, silent and lifeless, to exhaust its last heat into the eternal timelessness of outer space. Or perhaps it would crash on some barren asteroid, burst into a million fragments.

It was only a question of time.

"Your wife didn't remember anything?" Gross said.

"I told you. Only that he kept a goat, once."

"A hell of a lot of help that is."

Kramer shrugged. "It's not my fault."

"I wonder if we'll ever see him again." Gross stared down at the indicator dot, still hanging at the edge of the board. "I wonder if he'll ever move back this way."

"I wonder, too," Kramer said.

That night Kramer lay in bed, tossing from side to side, unable to sleep. The moon gravity, even artificially increased, was unfamiliar to him and it made him uncomfortable. A thousand thoughts wandered loose in his head as he lay, fully awake.

What did it all mean? What was the Professor's plan? Maybe they would never know. Maybe the ship was gone for good: the Old Man had left forever, shooting into outer space. They might never find out why he had done it, what purpose — if any — had been in his mind.

Kramer sat up in bed. He turned on the light and lit a cigarette. His quarters were small, a metal-lined bunk room, part of the moon station base.

The Old Man had wanted to talk to him. He had wanted to discuss things, hold a conversation, but in the hysteria and confusion all they had been able to think of was getting away. The ship was rushing off with them, carrying them into outer space. Kramer set his jaw. Could they be blamed for jumping? They had no idea where they were being taken, or why. They were helpless, caught in their own ship, and the pursuit ship standing by waiting to pick them up was their only chance. Another half hour and it would have been too late.

But what had the Old Man wanted to say? What had he intended to tell him, in those first confusing moments when the ship around them had come alive, each metal strut and wire suddenly animate, the body of a living creature, a vast metal organism?

It was weird, unnerving. He could not forget it, even now. He looked around the small room uneasily. What did it signify, the coming to life of metal and plastic? All at once they had found themselves inside a *living* creature, in its stomach, like Jonah inside the whale.

It had been alive, and it had talked to them, talked calmly and rationally, as it rushed them off, faster and faster into outer space. The wall speaker and circuit had become the vocal cords and mouth, the wiring the spinal cord and nerves, the hatches and relays and circuit breakers the muscles.

They had been helpless, completely helpless. The ship had, in a brief second, stolen their power away from them and left them defenseless, practically at its mercy. It was not right; it made him uneasy. All his life he had controlled machines, bent nature and the forces of nature to man and man's needs. The human race had slowly evolved until it was in a position to operate things, run them as it saw fit. Now all at once it had been plunged back down the ladder again, prostrate before a Power against which they were children.

Kramer got out of bed. He put on his bathrobe and began to search for a cigarette. While he was searching, the vidscreen rang.

He snapped the vidphone on. "Yes?"

The face of the immediate monitor appeared. "A call from Terra, Mr. Kramer. An emergency call."

"Emergency call? For me? Put it through." Kramer came awake, brushing his hair back out of his eyes. Alarm plucked at him.

From the speaker a strange voice came. "Philip Kramer? Is this Kramer?"

"Yes. Go on."

"This is General Hospital. New York City, Terra. Mr. Kramer, your wife is here. She has been critically injured in an accident. Your name was given to us to call. Is it possible for you to — "

"How badly?" Kramer gripped the vidphone stand. "Is it serious?"

"Yes, it's serious, Mr. Kramer. Are you able to come here? The quicker you can come the better."

"Yes." Kramer nodded. "I'll come. Thanks."

The screen died as the connection was broken. Kramer waited a moment. Then he tapped the button. The screen relit again. "Yes, sir," the monitor said.

"Can I get a ship to Terra at once? It's an emergency. My wife — "

"There's no ship leaving the moon for eight hours. You'll have to wait until the next period."

"Isn't there anything I can do?"

"We can broadcast a general request to all ships passing through this area. Sometimes cruisers pass by here returning to Terra for repairs."

"Will you broadcast that for me? I'll come down to the field."

"Yes, sir. But there may be no ship in the area for a while. It's a gamble." The screen died.

Kramer dressed quickly. He put on his coat and hurried out the lift. A moment later he was running across the general receiving lobby, past the rows of vacant desks and conference tables. At the door the sentries stepped aside and he went outside, onto the great concrete steps.

The face of the moon was in shadow. Below him the field stretched out in total darkness, a black void, endless, without form. He made his way carefully down the steps and along the ramp along the side of the field, to the control tower. A faint row of red lights showed him the way.

Two soldiers challenged him at the foot of the tower, standing in the shadows, their guns ready.

"Kramer?"

"Yes." A light was flashed in his face.

"Your call has been sent out already."

"Any luck?" Kramer asked.

"There's a cruiser nearby that has made contact with us. It has an injured jet and is moving slowly back toward Terra, away from the line."

"Good." Kramer nodded, a flood of relief rushing through him. He lit a cigarette and gave one to each of the soldiers. The soldiers lit up.

"Sir," one of them asked, "is it true about the experimental ship?"

"What do you mean?"

"It came to life and ran off?"

"No, not exactly," Kramer said. "It had a new type of control system instead of the Johnson units. It wasn't properly tested."

"But sir, one of the cruisers that was there got up close to it, and a buddy of mine says this ship acted funny. He never saw anything like it. It was like when he was fishing once on Terra, in Washington State, fishing for bass. The fish were smart, going this way and that — "

"Here's your cruiser," the other soldier said. "Look!"

An enormous vague shape was settling slowly down onto the field. They could make nothing out but its row of tiny green blinkers. Kramer stared at the shape.

"Better hurry, sir," the soldiers said. "They don't stick around here very long."

"Thanks." Kramer loped across the field, toward the black shape that rose above him, extended across the width of the field. The ramp was down from the side of the cruiser and he caught hold of it. The ramp rose, and a moment later Kramer was inside the hold of the ship. The hatch slid shut behind him.

As he made his way up the stairs to the main deck the turbines roared up from the moon, out into space.

Kramer opened the door to the main deck. He stopped suddenly, staring around him in surprise. There was nobody in sight. The ship was deserted.

"Good God," he said. Realization swept over him, numbing him. He sat down on a bench, his head swimming. "Good God."

The ship roared out into space leaving the moon and Terra farther behind each moment.

And there was nothing he could do.

"So it was you who put the call through," he said at last. "It was you who called me on the vidphone, not any hospital on Terra. It was all part of the plan." He looked up and around him. "And Dolores is really — "

"Your wife is fine," the wall speaker above him said tonelessly. "It was a fraud. I'm sorry to trick you that way, Philip, but it was all I could think of. Another day and you would have been back on Terra. I don't want to remain in this area any longer than necessary. They have been so certain of finding me out in deep space that I have been able to stay here without too much danger. But even the purloined letter was found eventually."

Kramer smoked his cigarette nervously. "What are you going to do? Where are we going?"

"First, I want to talk to you. I have many things to discuss. I was very disappointed when you left me, along with the others. I had hoped that you would remain." The dry voice chuckled. "Remember how we used to talk in the old days, you and I? That was a long time ago."

The ship was gaining speed. It plunged through space at tremendous speed, rushing through the last of the defense zone and out beyond. A rush of nausea made Kramer bend over for a moment.

When he straightened up the voice from the wall went on. "I'm sorry to step it up so quickly, but we are still in danger. Another few moments and we'll be free."

"How about yuk ships? Aren't they out here?"

"I've already slipped away from several of them. They're quite curious about me."

"Curious?"

"They sense that I'm different, more like their own organic mines. They don't like it. I believe they will begin to withdraw from this area, soon. Apparently they don't want to get involved with me. They're an odd race, Philip. I would have liked to study them closely, try to learn something about them. I'm of the opinion that they use no inert material. All their equipment and instruments are alive, in some form or other. They don't construct or build at all. The idea of *making* is foreign to them. They utilize existing forms. Even their ships — "

"Where are we going?" Kramer said. "I want to know where you are taking me."

"Frankly, I'm not certain."

"You're not certain?"

"I haven't worked some details out. There are a few vague spots in my program, still. But I think that in a short while I'll have them ironed out."

"What is your program?" Kramer said.

"It's really very simple. But don't you want to come into the control room and sit? The seats are much more comfortable than that metal bench."

Kramer went into the control room and sat down at the control board. Looking at the useless apparatus made him feel strange.

"What's the matter?" the speaker above the board rasped.

Kramer gestured helplessly. "I'm powerless. I can't do anything. And I don't like it. Do you blame me?"

"No. No, I don't blame you. But you'll get your control back, soon. Don't worry. This is only a temporary expedient, taking you off this way. It was something I didn't contemplate. I forgot that orders would be given out to shoot me on sight."

"It was Gross's idea."

"I don't doubt that. My conception, my plan, came to me as soon as you began to describe your project, that day at my house. I saw at once that you were wrong; you people have no understanding of the mind at all. I realized that the transfer of a human brain from an organic body to a complex artificial spaceship would not involve the loss of the intellectualization faculty of the mind. When a man thinks, he *is*.

"When I realized that, I saw the possibility of an age-old dream becoming real. I was quite elderly when I first met you, Philip. Even then my life-span had come pretty much to its end. I could look ahead to nothing but death, and with it the extinction of all my ideas. I had made no mark on the world, none at all. My students, one by one, passed from me into the world, to take up jobs in the great Research Project, the search for better and bigger weapons of war.

"The world has been fighting for a long time, first with itself, then with the Martians, then with these beings from Proxima Centauri, whom we know nothing about. The human society has evolved war as a cultural institution, like the science of astronomy, or mathematics. War is a part of our lives, a career, a respected vocation. Bright, alert young men and women move into it, putting their shoulders to the wheel as they did in the time of Nebuchadnezzar. It has always been so.

"But is it innate in mankind? I don't think so. No social custom is innate. There were many human groups that did not go to war; the Eskimos never grasped the idea at all, and the American Indians never took to it well.

"But these dissenters were wiped out, and a cultural pattern was established that became the standard for the whole planet. Now it has become ingrained in us.

"But if someplace along the line some other way of settling problems had arisen and taken hold, something different than the massing of men and to — "

"What's your plan?" Kramer said. "I know the theory. It was part of one of your lectures."

"Yes, buried in a lecture on plant selection, as I recall. When you came to me with this proposition I realized that perhaps my conception could be brought to life, after all. If my theory were right that war is only a habit, not an instinct, a society built up apart from Terra with a minimum of cultural roots might develop differently. If it failed to absorb our outlook, if it could start out on another foot, it might not arrive at the same point to which we have come: a dead end, with nothing but greater and greater wars in sight, until nothing is left but ruin and destruction everywhere.

"Of course, there would have to be a Watcher to guide the experiment, at first. A crisis would undoubtedly come very quickly, probably in the second generation. Cain would arise almost at once.

"You see, Kramer, I estimate that if I remain at rest most of the time, on some small planet or moon, I may be able to keep functioning for almost a hundred years. That would be time enough, sufficient to see the direction of the new colony. After that — Well, after that it would be up to the colony itself.

"Which is just as well, of course. Man must take control eventually, on his own. One hundred years, and after that they will have control of their destiny. Perhaps I am wrong, perhaps war is more than a habit. Perhaps it is a law of the universe, that things can only survive as groups by group violence.

"But I'm going ahead and taking the chance that it is only a habit, that I'm right, that war is something we're so accustomed to that we don't realize it is a very unnatural thing. Now as to the place! I'm still a little vague about that. We must find the place, still.

"That's what we're doing now. You and I are going to inspect a few systems off the beaten path, planets where the trading prospects are low enough to keep Terran ships away. I know of one planet that might be a good place. It was reported by the Fairchild expedition in their original manuscript. We may look into that, for a start."

The ship was silent.

Kramer sat for a time, staring down at the metal floor under him. The floor throbbed dully with the motion of the turbines. At last he looked up.

"You might be right. Maybe our outlook is only a habit." Kramer got to his feet. "But I wonder if something has occurred to you?"

"What is that?"

"If it's such a deeply ingrained habit, going back thousands of years, how are you going to get your colonists to make the break, leave Terra and Terran customs? How about *this* generation, the first ones, the people who found the colony? I think you're right that the next generation would be free of all this, if there were an — " He grinned. " — An Old Man Above to teach them something else instead."

Kramer looked up at the wall speaker. "How are you going to get the people to leave Terra and come with you, if by your own theory, this generation can't be saved, it all has to start with the next?"

The wall speaker was silent. Then it made a sound, the faint dry chuckle.

"I'm surprised at you, Philip. Settlers can be found. We won't need many, just a few." The speaker chuckled again. "I'll acquaint you with my solution."

At the far end of the corridor a door slid open. There was sound, a hesitant sound. Kramer turned.

"Dolores!"

Dolores Kramer stood uncertainly, looking into the control room. She blinked in amazement. "Phil! What are you doing here? What's going on?"

They stared at each other.

"What's happening?" Dolores said. "I received a vidcall that you had been hurt in a lunar explosion —"

The wall speaker rasped into life. "You see, Philip, that problem is already solved. We don't need so many people; even a single couple might do."

Kramer nodded slowly. "I see," he murmured thickly. "Just one couple. One man and woman."

"They might make it all right, if there were someone to watch and see that things went as they should. There will be quite a few things I can help you with, Philip. Quite a few. We'll get along very well, I think."

Kramer grinned wryly. "You could even help us name the animals," he said. "I understand that's the first step."

"I'll be glad to," the toneless, impersonal voice said. "As I recall, my part will be to bring them to you, one by one. Then you can do the actual naming."

"I don't understand," Dolores faltered. "What does he mean, Phil? Naming animals. What kind of animals? Where are we going?"

Kramer walked slowly over to the port and stood staring silently out, his arms folded. Beyond the ship myriad fragments of light gleamed, countless coals glowing in the dark void. Stars, suns, systems. Endless, without number. A universe of worlds. An infinity of planets, waiting for them, gleaming and winking from the darkness.

He turned back, away from the port. "Where are we going?" He smiled at his wife, standing nervous and frightened, her large eyes full of alarm. "I don't know where we are going," he said. "But somehow that doesn't seem important right now ... I'm beginning to see the Professor's point, it's the result that counts."

And for the first time in many months he put his arm around Dolores. At first she stiffened, the fright and nervousness still in her eyes. But then suddenly she relaxed against him and there were tears wetting her cheeks.

"Phil ... do you really think we can start over again — you and I?"

He kissed her tenderly, then passionately.

And the spaceship shot swiftly through the endless, trackless eternity of the void ...

PIPER IN THE WOODS

"WELL, Corporal Westerburg," Doctor Henry Harris said gently, "just why do you think you're a plant?"

As he spoke, Harris glanced down again at the card on his desk. It was from the Base Commander himself, made out in Cox's heavy scrawl: *Doc, this is the lad I told you about. Talk to him and try to find out how he got this delusion. He's from the new Garrison, the new check station on Asteroid Y-3, and we don't want anything to go wrong there. Especially a silly damn thing like this!*

Harris pushed the card aside and stared back up at the youth across the desk from him. The young man seemed ill at ease and appeared to be avoiding answering the question Harris had put to him. Harris frowned. Westerburg was a good looking chap, actually handsome in his Patrol uniform, a shock of blond hair over one eye. He was tall, almost six feet, a fine healthy lad, just two years out of Training, according to the card. Born in Detroit. Had measles when he was nine. Interested in jet engines, tennis, and girls. Twenty-six years old.

"Well, Corporal Westerburg," Doctor Harris said again. "Why do you think you're a plant?"

The Corporal looked up shyly. He cleared his throat. "Sir, I *am* a plant, I don't just think so. I've been a plant for several days now."

"I see." The Doctor nodded. "You mean that you weren't always a plant?"

"No sir. I just became a plant recently."

"And what were you before you became a plant?"

"Well, sir, I was just like the rest of you."

There was silence. Doctor Harris took up his pen and scratched a few lines, but nothing of importance came. A plant? And such a healthy-looking lad! Harris removed his steel-rimmed glasses and polished them with his

113

handkerchief. He put them on again and leaned back in his chair. "Care for a cigarette, Corporal?"

"No, sir."

The Doctor lit one for himself, resting his arm on the edge of the chair. "Corporal, you must realize that there are very few men who become plants, especially on such short notice. I have to admit you are the first person who has ever told me such a thing."

"Yes, sir, I realize it's quite rare."

"You can understand why I'm interested, then. When you say you're a plant, you mean you're not capable of mobility? Or do you mean you're a vegetable, as opposed to an animal? Or just what?"

The Corporal looked away. "I can't tell you any more," he murmured. "I'm sorry, sir."

"Well, would you mind telling me *how* you became a plant?"

Corporal Westerburg hesitated. He stared down at the floor, then out the window at the spaceport, then at a fly on the desk. At last he stood up, getting slowly to his feet. "I can't even tell you that, sir," he said.

"You can't? Why not?"

"Because — because I promised not to."

The room was silent. Doctor Harris rose, too, and they both stood facing each other. Harris frowned, rubbing his jaw. "Corporal, just *who* did you promise?"

"I can't even tell you that, sir. I'm sorry."

The Doctor considered this. At last he went to the door and opened it. "All right, Corporal. You may go now. And thanks for your time."

"I'm sorry I'm not more helpful." The Corporal went slowly out and Harris closed the door after him. Then he went across his office to the vidphone. He rang Commander Cox's letter. A moment later the beefy good-natured face of the Base Commander appeared.

"Cox, this is Harris. I talked to him, all right. All I could get is the statement that he's a plant. What else is there? What kind of behavior pattern?"

"Well," Cox said, "the first thing they noticed was that he wouldn't do any work. The Garrison Chief reported that this Westerburg would wander off outside the Garrison and just sit, all day long. Just sit."

"In the sun?"

"Yes. Just sit in the sun. Then at nightfall he would come back in. When they asked why he wasn't working in the jet repair building he told them he had to be out in the sun. Then he said — " Cox hesitated.

"Yes? Said what?"

"He said that work was unnatural. That it was a waste of time. That the only worthwhile thing was to sit and contemplate — outside."

"What then?"

"Then they asked him how he got that idea, and then he revealed to them that he had become a plant."

"I'm going to have to talk to him again, I can see," Harris said. "And he's applied for a permanent discharge from the Patrol? What reason did he give?"

"The same, that he's a plant now, and has no more interest in being a Patrolman. All he wants to do is sit in the sun. It's the damnedest thing I ever heard."

"All right. I think I'll visit him in his quarters." Harris looked at his watch. "I'll go over after dinner."

"Good luck," Cox said gloomily. "But who ever heard of a man turning into a plant? We told him it wasn't possible, but he just smiled at us."

"I'll let you know how I make out," Harris said.

Harris walked slowly down the hall. It was after six; the evening meal was over. A dim concept was coming into his mind, but it was much too soon to be sure. He increased his pace, turning right at the end of the hall. Two nurses passed, hurrying by. Westerburg was quartered with a buddy, a man who had been injured in a jet blast and who was now almost recovered. Harris came to the dorm wing and stopped, checking the numbers on the doors.

"Can I help you, sir?" the robot attendant said, gliding up.

"I'm looking for Corporal Westerburg's room."

"Three doors to the right."

Harris went on. Asteroid Y-3 had only recently been garrisoned and staffed. It had become the primary check-point to halt and examine ships entering the system from outer space. The Garrison made sure that no dangerous bacteria, fungus, or what-not arrived to infect the system. A nice asteroid it was, warm, well-watered, with trees and lakes and lots of sunshine. And the most modern Garrison in the nine planets. He shook his head, coming to the third door. He stopped, raising his hand and knocking.

"Who's there?" sounded through the door.

"I want to see Corporal Westerburg."

The door opened. A bovine youth with horn-rimmed glasses looked out, a book in his hand. "Who are you?"

"Doctor Harris."

"I'm sorry, sir. Corporal Westerburg is asleep."

"Would he mind if I woke him up? I want very much to talk to him." Harris peered inside. He could see a neat room, with a desk, a rug and lamp, and two bunks. On one of the bunks was Westerburg, lying face up, his arms folded across his chest, his eyes tightly closed.

"Sir," the bovine youth said, "I'm afraid I can't wake him up for you, much as I'd like to."

"You can't? Why not?"

"Sir, Corporal Westerburg won't wake up, not after the sun sets. He just won't. He can't be awakened."

"Cataleptic? Really?"

"But in the morning, as soon as the sun comes up, he leaps out of bed and goes outside. Stays the whole day."

"I see," the Doctor said. "Well, thanks anyhow." He went back out into the hall and the door shut after him. "There's more to this than I realized," he murmured. He went on back the way he had come.

It was a warm sunny day. The sky was almost free of clouds and a gentle wind moved through the cedars along the bank of the stream. There was a path leading from the hospital building down the slope to the stream. At the stream a small bridge led over to the other side, and a few patients were standing on the bridge, wrapped in their bathrobes, looking aimlessly down at the water.

It took Harris several minutes to find Westerburg. The youth was not with the other patients, near or around the bridge. He had gone farther down, past the cedar trees and out onto a strip of bright meadow, where poppies and grass grew everywhere. He was sitting on the stream bank, on a flat gray stone, leaning back and staring up, his mouth open a little. He did not notice the Doctor until Harris was almost beside him.

"Hello," Harris said softly.

Westerburg opened his eyes, looking up. He smiled and got slowly to his feet, a graceful, flowing motion that was rather surprising for a man of his size. "Hello, Doctor. What brings you out here?"

"Nothing. Thought I'd get some sun."

"Here, you can share my rock," Westerburg moved over and Harris sat down gingerly, being careful not to catch his trousers on the sharp edges of the rock. He lit a cigarette and gazed silently down at the water. Beside him, Westerburg had resumed his strange position, leaning back, resting on his hands, staring up with his eyes shut tight.

"Nice day," the Doctor said.

"Yes."

"Do you come here every day?"

"You like it better out here than inside."

"I can't stay inside," Westerburg said.

"You can't? How do you mean, 'can't'?"

"You would die without *air*, wouldn't you?" the Corporal said.

"And you'd die without sunlight?"

Westerburg nodded.

"Corporal, may I ask you something? Do you plan to do this the rest of your life, sit out in the sun on a flat rock? Nothing else?"

Westerburg nodded.

"How about your job? You went to school for years to become a Patrolman.

You wanted to enter the Patrol very badly. You were given a fine rating and a first-class position. How do you feel, giving all that up? You know, it won't be easy to get back in again. Do you realize that?"

"I realize it."

"And you're really going to give it all up?"

"That's right."

Harris was silent for a while. At last he put his cigarette out and turned toward the youth. "All right, let's say you give up your job and sit in the sun. Well, what happens, then? Someone else has to do the job instead of you. Isn't that true? The job has to be done, *your* job has to be done. And if you don't do it someone else has to."

"I suppose so."

"Westerburg, suppose everyone felt the way you do? Suppose everyone wanted to sit in the sun all day? What would happen? No one would check ships coming from outer space. Bacteria and toxic crystals would enter the system and cause mass death and suffering. Isn't that right?"

"If everyone felt the way I do they wouldn't be going into outer space."

"But they have to. They have to trade, they have to get minerals and products and new plants."

"Why?"

"To keep society going."

"Why?"

"Well — " Harris gestured. "People couldn't live without society."

Westerburg said nothing to that. Harris watched him, but the youth did not answer.

"Isn't that right?" Harris said.

"Perhaps. It's a peculiar business, Doctor. You know, I struggled for years to get through Training. I had to work and pay my own way. Washed dishes, worked in kitchens. Studied at night, learned, crammed, worked on and on. And you know what I think, now?"

"What?"

"I wish I'd become a plant earlier."

Doctor Harris stood up. "Westerburg, when you come inside, will you stop off at my office? I want to give you a few tests, if you don't mind."

"The shock box?" Westerburg smiled. "I knew that would be coming around. Sure, I don't mind."

Nettled, Harris left the rock, walking back up the bank a short distance. "About three, Corporal?"

The Corporal nodded.

Harris made his way up the hill, to the path, toward the hospital building. The whole thing was beginning to become more clear to him. A boy who had struggled all his life. Financial insecurity. Idealized goal, getting a Patrol assignment. Finally reached it, found the load too great. And on Asteroid Y-3 there was too much vegetation to look at all day. Primitive identification and projection on the flora of the asteroid. Concept of security involved in immobility and permanence. Unchanging forest.

He entered the building. A robot orderly stopped him almost at once. "Sir, Commander Cox wants you urgently, on the vidphone."

"Thanks." Harris strode to the office. He dialed Cox's letter and the Commander's face came presently into focus. "Cox? This is Harris. I've been out talking to the boy. I'm beginning to to get this lined up, now. I can see the pattern, too much load too long. Finally gets what he wants and the idealization shatters under the — "

"Harris!" Cox barked. "Shut up and listen. I just got a report from Y-3. They're sending an express rocket here. It's on the way."

"An express rocket?"

"Five more cases like Westerburg. All say they're plants! The Garrison Chief is worried as hell. Says we *must* find out what it is or the Garrison will fall apart, right away. Do you get me, Harris? Find out what it is!"

"Yes, sir," Harris murmured. "Yes, sir."

By the end of the week there were twenty cases, and all, of course, were from Asteroid Y-3.

Commander Cox and Harris stood together at the top of the hill, looking gloomily down at the stream below. Sixteen men and four women sat in the sun along the bank, none of them moving, none speaking. An hour had gone by since Cox and Harris appeared, and in all that time the twenty people below had not stirred.

"I don't get it," Cox said, shaking his head. "I just absolutely don't get it. Harris, is this the beginning of the end? Is everything going to start cracking around us? It gives me a hell of a strange feeling to see those people down there basking away in the sun, just sitting and basking."

"Who's that man there with the red hair?"

"That's Ulrich Deutsch. He was Second in Command at the Garrison. Now look at him! Sits and dozes with his mouth open and his eyes shut. A week ago that man was climbing, going right up to the top. When the Garrison Chief retires he was supposed to take over. Maybe another year, at the most. All his life he's been climbing to get up there."

"And now he sits in the sun," Harris finished.

"That woman. The brunette, with the short hair. Career woman. Head of the entire office staff of the Garrison. And the man beside her. Janitor. And that cute little gal there, with the bosom. Secretary, just out of school. All kinds. And I got a note this morning, three more coming in sometime today."

Harris nodded. "The strange thing is — they really *want* to sit down there. They're completely rational; they could do something else, but they just don't care to."

"Well?" Cox said. "What are you going to do? Have you found anything? We're counting on you. Let's hear it."

"I couldn't get anything out of them directly," Harris said, "but I've had some interesting results with the shock box. Let's go inside and I'll show you."

"Fine," Cox turned and started toward the hospital. "Show me anything you've got. This is serious. Now I know how Tiberius felt when Christianity showed up in high places."

Harris snapped off the light. The room was pitch black. "I'll run this first reel for you. The subject is one of the best biologists stationed at the Garrison. Robert Bradshaw. He came in yesterday. I got a good run from the shock box because Bradshaw's mind is so highly differentiated. There's a lot of repressed material of a non-rational nature, more than usual."

He pressed a switch. The projector whirred, and on the far wall a three-dimensional image appeared in color, so real that it might have been the man himself. Robert Bradshaw was a man of fifty, heavy-set, with iron-gray hair and a square jaw. He sat in the chair calmly, his hands resting on the arms, oblivious to the electrodes attached to his neck and wrist. "There I go," Harris said. "Watch."

His film-image appeared, approaching Bradshaw. "Now, Mr. Bradshaw," his image said, "this won't hurt you at all, and it'll help us a lot." The image rotated the controls on the shock box, Bradshaw stiffened, and his jaw set, but otherwise he gave no sign. The image of Harris regarded him for a time and then stepped away from the controls.

"Can you hear me, Mr. Bradshaw?" the image asked.

"Yes."

"What is your name?"

"Robert C. Bradshaw."

"What is your position?"

"Chief Biologist at the check station on Y-3."

"Are you there now?"

"No, I'm back on Terra. In a hospital."

"Why?"

"Because I admitted to the Garrison Chief that I had become a plant."

"Is that true? That you are a plant."

"Yes, in a non-biological sense. I retain the physiology of a human being, of course."

"What do you mean, then, that you're a plant?"

"The reference is to attitudinal response, to Weltanschauung."

"Go on."

"It is possible for a warm-blooded animal, an upper primate, to adopt the psychology of a plant, to some extent."

"Yes?"

"I refer to this."

"And the others? They refer to this also?"

"Yes."

"How did this occur, your adopting this attitude?

Bradshaw's image hesitated, the lips twisting. "See?" Harris said to Cox. "Strong conflict. He wouldn't have gone on, if he had been fully conscious."

"I — "

"Yes?"

"I was taught to become a plant."

The image of Harris showed surprise and interest. "What do you mean, you were *taught* to become a plant?"

"They realized my problems and taught me to become a plant. Now I'm free from them, the problems."

"Who? Who taught you?"

"The Pipers."

"Who? The Pipers? Who are the Pipers?"

There was no answer.

"Mr. Bradshaw, who are the Pipers?"

After a long, agonized pause, the heavy lips parted. "They live in the woods ... "

Harris snapped off the projector, and the lights came on. He and Cox blinked. "That was all I could get," Harris said. "But I was lucky to get that. He wasn't supposed to tell, not at all. That was the thing they all promised not to do, tell who taught them to become plants. The Pipers who live in the woods on Asteroid Y-3."

"You got this story from all twenty?"

"No." Harris grimaced. "Most of them put up too much fight. I couldn't even get *this* much from them."

Cox reflected. "The Pipers. Well? What do you propose to do? Just wait around until you can get the full story? Is that your program?"

"No." Harris said. "Not at all. I'm going to Y-3 and find out who the Pipers are, myself."

The small patrol ship made its landing with care and precision, its jets choking into final silence. The hatch slid back and Doctor Henry Harris found himself staring out at a field, a brown, sun-baked landing field. At the end of the field was a tall signal tower. Around the field on all sides were long gray buildings, the Garrison check station itself. Not far off a huge Venusian cruiser was parked, a vast green hulk, like an enormous lime. The technicians from the station were swarming all over it, checking and examining each inch of it for lethal life-forms and poisons that might have attached themselves to the hull.

"All out, sir," the pilot said.

Harris nodded. He took hold of his two suitcases and stepped carefully down. The ground was hot underfoot, and he blinked in the bright sunlight. Jupiter was in the sky, and the vast planet reflected considerable sunlight down onto the asteroid.

Harris started across the field, carrying his suitcase. A field attendant was already busy opening the storage compartment of the Patrol ship, extracting his trunk. The attendant lowered the trunk into a waiting dolly and came after him, manipulating the little truck with bored skill.

As Harris came to the entrance of the signal tower the gate slid back and a man came forward, an older man, large and robust, with white hair and a steady walk.

"How are you, Doctor?" he said, holding his hand out. "I'm Lawrence Watts, the Garrison Chief."

They shook hands. Watts smiled down at Harris. He was a huge old man, still regal and straight in his dark blue uniform, with his gold epaulets sparkling on his shoulders.

"Have a good trip?" Watts asked. "Come on inside and I'll have a drink fixed for you. It gets hot around here, with the Big Mirror up there."

"Jupiter?" Harris followed him inside the building. The signal tower was cool and dark, a welcome relief. "Why is the gravity so near Terra's? I expected to go flying off like a kangaroo. Is it artificial?"

"No. There's a dense core of some kind to the asteroid, some kind of metallic deposit. That's why we picked this asteroid out of all the others. It made the construction problem much simpler, and it also explains why the asteroid has natural air and water. Did you see the hills?"

"The hills?"

"When we get up higher in the tower we'll be able to see over the buildings. There's quite a natural park here, a regular little forest, complete with everything you'd want. Come in here, Harris. This is my office." The old man strode at quite a clip, around the corner and into a large, well-furnished apartment. "Isn't this pleasant? I intend to make my last year here as amiable as possible." He frowned. "Off course, with Deutsch gone, I may be here forever. Oh, well." He shrugged. "Sit down, Harris."

"Thanks." Harris took a chair, stretching his legs out. He watched Watts as he closed the door to the hall. "By the way, any more cases come up?"

"Two more today." Watts was grim. "Makes almost thirty, in all. We have three hundred men in this station. At the rate it's going — "

"Chief, you spoke about a forest on the asteroid. Do you allow the crew to go into the forest at will? Or do you restrict them to the buildings and grounds?"

Watts rubbed his jaw. "Well, it's a difficult situation, Harris. I have to let the men leave the grounds sometimes. They can *see* the forest from the buildings, and as long as you can see a nice place to stretch out and relax that does it. Once every ten days they have a full period of rest. Then they go out and fool around."

"And then it happens?"

"Yes, I suppose so. But as long as they can see the forest, they'll want to go. I can't help it."

"I know. I'm not censuring you. Well, what's your theory? What happens to them out there? What do they do?"

"What happens? Once they get out there and take it easy for a while they don't want to come back and work. It's boondoggling. Playing hookey. They don't want to work, so off they go."

"How about this business of their delusions?"

Watts laughed good-naturedly. "Listen, Harris. You know as well as I do that's a lot of poppycock. They're no more plants than you or I. They just don't want to work, that's all. When I was a cadet we had a few ways to make people work. I wish we could lay a few on their backs, like we used to."

"You think this is simple goldbricking, then?"

"Don't you think it is?"

"No," Harris said. "They really believe they're plants. I put them through the high-frequency shock treatment, the shock box. The whole nervous system is paralyzed, all inhibitions stopped cold. They tell the truth, then. And they said the same thing — and more."

Watts paced back and forth, his hands clasped behind his back. "Harris, you're a doctor, and I suppose you know what you're talking about. But look at the situation here. We have a garrison, a good modern garrison. We're probably the most modern outfit in the system. Every new device and gadget is here that science can produce. Harris, this garrison is one vast machine. The men are parts, and each has his job, the Maintenance Crew, the Biologists, the Office Crew, the Managerial Staff.

"Look what happens when one person steps away from his job. Everything else begins to creak. We can't service the bugs if no one services the machines. We can't order food to feed the crews if no one makes out reports, takes inventories. We can't direct any kind of activity if the Second in Command decides to go out and sit in the sun all day.

"Thirty people, one tenth of the Garrison. But we can't run without them. The Garrison is built that way. If you take the supports out the whole building falls. No one can leave. We're all tied here and these people know it. They know they have no right to do that, run off on their own. No one has that right anymore. We're all too tightly interwoven to suddenly start doing what we want. It's unfair to the rest, the majority."

Harris nodded. "Chief, can I ask you something?"

"What is it?"

"Are there any inhabitants on the asteroid? Any natives?"

"Natives?" Watts considered. "Yes, there's some kind of aborigines living out there." He waved vaguely toward the window.

"What are they like? Have you seen them?"

"Yes, I've seen them. At least, I saw them when we first came here. They hung around for a while, watching us, then after a time they disappeared."

"Did they die off? Diseases of some kind?"

"No. They just — just disappeared. Into their forest. They're still there, someplace."

"What kind of people are they?"

"Well, the story is that they're originally from Mars. They don't look much like Martians, though. They're dark, a kind of coppery color. Thin. Very agile, in their own way. They hunt and fish. No written language. We don't pay much attention to them."

"I see." Harris paused. "Chief, have you ever heard of anything called — The Pipers?"

"The Pipers?" Watts frowned. "No. Why?"

"The patients mentioned something called The Pipers. According to Bradshaw, the Pipers taught him to become a plant. He learned it from them, a kind of teaching."

"The Pipers. What are they?"

"I don't know," Harris admitted. "I thought maybe you might know. My first assumption, of course, was that they're the natives. But now I'm not so sure, after hearing your description of them."

"The natives are primitive savages. They don't have anything to teach anybody, especially a top-flight biologist."

Harris hesitated. "Chief, I'd like to go into the woods and look around. Is that possible?"

"Certainly. I can arrange it for you. I'll give you one of the men to show you around."

"I'd rather go alone. Is there any danger?"

"No, none that I know of. Except — "

"Except the Pipers," Harris finished. "I know. Well, there's only one way to find them, and that's it. I'll have to take my chances."

"If you walk in a straight line," Chief Watts said, "you'll find yourself back at the Garrison in about six hours. It's a damn small asteroid. There's a couple of streams and lakes, so don't fall in."

"How about snakes or poisonous insects?"

"Nothing like that reported. We did a lot of tramping around at first, but it's grown back now, the way it was. We never encountered anything dangerous."

"Thanks, Chief," Harris said. They shook hands. "I'll see you before nightfall."

"Good luck." The Chief and his two armed escorts turned and went back across the rise, down the other side toward the Garrison. Harris watched them go until they disappeared inside the building. Then he turned and started into the grove of trees.

The woods were very silent around him as he walked. Trees towered up on all sides of him, huge dark-green trees like eucalyptus. The ground underfoot was soft with endless leaves that had fallen and rotted into the soil. After awhile the grove of high trees fell behind and he found himself crossing a dry meadow, the grass and weeds burned brown in the sun. Insects buzzed around him, rising up from the dry weed-stalks. Something scuttled ahead, hurrying through the undergrowth. He caught sight of a gray ball with many legs, scampering furiously, its antennae weaving.

The meadow ended at the bottom of a hill. He was going up, now, going higher and higher. Ahead of him an endless expanse of green rose, acres of wild growth. He scrambled to the top finally, blowing and panting, catching his breath.

He went on. Now he was going down again, plunging into a deep gully. Tall ferns grew, as large as trees. He was entering a living Jurassic forest, ferns that stretched out endlessly ahead of him. Down he went, walking carefully. The air began to turn cold around him. The floor of the gully was damp and silent; underfoot the ground was almost wet.

He came out on a level table. It was dark, with the ferns growing up on all sides, dense growths of ferns, silent and unmoving. He came upon a natural path, an old stream bed, rough and rocky, but easy to follow. The air was thick and oppressive. Beyond the ferns he could see the side of the next hill, a green field rising up.

Something gray was ahead. Rocks, piled-up boulders, scattered and stacked here and there. The stream led directly to them. Apparently this had been a pool of some kind, a stream emptying from it. He climbed the first of the boulders awkwardly, feeling his way up. At the top he paused, resting again.

As yet he had had no luck. So far he had not met any of the natives. It would be through them that he would find the mysterious Pipers that were stealing the men away, if such really existed. If he could find the natives, talk to them, perhaps he could find out something. But as yet he had been unsuccessful. He looked around. The woods were very silent. A slight breeze moved through the ferns rustling them, but that was all. Where were the natives? Probably they had a settlement of some sort, huts, a clearing. The asteroid was small, he should be able to find them by nightfall.

He started down the rocks. More rocks rose up ahead and he climbed them. Suddenly he stopped, listening. Far off, he could hear a sound, the sound of water. Was he approaching a pool of some kind? He went on again, trying to locate the sound. He scrambled down rocks and up rocks, and all around him there was silence, except for the splashing of distant water. Maybe a waterfall, water in motion. A stream. If he found the stream he might find the natives.

The rocks ended and the stream bed began again, but this time it was wet, the bottom muddy and overgrown with moss. He was on the right track; not too long ago this stream had flowed, probably during the rainy season. He went up on the side of the stream, pushing through the ferns and vines. A golden snake slid expertly out of his path. Something glinted ahead, something sparkling through the ferns. Water. A pool. He hurried, pushing the vines aside and stepping out, leaving them behind.

He was standing on the edge of a pool, a deep pool sunk in a hollow of gray rocks, surrounded by ferns and vines. The water was clear and bright, and in motion, flowing in a waterfall at the far end. It was beautiful, and he stood watching, marveling at it, the undisturbed quality of it. Untouched, it was. Just as it had always been, probably. As long as the asteroid existed. Was he the first to see it? Perhaps. It was so hidden, so concealed by the ferns. It gave him a strange feeling, a feeling almost of ownership. He stepped down a little toward the water.

And it was then he noticed her.

The girl was sitting on the far edge of the pool, staring down into the water, resting her head on one drawn-up knee. She had been bathing; he could see that at once. Her coppery body was still wet and glistening with moisture, sparkling in the sun. She had not seen him. He stopped, holding his breath, watching her.

She was lovely, very lovely, with long dark hair that wound around her shoulders and arms. Her body was slim, very slender, with a supple grace to it that made him stare, accustomed as he was to various forms of anatomy. How silent she was! Silent and unmoving, staring down at the water. Time passed, strange, unchanging time, as he watched the girl. Time might even have ceased, with the girl sitting on the rock staring into the water, and the rows of great ferns behind her, as rigid as if they had been painted there.

All at once the girl looked up. Harris shifted, suddenly conscious of himself as an intruder. He stepped back. "I'm sorry," he murmured. "I'm from the Garrison. I didn't mean to come poking around."

She nodded without speaking.

"You don't mind?" Harris asked presently.

"No."

So she spoke Terran! He moved a little toward her, around the side of the pool. "I hope you don't mind my bothering you. I won't be on the asteroid very long. This is my first day here. I just arrived from Terra."

She smiled faintly.

"I'm a doctor. Henry Harris." He looked down at her, at the slim coppery body gleaming in the sunlight, a faint sheen of moisture on her arms and thighs. "You might be interested in why I'm here." He paused. "Maybe you can even help me."

She looked up a little. "Oh?"

"Would you like to help me?"

She smiled. "Yes. Of course."

"That's good. Mind if I sit down?" He looked around and found himself a flat rock. He sat down slowly, facing her. "Cigarette?"

"No."

"Well, I'll have one." He lit up, taking a deep breath. "You see, we have a problem at the Garrison. Something has been happening to some of the men, and it seems to be spreading. We have to find out what causes it or we won't be able to run the Garrison."

He waited for a moment. She nodded slightly. How silent she was! Silent and unmoving. Like the ferns.

"Well, I've been able to find out a few things from them, and one very interesting fact stands out. They keep saying that something called — called The Pipers are responsible for their condition. They say the Pipers taught them — " He stopped. A strange look had flitted across her dark, small face. "Do you know the Pipers?"

She nodded.

Acute satisfaction flooded over Harris. "You do? I was sure the natives would know." He stood up again. "I was sure they would, if the Pipers really existed. Then they do exist, do they?"

"They exist."

Harris frowned. "And they're here, in the woods?"

"Yes."

"I see." He ground his cigarette out impatiently. "You don't suppose there's any chance you could take me to them, do you?"

"Take you?"

"Yes. I have this problem and I have to solve it. You see, the Base Commander on Terra has assigned this to me, this business about the Pipers. It has to be solved. And I'm the one assigned to the job. So it's important to me to find them. Do you see? Do you understand?"

She nodded.

"Well, will you take me to them?"

The girl was silent. For a long time she sat, staring down into the water, resting her head against her knee. Harris began to become impatient. He fidgeted back and forth, resting first on one leg and then on the other.

"Well, will you?" he said again. "It's important to the whole Garrison. What do you say?" He felt around in his pockets. "Maybe I could give you something. What do I have ... " He brought out his lighter. "I could give you my lighter."

The girl stood up, rising slowly, gracefully, without motion or effort.

Harris' mouth fell open. How supple she was, gliding to her feet in a single motion! He blinked. Without effort she had stood, seemingly without *change*. All at once she was standing instead of sitting, standing and looking calmly at him, her small face expressionless.

"Will you?" he said.

"Yes. Come along." She turned away, moving toward the row of ferns.

Harris followed quickly, stumbling across the rocks. "Fine," he said. "Thanks a lot. I'm very interested to meet these Pipers. Where are you taking me, to your village? How much time do we have before nightfall?"

The girl did not answer. She had entered the ferns already, and Harris quickened his pace to keep from losing her. How silently she glided!

"Wait," he called. "Wait for me."

The girl paused, waiting for him, slim and lovely, looking silently back.

He entered the ferns, hurrying after her.

"Well I'll be damned!" Commander Cox said. "It sure didn't take you long." He leaped down the steps two at a time. "Let me give you a hand."

Harris grinned, lugging his heavy suitcases. He set them down and breathed a sigh of relief. "It isn't worth it," he said. "I'm going to give up taking so much."

"Come on inside. Soldier, give him a hand." A Patrolman hurried over and took one of the suitcases. The three men went inside and down the corridor to Harris' quarters. Harris unlocked the door and the Patrolman deposited his suitcase inside.

"Thanks," Harris said. He set the other down beside it. "It's good be be back, even for a little while."

"A little while?"

"I just came back to settle my affairs. I have to return to Y-3 tomorrow morning."

"Then you didn't solve the problem?"

"I solved it, but I haven't *cured* it. I'm going back and get to work right away. There's a lot to be done."

"But you found out what it is?"

"Yes. It was just what the men said. The Pipers."

"The Pipers do exist?"

"Yes." Harris nodded. "They do exist." He removed his coat and put it over the back of the chair. Then he went to the window and let it down. Warm spring air rushed into the room. He settled himself on the bed, leaning back.

"The Pipers exist, all right — in the minds of the Garrison crew! To the crew, the Pipers are real. The crew created them. It's a mass hypnosis, a group projection, and all the men there have it, to some degree."

"How did it start?"

"Those men on Y-3 were sent because they were skilled, highly-trained men with exceptional ability. All their lives they've been schooled by complex modern society, fast tempo and high integration between people. Constant pressure toward some goal, some job to be done.

"Those men are put down suddenly on an asteroid where there are natives living the most primitive of existence, completely vegetable lives. No concept of goal, no concept of purpose, and hence no ability to plan. The natives live the way the animals live, from day to day, sleeping, picking food from the trees. A kind of Garden-of-Eden existence, without struggle or conflict."

"So? But — "

"Each of the Garrison crew sees the natives and *unconsciously* thinks of his own early life, when he was a child, when *he* had no worries, no responsibilities, before he joined modern society. A baby lying in the sun.

"But he can't admit this to himself! He can't admit that he might *want* to live like the natives, to lie and sleep all day. So he invents The Pipers, the idea of a mysterious group living in the woods who trap him, lead him into their kind of life. Then he can blame *them*, not himself. They 'teach' him to become a part of the woods."

"What are you going to do? Have the woods burned?"

"No." Harris shook his head. "That's not the answer; the woods are harmless. The answer is psycho-therapy for the men. That's why I'm going right back, so I can begin work. They've got to be made to see that the Pipers are inside them, their own unconscious voices calling to them to give up their responsibilities. They've got to be made to realize that there are no Pipers, at least, not outside themselves. The woods are harmless and the natives have nothing to teach anyone. They're primitive savages, without even a written language. We're seeing a psychological projection by a whole Garrison of men who want to lay down their work and take it easy for a while."

The room was silent.

"I see," Cox said presently. "Well, it makes sense." He got to his feet. "I hope you can do something with the men you get back."

"I hope so, too," Harris agreed. "And I think I can. After all, it's just a question of increasing their self-awareness. When they have that the Pipers will vanish."

Cox nodded. "Well, you go ahead with your unpacking, Doc. I'll see you at dinner. And maybe before you leave, tomorrow."

"Fine."

Harris opened the door and the Commander went out into the hall. Harris closed the door after him and then went back across the room. He looked out the window for a moment, his hands in his pockets.

It was becoming evening, the air was turning cool. The sun was just setting as he watched, disappearing behind the buildings of the city surrounding the hospital. He watched it go down.

Then he went over to his two suitcases. He was tired, very tired from his trip. A great weariness was beginning to descend over him. There were so many things to do, so terribly many. How could he hope to do them all? Back to the asteroid. And then what?"

He yawned, his eyes closing. How sleepy he was! He looked over at the bed. Then he sat down on the edge of it and took his shoes off. So much to do, the next day.

He put his shoes in the corner of the room. Then he bent over, unsnapping one of the suitcases. He opened the suitcase. From it he took a bulging gunnysack. Carefully, he emptied the contents of the sack out on the floor. Dirt, rich soft dirt. Dirt he had collected during his last hours there, dirt he had carefully gathered up.

When the dirt was spread out on the floor he sat down in the middle of it. He stretched himself out, leaning back. When he was fully comfortable he folded his hands across his chest and closed his eyes. So much work to do — But later on, of course. Tomorrow. How warm the dirt was ...

He was sound asleep in a moment.

THE INFINITES

"I DON'T LIKE IT," Major Crispin Eller said. He stared through the port scope, frowning. "An asteroid like this with plenty of water, moderate temperature, an atmosphere similar to Terra's oxygen-nitrogen mix — "

"And no life." Harrison Blake, second in command, came up beside Eller. They both stared out. "No life, yet ideal conditions. Air, water, good temperature. Why?"

They looked at each other. Beyond the hull of the cruiser, the X-43y, the barren, level surface of the asteroid stretched away. The X-43y was a long way from home, half-way across the galaxy. Competition with the Mars-Venus-Jupiter Triumvirate had moved Terra to map and prospect every bit of rock in the galaxy, with the idea of claiming mining concessions later on. The X-43y had been out planting the blue and white flag for almost a year. The three-member crew had earned a rest, a vacation back on Terra and a chance to spend the pay they had accumulated. Tiny prospecting ships led a hazardous life, threading their way through the rubble-strewn periphery of the system, avoiding meteor swarms, clouds of hull-eating bacteria, space pirates, peanut-size empires on remote artificial planetoids —

"Look at it!" Eller said, jabbing angrily at the scope. "Perfect conditions for life. But nothing, just bare rock."

"Maybe it's an accident," Blake said, shrugging.

"You know there's no place where bacteria particles don't drift. There must be some reason why this asteroid isn't fertile. I sense something wrong."

"Well? What do we do?" Blake grinned humorlessly. "You're the captain. According to our instructions we're supposed to land and map every asteroid we encounter over Class-D diameter. This is a Class-C. Are we going outside and map it or not?"

Eller hesitated. "I don't like it. No one knows all the lethal factors floating out here in deep space. Maybe — "

"Could it be you'd like to go right on back to Terra?" Blake said. "Just think, no one would know we passed this last little bit of rock up. I wouldn't tip them off, Eller."

"That isn't it! I'm concerned with our safety, and that's all. You're the one who's been agitating to turn Terra-side." Eller studied the port scope. "If we only knew."

"Let out the pigs and see what shows. After they've run around for a while we should know something."

"I'm sorry I even landed."

Blake's face twisted in contempt. "You're sure getting cautious, now that we're almost ready to head home."

Eller moodily watched the gray barren rock, the gently moving water. Water and rock, a few clouds, even temperature. A perfect place for life. But there was no life. The rock was clean, smooth. Absolutely sterile, without growth or cover of any kind. The spectroscope showed nothing, not even one-celled water life, not even the familiar brown lichen encountered on countless rocks strewn through the galaxy.

"All right, then," Eller said. "Open one of the locks. I'll have Silv let out the pigs."

He picked up the com, dialing the laboratory. Down below them in the interior of the ship Silvia Simmons was working, surrounded by retorts and testing apparatus. Eller clicked the switch. "Silv?" he said.

Silvia's features formed on the vidscreen. "Yes?"

"Let the hamsters outside the ship for a short run, about half an hour. With line and collars, of course. I'm worried about this asteroid. There may be some toxic poisons around or radiation pits. When the pigs come back give them a rigid test. Throw the book at them."

"All right, Cris," Silvia smiled. "Maybe we can get out and stretch our legs after a while."

"Give me the results of the tests as soon as possible." Eller broke the circuit. He turned to Blake. "I assume you're satisfied. In a minute the pigs will be ready to go out."

Blake smiled faintly. "I'll be glad when we get back to Terra. One trip with you as captain is about all I can take."

Eller nodded. "Strange, that thirteen years in the Service hasn't taught you any more self-control. I guess you'll never forgive them for not giving you your stripes."

"Listen, Eller," Blake said. "I'm ten years older than you. I was serving when you were just a kid. You're still a pasty-faced squirt as far as I'm concerned. The next time — "

"CRIS!"

Eller turned quickly. The vidscreen was relit. On it, Silvia's face showed, frantic with fear.

"Yes?" He gripped the com. "What is it?"

"Cris, I went to the cages. The hamsters — They're cataleptic, stretched out, perfectly rigid. Every one of them is immobile. I'm afraid something — "

"Blake, get the ship up," Eller said.

"What?" Blake murmured, confused. "Are we — "

"Get the ship up! Hurry!" Eller raced toward the control board. "We have to get out of here!"

Blake came to him. "Is something — " he began, but abruptly he stopped, choked off. His face glazed over, his jaw slack. Slowly he settled to the smooth metal floor, falling like a limp sack. Eller stared, dazed. At last he broke away and reached toward the controls. All at once a numbing fire seared his skull, bursting inside his head. A thousand shafts of light exploded behind his eyes, blinding him. He staggered, groping for the switches. As darkness plucked at him his fingers closed over the automatic lift.

As he fell he pulled hard. Then the numbing darkness settled over him completely. He did not feel the smashing impact of the floor as it came up at him.

Out into space the ship rose, automatic relays pumping frantically. But inside no one moved.

Eller opened his eyes. His head throbbed with a deep, aching beat. He struggled to his feet, holding onto the hull railing. Harrison Blake was coming to life also, groaning and trying to rise. His dark face had turned sickly yellow, his eyes were blood-shot, his lips foam-flecked. He stared at Cris Eller, rubbing his forehead shakily.

"Snap out of it," Eller said, helping him up. Blake sat down in the control chair.

"Thanks." He shook his head. "What — what happened?"

"I don't know. I'm going to the lab and see if Silv is all right."

"Want me to come?" Blake murmured.

"No. Sit still. Don't strain your heart. Do you understand? Move as little as possible."

Blake nodded. Eller walked unsteadily across the control room to the corridor. He entered the drop lift and descended. A moment later he stepped out into the lab.

Silvia was slumped forward at one of the work tables, stiff and unmoving.

"Silv!" Eller ran toward her and caught hold of her, shaking her. Her flesh was hard and cold. "Silv!"

She moved a little.

"Wake up!" Eller got a stimulant tube from the supply cabinet. He broke the tube, holding it by her face. Silvia moaned. He shook her again.

"Cris?" Silvia said faintly. "Is it you? What — what happened? Is everything all right?" She lifted her head, blinking uncertainly. "I was talking to you on the vidscreen. I came over to the table, then all of a sudden — "

"It's all right." Eller frowned, deep in thought, his hand on her shoulder. "What could it have been? Some kind of radiation blast from the asteroid?" He glanced at his wristwatch. "Good Lord!"

"What's wrong?" Silvia sat up, brushing her hair back. "What is it, Cris?"

"We've been unconscious two whole days," Eller said slowly, staring at his watch. He put his hand to his chin. "Well, that explains this." He rubbed at the stubble.

"But we're all right now, aren't we?" Silvia pointed at the hamsters in their cages against the wall. "Look — they're up and running around again."

"Come on." Eller took her hand. "We're going up above and have a conference, the three of us. We're going over every dial and meter reading in the ship. I want to know what happened."

Blake scowled. "I have to agree. I was wrong. We never should have landed."

"Apparently the radiation came from the center of the asteroid." Eller traced a line on the chart. "This reading shows a wave building up quickly and then dying down. A sort of pulse wave from the asteroid's core, rhythmic."

"If we hadn't got into space we might have been hit by a second wave," Silvia said.

"The instruments picked up a subsequent wave about fourteen hours later. Apparently the asteroid has a mineral deposit that pulses regularly, throwing out radiation at fixed intervals. Notice how short the wave lengths are. Very close to cosmic ray patterns."

"But different enough to penetrate our screen."

"Right. It hit us full force." Eller leaned back in his seat. "That explains why there was no life on the asteroid. Bacteria landing would be withered by the first wave. Nothing would have a chance to get started."

"Cris?" Silvia said.

"Yes?"

"Cris, do you think the radiation might have done anything to us? Are we out of danger? Or — "

"I'm not certain. Look at this." Eller passed her a graph of lined foil, traced in red. "Notice that although our vascular systems have fully recovered, our neural responses are still not quite the same. There's been alteration there."

"In what way?"

"I don't know. I'm not a neurologist. I can see distinct differences from the original tracings, the characteristic test patterns we traced a month or two ago, but what it means I have no way to tell."

"Do you think it's serious?"

"Only time will tell. Our systems were jolted by an intense wave of unclassified radiation for a straight ten hours. What permanent effects it has left, I can't say. I feel all right at this moment. How do you feel?"

"Fine," Silvia said. She looked out through the port scope at the dark emptiness of deep space, at the endless fragments of light arranged in tiny unmoving specks. "Anyhow, we're finally heading Terra-side. I'll be glad to get home. We should have them examine us right away."

"At least our hearts survived without any obvious damage. No blood clots or cell destruction. That was what I was primarily worried about. Usually a dose of hard radiation of that general type will — "

"How soon will we reach the system?" Blake said.

"A week."

Blake set his lips. "That's a long time. I hope we're still alive."

"I'd advise against exercising too much," Eller said. "We'll take it easy the rest of the way and hope that whatever has been done to us can be undone back on Terra."

"I guess we actually got off fairly easy." Silvia said. She yawned. "Lord, I'm sleepy." She got slowly to her feet, pushing her chair back. "I think I'll turn in. Anyone object?"

"Go ahead," Eller said. "Blake, how about some cards? I want to relax. Blackjack?"

"Sure," Blake said. "Why not?" He slid a deck from his jacket pocket. "It'll make the time pass. Cut for deal."

"Fine." Eller took the deck. He cut, showing a seven of clubs. Blake won the deck with a jack of hearts.

They played listlessly, neither of them much interested. Blake was sullen and uncommunicative, still angry because Eller had been proved so right. Eller himself was tired and uncomfortable. His head throbbed dully in spite of the opiates he had taken. He removed his helmet and rubbed his forehead.

"Play," Blake murmured. Under them the jets rumbled, carrying them nearer and nearer Terra. In a week they would enter the system. They had not seen Terra in over a year. How would it look? Would it still be the same? The great green globe, with its vast oceans, all the tiny islands. Then down at New York Spaceport. San Francisco, for him. It would be nice, all right. The crowds of people, Terrans, good old frivolous, senseless Terrans, without a care in the world. Eller grinned up at Blake. His grin turned to a frown.

Blake's head had drooped. His eyes were slowly closing. He was going to sleep.

"Wake up," Eller said. "What's the matter?"

Blake grunted, pulling himself up straight. He went on dealing the next hand. Again his head sank lower and lower.

"Sorry," he murmured. He reached out to draw in his winnings. Eller fumbled in his pocket, getting out more credits. He looked up, starting to speak. But Blake had fallen completely asleep.

"I'll be damned!" Eller got to his feet. "This is strange." Blake's chest rose and fell evenly. He snored a little, his heavy body relaxed. Eller turned down the light and walked toward the door. What was the matter with Blake? It was unlike him to pass out during a game of cards.

Eller went down the corridor toward his own quarters. He was tired and ready for sleep. He entered his washroom, unfastening his collar. He removed his jacket and turned on the hot water. It would be good to get into bed, to forget everything that had happened to them, the sudden exploding blast of radiation, the painful awakening, the gnawing fear. Eller began to wash his face. Lord, how his head buzzed. Mechanically, he splashed water on his arms.

It was not until he had almost finished washing that he noticed it. He stood for a long time, water running over his hands, staring silently down, unable to speak.

His fingernails were gone.

He looked up in the mirror, breathing quickly. Suddenly he grabbed at his hair. Handfuls of hair came out, great bunches of light brown hair. Hair and nails —

He shuddered, trying to calm himself. Hair and nails. Radiation. Of course: radiation did that, killed both the hair and the nails. He examined his hands.

The nails were completely gone all right. There was no trace of them. He turned his hands over and over, studying the fingers. The ends were smooth and tapered. He fought down rising panic, moving unsteadily away from the mirror.

A thought struck him. Was he the only one? What about Silvia!

He put his jacket on again. Without nails his fingers were strangely deft and agile. Could there be anything else? They had to be prepared. He looked into the mirror again.

And sickened.

His head — What was happening? He clasped his hands to his temples. *His head.* Something was wrong, terribly wrong. He stared, his eyes wide. He was almost completely hairless, now, his shoulders and jacket covered with brown hair that had fallen. His scalp gleamed, bald and pink, a shocking pink. But there was something more.

His head had expanded. It was swelling into a full sphere. And his ears were shriveling, his ears and his nose. His nostrils were becoming thin and transparent even as he watched. He was changing, altering, faster and faster.

He reached a shaking hand into his mouth. His teeth were loose in the gums. He pulled. Several teeth came out easily. What was happening? Was he dying? Was he the only one? What about the others?

Eller turned and hurried out of the room. His breath came painfully, harshly. His chest seemed constricted, his ribs choking the air out of him. His heart labored, beating fitfully. And his legs were weak. He stopped, catching hold of the door. He started into the lift. Suddenly there was a sound, a deep bull roar. Blake's voice, raised in terror and agony.

"That answers that," Eller thought grimly, as the lift rose around him. "At least I'm not the only one!"

Harrison Blake gaped at him in horror. Eller had to smile. Blake, hairless, his skull pink and glistening, was not a very impressive sight. His cranium, too, had enlarged, and his nails were gone. He was standing by the control table, staring first at Eller and then down at his own body. His uniform was too large for his dwindling body. It bagged around him in slack folds.

"Well?" Eller said. "We'll be lucky if we get out of this. Space radiations can do strange things to a man's body. It was a bad day for us when we landed on that — "

"Eller," Blake whispered. "What'll we do? We can't live this way, not like this! Look at us."

"I know." Eller set his lips. He was having trouble speaking now that he was almost toothless. He felt suddenly like a baby. Toothless, without hair, a body growing more helpless each moment. Where would it end?

"We can't go back like this," Blake said. "We can't go back to Terra, not looking this way. Good heavens, Eller! We're freaks. Mutants. They'll — they'll lock us up like animals in cages. People will — "

"Shut up." Eller crossed to him. "We're lucky to be alive at all. Sit down." He drew a chair out. "I think we better get off our legs."

They both sat down. Blake took a deep, shuddering breath. He rubbed his smooth forehead, again and again.

"It's not us I'm worried about," Eller said, after a time. "It's Silvia. She'll suffer the most from this. I'm trying to decide whether we should go down at all. But if we don't, she may — "

There was a buzz. The vidscreen came to life, showing the white-walled laboratory, the retorts and rows of testing equipment, lined up neatly against the walls.

"Cris?" Silvia's voice came, thin and edged with horror. She was not visible on the screen. Apparently she was standing off to one side.

"Yes." Eller went to the screen. "How are you?"

"How am I?" A thrill of hysteria ran through the girl's voice. "Cris, has it hit you, too? I'm afraid to look." There was a pause. "It has, hasn't it? I can see you — but don't try to look at me. I don't want you to see me again. It's — it's horrible. What are we going to do?"

"I don't know. Blake says he won't go back to Terra this way."

"No! We can't go back! We can't!"

There was silence. "We'll decide later," Eller said finally. "We don't have to settle it now. These changes in our systems are due to radiation, so they may be only temporary. They may go away, in time. Or surgery may help. Anyhow, let's not worry about it now."

"Not worry? No, of course I won't worry. How could I worry about a little thing like this! Cris, don't you understand? We're monsters, hairless monsters. No hair, no teeth, no nails. Our heads — "

"I understand." Eller set his jaw. "You stay down in the lab. Blake and I will discuss it with you on the vidscreen. You won't have to show yourself to us."

Silvia took a deep breath. "Anything you say. You're still captain."

Eller turned away from the screen. "Well, Blake, do you feel well enough to talk?"

The great-domed figure in the corner nodded, the immense hairless skull moving slightly. Blake's once great body had shrunk, caved in. The arms were pipe stems, the chest hollow and sickly. Restlessly, the soft fingers tapped against the table. Eller studied him.

"What is it?" Blake said.

"Nothing. I was just looking at you."

"You're not very pleasant looking, either."

"I realize that." Eller sat down across from him. His heart was pounding, his breath coming shallowly. "Poor Silv! It's worse for her than it is for us."

Blake nodded. "Poor Silv. Poor all of us. She's right, Eller. We're monsters." His fragile lips curled. "They'll destroy us back on Terra. Or lock us up. Maybe a quick death would be better. Monsters, freaks, hairless hydrocephalics."

"Not hydrocephalics," Eller said. "Your brain isn't impaired. That's one thing to be thankful for. We can still think. We still have our minds."

"In any case we know why there isn't life on the asteroid," Blake said ironically. "We're a success as a scouting party. We got the information. Radiation, lethal radiation, destructive to organic tissue. Produces mutation and alteration in cell growth as well as changes in the structure and function of the organs."

Eller studied him thoughtfully. "That's quite learned talk for you, Blake."

"It's an accurate description." Blake looked up. "Let's be realistic. We're monstrous cancers blasted by hard radiation. Let's face it. We're not men, not human beings any longer. We're — "

"We're what?"

"I don't know." Blake lapsed into silence.

"It's strange," Eller said. He studied his fingers moodily. He experimented, moving his fingers about. Long, long and thin. He traced the surface of the table with them. The skin was sensitive. He could feel every indentation of the table, every line and mark.

"What are you doing?" Blake said.

"I'm curious." Eller held his fingers close to his eyes, studying them. His eyesight was dimming. Everything was vague and blurred. Across from him Blake was staring down. Blake's eyes had begun to recede, sinking slowly into the great hairless skull. It came to Eller all at once that they were losing their sight. They were going slowly blind. Panic seized him.

"Blake!" he said. "We're going blind. There's a progressive deterioration of our eyes, vision and muscles."

"I know," Blake said.

"But why? We're actually losing the eyes themselves! They're going away, drying up. Why?"

"Atrophied," Blake murmured.

"Perhaps." Eller brought out a log book from the table, and a writing beam. He traced a few notes on the foil. Sight diminishing, vision failing rapidly. But fingers much more sensitive. Skin response unusual. Compensation?

"What do you think of this?" he said. "We're losing some functions, gaining others."

"In our hands?" Blake studied his own hands. "The loss of the nails makes it possible to use the fingers in new ways." He rubbed his fingers against the cloth of his uniform. "I can feel individual fibers which was impossible before."

"Then the loss of nails was purposeful!"

"So?"

"We've been assuming this was all without purpose. Accidental burns, cell destruction, alteration. I wonder … " Eller moved the writing beam slowly across the log sheet. Fingers: new organs of perception. Heightened touch, more tactile response. But vision dimming. …

"Cris!" Silvia's voice came, sharp and frightened.

"What is it?" He turned toward the vidscreen.

"I'm losing my sight. I can't see."

"It's all right. Don't worry."

"I'm — I'm afraid."

Eller went over to the vidscreen. "Silv, I think we're losing some senses and gaining others. Examine your fingers. Do you notice anything? Touch something."

There was an agonizing pause. "I seem to be able to feel things much differently. Not the same as before."

"That's why our nails are gone."

"But what does it mean?"

Eller touched his bulging cranium, exploring the smooth skin thoughtfully. Suddenly he clenched his fists, gasping. "Silv! Can you still operate the X-ray equipment? Are you mobile enough to cross the lab?"

"Yes, I suppose so."

"Then I want an X-ray plate made. Make it right away. As soon as it's ready notify me."

"An X-ray plate? Of what?"

"Of your own cranium. I want to see what changes our brains have undergone. Especially the cerebrum. I'm beginning to understand, I think."

"What is it?"

"I'll tell you when I see the plate." A faint smile played across Eller's thin lips. "If I'm right, then we've been completely mistaken about what's happened to us!"

For a long time Eller stared at the X-ray plate framed in the vidscreen. Dimly he made out the lines of the skull, struggling to see with his fading eyesight. The plate trembled in Silvia's hands.

"What do you see?" she whispered.

"I was right. Blake, look at this, if you can."

Blake came slowly over, supporting himself with one of the chairs. "What is it?" He peered at the plate, blinking. "I can't see well enough."

"The brain has changed enormously. Notice how much enlargement there is here." Eller traced the frontal lobe outline. "Here, and here. There's been growth, amazing growth. And greater convolution. Notice this odd bulge off the frontal lobe. A kind of projection. What do you suppose it might be?"

"I have no idea," Blake said. "Isn't that area mainly concerned with higher processes of thought?"

"The most developed cognitive faculties are located there. And that's where the most growth has taken place." Eller moved slowly away from the screen.

"What do you make of it?" Silvia's voice came.

"I have a theory. It may be wrong, but this fits in perfectly. I thought of it almost at first, when I saw that my nails were gone."

"What's your theory?"

Eller sat down at the control table. "Better get off your feet, Blake. I don't think our hearts are too strong. Our body mass is decreasing, so perhaps later on — "

"Your theory! What is it?" Blake came toward him, his thin bird-like chest rising and falling. He peered down intently at Eller. "What is it?"

"We've evolved," Eller said. "The radiation from the asteroid speeded up cell growth, like cancer. But not without design. There's purpose and direction to these changes, Blake. We're changing rapidly, moving through centuries in a few seconds."

Blake stared at him.

"It's true," Eller said. "I'm sure of it. The enlarged brain, diminished powers of sight, loss of hair, teeth. Increased dexterity and tactile sense. Our bodies have lost, for the most part. But our minds have benefited. We're developing greater cognitive powers, greater conceptual capacity. Our minds are moving ahead into the future. Our minds are evolving."

"Evolving!" Blake sat down slowly. "Can this be true?"

"I'm certain of it. We'll take more X-rays, of course. I'm anxious to see changes in the internal organs, kidneys, stomach. I imagine we've lost portions of our — "

"Evolved! But that means that evolution is not the result of accidental external stresses. Competition and struggle. Natural selection, aimless, without direction. It implies that every organism carries the thread of its evolution within it. Then evolution is teleological, with a goal, not determined by chance."

Eller nodded. "Our evolution seems to be more of an internal growth and change along distinct lines. Certainly not at random. It would be interesting to know what the directing force is."

"This throws a new light on things," Blake murmured. "Then we're not monsters, after all. We're not monsters. We're — we're men of the future."

Eller glanced at him. There was a strange quality in Blake's voice. "I suppose you might say that," he admitted. "Of course, we'll still be considered freaks on Terra."

"But they'll be wrong," Blake said. "Yes, they'll look at us and say we're freaks. But we're not freaks. In another few million years the rest of mankind will catch up to us. We're moving ahead of our own time, Eller."

Eller studied Blake's great bulging head. He could only dimly make out its lines. Already, the well-lighted control room was turning almost dark. Their sight was virtually gone. All he could make out was vague shadows, nothing more.

"Men of the future," Blake said. "Not monsters, but men from tomorrow. Yes, this certainly throws a new light on things." He laughed nervously. "A few minutes ago I was ashamed of my new appearance! But now — "

"But now what?"

"But now I'm not so sure."

"What do you mean?"

Blake did not answer. He had got slowly to his feet, holding onto the table.

"Where are you going?" Eller said.

Blake crossed the control room painfully, feeling his way toward the door. "I must think this over. There are astonishing new elements to be considered. I agree, Eller. You're quite right. We have evolved. Our cognitive faculties are greatly improved. There's considerable deterioration in body functions, of course. But that's to be expected. I think we're actually the gainers, everything considered." Blake touched his great skull cautiously. "Yes, I think that in the long run we may have gained. We will look back on this as a great day,

Eller. A great day in our lives. I'm sure your theory is correct. As the process continues I can sense changes in my conceptual abilities. The Gestalt faculty has risen amazingly. I can intuit certain relationships that — "

"Stop!" Eller said. "Where are you going? Answer me. I'm still captain of this ship."

"Going? I'm going to my quarters. I must rest. This body is highly inadequate. It may be necessary to devise mobile carts and perhaps even artificial organs as mechanical lungs and hearts. I'm certain the pulmonary and vascular systems are not going to stand up long. The life expectancy is no doubt greatly diminished. I'll see you later, Major Eller. But perhaps I should not use the word *see*." He smiled faintly. "We will not see much any more." He raised his hands. "But *these* will take the place of vision." He touched his skull. "And *this* will take the place of many, many things."

He disappeared, closing the door behind him. Eller heard him going slowly, determinedly down the corridor, feeling his way along with careful, feeble steps.

Eller crossed to the vidscreen. "Silv! Can you hear me? Did you listen to our conversation?"

"Yes."

"Then you know what has happened to us."

"Yes, I know. Cris, I'm almost completely blind now. I can see virtually nothing."

Eller grimaced, remembering Silvia's keen, sparkling eyes. "I'm sorry, Silv. I wish this had never happened. I wish we were back the way we were. It's not worth it."

"Blake thinks it's worth it."

"I know. Listen, Silv. I want you to come here to the control room, if you can. I'm worried about Blake, and I want you here with me."

"Worried? How?"

"He's got something on his mind. He's not going to his quarters merely to rest. Come here with me and we'll decide what to do. A few minutes ago I was the one who said we should go back to Terra. But now I think I'm beginning to change my mind."

"Why? Because of Blake? You don't suppose Blake would — "

"I'll discuss it with you when you get here. Make your way along with your hands. Blake did it, so probably you can. I think perhaps we won't return to Terra after all. But I want to give you my reasons."

"I'll be there as soon as I can," Silvia said. "But be patient. And Cris — Don't look at me. I don't want you to see me this way."

"I won't see you," Eller said grimly. "By the time you get here I won't be able to see much at all."

Silvia sat down at the control table. She had put on one of the spacesuits from the lab locker so that her body was hidden by the plastic and metal suit. Eller waited until she had caught her breath.

"Go on," Silvia said.

"The first thing we must do is collect all the weapons on the ship. When Blake comes back I'm going to announce that we are not returning to Terra. I think he will be angry, perhaps enough to start trouble. If I'm not mistaken, he very much wants to keep moving Terra-side now, as he begins to understand the implications of our change."

"And you don't want to go back."

"No." Eller shook his head. "We must not go back to Terra. There's danger, great danger. You can see what kind of danger already."

"Blake is fascinated by the new possibilities," Silvia said thoughtfully. "We're ahead of other men, several millions of years, advancing each moment. Our brains, our powers of thought, are far in advance of other Terrans."

"Blake will want to go back to Terra, not as an ordinary man, but as a man of the future. We may find ourselves in relation to other Terrans as geniuses among idiots. If the process of change keeps up, we may find them nothing more than higher primates, animals in comparison to us."

They both were silent.

"If we go back to Terra we'll find human beings nothing more than animals," Eller went on. "Under the circumstances, what would be more natural than for us to help them? After all, we're millions of years ahead of them. We could do a lot for them if they'd let us direct them, lead them, do their planning for them."

"And if they resist we probably could find ways of gaining control of them," Silvia said. "And everything, of course, would be for their own good. That goes without saying. You're right, Cris. If we go back to Terra we'll soon find ourselves contemptuous of mankind. We'll want to lead them, show them how to live, whether they want us to or not. Yes, it'll be a strong temptation."

Eller got to his feet. He went over to the weapons locker and opened it. Carefully, he removed the heavy-duty Boris guns and brought them over to the table, one by one.

"The first thing is to destroy these. After that, you and I have to see to it that Blake is kept away from the control room. Even if we have to barricade ourselves in, it has to be done. I'll reroute the ship. We'll move away from the system, toward some remote region. It's the only way."

He opened the Boris guns and removed the firing controls. One by one he broke the controls, crunching them under foot.

There was a sound. Both turned, straining to see.

"Blake!" Eller said. "It must be you. I can't see you, but — "

"You're correct," Blake's voice came. "No, Eller, we're all of us blind, or almost blind. So you destroyed the Boris guns! I'm afraid that won't keep us from returning to Terra."

"Go back to your quarters," Eller said. "I'm the captain, and I'm giving you an order to — "

Blake laughed. "You're ordering me? You're almost blind, Eller, but I think you'll be able to see — this!"

Something rose up into the air around Blake, a soft pale cloud of blue. Eller gasped, cringing, as the cloud swirled around him. He seemed to be dissolving, breaking into countless fragments, rushed and carried away, drifting —

Blake withdrew the cloud into the tiny disc that he held. "If you'll remember," he said calmly, "I received the *first* bath of radiation. I'm a little ahead of you two, by only a short time, perhaps, but enough. In any case, the Boris guns would have been useless, compared to what I have. Remember, everything in this ship is a million years antiquated. What I hold — "

"Where did you get it, that disc?"

"I got it nowhere. I constructed it, as soon as I realized that you would turn the ship away from Terra. I found it easy to make. In a short time the two of you will also begin to realize our new powers. But right now, I'm afraid, you're just a bit behind."

Eller and Silvia struggled to breathe. Eller sank against the hull railing, exhausted, his heart laboring. He stared at the disc in Blake's hand.

"We'll continue moving toward Terra," Blake went on. "Neither of you is going to change the control settings. By the time we arrive at the New York Spaceport you both will have come to see things differently. When you've caught up with me you'll see things as I see them. We must go back, Eller. It's our duty to mankind."

"Our duty?"

There was a faint mocking quality in Blake's voice. "Of course it's our duty! Mankind needs us. It needs us very much. There's much we can do for Terra. You see, I was able to catch some of your thoughts. Not all of them, but enough to know what you were planning. You'll find that from now on we'll begin to lose speech as a method of communication. We'll soon begin to rely directly on — "

"If you can see into my mind then you can see why we mustn't return to Terra," Eller said.

"I can see what you're thinking but you're wrong. We must go back for their good." Blake laughed softly. "We can do a lot for them. Their science will change in our hands. They will change, altered by us. We'll remake Terra, make her strong. The Triumvirate will be helpless before the new Terra, the Terra that we will build. The three of us will transform the race, make it rise, burst across the entire galaxy. Mankind will be material for us to mold. The blue and white will be planted everywhere, on all the planets of the galaxy, not on mere bits of rock. We'll make Terra strong, Eller. Terra will rule everywhere."

"So that's what you have in mind," Eller said. "And if Terra doesn't want to go along with us? What then?"

"It is possible they won't understand," Blake admitted. "After all, we must begin to realize that we're millions of years ahead of them. They're a long way behind us, and many times they may not understand the purpose of our orders. But you know that orders must be carried out, even if their meaning is not comprehended. You've commanded ships, you know that. For Terra's own good, and for — "

Eller leaped. But the fragile, brittle body betrayed him. He fell short, grasping frantically, blindly, for Blake. Blake cursed, stepping back.

"You fool! Don't you — "

The disc glinted, the blue cloud bursting into Eller's face. He staggered to one side, his hands up. Abruptly he fell, crashing to the metal floor. Silvia lumbered to her feet, coming toward Blake, slow and awkward in the heavy spacesuit. Blake turned toward her, the disc raised. A second cloud rose up. Silvia screamed. The cloud devoured her.

"Blake!" Eller struggled to his knees. The tottering figure that had been Silvia lurched and fell. Eller caught hold of Blake's arms. The two figures swayed back and forth. Blake trying to pull away. Suddenly Eller's strength gave out. He slipped back down, his head striking the metal floor. Nearby, Silvia lay, silent and inert.

"Get away from me," Blake snarled, waving the disc. "I can destroy you the way I did her. Do you understand?"

"You killed her," Eller screamed.

"It's your own fault. You see what you gained by fighting? Stay away from me! If you come near me I'll turn the cloud on you again. It'll be the end of you."

Eller did not move. He stared at the silent form.

"All right," Blake's voice came to him, as if from a great distance. "Now listen to me. We're continuing toward Terra. You'll guide the ship for me while I work down in the laboratory. I can follow your thoughts, so if you attempt to change course I'll know at once. Forget about her! It still leaves two of us, enough to do what we must. We'll be within the system in a few days. There's much to accomplish, first." Blake's voice was calm, matter of fact. "Can you get up?"

Eller rose slowly, holding onto the hull railing.

"Good," Blake said. "We must work everything out very carefully. We may have difficulties with the Terrans at first. We must be prepared for that. I think that in the time remaining I will be able to construct the necessary equipment that we will need. Later on, when your development catches up with my own, we will be able to work together to produce the things we need."

Eller stared at him. "Do you think I'll ever go along with you?" he said. His glance moved toward the figure on the floor, the silent, unmoving figure. "Do you think after that I could ever — '

"Come, come, Eller," Blake said impatiently. "I'm surprised at you. You must begin to see things from a new position. There is too much involved to consider — "

"So this is how mankind will be treated! This is the way you'll save them, by ways like this!"

"You'll come around to a realistic attitude," Blake said calmly. "You'll see that as men of the future — "

"Do you really think I will?"

The two men faced each other.

Slowly a flicker of doubt passed over Blake's face. "You must, Eller! It's our duty to consider things in a new way. Of course you will." He frowned, raising the disc a little. "How can there be any doubt of that?"

Eller did not answer.

"Perhaps," Blake said thoughtfully, "you will hold a grudge against me. Perhaps your vision will be clouded by this incident. It is possible ... " The disc moved. "In that case I must adjust myself as soon as possible to the realization that I will have to go on alone. If you won't join me to do the things that must be done then I will have to do them without you." His fingers tightened against the disc. "I will do it all alone, Eller, if you won't join me. Perhaps this is the best way. Sooner or later this moment might come, in any case. It is better for me to — "

Blake screamed.

From the wall a vast, transparent shape moved slowly, almost leisurely, out into the control room. Behind the shape came another, and then another, until at last there were five of them. The shapes pulsed faintly, glimmering with a vague, internal glow. All were identical, featureless.

In the center of the control room the shapes came to rest, hovering a little way up from the floor, soundlessly, pulsing gently, as if waiting.

Eller stared at them. Blake had lowered his disc and was standing, pale and tense, gaping in astonishment. Suddenly Eller realized something that made chill fear rush through him. He was not seeing the shapes at all. He was almost completely blind. He was sensing them in some new way, through some new mode of perception. He struggled to comprehend, his mind racing. Then, all at once, he understood. And he knew why they had no distinct shapes, no features.

They were pure energy.

Blake pulled himself together, coming to life. "What — " he stammered, waving the disc. "Who — "

A thought flashed, cutting Blake off. The thought seared through Eller's mind, hard and sharp, a cold, impersonal thought, detached and remote.

"The girl. First."

Two of the shapes moved toward Silvia's inert form, lying silently beside Eller. They paused a slight distance above her, glowing and pulsing. Then part of the glimmering corona leaped out, hurtling toward the girl's body, bathing her in a shimmering fire.

"That will suffice," a second thought came, after a few moments. The corona retreated. "Now, the one with the weapon."

A shape moved toward Blake. Blake retreated toward the door behind him. His withered body shook with fear.

"What are you?" he demanded, raising the disc. "Who are you? Where did you come from?"

The shape came on.

"Get away!" Blake cried. "Get back! If you don't — "

He fired. The blue cloud entered the shape. The shape quivered for a moment, absorbing the cloud. Then it came on again. Blake's jaw fell. He scrambled into the corridor, stumbling and falling. The shape hesitated at the door. Then it was joined by a second shape which moved up beside it.

A ball of light left the first shape, moving toward Blake. It enveloped him. The light winked out. There was nothing where Blake had stood. Nothing at all.

"That was unfortunate," a thought came. "But necessary. Is the girl reviving?"

"Yes."

"Good."

"Who are you?" Eller asked. "What are you? Will Silv be all right? Is she alive?"

"The girl will recover." The shapes moved toward Eller, surrounding him. "We should perhaps have intervened before she was injured but we preferred to wait until we were certain the one with the weapon was going to gain control."

"Then you knew what was happening?"

"We saw it all."

"Who are you? Where did you — where did you come from?"

"We were here," the thought came.

"Here?"

"On the ship. We were here from the start. You see, *we* were the first to receive the radiation; Blake was wrong. So our transformation began even before his did. And in addition, we had much farther to go. Your race has little evolution ahead of it. A few more inches of cranium, a little less hair, perhaps. But not really so much. Our race, on the other hand, had just begun."

"Your race? First to receive the radiation?" Eller stared around him in dawning realization. "Then you must be — "

"Yes," the calm, inflexible thought came. "You are right. We are the hamsters from the laboratory. The pigs carried for your experiments and tests." There was almost a note of humor in the thought. "However, we hold nothing against you, I assure you. In fact, we have very little interest in your race, one way or another. We owe you a slight debt for helping us along our path, bringing our destiny onto us in a few short minutes instead of another fifty million years.

"For that we are thankful. And I think we have already repaid you. The girl will be all right. Blake is gone. You will be allowed to continue on your way back to your own planet."

"Back to Terra?" Eller faltered. "But — "

"There is one more thing that we will do before we go," the calm thought came. "We have discussed the matter and we are in complete agreement on this. Eventually your race will achieve its rightful position through the natural course of time. There is no value in hurrying it prematurely. For the sake of your race and the sake of you two, we will do one last thing before we depart. You will understand."

A swift ball of flame rose from the first shape. It hovered over Eller. It touched him and passed on to Silvia. "It is better," the thought came. "There is no doubt."

They watched silently, staring through the port scope. From the side of the ship the first ball of light moved, flashing out into the void.

"Look!" Silvia exclaimed.

The ball of light increased speed. It shot away from the ship, moving at incredible velocity. A second ball oozed through the hull of the ship, out into space behind the first.

After it came a third, a fourth, and finally a fifth. One by one the balls of light hurtled out into the void, out into deep space.

When they were gone Silvia turned to Eller, her eyes shining. "That's that," she said. "Where are they going?"

"No way to tell. A long way, probably. Maybe not anywhere in this galaxy. Some remote place." Eller reached out suddenly, touching Silvia's dark-brown hair. He grinned. "You know, your hair is really something to see. The most beautiful hair in the whole universe."

Silvia laughed. "Any hair looks good to us, now." She smiled up at him, her red lips warm. "Even yours, Cris."

Eller gazed down at her a long time. "They were right," he said at last.

"Right?"

"It *is* better." Eller nodded, gazing down at the girl beside him, at her hair and dark eyes, the familiar lithe, supple form. "I agree — There is no doubt of it."

THE PRESERVING MACHINE

DOC LABYRINTH LEANED BACK in his lawn chair, closing his eyes gloomily. He pulled his blanket up around his knees.

"Well?" I said. I was standing by the barbecue pit, warming my hands. It was a clear cold day. The sunny Los Angeles sky was almost cloud-free. Beyond Labyrinth's modest house a gently undulating expanse of green stretched off until it reached the mountains — a small forest that gave the illusion of wilderness within the very limits of the city. "Well?" I said. "Then the Machine did work the way you expected?"

Labyrinth did not answer. I turned around. The old man was staring moodily ahead, watching an enormous dun-colored beetle that was slowly climbing the side of his blanket. The beetle rose methodically, its face blank with dignity. It passed over the top and disappeared down the far side. We were alone again.

Labyrinth sighed and looked up at me. "Oh, it worked well enough."

I looked after the beetle, but it was nowhere to be seen. A faint breeze eddied around me, chill and thin in the fading afternoon twilight. I moved nearer the barbecue pit.

"Tell me about it," I said.

Doctor Labyrinth, like most people who read a great deal and who have too much time on their hands, had become convinced that our civilization was going the way of Rome. He saw, I think, the same cracks forming that had sundered the ancient world, the world of Greece and Rome; and it was his conviction that presently our world, our society, would pass away as theirs did, and a period of darkness would follow.

Now Labyrinth, having thought this, began to brood over all the fine and lovely things that would be lost in the reshuffling of societies. He thought of the art, the literature, the manners, the music, everything that would be lost. And it seemed to him that of all these grand and noble things, music would probably be the most lost, the quickest forgotten.

Music is the most perishable of things, fragile and delicate, easily destroyed.

Labyrinth worried about this, because he loved music, because he hated the idea that some day there would be no more Brahms and Mozart, no more gentle chamber music that he could dreamily associate with powdered wigs and resined bows, with long, slender candles, melting away in the gloom.

What a dry and unfortunate world it would be, without music! How dusty and unbearable.

This is how he came to think of the Preserving Machine. One evening as he sat in his living room in his deep chair, the gramophone on low, a vision came to him. He perceived in his mind a strange sight, the last score of a Schubert trio, the last copy, dog-eared, well-thumbed, lying on the floor of some gutted place, probably a museum.

A bomber moved overhead. Bombs fell, bursting the museum to fragments, bringing the walls down in a roar of rubble and plaster. In the debris the last score disappeared, lost in the rubbish, to rot and mold.

And then, in Doc Labyrinth's vision, he saw the score come burrowing out, like some buried mole. Quick like a mole, in fact, with claws and sharp teeth and a furious energy.

If music had that faculty, the ordinary, everyday instinct of survival which every worm and mole has, how different it would be! If music could be transformed into living creatures, animals with claws and teeth, then music might survive. If only a Machine could be built, a Machine to process musical scores into living forms.

But Doc Labyrinth was no mechanic. He made a few tentative sketches and sent them hopefully around to the research laboratories. Most of them were much too busy with war contracts, of course. But at last he found the people he wanted. A small midwestern university was delighted with his plans, and they were happy to start work on the Machine at once.

Weeks passed. At last Labyrinth received a postcard from the university. The Machine was coming along fine; in fact, it was almost finished. They had given it a trial run, feeding a couple of popular songs into it. The results? Two small mouse-like animals had come scampering out, rushing around the laboratory until the cat caught and ate them. But the Machine was a success.

It came to him shortly after, packed carefully in a wood crate, wired together and fully insured. He was quite excited as he set to work, taking the slats from it. Many fleeting notions must have coursed through his mind as he adjusted the controls and made ready for the first transformation. He had selected a priceless score to begin with, the score of the Mozart G Minor

Quintet. For a time he turned the pages, lost in thought, his mind far away. At last he carried it to the Machine and dropped it in.

Time passed. Labyrinth stood before it, waiting nervously, apprehensive and not really certain what would greet him when he opened the compartment. He was doing a fine and tragic work, it seemed to him, preserving the music of the great composers for all eternity. What would his thanks be? What would he find? What form would this all take, before it was over?

There were many question unanswered. The red light of the Machine was glinting, even as he meditated. The process was over, the transformation had already taken place. He opened the door.

"Good Lord!" he said. "This is very odd."

A bird, not an animal, stepped out. The mozart bird was pretty, small and slender, with the flowing plumage of a peacock. It ran a little way across the room and then walked back to him, curious and friendly. Trembling, Doc Labyrinth bent down, his hand out. The mozart bird came near. Then, all at once, it swooped up into the air.

"Amazing," he murmured. He coaxed the bird gently, patiently, and at last it fluttered down to him. Labyrinth stroked it for a long time, thinking. What would the rest of them be like? He could not guess. He carefully gathered up the mozart bird and put it into a box.

He was even more surprised the next day when the beethoven beetle came out, stern and dignified. That was the beetle I saw myself, climbing along his red blanket, intent and withdrawn, on some business of its own.

After that came the schubert animal. The schubert animal was silly, an adolescent sheep-creature that ran this way and that, foolish and wanting to play. Labyrinth sat down right then and there and did some heavy thinking.

Just what *were* survival factors? Was a flowing plume better than claws, better than sharp teeth? Labyrinth was stumped. He had expected an army of stout badger creatures, equipped with claws and scales, digging, fighting, ready to gnaw and kick. Was he getting the right thing? Yet who could say what was good for survival? — the dinosaurs had been well armed, but there were none of them left. In any case the Machine was built; it was too late to turn back, now.

Labyrinth went ahead, feeding the music of many composers into the Preserving Machine, one after another, until the woods behind his house was filled with creeping, bleating things that screamed and crashed in the night. There were many oddities that came out, creations that startled and astonished him. The brahms insect had many legs sticking in all directions, a vast, platter-shaped centipede. It was low and flat, with a coating of uniform fur. The brahms insect liked to be by itself, and it went off promptly, taking great pains to avoid the wagner animal who had come just before.

The wagner animal was large and splashed with deep colors. It seemed to have quite a temper, and Doc Labyrinth was a little afraid of it, as were the bach bugs, the round ball-like creatures, a whole flock of them, some large, some small, that had been obtained for the Forty-Eight Preludes and Fugues. And there was the stravinsky bird, made up of curious fragments and bits, and many others besides.

So he let them go, off into the woods, and away they went, hopping and rolling and jumping as best they could. But already a sense of failure hung over him. Each time a creature came out he was astonished; he did not seem to have control over the results at all. It was out of his hands, subject to some strong, invisible law that had subtly taken over, and this worried him greatly. The creatures were bending, changing before a deep, impersonal force, a force that Labyrinth could neither see nor understand. And it made him afraid.

Labyrinth stopped talking. I waited for a while but he did not seem to be going on. I looked around at him. The old man was staring at me in a strange, plaintive way.

"I don't really know much more," he said. "I haven't been back there for a long time, back in the woods. I'm afraid to. I know something is going on, but — "

"Why don't we both go and take a look?"

He smiled with relief. "You wouldn't mind, would you? I was hoping you might suggest that. This business is beginning to get me down." He pushed his blanket aside and stood up, brushing himself off. "Let's go then."

We walked around the side of the house and along a narrow path, into the woods. Everything was wild and chaotic, overgrown and matted, an unkempt, unattended sea of green. Doc Labyrinth went first, pushing the branches off the path, stooping and wriggling to get through.

"Quite a place," I observed. We made our way for a time. The woods were dark and damp; it was almost sunset now, and a light mist was descending on us, drifting down through the leaves above.

"No one comes here." Then Doc stopped suddenly, looking around. "Maybe we'd better go and find my gun. I don't want anything to happen."

"You seem certain that things have got out of hand." I came up beside him and we stood together. "Maybe it's not as bad as you think."

Labyrinth looked around. He pushed some shrubbery back with his foot. "They're all around us, everywhere, watching us. Can't you feel it?"

I nodded absently. "What's this?" I lifted up a heavy, moldering branch, particles of fungus breaking from it. I pushed it out of the way. A mound lay outstretched, shapeless and indistinct, half buried in the soft ground.

"What is it?" I said again. Labyrinth stared down, his face tight and forlorn. He began to kick at the mound aimlessly. I felt uncomfortable. "What is it, for heaven's sake?" I said. "Do you know?"

Labyrinth looked slowly up at me. "It's the schubert animal," he murmured. "Or it was, once. There isn't much left of it, any more."

The schubert animal — that was the one that had run and leaped like a puppy, silly and wanting to play. I bent down, staring at the mound, pushing a few leaves and twigs from it. It was dead all right. Its mouth was open, its body had been ripped wide. Ants and vermin were already working on it, toiling endlessly away. It had begun to stink.

"But what happened?" Labyrinth said. He shook his head. "What could have done it?"

There was a sound. We turned quickly.

For a moment we saw nothing. Then a bush moved, and for the first time we made out its form. It must have been standing there watching us all the time. The creature was immense, thin and extended, with bright, intense eyes. To me, it looked something like a coyote, but much heavier. Its coat was matted and thick, its muzzle hung partly open as it gazed at us silently, studying us as if astonished to find us there.

"The wagner animal," Labyrinth said thickly. "But it's changed. It's changed. I hardly recognize it."

The creature sniffed the air, its hackles up. Suddenly it moved back, into the shadows, and a moment later it was gone.

We stood for a while, not saying anything. At last Labyrinth stirred. "So, that's what it was," he said. "I can hardly believe it. But why? What — "

"Adaptation," I said. "When you toss an ordinary house cat out it becomes wild. Or a dog."

"Yes." He nodded. "A dog becomes a wolf again, to stay alive. The law of the forest. I should have expected it. It happens to everything."

I looked down at the corpse on the ground, and then around at the silent bushes. Adaptation — or maybe something worse. An idea was forming in my mind, but I said nothing, not right away.

"I'd like to see some more of them," I said. "Some of the others. Let's look around some more."

He agreed. We began to poke slowly through the grass and weeds, pushing branches and foliage out of the way. I found a stick, but Labyrinth got down on his hands and knees, reaching and feeling, staring near-sightedly down.

"Even children turn into beasts," I said. "You remember the wolf children of India? No one could believe they had been ordinary children."

Labyrinth nodded. He was unhappy, and it was not hard to understand why. He had been wrong, mistaken in his original idea, and the consequences of it were just now beginning to become apparent to him. Music would survive as living creatures, but he had forgotten the lesson of the Garden of Eden: that once a thing has been fashioned it begins to exist on its own, and thus ceases to be the property of its creator to mold and direct as he wishes. God, watching man's development, must have felt the same sadness — and the same humiliation — as Labyrinth, to see His creatures alter and change to meet the needs of survival.

That his musical creatures should survive could mean nothing to him any more, for the very thing he had created them to prevent, the brutalization of beautiful things, was happening in *them*, before his own eyes. Doc Labyrinth looked up at me suddenly, his face full of misery. He had ensured their survival, all right, but in so doing he had erased any meaning, any value in it. I tried to smile a little at him, but he promptly looked away again.

"Don't worry so much about it," I said. "It wasn't much of a change for the wagner animal. Wasn't it pretty much that way anyhow, rough and temperamental? Didn't it have a proclivity towards violence — "

I broke off. Doc Labyrinth had leaped back, jerking his hand out of the grass. He clutched his wrist, shuddering with pain.

"What is it?" I hurried over. Trembling, he held his little old hand out to me. "What is it? What happened?"

I turned the hand over. All across the back of it were marks, red cuts that swelled even as I watched. He had been stung, stung or bitten by something in the grass. I looked down, kicking the grass with my foot.

There was a stir. A little golden ball rolled quickly away, back toward the bushes. It was covered with spines like a nettle.

"Catch it!" Labyrinth cried. "Quick!"

I went after it, holding out my handkerchief, trying to avoid the spines. The sphere rolled frantically, trying to get away, but finally I got it into the handkerchief.

Labyrinth stared at the struggling handkerchief as I stood up. "I can hardly believe it," he said. "We'd better go back to the house."

"What is it?"

"One of the bach bugs. But it's changed. . . . "

We made our way back along the path, toward the house, feeling our way through the darkness. I went first, pushing the branches aside, and Labyrinth followed behind, moody and withdrawn, rubbing his hand from time to time.

We entered the yard and went up to the back steps of the house, onto the porch. Labyrinth unlocked the door and we went into the kitchen. He snapped on the light and hurried to the sink to bathe his hand.

I took an empty fruit jar from the cupboard and carefully dropped the bach bug into it. The golden ball rolled testily around as I clamped the lid on. I sat down at the table. Neither of us spoke, Labyrinth at the sink, running cold water over his stung hand, I at the table, uncomfortably watching the golden ball in the fruit jar trying to find some way to escape.

"Well?" I said at last.

"There's no doubt." Labyrinth came over and sat down opposite me. "It's undergone some metamorphosis. It certainly didn't have poisoned spines to start with. You know, it's a good thing that I played my Noah role carefully."

"What do you mean?"

"I made them all neuter. They can't reproduce. There will be no second generation. When these die, that will be the end of it."

"I must say I'm glad you thought of that."

"I wonder," Labyrinth murmured. "I wonder how it would sound, now, this way."

"What?"

"The sphere, the bach bug. That's the real test, isn't it? I could put it back through the Machine. We could see. Do you want to find out?"

"Whatever you say, Doc," I said. "It's up to you. But don't get your hopes up too far."

He picked up the fruit jar carefully and we walked downstairs, down the steep flights of steps to the cellar. I made out an immense column of dull metal rising up in the corner, by the laundry tubs. A strange feeling went through me. It was the Preserving Machine.

"So this is it," I said.

"Yes, this is it." Labyrinth turned the controls on and worked with them for a time. At last he took the jar and held it over the hopper. He removed the lid carefully, and the bach bug dropped reluctantly from the jar, into the Machine. Labyrinth closed the hopper after it.

"Here we go," he said. He threw the control and the Machine began to operate. Labyrinth folded his arms and we waited. Outside the night came on, shutting out the light, squeezing it out of existence. At last an indicator on the face of the Machine blinked red. The Doc turned the control to OFF and we stood in silence, neither of us wanting to be the one who opened it.

"Well?" I said finally. "Which one of us is going to look?"

Labyrinth stirred. He pushed the slot-piece aside and reached into the Machine. His fingers came out grasping a slim sheet, a score of music. He handed it to me. "This is the result," he said. "We can go upstairs and play it."

We went back up to the music room. Labyrinth sat down before the grand piano and I passed him back the score. He opened it and studied it for a moment, his face blank, without expression. Then he began to play.

I listened to the music. It was hideous. I have never heard anything like it. It was distorted, diabolical, without sense or meaning, except, perhaps, an alien, disconcerting meaning that should never have been there. I could believe only with the greatest effort that it had once been a Bach Fugue, part of a most orderly and respected work.

"That settles it," Labyrinth said. He stood up, took the score in his hands, and tore it to shreds.

As we made our way down the path to my car I said, "I guess the struggle for survival is a force bigger than any human ethos. It makes our precious morals and manners look a little thin."

Labyrinth agreed. "Perhaps nothing can be done, then, to save those manners and morals."

"Only time will tell," I said. "Even though this method failed, some other may work; something that we can't foresee or predict now may come along, some day."

I said good night and got into my car. It was pitch dark; night had fallen completely. I switched on my headlights and moved off down the road, driving into the utter darkness. There were no other cars in sight anywhere. I was alone, and very cold.

At the corner I stopped, slowing down to change gears. Something moved suddenly at the curb, something by the base of a huge sycamore tree, in the darkness. I peered out, trying to see what it was.

At the base of the sycamore tree a huge dun-colored beetle was building something, putting a bit of mud into place on a strange, awkard structure. I watched the beetle for a time, puzzled and curious, until at last it noticed me and stopped. The beetle turned abruptly and entered its building, snapping the door firmly shut behind it.

I drove away.

EXPENDABLE

THE MAN CAME OUT on the front porch and examined the day. Bright and cold — with dew on the lawns. He buttoned his coat and put his hands in his pockets.

As the man started down the steps the two caterpillars waiting by the mailbox twitched with interest.

"There he goes," the first one said. "Send in your report."

As the other began to rotate his vanes the man stopped, turning quickly.

"I heard that," he said. He brought his foot down against the wall, scraping the caterpillars off, onto the concrete. He crushed them.

Then he hurried down the path to the sidewalk. As he walked he looked around him. In the cherry tree a bird was hopping, pecking bright-eyed at the cherries. The man studied him. All right? Or — The bird flew off. Birds all right. No harm from them.

He went on. At the corner he brushed against a spider web, crossed from the bushes to the telephone pole. His heart pounded. He tore away, batting the air. As he went on he glanced over his shoulder. The spider was coming slowly down the bush, feeling out the damage to his web.

Hard to tell about spiders. Difficult to figure out. More facts needed — No contact, yet.

He waited at the bus stop, stomping his feet to keep them warm.

The bus came and he boarded it, feeling a sudden pleasure as he took his seat with all the warm, silent people, staring indifferently ahead. A vague flow of security poured through him.

He grinned, and relaxed, the first time in days.

The bus went down the street.

*   *   *

Tirmus waved his antennae excitedly.

"Vote, then, if you want." He hurried past them, up onto the mound. "But let me say what I said yesterday, before you start."

"We already know it all," Lala said impatiently. "Let's get moving. We have the plans worked out. What's holding us up?"

"More reason for me to speak." Tirmus gazed around at the assembled gods. "The entire Hill is ready to march against the giant in question. Why? We know he can't communicate to his fellows — It's out of the question. The type of vibration, the language they use, makes it impossible to convey such ideas as he holds about us, about our — "

"Nonsense." Lala stepped up. "Giants communicate well enough."

"There is no record of a giant having made known information about us!" The army moved restlessly.

"Go ahead," Tirmus said. "But it's a waste of effort. He's harmless — cut off. Why take all the time and — "

"Harmless?" Lala stared at him. "Don't you understand? He knows!"

Tirmus walked away from the mound. "I'm against unnecessary violence. We should save our strength. Someday we'll need it."

The vote was taken. As expected, the army was in favor of moving against the giant. Tirmus sighed and began stroking out the plans on the ground.

"This is the location that he takes. He can be expected to appear there at period-end. Now, as I see the situation — "

He went on, laying out the plans in the soft soil.

One of the gods leaned toward another, antennae touching. "This giant. He doesn't stand a chance. In a way, I feel sorry for him. How'd he happen to butt in?"

"Accident." The other grinned. "You know, the way they do, barging around."

"It's too bad for him, though."

It was nightfall. The street was dark and deserted. Along the sidewalk the man came, newspaper under his arm. He walked quickly, glancing around him. He skirted around the big tree growing by the curb and leaped agilely into the street. He crossed the street and gained the opposite side. As he turned the corner he entered the web, sewn from bush to telephone pole. Automatically he fought it, brushing it off him. As the strands broke a thin humming came to him, metallic and wiry.

" … wait!"

He paused.

" … careful … inside … wait … "

His jaw set. The last strands broke in his hands and he walked on. Behind him the spider moved in the fragment of his web, watching. The man looked back.

"Nuts to you," he said. "I'm not taking any chances, standing there all tied up."

He went on, along the sidewalk, to his path. He skipped up the path, avoiding the darkening bushes. On the porch he found his key, fitting it into the lock.

He paused. Inside? Better than outside, especially at night. Night a bad time. Too much movement under the bushes. Not good. He opened the door and stepped inside. The rug lay ahead of him, a pool of blackness. Across on the other side he made out the form of the lamp.

Four steps to the lamp. His foot came up. He stopped.

What did the spider say? Wait? He waited, listening. Silence.

He took his cigarette lighter and flicked it on.

The carpet of ants swelled toward him, rising up in a flood. He leaped aside, out onto the porch. The ants came rushing, hurrying, scratching across the floor in the half light.

The man jumped down to the ground and around the side of the house. When the first ants came flowing over the porch he was already spinning the faucet handle rapidly, gathering up the hose.

The burst of water lifted the ants up and scattered them, flinging them away. The man adjusted the nozzle, squinting through the mist. He advanced, turning the hard stream from side to side.

"God damn you," he said, his teeth locked. "Waiting inside — "

He was frightened. Inside — never before! In the night cold sweat came out on his face. Inside. They had never got inside before. Maybe a moth or two, and flies, of course. But they were harmless, fluttery, noisy —

A carpet of ants!

Savagely, he sprayed them until they broke rank and fled into the lawn, into the bushes, under the house.

He sat down on the walk, holding the hose, trembling from head to foot.

They really meant it. Not an anger raid, annoyed, spasmodic; but planned, an attack, worked out. They had waited for him. One more step.

Thank God for the spider.

Presently he shut the hose off and stood up. No sound; silence everywhere. The bushes rustled suddenly. Beetle? Something black scurried — he put his foot on it. A messenger, probably. Fast runner. He went gingerly inside the dark house, feeling his way by the cigarette lighter.

Later, he sat at his desk, the spray gun beside him, heavy-duty steel and copper. He touched its damp surface with his fingers.

Seven o'clock. Behind him the radio played softly. He reached over and moved the desk lamp so that it shone on the floor beside the desk.

He lit a cigarette and took some writing paper and his fountain pen. He paused, thinking.

So they really wanted him, badly enough to plan it out. Bleak despair descended over him like a torrent. What could he do? Whom could he go to? Or tell. He clenched his fists, sitting bolt upright in the chair.

The spider slid down beside him onto the desk top. "Sorry. Hope you aren't frightened, as in the poem."

The man stared. "Are you the same one? The one at the corner? The one who warned me?"

"No. That's somebody else. A Spinner. I'm strictly a Cruncher. Look at my jaws." He opened and shut his mouth. "I bite them up."

The man smiled. "Good for you."

"Sure. Do you know how many there are of us in — say — an acre of land. Guess."

"A thousand."

"No. Two and a half million. Of all kinds. Crunchers, like me, or Spinners, or Stingers."

"Stingers?"

"The best. Let's see." The spider thought. "For instance, the black widow, as you call her. Very valuable." He paused. "Just one thing."

"What's that?"

"We have our problems. The gods — "

"Gods!"

"Ants, as you call them. The leaders. They're beyond us. Very unfortunate. They have an awful taste — makes one sick. We have to leave them for the birds."

The man stood up. "Birds? Are they — "

"Well, we have an arrangement. This has been going on for ages. I'll give you the story. We have some time left."

The man's heart contracted. "Time left? What do you mean?"

"Nothing. A little trouble later on, I understand. Let me give you the background. I don't think you know it."

"Go ahead. I'm listening." He stood up and began to walk back and forth.

"*They* were running the Earth pretty well, about a billion years ago. You see, men came from some other planet. Which one? I don't know. They landed and found the Earth quite well cultivated by them. There was a war."

"So we're the invaders," the man murmured.

"Sure. The war reduced both sides to barbarism, them and yourselves. You forgot how to attack, and they degenerated into closed social factions, ants, termites — "

"I see."

"The last group of you that knew the full story started us going. We were bred" — the spider chuckled in its own fashion — "bred some place for this worthwhile purpose. We keep them down very well. You know what they call us? The Eaters. Unpleasant, isn't it?

Two more spiders came drifting down on their webstrands, alighting on the desk. The three spiders went into a huddle.

"More serious than I thought," the Cruncher said easily. "Didn't know the whole dope. The Stinger here —"

The black widow came to the edge of the desk. "Giant," she piped, metallically. "I'd like to talk with you."

"Go ahead," the man said.

"There's going to be some trouble here. They're moving, coming here, a lot of them. We thought we'd stay with you awhile. Get in on it."

"I see." The man nodded. He licked his lips, running his fingers shakily through his hair. "Do you think — that is, what are the chances —"

"Chances?" The Stinger undulated thoughtfully. "Well, we've been in this work a long time. Almost a million years. I think that we have the edge over them, in spite of the drawbacks. Our arrangements with the birds, and of course, with the toads —"

"I think we can save you," the Cruncher put in cheerfully. "As a matter of fact, we look forward to events like this."

From under the floorboards came a distant scratching sound, the noise of a multitude of tiny claws and wings, vibrating faintly, remotely. The man heard. His body sagged all over.

"You're really certain? You think you can do it?" He wiped the perspiration from his lips and picked up the spray gun, still listening.

The sound was growing, swelling beneath them, under the floor, under their feet. Outside the house bushes rustled and a few moths flew up against the window. Louder and louder the sound grew, beyond and below, everywhere, a rising hum of anger and determination. The man looked from side to side.

"You're sure you can do it?" he murmured. "You can really save me?"

"Oh," the Stinger said, embarrassed. "I didn't mean *that*. I meant the species, the race ... not you as an individual."

The man gaped at him and the three Eaters shifted uneasily. More moths burst against the window. Under them the floor stirred and heaved.

"I see," the man said. "I'm sorry I misunderstood you."

THE VARIABLE MAN

I

SECURITY COMMISSIONER REINHART rapidly climbed the front steps and entered the Council building. Council guards stepped quickly aside and he entered the familiar place of great whirring machines. His thin face rapt, eyes alight with emotion, Reinhart gazed intently up at the central SRB computer, studying its reading.

"Straight gain for the last quarter," observed Kaplan, the lab organizer. He grinned proudly as if personally responsible. "Not bad, Commissioner."

"We're catching up to them," Reinhart retorted. "But too damn slowly. We must finally go over — and soon."

Kaplan was in a talkative mood. "We design new offensive weapons, they counter with improved defenses. And nothing is actually made! Continual improvement, but neither we nor Centaurus can stop designing long enough to stabilize for production."

"It will end," Reinhart stated coldly, "as soon as Terra turns out a weapon for which Centaurus can build no defense."

"Every weapon has a defense. Design and discord. Immediate obsolescence. Nothing lasts long enough to — "

"What we count on is the *lag*," Reinhart broke in, annoyed. His hard gray eyes bored into the lab organizer and Kaplan slunk back. "The time lag between our offensive design and their counter development. The lag varies." He waved impatiently toward the massed banks of SRB machines. "As you well know."

At this moment, 9:30 AM, May 7, 2136, the statistical ratio on the SRB machines stood at 21–17 on the Centauran side of the ledger. All facts consid-

163

ered, the odds favored a successful repulsion by Proxima Centaurus of a Terran military attack. The ratio was based on the total information known to the SRB machines, on a gestalt of the vast flow of data that poured in endlessly from all sectors of the Sol and Centaurus systems.

21–17 on the Centauran side. But a month ago it had been 24–18 in the enemy's favor. Things were improving, slowly but steadily. Centaurus, older and less virile than Terra, was unable to match Terra's rate of technocratic advance. Terra was pulling ahead.

"If we went to war now," Reinhart said thoughtfully, "we would lose. We're not far enough along to risk an overt attack." A harsh, ruthless glow twisted across his handsome features, distorting them into a stern mask. "But the odds are moving in our favor. Our offensive designs are gradually gaining on their defenses."

"Let's hope the war comes soon," Kaplan agreed. "We're all on edge. This damn waiting. ... "

The war would come soon. Reinhart knew it intuitively. The air was full of tension, the *élan*. He left the SRB rooms and hurried down the corridor to his own elaborately guarded office in the Security wing. It wouldn't be long. He could practically feel the hot breath of destiny on his neck — for him a pleasant feeling. His thin lips set in a humorless smile, showing an even line of white teeth against his tanned skin. It made him feel good, all right. He'd been working at it a long time.

First contact, a hundred years earlier, had ignited instant conflict between Proxima Centauran outposts and exploring Terran raiders. Flash fights, sudden eruptions of fire and energy beams.

And then the long, dreary years of inaction between enemies where contact required years of travel, even at nearly the speed of light. The two systems were evenly matched. Screen against screen. Warship against power station. The Centauran Empire surrounded Terra, an iron ring that couldn't be broken, rusty and corroded as it was. New weapons had to be conceived, if Terra was to break out.

Through the windows of his office, Reinhart could see endless buildings and streets. Terrans hurrying back and forth. Bright specks that were commute ships, little eggs that carried businessmen and white-collar workers around. The huge transport tubes that shot masses of workmen to factories and labor camps from their housing units. All these people, waiting to break out. Waiting for the day.

Reinhart snapped on his vidscreen, the confidential channel. "Give me Military Designs," he ordered sharply.

He sat tense, his wiry body taut, as the vidscreen warmed into life. Abruptly he was facing the hulking image of Peter Sherikov, director of the vast network of labs under the Ural Mountains.

Sherikov's great bearded features hardened as he recognized Reinhart.

His bushy black eyebrows pulled up in a sullen line. "What do you want? You know I'm busy. We have too much work to do, as it is. Without being bothered by — politicians."

"I'm dropping over your way," Reinhart answered lazily. He adjusted the cuff of his immaculate gray cloak. "I want a full description of your work and whatever progress you've made."

"You'll find a regular departmental report plate filed in the usual way, around your office someplace. If you'll refer to that you'll know exactly what we — "

"I'm not interested in that. I want to *see* what you're doing. And I expect you to be prepared to describe your work fully. I'll be there shortly. Half an hour."

Reinhart cut the circuit. Sherikov's heavy features dwindled and faded. Reinhart relaxed, letting his breath out. Too bad he had to work with Sherikov. He had never liked the man. The big Polish scientist was an individualist, refusing to integrate himself with society. Independent, atomistic in outlook. He held concepts of the individual as an end, diametrically contrary to the accepted organic state Weltansicht.

But Sherikov was the leading research scientist, in charge of the Military Designs Department. And on Designs the whole future of Terra depended. Victory over Centaurus — or more waiting, bottled up in the Sol system, surrounded by a rotting, hostile Empire, now sinking into ruin and decay, yet still strong.

Reinhart got quickly to his feet and left the office. He hurried down the hall and out of the Council building.

A few minutes later he was heading across the mid-morning sky in his highspeed cruiser, toward the Asiatic landmass, the vast Ural mountain range. Toward the Military Designs labs.

Sherikov met him at the entrance. "Look here, Reinhart. Don't think you're going to order me around. I'm not going to — "

"Take it easy." Reinhart fell into step beside the bigger man. They passed through the check and into the auxiliary labs. "No immediate coercion will be exerted over you or your staff. You're free to continue your work as you see fit — for the present. Let's get this straight. My concern is to integrate your work with our total social needs. As long as your work is sufficiently productive — "

Reinhart stopped in his tracks.

"Pretty, isn't he?" Sherikov said ironically.

"What the hell is it?"

"Icarus, we call him. Remember the Greek myth? The legend of Icarus. Icarus flew ... This Icarus is going to fly, one of these days." Sherikov shrugged. "You can examine him, if you want. I suppose this is what you came here to see."

Reinhart advanced slowly. "This is the weapon you've been working on?"

"How does he look?"

Rising up in the center of the chamber was a squat metal cylinder, a great ugly cone of dark gray. Technicians circled around it, wiring up the exposed relay banks. Reinhart caught a glimpse of endless tubes and filaments, a maze of wires and terminals and parts criss-crossing each other, layer on layer.

"What is it?" Reinhart perched on the edge of a workbench, leaning his big shoulders against the wall.

"An idea of Jamison Hedge — the same man who developed our instantaneous interstellar vidcasts forty years ago. He was trying to find a method of faster than light travel when he was killed, destroyed along with most of his work. After that ftl research was abandoned. It looked as if there were no future in it."

"Wasn't it shown that nothing could travel faster than light?"

"The interstellar vidcasts do! No, Hedge developed a valid ftl drive. He managed to propel an object at fifty times the speed of light. But as the object gained speed, its length began to diminish and its mass increased. This was in line with familiar twentieth-century concepts of mass-energy transformation. We conjectured that as Hedge's object gained velocity it would continue to lose length and gain mass until its length became nil and its mass infinite. Nobody can imagine such an object."

"Go on."

"But what actually occurred is this. Hedge's object continued to lose length and gain mass until it reached the theoretical limit of velocity, the speed of light. At that point the object, still gaining speed, simply ceased to exist. Having no length, it ceased to occupy space. It disappeared. However, the object had not been *destroyed*. It continued on its way, gaining momentum each moment, moving in an arc across the galaxy, away from the Sol system. Hedge's object entered some other realm of being, beyond our powers of conception. The next phase of Hedge's experiment consisted in a search for some way to slow the ftl object down, back to a sub-ftl speed, hence back into our universe. This counterprinciple was eventually worked out."

"With what result?"

"The death of Hedge and destruction of most of his equipment. His experimental object, in re-entering the space-time universe, came into being in space already occupied by matter. Possessing an incredible mass, just below infinity level, Hedge's object exploded in a titanic cataclysm. It was obvious that no space travel was possible with such a drive. Virtually all space contains *some* matter. To re-enter space would bring automatic destruction. Hedge had found his ftl drive and his counterprinciple, but no one before this has been able to put them to any use."

Reinhart walked over toward the great metal cylinder. Sherikov jumped down and followed him. "I don't get it," Reinhart said. "You said the principle is no good for space travel."

"That's right."

"What's this for, then? If the ship explodes as soon as it returns to our universe — "

"This is not a ship." Sherikov grinned slyly. "Icarus is the first practical application of Hedge's principles. Icarus is a bomb."

"So this is our weapon," Reinhart said. "A bomb. An immense bomb."

"A bomb, moving at a velocity greater than light. A bomb which will not exist in our universe. The Centaurans won't be able to detect or stop it. How could they? As soon as it passes the speed of light it will cease to exist — beyond all detection."

"But — "

"Icarus will be launched outside the lab, on the surface. He will align himself with Proxima Centaurus, gaining speed rapidly. By the time he reaches his destination he will be traveling at ftl-100. Icarus will be brought back to this universe within Centaurus itself. The explosion should destroy the star and wash away most of its planets — including their central hub-planet, Armun. There is no way they can halt Icarus, once he has been launched. No defense is possible. Nothing can stop him. It is a real fact."

"When will it be ready?"

Sherikov's eyes flickered. "Soon."

"Exactly how soon?"

The big Pole hesitated. "As a matter of fact, there's only one thing holding us back."

Sherikov led Reinhart around to the other side of the lab. He pushed a lab guard out of the way.

"See this?" He tapped a round globe, open at one end, the size of a grapefruit. "This is holding us up."

"What is it?"

"The central control turret. This thing brings Icarus back to sub-ftl flight at the correct moment. It must be absolutely accurate. Icarus will be within the star only a matter of a microsecond. If the turret does not function exactly, Icarus will pass out the other side and shoot beyond the Centauran system."

"How near completed is this turret?"

Sherikov hedged uncertainly, spreading out his big hands. "Who can say? It must be wired with infinitely minute equipment — microscope grapples and wires invisible to the naked eye."

"Can you name any completion date?"

Sherikov reached into his coat and brought out a manila folder. "I've drawn up the data for the SRB machines, giving a date of completion. You can go ahead and feed it. I entered ten days as the maximum period. The machines can work from that."

Reinhart accepted the folder cautiously. "You're sure about the date? I'm not convinced I can trust you, Sherikov."

Sherikov's features darkened. "You'll have to take a chance, Commissioner. I don't trust you any more than you trust me. I know how much you'd like an excuse to get me out of here and one of your puppets in."

Reinhart studied the huge scientist thoughtfully. Sherikov was going to be a hard nut to crack. Designs was responsible to Security, not the Council. Sherikov was losing ground — but he was still a potential danger. Stubborn, individualistic, refusing to subordinate his welfare to the general good.

"All right." Reinhart put the folder slowly away in his coat. "I'll feed it. But you better be able to come through. There can't be any slip-ups. Too much hangs on the next few days."

"If the odds change in our favor are you going to give the mobilization order?"

"Yes," Reinhart stated. "I'll give the order the moment I see the odds change."

Standing in front of the machines, Reinhart waited nervously for the results. It was two o'clock in the afternoon. The day was warm, a pleasant May afternoon. Outside the building the daily life of the planet went on as usual.

As usual? Not exactly. The feeling was in the air, an expanding excitement growing every day. Terra had waited a long time. The attack on Proxima Centaurus had to come — and the sooner the better. The ancient Centauran Empire hemmed in Terra, bottled the human race up in its one system. A vast, suffocating net draped across the heavens, cutting Terra off from the bright diamonds beyond ... And it had to end.

The SRB machines whirred, the visible combination disappearing. For a time no ratio showed. Reinhart tensed, his body rigid. He waited.

The new ratio appeared.

Reinhart gasped. 7–6. Toward Terra!

Within five minutes the emergency mobilization alert had been flashed to all Government departments. The Council and President Duffe had been called to immediate session. Everything was happening fast.

But there was no doubt. 7–6. In Terra's favor. Reinhart hurried frantically to get his papers in order, in time for the Council session.

At histo-research the message plate was quickly pulled from the confidential slot and rushed across the central lab to the chief official.

"Look at this!" Fredman dropped the plate on his superior's desk. "Look at it!"

Harper picked up the plate, scanning it rapidly. "Sounds like the real thing. I didn't think we'd live to see it."

Fredman left the room, hurrying down the hall. He entered the time bubble office. "Where's the bubble?" he demanded, looking around.

One of the technicians looked slowly up. "Back about two hundred years. We're coming up with interesting data on the War of 1914. According to material the bubble has already brought up — "

"Cut it. We're through with routine work. Get the bubble back to the present. From now on all equipment has to be free for Military work."

"But — the bubble is regulated automatically."

"You can bring it back manually."

"It's risky." The technician hedged. "If the emergency requires it, I suppose we could take a chance and cut the automatic."

"The emergency requires *everything*," Fredman said feelingly.

"But the odds might change back," Margaret Duffe, President of the Council, said nervously. "Any minute they can revert."

"This is our chance!" Reinhart snapped, his temper rising. "What the hell's the matter with you? We've waited years for this."

The Council buzzed with excitement. Margaret Duffe hesitated uncertainly, her blue eyes clouded with worry. "I realize the opportunity is here. At least, statistically. But the new odds have just appeared. How do we know they'll last? They stand on the basis of a single weapon."

"You're wrong. You don't grasp the situation." Reinhart held himself in check with great effort. "Sherikov's weapon tipped the ratio in our favor. But the odds have been moving in our direction for months. It was only a question of time. The new balance was inevitable, sooner or later. It's not just Sherikov. He's only one factor in this. It's all nine planets of the Sol system — not a single man."

One of the Councilmen stood up. "The President must be aware the entire planet is eager to end this waiting. All our activities for the past eighty years have been directed toward — "

Reinhart moved close to the slender President of the Council. "If you don't approve the war, there probably will be mass rioting. Public reaction will be strong. Damn strong. And you know it."

Margaret Duffe shot him a cold glance. "You sent out the emergency order to force my hand. You were fully aware of what you were doing. You knew once the order was out there'd be no stopping things."

A murmur rushed through the Council, gaining volume. "We have to approve the war! ... We're committed! ... It's too late to turn back!"

Shouts, angry voices, insistent waves of sound lapped around Margaret Duffe. "I'm as much for the war as anybody," she said sharply. "I'm only urging moderation. An inter-system war is a big thing. We're going to war because a machine says we have a statistical chance of winning."

"There's no use starting the war unless we can win it," Reinhart said. "The SRB machines tell us whether we can win."

"They tell us our *chance* of winning. They don't guarantee anything."

"What more can we ask, besides a good chance of winning?"

Margaret Duffe clamped her jaw together tightly. "All right. I hear all the clamor. I won't stand in the way of Council approval. The vote can go ahead." Her cold, alert eyes appraised Reinhart. "Especially since the emergency order has already been sent out to all Government departments."

"Good." Reinhart stepped away with relief. "Then it's settled. We can finally go ahead with full mobilization."

Mobilization proceeded rapidly. The next forty-eight hours were alive with activity.

Reinhart attended a policy-level Military briefing in the Council rooms, conducted by Fleet Commander Carleton.

"You can see our strategy," Carleton said. He traced a diagram on the blackboard with a wave of his hand. "Sherikov states it'll take eight more days to complete the ftl bomb. During that time the fleet we have near the Centauran system will take up positions. As the bomb goes off the fleet will begin operations against the remaining Centauran ships. Many will no doubt survive the blast, but with Armun gone we should be able to handle them."

Reinhart took Commander Carleton's place. "I can report on the economic situation. Every factory on Terra is converted to arms production. With Armun out of the way we should be able to promote mass insurrection among the Centauran colonies. An inter-system Empire is hard to maintain, even with ships that approach light speed. Local war-lords should pop up all over the place. We want to have weapons available for them and ships starting *now* to reach them in time. Eventually we hope to provide a unifying principle around which the colonies can all collect. Our interest is more economic than political. They can have any kind of government they want, as long as they act as supply areas for us. As our eight system planets act now."

Carleton resumed his report. "Once the Centauran fleet has been scattered we can begin the crucial stage of the war. The landing of men and supplies from the ships we have waiting in all key areas throughout the Centauran system. In this stage — "

Reinhart moved away. It was hard to believe only two days had passed since the mobilization order had been sent out. The whole system was alive, functioning with feverish activity. Countless problems were being solved — but much remained.

He entered the lift and ascended to the SRB room, curious to see if there had been any change in the machines' reading. He found it the same. So far so good. Did the Centaurans know about Icarus? No doubt; but there wasn't anything they could do about it. At least, not in eight days.

Kaplan came over to Reinhart, sorting a new batch of data that had come in. The lab organizer searched through his data. "An amusing item came in. It might interest you." He handed a message plate to Reinhart.

It was from histo-research:

May 9, 2136

This is to report that in bringing the research time bubble up to the present the manual return was used for the first time. Therefore a clean break was not made and a quantity of material from the past was brought forward. This material included an individual from the early twentieth century who escaped from the lab immediately. He has not yet been taken into protective custody. Histo-research regrets this incident, but attributes it to the emergency.

E. Fredman

Reinhart handed the plate back to Kaplan. "Interesting. A man from the past — hauled into the middle of the biggest war the universe has seen."

"Strange things happen. I wonder what the machines will think."

"Hard to say. Probably nothing." Reinhart left the room and hurried along the corridor to his own office.

As soon as he was inside he called Sherikov on the vidscreen, using the confidential line.

The Pole's heavy features appeared. "Good day, Commissioner. How's the war effort?"

"Fine. How's the turret wiring proceeding?"

A faint frown flickered across Sherikov's face. "As a matter of fact, Commissioner — "

"What's the matter?" Reinhart said sharply.

Sherikov floundered. "You know how these things are. I've taken my crew off it and tried robot workers. They have greater dexterity, but they can't make decisions. This calls for more than mere dexterity. This calls for — " He searched for the word. " — for an *artist.*"

Reinhart's face hardened. "Listen, Sherikov. You have eight days left to complete the bomb. The data given to the SRB machines contained that information. The 7–6 ratio is based on that estimate. If you don't come through — "

Sherikov twisted in embarrassment. "Don't get excited, Commissioner. We'll complete it."

"I hope so. Call me as soon as it's done." Reinhart snapped off the connection. If Sherikov let them down he'd have him taken out and shot. The whole war depended on the ftl bomb.

The vidscreen glowed again. Reinhart snapped it on. Kaplan's face formed on it. The lab organizer's face was pale and frozen. "Commissioner, you better come up to the SRB office. Something's happened."

"What is it?"

"I'll show you."

Alarmed, Reinhart hurried out of his office and down the corridor. He found Kaplan standing in front of the SRB machines. "What's the story?" Reinhart demanded. He glanced down at the reading. It was unchanged.

Kaplan held up a message plate nervously. "A moment ago I fed this into the machines. After I saw the results I quickly removed it. It's that item I showed you. From histo-research. About the man from the past."

"What happened when you fed it?"

Kaplan swallowed unhappily. "I'll show you. I'll do it again. Exactly as before." He fed the plate into a moving intake belt. "Watch the visible figures," Kaplan muttered.

Reinhart watched, tense and rigid. For a moment nothing happened. 7–6 continued to show. Then— The figures disappeared. The machines faltered. New figures showed briefly. 4–24 for Centaurus. Reinhart gasped, suddenly sick with apprehension. But the figures vanished. New figures appeared. 16–38 for Centaurus. Then 48–86. 79–15 in Terra's favor. Then nothing. The machines whirred, but nothing happened.

Nothing at all. No figures. Only a blank.

"What's it mean?" Reinhart muttered, dazed.

"It's fantastic. We didn't think this could—"

"What's happened?"

"The machines aren't able to handle the item. No reading can come. It's data they can't integrate. They can't use it for prediction material, and it throws off all their other figures."

"Why?"

"It's—it's a variable." Kaplan was shaking, white-lipped and pale. "Something from which no inference can be made. The man from the past. The machines can't deal with him. The variable man!"

II

Thomas Cole was sharpening a knife with his whetstone when the tornado hit.

The knife belonged to the lady in the big green house. Every time Cole came by with his Fixit cart the lady had something to be sharpened. Once in a while she gave him a cup of coffee, hot black coffee from an old bent pot. He liked that fine; he enjoyed good coffee.

The day was drizzly and overcast. Business had been bad. An automobile had scared his two horses. On bad days less people were outside and he had to get down from the cart and go to ring doorbells.

But the man in the yellow house had given him a dollar for fixing his electric refrigerator. Nobody else had been able to fix it, not even the factory man. The dollar would go a long way. A dollar was a lot.

He knew it was a tornado even before it hit him. Everything was silent. He was bent over his whetstone, the reins between his knees, absorbed in his work.

He had done a good job on the knife; he was almost finished. He spat on the blade and was holding it up to see — and then the tornado came.

All at once it was there, completely around him. Nothing but grayness. He and the cart and horses seemed to be in a calm spot in the center of the tornado. They were moving in a great silence, gray mist everywhere.

And while he was wondering what to do, and how to get the old lady's knife back to her, all at once there was a bump and the tornado tipped him over, sprawled out on the ground. The horses screamed in fear, struggling to pick themselves up. Cole got quickly to his feet.

Where was he?

The grayness was gone. White walls stuck up on all sides. A deep light gleamed down, not daylight but something like it. The team was pulling the cart on its side, dragging it along, tools and equipment falling out. Cole righted the cart, leaping up onto the seat.

And for the first time saw the people.

Men, with astonished white faces, in some sort of uniforms. And a feeling of danger!

Cole headed the team toward the door. Hoofs thundered steel against steel as they pounded through the doorway, scattering the astonished men in all directions. He was out in a wide hall. A building, like a hospital.

The hall divided. More men were coming, spilling from all sides.

Shouting and milling in excitement, like white ants. Something cut past him, a beam of dark violet. It seared off a corner of the cart, leaving the wood smoking.

Cole felt fear. He kicked at the terrified horses. They reached a big door, crashing wildly against it. The door gave — and they were outside, bright sunlight blinking down on them. For a sickening second the cart tilted, almost turning over. Then the horses gained speed, racing across an open field, toward a distant line of green, Cole holding tightly to the reins.

Behind him the little white-faced men had come out and were standing in a group, gesturing frantically. He could hear their faint shrill shouts.

But he had got away. He was safe. He slowed the horses down and began to breathe again.

The woods were artificial. Some kind of park. But the park was wild and overgrown. A dense jungle of twisted plants. Everything growing in confusion.

The park was empty. No one was there. By the position of the sun he could tell it was either early morning or late afternoon. The smell of the flowers and grass, the dampness of the leaves, indicated morning. It had been late afternoon when the tornado had picked him up. And the sky had been overcast and cloudy.

Cole considered. Clearly, he had been carried a long way. The hospital, the men with white faces, the odd lighting, the accented words he had caught — everything indicated he was no longer in Nebraska — maybe not even in the United States.

Some of his tools had fallen out and gotten lost along the way. Cole collected everything that remained, sorting them, running his fingers over each tool with affection. Some of the little chisels and wood gouges were gone. The bit box had opened, and most of the smaller bits had been lost. He gathered up those that remained and replaced them tenderly in the box. He took a keyhole saw down, and with an oil rag wiped it carefully and replaced it.

Above the cart the sun rose slowly in the sky. Cole peered up, his horny hand over his eyes. A big man, stoop-shouldered, his chin gray and stubbled. His clothes wrinkled and dirty. But his eyes were clear, a pale blue, and his hands were finely made.

He could not stay in the park. They had seen him ride that way; they would be looking for him.

Far above something shot rapidly across the sky. A tiny black dot moving with incredible haste. A second dot followed. The two dots were gone almost before he saw them. They were utterly silent.

Cole frowned, perturbed. The dots made him uneasy. He would have to keep moving — and looking for food. His stomach was already beginning to rumble and groan.

Work. There was plenty he could do: gardening, sharpening, grinding, repair work on machines and clocks, fixing all kinds of household things. Even painting and odd jobs and carpentry and chores.

He could do anything. Anything people wanted done. For a meal and pocket money.

Thomas Cole urged the team into life, moving forward. He sat hunched over in the seat, watching intently, as the Fixit cart rolled slowly across the tangled grass, through the jungle of trees and flowers.

Reinhart hurried, racing his cruiser at top speed, followed by a second ship, a military escort. The ground sped by below him, a blur of gray and green.

The remains of New York lay spread out, a twisted, blunted ruin overgrown with weeds and grass. The great atomic wars of the twentieth century had turned virtually the whole seaboard area into an endless waste of slag.

Slag and weeds below him. And then the sudden tangle that had been Central Park.

Histo-research came into sight. Reinhart swooped down, bringing his cruiser to rest at the small supply field behind the main buildings.

Harper, the chief official of the department, came over quickly as soon as Reinhart's ship landed.

"Frankly, we don't understand why you consider this matter important," Harper said uneasily.

Reinhart shot him a cold glance. "I'll be the judge of what's important. Are you the one who gave the order to bring the bubble back manually?"

"Fredman gave the actual order. In line with your directive to have all facilities ready for — "

Reinhart headed toward the entrance of the research building. "Where is Fredman?"

"Inside."

"I want to see him. Let's go."

Fredman met them inside. He greeted Reinhart calmly, showing no emotion. "Sorry to cause you trouble, Commissioner. We were trying to get the station in order for the war. We wanted the bubble back as quickly as possible." He eyed Reinhart curiously. "No doubt the man and his cart will soon be picked up by your police."

"I want to know everything that happened, in exact detail."

Fredman shifted uncomfortably. "There's not much to tell. I gave the order to have the automatic setting canceled and the bubble brought back manually. At the moment the signal reached it, the bubble was passing through the spring of 1913. As it broke loose, it tore off a piece of ground on which this person and his cart were located. The person naturally was brought up to the present, inside the bubble."

"Didn't any of your instruments tell you the bubble was loaded?"

"We were too excited to take any readings. Half an hour after the manual control was thrown, the bubble materialized in the observation room. It was de-energized before anyone noticed what was inside. We tried to stop him but he drove the cart out into the hall, bowling us out of the way. The horses were in a panic."

"What kind of cart was it?"

"There was some kind of sign on it. Painted in black letters on both sides. No one saw what it was."

"Go ahead. What happened then?"

"Somebody fired a Slem-ray after him, but it missed. The horses carried him out of the building and onto the grounds. By the time we reached the exit the cart was halfway to the park."

Reinhart reflected. "If he's still in the park we should have him shortly. But we must be careful." He was already starting back toward his ship, leaving Fredman behind. Harper fell in beside him.

Reinhart halted by his ship. He beckoned some Government guards over.

"Put the executive staff of this department under arrest. I'll have them tried on a treason count, later on." He smiled ironically as Harper's face blanched sickly pale. "There's a war going on. You'll be lucky if you get off alive."

Reinhart entered his ship and left the surface, rising rapidly into the sky. A second ship followed after him, a military escort. Reinhart flew high above the sea of gray slag, the unrecovered waste area. He passed over a sudden square of green set in the ocean of gray. Reinhart gazed back at it until it was gone.

Central Park. He could see police ships racing through the sky, ships and transports loaded with troops, heading toward the square of green. On the ground some heavy guns and surface cars rumbled along, lines of black approaching the park from all sides.

They would have the man soon. But meanwhile, the SRB machines were blank. And on the SRB machines' readings the whole war depended.

About noon the cart reached the edge of the park. Cole rested for a moment, allowing the horses time to crop at the thick grass. The silent expanse of slag amazed him. What had happened? Nothing stirred. No buildings, no sign of life. Grass and weeds poked up occasionally through it, breaking the flat surface here and there, but even so, the sight gave him an uneasy chill.

Cole drove the cart slowly out onto the slag, studying the sky above him. There was nothing to hide him, now that he was out of the park. The slag was bare and uniform, like the ocean. If he were spotted —

A horde of tiny black dots raced across the sky, coming rapidly closer. Presently they veered to the right and disappeared. More planes, wingless metal planes. He watched them go, driving slowly on.

Half an hour later something appeared ahead. Cole slowed the cart down, peering to see. The slag came to an end. He had reached its limits. Ground appeared, dark soil and grass. Weeds grew everywhere. Ahead of him, beyond the end of the slag, was a line of buildings, houses of some sort. Or sheds.

Houses, probably. But not like any he had ever seen.

The houses were uniform, all exactly the same. Like little green shells, rows of them, several hundred. There was a little lawn in front of each. Lawn, a path, a front porch, bushes in a meager row around each house. But the houses were all alike and very small.

Little green shells in precise, even rows. He urged the cart cautiously forward, toward the houses.

No one seemed to be around. He entered a street between two rows of houses, the hoofs of his two horses sounding loudly in the silence. He was in some kind of town. But there were no dogs or children. Everything was neat and silent. Like a model. An exhibit. It made him uncomfortable.

A young man walking along the pavement gaped at him in wonder. An oddly-dressed youth, in a toga-like cloak that hung down to his knees. A single piece of fabric. And sandals.

Or what looked like sandals. Both the cloak and the sandals were of some strange half-luminous material. It glowed faintly in the sunlight. Metallic, rather than cloth.

A woman was watering flowers at the edge of a lawn. She straightened up as his team of horses came near. Her eyes widened in astonishment — and then fear. Her mouth fell open in a soundless *O* and her sprinkling can slipped from her fingers and rolled silently onto the lawn.

Cole blushed and turned his head quickly away. The woman was scarcely dressed! He flicked the reins and urged the horses to hurry.

Behind him, the woman still stood. He stole a brief, hasty look back — and then shouted hoarsely to his team, ears scarlet. He had seen right. She wore only a pair of translucent shorts. Nothing else. A mere fragment of the same half-luminous material that glowed and sparkled. The rest of her small body was utterly naked.

He slowed the team down. She had been pretty. Brown hair and eyes, deep red lips. Quite a good figure. Slender waist, downy legs, bare and supple, full breasts — He clamped the thought furiously off. He had to get to work. Business.

Cole halted the Fixit cart and leaped down onto the pavement. He selected a house at random and approached it cautiously. The house was attractive. It had a certain simple beauty. But it looked frail — and exactly like the others.

He stepped up on the porch. There was no bell. He searched for it, running his hand uneasily over the surface of the door. All at once there was a click, a sharp snap on a level with his eyes. Cole glanced up, startled. A lens was vanishing as the door section slid over it. He had been photographed.

While he was wondering what it meant, the door swung suddenly open. A man filled up the entrance, a big man in a tan uniform, blocking the way ominously.

"What do you want?" the man demanded.

"I'm looking for work," Cole murmured. "Any kind of work. I can do anything, fix any kind of thing. I repair broken objects. Things that need mending." His voice trailed off uncertainly. "Anything at all."

"Apply to the Placement Department of the Federal Activities Control Board," the man said crisply. "You know all occupational therapy is handled through them." He eyed Cole curiously. "Why have you got on those ancient clothes?"

"Ancient? Why, I — "

The man gazed past him at the Fixit cart and the two dozing horses. "What's that? What are those two animals? *Horses?*" The man rubbed his jaw, studying Cole intently. "That's strange," he said.

"Strange?" Cole murmured uneasily. "Why?"

"There haven't been any horses for over a century. All the horses were wiped out during the Fifth Atomic War. That's why it's strange."

Cole tensed, suddenly alert. There was something in the man's eyes, a hardness, a piercing look. Cole moved back off the porch, onto the path. He had to be careful. Something was wrong.

"I'll be going," he murmured.

"There haven't been any horses for over a hundred years." The man came toward Cole. "Who are you? Why are you dressed up like that? Where did you get that vehicle and pair of horses?"

"I'll be going," Cole repeated, moving away.

The man whipped something from his belt, a thin metal tube. He stuck it toward Cole.

It was a rolled-up paper, a thin sheet of metal in the form of a tube. Words, some kind of script. He could not make any of them out. The man's picture, rows of numbers, figures —

"I'm Director Winslow," the man said. "Federal Stockpile Conservation. You better talk fast, or there'll be a Security car here in five minutes."

Cole moved — fast. He raced, head down, back along the path to the cart, toward the street.

Something hit him. A wall of force, throwing him down on his face. He sprawled in a heap, numb and dazed. His body ached, vibrating wildly, out of control. Waves of shock rolled over him, gradually diminishing.

He got shakily to his feet. His head spun. He was weak, shattered, trembling violently. The man was coming down the walk after him. Cole pulled himself onto the cart, gasping and retching. The horses jumped into life. Cole rolled over against the seat, sick with the motion of the swaying cart.

He caught hold of the reins and managed to drag himself up in a sitting position. The cart gained speed, turning a corner. Houses flew past. Cole urged the team weakly, drawing great shuddering breaths. Houses and streets, a blur of motion, as the cart flew faster and faster along.

Then he was leaving the town, leaving the neat little houses behind. He was on some sort of highway. Big buildings, factories, on both sides of the highway. Figures, men watching in astonishment.

After a while the factories fell behind. Cole slowed the team down. What had the man meant? Fifth Atomic War. Horses destroyed. It didn't make sense. And they had things he knew nothing about. Force fields. Planes without wings — soundless.

Cole reached around in his pockets. He found the identification tube the man had handed him. In the excitement he had carried it off. He unrolled the tube slowly and began to study it. The writing was strange to him.

For a long time he studied the tube. Then, gradually, he became aware of something. Something in the top right-hand corner.

A date. October 6, 2128.

Cole's vision blurred. Everything spun and wavered around him. October, 2128. Could it be?

But he held the paper in his hand. Thin, metal paper. Like foil. And it had to be. It said so, right in the corner, printed on the paper itself.

Cole rolled the tube up slowly, numbed with shock. Two hundred years. It didn't seem possible. But things were beginning to make sense. He was in the future, two hundred years in the future.

While he was mulling this over, the swift black Security ship appeared overhead, diving rapidly toward the horse-drawn cart, as it moved slowly along the road.

Reinhart's vidscreen buzzed. He snapped it quickly on. "Yes?"

"Report from Security."

"Put it through." Reinhart waited tensely as the lines locked in place. The screen re-lit.

"This is Dixon. Western Regional Command." The officer cleared his throat, shuffling his message plates. "The man from the past has been reported, moving away from the New York area."

"Which side of your net?"

"Outside. He evaded the net around Central Park by entering one of the small towns at the rim of the slag area."

"*Evaded?*"

"We assumed he would avoid the towns. Naturally the net failed to encompass any of the towns."

Reinhart's jaw stiffened. "Go on."

"He entered the town of Petersville a few minutes before the net closed around the park. We burned the park level, but naturally found nothing. He had already gone. An hour later we received a report from a resident in Petersville, an official of the Stockpile Conservation Department. The man from the past had come to his door, looking for work. Winslow, the official, engaged him in conversation, trying to hold onto him, but he escaped, driving his cart off. Winslow called Security right away, but by then it was too late."

"Report to me as soon as anything more comes in. We must have him — and damn soon." Reinhart snapped the screen off. It died quickly.

He sat back in his chair, waiting.

Cole saw the shadow of the Security ship. He reacted at once. A second after the shadow passed over him, Cole was out of the cart, running and falling. He rolled, twisting and turning, pulling his body as far away from the cart as possible.

There was a blinding roar and flash of white light. A hot wind rolled over Cole, picking him up and tossing him like a leaf. He shut his eyes, letting his body relax. He bounced, falling and striking the ground. Gravel and stones tore into his face, his knees, the palms of his hands.

Cole cried out, shrieking in pain. His body was on fire. He was being consumed, incinerated by the blinding white orb of fire. The orb expanded, growing in size, swelling like some monstrous sun, twisted and bloated. The end had come. There was no hope. He gritted his teeth —

The greedy orb faded, dying down. It sputtered and winked out, blackening into ash. The air reeked, a bitter acrid smell. His clothes were burning and smoking. The ground under him was hot, baked dry, seared by the blast. But he was alive. At least, for a while.

Cole opened his eyes slowly. The cart was gone. A great hole gaped where it had been, a shattered sore in the center of the highway. An ugly cloud hung above the hole, black and ominous. Far above, the wingless plane circled, watching for any signs of life.

Cole lay, breathing shallowly, slowly. Time passed. The sun moved across the sky with agonizing slowness. It was perhaps four in the afternoon. Cole calculated mentally. In three hours it would be dark. If he could stay alive until then —

Had the plane seen him leap from the cart?

He lay without moving. The late afternoon sun beat down on him. He felt sick, nauseated and feverish. His mouth was dry.

Some ants ran over his outstretched hand. Gradually, the immense black cloud was beginning to drift away, dispersing into a formless blob.

The cart was gone. The thought lashed against him, pounding at his brain, mixing with his labored pulsebeat. *Gone*. Destroyed. Nothing but ashes and debris remained. The realization dazed him.

Finally the plane finished its circling, winging its way toward the horizon. At last it vanished. The sky was clear.

Cole got unsteadily to his feet. He wiped his face shakily. His body ached and trembled. He spat a couple of times, trying to clear his mouth. The plane would probably send in a report. People would be coming to look for him. Where could he go?

To his right a line of hills rose up, a distant green mass. Maybe he could reach them. He began to walk slowly. He had to be very careful. They were looking for him — and they had weapons. Incredible weapons.

He would be lucky to still be alive when the sun set. His team and Fixit cart were gone — and all his tools. Cole reached into his pockets, searching through them hopefully. He brought out some small screwdrivers, a little pair of cutting pliers, some wire, some solder, the whetstone, and finally the lady's knife.

Only a few small tools remained. He had lost everything else. But without the cart he was safer, harder to spot. They would have more trouble finding him, on foot.

Cole hurried along, crossing the level fields toward the distant range of hills.

The call came through to Reinhart almost at once. Dixon's features formed on the vidscreen. "I have a further report, Commissioner." Dixon scanned the plate. "Good news. The man from the past was sighted moving away from Petersville, along highway 13, at about ten miles an hour, on his horse-drawn cart. Our ship bombed him immediately."

"Did — did you get him?"

"The pilot reports no sign of life after the blast."

Reinhart's pulse almost stopped. He sank back in his chair. "Then he's dead!"

"Actually, we won't know for certain until we can examine the debris. A surface car is speeding toward the spot. We should have the complete report in a short time. We'll notify you as soon as the information comes in."

Reinhart reached out and cut the screen. It faded into darkness. Had they got the man from the past? Or had he escaped again? Weren't they ever going to get him? Couldn't he be captured? And meanwhile, the SRB machines were silent, showing nothing at all.

Reinhart sat brooding, waiting impatiently for the report of the surface car to come.

It was evening.

"Come on!" Steven shouted, running frantically after his brother. "Come on back!"

"Catch me." Earl ran and ran, down the side of the hill, over behind a military storage depot, along a neotex fence, jumping finally down into Mrs. Norris' back yard.

Steven hurried after his brother, sobbing for breath, shouting and gasping as he ran. "Come back! You come back with that!"

"What's he got?" Sally Tate demanded, stepping out suddenly to block Steven's way.

Steven halted, his chest rising and falling. "He's got my inter-system vidsender." His small face twisted with rage and misery. "He better give it back!"

Earl came circling around from the right. In the warm gloom of evening he was almost invisible. "Here I am," he announced. "What are you going to do?"

Steven glared at him hotly. His eyes made out the square box in Earl's hands. "You give that back! Or — or I'll tell Dad."

Earl laughed. "Make me."

"Dad'll make you."

"You better give it to him," Sally said.

"Catch me." Earl started off. Steven pushed Sally out of the way, lashing wildly at his brother. He collided with him, throwing him sprawling. The box fell from Earl's hands. It skidded to the pavement, crashing into the side of a guide-light post.

Earl and Steven picked themselves up slowly. They gazed down at the broken box.

"See?" Steven shrilled, tears filling his eyes. "See what you did?"

"You did it. You pushed into me."

"You did it!" Steven bent down and picked up the box. He carried it over to the guide-light, sitting down on the curb to examine it.

Earl came slowly over. "If you hadn't pushed me it wouldn't have got broken."

Night was descending rapidly. The line of hills rising above the town were already lost in darkness. A few lights had come on here and there. The evening was warm. A surface car slammed its doors, some place off in the distance. In the sky ships droned back and forth, weary commuters coming home from work in the big underground factory units.

Thomas Cole came slowly toward the three children grouped around the guide-light. He moved with difficulty, his body sore and bent with fatigue. Night had come, but he was not safe yet.

He was tired, exhausted and hungry. He had walked a long way. And he had to have something to eat — soon.

A few feet from the children Cole stopped. They were all intent and absorbed by the box on Steven's knees. Suddenly a hush fell over the children. Earl looked up slowly.

In the dim light the big stooped figure of Thomas Cole seemed extra menacing. His long arms hung down loosely at his sides. His face was lost in shadow. His body was shapeless, indistinct. A big unformed statue, standing silently a few feet away, unmoving in the half-darkness.

"Who are you?" Earl demanded, his voice low.

"What do you want?" Sally said. The children edged away nervously. "Get away."

Cole came toward them. He bent down a little. The beam from the guide-light crossed his features. Lean, prominent nose, beak-like, faded blue eyes —

Steven scrambled to his feet, clutching the vidsender box. "You get out of here!"

"Wait." Cole smiled crookedly at them. His voice was dry and raspy. "What do you have there?" He pointed with his long, slender fingers. "The box you're holding."

The children were silent. Finally Steven stirred. "It's my inter-system vidsender."

"Only it doesn't work," Sally said.

"Earl broke it." Steven glared at his brother bitterly. "Earl threw it down and broke it."

Cole smiled a little. He sank down wearily on the edge of the curb, sighing with relief. He had been walking too long. His body ached with fatigue. He was hungry and tired. For a long time he sat, wiping perspiration from his neck and face, too exhausted to speak.

"Who are you?" Sally demanded, at last. "Why do you have on those funny clothes? Where did you come from?"

"Where?" Cole looked around at the children. "From a long way off. A long way." He shook his head slowly from side to side, trying to clear it.

"What's your therapy?" Earl said.

"My therapy?"

"What do you do? Where do you work?"

Cole took a deep breath and let it out again slowly. "I fix things. All kinds of things. Any kind."

Earl sneered. "Nobody fixes things. When they break you throw them away."

Cole didn't hear him. Sudden need had roused him, getting him suddenly to his feet. "You know any work I can find?" he demanded. "Things I could do? I can fix anything. Clocks, typewriters, refrigerators, pots and pans. Leaks in the roof. I can fix anything there is."

Steven held out his inter-system vidsender. "Fix this."

There was silence. Slowly, Cole's eyes focused on the box. "That?"

"My sender. Earl broke it."

Cole took the box slowly. He turned it over, holding it up to the light. He frowned, concentrating on it. His long, slender fingers moved carefully over the surface, exploring it.

"He'll steal it!" Earl said suddenly.

"No." Cole shook his head vaguely. "I'm reliable." His sensitive fingers found the studs that held the box together. He depressed the studs, pushing them expertly in. The box opened, revealing its complex interior.

"He got it open," Sally whispered.

"Give it back!" Steven demanded, a little frightened. He held out his hand. "I want it back."

The three children watched Cole apprehensively. Cole fumbled in his pocket. Slowly he brought out his tiny screwdrivers and pliers. He laid them in a row beside him. He made no move to return the box.

"I want it back," Steven said feebly.

Cole looked up. His faded blue eyes took in the sight of the three children standing before him in the gloom. "I'll fix it for you. You said you wanted it fixed."

"I want it back." Steven stood on one foot, then the other, torn by doubt and indecision. "Can you really fix it? Can you make it work again?"

"Yes."

"All right. Fix it for me, then."

A sly smile flickered across Cole's tired face. "Now, wait a minute. If I fix it, will you bring me something to eat? I'm not fixing it for nothing."

"Something to eat?"

"Food. I need hot food. Maybe some coffee."

Steven nodded. "Yes. I'll get it for you."

Cole relaxed. "Fine. That's fine." He turned his attention back to the box resting between his knees. "Then I'll fix it for you. I'll fix it for you good."

His fingers flew, working and twisting, tracing down wires and relays, exploring and examining. Finding out about the inter-system vidsender. Discovering how it worked.

Steven slipped into the house through the emergency door. He made his way to the kitchen with great care, walking on tip-toe. He punched the kitchen controls at random, his heart beating excitedly. The stove began to whirr, purring into life. Meter readings came on, crossing toward the completion marks.

Presently the stove opened, sliding out a tray of steaming dishes. The mechanism clicked off, dying into silence. Steven grabbed up the contents of the tray, filling his arms. He carried everything down the hall, out the emergency door and into the yard. The yard was dark. Steven felt his way carefully along.

He managed to reach the guide-light without dropping anything at all.

Thomas Cole got slowly to his feet as Steven came into view. "Here," Steven said. He dumped the food onto the curb, gasping for breath. "Here's the food. Is it finished?"

Cole held out the inter-system vidsender. "It's finished. It was pretty badly smashed."

Earl and Sally gazed up, wide-eyed. "Does it work?" Sally asked.

"Of course not," Earl stated. "How could it work? He couldn't — "

"Turn it on!" Sally nudged Steven eagerly. "See if it works."

Steven was holding the box under the light, examining the switches. He flicked the main switch on. The indicator light gleamed. "It lights up," Steven said.

"Say something into it."

Steven spoke into the box. "Hello! Hello! This is operator 6-Z75 calling. Can you hear me? This is operator 6-Z75. Can you hear me?"

In the darkness, away from the beam of the guide-light, Thomas Cole sat crouched over the food. He ate gratefully, silently. It was good food, well cooked and seasoned. He drank a container of orange juice and then a sweet drink he didn't recognize. Most of the food was strange to him, but he didn't care. He had walked a long way and he still had a long way to go, before morning. He had to be deep in the hills before the sun came up. Instinct told him that he would be safe among the trees and tangled growth — at least, as safe as he could hope for.

He ate rapidly, intent on the food. He did not look up until he was finished. Then he got slowly to his feet, wiping his mouth with the back of his hand.

The three children were standing around in a circle, operating the intersystem vidsender. He watched them for a few minutes. None of them looked up from the small box. They were intent, absorbed in what they were doing.

"Well?" Cole said, at last. "Does it work all right?"

After a moment Steven looked up at him. There was a strange expression on his face. He nodded slowly. "Yes. Yes, it works. It works fine."

Cole grunted. "All right." He turned and moved away from the light. "That's fine."

The children watched silently until the figure of Thomas Cole had completely disappeared. Slowly, they turned and looked at each other. Then down at the box in Steven's hands. They gazed at the box in growing awe. Awe mixed with dawning fear.

Steven turned and edged toward his house. "I've got to show it to my Dad," he murmured, dazed. "He's got to know. *Somebody's* got to know!"

III

Eric Reinhart examined the vidsender box carefully, turning it around and around.

"Then he did escape from the blast," Dixon admitted reluctantly. "He must have leaped from the cart just before the concussion."

Reinhart nodded. "He escaped. He got away from you — twice." He pushed the vidsender box away and leaned abruptly toward the man standing uneasily in front of his desk. "What's your name again?"

"Elliot. Richard Elliot."

"And your son's name?"

"Steven."

"It was last night this happened?"

"About eight o'clock."

"Go on."

"Steven came into the house. He acted queerly. He was carrying his intersystem vidsender." Elliot pointed at the box on Reinhart's desk. "That. He was nervous and excited. I asked what was wrong. For a while he couldn't tell me. He was quite upset. Then he showed me the vidsender." Elliot took a deep, shaky breath. "I could see right away it was different. You see I'm an electrical engineer. I had opened it once before, to put in a new battery. I had a fairly good idea how it should look." Elliot hesitated. "Commissioner, it had been *changed*. A lot of the wiring was different. Moved around. Relays connected differently. Some parts were missing. New parts had been jury rigged out of old. Then I discovered the thing that made me call Security. The vidsender — it really *worked*."

"Worked?"

"You see, it never was anything more than a toy. With a range of a few city blocks. So the kids could call back and forth from their rooms. Like a sort of portable vidscreen. Commissioner, I tried out the vidsender, pushing the call button and speaking into the microphone. I — I got a ship of the line. A battleship operating beyond Proxima Centaurus — over eight light years away. As far out as the actual vidsenders operate. Then I called Security. Right away."

For a time Reinhart was silent. Finally he tapped the box lying on the desk. "You got a ship of the line — with *this*?"

"That's right."

"How big are the regular vidsenders?"

Dixon supplied the information. "As big as a twenty-ton safe."

"That's what I thought." Reinhart waved his hand impatiently. "All right, Elliot. Thanks for turning the information over to us. That's all."

Security police led Elliot outside the office.

Reinhart and Dixon looked at each other. "This is bad," Reinhart said harshly. "He has some ability, some kind of mechanical ability. Genius, perhaps, to do a thing like this. Look at the period he came from, Dixon. The early part of the twentieth century. Before the wars began. That was a unique period. There was a certain vitality, a certain ability. It was a period of incredible growth and discovery. Edison. Pasteur. Burbank. The Wright brothers. Inventions and machines. People had an uncanny ability with machines. A kind of intuition about machines — which we don't have."

"You mean — "

"I mean a person like this coming into our own time is bad in itself, war or no war. He's too different. He's oriented along different lines. He has abilities we lack. This fixing skill of his. It throws us off, out of kilter. And with the war. . . .

"Now I'm beginning to understand why the SRB machines couldn't factor him. It's impossible for us to understand this kind of person. Winslow says he asked for work, any kind of work. The man said he could do anything, fix anything. Do you understand what that means?"

"No," Dixon said. "What does it mean?"

"Can any of us fix anything? No. None of us can do that. We're specialized. Each of us has his own line, his own work. I understand my work, you understand yours. The tendency in evolution is toward greater and greater specialization. Man's society is an ecology that forces adaptation to it. Continual complexity makes it impossible for any of us to know anything outside our own personal field — I can't follow the work of the man sitting at the next desk over from me. Too much knowledge has piled up in each field. And there are too many fields.

"This man is different. He can fix anything, do anything. He doesn't work with knowledge, with science — the classified accumulation of facts. He *knows* nothing. It's not in his head, a form of learning. He works by intuition — his power is in his hands, not his head. Jack-of-all-trades. His hands! Like a painter, an artist. In his hands — and he cuts across our lives like a knife-blade."

"And the other problem?"

"The other problem is that this man, this variable man, has escaped into the Albertine Mountain Range. Now we'll have one hell of a time finding him. He's clever — in a strange kind of way. Like some sort of animal. He's going to be hard to catch."

Reinhart sent Dixon out. After a moment he gathered up the handful of reports on his desk and carried them up to the SRB room. The SRB room was closed up, sealed off by a ring of armed Security police. Standing angrily before the ring of police was Peter Sherikov, his beard waggling angrily, his immense hands on his hips.

"What's going on?" Sherikov demanded. "Why can't I go in and peep at the odds?"

"Sorry." Reinhart cleared the police aside. "Come inside with me. I'll explain." The doors opened for them and they entered. Behind them the doors shut and the ring of police formed outside. "What brings you away from your lab?" Reinhart asked.

Sherikov shrugged. "Several things. I wanted to see you. I called you on the vidphone and they said you weren't available. I thought maybe something had happened. What's up?"

"I'll tell you in a few minutes." Reinhart called Kaplan over. "Here are some new items. Feed them in right away. I want to see if the machines can total them."

"Certainly, Commissioner." Kaplan took the message plates and placed them on an intake belt. The machines hummed into life.

"We'll know soon," Reinhart said, half aloud.

Sherikov shot him a keen glance. "We'll know what? Let me in on it. What's taking place?"

"We're in trouble. For twenty-four hours the machines haven't given any reading at all. Nothing but a blank. A total blank."

Sherikov's features registered disbelief. "But that isn't possible. *Some* odds exist at all times."

"The odds exist, but the machines aren't able to calculate them."

"Why not?"

"Because a variable factor has been introduced. A factor which the machines can't handle. They can't make any predictions from it."

"Can't they reject it?" Sherikov said slyly. "Can't they just — just *ignore* it?"

"No. It exists, as real data. Therefore it affects the balance of the material, the sum total of all other available data. To reject it would be to give a false reading. The machines can't reject any data that's known to be true."

Sherikov pulled moodily at his black beard. "I would be interested in knowing what sort of factor the machines can't handle. I thought they could take in all data pertaining to contemporary reality."

"They can. This factor has nothing to do with contemporary reality. That's the trouble. Histo-research in bringing its time bubble back from the past got overzealous and cut the circuit too quickly. The bubble came back loaded — with a man from the twentieth century. A man from the past."

"I see. A man from two centuries ago." The big Pole frowned. "And with a radically different Weltanschauung. No connection with our present society. Not integrated along our lines at all. Therefore the SRB machines are perplexed."

Reinhart grinned. "Perplexed? I suppose so. In any case, they can't do anything with the data about this man. The variable man. No statistics at all have been thrown up — no predictions have been made. And it knocks everything else out of phase. We're dependent on the constant showing of these odds. The whole war effort is geared around them."

"The horse-shoe nail. Remember the old poem? 'For want of a nail the shoe was lost. For want of the shoe the horse was lost. For want of the horse the rider was lost. For want — ' "

"Exactly. A single factor coming along like this, one single individual, can throw everything off. It doesn't seem possible that one person could knock an entire society out of balance — but apparently it is."

"What are you doing about this man?"

"The Security police are organized in a mass search for him."

"Results?"

"He escaped into the Albertine Mountain Range last night. It'll be hard to find him. We must expect him to be loose for another forty-eight hours. It'll take that long for us to arrange the annihilation of the range area. Perhaps a trifle longer. And meanwhile — "

"Ready, Commissioner," Kaplan interrupted. "The new totals."

The SRB machines had finished factoring the new data. Reinhart and Sherikov hurried to take their places before the view windows.

For a moment nothing happened. Then odds were put up, locking in place. Sherikov gasped. 99–2. In favor of Terra. "That's wonderful! Now we — "

The odds vanished. New odds took their places. 97–4. In favor of Centaurus. Sherikov groaned in astonished dismay. "Wait," Reinhart said to him. "I don't think they'll last."

The odds vanished. A rapid series of odds shot across the screen, a violent stream of numbers, changing almost instantly. At last the machines became silent.

Nothing showed. No odds. No totals at all. The view windows were blank.

"You see?" Reinhart murmured. "The same damn thing!"

Sherikov pondered. "Reinhart, you're too Anglo-Saxon, too impulsive. Be more Slavic. This man will be captured and destroyed within two days. You said so yourself. Meanwhile, we're all working night and day on the war effort. The warfleet is waiting near Proxima, taking up positions for the attack on the Centaurans. All our war plants are going full blast. By the time the attack date comes we'll have a full-sized invasion army ready to take off for the long trip to the Centauran colonies. The whole Terran population has been mobilized. The eight supply planets are pouring in material. All this is going on day and night, even without odds showing. Long before the attack comes this man will certainly be dead, and the machines will be able to show odds again."

Reinhart considered. "But it worries me, a man like that out in the open. Loose. A man who can't be predicted. It goes against science. We've been making statistical reports on society for two centuries. We have immense files of data. The machines are able to predict what each person and group will do at a given time, in a given situation. But this man is beyond all prediction. He's a variable. It's contrary to science."

"The indeterminate particle."

"What's that?"

"The particle that moves in such a way that we can't predict what position it will occupy at a given second. Random. The random particle."

"Exactly. It's — it's *unnatural*."

Sherikov laughed sarcastically. "Don't worry about it, Commissioner. The man will be captured and things will return to their natural state. You'll be able to predict people again, like laboratory rats in a maze. By the way — why is this room guarded?"

"I don't want anyone to know the machines show no totals. It's dangerous to the war effort."

"Margaret Duffe, for example?"

Reinhart nodded reluctantly. "They're too timid, these parliamentarians. If they discover we have no SRB odds they'll want to shut down the war planning and go back to waiting."

"Too slow for you, Commissioner? Laws, debates, council meetings, discussions. ... Saves a lot of time if one man has all the power. One man to tell people what to do, think for them, lead them around."

Reinhart eyed the big Pole critically. "That reminds me. How is Icarus coming? Have you continued to make progress on the control turret?"

A scowl crossed Sherikov's broad features. "The control turret?" He waved his big hand vaguely. "I would say it's coming along all right. We'll catch up in time."

Instantly Reinhart became alert. "Catch up? You mean you're still behind?"

"Somewhat. A little. But we'll catch up." Sherikov retreated toward the door. "Let's go down to the cafeteria and have a cup of coffee. You worry too much, Commissioner. Take things more in your stride."

"I suppose you're right." The two men walked out into the hall. "I'm on edge. This variable man. I can't get him out of my mind."

"Has he done anything yet?"

"Nothing important. Rewired a child's toy. A toy vidsender."

"Oh?" Sherikov showed interest. "What do you mean? What did he do?"

"I'll show you." Reinhart led Sherikov down the hall to his office. They entered and Reinhart locked the door. He handed Sherikov the toy and roughed in what Cole had done. A strange look crossed Sherikov's face. He found the studs on the box and depressed them. The box opened. The big Pole sat down at the desk and began to study the interior of the box. "You're sure it was the man from the past who rewired this?"

"Of course. On the spot. The boy damaged it playing. The variable man came along and the boy asked him to fix it. He fixed it, all right."

"Incredible." Sherikov's eyes were only an inch from the wiring. "Such tiny relays. How could he — "

"What?"

"Nothing." Sherikov got abruptly to his feet, closing the box carefully. "Can I take this along? To my lab? I'd like to analyze it more fully."

"Of course. But why?"

"No special reason. Let's go get our coffee." Sherikov headed toward the door. "You say you expect to capture this man in a day or so?"

"*Kill* him, not capture him. We've got to eliminate him as a piece of data. We're assembling the attack formations right now. No slip-ups, this time. We're in the process of setting up a cross-bombing pattern to level the entire Albertine Range. He must be destroyed, within the next forty-eight hours."

Sherikov nodded absently. "Of course," he murmured. A preoccupied expression still remained on his broad features. "I understand perfectly."

Thomas Cole crouched over the fire he had built, warming his hands. It was almost morning. The sky was turning violet gray. The mountain air was crisp and chilly. Cole shivered and pulled himself closer to the fire.

The heat felt good against his hands. *His hands.* He gazed down at them, glowing yellow-red in the firelight. The nails were black and chipped. Warts and endless calluses on each finger, and the palms. But they were good hands, the fingers were long and tapered. He respected them, although in some ways he didn't understand them.

Cole was deep in thought, meditating over his situation.

He had been in the mountains two nights and a day. The first night had been the worst. Stumbling and falling, making his way uncertainly up the steep slopes, through the tangled brush and undergrowth —

But when the sun came up he was safe, deep in the mountains, between two great peaks. And by the time the sun had set again he had fixed himself a shelter and a means of making a fire. Now he had a neat little box trap, operated by a plaited grass rope and pit, a notched stake. One rabbit already hung by his hind legs and the trap was waiting for another.

The sky turned from violet gray to a deep cold gray, a metallic color. The mountains were silent and empty. Far off someplace a bird sang, its voice echoing across the vast slopes and ravines. Other birds began to sing. Off to his right something crashed through the brush, an animal pushing its way along.

Day was coming. His second day. Cole got to his feet and began to unfasten the rabbit. Time to eat. And then? After that he had no plans. He knew instinctively that he could keep himself alive indefinitely with the tools he had retained, and the genius of his hands. He could kill game and skin it. Eventually he could build himself a permanent shelter, even make clothes out of hides. In winter —

But he was not thinking that far ahead. Cole stood by the fire, staring up at the sky, his hands on his hips. He squinted, suddenly tense. Something was moving. Something in the sky, drifting slowly through the grayness. A black dot.

He stamped out the fire quickly. What was it? He strained, trying to see. A bird?

A second dot joined the first. Two dots. Then three. Four. Five. A fleet of them, moving rapidly across the early morning sky. Toward the mountains.

Toward him.

Cole hurried away from the fire. He snatched up the rabbit and carried it along with him, into the tangled shelter he had built. He was invisible, inside the shelter. No one could find him. But if they had seen the fire —

He crouched in the shelter, watching the dots grow larger. They were planes, all right. Black wingless planes, coming closer each moment. Now he could hear them, a faint dull buzz, increasing until the ground shook under him.

The first plane dived. It dropped like a stone, swelling into a great black shape. Cole gasped, sinking down. The plane roared in an arch, swooping low over the ground. Suddenly bundles tumbled out, white bundles falling and scattering like seeds.

The bundles drifted rapidly to the ground. They landed. They were men. Men in uniform.

Now the second plane was diving. It roared overhead, releasing its load.

More bundles tumbled out, filling the sky. The third plane dived, then the fourth. The air was thick with drifting bundles of white, a blanket of descending weed spores, settling to earth.

On the ground the soldiers were forming into groups. Their shouts carried to Cole, crouched in his shelter. Fear leaped through him. They were landing on all sides of him. He was cut off. The last two planes had dropped men behind him.

He got to his feet, pushing out of the shelter. Some of the soldiers had found the fire, the ashes and coals. One dropped down, feeling the coals with his hand. He waved to the others. They were circling all around, shouting and gesturing. One of them began to set up some kind of gun. Others were unrolling coils of tubing, locking a collection of strange pipes and machinery in place.

Cole ran. He rolled down a slope, sliding and falling. At the bottom he leaped to his feet and plunged into the brush. Vines and leaves tore at his face, slashing and cutting him. He fell again, tangled in a mass of twisted shrubbery. He fought desperately, trying to free himself. If he could reach the knife in his pocket —

Voices. Footsteps. Men were behind him, running down the slope. Cole struggled frantically, gasping and twisting, trying to pull loose. He strained, breaking the vines, clawing at them with his hands.

A soldier dropped to his knee, leveling his gun. More soldiers arrived, bringing their rifles and aiming.

Cole cried out. He closed his eyes, his body suddenly went limp. He waited, his teeth locked together, sweat dripping down his neck, into his shirt, sagging against the mesh of vines and branches coiled around him.

Silence.

Cole opened his eyes slowly. The soldiers had regrouped. A huge man was striding down the slope toward them, barking orders as he came.

Two soldiers stepped into the brush. One of them grabbed Cole by the shoulder.

"Don't let go of him." The huge man came over, his black beard jutting out. "Hold on."

Cole gasped for breath. He was caught. There was nothing he could do. More soldiers were pouring down into the gully, surrounding him on all sides. They studied him curiously, murmuring together. Cole shook his head wearily and said nothing.

The huge man with the beard stood directly in front of him, his hands on his hips, looking him up and down. "Don't try to get away," the man said. "You can't get away. Do you understood?"

Cole nodded.

"All right. Good." The man waved. Soldiers clamped metal bands around Cole's arms and wrists. The metal dug into his flesh, making him gasp with pain. More clamps locked around his legs. "Those stay there until we're out of here. A long way out."

"Where — where are you taking me?"

Peter Sherikov studied the variable man for a moment before he answered. "Where? I'm taking you to my labs. Under the Urals." He glanced suddenly up at the sky. "We better hurry. The Security police will be starting their demolition attack in a few hours. We want to be a long way from here when that begins."

Sherikov settled down in his comfortable reinforced chair with a sigh. "It's good to be back." He signaled to one of his guards. "All right. You can unfasten him."

The metal clamps were removed from Cole's arms and legs. He sagged, sinking down in a heap. Sherikov watched him silently.

Cole sat on the floor, rubbing his wrists and legs, saying nothing.

"What do you want?" Sherikov demanded. "Food? Are you hungry?"

"No."

"Medicine? Are you sick? Injured?"

"No."

Sherikov wrinkled his nose. "A bath wouldn't hurt you any. We'll arrange that later." He lit a cigar, blowing a cloud of gray smoke around him. At the door of the room two lab guards stood with guns ready. No one else was in the room beside Sherikov and Cole.

Thomas Cole sat huddled in a heap on the floor, his head sunk down against his chest. He did not stir. His bent body seemed more elongated and stooped than ever, his hair tousled and unkempt, his chin and jowls a rough stubbled gray. His clothes were dirty and torn from crawling through the brush. His skin was cut and scratched; open sores dotted his neck and cheeks and forehead. He said nothing. His chest rose and fell. His faded blue eyes were almost closed. He looked quite old, a withered, dried-up old man.

Sherikov waved one of the guards over. "Have a doctor brought up here. I want this man checked over. He may need intravenous injections. He may not have had anything to eat for awhile."

The guard departed.

"I don't want anything to happen to you," Sherikov said. "Before we go on I'll have you checked over. And deloused at the same time."

Cole said nothing.

Sherikov laughed. "Buck up! You have no reason to feel bad." He leaned toward Cole, jabbing an immense finger at him. "Another two hours and you'd have been dead, out there in the mountains. You know that?"

Cole nodded.

"You don't believe me. Look." Sherikov leaned over and snapped on the vidscreen mounted in the wall. "Watch this. The operation should still be going on."

The screen lit up. A scene gained form.

"This is a confidential Security channel. I had it tapped several years ago — for my own protection. What we're seeing now is being piped in to Eric Reinhart." Sherikov grinned. "Reinhart arranged what you're seeing on the screen. Pay close attention. You were there, two hours ago."

Cole turned toward the screen. At first he could not make out what was happening. The screen showed a vast foaming cloud, a vortex of motion. From the speaker came a low rumble, a deep-throated roar. After a time the screen shifted, showing a slightly different view. Suddenly Cole stiffened.

He was seeing the destruction of a whole mountain range.

The picture was coming from a ship, flying above what had once been the Albertine Mountain Range. Now there was nothing but swirling clouds of gray and columns of particles and debris, a surging tide of restless material gradually sweeping off and dissipating in all directions.

The Albertine Mountains had been disintegrated. Nothing remained but these vast clouds of debris. Below, on the ground, a ragged plain stretched out, swept by fire and rain. Gaping wounds yawned, immense holes without bottoms, craters side by side as far as the eye could see. Craters and debris. Like the blasted, pitted surface of the moon. Two hours ago it had been rolling peaks and gulleys, brush and green bushes and trees.

Cole turned away.

"You see?" Sherikov snapped the screen off. "You were down there, not so long ago. All that noise and smoke — all for you. All for you, Mr. Variable Man from the past. Reinhart arranged that, to finish you off. I want you to understand that. It's very important that you realize that."

Cole said nothing.

Sherikov reached into a drawer of the table before him. He carefully brought out a small square box and held it out to Cole. "You wired this, didn't you?"

Cole took the box in his hands and held it. For a time his tired mind failed to focus. What did he have? He concentrated on it. The box was the children's toy. The inter-system vidsender, they had called it.

"Yes. I fixed this." He passed it back to Sherikov. "I repaired that. It was broken."

Sherikov gazed down at him intently, his large eyes bright. He nodded, his black beard and cigar rising and falling. "Good. That's all I wanted to know." He got suddenly to his feet, pushing his chair back. "I see the doctor's here. He'll fix you up. Everything you need. Later on I'll talk to you again."

Unprotesting, Cole got to his feet, allowing the doctor to take hold of his arm and help him up.

After Cole had been released by the medical department, Sherikov joined him in his private dining room, a floor above the actual laboratory.

The Pole gulped down a hasty meal, talking as he ate. Cole sat silently across from him, not eating or speaking. His old clothing had been taken away and new clothing given to him. He was shaved and rubbed down. His sores and cuts were healed, his body and hair washed. He looked much healthier and younger, now. But he was still stooped and tired, his blue eyes worn and faded. He listened to Sherikov's account of the world of 2136 AD without comment.

"You can see," Sherikov said finally, waving a chicken leg, "that your appearance here has been very upsetting to our program. Now that you know more about us you can see why Commissioner Reinhart was so interested in destroying you."

Cole nodded.

"Reinhart, you realize, believes that the failure of the SRB machines is the chief danger to the war effort. But that is nothing!" Sherikov pushed his plate away noisily, draining his coffee mug. "After all, wars *can* be fought without statistical forecasts. The SRB machines only describe. They're nothing more than mechanical onlookers. In themselves, they don't affect the course of the war. *We* make the war. They only analyze."

Cole nodded.

"More coffee?" Sherikov asked. He pushed the plastic container toward Cole. "Have some."

Cole accepted another cupful. "Thank you."

"You can see that our real problem is another thing entirely. The machines only do figuring for us in a few minutes that eventually we could do for our own selves. They're our servants, tools. Not some sort of gods in a temple which we go and pray to. Not oracles who can see into the future for us. They don't see into the future. They only make statistical predictions — not prophecies. There's a big difference there, but Reinhart and his kind have made such things as the SRB machines into gods. But I have no gods. At least, not any I can see."

Cole nodded, sipping his coffee.

"I'm telling you all these things because you must understand what we're up against. Terra is hemmed in on all sides by the ancient Centauran Empire. It's been out there for centuries, thousands of years. No one knows how long. It's old — crumbling and rotting. Corrupt and venal. But it holds most of the galaxy around us, and we can't break out of the Sol system. I told you about Icarus, and Hedge's work in ftl flight. We must win the war against Centaurus. We've waited and worked a long time for this, the moment when we can break out and get room among the stars for ourselves. Icarus is the deciding weapon. The data on Icarus tipped the SRB odds in our favor — for the first time in history. Success in the war against Centaurus will depend on Icarus, not on the SRB machines. You see?"

Cole nodded.

"However, there is a problem. The data on Icarus which I turned over to the machines specified that Icarus would be completed in ten days. More than half that time has already passed. Yet, we are no closer to wiring up the control turret than we were then. The turret baffles us." Sherikov grinned ironically. "Even *I* have tried my hand on the wiring, but with no success. It's intricate — and small. Too many technical buts not worked out. We are building only once, you understand. If we had many experimental models worked out before — "

"'But this is the experimental model," Cole said.

"And built from the designs of a man dead four years — who isn't here to correct us. We've made Icarus with our own hands down here in the labs. And he's giving us plenty of trouble." All at once Sherikov got to his feet. "Let's go down to the lab and look at him."

They descended to the floor below, Sherikov leading the way. Cole stopped short at the lab door.

"Quite a sight," Sherikov agreed. "We keep him down here at the bottom for safety's sake. He's well protected. Come on in. We have work to do."

In the center of the lab Icarus rose up, the gray squat cylinder that someday would flash through space at a speed of thousands of times that of light, toward the heart of Proxima Centaurus, over four light years away. Around the cylinder groups of men in uniform were laboring feverishly to finish the remaining work.

"Over here. The turret." Sherikov led Cole over to one side of the room. "It's guarded. Centauran spies are swarming everywhere on Terra. They see into everything. But so do we. That's how we get information for the SRB machines. Spies in both systems."

The translucent globe that was the control turret reposed in the center of a metal stand, an armed guard standing at each side. They lowered their guns as Sherikov approached.

"We don't want anything to happen to this," Sherikov said. "Everything depends on it." He put out his hand for the globe. Halfway to it his hand stopped, striking against an invisible presence in the air.

Sherikov laughed. "The wall. Shut it off. It's still on."

One of the guards pressed a stud at his wrist. Around the globe the air shimmered and faded.

"Now." Sherikov's hand closed over the globe. He lifted it carefully from its mount and brought it out for Cole to see. "This is the control turret for our enormous friend here. This is what will slow him down when he's inside Centaurus. He slows down and re-enters this universe. Right in the heart of the star. Then — no more Centaurus." Sherikov beamed. "And no more Armun."

But Cole was not listening. He had taken the globe from Sherikov and was turning it over and over, running his hands over it, his face close to its surface. He peered down into its interior, his face rapt and intent.

"You can't see the wiring. Not without lenses." Sherikov signalled for a pair of micro-lenses to be brought. He fitted them on Cole's nose, hooking them behind his ears. "Now try it. You can control the magnification. It's set for 1000X right now. You can increase or decrease it."

Cole gasped, swaying back and forth. Sherikov caught hold of him. Cole gazed down into the globe, moving his head slightly, focussing the glasses.

"It takes practice. But you can do a lot with them. Permits you to do microscopic wiring. There are tools to go along, you understand." Sherikov paused, licking his lip. "We can't get it done correctly. Only a few men can wire circuits using the micro-lenses and the little tools. We've tried robots, but there are too many decisions to be made. Robots can't make decisions. They just react."

Cole said nothing. He continued to gaze into the interior of the globe, his lips tight, his body taut and rigid. It made Sherikov feel strangely uneasy.

"You look like one of those old fortunetellers," Sherikov said jokingly, but a cold shiver crawled up his spine. "Better hand it back to me." He held out his hand.

Slowly, Cole returned the globe. After a time he removed the micro-lenses, still deep in thought.

"Well?" Sherikov demanded. "You know what I want. I want you to wire this damn thing up." Sherikov came close to Cole, his big face hard. "You can do it, I think. I could tell by the way you held it — and the job you did on the children's toy, of course. You could wire it up right, and in five days. Nobody else can. And if it's not wired up Centaurus will keep on running the galaxy and Terra will have to sweat it out here in the Sol system. One tiny mediocre sun, one dust mote out of a whole galaxy."

Cole did not answer.

Sherikov became impatient. "Well? What do you say?"

"What happens if I don't wire this control for you? I mean, what happens to *me*?"

"Then I turn you over to Reinhart. Reinhart will kill you instantly. He thinks you're dead, killed when the Albertine Range was annihilated. If he had any idea I had saved you — "

"I see."

"I brought you down here for one thing. If you wire it up I'll have you sent back to your own time continuum. If you don't — "

Cole considered, his face dark and brooding.

"What do you have to lose? You'd already be dead, if we hadn't pulled you out of those hills."

"Can you really return me to my own time?"

"Of course!"

"Reinhart won't interfere?"

Sherikov laughed. "What can he do? How can he stop me? I have my own men. You saw them. They landed all around you. You'll be returned."

"Yes. I saw your men."

"Then you agree?"

"I agree," Thomas Cole said. "I'll wire it for you. I'll complete the control turret — within the next five days."

IV

Three days later Joseph Dixon slid a closed-circuit message plate across the desk to his boss.

"Here. You might be interested in this."

Reinhart picked the plate up slowly. "What is it? You came all the way here to show me this?"

"That's right."

"Why didn't you vidscreen it?"

Dixon smiled grimly. "You'll understand when you decode it. It's from Proxima Centaurus."

"Centaurus!"

"Our counter-intelligence service. They sent it direct to me. Here, I'll decode it for you. Save you the trouble."

Dixon came around behind Reinhart's desk. He leaned over the Commissioner's shoulder, taking hold of the plate and breaking the seal with his thumb nail.

"Hang on," Dixon said. "This is going to hit you hard. According to our agents on Armun, the Centauran High Council has called an emergency session to deal with the problem of Terra's impending attack. Centauran replay couriers have reported to the High Council that the Terran bomb Icarus is virtually complete. Work on the bomb has been rushed through final stages in the underground laboratories under the Ural Range, directed by the Terran physicist Peter Sherikov."

"So I understand from Sherikov himself. Are you surprised the Centaurans know about the bomb? They have spies swarming over Terra. That's no news."

"There's more." Dixon traced the message plate grimly, with an unsteady finger. "The Centauran replay couriers reported that Peter Sherikov brought an expert mechanic out of a previous time continuum to complete the wiring of the turret!"

Reinhart staggered, holding on tight to the desk. He closed his eyes, gasping.

"The variable man is still alive," Dixon murmured. "I don't know how. Or why. There's nothing left of the Albertines. And how the hell did the man get halfway around the world?"

Reinhart opened his eyes slowly, his face twisting. "Sherikov! He must have removed him before the attack was forthcoming. I gave him the exact hour. He had to get help — from the variable man. He couldn't meet his promise otherwise."

Reinhart leaped up and began to pace back and forth. "I've already informed the SRB machines that the variable man has been destroyed. The machines now show the original 7–6 ratio in our favor. But the ratio is based on false information."

"Then you'll have to withdraw the false data and restore the original situation."

"No." Reinhart shook his head. "I can't do that. The machines must be kept functioning. We can't allow them to jam again. It's too dangerous. If Duffe should become aware that — "

"What are you going to do, then?" Dixon picked up the message plate. "You can't leave the machines with false data. That's treason."

"The data can't be withdrawn! Not unless equivalent data exists to take its place." Reinhart paced angrily back and forth. "Damn it, I was *certain* the man was dead. This is an incredible situation. He must be eliminated — at any cost."

Suddenly Reinhart stopped pacing. "The turret. It's probably finished by this time. Correct?"

Dixon nodded slowly in agreement. "With the variable man helping, Sherikov has undoubtedly completed work well ahead of schedule."

Reinhart's gray eyes flickered. "Then he's no longer of any use — even to Sherikov. We could take a chance ... Even if there were active opposition ... "

"What's this?" Dixon demanded. "What are you thinking about?"

"How many units are ready for immediate action? How large a force can we raise without notice?"

"Because of the war we're mobilized on a twenty-four hour basis. There are seventy air units and about two hundred surface units. The balance of the Security forces have been transferred to the line, under military control."

"Men?"

"We have about five thousand men ready to go, still on Terra. Most of them in the process of being transferred to military transports. I can hold it up at any time."

"Missiles?"

"Fortunately, the launching tubes have not yet been disassembled.

They're still here on Terra. In another few days they'll be moving out for the Colonial fracas."

"Then they're available for immediate use?"

"Yes."

"Good." Reinhart locked his hands, knotting his fingers harshly together in sudden decision. "That will do exactly. Unless I am completely wrong, Sherikov has only a half-dozen air units and no surface cars. And only about two hundred men. Some defense shields, of course — "

"What are you planning?"

Reinhart's face was gray and hard, like stone. "Send out orders for all available Security units to be unified under your immediate command. Have them ready to move by four o'clock this afternoon. We're going to pay a visit," Reinhart stated grimly. "A surprise visit. On Peter Sherikov."

"Stop here," Reinhart ordered.

The surface car slowed to a halt. Reinhart peered cautiously out, studying the horizon ahead.

On all sides a desert of scrub grass and sand stretched out. Nothing moved or stirred. To the right the grass and sand rose up to form immense peaks, a range of mountains without end, disappearing finally into the distance. The Urals.

"Over there," Reinhart said to Dixon, pointing. "See?"

"No."

"Look hard. It's difficult to spot unless you know what to look for. Vertical pipes. Some kind of vent. Or periscopes."

Dixon saw them finally. "I would have driven past without noticing."

"It's well concealed. The main labs are a mile down. Under the range itself. It's virtually impregnable. Sherikov had it built years ago, to withstand any attack. From the air, by surface cars, bombs, missiles — "

"He must feel safe down there."

"No doubt." Reinhart gazed up at the sky. A few faint black dots could be seen, moving lazily about, in broad circles. "Those aren't ours, are they? I gave orders — "

"No. They're not ours. All our units are out of sight. Those belong to Sherikov. His patrol."

Reinhart relaxed. "Good." He reached over and flicked on the vidscreen over the board of the car. "This screen is shielded? It can't be traced?"

"There's no way they can spot it back to us. It's nondirectional."

The screen glowed into life. Reinhart punched the combination keys and sat back to wait.

After a time an image formed on the screen. A heavy face, bushy black beard and large eyes.

Peter Sherikov gazed at Reinhart with surprised curiosity. "Commissioner! Where are you calling from? What — "

"How's the work progressing?" Reinhart broke in coldly. "Is Icarus almost complete?"

Sherikov beamed with expansive pride. "He's done, Commissioner. Two days ahead of time. Icarus is ready to be launched into space. I tried to call your office, but they told me — "

"I'm not at my office." Reinhart leaned toward the screen. "Open your entrance tunnel at the surface. You're about to receive visitors."

Sherikov blinked. "Visitors?"

"I'm coming down to see you. About Icarus. Have the tunnel opened for me at once."

"Exactly where are you, Commissioner?"

"On the surface."

Sherikov's eyes flickered. "Oh? But — "

"Open up!" Reinhart snapped. He glanced at his wristwatch. "I'll be at the entrance in five minutes. I expect to find it ready for me."

"Of course." Sherikov nodded in bewilderment. "I'm always glad to see you, Commissioner. But I — "

"Five minutes, then." Reinhart cut the circuit. The screen died. He turned quickly to Dixon. "You stay up here, as we arranged. I'll go down with one company of police. You understand the necessity of exact timing on this?"

"We won't slip up. Everything's ready. All units are in their places."

"Good." Reinhart pushed the door open for him. "You join your directional staff. I'll proceed toward the entrance tunnel."

"Good luck." Dixon leaped out of the car, onto the sandy ground. A gust of dry air swirled into the car around Reinhart. "I'll see you later."

Reinhart slammed the door. He turned to the group of police crouched in the rear of the car, their guns held tightly. "Here we go," Reinhart murmured. "Hold on."

The car raced across the sandy ground, toward the entrance tunnel to Sherikov's underground fortress.

Sherikov met Reinhart at the bottom end of the tunnel, where the tunnel opened up onto the main floor of the lab.

The big Pole approached, his hand out, beaming with pride and satisfaction. "It's a pleasure to see you, Commissioner."

Reinhart got out of the car, with his group of armed Security police. "Calls for a celebration, doesn't it?" he said.

"That's a good idea! We're two days ahead, Commissioner. The SRB machines will be interested. The odds should change abruptly at the news."

"Let's go down to the lab. I want to see the control turret myself."

A shadow crossed Sherikov's face. "I'd rather not bother the workmen right now, Commissioner. They've been under a great load, trying to complete the turret in time. I believe they're putting a few last finishes on it at this moment."

"We can view them by vidscreen. I'm curious to see them at work. It must be difficult to wire such minute relays."

Sherikov shook his head. "Sorry, Commissioner. No vidscreen on them. I won't allow it. This is too important. Our whole future depends on it."

Reinhart snapped a signal to his company of police. "Put this man under arrest."

Sherikov blanched. His mouth fell open. The police moved quickly around him, their gun-tubes up, jabbing into him. He was searched rapidly, efficiently. His gun belt and concealed energy screen were yanked off.

"What's going on?" Sherikov demanded, some color returning to his face. "What are you doing?"

"You're under arrest for the duration of the war. You're relieved of all authority. From now on one of my men will operate Designs. When the war is over you'll be tried before the Council and President Duffe."

Sherikov shook his head, dazed. "I don't understand. What's this all about? Explain it to me, Commissioner. What's happened?"

Reinhart signalled to his police. "Get ready. We're going into the lab. We may have to shoot our way in. The variable man should be in the area of the bomb, working on the control turret."

Instantly Sherikov's face hardened. His black eyes glittered, alert and hostile.

Reinhart laughed harshly. "We received a counter-intelligence report from Centaurus. I'm surprised at you, Sherikov. You know the Centaurans are everywhere with their relay couriers. You should have known — "

Sherikov moved. Fast. All at once he broke away from the police, throwing his massive body against them. They fell, scattering. Sherikov ran — directly at the wall. The police fired wildly. Reinhart fumbled frantically for his gun tube, pulling it up.

Sherikov reached the wall, running head down, energy beams flashing around him. He struck against the wall — and vanished.

"Down!" Reinhart shouted. He dropped to his hands and knees. All around him his police dived for the floor. Reinhart cursed wildly, dragging himself quickly toward the door. They had to get out, and right away. Sherikov had escaped. A false wall, an energy barrier set to respond to his pressure. He had dashed through it to safety. He —

From all sides an inferno burst, a flaming roar of death surging over them, around them, on every side. The room was alive with blazing masses of destruction, bouncing from wall to wall. They were caught between four banks of power, all of them open to full discharge. A trap — a death trap.

Reinhart reached the hall gasping for breath. He leaped to his feet. A few Security police followed him. Behind them, in the flaming room, the rest of the company screamed and struggled, blasted out of existence by the leaping bursts of power.

Reinhart assembled his remaining men. Already, Sherikov's guards were forming. At one end of the corridor a snub-barreled robot gun was maneuvering into position. A siren wailed. Guards were running on all sides, hurrying to battle stations.

The robot gun opened fire. Part of the corridor exploded, bursting into fragments. Clouds of choking debris and particles swept around them. Reinhart and his police retched, moving back along the corridor.

They reached a junction. A second robot gun was rumbling toward them, hurrying to get within range. Reinhart fired carefully, aiming at its delicate control. Abruptly the gun spun convulsively. It lashed against the wall, smashing itself into the unyielding metal. Then it collapsed in a heap, gears still whining and spinning.

"Come on." Reinhart moved away, crouching and running. He glanced at his watch. *Almost time.* A few more minutes. A group of lab guards appeared ahead of them. Reinhart fired. Behind him his police fired past him, violet shafts of energy catching the group of guards as they entered the corridor. The guards spilled apart, falling and twisting. Part of them settled into dust, drifting down the corridor. Reinhart made his way toward the lab, crouching and leaping, pushing past heaps of debris and remains, followed by his men. "Come on! Don't stop!"

Suddenly from around them the booming, enlarged voice of Sherikov thundered, magnified by rows of wall speakers along the corridor. Reinhart halted, glancing around.

"Reinhart! You haven't got a chance. You'll never get back to the surface. Throw down your guns and give up. You're surrounded on all sides. You're a mile under the surface."

Reinhart threw himself into motion, pushing into billowing clouds of particles drifting along the corridor. "Are you sure, Sherikov?" he grunted.

Sherikov laughed, his harsh, metallic peals rolling in waves against Reinhart's eardrums. "I don't want to have to kill you, Commissioner. You're vital to the war. I'm sorry you found out about the variable man. I admit we overlooked the Centauran espionage as a factor in this. But now that you know about him — "

Suddenly Sherikov's voice broke off. A deep rumble had shaken the floor, a lapping vibration that shuddered through the corridor.

Reinhart sagged with relief. He peered through the clouds of debris, making out the figures on his watch. Right on time. Not a second late.

The first of the hydrogen missiles, launched from the Council buildings on the other side of the world, were beginning to arrive. The attack had begun.

*   *   *

At exactly six o'clock Joseph Dixon, standing on the surface four miles from the entrance tunnel, gave the sign to the waiting units.

The first job was to break down Sherikov's defense screens. The missiles had to penetrate without interference. At Dixon's signal a fleet of thirty Security ships dived from a height of ten miles, swooping above the mountains, directly over the underground laboratories. Within five minutes the defense screens had been smashed, and all the tower projectors leveled flat. Now the mountains were virtually unprotected.

"So far so good," Dixon murmured, as he watched from his secure position. The fleet of Security ships roared back, their work done. Across the face of the desert the police surface cars were crawling rapidly toward the entrance tunnel, snaking from side to side.

Meanwhile, Sherikov's counter-attack had begun to go into operation.

Guns mounted among the hills opened fire. Vast columns of flames burst up in the path of the advancing cars. The cars hesitated and retreated, as the plain was churned up by a howling vortex, a thundering chaos of explosions. Here and there a car vanished in a cloud of particles. A group of cars moving away suddenly scattered, caught up by a giant wind that lashed across them and swept them up into the air.

Dixon gave orders to have the cannon silenced. The police air arm again swept overhead, a sullen roar of jets that shook the ground below. The police ships divided expertly and hurtled down on the cannon protecting the hills.

The cannon forgot the surface cars and lifted their snouts to meet the attack. Again and again the airships came, rocking the mountains with titanic blasts.

The guns became silent. Their echoing boom diminished, died away reluctantly, as bombs took critical toll of them.

Dixon watched with satisfaction as the bombing came to an end. The airships rose in a thick swarm, black gnats shooting up in triumph from a dead carcass. They hurried back as emergency anti-aircraft robot guns swung into position and saturated the sky with blazing puffs of energy.

Dixon checked his wristwatch. The missiles were already on the way from North America. Only a few minutes remained.

The surface cars, freed by the successful bombing, began to regroup for a new frontal attack. Again they crawled forward, across the burning plain, bearing down cautiously on the battered wall of mountains, heading toward the twisted wrecks that had been the ring of defense guns. Toward the entrance tunnel.

An occasional cannon fired feebly at them. The cars came grimly on. Now, in the hollows of the hills, Sherikov's troops were hurrying to the surface to meet the attack. The first car reached the shadow of the mountains . . .

A deafening hail of fire burst loose. Small robot guns appeared everywhere, needle barrels emerging from behind hidden screens, trees, shrubs, rocks, and stones. The police cars were caught in a withering cross-fire, trapped at the base of the hills.

Down the slopes Sherikov's guards raced, toward the stalled cars. Clouds of heat rose up and boiled across the plain as the cars fired up at the running men. A robot gun dropped like a slug onto the plain and screamed toward the cars, firing as it came.

Dixon twisted nervously. Only a few minutes. Any time, now. He shaded his eyes and peered up at the sky. No sign of them yet. He wondered about Reinhart. No signal had come from below. Clearly, Reinhart had run into trouble. No doubt there was desperate fighting going on in the maze of underground tunnels, the intricate web of passages that honeycombed the earth below the mountains.

In the air, Sherikov's few defense ships darted rapidly, wildly, putting up a futile fight.

Sherikov's guards streamed out onto the plain. Crouching and running, they advanced toward the stalled cars. The police airships screeched down at them, guns thundering.

Dixon held his breath. When the missiles arrived —

The first missile struck. A section of the mountain vanished, turned to smoke and foaming gases. The wave of heat slapped Dixon across the face, spinning him around. Quickly he re-entered his ship and took off, shooting rapidly away from the scene. He glanced back. A second and third missile had arrived. Great gaping pits yawned among the mountains, vast sections missing like broken teeth. Now the missiles could penetrate to the underground laboratories below.

On the ground, the surface cars halted beyond the danger area, waiting for the missile attack to finish. When the eighth missile had struck, the cars again moved forward. No more missiles fell.

Dixon swung his ship around, heading back toward the scene. The laboratory was exposed. The top sections of it had been ripped open. The laboratory lay like a tin can, torn apart by mighty explosions, its first floors visible from the air. Men and cars were pouring down into it, fighting with the guards swarming to the surface.

Dixon watched intently. Sherikov's men were bringing up heavy guns, big robot artillery. But the police ships were diving again. Sherikov's defensive patrols had been cleaned from the sky. The police ships whined down, arcing over the exposed laboratory. Small bombs fell, whistling down, pinpointing the artillery rising to the surface on the remaining lift stages.

Abruptly Dixon's vidscreen clicked. Dixon turned toward it.

Reinhart's features formed. "Call off the attack." His uniform was torn. A deep bloody gash crossed his cheek. He grinned sourly at Dixon, pushing his tangled hair back out of his face. "Quite a fight."

"Sherikov — "

"He's called off his guards. We've agreed to a truce. It's all over. No more needed." Reinhart gasped for breath, wiping grime and sweat from his neck. "Land your ship and come down here at once."

"The variable man?"

"That comes next," Reinhart said grimly. He adjusted his gun tube. "I want you down here, for that part. I want you to be in on the kill."

Reinhart turned away from the vidscreen. In the corner of the room Sherikov stood silently, saying nothing. "Well?" Reinhart barked. "Where is he? Where will I find him?"

Sherikov licked his lips nervously, glancing up at Reinhart. "Commissioner, are you sure — "

"The attack has been called off. Your labs are safe. So is your life. Now it's your turn to come through." Reinhart gripped his gun, moving toward Sherikov. *"Where is he?"*

For a moment Sherikov hesitated. Then slowly his huge body sagged, defeated. He shook his head wearily. "All right. I'll show you where he is." His voice was hardly audible, a dry whisper. "Down this way. Come on."

Reinhart followed Sherikov out of the room, into the corridor. Police and guards were working rapidly, clearing the debris and ruins away, putting out the hydrogen fires that burned everywhere. "No tricks, Sherikov."

"No tricks." Sherikov nodded resignedly. "Thomas Cole is by himself. In a wing lab off the main rooms."

"Cole?"

"The variable man. That's his name." The Pole turned his massive head a little. "He has a name."

Reinhart waved his gun. "Hurry up. I don't want anything to go wrong. This is the part I came for."

"You must remember something, Commissioner."

"What is it?"

Sherikov stopped walking. "Commissioner, nothing must happen to the globe. The control turret. Everything depends on it, the war, our whole — "

"I know. Nothing will happen to the damn thing. Let's go."

"If it should get damaged — "

"I'm not after the globe. I'm interested only in — in Thomas Cole."

They came to the end of the corridor and stopped before a metal door. Sherikov nodded at the door. "In there."

Reinhart moved back. "Open the door."

"Open it yourself. I don't want to have anything to do with it."

Reinhart shrugged. He stepped up to the door. Holding his gun level he raised his hand, passing it in front of the eye circuit. Nothing happened.

Reinhart frowned. He pushed the door with his hand. The door slid open. Reinhart was looking into a small laboratory. He glimpsed a workbench, tools, heaps of equipment, measuring devices, and in the center of the bench the transparent globe, the control turret.

"Cole?" Reinhart advanced quickly into the room. He glanced around him, suddenly alarmed. "Where — "

The room was empty. Thomas Cole was gone.

When the first missile struck, Cole stopped work and sat listening.

Far off, a distant rumble rolled through the earth, shaking the floor under him. On the bench, tools and equipment danced up and down. A pair of pliers fell crashing to the floor. A box of screws tipped over, spilling its minute contents out.

Cole listened for a time. Presently he lifted the transparent globe from the bench. With carefully controlled hands he held the globe up, running his fingers gently over the surface, his faded blue eyes thoughtful. Then, after a time, he placed the globe back on the bench, in its mount.

The globe was finished. A faint glow of pride moved through the variable man. The globe was the finest job he had ever done.

The deep rumblings ceased. Cole became instantly alert. He jumped down from his stool, hurrying across the room to the door. For a moment he stood by the door listening intently. He could hear noise on the other side, shouts, guards rushing past, dragging heavy equipment, working frantically.

A rolling crash echoed down the corridor and lapped against his door. The concussion spun him around. Again a tide of energy shook the walls and floor and sent him down on his knees.

The lights flickered and winked out.

Cole fumbled in the dark until he found a flashlight. Power failure. He could hear crackling flames. Abruptly the lights came on again, an ugly yellow, then faded back out. Cole bent down and examined the door with his flashlight. A magnetic lock. Dependent on an externally induced electric flux. He grabbed a screwdriver and pried at the door. For a moment it held. Then it fell open.

Cole stepped warily out into the corridor. Everything was in shambles. Guards wandered everywhere, burned and half blinded. Two lay groaning under a pile of wrecked equipment. Fused guns, reeking metal. The air was heavy with the smell of burning wiring and plastic. A thick cloud that choked him and made him bend double as he advanced.

"Halt," a guard gasped feebly, struggling to rise. Cole pushed past him and down the corridor. Two small robot guns, still functioning, glided past him hurriedly toward the drumming chaos of battle. He followed.

At a major intersection the fight was in full swing. Sherikov's guards fought Security police, crouched behind pillars and barricades, firing wildly, desperately. Again the whole structure shuddered as a great booming blast ignited some place above. Bombs? Shells?

Cole threw himself down as a violet beam cut past his ear and disintegrated the wall behind him. A Security policeman, wild-eyed, firing erratically. One of Sherikov's guards winged him and his gun skidded to the floor.

A robot cannon turned toward him as he made his way past the intersection. He began to run. The cannon rolled along behind him, aiming itself uncertainly. Cole hunched over as he shambled rapidly along, gasping for breath. In the flickering yellow light he saw a handful of Security police advancing, firing expertly, intent on a line of defense Sherikov's guards had hastily set up.

The robot cannon altered its course to take them on, and Cole escaped around a corner.

He was in the main lab, the big chamber where Icarus himself rose, the vast squat column.

Icarus! A solid wall of guards surrounded him, grim-faced, hugging guns and protection shields. But the Security police were leaving Icarus alone. Nobody wanted to damage him. Cole evaded a lone guard tracking him and reached the far side of the lab.

It took him only a few seconds to find the force field generator. There was no switch. For a moment that puzzled him — and then he remembered. The guard had controlled it from his wrist.

Too late to worry about that. With his screwdriver he unfastened the plate over the generator and ripped out the wiring in handfuls. The generator came loose and he dragged it away from the wall. The screen was off, thank God. He managed to carry the generator into a side corridor.

Crouched in a heap, Cole bent over the generator, deft fingers flying. He pulled the wiring to him and laid it out on the floor, tracing the circuits with feverish haste.

The adaptation was easier than he had expected. The screen flowed at right angles to the wiring, for a distance of six feet. Each lead was shielded on one side; the field radiated outward, leaving a hollow cone in the center. He ran the wiring through his belt, down his trouser legs, under his shirt, all the way to his wrists and ankles.

He was just snatching up the heavy generator when two Security police appeared. They raised their blasters and fired point-blank.

Cole clicked on the screen. A vibration leaped through him that snapped his jaw and danced up his body. He staggered away, half-stupefied by the surging force that radiated out from him. The violet rays struck the field and deflected harmlessly.

He was safe.

He hurried on down the corridor, past a ruined gun and sprawled bodies still clutching blasters. Great drifting clouds of radioactive particles billowed around him. He edged by one cloud nervously. Guards lay everywhere, dying and dead, partly destroyed, eaten and corroded by the hot metallic salts in the air. He had to get out — and fast.

At the end of the corridor a whole section of the fortress was in ruins. Towering flames leaped on all sides. One of the missiles had penetrated below ground level.

Cole found a lift that still functioned. A load of wounded guards was being raised to the surface. None of them paid any attention to him. Flames surged around the lift, licking at the wounded. Workmen were desperately trying to get the lift into action. Cole leaped onto the lift. A moment later it began to rise, leaving the shouts and the flames behind.

The lift emerged on the surface and Cole jumped off. A guard spotted him and gave chase. Crouching, Cole dodged into a tangled mass of twisted metal, still white-hot and smoking. He ran for a distance, leaping from the side of a ruined defense-screen tower, onto the fused ground and down the side of a hill. The ground was hot underfoot. He hurried as fast as he could, gasping for breath. He came to a long slope and scrambled up the side.

The guard who had followed was gone, lost behind in the rolling clouds of ash that drifted from the ruins of Sherikov's underground fortress.

Cole reached the top of the hill. For a brief moment he halted to get his breath and figure where he was. It was almost evening. The sun was beginning to set. In the darkening sky a few dots still twisted and rolled, black specks that abruptly burst into flame and fused out again.

Cole stood up cautiously, peering around him. Ruins stretched out below, on all sides, the furnace from which he had escaped. A chaos of incandescent metal and debris, gutted and wrecked beyond repair. Miles of tangled rubbish and half-vaporized equipment.

He considered. Everyone was busy putting out the fires and pulling the wounded to safety. It would be a while before he was missed. But as soon as they realized he was gone they'd be after him. Most of the laboratory had been destroyed. Nothing lay back that way.

Beyond the ruins lay the great Ural peaks, the endless mountains, stretching out as far as the eye could see.

Mountains and green forests. A wilderness. They'd never find him there.

Cole started along the side of the hill, walking slowly and carefully, his screen generator under his arm. Probably in the confusion he could find enough food and equipment to last him indefinitely. He could wait until early morning then circle back toward the ruins and load up. With a few tools and his own innate skill he would get along fine. A screwdriver, hammer, nails, odds and ends —

A great hum sounded in his ears. It swelled to a deafening roar. Startled, Cole whirled around. A vast shape filled the sky behind him, growing each moment. Cole stood frozen, utterly transfixed. The shape thundered over him, above his head, as he stood stupidly, rooted to the spot.

Then, awkwardly, uncertainly, he began to run. He stumbled and fell and rolled a short distance down the side of the hill. Desperately, he struggled to hold onto the ground. His hands dug wildly, futilely, into the soft soil, trying to keep the generator under his arm at the same time.

A flash, and a blinding spark of light around him.

The spark picked him up and tossed him like a dry leaf. He grunted in agony as searing fire crackled about him, a blazing inferno that gnawed and ate hungrily through his screen. He spun dizzily and fell through the cloud of fire, down into a pit of darkness, a vast gulf between two hills. His wiring ripped off. The generator tore out of his grip and was lost behind. Abruptly, his force field ceased.

Cole lay in the darkness at the bottom of the hill. His whole body shrieked in agony as the unholy fire played over him. He was a blazing cinder, a half-consumed ash flaming in a universe of darkness. The pain made him twist and crawl like an insect, trying to burrow into the ground. He screamed and shrieked and struggled to escape, to get away from the hideous fire. To reach the curtain of darkness beyond, where it was cool and silent, where the flames couldn't crackle and eat at him.

He reached imploringly out, into the darkness, groping feebly toward it, trying to pull himself into it. Gradually, the glowing orb that was his own body faded. The impenetrable chaos of night descended. He allowed the tide to sweep over him, to extinguish the searing fire.

Dixon landed his ship expertly, bringing it to a halt in front of an over-turned defense tower. He leaped out and hurried across the smoking ground.

From a lift Reinhart appeared, surrounded by his Security police. "He got away from us! He escaped!"

"He didn't escape," Dixon answered. "I got him myself."

Reinhart quivered violently. "What do you mean?"

"Come along with me. Over in this direction." He and Reinhart climbed the side of a demolished hill, both of them panting for breath. "I was landing. I saw a figure emerge from a lift and run toward the mountains, like some sort of animal. When he came out in the open I dived on him and released a phosphorous bomb."

"Then he's — *dead?*"

"I don't see how anyone could have lived through a phosphorous bomb." They reached the top of the hill. Dixon halted, then pointed excitedly down into the pit beyond the hill. "There!"

They descended cautiously. The ground was singed and burned clean. Clouds of smoke hung heavily in the air. Occasional fires still flickered here and there. Reinhart coughed and bent over to see. Dixon flashed on a pocket flare and set it beside the body.

The body was charred, half destroyed by the burning phosphorous. It lay motionless, one arm over its face, mouth open, legs sprawled grotesquely.

Like some abandoned rag doll, tossed in an incinerator and consumed almost beyond recognition.

"He's alive!" Dixon muttered. He felt around curiously. "Must have had some kind of protection screen. Amazing that a man could — "

"It's him? It's really him?"

"Fits the description." Dixon tore away a handful of burned clothing. "This is the variable man. What's left of him, at least."

Reinhart sagged with relief. "Then we've finally got him. The data is accurate. He's no longer a factor."

Dixon got out his blaster and released the safety catch thoughtfully. "If you want, I can finish the job right now."

At that moment Sherikov appeared, accompanied by two armed Security police. He strode grimly down the hillside, black eyes snapping. "Did Cole — " He broke off. "Good God."

"Dixon got him with a phosphorous bomb," Reinhart said noncommittally. "He had reached the surface and was trying to get into the mountains."

Sherikov turned wearily away. "He was an amazing person. During the attack he managed to force the lock on his door and escape. The guards fired at him, but nothing happened. He had rigged up some kind of force field around him. Something he adapted."

"Anyhow, it's over with," Reinhart answered. "Did you have SRB plates made up on him?"

Sherikov reached slowly into his coat. He drew out a manila envelope. "Here's all the information I collected about him, while he was with me."

"Is it complete? Everything previous has been merely fragmentary."

"As near complete as I could make it. It includes photographs and diagrams of the interior of the globe. The turret wiring he did for me. I haven't had a chance even to look at them." Sherikov fingered the envelope. "What are you going to do with Cole?"

"Have him loaded up, taken back to the city — and officially put to sleep by the Euthanasia Ministry."

"Legal murder?" Sherikov's lips twisted. "Why don't you simply do it right here and get it over with?"

Reinhart grabbed the envelope and stuck it in his right pocket. "I'll turn this right over to the machines." He motioned to Dixon. "Let's go. Now we can notify the fleet to prepare for the attack on Centaurus." He turned briefly back to Sherikov. "When can Icarus be launched?"

"In an hour or so, I suppose. They're locking the control turret in place. Assuming it functions correctly, that's all that's needed."

"Good. I'll notify Duffe to send out the signal to the warfleet." Reinhart nodded to the police to take Sherikov to the waiting Security ship. Sherikov moved off dully, his face gray and haggard. Cole's inert body was picked up and tossed onto a freight cart. The cart rumbled into the hold of the Security ship and the lock slid shut after it.

"It'll be interesting to see how the machines respond to the additional data," Dixon said.

"It should make quite an improvement in the odds," Reinhart agreed. He patted the envelope bulging in his inside pocket. "We're two days ahead of time."

Margaret Duffe got up slowly from her desk. She pushed her chair automatically back. "Let me get all this straight. You mean the bomb is finished? Ready to go?"

Reinhart nodded impatiently. "That's what I said. The Technicians are checking the turret locks to make sure it's properly attached. The launching will take place in half an hour."

"Thirty minutes! Then — "

"Then the attack can begin at once. I assume the fleet is ready for action."

"Of course. It's been ready for several days. But I can't believe the bomb is ready so soon." Margaret Duffe moved numbly toward the door of her office. "This is a great day, Commissioner. An old era lies behind us. This time tomorrow Centaurus will be gone. And eventually the colonies will be ours."

"It's been a long climb," Reinhart murmured.

"One thing. Your charge against Sherikov. It seems incredible that a person of his caliber could ever — "

"We'll discuss that later," Reinhart interrupted coldly. He pulled the manila envelope from his coat. "I haven't had an opportunity to feed the additional data to the SRB machines. If you'll excuse me, I'll do that now."

For a moment Margaret Duffe stood at the door. The two of them faced each other silently, neither speaking, a faint smile on Reinhart's thin lips, hostility in the woman's blue eyes.

"Reinhart, sometimes I think perhaps you'll go too far. And sometimes I think you've *already* gone too far ... "

"I'll inform you of any change in the odds showing." Reinhart strode past her, out of the office and down the hall. He headed toward the SRB room, an intense thalamic excitement rising up inside him.

A few moments later he entered the SRB room. He made his way to the machines. The odds 7–6 showed in the view windows. Reinhart smiled a little. 7–6. False odds, based on incorrect information. Now they could be removed.

Kaplan hurried over. Reinhart handed him the envelope, and moved over to the window, gazing down at the scene below. Men and cars scurried frantically everywhere. Officials coming and going like ants, hurrying in all directions.

The war was on. The signal had been sent out to the warfleet that had waited so long near Proxima Centaurus. A feeling of triumph raced through Reinhart. He had won. He had destroyed the man from the past and broken Peter Sherikov. The war had begun as planned. Terra was breaking out. Reinhart smiled thinly. He had been completely successful.

"Commissioner."

Reinhart turned slowly. "All right."

Kaplan was standing in front of the machines, gazing down at the reading. "Commissioner — "

Sudden alarm plucked at Reinhart. There was something in Kaplan's voice. He hurried quickly over. "What is it?"

Kaplan looked up at him, his face white, his eyes wide with terror. His mouth opened and closed, but no sound came.

"What is it?" Reinhart demanded, chilled. He bent toward the machines, studying the reading.

And sickened with horror.

100–1. *Against* Terra!

He could not tear his gaze away from the figures. He was numb, shocked with disbelief. 100–1. *What had happened?* What had gone wrong? The turret was finished, Icarus was ready, the fleet had been notified —

There was a sudden deep buzz from outside the building. Shouts drifted up from below. Reinhart turned his head slowly toward the window, his heart frozen with fear.

Across the evening sky a trail moved, rising each moment. A thin line of white. Something climbed, gaining speed each moment. On the ground, all eyes were turned toward it, awed faces peering up.

The object gained speed. Faster and faster. Then it vanished. Icarus was on his way. The attack had begun; it was too late to stop, now.

And on the machines the odds read a hundred to one — for failure.

At eight o'clock in the evening of May 15, 2136, Icarus was launched toward the star Centaurus. A day later, while all Terra waited, Icarus entered the star, traveling at thousands of times the speed of light.

Nothing happened. Icarus disappeared into the star. There was no explosion. The bomb failed to go off.

At the same time the Terran warfleet engaged the Centauran outer fleet, sweeping down in a concentrated attack. Twenty major ships were seized. A good part of the Centauran fleet was destroyed. Many of the captive systems began to revolt, in the hope of throwing off the Imperial bonds.

Two hours later the massed Centauran warfleet from Armun abruptly appeared and joined battle. The great struggle illuminated half the Centauran system. Ship after ship flashed briefly and then faded to ash. For a whole day the two fleets fought, strung out over millions of miles of space. Innumerable fighting men died — on both sides.

At last the remains of the battered Terran fleet turned and limped toward

Armun — defeated. Little of the once impressive armada remained. A few blackened hulks, making their way uncertainly toward captivity.

Icarus had not functioned. Centaurus had not exploded. The attack was a failure.

The war was over.

"We've lost the war," Margaret Duffe said in a small voice, wondering and awed. "It's over. Finished."

The Council members sat in their places around the conference table, gray-haired elderly men, none of them speaking or moving. All gazed up mutely at the great stellar maps that covered two walls of the chamber.

"I have already empowered negotiators to arrange a truce," Margaret Duffe murmured. "Orders have been sent out to Vice-Commander Jessup to give up the battle. There's no hope. Fleet Commander Carleton destroyed himself and his flagship a few minutes ago. The Centauran High Council has agreed to end the fighting. Their whole Empire is rotten to the core. Ready to topple of its own weight."

Reinhart was slumped over at the table, his head in his hands. "I don't understand ... *Why?* Why didn't the bomb explode?" He mopped his forehead shakily. All his poise was gone. He was trembling and broken. *"What went wrong?"*

Gray-faced, Dixon mumbled an answer. "The variable man must have sabotaged the turret. The SRB machines knew ... They analyzed the data. *They knew!* But it was too late."

Reinhart's eyes were bleak with despair as he raised his head a little. "I knew he'd destroy us. We're finished. A century of work and planning." His body knotted in a spasm of furious agony. "All because of Sherikov!"

Margaret Duffe eyed Reinhart coldly. "Why because of Sherikov?"

"He kept Cole alive! I wanted him killed from the start." Suddenly Reinhart jumped from his chair. His hand clutched convulsively at his gun. "And he's *still* alive! Even if we've lost I'm going to have the pleasure of putting a blast beam through Cole's chest!"

"Sit down!" Margaret Duffe ordered.

Reinhart was halfway to the door. "He's still at the Euthanasia Ministry, waiting for the official — "

"No, he's not," Margaret Duffe said.

Reinhart froze. He turned slowly, as if unable to believe his sense. *"What?"*

"Cole isn't at the Ministry. I ordered him transferred and your instructions cancelled."

"Where — where is he?"

There was unusual hardness in Margaret Duffe's voice as she answered. "With Peter Sherikov. In the Urals. I had Sherikov's full authority restored. I then had Cole transferred there, put in Sherikov's safekeeping. I want to make sure Cole recovers, so we can keep our promise to him — our promise to return him to his own time."

Reinhart's mouth opened and closed. All the color had drained from his face. His cheek muscles twitched spasmodically. At last he managed to speak. "You've gone insane! The traitor responsible for Earth's greatest defeat — "

"We have lost the war," Margaret Duffe stated quietly. "But this is not a day of defeat. It is a day of victory. The most incredible victory Terra has ever had."

Reinhart and Dixon were dumbfounded. "What — " Reinhart gasped. "What do you — " The whole room was in an uproar. All the Council members were on their feet. Reinhart's words were drowned out.

"Sherikov will explain when he gets here," Margaret Duffe's calm voice came. "He's the one who discovered it." She looked around the chamber at the incredulous Council members. "Everyone stay in his seat. You are all to remain here until Sherikov arrives. It's vital you hear what he has to say. His news transforms this whole situation."

Peter Sherikov accepted the briefcase of papers from his armed technician. "Thanks." He pushed his chair back and glanced thoughtfully around the Council chamber. "Is everybody ready to hear what I have to say?"

"We're ready," Margaret Duffe answered. The Council members sat alertly around the table. At the far end, Reinhart and Dixon watched uneasily as the big Pole removed papers from his briefcase and carefully examined them.

"To begin, I recall to you the original work behind the ftl bomb. Jamison Hedge was the first human to propel an object at a speed greater than light. As you know, that object diminished in length and gained in mass as it moved toward light speed. When it reached that speed it vanished. It ceased to exist in our terms. Having no length it could not occupy space. It rose to a different order of existence.

"When Hedge tried to bring the object back, an explosion occurred. Hedge was killed, and all his equipment was destroyed. The force of the blast was beyond calculation. Hedge had placed his observation ship many millions of miles away. It was not far enough, however. Originally, he had hoped his drive might be used for space travel. But after his death the principle was abandoned.

"That is — until Icarus. I saw the possibilities of a bomb, an incredibly powerful bomb to destroy Centaurus and all the Empire's forces. The reappearance of Icarus would mean the annihilation of their System. As Hedge had shown, the object would re-enter space already occupied by matter, and the cataclysm would be beyond belief."

"But Icarus never came back," Reinhart cried. "Cole altered the wiring so the bomb kept on going. It's probably still going."

"Wrong," Sherikov boomed. "The bomb *did* reappear. But it didn't explode."

Reinhart reacted violently. "You mean — "

"The bomb came back, dropping below the ftl speed as soon as it entered the star Proxima. But it did not explode. There was no cataclysm. It reappeared and was absorbed by the sun, turned into gas at once."

"Why didn't it explode?" Dixon demanded.

"Because Thomas Cole solved Hedge's problem. He found a way to bring the ftl object back into this universe without collision. Without an explosion. The variable man found what Hedge was after. ... "

The whole Council was on its feet. A growing murmur filled the chamber, a rising pandemonium breaking out on all sides.

"I don't believe it!" Reinhart gasped. "It isn't possible. If Cole solved Hedge's problem that would mean — " He broke off, staggered.

"Faster than light drive can now be used for space travel," Sherikov continued, waving the noise down. "As Hedge intended. My men have studied the photographs of the control turret. They don't know *how* or *why*, yet. But we have complete records of the turret. We can duplicate the wiring, as soon as the laboratories have been repaired."

Comprehension was gradually beginning to settle over the room. "Then it'll be possible to build ftl ships," Margaret Duffe murmured, dazed. "And if we can do that — "

"When I showed him the control turret, Cole understood its purpose. Not *my* purpose, but the original purpose Hedge had been working toward. Cole realized Icarus was actually an incomplete spaceship, not a bomb at all. He saw what Hedge had seen, an ftl space drive. He set out to make Icarus work."

"We can go *beyond* Centaurus," Dixon murmured. His lips twisted. "Then the war was trivial. We can leave the Empire completely behind. We can go beyond the galaxy."

"The whole universe is open to us," Sherikov agreed. "Instead of taking over an antiquated Empire, we have the entire cosmos to map and explore, God's total creation."

Margaret Duffe got to her feet and moved slowly toward the great stellar maps that towered above them at the far end of the chamber. She stood for a long time, gazing up at the myriad suns, the legions of systems, awed by what she saw.

"Do you suppose he realized all this?" she asked suddenly. "What we can see, here on these maps?"

"Thomas Cole is a strange person," Sherikov said, half to himself. "Apparently he has a kind of intuition about machines, the way things are supposed to work. An intuition more in his hands than in his head. A kind of genius, such as a painter or a pianist has. Not a scientist. He has no verbal knowledge about things, no semantic references. He deals with the things themselves. Directly.

"I doubt very much if Thomas Cole understood what would come about. He looked into the globe, the control turret. He saw unfinished wiring and relays. He saw a job half done. An incomplete machine."

"Something to be fixed," Margaret Duffe put in.

"Something to be fixed. Like an artist, he saw his work ahead of him. He was interested in only one thing: turning out the best job he could, with the skill he possessed. For us, that skill has opened up a whole universe, endless galaxies and systems to explore. Worlds without end. Unlimited, *untouched* worlds."

Reinhart got unsteadily to his feet. "We better get to work. Start organizing construction teams. Exploration crews. We'll have to reconvert from war production to ship designing. Begin the manufacture of mining and scientific instruments for survey work."

"That's right," Margaret Duffe said. She looked reflectively up at him. "But you're not going to have anything to do with it."

Reinhart saw the expression on her face. His hands flew to his gun and he backed quickly toward the door. Dixon leaped up and joined him. "Get back!" Reinhart shouted.

Margaret Duffe signaled and a phalanx of Government troops closed in around the two men. Grim-faced, efficient soldiers with magnetic grapples ready.

Reinhart's blaster wavered — toward the Council members sitting shocked in their seats, and toward Margaret Duffe, straight at her blue eyes. Reinhart's features were distorted with insane fear. "Get back! Don't anybody come near me or she'll be the first to get it!"

Peter Sherikov slid from the table and with one great stride swept his immense bulk in front of Reinhart. His huge black-furred fist rose in a smashing arc. Reinhart sailed against the wall, struck with ringing force and then slid slowly to the floor.

The Government troops threw their grapples quickly around him and jerked him to his feet. His body was frozen rigid. Blood dripped from his mouth. He spat bits of tooth, his eyes glazed over. Dixon stood dazed, mouth open, uncomprehending, as the grapples closed around his arms and legs.

Reinhart's gun skidded to the floor as he was yanked toward the door. One of the elderly Council members picked the gun up and examined it curiously. He laid it carefully on the table. "Fully loaded," he murmured. "Ready to fire."

Reinhart's battered face was dark with hate. "I should have killed all of you. *All* of you!" An ugly sneer twisted across his shredded lips. "If I could get my hands loose — "

"You won't," Margaret Duffe said. "You might as well not even bother to think about it." She signaled to the troops and they pulled Reinhart and Dixon roughly out of the room, two dazed figures, snarling and resentful.

For a moment the room was silent. Then the Council members shuffled nervously in their seats, beginning to breathe again.

Sherikov came over and put his big paw on Margaret Duffe's shoulder. "Are you all right, Margaret?"

She smiled faintly. "I'm fine. Thanks. ... "

Sherikov touched her soft hair briefly. Then he broke away and began to pack up his briefcase busily. "I have to go. I'll get in touch with you later."

"Where are you going?" she asked hesitantly. "Can't you stay and — "

"I have to get back to the Urals." Sherikov grinned at her over his bushy black beard as he headed out of the room. "Some very important business to attend to."

Thomas Cole was sitting up in bed when Sherikov came to the door. Most of his awkward, hunched-over body was sealed in a thin envelope of transparent air-proof plastic. Two robot attendants whirred ceaselessly at his side, their leads contacting his pulse, blood-pressure, respiration, and body temperature.

Cole turned a little as the huge Pole tossed down his briefcase and seated himself on the window ledge.

"How are you feeling?" Sherikov asked him.

"Better."

"You see we've quite advanced therapy. Your burns should be healed in a few months."

"How is the war coming?"

"The war is over."

Cole's lips moved. "Icarus — "

"Icarus went as expected. As *you* expected." Sherikov leaned toward the bed. "Cole, I promised you something, I mean to keep my promise — as soon as you're well enough."

"To return me to my own time?"

"That's right. It's a relatively simple matter, now that Reinhart has been removed from power. You'll be back home again, back in your own time, your own world. We can supply you with some discs of platinum or something of the kind to finance your business. You need a new Fixit truck. Tools. And clothes. A few thousand dollars ought to do it."

Cole was silent.

"I've already contacted histo-research," Sherikov continued. "The time bubble is ready as soon as you are. We're somewhat beholden to you, as you probably realize. You've made it possible for us to actualize our greatest dream. The whole planet is seething with excitement. We're changing our economy over from war to — "

"They don't resent what happened? The dud must have made an awful lot of people feel downright bad."

"At first. But they got over it — as soon as they understood what was ahead. Too bad you won't be here to see it, Cole. A whole world breaking loose. Bursting out into the universe. They want me to have an ftl ship ready by the end of the week! Thousands of applications are already on file, men and women wanting to get in on the initial flight."

Cole smiled a little. "There won't be any band, there. No parade or welcoming committee waiting for them."

"Maybe not. Maybe the first ship will wind up on some dead world, nothing but sand and dried salt. But everyone wants to go. It's almost like a holiday. People running around and shouting and throwing things in the streets.

"Afraid I must get back to the labs. Lots of reconstruction work being started." Sherikov dug into his bulging briefcase. "By the way ... One little thing. While you're recovering here, you might like to look at these." He tossed a handful of schematics on the bed.

Cole picked them up slowly. "What's this?"

"Just a little thing I designed." Sherikov arose and lumbered toward the door. "We're realigning our political structure to eliminate any recurrence of the Reinhart affair. This will block any more one-man power grabs." He jabbed a thick finger at the schematics. "It'll turn power over to all of us, not to just a limited number one person could dominate — the way Reinhart dominated the Council.

"This gimmick makes it possible for citizens to raise and decide issues directly. They won't have to wait for the Council to verbalize a measure. Any citizen can transmit his will with one of these, make his needs register on a central control that automatically responds. When a large enough segment of the population wants a certain thing done, these little gadgets set up an active field that touches all the others. An issue won't have to go through a formal Council. The citizens can express their will long before any bunch of gray-haired old men could get around to it."

Sherikov broke off, frowning. "Of course," he continued slowly, "there's one little detail ... "

"What's that?"

"I haven't been able to get a model to function. A few bugs ... Such intricate work never was in my line." He paused at the door. "Well, I hope I'll see you again before you go. Maybe if you feel well enough later on we could get together for one last talk. Maybe have dinner sometime. Eh?"

But Thomas Cole wasn't listening. He was bent over the schematics, an intense frown on his weathered face. His long fingers moved restlessly over the schematics, tracing wiring and terminals. His lips moved as he calculated.

Sherikov waited a moment. Then he stepped out into the hall and softly closed the door after him.

He whistled merrily as he strode off down the corridor.

THE INDEFATIGABLE FROG

"ZENO WAS THE FIRST great scientist," Professor Hardy stated, looking sternly around his classroom. "For example, take his paradox of the frog and the well. As Zeno showed, the frog will never reach the top of the well. Each jump is half the previous jump; a small but very real margin always remains for him to travel."

There was silence, as the afternoon Physics 3-A Class considered Hardy's oracular utterance. Then, in the back of the room, a hand slowly went up.

Hardy stared at the hand in disbelief. "Well?" he said. "What is it, Pitner?"

"But in Logic we were told the frog *would* reach the top of the well. Professor Grote said — "

"The frog will not!"

"Professor Grote says he will."

Hardy folded his arms. "In this class the frog will never reach the top of the well. I have examined the evidence myself. I am satisfied that he will always be a small distance away. For example, if he jumps — "

The bell rang.

All the students rose to their feet and began to move towards the door. Professor Hardy stared after them, his sentence half finished. He rubbed his jaw with displeasure, frowning at the horde of young men and women with their bright, vacant faces.

When the last of them had gone, Hardy picked up his pipe and went out of the room into the hall. He looked up and down. Sure enough, not far off was Grote, standing by the drinking fountain, wiping his chin.

"Grote!" Hardy said. "Come here!"

Professor Grote looked up, blinking, "What?"

221

"Come here," Hardy strode up to him. "How dare you try to teach Zeno? He was a scientist, and as such he's my property to teach, not yours. Leave Zeno to me!"

"Zeno was a philosopher." Grote stared up indignantly at Hardy. "I know what's on your mind. It's that paradox about the frog and the well. For your information, Hardy, the frog will easily get out. You've been misleading your students. Logic is on my side."

"Logic, bah!" Hardy snorted, his eyes blazing. "Old dusty maxims. It's obvious that the frog is trapped forever, in an eternal prison and can never get away!"

"He will escape."

"He will not."

"Are you gentlemen quite through?" a calm voice said. They turned quickly around. The Dean was standing quietly behind them, smiling gently. "If you are through, I wonder if you'd mind coming into my office for a moment." He nodded towards his door. "It won't take too long."

Grote and Hardy looked at each other. "See what you've done?" Hardy whispered, as they filed into the Dean's office. "You've got us into trouble again."

"You started it — you and your frog!"

"Sit down, gentlemen." The Dean indicated two stiff-backed chairs. "Make yourselves comfortable. I'm sorry to trouble you when you're so busy, but I do wish to speak to you for a moment." He studied them moodily. "May I ask what is the nature of your discussion this time?"

"It's about Zeno," Grote murmured.

"Zeno?"

"The paradox about the frog and the well."

"I see." The Dean nodded. "I see. The frog and the well. A two thousand-year-old saw. An ancient puzzle. And you two grown men stand in the hall arguing like a — "

"The difficulty," Hardy said, after a time, "is that no one has ever performed the experiment. The paradox is a pure abstraction."

"Then you two are going to be the first to lower the frog into his well and actually see what happens."

"But the frog won't jump in conformity to the conditions of the paradox."

"Then you'll have to make him, that's all. I'll give you two weeks to set up control conditions and determine the truth of this miserable puzzle. I want no more wrangling, month after month. I want this settled, once and for all."

Hardy and Grote were silent.

"Well, Grote," Hardy said at last, "let's get it started."

"We'll need a net," Grote said.

"A net and a jar." Hardy sighed. "We might as well be at it as soon as possible."

The "Frog Chamber," as it got to be called, was quite a project. The University donated most of the basement to them, and Grote and Hardy set to work at once, carrying parts and materials downstairs. There wasn't a soul who didn't know about it before long. Most of the science majors were on Hardy's side; they formed a Failure Club and denounced the frog's efforts. In the philosophy and art departments there was some agitation for a Success Club, but nothing ever came of it.

Grote and Hardy worked feverishly on the project. They were absent from their classes more and more of the time, as the two weeks wore on. The Chamber itself grew and developed, resembling more and more a long section of sewer pipe running the length of the basement. One end of it disappeared into a maze of wires and tubes: at the other there was a door.

One day when Grote went downstairs there was Hardy already, peering into the tube.

"See here," Grote said, "we agreed to keep hands off unless both of us were present."

"I'm just looking inside. It's dark in there." Hardy grinned. "I hope the frog will be able to see."

"Well, there's only one way to go."

Hardy lit his pipe. "What do you think of trying out a sample frog? I'm itching to see what happens."

"It's too soon." Grote watched nervously as Hardy searched about for his jar. "Shouldn't we wait a bit?"

"Can't face reality, eh? Here, give me a hand."

There was a sudden sound, a scraping at the door. They looked up. Pitner was standing there, looking curiously into the room, at the elongated Frog Chamber.

"What do you want?" Hardy said. "We're very busy."

"Are you going to try it out?" Pitner came into the room. "What are all the coils and relays for?"

"It's very simple," Grote said, beaming. "Something I worked out myself. This end here — "

"I'll show him," Hardy said. "You'll only confuse him. Yes, we were about to run the first trial frog. You can stay, boy, if you want." He opened the jar and took a damp frog from it. "As you can see, the big tube has an entrance and an exit. The frog goes in the entrance. Look inside the tube, boy. Go on."

Pitner peered into the open end of the tube. He saw a long black tunnel. "What are the lines?"

"Measuring lines. Grote, turn it on."

The machinery came on, humming softly. Hardy took the frog and dropped him into the tube. He swung the metal door shut and snapped it tight. "That's so the frog won't get out again, at this end."

"How big a frog were you expecting?" Pitner said. "A full-grown man could get into that."

"Now watch." Hardy turned the gas cock up. "This end of the tube is warmed. The heat drives the frog up the tube. We'll watch through the window."

They looked into the tube. The frog was sitting quietly in a little heap, staring sadly ahead.

"Jump, you stupid frog," Hardy said. He turned the gas up.

"Not so high, you maniac!" Grote shouted. "Do you want to stew him?"

"Look!" Pitner cried. "There he goes."

The frog jumped. "Conduction carries the heat along the tube bottom," Hardy explained. "He has to keep on jumping to get away from it. Watch him go."

Suddenly Pitner gave a frightened rattle. "My God, Hardy. The frog has shrunk. He's only half as big as he was."

Hardy beamed. "That is the miracle. You see, at the far end of the tube there is a force field. The frog is compelled to jump towards it by the heat. The effect of the field is to reduce animal tissue to its proximity. The frog is made smaller the farther he goes."

"Why?"

"It's the only way the jumping span of the frog can be reduced. As the frog leaps he diminishes in size, and hence each leap is proportionally reduced. We have arranged it so that the diminution is the same as in Zeno's paradox."

"But where does it all end?"

"That," Hardy said, "is the question to which we are devoted. At the far end of the tube there is a photon beam which the frog would pass through, if he ever got that far. If he could reach it, he would cut off the field."

"He'll reach it," Grote muttered.

"No. He'll get smaller and smaller, and jump shorter and shorter. To him, the tube will lengthen more and more, endlessly. He will never get there."

They glared at each other. "Don't be so sure," Grote said.

They peered through the window into the tube. The frog had gone quite a distance up. He was almost invisible, now, a tiny speck no larger than a fly, moving imperceptibly along the tube. He became smaller. He was a pin point. He disappeared.

"Gosh," Pitner said.

"Pitner, go away," Hardy said. He rubbed his hands together. "Grote and I have things to discuss."

He locked the door after the boy.

"All right," Grote said. "You designed this tube. What became of the frog?"

"Why, he's still hopping, somewhere in a sub-atomic world."

"You're a swindler. Some place along that tube the frog met with misfortune."

"Well," Hardy said. "If you think that, perhaps you should inspect the tube personally."

"I believe I will. I may find a — trap door."

"Suit yourself," Hardy said, grinning. He turned off the gas and opened the big metal door.

"Give me the flashlight," Grote said. Hardy handed him the flashlight and he crawled into the tube, grunting. His voice echoed hollowly. "No tricks, now."

Hardy watched him disappear. He bent down and looked into the end of the tube. Grote was half-way down, wheezing and struggling. "What's the matter?" Hardy said.

"Too tight. ... "

"Oh?" Hardy's grin broadened. He took his pipe from his mouth and set it on the table. "Well, maybe we can do something about that."

He slammed the metal door shut. He hurried to the other end of the tube and snapped the switches. Tubes lit up, relays clicked into place.

Hardy folded his arms. "Start hopping, my dear frog," he said. "Hop for all you're worth."

He went to the gas cock and turned it on.

It was very dark. Grote lay for a long time without moving. His mind was filled with drifting thoughts. What was the matter with Hardy? What was he up to? At last he pulled himself on to his elbows. His head cracked against the roof of the tube.

It began to get warm. "Hardy!" His voice thundered around him, loud and panicky. "Open the door. What's going on?"

He tried to turn around in the tube, to reach the door, but he couldn't budge. There was nothing to do but go forward. He began to crawl, muttering under his breath. "Just wait, Hardy. You and your jokes. I don't see what you expect to — "

Suddenly the tube leaped. He fell, his chin banging against the metal. He blinked. The tube had grown; now there was more than enough room. And his clothing! His shirt and pants were like a tent around him.

"Oh, heavens," Grote said in a tiny voice. He rose to his knees. Laboriously he turned around. He pulled himself back through the tube the way he had come, towards the metal door. He pushed against it, but nothing happened. It was now too large for him to force.

He sat for a long time. When the metal floor under him became too warm he crawled reluctantly along the tube to a cooler place. He curled himself up and stared dismally into the darkness. "What am I going to do," he asked himself.

After a time a measure of courage returned to him. "I must think logically. I've already entered the force field once, therefore I'm reduced in size by one-half. I must be about three feet high. That makes the tube twice as long."

He got out the flashlight and some paper from his immense pocket and did some figuring. The flashlight was almost unmanageable.

Underneath him the floor became warm. Automatically he shifted, a little up the tube to avoid the heat. "If I stay here long enough," he murmured, "I might be — "

The tube leaped again, rushing off in all directions. He found himself floundering in a sea of rough fabric, choking and gasping. At last he struggled free.

"One and a half feet," Grote said, staring around him. "I don't dare move any more, not at all."

But when the floor heated under him he moved some more. "Three-quarters of a foot." Sweat broke out on his face. "Three-quarters of one foot." He looked down the tube. Far, far down at the end was a spot of light, the photon beam crossing the tube. If he could reach it, if only he could reach it, if only he could reach it!

He meditated over his figures for a time. "Well," he said at last, "I hope I'm correct. According to my calculations I should reach the beam of light in about nine hours and thirty minutes, if I keep walking steadily." He took a deep breath and lifted the flashlight to his shoulder.

"However," he murmured, "I may be rather small by that time...." He started walking, his chin up.

Professor Hardy turned to Pitner. "Tell the class what you saw this morning."

Everyone turned to look. Pitner swallowed nervously. "Well, I was downstairs in the basement. I was asked in to see the Frog Chamber. By Professor Grote. They were going to start the experiment."

"What experiment do you refer to?"

"The Zeno one," he explained nervously. "The frog. He put the frog in the tube and closed the door. And then Professor Grote turned on the power."

"What occurred?"

"The frog started to hop. He got smaller."

"He got smaller, you say. And then what?"

"He disappeared."

Professor Hardy sat back in his chair. "The frog did not reach the end of the tube, then?"

"No."

"That's all." There was a murmuring from the class. "So you see, the frog did not reach the end of the tube, as expected by my colleague, Professor

Grote. He will never reach the end. Alas, we shall not see the unfortunate frog again."

There was a general stir. Hardy tapped with his pencil. He lit his pipe and puffed calmly, leaning back in his chair. "This experiment was quite an awakener to poor Grote, I'm afraid. He has had a blow of some unusual proportion. As you may have noticed, he hasn't appeared for his afternoon classes. Professor Grote, I understand, has decided to go on a long vacation to the mountains. Perhaps after he has had time to rest and enjoy himself, and to forget — "

Grote winced. But he kept on walking. "Don't get frightened," he said to himself. "Keep on."

The tube jumped again. He staggered. The flashlight crashed to the floor and went out. He was alone in the enormous cave, an immense void that seemed to have no end, no end at all.

He kept walking.

After a time he began to get tired again. It was not the first time. "A rest wouldn't do any harm." He sat down. The floor was rough under him, rough and uneven. "According to my figures it will be more like two days, or so. Perhaps a little longer. ... "

He rested, dozing a little. Later on he began to walk again. The sudden jumping of the tube had ceased to frighten him; he had grown accustomed to it. Sooner or later he would reach the photon beam and cut through it. The force field would go off and he would resume his normal size. Grote smiled a little to himself. Wouldn't Hardy be surprised to —

He stubbed his toe and fell, headlong into the blackness around him. A deep fear ran through him and he began to tremble. He stood up, staring around him.

Which way?

"My God," he said. He bent down and touched the floor under him. Which way? Time passed. He began to walk slowly, first one way, then another. He could make out nothing, nothing at all.

Then he was running, hurrying through the darkness, this way and that, slipping and falling. All at once he staggered. The familiar sensation: he breathed a sobbing sigh of relief. He was moving in the right direction! He began to run again, calmly, taking deep breaths, his mouth open. Then once more the staggering shudder as he shrank down another notch; but he was going the right way. He ran on and on.

And as he ran the floor became rougher and rougher. Soon he was forced to stop, falling over boulders and rocks. Hadn't they smoothed the pipe down? What had gone wrong with the sanding, the steel wool —

"Of course," he murmured. "Even the surface of a razor blade ... if one is small. ... "

He walked ahead, feeling his way along. There was a dim light over every-thing, rising up from the great stones around him, even from his own body. What was it? He looked at his hands. They glittered in the darkness.

"Heat," he said. "Of course. Thanks, Hardy." In the half light he leaped from stone to stone. He was running across an endless plain of rocks and boulders, jumping like a goat, from crag to crag. "Or like a frog," he said. He jumped on, stopping once in a while for breath. How long would it be? He looked at the size of the great blocks of ore piled up around him. Suddenly a terror rushed through him.

"Maybe I shouldn't figure it out," he said. He climbed up the side of one towering cliff and leaped across to the other side. The next gulf was even wider. He barely made it, gasping and struggling to catch hold.

He jumped endlessly, again and again. He forgot how many times.

He stood on the edge of a rock and leaped.

Then he was falling, down, down, into the cleft, into the dim light. There was no bottom. On and on he fell.

Professor Grote closed his eyes. Peace came over him, his tired body relaxed.

"No more jumping," he said, drifting down, down. "A certain law regard-ing falling bodies ... the smaller the body the less the effect of gravity. No wonder bugs fall so lightly ... certain characteristics. ... "

He closed his eyes and allowed the darkness to take him over, at last.

"And so," Professor Hardy said, "we can expect to find that this experi-ment will go down in science as — "

He stopped, frowning. The class was staring towards the door. Some of the students were smiling, and one began to laugh. Hardy turned to see what it was.

"Shades of Charles Fort," he said.

A frog came hopping into the room.

Pitner stood up. "Professor," he said excitedly. "This confirms a theory I've worked out. The frog became so reduced in size that he passed through the spaces — "

"What?" Hardy said. "This is another frog."

" — through the spaces between the molecules which form the floor of the Frog Chamber. The frog would then drift slowly to the floor, since he would be proportionally less affected by the law of acceleration. And leaving the force field, he would regain his original size."

Pitner beamed down at the frog as the frog slowly made his way across the room.

"Really," Professor Hardy began. He sat down at his desk weakly. At that moment the bell rang, and the students began to gather their books and papers together. Presently Hardy found himself alone, staring down at the frog. He shook his head. "It can't be," he murmured. "The world is full of frogs. It can't be the same frog."

A student came up to the desk. "Professor Hardy — "

Hardy looked up.

"Yes? What is it?"

"There's a man outside in the hall wants to see you. He's upset. He has a blanket on."

All right," Hardy said. He sighed and got to his feet. At the door he paused, taking a deep breath. Then he set his jaw and went out into the hall.

Grote was standing there, wrapped in a red-wool blanket, his face flushed with excitement. Hardy glanced at him apologetically.

"We still don't know!" Grote cried.

"What?" Hardy murmured. "Say, er, Grote — "

"We still don't know whether the frog would have reached the end of the tube. He and I fell out between the molecules. We'll have to find some other way to test the paradox. The Chamber's no good."

"Yes, true," Hardy said. "Say, Grote — "

"Let's discuss it later," Grote said. "I have to get to my classes. I'll look you up this evening."

And he hurried off down the hall clutching his blanket.

THE CRYSTAL CRYPT

"ATTENTION Inner-Flight ship! Attention! You are ordered to land at the Control Station on Deimos for inspection. Attention! You are to land at once!"

The metallic rasp of the speaker echoed through the corridors of the great ship. The passengers glanced at each other uneasily, murmuring and peering out the port windows at the small speck below, the dot of rock that was the Martian checkpoint, Deimos.

"What's up?" an anxious passenger asked one of the pilots, hurrying through the ship to check the escape lock.

"We have to land. Keep seated." The pilot went on.

"Land? But why?" They all looked at each other. Hovering above the bulging Inner-Flight ship were three slender Martian pursuit craft, poised and alert for any emergency. As the Inner-Flight ship prepared to land the pursuit ships dropped lower, carefully maintaining themselves a short distance away.

"There's something going on," a woman passenger said nervously. "Lord, I thought we were finally through with those Martians. Now what?"

"I don't blame them for giving us one last going over," a heavy set business man said to his companion. "After all, we're the last ship leaving Mars for Terra. We're damn lucky they let us go at all."

"You think there really will be war?" a young man said to the girl sitting in the seat next to him. "Those Martians won't dare fight, not with our weapons and ability to produce. We could take care of Mars in a month. It's all talk."

The girl glanced at him. "Don't be so sure. Mars is desperate. They'll fight tooth and nail. I've been on Mars three years." She shuddered. "Thank goodness I'm getting away. If — "

"Prepare to land!" the pilot's voice came. The ship began to settle slowly, dropping down toward the tiny emergency field on the seldom visited moon. Down, down the ship dropped. There was a grinding sound, a sickening jolt. Then silence.

"We've landed," the heavy set business man said. "They better not do anything to us! Terra will rip them apart if they violate one Space Article."

"Please keep your seats," the pilot's voice came. "No one is to leave the ship, according to the Martian authorities. We are to remain here."

A restless stir filled the ship. Some of the passengers began to read uneasily, others stared out at the deserted field, nervous and on edge, watching the three Martian pursuit ships land and disgorge groups of armed men.

The Martian soldiers were crossing the field quickly, moving toward them, running double time.

This Inner-Flight spaceship was the last passenger vessel to leave Mars for Terra. All other ships had long since left, returning to safety before the outbreak of hostilities. The passengers were the very last to go, the final group of Terrans to leave the grim red planet, business men, expatriates, tourists, any and all Terrans who had not already gone home.

"What do you suppose they want?" the young man said to the girl. "It's hard to figure Martians out, isn't it? First they give the ship clearance, let us take off, and now they radio us to set down again. By the way, my name's Thacher, Bob Thacher. Since we're going to be here awhile — "

The port lock opened. Talking ceased abruptly, as everyone turned. A black-clad Martian official, a Province Leiter, stood framed against the bleak sunlight, staring around the ship. Behind him a handful of Martian soldiers stood waiting, their guns ready.

"This will not take long," the Leiter said, stepping into the ship, the soldiers following him. "You will be allowed to continue your trip shortly."

An audible sigh of relief went through the passengers.

"Look at him," the girl whispered to Thacher. "How I hate those black uniforms!"

"He's just a Provincial Leiter," Thacher said. "Don't worry."

The Leiter stood for a moment, his hands on his hips, looking around at them without expression. "I have ordered your ship grounded so that an inspection can be made of all persons aboard," he said. "You Terrans are the last to leave our planet. Most of you are ordinary and harmless — I am not interested in you. I am interested in finding three saboteurs, three Terrans, two men and a woman, who have committed an incredible act of destruction and violence. They are said to have fled to this ship."

Murmurs of surprise and indignation broke out on all sides. The Leiter motioned the soldiers to follow him up the aisle.

"Two hours ago a Martian city was destroyed. Nothing remains, only a depression in the sand where the city was. The city and all its people have completely vanished. An entire city destroyed in a second! Mars will never rest until the saboteurs are captured. And we know they are aboard this ship."

"It's impossible," the heavy set business man said. "There aren't any saboteurs here."

"We'll begin with you," the Leiter said to him, stepping up beside the man's seat. One of the soldiers passed the Leiter a square metal box. "This will soon tell us if you're speaking the truth. Stand up. Get on your feet."

The man rose slowly, flushing. "See here — "

"Are you involved in the destruction of the city? Answer!"

The man swallowed angrily. "I know nothing about any destruction of any city. And furthermore — "

"He is telling the truth," the metal box said tonelessly.

"Next person." The Leiter moved down the aisle.

A thin bald headed man stood up nervously. "No sir," he said. "I don't know a thing about it."

"He is telling the truth," the box affirmed.

"Next person! Stand up!"

One person after another stood, answered, and sat down again in relief. At last there were only a few people left who had not been questioned. The Leiter paused, studying them intently.

"Only five left. The three must be among you. We have narrowed it down." His hand moved to his belt. Something flashed, a rod of pale fire. He raised the rod, pointing it steadily at the five people. "All right, the first one of you. What do you know about this destruction? Are you involved with the destruction of our city?"

"No, not at all," the man murmured.

"Yes, he's telling the truth," the box intoned.

"Next!"

"Nothing — I know nothing. I had nothing to do with it."

"True," the box said.

The ship was silent. Three people remained, a middle-aged man and his wife and their son, a boy of about twelve. They stood in the corner, staring white-faced at the Leiter, at the rod in his dark fingers.

"It must be you," the Leiter grated, moving toward them. The Martian soldiers raised their guns. "It *must* be you. You there, the boy. What do you know about the destruction of our city? Answer!"

The boy shook his head. "Nothing," he whispered.

The box was silent for a moment. "He is telling the truth," it said reluctantly.

"Next!"

"Nothing," the woman muttered. "Nothing."

"The truth."

"Next!"

"I had nothing to do with blowing up your city," the man said. "You're wasting your time."

"It is the truth," the box said.

For a long time the Leiter stood, toying with his rod. At last he pushed it back in his belt and signalled the soldiers toward the exit lock.

"You may proceed on your trip," he said. He walked after the soldiers. At the hatch he stopped, looking back at the passengers, his face grim. "You may go — But Mars will not allow her enemies to escape. The three saboteurs will be caught, I promise you." He rubbed his dark jaw thoughtfully. "It is strange. I was certain they were on this ship."

Again he looked coldly around at the Terrans.

"Perhaps I was wrong. All right, proceed! But remember: the three will be caught, even if it takes endless years. Mars will catch them and punish them! I swear it!"

For a long time no one spoke. The ship lumbered through space again, its jets firing evenly, calmly, moving the passengers toward their own planet, toward home. Behind them Deimos and the red ball that was Mars dropped farther and farther away each moment, disappearing and fading into the distance.

A sigh of relief passed through the passengers. "What a lot of hot air that was," one grumbled.

"Barbarians!" a woman said.

A few of them stood up, moving out into the aisle, toward the lounge and the cocktail bar. Beside Thacher the girl got to her feet, pulling her jacket around her shoulders.

"Pardon me," she said, stepping past him.

"Going to the bar?" Thacher said. "Mind if I come along?"

"I suppose not."

They followed the others into the lounge, walking together up the aisle. "You know," Thacher said, "I don't even know your name, yet."

"My name is Mara Gordon."

"Mara? That's a nice name. What part of Terra are you from? North America? New York?"

"I've been in New York," Mara said. "New York is very lovely." She was slender and pretty, with a cloud of dark hair tumbling down her neck, against her leather jacket.

They entered the lounge and stood undecided.

"Let's sit at a table," Mara said, looking around at the people at the bar, mostly men. "Perhaps over there."

"But someone's there already," Thacher said. The heavy set business man had sat down at the table and deposited his sample case on the floor. "Do we want to sit with *him*?"

"Oh, it's all right," Mara said, crossing to the table. "May we sit here?" she said to the man.

The man looked up, half-rising. "It's a pleasure," he murmured. He studied Thacher intently. "However, a friend of mine will be joining me in a moment."

"I'm sure there's room enough for us all," Mara said. She seated herself and Thacher helped her with her chair. He sat down, too, glancing up suddenly at Mara and the business man. They were looking at each other almost as if something had passed between them. The man was middle-aged, with a florid face and tired, grey eyes. His hands were mottled with the veins showing thickly. At the moment he was tapping nervously.

"My name's Thacher," Thacher said to him, holding out his hand. "Bob Thacher. Since we're going to be together for a while we might as well get to know each other."

The man studied him. Slowly his hand came out. "Why not? My name's Erickson. Ralf Erickson."

"Erickson?" Thacher smiled. "You look like a commercial man, to me." He nodded toward the sample case on the floor. "Am I right?"

The man named Erickson started to answer, but at that moment there was a stir. A thin man of about thirty had come up to the table, his eyes bright, staring down at them warmly. "Well, we're on our way," he said to Erickson.

"Hello, Mara." He pulled out a chair and sat down quickly, folding his hands on the table before him. He noticed Thacher and drew back a little. "Pardon me," he murmured.

"Bob Thacher is my name," Thacher said. "I hope I'm not intruding here." He glanced around at the three of them, Mara, alert, watching him intently, heavyset Erickson, his face blank, and this person. "Say, do you three know each other?" he asked suddenly.

There was silence.

The robot attendant slid over soundlessly, poised to take their orders. Erickson roused himself. "Let's see," he murmured. "What will we have? Mara?"

"Whiskey and water."

"You, Jan?"

The bright slim man smiled. "The same."

"Thacher?"

"Gin and tonic."

"Whiskey and water for me, also," Erickson said. The robot attendant went off. It returned at once with the drinks, setting on the table. Each took his own. "Well," Erickson said, holding his glass up. "To our mutual success."

All drank, Thacher and the three of them, heavy set Erickson, Mara, her eyes nervous and alert, Jan, who had just come. Again a look passed between

Mara and Erickson, a look so swift that he would have not caught it had he not been looking directly at her.

"What line do you represent, Mr. Erickson?" Thacher asked.

Erickson glanced at him, then down at the sample case on the floor. He grunted. "Well, as you can see, I'm a salesman."

Thacher smiled. "I knew it! You get so you can always spot a salesman right off by his sample case. A salesman always has to carry something to show. What are you in, sir?"

Erickson paused. He licked his thick lips. his eyes blank and lidded, like a toad's. At last he rubbed his mouth with his hand and reached down, lifting up the sample case. He set it on the table in front of him.

"Well?" he said. "Perhaps we might even show Mr. Thacher."

They all stared down at the sample case. It seemed to be an ordinary leather case, with a metal handle and a snap lock. "I'm getting curious," Thacher said. "What's in there? You're all so tense. Diamonds? Stolen jewels?"

Jan laughed harshly, mirthlessly. "Erick, put it down. We're not far enough away, yet."

"Nonsense," Erick rumbled. "We're away, Jan."

"Please," Mara whispered. "Wait, Erick."

"Wait? Why? What for? You're so accustomed to — "

"Erick," Mara said. She nodded toward Thacher. "We don't know him, Erick. Please!"

"He's a Terran, isn't he?" Erickson said. "All Terrans are together in these times." He fumbled suddenly at the catch lock on the case. "Yes, Mr. Thacher. I'm a salesman. We're all salesmen, the three of us."

"Then you do know each other."

"Yes." Erickson nodded. His two companions sat rigidly, staring down. "Yes, we do. Here, I'll show you our line."

He opened the case. From it he took a letter-knife, a pencil sharpener, a glass globe paperweight, a box of thumb tacks, a stapler, some clips, a plastic ashtray, and some things Thacher could not identify. He placed the objects in a row in front of him on the table top. Then he closed the sample case.

"I gather you're in office supplies," Thacher said. He touched the letter knife with his finger. "Nice quality steel. Looks like Swedish steel, to me."

Erickson nodded, looking into Thacher's face. "Not really an impressive business, is it? Office supplies. Ashtrays, paper clips." He smiled.

"Oh — " Thacher shrugged. "Why not? They're a necessity in modern business. The only thing I wonder — "

"What's that?"

"Well, I wonder how you'd ever find enough customers on Mars to make it worth your while." He paused, examining the glass paperweight. He lifted it, holding it to the light, staring at the scene within until Erickson took it out of his hand and put it back in the sample case. "And another thing. If you three know each other, why did you sit apart when you got on?"

They looked at him quickly.

"And why didn't you speak to each other until we left Deimos?" He leaned toward Erickson, smiling at him. "Two men and a woman. Three of you. Sitting apart in the ship. Not speaking, not until the check-station was past. I find myself thinking over what the Martian said. Three saboteurs. A woman and two men."

Erickson put the things back in the sample case. He was smiling, but his face had gone chalk white. Mara stared down, playing with a drop of water on the edge of her glass. Jan clenched his hands together nervously, blinking rapidly.

"You three are the ones the Leiter was after," Thacher said softly. "You are the destroyers, the saboteurs. But their lie detector — Why didn't it trap you? How did you get by that? And now you're safe, outside the check-station." He grinned, staring around at them. "I'll be damned! And I really thought you were a salesman, Erickson. You really fooled me."

Erickson relaxed a little. "Well, Mr. Thacher, it's in a good cause. I'm sure you have no love for Mars, either. No Terran does. And I see you're leaving with the rest of us."

"True," Thacher said. "You must certainly have an interesting account to give, the three of you." He looked around the table.

"We still have an hour or so of travel. Sometimes it gets dull, this Mars-Terra run. Nothing to see, nothing to do but sit and drink in the lounge." He raised his eyes slowly. "Any chance you'd like to spin a story to keep us awake?"

Jan and Mara looked at Erickson. "Go on," Jan said. "He knows who we are. Tell him the rest of the story."

"You might as well," Mara said.

Jan let out a sigh suddenly, a sigh of relief. "Let's put the cards on the table, get this weight off us. I'm tired of sneaking around, slipping — "

"Sure," Erickson said expansively. "Why not?" He settled back in his chair, unbuttoning his vest. "Certainly, Mr. Thacher. I'll be glad to spin you a story. And I'm sure it will be interesting enough to keep you awake."

They ran through the groves of dead trees, leaping across the sun-baked Martian soil, running silently together. They went up a little rise, across a narrow ridge. Suddenly Erick stopped, throwing himself down flat on the ground. The others did the same, pressing themselves against the soil, gasping for breath.

"Be silent," Erick muttered. He raised himself a little. "No noise. There'll be Leiters nearby, from now on. We don't dare take any chances."

Between the three people lying in the grove of dead trees and the City was a barren, level waste of desert, over a mile of blasted sand. No trees or bushes marred the smooth, parched surface. Only an occasional wind, a dry wind eddying and twisting, blew the sand up into little rills. A faint odor came to them, a bitter smell of heat and sand, carried by the wind.

Erick pointed. "Look. The City — There it is."

They stared, still breathing deeply from their race through the trees. The City was close, closer than they had ever seen it before. Never had they gotten so close to it in times past. Terrans were never allowed near the great Martian cities, the centers of Martian life. Even in ordinary times, when there was no threat of approaching war, the Martians shrewdly kept all Terrans away from their citadels, partly from fear, partly from a deep, innate sense of hostility toward the white-skinned visitors whose commercial ventures had earned them the respect, and the dislike, of the whole system.

"How does it look to you?" Erick said.

The City was huge, much larger than they had imagined from the drawings and models they had studied so carefully back in New York, in the War Ministry Office. Huge it was, huge and stark, black towers rising up against the sky, incredibly thin columns of ancient metal, columns that had stood wind and sun for centuries. Around the City was a wall of stone, red stone, immense bricks that had been lugged there and fitted into place by slaves of the early Martian dynasties, under the whiplash of the first great Kings of Mars.

An ancient, sun-baked City, a City set in the middle of a wasted plain, beyond groves of dead trees, a City seldom seen by Terrans — but a City studied on maps and charts in every War Office on Terra. A City that contained, for all its ancient stone and archaic towers, the ruling group of all Mars, the Council of Senior Leiters, black-clad men who governed and ruled with an iron hand.

The Senior Leiters, twelve fanatic and devoted men, black priests, but priests with flashing rods of fire, lie detectors, rocket ships, intra-space cannon, many more things the Terran Senate could only conjecture about. The Senior Leiters and their subordinate Province Leiters — Erick and the two behind him suppressed a shudder.

"We've got to be careful," Erick said again. "We'll be passing among them, soon. If they guess who we are, or what we're here for — "

He snapped open the case he carried, glancing inside for a second. Then he closed it again, grasping the handle firmly. "Let's go," he said. He stood up slowly. "You two come up beside me. I want to make sure you look the way you should."

Mara and Jan stepped quickly ahead. Erick studied them critically as the three of them walked slowly down the slope, onto the plain, toward the towering black spires of the City.

"Jan," Erick said. "Take hold of her hand! Remember, you're going to marry her; she's your bride. And Martian peasants think a lot of their brides."

Jan was dressed in the short trousers and coat of the Martian farmer, a knotted rope tied around his waist, a hat on his head to keep off the sun. His skin was dark, colored by dye until it was almost bronze.

"You look fine," Erick said to him. He glanced at Mara. Her black hair was tied in a knot, looped through a hollowed-out yuke bone. Her face was dark, too, dark and lined with colored ceremonial pigment, green and orange stripes across her cheeks. Earrings were strung through her ears. On her feet were tiny slippers of perruh hide, laced around her ankles, and she wore long translucent Martian trousers with a bright sash tied around her waist. Between her small breasts a chain of stone beads rested, good-luck charms for the coming marriage.

"All right," Erick said. He, himself, wore the flowing gray robe of a Martian priest, dirty robes that were supposed to remain on him all his life, to be buried around him when he died. "I think we'll get past the guards. There should be heavy traffic on the road."

They walked on, the hard sand crunching under their feet. Against the horizon they could see specks moving, other persons going toward the City, farmers and peasants and merchants, bringing their crops and goods to market.

"See the cart!" Mara exclaimed.

They were nearing a narrow road, two ruts worn into the sand. A Martian hufa was pulling the cart, its great sides wet with perspiration, its tongue hanging out. The cart was piled high with bales of cloth, rough country cloth, hand dipped. A bent farmer urged the hufa on.

"And there." She pointed, smiling.

A group of merchants riding small animals were moving along behind the cart, Martians in long robes, their faces hidden by sand masks. On each animal was a pack, carefully tied on with rope. And beyond the merchants, plodding dully along, were peasants and farmers in an endless procession, some riding carts or animals, but mostly on foot.

Mara and Jan and Erick joined the line of people, melting in behind the merchants. No one noticed them; no one looked up or gave any sign. The march continued as before. Neither Jan nor Mara said anything to each other. They walked a little behind Erick, who paced with a certain dignity, a certain bearing becoming his position.

Once he slowed down, pointing up at the sky. "Look," he murmured, in the Martian hill dialect. "See that?"

Two black dots circled lazily. Martian patrol craft, the military on the outlook for any sign of unusual activity. War was almost ready to break out with Terra. Any day, almost any moment.

"We'll be just in time," Erick said. "Tomorrow will be too late. The last ship will have left Mars."

"I hope nothing stops us," Mara said. "I want to get back home when we're through."

Half an hour passed. They neared the City, the wall growing as they walked, rising higher and higher until it seemed to blot out the sky itself. A vast wall, a wall of eternal stone that had felt the wind and sun for centuries. A group of Martian soldiers were standing at the entrance, the single passage-gate hewn into the rock, leading to the City. As each person went through the soldiers examined him, poking his garments, looking into his load.

Erick tensed. The line had slowed almost to a halt. "It'll be our turn, soon," he murmured. "Be prepared."

"Let's hope no Leiters come around," Jan said. "The soldiers aren't so bad."

Mara was staring up at the wall and the towers beyond. Under their feet the ground trembled, vibrating and shaking. She could see tongues of flame rising from the towers, from the deep underground factories and forges of the City. The air was thick and dense with particles of soot. Mara rubbed her mouth, coughing.

"Here they come," Erick said softly.

The merchants had been examined and allowed to pass through the dark gate, the entrance through the wall into the City. They and their silent animals had already disappeared inside. The leader of the group of soldiers was beckoning impatiently to Erick, waving him on.

"Come along!" he said. "Hurry up there, old man."

Erick advanced slowly, his arms wrapped around his body, looking down at the ground.

"Who are you and what's your business here?" the soldier demanded, his hands on his hips, his gun hanging idly at his waist. Most of the soldiers were lounging lazily, leaning against the wall, some even squatting in the shade. Flies crawled on the face of one who had fallen asleep, his gun on the ground beside him.

"My business?" Erick murmured. "I am a village priest."

"Why do you want to enter the City?"

"I must bring these two people before the magistrate to marry them." He indicated Mara and Jan, standing a little behind him. "That is the Law the Leiters have made."

The soldier laughed. He circled around Erick. "What do you have in that bag you carry?"

"Laundry. We stay the night."

"What village are you from?"

"Kranos."

"Kranos?" The soldier looked to a companion. "Ever heard of Kranos?"

"A backward pig sty. I saw it once on a hunting trip."

The leader of the soldiers nodded to Jan and Mara. The two of them advanced, their hands clasped, standing close together. One of the soldiers put his hand on Mara's bare shoulder, turning her around.

"Nice little wife you're getting," he said. "Good and firm looking." He winked, grinning lewdly.

Jan glanced at him in sullen resentment. The soldiers guffawed. "All right," the leader said to Erick. "You people can pass."

Erick took a small purse from his robes and gave the soldier a coin. Then the three of them went into the dark tunnel that was the entrance, passing through the wall of stones, into the City beyond.

They were within the City!

"Now," Erick whispered. "Hurry."

Around them the City roared and cracked, the sound of a thousand vents and machines, shaking the stones under their feet. Erick led Mara and Jan into a corner, by a row of brick warehouses. People were everywhere, hurrying back and forth, shouting above the din, merchants, peddlers, soldiers, street women. Erick bent down and opened the case he carried. From the case he quickly took three small coils of fine metal, intricate meshed wires and vanes worked together into a small cone. Jan took one and Mara took one. Erick put the remaining cone into his robe and snapped the case shut again.

"Now remember, the coils must be buried in such a way that the line runs through the center of the City. We must trisect the main section, where the largest concentration of buildings is. Remember the maps! Watch the alleys and streets carefully. Talk to no one if you can help it. Each of you has enough Martian money to buy your way out of trouble. Watch especially for cut-purses, and for heaven's sake, don't get lost."

Erick broke off. Two black-clad Leiters were coming along the inside of the wall, strolling together with their hands behind their backs. They noticed the three who stood in the corner by the warehouses and stopped.

"Go," Erick muttered. "And be back here at sundown." He smiled grimly. "Or never come back."

Each went off in a different way, walking quickly without looking back. The Leiters watched them go. "The little bride was quite lovely," one Leiter said. "Those hill people have the stamp of nobility in their blood, from the old times."

"A very lucky young peasant to possess her," the other said. They went on. Erick looked after them, still smiling a little. Then he joined the surging mass of people that milled eternally through the streets of the City.

At dusk they met outside the gate. The sun was soon to set, and the air had turned thin and frigid. It cut through their clothing like knives.

Mara huddled against Jan, trembling and rubbing her bare arms.

"Well?" Erick said. "Did you both succeed?"

Around them peasants and merchants were pouring from the entrance, leaving the City to return to their farms and villages, starting the long trip back across the plain toward the hills beyond. None of them noticed the shivering girl and the young man and the old priest standing by the wall.

"Mine's in place," Jan said. "On the other side of the City, on the extreme edge. Buried by a well."

"Mine's in the industrial section," Mara whispered, her teeth chattering. "Jan, give me something to put over me! I'm freezing."

"Good," Erick said. "Then the three coils should trisect dead center, if the models were correct." He looked up at the darkening sky. Already, stars were beginning to show. Two dots, the evening patrol, moved slowly toward the horizon. "Let's hurry. It won't be long."

They joined the line of Martians moving along the road, away from the City. Behind them the City was losing itself in the somber tones of night, its black spires disappearing into darkness.

They walked silently with the country people until the flat ridge of dead trees became visible on the horizon. Then they left the road and turned off, walking toward the trees.

"Almost time!" Erick said. He increased his pace, looking back at Jan and Mara impatiently.

"Come on!"

They hurried, making their way through the twilight, stumbling over rocks and dead branches, up the side of the ridge. At the top Erick halted, standing with his hands on his hips, looking back.

"See," he murmured. "The City. The last time we'll ever see it this way."

"Can I sit down," Mara said. "My feet hurt me."

Jan pulled at Erick's sleeve. "Hurry, Erick! Not much time left." He laughed nervously. "If everything goes right we'll be able to look at it — forever."

"But not like this," Erick murmured. He squatted down, snapping his case open. He took some tubes and wiring out and assembled them together on the ground, at the peak of the ridge. A small pyramid of wire and plastic grew, shaped by his expert hands.

At last he grunted, standing up. "All right."

"Is it pointed directly at the City?" Mara asked anxiously, looking down at the pyramid.

Erick nodded. "Yes, it's placed according — " He stopped, suddenly stiffening. "Get back! It's time! *Hurry!*"

Jan ran, down the far side of the slope, away from the City, pulling Mara with him. Erick came quickly after, still looking back at the distant spires, almost lost in the night sky.

"Down."

Jan sprawled out, Mara beside him, her trembling body pressed against his. Erick settled down into the sand and dead branches, still trying to see. "I want to see it," he murmured. "A miracle. I want to see — "

A flash, a blinding burst of violet light, lit up the sky. Erick clapped his hands over his eyes. The flash whitened, growing larger, expanding. Suddenly there was a roar, and a furious hot wind rushed past him, throwing him on his face in the sand. The hot dry wind licked and seared at them, crackling the bits of branches into flame. Mara and Jan shut their eyes, pressed tightly together.

"God — " Erick muttered.

The storm passed. They opened their eyes slowly. The sky was still alive with fire, a drifting cloud of sparks that was beginning to dissipate with the night wind. Erick stood up unsteadily, helping Jan and Mara to their feet. The three of them stood, staring silently across the dark waste, the black plain, none of them speaking.

The City was gone.

At last Erick turned away. "That part's done," he said. "Now the rest! Give me a hand, Jan. There'll be a thousand patrol ships around here in a minute."

"I see one already," Mara said, pointing up. A spot winked in the sky, a rapidly moving spot. "They're coming, Erick." There was a throb of chill fear in her voice.

"I know." Erick and Jan squatted on the ground around the pyramid of tubes and plastic, pulling the pyramid apart. The pyramid was fused, fused together like molten glass. Erick tore the pieces away with trembling fingers. From the remains of the pyramid he pulled something forth, something he held up high, trying to make it out in the darkness. Jan and Mara came close to see, both staring up intently, almost without breath.

"There it is," Erick said. "There!"

In his hand was a globe, a small transparent globe of glass. Within the glass something moved, something minute and fragile, spires almost too small to be seen, microscopic, a complex web swimming within the hollow glass globe. A web of spires. A city.

Erick put the globe into the case and snapped it shut. "Let's go," he said. They began to lope back through the trees, back the way they had come before. "We'll change in the car," he said as they ran. "I think we should keep these clothes on until we're actually inside the car. We still might encounter someone."

"I'll be glad to get my own clothing on again," Jan said. "I feel funny in these little pants."

"How do you think I feel?" Mara gasped. "I'm freezing in this, what there is of it."

"All young Martian brides dress that way," Erick said. He clutched the case tightly as they ran. "I think it looks fine."

"Thank you," Mara said. "But it is cold."

"What do you suppose they'll think?" Jan asked. "They'll assume the City was destroyed, won't they? That's certain."

"Yes," Erick said. "They'll be sure it was blown up. We can count on that. And it will be damn important to us that they think so!"

"The car should be around here, someplace," Mara said, slowing down.

"No. Farther on," Erick said. "Past that little hill over there. In the ravine, by the trees. It's so hard to see where we are."

"Shall I light something?" Jan said.

"No. There may be patrols around who — "

He halted abruptly. Jan and Mara stopped beside him. "What — " Mara begin.

A light glimmered. Something stirred in the darkness. There was a sound.

"Quick!" Erick rasped. He dropped, throwing the case far away from him into the bushes. He straightened up tensely.

A figure loomed up, moving through the darkness, and behind it came more figures, men, soldiers in uniform. The light flashed up brightly, blinding them. Erick closed his eyes. The light left him, touching Mara and Jan, standing silently together, clasping hands. Then it flicked down to the ground and around in a circle.

A Leiter stepped forward, a tall figure in black, with his soldiers close behind him, their guns ready. "You three," the Leiter said. "Who are you? Don't move. Stand where you are."

He came up to Erick, peering at him intently, his hard Martian face without expression. He went all around Erick, examining his robes, his sleeves.

"Please — " Erick began in a quavering voice, but the Leiter cut him off.

"I'll do the talking. Who are you three? What are you doing here? Speak up."

"We — we are going back to our village," Erick muttered, staring down, his hands folded. "We were in the City, and now we are going home."

One of the soldiers spoke into a mouthpiece. He clicked it off and put it away.

"Come with me," the Leiter said. "We're taking you in. Hurry along."

"In? Back to the City?"

One of the soldiers laughed. "The City is gone," he said. "All that's left of it you can put in the palm of your hand."

"But what happened?" Mara said.

"No one knows. Come on, hurry it up!"

There was a sound. A soldier came quickly out of the darkness. "A Senior Leiter," he said. "Coming this way." He disappeared again.

"A Senior Leiter." The soldiers stood waiting, standing at a respectful attention. A moment later the Senior Leiter stepped into the light, a black-clad old man, his ancient face thin and hard, like a bird's, eyes bright and alert. He looked from Erick to Jan.

"Who are these people?" he demanded.

"Villagers going back home."

"No they're not. They don't stand like villagers. Villagers slump — diet poor food. These people are not villagers. I myself came from the hills, and I know."

He stepped close to Erick, looking keenly into his face. "Who are you? Look at his chin — he never shaved with a sharpened stone! Something is wrong here."

In his hand a rod of pale fire flashed. "The City is gone, and with it at least half the Leiter Council. It is very strange, a flash, then heat, and a wind. But it was not fission. I am puzzled. All at once the City has vanished. Nothing is left but a depression in the sand."

"We'll take them in," the other Leiter said. "Soldiers, surround them. Make certain that — "

"Run!" Erick cried. He struck out, knocking the rod from the Senior Leiter's hand. They were all running, soldiers shouting, flashing their lights, stumbling against each other in the darkness. Erick dropped to his knees, groping frantically in the bushes. His fingers closed over the handle of the case and he leaped up. In Terran he shouted to Mara and Jan.

"Hurry! To the car! Run!" He set off, down the slope, stumbling through the darkness. He could hear soldiers behind him, soldiers running and falling. A body collided against him and he struck out. Someplace behind him there was a hiss, and a section of the slope went up in flames. The Leiter's rod —

"Erick," Mara cried from the darkness. He ran toward her. Suddenly he slipped, falling on a stone. Confusion and firing. The sound of excited voices.

"Erick, is that you?" Jan caught hold of him, helping him up. "The car. It's over here. Where's Mara?"

"I'm here," Mara's voice came. "Over here, by the car."

A light flashed. A tree went up in a puff of fire, and Erick felt the singe of the heat against his face. He and Jan made their way toward the girl. Mara's hand caught his in the darkness.

"Now the car," Erick said. "If they haven't got to it." He slid down the slope into the ravine, fumbling in the darkness, reaching and holding onto the handle of the case. Reaching, reaching —

He touched something cold and smooth. Metal, a metal door handle. Relief flooded through him. "I've found it! Jan, get inside. Mara, come on." He pushed Jan past him, into the car. Mara slipped in after Jan, her small agile body crowding in beside him.

"Stop!" a voice shouted from above. "There's no use hiding in that ravine. We'll get you! Come up and — "

The sound of voices was drowned out by the roar of the car's motor. A moment later they shot into the darkness, the car rising into the air. Treetops broke and cracked under them as Erick turned the car from side to side, avoiding the groping shafts of pale light from below, the last furious thrusts from the two Leiters and their soldiers.

Then they were away, above the trees, high in the air, gaining speed each moment, leaving the knot of Martians far behind.

"Toward Marsport," Jan said to Erick. "Right?"

Erick nodded. "Yes. We'll land outside the field, in the hills. We can change back to our regular clothing there, our commercial clothing. Damn it — we'll be lucky if we can get there in time for the ship."

"The last ship," Mara whispered, her chest rising and falling. "What if we don't get there in time?"

Erick looked down at the leather case in his lap. "We'll have to get there," he murmured. "We must!"

For a long time there was silence. Thacher stared at Erickson. The older man was leaning back in his chair, sipping a little of his drink. Mara and Jan were silent.

"So you didn't destroy the City," Thacher said. "You didn't destroy it at all. You shrank it down and put it in a glass globe, in a paperweight. And now you're salesmen again, with a sample case of office supplies!"

Erickson smiled. He opened the briefcase and reaching into it he brought out the glass globe paperweight. He held it up, looking into it. "Yes, we stole the City from the Martians. That's how we got by the lie detector. It was true that we knew nothing about a *destroyed* City."

"But why?" Thacher said. "Why steal a City? Why not merely bomb it?"

"Ransom," Mara said fervently, gazing into the globe, her dark eyes bright. "Their biggest City, half of the Council — in Erick's hand!"

"Mars will have to do what Terra asks," Erickson said. "Now Terra will be able to make her commercial demands felt. Maybe there won't even be a war. Perhaps Terra will get her way without fighting." Still smiling, he put the globe back into the briefcase and locked it.

"Quite a story," Thacher said. "What an amazing process, reduction of size — A whole City reduced to microscopic dimensions. Amazing. No wonder you were able to escape. With such daring as that, no one could hope to stop you."

He looked down at the briefcase on the floor. Underneath them the jets murmured and vibrated evenly, as the ship moved through space toward distant Terra.

"We still have quite a way to go," Jan said. "You've heard our story, Thacher. Why not tell us yours? What sort of line are you in? What's your business?"

"Yes," Mara said. "What do you do?"

"What do I do?" Thacher said. "Well, if you like, I'll show you." He reached into his coat and brought out something. Something that flashed and glinted, somethig slender. A rod of pale fire.

The three stared at it. Sickened shock settled over them slowly.

Thacher held the rod loosely, calmly, pointing it at Erickson. "We knew you three were on this ship," he said. "There was not doubt of that. But we did not know what had become of the City. My theory was that the City had not been destroyed at all, that something else had happened to it. Council instruments measured a sudden loss of mass in that area, a decrease equal to the mass of the City. Somehow the City had been spirited away, not destroyed. But I could not convince the other Council Leiters of it. I had to follow you alone."

Thacher turned a little, nodding to the men sitting at the bar. The men rose at once, coming toward the table.

"A very interesting process you have. Mars will benefit a great deal from it. Perhaps it will even turn the tide in our favor. When we return to Marsport I wish to begin work on it at once. And now, if you will please pass me the briefcase — "

THE SHORT HAPPY LIFE
OF THE BROWN OXFORD

"I HAVE SOMETHING to show you," Doc Labyrinth said. From his coat pocket he gravely drew forth a matchbox. He held the matchbox tightly, his eyes fixed on it. "You're about to see the most momentous thing in all modern science. The world will shake and shudder."

"Let me see," I said. It was late, past midnight. Outside my house rain was falling on the deserted streets. I watched Doc Labyrinth as he carefully pushed the matchbox open with his thumb, just a crack. I leaned over to see.

There was a brass button in the matchbox. It was alone, except for a bit of dried grass and what looked like a bread crumb.

"Buttons have already been invented," I said. "I don't see much to this." I reached out my hand to touch the button but Labyrinth jerked the box away, frowning furiously.

"This isn't just a button," he said. Looking down at the button he said, "Go on! Go on!" He nudged the button with his finger. "Go on!"

I watched with curiosity. "Labyrinth, I wish you'd explain. You come here in the middle of the night, show me a button in a matchbox, and — "

Labyrinth settled back against the couch, sagging with defeat. He closed the matchbox and resignedly put it back in his pocket. "It's no use pretending," he said. "I've failed. The button is dead. There's no hope."

"Is that so unusual? What did you expect?"

"Bring me something." Labyrinth gazed hopelessly around the room. "Bring me — bring me *wine.*"

"All right, Doc," I said getting up. "But you know what wine does to people." I went into the kitchen and poured two glasses of sherry. I brought them back and gave one to him. We sipped for a time. "I wish you'd let me in on this."

Doc put his glass down, nodding absently. He crossed his legs and took out his pipe. After he had lit his pipe he carefully looked once more into the matchbox. He sighed and put it away again.

"No use," he said. "The Animator will never work, the Principle itself is wrong. I refer to the Principle of Sufficient Irritation, of course."

"And what is that?"

"The Principle came to me this way. One day I was sitting on a rock at the beach. The sun was shining and it was very hot. I was perspiring and quite uncomfortable. All at once a pebble next to me got up and crawled off. The heat of the sun had annoyed it."

"Really? A pebble?"

"At once the realization of the Principle of Sufficient Irritation came to me. Here was the origin of life. Eons ago, in the remote past, a bit of inanimate matter had become so irritated by something that it crawled away, moved by indignation. Here was my life work: to discover the perfect irritant, annoying enough to bring inanimate matter to life, and to incorporate it into a workable machine. The machine, which is at present in the back seat of my car, is called The Animator. But it doesn't work."

We were silent for a time. I felt my eyes slowly begin to close. "Say, Doc," I began, "isn't it time we — "

Doc Labyrinth leaped abruptly to his feet. "You're right," he said. "It's time for me to go. I'll leave."

He headed for the door. I caught up with him. "About the machine," I said. "Don't give up hope. Maybe you'll get it to work some other time."

"The machine?" He frowned. "Oh, the Animator. Well, I'll tell you what. I'll sell it to you for five dollars."

I gaped. There was something so forlorn about him that I didn't feel like laughing. "For how much?" I said.

"I'll bring it inside the house. Wait here." He went outside, down the steps and up the dark sidewalk. I heard him open the car door, and then grunt and mutter.

"Hold on," I said. I hurried after him. He was struggling with a bulky square box, trying to get it out of the car. I caught hold of one side, and together we lugged it into the house. We set it down on the dining table.

"So this is the Animator," I said. "It looks like a Dutch oven."

"It is, or it was. The Animator throws out a heat beam as an irritant. But I'm through with it forever."

I took out my wallet. "All right. If you want to sell it, I might as well be the one who buys it." I gave him the money and he took it. He showed me where to put in the inanimate matter, how to adjust the dials and meters, and then, without any warning, he put on his hat and left.

I was alone, with my new Animator. While I was looking at it my wife came downstairs in her bathrobe.

"What's going on?" she said. "Look at you, your shoes are soaked. Were you outside in the gutter?"

"Not quite. Look at this oven. I just paid five dollars for it. It animates things."

Joan stared down at my shoes. "It's one o'clock in the morning. You put your shoes in the oven and come to bed."

"But don't you realize —"

"Get those shoes in the oven," Joan said, going back upstairs again. "Do you hear me?"

"All right," I said.

It was at breakfast, while I was sitting staring moodily down at a plate of cold eggs and bacon, that he came back. The doorbell commenced to ring furiously.

"Who can that be?" Joan said. I got up and went down the hall, into the living room. I opened the door.

"Labyrinth!" I said. His face was pale, and there were dark circles under his eyes.

"Here's your five dollars," he said. "I want my Animator back."

I was dazed. "All right, Doc. Come on in and I'll get it."

He came inside and stood, tapping his foot. I went over and got the Animator. It was still warm. Labyrinth watched me carrying it toward him. "Set it down," he said. "I want to make sure it's all right."

I put it on the table and the Doc went over it lovingly, carefully, opening the little door and peering inside. "There's a shoe in it," he said.

"There should be two shoes," I said, suddenly remembering last night. "My God, I put my shoes in it."

"Both of them? There's only one now."

Joan came from the kitchen. "Hello, Doctor," she said. "What brings you out so early?"

Labyrinth and I were staring at each other. "Only one?" I said. I bent down to look. Inside was a single muddy shoe, quite dry, now, after its night in Labyrinth's Animator. A single shoe — but I had put two in. Where was the other?

I turned around but the expression on Joan's face made me forget what I was going to say. She was staring in horror at the floor, her mouth open.

Something small and brown was moving, sliding toward the couch. It went under the couch and disappeared. I had seen only a glimpse of it, a momentary flash of motion, but I knew what it was.

"My God," Labyrinth said. "Here, take the five dollars." He pushed the bill into my hands. "I really want it back, now!"

"Take it easy," I said. "Give me a hand. We have to catch the damn thing before it gets outdoors."

Labyrinth went over and shut the door to the living room. "It went under the couch." He squatted down and peered under. "I think I see it. Do you have a stick or something?"

"Let me out of here," Joan said. "I don't want to have anything to do with this."

"You can't leave," I said. I yanked down a curtain rod from the window and pulled the curtain from it. "We can use this." I joined Labyrinth on the floor. "I'll get it out, but you'll have to help me catch it. If we don't work fast we'll never see it again."

I nudged the shoe with the end of the rod. The shoe retreated, squeezing itself back toward the wall. I could see it, a small mound of brown, huddled and silent, like some wild animal at bay, escaped from its cage. It gave me an odd feeling.

"I wonder what we can do with it?" I murmured. "Where the hell are we going to keep it?"

"Could we put it in the desk drawer?" Joan said, looking around. "I'll take the stationery out."

"There it goes!" Labyrinth scrambled to his feet. The shoe had come out, fast. It went across the room, heading for the big chair. Before it could get underneath, Labyrinth caught hold of one of its laces. The shoe pulled and tugged, struggling to get free, but the old Doc had a firm hold of it.

Together we got the shoe into the desk and closed the drawer. We breathed a sigh of relief.

"That's that," Labyrinth said. He grinned foolishly at us. "Do you see what this means? We've done it, we've really done it! The Animator worked. But I wonder why it didn't work with the button."

"The button was brass," I said. "And the shoe was hide and animal glue. A natural. And it was wet."

We looked toward the drawer. "In that desk," Labyrinth said, "is the most momentous thing in modern science."

"The world will shake and shudder," I finished. "I know. Well, you can consider it yours." I took hold of Joan's hand. "I give you the shoe along with your Animator."

"Fine." Labyrinth nodded. "Keep watch here, don't let it get away." He went to the front door. "I must get the proper people, men who will — "

"Can't you take it with you?" Joan said nervously.

Labyrinth paused at the door. "You must watch over it. It is proof, proof the Animator works. The Principle of Sufficient Irritation." He hurried down the walk.

"Well?" Joan said. "What now? Are you really going to stay here and watch over it?"

I looked at my watch. "I have to get to work."

"Well, I'm not going to watch it. If you leave, I'm leaving with you. I won't stay here."

"It should be all right in the drawer," I said. "I guess we could leave it for a while."

"I'll visit my family. I'll meet you downtown this evening and we can come back home together."

"Are you really that afraid of it?"

"I don't like it. There's something about it."

"It's only an old shoe."

Joan smiled thinly. "Don't kid me," she said. "There never was another shoe like this."

I met her downtown, after work that evening, and we had dinner. We drove home, and I parked the car in the driveway. We walked slowly up the walk.

On the porch Joan paused. "Do we really have to go inside? Can't we go to a movie or something?"

"We have to go in. I'm anxious to see how it is. I wonder what we'll have to feed it." I unlocked the door and pushed it open.

Something rushed past me, flying down the walk. It disappeared into the bushes.

"What was that?" Joan whispered, stricken.

"I can guess." I hurried to the desk. Sure enough, the drawer was standing open. The shoe had kicked its way out. "Well, that's that," I said. "I wonder what we're going to tell Doc?"

"Maybe you could catch it again," Joan said. She closed the front door after us. "Or animate another. Try working on the other shoe, the one that's left."

I shook my head. "It didn't respond. Creation is funny. Some things don't react. Or maybe we could — "

The telephone rang. We looked at each other. There was something in the ring. "It's him," I said. I picked up the receiver.

"This is Labyrinth," the familiar voice said. "I'll be over early tomorrow. They're coming with me. We'll get photographs and a good write-up. Jenkins from the lab — "

"Look, Doc," I began.

"I'll talk later. I have a thousand things to do. We'll see you tomorrow morning." He clicked off.

"Was it the Doctor?" Joan said.

I looked at the empty desk drawer, hanging open. "It was. It was him, all right." I went to the hall closet, taking my coat off. Suddenly I had an eerie feeling. I stopped, turning around. Something was watching me. But what? I saw nothing. It gave me the creeps.

"What the hell," I said. I shrugged it off and hung my coat up. As I started back toward the living room I thought I saw something move, out of the corner of my eye.

"Damn," I said.

"What is it?"

"Nothing. Nothing at all." I looked all around me, but I could not pin anything down. There was the bookcase, the rugs, the pictures on the walls, everything as it always was. But something had moved.

I entered the living room. The Animator was sitting on the table. As I passed it I felt a surge of warmth. The Animator was still on, and the door was open! I snapped the switch off, and the dial light died. Had we left it on all day? I tried to remember, but I couldn't be sure.

"We've got to find the shoe before nightfall," I said.

We looked, but we found nothing. The two of us went over every inch of the yard, examining each bush, looking under the hedge, even under the house, but without any luck.

When it got too dark to see we turned on the porch light and worked for a time by it. At last I gave up. I went over and sat down on the porch steps. "It's no use," I said. "Even in the hedge there are a million places. And while we're beating one end, it could slip out the other. We're licked. We might as well face it."

"Maybe it's just as well," Joan said.

I stood up. "We'll leave the front door open tonight. There's a chance it might come back in."

We left it open, but the next morning when we came downstairs the house was silent and empty. I knew at once the shoe was not there. I poked around, examining things. In the kitchen eggshells were strewn around the garbage pail. The shoe had come in during the night, but after helping itself it had left again.

I closed the front door and we stood silently, looking at each other. "He'll be here any time," I said. "I guess I better call the office and tell them I'll be late."

Joan touched the Animator. "So this is what did it. I wonder if it'll ever happen again."

We went outside and looked around hopefully for a time. Nothing stirred the bushes, nothing at all. "That's that," I said. I looked up. "Here comes a car, now."

A dark Plymouth coasted up in front of the house. Two elderly men got out and came up the path toward us, studying us curiously.

"Where is Rupert?" one of them asked.

"Who? You mean Doc Labyrinth? I suppose he'll be along any time."

"Is it inside?" the man said. "I'm Porter, from the University. May I take a peek at it?"

"You'd better wait," I said unhappily. "Wait until the Doc is here."

Two more cars pulled up. More old men got out and started up the walk, murmuring and talking together. "Where's the Animator?" one asked me, a codger with bushy whiskers. "Young man, direct us to the exhibit."

"The exhibit is inside," I said. "If you want to see the Animator, go on in."

They crowded inside. Joan and I followed them. They were standing around the table, studying the square box, the Dutch oven, talking excitedly.

"This is it!" Porter said. "The Principle of Sufficient Irritation will go down in — "

"Nonsense," another said. "It's absurd. I want to see this hat, or shoe, or whatever it is."

"You'll see it," Porter said. "Rupert knows what he's doing. You can count on that."

They fell into controversy, quoting authorities and citing dates and places. More cars were arriving, and some of them were press cars.

"Oh, God," I said. "This will be the end of him."

"Well, he'll just have to tell them what happened," Joan said. "About its getting away."

"We're going to, not him. We let the thing go."

"I had nothing to do with it. I never liked that pair from the start. Don't you remember, I wanted you to get those ox-blood ones?"

I ignored her. More and more old men were assembling on the lawn, standing around talking and discussing. All at once I saw Labyrinth's little blue Ford pull up, and my heart sank. He had come, he was here, and in a minute we would have to tell him.

"I can't face him," I said to Joan. "Let's slip out the back way."

At the sight of Doc Labyrinth all the scientists began streaming out of the house, surrounding him in a circle. Joan and I looked at each other. The house was deserted, except for the two of us. I closed the front door. Sounds of talk filtered through the windows; Labyrinth was expounding the Principle of Sufficient Irritation. In a moment he would come inside and demand the shoe.

"Well, it was his own fault for leaving it," Joan said. She picked up a magazine and thumbed through it.

Doc Labyrinth waved at me through the window. His old face was wreathed with smiles. I waved back halfheartedly. After a while I sat down beside Joan.

Time passed. I stared down at the floor. What was there to do? Nothing but wait, wait for the Doc to come triumphantly into the house, surrounded by scientists, learned men, reporters, historians, demanding the proof of his theory, the shoe. On my old shoe rested Labyrinth's whole life, the proof of his Principle, of the Animator, of everything.

And the damn shoe was gone, outside someplace!

"It won't be long now," I said.

We waited, without speaking. After a time I noticed a peculiar thing. The talk outside had died away. I listened, but I heard nothing.

"Well?" I said. "Why don't they come in?"

The silence continued. What was going on? I stood up and went to the front door. I opened it and looked out.

"What's the matter?" Joan said. "Can you see?"

"No," I said. "I don't get it." They were all standing silently, staring down at something, none of them speaking. I was puzzled. I could not make sense out of it. "What's happening?" I said.

"Let's go and look." Joan and I went slowly down the steps, onto the lawn. We pushed through the row of old men and made our way to the front.

"Good Lord," I said. "Good Lord."

Crossing the lawn was a strange little procession, making its way through the grass. Two shoes, my old brown shoe, and just ahead of it, leading the way, another shoe, a tiny white high-heeled slipper. I stared at it. I had seen it someplace before.

"That's mine!" Joan cried. Everyone looked at her. "That belongs to me! My party shoes — "

"Not any more," Labyrinth said. His old face was pale with emotion. "It is beyond us all, forever."

"Amazing," one of the learned men said. "Look at them. Observe the female. Look at what she is doing."

The little white shoe was keeping carefully ahead of my old shoe, a few inches away, leading him coyly on. As my old shoe approached she backed away, moving in a half circle. The two shoes stopped for a moment, regarding each other. Then, all at once, my old shoe began to hop up and down, first on his heel, then on his toe. Solemnly, with great dignity, the shoe danced around her, until he reached his starting point.

The little white shoe hopped once, and then she began again to move away, slowly, hesitantly, letting my shoe almost catch up to her before she went on.

"This implies a developed sense of mores," an old gentleman said. "Perhaps even a racial unconscious. The shoes are following a rigid pattern of ritual, probably laid down centuries — "

"Labyrinth, what does this mean?" Porter said. "Explain it to us."

"So that's what it was," I murmured. "While we were away the shoe got her out of the closet and used the Animator on her. I knew something was watching me, that night. She was still in the house."

"That's what he turned on the Animator for," Joan said. She sniffed. "I'm not sure I think much of it."

The two shoes had almost reached the hedge, the white slipper still just beyond the laces of the brown shoe. Labyrinth moved toward them.

"So, gentlemen, you can see that I did not exaggerate. This is the greatest moment in science, the creation of a new race. Perhaps, when mankind has fallen into ruin, society destroyed, this new life form — "

He started to reach for the shoes, but at that moment the lady shoe disappeared into the hedge, backing into the obscurity of the foliage. With one bound the brown shoe popped in after her. There was a rustling, then silence.

"I'm going indoors," Joan said, walking away.

"Gentlemen," Labyrinth said, his face a little red, "this is incredible. We are witnessing one of the most profound and far-reaching moments of science."

"Well, *almost* witnessing," I said.

THE BUILDER

"E.J. ELWOOD!" Liz said anxiously. "You aren't listening to anything we're saying. And you're not eating a bit. What in the world is the matter with you? Sometimes I just can't understand you."

For a long time there was no response. Ernest Elwood continued to stare past them, staring out the window at the semi-darkness beyond, as if hearing something they did not hear. At last he sighed, drawing himself up in his chair, almost as if he were going to say something. But then his elbow knocked against his coffee cup and he turned instead to steady the cup, wiping spilled brown coffee from its side.

"Sorry," he murmured. "What were you saying?"

"Eat, dear," his wife said. She glanced at the two boys as she spoke to see if they had stopped eating also. "You know, I go to a great deal of trouble to fix your food." Bob, the older boy, was going right ahead, cutting his liver and bacon carefully into bits. But sure enough, little Toddy had put down his knife and fork as soon as E.J. had, and now he, too, was sitting silently, staring down at his plate.

"See?" Liz said. "You're not setting a very good example for the boys. Eat up your food. It's getting cold. You don't want to eat cold liver, do you? There's nothing worse than liver when it gets cold and the fat all over the bacon hardens. It's harder to digest cold fat than anything else in the world. Especially lamb fat. They say a lot of people can't eat lamb fat at all. Dear, please eat."

Elwood nodded. He lifted his fork and spooned up some peas and potatoes, carrying them to his mouth. Little Toddy did the same, gravely and seriously, a small edition of his father.

"Say," Bob said. "We had an atomic bomb drill at school today. We lay under the desks."

"Is that right?" Liz said.

"But Mr. Pearson our science teacher says that if they drop a bomb on us the whole town'll be demolished, so I can't see what good getting under the desk will do. I think they ought to realize what advances science has made. There are bombs now that'll destroy miles, leaving nothing standing."

"You sure know a lot," Toddy muttered.

"Oh, shut up."

"Boys," Liz said.

"It's true," Bob said earnestly. "A fellow I know is in the Marine Corps Reserve and he says they have new weapons that will destroy wheat crops and poison water supplies. It's some kind of crystals."

"Heavens," Liz said.

"They didn't have things like that in the last war. Atomic development came almost at the end without there really being an opportunity to make use of it on a full scale." Bob turned to his father. "Dad, isn't that true? I'll bet when you were in the Army you didn't have any of the fully atomic — "

Elwood threw down his fork. He pushed his chair back and stood up. Liz stared up in astonishment at him, her cup half raised. Bob's mouth hung open, his sentence unfinished. Little Toddy said nothing.

"Dear, what's the matter?" Liz said.

"I'll see you later."

They gazed after him in amazement as he walked away from the table, out of the dining-room. They heard him go into the kitchen and pull open the back door. A moment later the back door slammed behind him.

"He went out in the back yard," Bob said. "Mom, was he always like this? Why does he act so funny? It isn't some kind of war psychosis he got in the Philippines, is it? In the First World War they called it shell shock, but now they know it's a form of war psychosis. Is it something like that?"

"Eat your food," Liz said, red spots of anger burning in her cheeks. She shook her head. "Darn that man. I just can't imagine — "

The boys ate their food.

It was dark out in the back yard. The sun had set and the air was cool and thin, filled with dancing specks of night insects. In the next yard Joe Hunt was working, raking leaves from under his cherry tree. He nodded to Elwood.

Elwood walked slowly down the path, across the yard towards the garage. He stopped, his hands in his pockets. By the garage something immense and white loomed up, a vast pale shape in the evening gloom. As he stood gazing at it a kind of warmth began to glow inside him. It was a strange warmth, something like pride, a little pleasure mixed in, and — and excitement. Looking at the boat always made him excited. Even when he was first starting on it he had felt the sudden race of his heart, the shaking of his hands, sweat on his face.

His boat. He grinned, walking closer. He reached up and thumped the solid side. What a fine boat it was, and coming along damn well. Almost done. A lot of work had gone into that, a lot of work and time. Afternoons off from work, Sundays, and even sometimes early in the morning before work.

That was best, early in the morning, with the bright sun shining down and the air good-smelling and fresh, and everything wet and sparkling. He liked that time best of all, and there was no one else up to bother him and ask him questions. He thumped the solid side again. A lot of work and material, all right. Lumber and nails, sawing and hammering and bending. Of course, Toddy had helped him. He certainly couldn't have done it alone; no doubt of that. If Toddy hadn't drawn the lines on the board and —

"Hey," Joe Hunt said.

Elwood started, turning. Joe was leaning on the fence, looking at him.

"Sorry," Elwood said. "What did you say?"

"Your mind was a million miles away," Hunt said. He took a puff on his cigar. "Nice night."

"Yes."

"That's some boat you got there, Elwood."

"Thanks," Elwood murmured. He walked away from it, back towards the house. "Goodnight, Joe."

"How long is it you've been working on that boat?" Hunt reflected. "Seems like about a year in all, doesn't it? About twelve months. You sure put a lot of time and effort into it. Seems like every time I see you you're carting lumber back here and sawing and hammering away."

Elwood nodded, moving towards the back door.

"You even got your kids working. At least, the little tyke. Yes, it's quite a boat." Hunt paused. "You sure must be going to go quite a way with it, by the size of it. Now just exactly where was it you told me you're going? I forget."

There was silence.

"I can't hear you, Elwood," Hunt said. "Speak up. A boat that big, you must be — "

"Lay off."

Hunt laughed easily. "What's the matter, Elwood? I'm just having a little harmless fun, pulling your leg. But seriously, where are you going with that? You going to drag it down to the beach and float it? I know a guy has a little sail-boat he fits on to a trailer cart, hooks it up to his car. He drives down to the yacht harbor every week or so. But my God, you can't get that big thing on a trailer. You know, I heard about a guy built a boat in his cellar. Well, he got done and you know what he discovered? He discovered that the boat was so big when he tried to get it out the door — "

Liz Elwood came to the back door, snapping on the kitchen light and pushing the door open. She stepped out on to the grass, her arms folded.

"Good evening, Mrs. Elwood," Hunt said, touching his hat. "Sure a nice night."

"Good evening." Liz turned to E.J. "For heaven's sake, are you going to come in?" Her voice was low and hard.

"Sure." Elwood reached out listlessly for the door. "I'm coming in. Goodnight, Joe."

"Goodnight," Hunt said. He watched the two of them go inside. The door closed, the light went off. Hunt shook his head. "Funny guy," he murmured. "Getting funnier all the time. Like he's in a different world. Him and his boat!"

He went indoors.

"She was just eighteen," Jack Fredericks said, "but she sure knew what it was all about."

"Those southern girls are that way," Charlie said. "It's like fruit, nice soft, ripe, slightly damp fruit."

"There's a passage in Hemingway like that," Ann Pike said. "I can't remember what it's from. He compares a — "

"But the way they talk," Charlie said. "Who can stand the way those southern girls talk?"

"What's the matter with the way they talk?" Jack demanded. "They talk different, but you get used to it."

"Why can't they talk right?"

"What do you mean?"

"They talk like — colored people."

"It's because they all come from the same region," Ann said.

"Are you saying this girl was colored?" Jack said.

"No, of course not. Finish your pie." Charlie looked at his wristwatch. "Almost one. We have to be getting on back to the office."

"I'm not finished eating," Jack said. "Hold on!"

"You know, there's a lot of colored people moving into my area," Ann said. "There's a real estate sign up on a house about a block from me. 'All races welcomed.' I almost fell over dead when I saw it."

"What did you do?"

"I didn't do anything. What can we do?"

"You know, if you work for the Government they can put a colored man or a Chinese next to you," Jack said, "and you can't do anything about it."

"Except quit."

"It interferes with your right to work," Charlie said. "How can you work like that? Answer me."

"There's too many pinks in the Government," Jack said. "That's how they got that, about hiring people for Government jobs without looking to see what race they belong to. During WPA days, when Harry Hopkins was in."

"You know where Harry Hopkins was born?" Ann said. "He was born in Russia."

"That was Sidney Hillman," Jack said.

"It's all the same," Charlie said. "They all ought to be sent back there."

Ann looked curiously at Ernest Elwood. He was sitting quietly, reading his newspaper, not saying anything. The cafeteria was alive with movement and noise. Everyone was eating and talking, coming and going, back and forth.

"E.J., are you all right?" Ann said.

"Yes."

"He's reading about the White Sox," Charlie said. "He has that intent look. Say, you know, I took my kids to the game the other night, and — "

"Come on," Jack said, standing up. "We have to get back."

They all rose. Elwood folded his newspaper up silently, putting it into his pocket.

"Say, you're not talking much," Charlie said to him as they went up the aisle. Elwood glanced up.

"Sorry."

"I've been meaning to ask you something. Do you want to come over Saturday night for a little game? You haven't played with us for a hell of a long time."

"Don't ask him," Jack said, paying for his meal at the cash register. "He always wants to play queer games like deuces wild, baseball, spit in the ocean — "

"Straight poker for me," Charlie said. "Come on, Elwood. The more the better. Have a couple of beers, chew the fat, get away from the wife, eh?" He grinned.

"One of these days we're going to have a good old stag party," Jack said, pocketing his change. He winked at Elwood. "You know the kind I mean? We get some gals together, have a little show — " He made a motion with his hand.

Elwood moved off. "Maybe. I'll think it over." He paid for his lunch. Then he went outside, out on to the bright pavement. The others were still inside, waiting for Ann. She had gone into the powder room.

Suddenly Elwood turned and walked hurriedly down the pavement, away from the cafeteria. He turned the corner quickly and found himself on Cedar Street, in front of a television store. Shoppers and clerks out on their lunch hour pushed and crowded past him, laughing and talking, bits of their conversations rising and falling around him like waves of the sea. He stepped into the doorway of the television shop and stood, his hands in his pockets, like a man hiding from the rain.

What was the matter with him? Maybe he should go see a doctor. The sounds, the people, everything bothered him. Noise and motion everywhere. He wasn't sleeping enough at night. Maybe it was something in his diet. And he was working so damn hard out in the yard. By the time he went to bed at night he was exhausted. Elwood rubbed his forehead. People and sounds, talking, streaming past him, endless shapes moving in the streets and stores.

In the window of the television shop a big television set blinked and winked a soundless program, the images leaping merrily. Elwood watched passively. A woman in tights was doing acrobatics, first a series of splits, then cartwheels and spins. She walked on her hands for a moment, her legs waving above her, smiling at the audience. Then she disappeared and a brightly dressed man came on, leading a dog.

Elwood looked at his watch. Five minutes to one. He had five minutes to get back to the office. He went back to the pavement and looked around the corner. Ann and Charlie and Jack were no place to be seen. They had gone on. Elwood walked slowly along, past the stores, his hands in his pockets. He stopped for a moment in front of the ten cent store, watching the milling women pushing and shoving around the imitation jewelry counters, touching things, picking them up, examining them. In the window of a drugstore he stared at an advertisement for athlete's foot, some kind of a powder, being sprinkled between two cracked and blistered toes. He crossed the street.

On the other side he paused to look at a display of women's clothing, skirts and blouses and wool sweaters. In a color photograph a handsomely dressed girl was removing her blouse to show the world her elegant bra. Elwood passed on. The next window was suitcases, luggage and trunks.

Luggage. He stopped, frowning. Something wandered through his mind, some loose vague thought, too nebulous to catch. He felt, suddenly, a deep inner urgency. He examined his watch. Ten past one. He was late. He hurried to the corner and stood waiting impatiently for the light to change. A handful of men and women pressed past him, moving out to the curb to catch an oncoming bus. Elwood watched the bus. It halted, its doors opening. The people rushed on to it. Suddenly Elwood joined them, stepping up the steps of the bus. The doors closed behind him as he fished out change from his pocket.

A moment later he took his seat, next to an immense old woman with a child on her lap. Elwood sat quietly, his hands folded, staring ahead and waiting, as the bus moved off down the street, moving towards the residential district.

When he got home there was no one there. The house was dark and cool. He went to the bedroom and got his old clothes from the closet. He was just going out into the back yard when Liz appeared in the driveway, her arms loaded with groceries.

"E.J.!" she said. "What's the matter? Why are you home?"

"I don't know. I took some leave. It's all right."

Liz put her packages down on the fence. "For heaven's sake," she said irritably. "You frightened me." She stared at him intently. "You took *leave*."

"Yes."

"How much does that make, this year? How much leave have you taken in all?"

"I don't know."

"You don't know? Well, is there any left?"

"Left for what?"

Liz stared at him. Then she picked up her packages and went inside the house, the back door banging after her. Elwood frowned. What was the matter? He went on into the garage and began to drag lumber and tools out on to the lawn, beside the boat.

He gazed up at it. It was square, big and square, like some enormous solid packing crate. Lord, but it was solid. He had put endless beams into it. There was a covered cabin with a big window, the roof tarred over. Quite a boat.

He began to work. Presently Liz came out of the house. She crossed the yard silently, so that he did not notice her until he came to get some large nails.

"Well?" Liz said.

Elwood stopped for a moment. "What is it?"

Liz folded her arms.

Elwood became impatient. "What is it? Why are you looking at me?"

"Did you really take more leave? I can't believe it. You really came home again to work on — on that."

Elwood turned away.

"Wait." She came up beside him. "Don't walk off from me. Stand still."

"Be quiet. Don't shout."

"I'm not shouting. I want to talk to you. I want to ask you something. May I? May I ask you something? You don't mind talking to me?"

Elwood nodded.

"*Why?*" Liz said, her voice low and intense. "Why? Will you tell me that? Why?"

"Why what?"

"That. That — that thing. What is it for? Why are you here in the yard in the middle of the day? For a whole year it's been like this. At the table last night, all of a sudden you got up and walked out. Why? What's it all for?"

"It's almost done," Elwood murmured. "A few more licks here and there and it'll be — "

"And then what?" Liz came around in front of him, standing in his path. "And then what? What are you going to do with it? Sell it? Float it? All the neighbors are laughing at you. Everybody in the block knows — " Her voice broke suddenly. " — Knows about you, and this. The kids at school make fun of Bob and Toddy. They tell them their father is — That he's — "

"That he's crazy?"

"Please, E.J. Tell me what it's for. Will you do that? Maybe I can understand. You never told me. Wouldn't it help? Can't you even do that?"

"I can't," Elwood said.

"You can't! Why not?"

"Because I don't know," Elwood said. "I don't know what it's for. Maybe it isn't for anything."

"But if it isn't for anything why do you work on it?"

"I don't know. I like to work on it. Maybe it's like whittling." He waved his hand impatiently. "I've always had a workshop of some kind. When I was a kid I used to build model airplanes. I have tools. I've always had tools."

"But why do you come home in the middle of the day?"

"I get restless."

"Why?"

"I — I hear people talking, and it makes me uneasy. I want to get away from them. There's something about it all, about them. Their ways. Maybe I have claustrophobia."

"Shall I call Doctor Evans and make an appointment?"

"No. No, I'm all right. Please, Liz, get out of the way so I can work. I want to finish."

"And you don't even know what it's for." She shook her head. "So all this time you've been working without knowing why. Like some animal that goes out at night and fights, like a cat on the back fence. You leave your work and us to — "

"Get out of the way."

"Listen to me. You put down that hammer and come inside. You're putting your suit on and going right back to the office. Do you hear? If you don't I'm never going to let you inside the house again. You can break down the door if you want, with your hammer. But it'll be locked for you from now on, if you don't forget that boat and go back to work."

There was silence.

"Get out of the way," Elwood said. "I have to finish."

Liz stared at him. "You're going on?" The man pushed past her. "You're going to go ahead? There's something wrong with you. Something wrong with your mind. You're — "

"Stop," Elwood said, looking past her. Liz turned.

Toddy was standing silently in the driveway, his lunch pail under his arms. His small face was grave and solemn. He did not say anything to them.

"Tod!" Liz said. "Is it that late already?"

Toddy came across the grass to his father. "Hello, boy," Elwood said. "How was school?"

"Fine."

"I'm going in the house," Liz said. "I meant it, E.J. Remember that I meant it."

She went up the walk. The back door slammed behind her.

Elwood sighed. He sat down on the ladder leading up the side of the boat and put his hammer down. He lit a cigarette and smoked silently. Toddy waiting without speaking.

"Well, boy?" Elwood said at last. "What do you say?"

"What do you want done, Dad?"

"Done?" Elwood smiled. "Well, there's not too much left. A few things here and there. We'll be through, soon. You might look around for boards we didn't nail down on the deck." He rubbed his jaw. "Almost done. We've been working a long time. You could paint, if you want. I want to get the cabin painted. Red, I think. How would red be?"

"Green."

"Green? All right. There's some green porch paint in the garage. Do you want to start stirring it up?"

"Sure," Toddy said. He headed towards the garage.

Elwood watched him go. "Toddy — "

The boy turned. "Yes?"

"Toddy, wait." Elwood went slowly towards him. "I want to ask you something."

"What is it, Dad?"

"You — you don't mind helping me, do you? You don't mind working on the boat?"

Toddy looked up gravely into his father's face. He said nothing. For a long time the two of them gazed at each other.

"Okay!" Elwood said suddenly. "You run along and get the paint started."

Bob came swinging along the driveway with two of the kids from the junior high school. "Hi, Dad," Bob called, grinning. "Say, how's it coming?"

"Fine," Elwood said.

"Look," Bob said to his pals, pointing to the boat. "You see that? You know what that is?"

"What is it?" one of them said.

Bob opened the kitchen door. "That's an atomic powered sub." He grinned, and the two boys grinned. "It's full of Uranium 235. Dad's going all the way to Russia with it. When he gets through, there won't be a thing left of Moscow."

The boys went inside, the door slamming behind them.

Elwood stood looking up at the boat. In the next yard Mrs. Hunt stopped for a moment with taking down her washing, looking at him and the big square hull rising above him.

"Is it really atomic powered, Mr. Elwood?" she said.

"No."

"What makes it run, then? I don't see any sails. What kind of motor is in it? Steam?"

Elwood bit his lip. Strangely, he had never thought of that part. There was no motor in it, no motor at all. There were no sails, no boiler. He had put no engine into it, no turbines, no fuel. Nothing. It was a wood hull, an immense box, and that was all. He had never thought of what would make it go, never in all the time he and Toddy had worked on it.

Suddenly a torrent of despair descended over him. There was no engine, nothing. It was not a boat, it was only a great mass of wood and tar and nails. It would never go, never never leave the yard. Liz was right: he was like some animal going out into the yard at night, to fight and kill in the darkness, to struggle dimly, without sight or understanding, equally blind, equally pathetic.

What had he built it for? He did not know. Where was it going? He did not know that either. What would make it run? How would he get it out of the yard? What was it all for, to build without understanding, darkly, like a creature in the night?

Toddy had worked alongside him, the whole time. Why had *he* worked? Did he know? Did the boy know what the boat was for, why they were building? Toddy had never asked because he trusted his father to know.

But he did not know. He, the father, he did not know either, and soon it would be done, finished, ready. And then what? Soon Toddy would lay down his paint brush, cover the last can of paint, put away the nails, the scraps of wood, hang the saw and hammer up in the garage again. And *then* he would ask, ask the question he had never asked before but which must come finally.

And he could not answer him.

Elwood stood, staring up at it, the great hulk they had built, struggling to understand. Why had he worked? What was it all for? When would he know? Would he *ever* know? For an endless time he stood there, staring up.

It was not until the first great black drops of rain began to splash about him that he understood.

MEDDLER

THEY ENTERED the great chamber. At the far end, technicians hovered around an immense illuminated board, following a complex pattern of lights that shifted rapidly, flashing through seemingly endless combinations. At long tables machines whirred — computers, human-operated and robot. Wall-charts covered every inch of vertical space. Hasten gazed around him in amazement.

Wood laughed. "Come over here and I'll really show you something. You recognize *this*, don't you?" He pointed to a hulking machine surrounded by silent men and women in white lab robes.

"I recognize it," Hasten said slowly. "It's something like our own Dip, but perhaps twenty times larger. What do you haul up? And *when* do you haul?" He fingered the surface-plate of the Dip, then squatted down, peering into the maw. The maw was locked shut; the Dip was in operation. "You know, if we had any idea this existed, Histo-Research would have — "

"You know now." Wood bent down beside him. "Listen. Hasten, you're the first man from outside the Department ever to get into this room. You saw the guards. No one gets in here unauthorized; the guards have orders to kill anyone trying to enter illegally."

"To hide this? A machine? You'd shoot to — "

They stood, Wood facing him, his jaw hard. "*Your* Dip digs back into antiquity. Rome. Greece. Dust and old volumes." Wood touched the big Dip beside them. "This Dip is different. We guard it with our lives, and anyone else's lives; do you know why?"

Hasten stared at it.

"This Dip is set, not for antiquity, but — for the future." Wood looked directly into Hasten's face. "Do you understand? The future."

"You're dredging the future? But you can't! It's forbidden by law; you know that!" Hasten drew back. "If the Executive Council knew this they'd break this building apart. You know the dangers. Berkowsky himself demonstrated them in his original thesis."

Hasten paced angrily. "I can't understand you, using a future oriented Dip. When you pull material from the future you automatically introduce new factors into the present; the future is altered — you start a never-ending shift. The more you dip the more new factors are brought in. You create unstable conditions for centuries to come. That's why the law was passed."

Wood nodded. "I know."

"And you still keep dipping?" Hasten gestured at the machine and the technicians. "Stop, for God's sake! Stop before you introduce some lethal element that can't be erased. Why do you keep — "

Wood sagged suddenly. "All right, Hasten, don't lecture us. It's too late; it's already happened. A lethal factor was introduced in our first experiments. We thought we knew what we were doing ... " He looked up. "And that's why you were brought here. Sit down — you're going to hear all about it."

They faced each other across the desk. Wood folded his hands. "I'm going to put it straight on the line. You are considered an expert, *the* expert at Histo-Research. You know more about using a Time Dip than anyone alive; that's why you've been shown our work, our illegal work."

"And you've already got into trouble?"

"Plenty of trouble, and every attempt to meddle further makes it that much worse. Unless we do something, we'll be the most culpable organization in history."

"Please start at the beginning," Hasten said.

"The Dip was authorized by the Political Science Council; they wanted to know the results of some of their decisions. At first we objected, giving Berkowsky's theory; but the idea is hypnotic, you know. We gave in, and the Dip was built — secretly, of course.

"We made our first dredge about one year hence. To protect ourselves against Berkowsky's factor we tried a subterfuge; we actually brought nothing back. This Dip is geared to pick up nothing. No object is scooped; it merely photographs from a high altitude. The film comes back to us and we make enlargements and try to gestalt the conditions.

"Results were all right, at first. No more wars, cities growing, much better looking. Blow-ups of street scenes show many people, well-content, apparently. Pace a little slower.

"Then we went ahead fifty years. Even better: cities on the decrease. People not so dependent on machines. More grass, parks. Same general conditions, peace, happiness, much leisure. Less frenetic waste, hurry.

"We went on, skipping ahead. Of course, with such an indirect viewing method we couldn't be certain of anything, but it all looked fine. We relayed our information to the Council and they went ahead with their planning. And then it happened."

"What, exactly?" Hasten said, leaning forward.

"We decided to revisit a period we had already photographed, about a hundred years hence. We sent out the Dip, got it back with a full reel. The men developed it and we watched the run." Wood paused.

"And?"

"And it wasn't the same. It was different. Everything was changed. War — war and destruction everywhere." Wood shuddered. "We were appalled; we sent the Dip back at once to make absolutely certain."

"And what did you find this time?"

Wood's fists clenched. "Changed again, and for worse! Ruins, vast ruins. People poking around. Ruin and death everywhere. Slag. The *end* of war, the last phase."

"I see," Hasten said, nodding.

"That's not the worst! We conveyed the news to the Council. It ceased all activity and went into a two-week conference; it canceled all ordinances and withdrew every plan formed on the basis of our reports. It was a month before the Council got in touch with us again. The members wanted us to try once more, take one more Dip to the same period. We said no, but they insisted. It could be no worse, they argued.

"So we sent the Dip out again. It came back and we ran the film. Hasten, there are things worse than war. You wouldn't believe what we saw. There was no human life; none at all, not a single human being."

"Everything was destroyed?"

"No! No destruction, cities big and stately, roads, buildings, lakes, fields. But no human life; the cities empty, functioning mechanically, every machine and wire untouched. But no living people."

"What was it?"

"We sent the Dip on ahead, at fifty year leaps. Nothing. Nothing each time. Cities, roads, buildings, but no human life. Everyone dead. Plague, radiation, or what, we don't know. But *something* killed them. Where did it come from? We don't know. It wasn't there at first, not in our original dips.

"Somehow, *we* introduced it, the lethal factor. *We* brought it, with our meddling. It wasn't there when we started; it was done by us, Hasten." Wood stared at him, his face a white mask. "We brought it and now we've got to find what it is and get rid of it."

"How are you going to do that?"

"We've built a Time Car, capable of carrying one human observer into the future. We're sending a man there to see what it is. Photographs don't tell us enough; we have to know more! When did it first appear? How? What were the first signs? *What is it?* Once we know, maybe we can eliminate it, the factor, trace it down and remove it. Someone must go into the future and find out what it was we began. It's the only way."

Woods stood up, and Hasten rose, too.

"You're that person," Wood said. "You're going, the most competent person available. The Time Car is outside, in an open square, carefully guarded." Wood gave a signal. Two soldiers came toward the desk.

"Sir?"

"Come with us," Wood said. "We're going outside to the square; make sure no one follows after us." He turned to Hasten. "Ready?"

Hasten hesitated. "Wait a minute. I'll have to go over your work, study what's been done. Examine the Time Car itself. I can't — "

The two soldiers moved closer, looking to Wood. Wood put his hand on Hasten's shoulder. "I'm sorry," he said, "we have no time to waste; come along with me."

All around him blackness moved, swirling toward him and then receding. He sat down on the stool before the bank of controls, wiping the perspiration from his face. He was on his way, for better or worse. Briefly, Wood had outlined the operation of the Time Car. A few moments of instruction, the controls set for him, and then the metal door slammed behind him.

Hasten looked around him. It was cold in the sphere; the air was thin and chilly. He watched the moving dials for a while, but presently the cold began to make him uncomfortable. He went over to the equipment-locker and slid the door back. A jacket, a heavy jacket, and a flash gun. He held the gun for a minute, studying it. And tools, all kinds of tools and equipment. He was just putting the gun away when the dull chugging under him suddenly ceased. For one terrible second he was floating, drifting aimlessly, then the feeling was gone.

Sunlight flowed through the window, spreading out over the floor. He snapped the artificial lights off and went to the window to see. Wood had set the controls for a hundred years hence; bracing himself, he looked out.

A meadow, flowers and grass, rolling off into the distance. Blue sky and wandering clouds. Some animals grazed a long way off, standing together in the shade of a tree. He went to the door and unlocked it, stepping out. Warm sunlight struck him, and he felt better at once. Now he could see the animals were cows.

He stood for a long time at the door, his hands on his hips. Could the plague have been bacterial? Air-carried? If it *were* a plague. He reached up, feeling the protective helmet on his shoulders. Better to keep it on.

He went back and got the gun from the locker. Then he returned to the lip of the sphere, checked the door-lock to be certain it would remain closed during his absence. Only then, Hasten stepped down onto the grass of the meadow. He closed the door and looked around him. Presently he began to walk quickly away from the sphere, toward the top of a long hill that stretched out half a mile away. As he strode along, he examined the click-band on his wrist which would guide him back to the metal sphere, the Time Car, if he could not find the way himself.

He came to the cows, passing by their tree. The cows got up and moved away from him. He noticed something that gave him a sudden chill; their udders were small and wrinkled. Not herd cows.

When he reached the top of the hill he stopped, lifting his glasses from his waist. The earth fell away, mile after mile of it, dry green fields without pattern or design, rolling like waves as far as the eye could see. Nothing else? He turned, sweeping the horizon.

He stiffened, adjusting the sight. Far off to the left, at the very limit of vision, the vague perpendiculars of a city rose up. He lowered the glasses and hitched up his heavy boots. Then he walked down the other side of the hill, taking big steps; he had a long way to go.

Hasten had not walked more than half an hour when he saw butterflies. They rose up suddenly a few yards in front of him, dancing and fluttering in the sunlight. He stopped to rest, watching them. They were all colors, red and blue, with splashes of yellow and green. They were the largest butterflies he had ever seen. Perhaps they had come from some zoo, escaped and bred wild after man left the scene. The butterflies rose higher and higher in the air. They took no notice of him but struck out toward the distant spires of the city; in a moment they were gone.

Hasten started up again. It was hard to imagine the death of man in such circumstances, butterflies and grass and cows in the shade. What a quiet and lovely world was left, without the human race!

Suddenly one last butterfly fluttered up, almost in his face, rising quickly from the grass. He put his arm up automatically, batting at it. The butterfly dashed against his hand. He began to laugh —

Pain made him sick; he fell half to his knees, gasping and retching. He rolled over on his face, hunching himself up, burying his face in the ground. His arm ached, and pain knotted him up; his head swam and he closed his eyes.

When Hasten turned over at last, the butterfly was gone; it had not lingered.

He lay for a time in the grass, then he sat up slowly, getting shakily to his feet. He stripped off his shirt and examined his hand and wrist. The flesh was black, hard and already swelling. He glanced down at it and then at the distant city. The butterflies had gone there ...

He made his way back to the Time Car.

Hasten reached the sphere a little after the sun had begun to drop into evening darkness. The door slid back to his touch and he stepped inside. He dressed his hand and arm with salve from the medicine kit and then sat down on the stool, deep in thought, staring at his arm. A small sting, accidental, in fact. The butterfly had not even noticed. Suppose the whole pack —

He waited until the sun had completely set and it was pitch black outside the sphere. At night all the bees and butterflies disappeared; or at least, those he knew did. Well, he would have to take a chance. His arm still ached dully, throbbing without respite. The salve had done no good; he felt dizzy, and there was a fever taste in his mouth.

Before he went out he opened the locker and brought all the things out. He examined the flash gun but put it aside. A moment later he found what he wanted. A blowtorch, and a flashlight. He put all the other things back and stood up. Now he was ready — if that were the word for it. As ready as he would ever be.

He stepped out into the darkness, flashing the light ahead of him. He walked quickly. It was a dark and lonely night; only a few stars shone above him, and his was the only earthly light. He passed up the hill and down the other side. A grove of trees loomed up, and then he was on a level plain, feeling his way toward the city by the beam of the flashlight.

When he reached the city he was very tired. He had gone a long way, and his breath was beginning to come hard. Huge ghostly outlines rose up ahead of him, disappearing above, vanishing into darkness. It was not a large city, apparently, but its design was strange to Hasten, more vertical and slim than he was used to.

He went through the gate. Grass was growing from the stone pavement of the streets. He stopped, looking down. Grass and weeds everywhere; and in the corners, by the buildings were bones, little heaps of bones and dust. He walked on, flashing his light against the sides of the slender buildings. His footsteps echoed hollowly. There was no light except his own.

The buildings began to thin out. Soon he found himself entering a great tangled square, overgrown with bushes and vines. At the far end a building larger than the others rose. He walked toward it, across the empty, desolate square, flashing his light from side to side. He walked up a half-buried step and onto a concrete plaza. All at once he stopped. To his right, another building reared up, catching his attention. His heart thudded. Above the doorway his light made out a word cut expertly into the arch:

Bibliotheca

This was what he wanted, the library. He went up the steps toward the dark entrance. Wood boards gave under his feet. He reached the entrance and found himself facing a heavy wood door with metal handles. When he took hold of the handles the door fell toward him, crashing past him, down the steps and into the darkness. The odor of decay and dust choked him.

He went inside. Spider webs brushed against his helmet as he passed along silent halls. He chose a room at random and entered it. Here were more heaps of dust and gray bits of bones. Low tables and shelves ran along the walls. He went to the shelves and took down a handful of books. They powdered and broke in his hands, showering bits of paper and thread onto him. Had only a century passed since his own time?

Hasten sat down at one of the tables and opened one of the books that was in better condition. The words were no language he knew, a Romance language that he knew must be artificial. He turned page after page. At last he took a handful of books at random and moved back toward the door. Suddenly his heart jumped. He went over to the wall, his hands trembling. Newspapers.

He took the brittle, cracking sheets carefully down, holding them to the light. The same language, of course. Bold, black headlines. He managed to roll some of the papers together and add them to his load of books. Then he went through the door, out into the corridor, back the way he had come.

When he stepped out onto the steps cold fresh air struck him, tingling his nose. He looked around at the dim outlines rising up on all sides of the square. Then he walked down and across the square, feeling his way carefully along. He came to the gate of the city, and a moment later he was outside, on the flat plain again, heading back toward the Time Car.

For an endless time he walked, his head bent down, plodding along. Finally fatigue made him stop, swaying back and forth, breathing deeply. He set down his load and looked around him. Far off, at the edge of the horizon, a long streak of gray had appeared, silently coming into existence while he was walking. Dawn. The sun coming up.

A cold wind moved through the air, eddying against him. In the forming gray light the trees and hills were beginning to take shape, a hard, unbending outline. He turned toward the city. Bleak and thin, the shafts of the deserted buildings stuck up. For a moment he watched, fascinated by the first color of day as it struck the shafts and towers. Then the color faded, and a drifting mist moved between him and the city. All at once he bent down and grabbed up his load. He began to walk, hurrying as best he could, chill fear moving through him.

From the city a black speck had leaped up into the sky and was hovering over it.

After a time, a long time, Hasten looked back. The speck was still there — but it had grown. And it was no longer black; in the clear light of day the speck was beginning to flash, shining with many colors.

He increased his pace; he went down the side of a hill and up another. For a second he paused to snap on his click-band. It spoke loudly; he was not far from the sphere. He waved his arm and the clicks rose and fell. To the right. Wiping the perspiration from his hands he went on.

A few minutes later he looked down from the top of a ridge and saw a gleaming metal sphere resting silently on the grass, dripping with cold dew from the night. The Time Car; sliding and running, he leaped down the hill toward it.

He was just pushing the door open with his shoulder when the first cloud of butterflies appeared at the top of the hill, moving quietly toward him.

He locked the door and set his armload down, flexing his muscles. His hand ached, burning now with an intense pain. He had no time for that — he hurried to the window and peered out. The butterflies were swarming toward the sphere, darting and dancing above him, flashing with color. They began to settle down onto the metal, even onto the window. Abruptly, his gaze was cut off by gleaming bodies, soft and pulpy, their beating wings mashed together. He listened. He could hear them, a muffled, echoing sound that came from all sides of him. The interior of the sphere dimmed into darkness as the butterflies sealed off the window. He lit the artificial lights.

Time passed. He examined the newspapers, uncertain of what to do. Go back? Or ahead? Better jump ahead fifty years or so. The butterflies were dangerous, but perhaps not the real thing, the lethal factor that he was looking for. He looked at his hand. The skin was black and hard, a dead area was increasing. A faint shadow of worry went through him; it was getting worse, not better.

The scratching sound on all sides of him began to annoy him, filling him with an uneasy restlessness. He put down the books and paced back and forth. How could insects, even immense insects such as these, destroy the human race? Surely human beings could combat them. Dusts, poisons, sprays.

A bit of metal, a little particle drifted down onto his sleeve. He brushed it off. A second particle fell, and then some tiny fragments. He leaped, his head jerking up.

A circle was forming above his head. Another circle appeared to the right of it, and then a third. All around him circles were forming in the walls and roof of the sphere. He ran to the control board and closed the safety switch. The board hummed into life. He began to set the indicator panel, working rapidly, frantically. Now pieces of metal were dropping down, a rain of metal fragments onto the floor. Corrosive, some kind of substance exuded from them. Acid? Natural secretion of some sort. A large piece of metal fell; he turned.

Into the sphere the butterflies came, fluttering and dancing toward him. The piece that had fallen was a circle of metal, cut cleanly through. He did not have time even to notice it; he snatched up the blowtorch and snapped it on. The flame sucked and gurgled. As the butterflies came toward him he pressed the handle and held the spout up. The air burst alive with burning particles that rained down all over him, and a furious odor reeked through the sphere.

He closed the last switches. The indicator lights flickered, the floor chugged under him. He threw the main lever. More butterflies were pushing in, crowding each other eagerly, struggling to get through. A second circle of metal crashed to the floor suddenly, emitting a new horde. Hasten cringed, backing away, the blowtorch up, spouting flame. The butterflies came on, more and more of them.

Then sudden silence settled over everything, a quiet so abrupt that he blinked. The endless, insistent scratching had ceased. He was alone, except for a cloud of ashes and particles over the floor and walls, the remains of the butterflies that had got into the sphere. Hasten sat down on the stool, trembling. he was safe, on his way back to his own time; and there was no doubt, no possible doubt that he had found the lethal factor. It was there, in the heap of ashes on the floor, in the circles neatly cut in the hull of the car. Corrosive secretion? He smiled grimly.

His last vision of them, of the swelling horde had told him what he wanted to know. Clutched carefully against the first butterflies through the circles were tools, tiny cutting tools. They had cut their way in, bored through; they had come carrying their own equipment.

He sat down, waiting for the Time Car to complete its journey.

Department guards caught hold of him, helping him from the Car. He stepped down unsteadily, leaning against them. "Thanks," he murmured.

Wood hurried up. "Hasten, you're all right?"

He nodded. "Yes. Except my hand."

"Let's get inside at once." They went through the door, into the great chamber. "Sit down." Wood waved his hand impatiently, and a soldier hurried a chair over. "Get him some hot coffee."

Coffee was brought. Hasten sat sipping. At last he pushed the cup away and leaned back.

"Can you tell us now?" Wood asked.

"Yes."

"Fine." Wood sat down across from him. A tape recorder whirred into life and a camera began to photograph Hasten's face as he talked. "Go on. What did you find?"

When he had finished the room was silent. None of the guards or technicians spoke.

Wood stood up, trembling. "God. So it's a form of toxic life that got them. I thought it was something like that. But butterflies? And intelligent. Planning attacks. Probably rapid breeding, quick adaptation."

"Maybe the books and newspapers will help us."

"But where did they come from? Mutation of some existing form? Or from some other planet. Maybe space travel brought them in. We've got to find out."

"They attacked only human beings," Hasten said. "They left the cows. Just people."

"Maybe we can stop them." Wood snapped on the vidphone. "I'll have the Council convene an emergency session. We'll give them your description and recommendations. We'll start a program, organize units all over the planet. Now that we know what it is, we have a chance. Thanks to you, Hasten, maybe we can stop them in time!"

The operator appeared and Wood gave the Council's code letter. Hasten watched dully. At last he got to his feet and wandered around the room. His arm throbbed unmercifully. Presently he went back outside, through the doorway into the open square. Some soldiers were examining the Time Car curiously. Hasten watched them without feeling, his mind blank.

"What is it, sir?" one asked.

"That?" Hasten roused himself, going slowly over. "That's a Time Car."

"No, I mean this." The soldier pointed to something on the hull. "This, sir; it wasn't on there when the Car went out."

Hasten's heart stopped beating. He pushed past them, staring up. At first he saw nothing on the metal hull, only the corroded metal surface. Then chill fright rushed through him.

Something small and brown and furry was there, on the surface. He reached out, touching it. A sack, a stiff little brown sack. It was dry, dry and empty. There was nothing in it; it was open at one end. He stared up. All across the hull of the Car were little brown sacks, some still full, but most of them already empty.

Cocoons.

PAYCHECK

ALL AT ONCE he was in motion. Around him smooth jets hummed. He was on a small private rocket cruiser, moving leisurely across the afternoon sky, between cities.

"Ugh!" he said, sitting up in his seat and rubbing his head. Beside him Earl Rethrick was staring keenly at him, his eyes bright.

"Coming around?"

"Where are we?" Jennings shook his head, trying to clear the dull ache. "Or maybe I should ask that a different way." Already, he could see that it was not late fall. It was spring. Below the cruiser the fields were green. The last thing he remembered was stepping into an elevator with Rethrick. And it was late fall. And in New York.

"Yes," Rethrick said. "It's almost two years later. You'll find a lot of things have changed. The Government fell a few months ago. The new Government is even stronger. The SP, Security Police, have almost unlimited power. They're teaching the schoolchildren to inform, now. But we all saw that coming. Let's see, what else? New York is larger. I understand they've finished filling in San Francisco Bay."

"What I want to know is what the hell I've been doing the last two years!" Jennings lit a cigarette nervously, pressing the strike end. "Will you tell me that?"

"No. Of course I won't tell you that."

"Where are we going?"

"Back to the New York Office. Where you first met me. Remember? You probably remember it better than I. After all, it was just a day or so ago for you."

Jennings nodded. Two years! Two years out of his life, gone forever. It didn't seem possible. He had still been considering, debating, when he stepped into the elevator. Should he change his mind? Even if he were getting that much money—and it was a lot, even for him—it didn't really seem worth it. He would always wonder what work he had been doing. Was it legal? Was it—But that was past speculation, now. Even while he was trying to make up his mind the curtain had fallen. He looked ruefully out the window at the afternoon sky. Below, the earth was moist and alive. Spring, spring two years later. And what did he have to show for the two years?

"Have I been paid?" he asked. He slipped his wallet out and glanced into it. "Apparently not."

"No. You'll be paid at the Office. Kelly will pay you."

"The whole works at once?"

"Fifty thousand credits."

Jennings smiled. He felt a little better, now that the sum had been spoken aloud. Maybe it wasn't so bad, after all. Almost like being paid to sleep. But he was two years older; he had just that much less to live. It was like selling part of himself, part of his life. And life was worth plenty, these days. He shrugged. Anyhow, it was in the past.

"We're almost there," the older man said. The robot pilot dropped the cruiser down, sinking toward the ground. The edge of New York City became visible below them. "Well, Jennings, I may never see you again." He held out his hand. "It's been a pleasure working with you. We did work together, you know. Side by side. You're one of the best mechanics I've ever seen. We were right in hiring you, even at that salary. You paid us back many times— although you don't realize it."

"I'm glad you got your money's worth."

"You sound angry."

"No. I'm just trying to get used to the idea of being two years older."

Rethrick laughed. "You're still a very young man. And you'll feel better when she gives you your pay."

They stepped out onto the tiny rooftop field of the New York office building. Rethrick led him over to an elevator. As the doors slid shut Jennings got a mental shock. This was the last thing he remembered, this elevator. After that he had blacked out.

"Kelly will be glad to see you," Rethrick said, as they came out into a lighted hall. "She asks about you, once in a while."

"Why?"

"She says you're good-looking." Rethrick pushed a code key against a door. The door responded, swinging wide. They entered the luxurious office of Rethrick Construction. Behind a long mahogany desk a young woman was sitting, studying a report.

"Kelly," Rethrick said, "look whose time finally expired."

The girl looked up, smiling. "Hello, Mr. Jennings. How does it feel to be back in the world?"

"Fine." Jennings walked over to her. "Rethrick says you're the paymaster."

Rethrick clapped Jennings on the back. "So long, my friend. I'll go back to the plant. If you ever need a lot of money in a hurry come around and we'll work out another contract with you."

Jennings nodded. As Rethrick went back out he sat down beside the desk, crossing his legs. Kelly slid a drawer open, moving her chair back. "All right. Your time is up, so Rethrick Construction is ready to pay. Do you have your copy of the contract?"

Jennings took an envelope from his pocket and tossed it on the desk. "There it is."

Kelly removed a small cloth sack and some sheets of handwritten paper from the desk drawer. For a time she read over the sheets, her small face intent.

"What is it?"

"I think you're going to be surprised." Kelly handed him his contract back. "Read that over again."

"Why?" Jennings unfastened the envelope.

"There's an alternate clause. 'If the party of the second part so desires, at any time during his time of contract to the aforesaid Rethrick Construction Company — ' "

" 'If he so desires, instead of the monetary sum specified, he may choose instead, according to his own wish, articles or products which, in his own opinion, are of sufficient value to stand in lieu of the sum — ' "

Jennings snatched up the cloth sack, pulling it open. He poured the contents into his palm. Kelly watched.

"Where's Rethrick?" Jennings stood up. "If he has an idea that this — "

"Rethrick has nothing to do with it. It was your own request. Here, look at this." Kelly passed him the sheets of paper. "In your own hand. Read them. It was your idea, not ours. Honest." She smiled up at him. "This happens every once in a while with people we take on contract. During their time they decide to take something else instead of money. Why, I don't know. But they come out with their minds clean, having agreed — "

Jennings scanned the pages. It was his own writing. There was no doubt of it. His hands shook. "I can't believe it. Even if it is my own writing." He folded up the paper, his jaw set. "Something was done to me while I was back there. I never would have agreed to this."

"You must have had a reason. I admit it doesn't make sense. But you don't know what factors might have persuaded you, before your mind was cleaned. You aren't the first. There have been several others before you."

Jennings stared down at what he held in his palm. From the cloth sack he had spilled a little assortment of items. A code key. A ticket stub. A parcel receipt. A length of fine wire. Half a poker chip, broken across. A green strip of cloth. A bus token.

"This, instead of fifty thousand credits," he murmured. "Two years ... "

He went out of the building, onto the busy afternoon street. He was still dazed, dazed and confused. Had he been swindled? He felt in his pocket for the little trinkets, the wire, the ticket stub, all the rest. *That*, for two years of work! But he had seen his own handwriting, the statement of waiver, the request for the substitution. Like Jack and the Beanstalk. Why? What for? What had made him do it?

He turned, starting down the sidewalk. At the corner he stopped for a surface cruiser that was turning.

"All right, Jennings. Get in."

His head jerked up. The door of the cruiser was open. A man was kneeling, pointing a heat-rifle straight at his face. A man in blue-green. The Security Police.

Jennings got in. The door closed, magnetic locks slipping into place behind him. Like a vault. The cruiser glided off down the street. Jennings sank back against the seat. Beside him the SP man lowered his gun. On the other side a second officer ran his hands expertly over him, searching for weapons. He brought out Jenning's wallet and the handful of trinkets. The envelope and contract.

"What does he have?" the driver said.

"Wallet, money. Contract with Rethrick Construction. No weapons." He gave Jennings back his things.

"What's this all about?" Jennings said.

"We want to ask you a few questions. That's all. You've been working for Rethrick?"

"Yes."

"Two years?"

"Almost two years."

"At the Plant?"

Jennings nodded. "I suppose so."

The officer leaned toward him. "Where is that Plant, Mr. Jennings. Where is it located?"

"I don't know."

The two officers looked at each other. The first one moistened his lips, his face sharp and alert. "You don't know? The next question. The last. In those two years, what kind of work did you do? What was your job?"

"Mechanic. I repaired electronic machinery."

"What *kind* of electronic machinery?"

"I don't know." Jennings looked up at him. He could not help smiling, his lips twisting ironically. "I'm sorry, but I don't know. It's the truth."

There was silence.

"What do you mean, you don't know? You mean you worked on machinery for two years without knowing what it was? Without even knowing where you were?"

Jennings roused himself. "What is all this? What did you pick me up for? I haven't done anything. I've been — "

"We know. We're not arresting you. We only want to get information for our records. About Rethrick Construction. You've been working for them, in their Plant. In an important capacity. You're an electronic mechanic?"

"Yes."

"You repair high-quality computers and allied equipment?" The officer consulted his notebook. "You're considered one of the best in the country, according to this."

Jennings said nothing.

"Tell us the two things we want to know, and you'll be released at once. Where is Rethrick's Plant? What kind of work are they doing? You serviced their machines for them, didn't you? Isn't that right? For two years."

"I don't know. I suppose so. I don't have any idea what I did during the two years. You can believe me or not." Jennings stared wearily down at the floor.

"What'll we do?" the driver said finally. "We have no instructions past this."

"Take him to the station. We can't do any more questioning here." Beyond the cruiser, men and women hurried along the sidewalk. The streets were choked with cruisers, workers going to their homes in the country.

"Jennings, why don't you answer us? What's the matter with you? There's no reason why you can't tell us a couple of simple things like that. Don't you want to cooperate with your Government? Why should you conceal information from us?"

"I'd tell you if I knew."

The officer grunted. No one spoke. Presently the cruiser drew up before a great stone building. The driver turned the motor off, removing the control cap and putting it in his pocket. He touched the door with a code key, releasing the magnetic lock.

"What shall we do, take him in? Actually, we don't — "

"Wait." The driver stepped out. The other two went with him, closing and locking the doors behind them. They stood on the pavement before the Security Station, talking.

Jennings sat silently, staring down at the floor. The SP wanted to know about Rethrick Construction. Well, there was nothing he could tell them. They had come to the wrong person, but how could he prove that? The whole thing was impossible. Two years wiped clean from his mind. Who would believe him? It seemed unbelievable to him, too.

His mind wandered, back to when he had first read the ad. It had hit home, hit him direct. *Mechanic wanted*, and a general outline of the work, vague, indirect, but enough to tell him that it was right up his line. And the pay! Interviews at the Office. Tests, forms. And then the gradual realization that Rethrick Construction was finding all about him while he knew nothing about them. What kind of work did they do? Construction, but what kind? What sort of machines did they have? Fifty thousand credits for two years...

And he had come out with his mind washed clean. Two years, and he remembered nothing. It took him a long time to agree to that part of the contract. But he *had* agreed.

Jennings looked out the window. The three officers were still talking on the sidewalk, trying to decide what to do with him. He was in a tough spot. They wanted information he couldn't give, information he didn't know. But how could he prove it? How could he prove that he had worked two years and come out knowing no more than when he had gone in! The SP would work him over. It would be a long time before they'd believe him, and by that time —

He glanced quickly around. Was there any escape? In a second they would be back. He touched the door. Locked, the triple-ring magnetic locks. He had worked on magnetic locks many times. He had even designed part of a trigger core. There was no way to open the doors without the right code key. No way, unless by some chance he could short out the lock. But with what?

He felt in his pockets. What could he use? If he could short the locks, blow them out, there was a faint chance. Outside, men and women were swarming by, on their way home from work. It was past five; the great office buildings were shutting down, the streets were alive with traffic. If he once got out they wouldn't dare fire. — If he could get out.

The three officers separated. One went up the steps into the Station building. In a second the others would reenter the cruiser. Jennings dug into his pocket, bringing out the code key, the ticket stub, the wire. The wire! Thin wire, thin as human hair. Was it insulated? He unwound it quickly. No.

He knelt down, running his fingers expertly across the surface of the door. At the edge of the lock was a thin line, a groove between the lock and the door. He brought the end of the wire up to it, delicately maneuvering the wire into the almost invisible space. The wire disappeared an inch or so. Sweat rolled down Jennings' forehead. He moved the wire a fraction of an inch, twisting it. He held his breath. The relay should be —

A flash.

Half blinded, he threw his weight against the door. The door fell open, the lock fused and smoking. Jennings tumbled into the street and leaped to his feet. Cruisers were all around him, honking and sweeping past. He ducked behind a lumbering truck, entering the middle lane of traffic. On the sidewalk he caught a momentary glimpse of the SP men starting after him.

A bus came along, swaying from side to side, loaded with shoppers and workers. Jennings caught hold of the back rail, pulling himself up onto the platform. Astonished faces loomed up, pale moons thrust suddenly at him. The robot conductor was coming toward him, whirring angrily. "Sir — " the conductor began. The bus was slowing down. "Sir, it is not allowed — "

"It's all right," Jennings said. He was filled, all at once, with a strange elation. A moment ago he had been trapped, with no way to escape. Two years of his life had been lost for nothing. The Security Police had arrested him, demanding information he couldn't give. A hopeless situation! But now things were beginning to click in his mind.

He reached into his pocket and brought out the bus token. He put it calmly into the conductor's coin slot.

"Okay?" he said. Under his feet the bus wavered, the driver hesitating. Then the bus resumed pace, going on. The conductor turned away, its whirrs subsiding. Everything was all right. Jennings smiled. He eased past the standing people, looking for a seat, some place to sit down. Where he could think.

He had plenty to think about. His mind was racing.

The bus moved on, flowing with the restless stream of urban traffic. Jennings only half saw the people sitting around him. There was no doubt of it: he had not been swindled. It was on the level. The decision had actually been his. Amazingly, after two years of work he had preferred a handful of trinkets instead of fifty thousand credits. But more amazingly, the handful of trinkets were turning out to be worth more than the money.

With a piece of wire and a bus token he had escaped from the Security Police. That was worth plenty. Money would have been useless to him once he disappeared inside the great stone Station. Even fifty thousand credits wouldn't have helped him. And there were five trinkets left. He felt around in his pocket. Five more things. He had used two. The others — what were they for? Something as important?

But the big puzzle: how had *he* — his earlier self — known that a piece of wire and a bus token would save his life?" *He* had known, all right. Known in advance. But how? And the other five. Probably they were just as precious, or would be.

The *he* of those two years had known things that he did not know now, things that had been washed away when the company cleaned his mind. Like an adding machine which had been cleared. Everything was slate-clean. What *he* had known was gone, now. Gone, except for seven trinkets, five of which were still in his pocket.

But the real problem right now was not a problem of speculation. It was very concrete. The Security Police were looking for him. They had his name and description. There was no use thinking of going to his apartment — if he even still had an apartment. But where, then? Hotels? The SP combed them daily. Friends? That would mean putting them in jeopardy, along with him. It was only a question of time before the SP found him, walking along the street, eating in a restaurant, in a show, sleeping in some rooming house. The SP were everywhere.

Everywhere? Not quite. When an individual person was defenseless, a business was not. The big economic forces had managed to remain free, although virtually everything else had been absorbed by the Government. Laws that had been eased away from the private person still protected property and industry. The SP could pick up any given person, but they could not enter and seize a company, a business. That had been clearly established in the middle of the twentieth century.

Business, industry, corporations, were safe from the Security Police. Due process was required. Rethrick Construction was a target of SP interest, but they could do nothing until some statute was violated. If he could get back to the Company, get inside its doors, he would be safe. Jennings smiled grimly. The modern church, sanctuary. It was the Government against the corporation, rather than the State against the Church. The new Notre Dame of the world. Where the law could not follow.

Would Rethrick take him back? Yes, on the old basis. He had already said so. Another two years sliced from him, and then back onto the streets. Would that help him? He felt suddenly in his pocket. And there were the remaining trinkets. Surely *he* had intended them to be used! No, he could not go back to Rethrick and work another contract time. Something else was indicated. Something more permanent. Jennings pondered. Rethrick Construction. What did it construct? What had *he* known, found out, during those two years? And why were the SP so interested?

He brought out the five objects and studied them. The green strip of cloth. The code key. The ticket stub. The parcel receipt. The half poker chip. Strange, that little things like that could be important.

And Rethrick Construction was involved.

There was no doubt. The answer, all the answers, lay at Rethrick. But where *was* Rethrick? He had no idea where the plant was, no idea at all. He knew where the Office was, the big, luxurious room with the young woman and her desk. But that was not Rethrick Construction. Did anyone know, beside Rethrick? Kelly didn't know. Did the SP know?

It was out of town. That was certain. He had gone there by rocket. It was probably in the United States, maybe in the farmlands, the country, between cities. What a hell of a situation! Any moment the SP might pick him up. The next time he might not get away. His only chance, his own real chance for safety, lay in reaching Rethrick. And his only chance to find out the things he had to know. The plant — a place where he had been, but which he could not recall. He looked down at the five trinkets. Would any of them help?

A burst of despair swept through him. Maybe it was just coincidence, the wire and the token. Maybe —

He examined the parcel receipt, turning it over and holding it up to the light. Suddenly his stomach muscles knotted. His pulse changed. He had been right. No, it was not a coincidence, the wire and the token. The parcel receipt was dated two days hence. The parcel, whatever it might be, had not even been deposited yet. Not for forty-eight more hours.

He looked at the other things. The ticket stub. What good was a ticket stub? It was creased and bent, folded over, again and again. He couldn't go anyplace with that. A stub didn't take you anywhere. It only told you where you had been.

Where you had been!

He bent down, peering at it, smoothing the creases. The printing had been torn through the middle. Only part of each word could be made out.

PORTOLA T
STUARTSVI
IOW

He smiled. That was it. Where he had been. He could fill in the missing letters. It was enough. There was no doubt: *he* had foreseen this, too. Three of the seven trinkets used. Four left. Stuartsville, Iowa. Was there such a place? He looked out the window of the bus. The Intercity rocket station was only a block or so away. He could be there in a second. A quick sprint from the bus, hoping the Police wouldn't be there to stop him —

But somehow he knew they wouldn't. Not with the other four things in his pocket. And once he was on the rocket he would be safe. Intercity was big, big enough to keep free of the SP. Jennings put the remaining trinkets back into his pocket and stood up, pulling the bellcord.

A moment later he stepped gingerly out onto the sidewalk.

The rocket let him off at the edge of town, at a tiny brown field. A few disinterested porters moved about, stacking luggage, resting from the heat of the sun.

Jennings crossed the field to the waiting room, studying the people around him. Ordinary people, workmen, businessmen, housewives. Stuartsville was a small middle Western town. Truck drivers. High school kids.

He went through the waiting room, out onto the street. So this was where Rethrick's Plant was located — perhaps. If he had used the stub correctly. Anyhow, *something* was here, or *he* wouldn't have included the stub with the other trinkets.

Stuartsville, Iowa. A faint plan was beginning to form in the back of his mind, still vague and nebulous. He began to walk, his hands in his pockets, looking around him. A newspaper office, lunch counters, hotels, poolrooms, a barber shop, a television repair shop. A rocket sales store with huge showrooms of gleaming rockets. Family size. And at the end of the block the Portola Theater.

The town thinned out. Farms, fields. Miles of green country. In the sky above a few transport rockets lumbered, carrying farm supplies and equipment back and forth. A small, unimportant town. Just right for Rethrick Construction. The Plant would be lost here, away from the city, away from the SP.

Jennings walked back. He entered a lunchroom, BOB'S PLACE. A young man with glasses came over as he sat down at the counter, wiping his hands on his white apron.

"Coffee," Jennings said.

"Coffee." The man brought the cup. There were only a few people in the lunchroom. A couple of flies buzzed, against the window.

Outside in the street shoppers and farmers moved leisurely by.

"Say," Jennings said, stirring his coffee. "Where can a man get work around here? Do you know?"

"What kind of work?" The young man came back, leaning against the counter.

"Electrical wiring. I'm an electrician. Television, rockets, computers. That sort of stuff."

"Why don't you try the big industrial areas? Detroit. Chicago. New York."

Jennings shook his head. "Can't stand the big cities. I never liked cities."

The young man laughed. "A lot of people here would be glad to work in Detroit. You're an electrician?"

"Are there any plants around here? Any repair shops or plants?"

"None that I know of." The young man went off to wait on some men that had come in. Jennings sipped his coffee. Had he made a mistake? Maybe he should go back and forget about Stuartsville, Iowa. Maybe he had made the wrong inference from the ticket stub. But the ticket meant something, unless he was completely wrong about everything. It was a little late to decide that, though.

The young man came back. "Is there *any* kind of work I can get here?" Jennings said. "Just to tide me over."

"There's always farm work."

"How about the retail repair shops? Garages. TV."

"There's a TV repair shop down the street. Maybe you might get something there. You could try. Farm work pays good. They can't get many men, anymore. Most men in the military. You want to pitch hay?"

Jennings laughed. He paid for his coffee. "Not very much. Thanks."

"Once in a while some of the men go up the road and work. There's some sort of Government station."

Jennings nodded. He pushed the screen door open, stepping outside onto the hot sidewalk. He walked aimlessly for a time, deep in thought, turning his nebulous plan over and over. It was a good plan; it would solve everything, all his problems at once. But right now it hinged on one thing: finding Rethrick Construction. And he had only one clue, if it really was a clue. The ticket stub, folded and creased, in his pocket. And a faith that *he* had known what he was doing.

A Government station. Jennings paused, looking around him. Across the street was a taxi stand, a couple of cabbies sitting in their cabs, smoking and reading the newspaper. It was worth a try, at least. There wasn't much else to do. Rethrick would be something else, on the surface. If it posed as a Government project no one would ask any questions. They were all too accustomed to Government projects working without explanation, in secrecy.

He went over to the first cab. "Mister," he said, "can you tell me something?"

The cabbie looked up. "What do you want?"

"They tell me there's work to be had, out at the Government station. Is that right?"

The cabbie studied him. He nodded.

"What kind of work is it?"

"I don't know."

"Where do they do the hiring?"

"I don't know." The cabbie lifted his paper.

"Thanks." Jennings turned away.

"They don't do any hiring. Maybe once in a long while. They don't take many on. You better go someplace else if you're looking for work."

"All right."

The other cabbie leaned out of his cab. "They use only a few day laborers, buddy. That's all. And they're very choosy. They don't hardly let anybody in. Some kind of war work."

Jennings pricked up his ears. "Secret?"

"They come into town and pick up a load of construction workers. Maybe a truck full. That's all. They're real careful who they pick."

Jennings walked back toward the cabbie. "That right?"

"It's a big place. Steel wall. Charged. Guards. Work going on day and night. But nobody gets in. Set up on top of a hill, out the old Henderson Road. About two miles and a half." The cabbie poked at his shoulder. "You can't get in unless you're identified. They identify their laborers, after they pick them out. You know."

Jennings stared at him. The cabbie was tracing a line on his shoulder. Suddenly Jennings understood. A flood of relief rushed over him.

"Sure," he said. "I understand what you mean. At least, I think so." He reached into his pocket, bringing out the four trinkets. Carefully, he unfolded the strip of green cloth, holding it up. "Like this?"

The cabbies stared at the cloth. "That's right," one of them said slowly, staring at the cloth. "Where did you get it?"

Jennings laughed. "A friend." He put the cloth back in his pocket. "A friend gave it to me."

He went off, toward the Intercity field. He had plenty to do, now that the first step was over. Rethrick was here, all right. And apparently the trinkets were going to see him through. One for every crisis. A pocketful of miracles, from someone who knew the future!

But the next step couldn't be done alone. He needed help. Somebody else was needed for this part. But who? He pondered, entering the Intercity waiting room. There was only one person he could possibly go to. It was a long chance, but he had to take it. He couldn't work alone, here on out. If the Rethrick plant was here then Kelly would be too ...

The street was dark. At the corner a lamppost cast a fitful beam. A few cruisers moved by.

From the apartment building entrance a slim shape came, a young woman in a coat, a purse in her hand. Jennings watched as she passed under the streetlamp. Kelly McVane was going someplace, probably to a party. Smartly dressed, high heels tap-tapping on the pavement, a little coat and hat.

He stepped out behind her. "Kelly."

She turned quickly, her mouth open. "Oh!"

Jennings took her arm. "Don't worry. It's just me. Where are you going, all dressed up?"

"No place." She blinked. "My golly, you scared me. What is it? What's going on?"

"Nothing. Can you spare a few minutes? I want to talk to you."

Kelly nodded. "I guess so." She looked around. "Where'll we go?"

"Where's a place we can talk? I don't want anyone to overhear us."

"Can't we just walk along?"

"No. The Police."

"The Police?"

"They're looking for me."

"For you? But why?"

"Let's not stand here," Jennings said grimly. "Where can we go?"

Kelly hesitated. "We can go up to my apartment. No one's there."

They went up to the elevator. Kelly unlocked the door, pressing the code key against it. The door swung open and they went inside, the heater and lights coming on automatically at her step. She closed the door and took off her coat.

"I won't stay long." Jennings said.

"That's all right. I'll fix you a drink." She went into the kitchen. Jennings sat down on the couch, looking around at the neat little apartment. Presently the girl came back. She sat down beside him and Jennings took his drink. Scotch and water, cold.

"Thanks."

Kelly smiled. "Not at all." The two of them sat silently for a time. "Well?" she said at last. "What's this all about? Why are the Police looking for you?"

"They want to find out about Rethrick Construction. I'm only a pawn in this. They think I know something because I worked two years at Rethrick's Plant."

"But you don't!"

"I can't prove that."

Kelly reached out, touching Jennings' head, just above the ear. "Feel there. That spot."

Jennings reached up. Above his ear, under the hair, was a tiny hard spot. "What is it?"

"They burned through the skull there. Cut a tiny wedge from the brain. All your memories of the two years. They located them and burned them out. The SP couldn't possibly make you remember. It's gone. You don't have it."

"By the time they realize that there won't be much left of me."

Kelly said nothing.

"You can see the spot I'm in. It would be better for me if I did remember. Then I could tell them and they'd — "

"And destroy Rethrick!"

Jennings shrugged. "Why not? Rethrick means nothing to me. I don't even know what they're doing. And why are the Police so interested? From the very start, all the secrecy, cleaning my mind — "

"There's reason. Good reason."

"Do you know why?"

"No." Kelly shook her head. "But I'm sure there's a reason. If the SP are interested, there's reason." She set down her drink, turning toward him. "I hate the Police. We all do, every one of us. They're after us all the time. I don't know anything about Rethrick. If I did my life wouldn't be safe. There's not much standing between Rethrick and them. A few laws, a handful of laws. Nothing more."

"I have the feeling Rethrick is a great deal more than just another construction company the SP wants to control."

"I suppose it is. I really don't know. I'm just a receptionist. I've never been to the Plant. I don't even know where it is."

"But you wouldn't want anything to happen to it."

"Of course not! They're fighting the Police. Anyone that's fighting the Police is on our side."

"Really? I've heard that kind of logic before. Anyone fighting communism was automatically good, a few decades ago. Well, time will tell. As far as I'm concerned I'm an individual caught between two ruthless forces. Government and business. The Government has men and wealth. Rethrick Construction has its technocracy. What they've done with it, I don't know. I did, a few weeks ago. All I have now is a faint glimmer, a few references. A theory."

Kelly glanced at him. "A theory?"

"And my pocketful of trinkets. Seven. Three or four now. I've used some. They're the basis of my theory. If Rethrick is doing what I think it's doing, I can understand the SP's interest. As a matter of fact, I'm beginning to share their interest."

"What is Rethrick doing?"

"It's developed a time scoop."

"What?"

"A time scoop. It's been theoretically possible for several years. But it's illegal to experiment with time scoops and mirrors. It's a felony, and if you're caught, all your equipment and data becomes the property of the Government." Jennings smiled crookedly. "No wonder the Government's interested. If they can catch Rethrick with the goods — "

"A time scoop. It's hard to believe."

"Don't you think I'm right?"

"I don't know. Perhaps. Your trinkets. You're not the first to come out with a little cloth sack of odds and ends. You've used some? How?"

"First, the wire and the bus token. Getting away from the Police. It seems funny, but if I hadn't had them, I'd be there yet. A piece of wire and a ten-cent token. But I don't usually carry such things. That's the point."

"Time travel."

"No. Not time travel. Berkowsky demonstrated that time travel is impossible. This is a time scoop, a mirror to see and a scoop to pick up things. These trinkets. At least one of them is from the future. Scooped up. Brought back."

"How do you know?"

"It's dated. The others, perhaps not. Things like tokens and wire belong to classes of things. Any one token is as good as another. There, *he* must have used a mirror."

"*He?*"

"When I was working with Rethrick. I must have used the mirror. I looked into my own future. If I was repairing their equipment I could hardly keep from it! I must have looked ahead, seen what was coming. The SP picking me up. I must have seen that, and seen what a piece of thin wire and a bus token would do — if I had them with me at the exact moment."

Kelly considered. "Well? What do you want me for?"

"I'm not sure, now. Do you really look on Rethrick as a benevolent institution, waging war against the Police? A sort of Roland at Roncesvalles — "

"What does it matter how I feel about the Company?"

"It matters a lot." Jennings finished his drink, pushing the glass aside. "It matters a lot, because I want you to help me. I'm going to blackmail Rethrick Construction."

Kelly stared at him.

"It's my one chance to stay alive, I've got to get a hold over Rethrick, a big hold. Enough of a hold so they'll let me in, on my own terms. There's no other place I can go. Sooner or later the Police are going to pick me up. If I'm not inside the Plant, and soon — "

"Help you blackmail the Company? Destroy Rethrick?"

"No. Not destroy. I don't want to destroy it — my life depends on the Company. My life depends on Rethrick being strong enough to defy the SP. But if I'm on the *outside* it doesn't much matter how strong Rethrick is. Do you see? I want to get in. I want to get inside before it's too late. And I want in on my own terms, not as a two-year worker who gets pushed out again afterward."

"For the Police to pick up."

Jennings nodded. "Exactly."

"How are you going to blackmail the Company?"

"I'm going to enter the Plant and carry out enough material to prove Rethrick is operating a time scoop."

Kelly laughed. "Enter the Plant? Let's see you *find* the Plant. The SP have been looking for it for years."

"I've already found it." Jennings leaned back, lighting a cigarette. "I've located it with my trinkets. And I have four left, enough to get me inside, I think. And to get me what I want. I'll be able to carry out enough papers and photographs to hang Rethrick. But I don't want to hang Rethrick. I only want to bargain. That's where you come in."

"I?"

"You can be trusted not to go to the Police. I need someone I can turn the material over to. I don't dare keep it myself. As soon as I have it I must turn it over to someone else, someone who'll hide it where I won't be able to find it."

"Why?"

"Because," Jennings said calmly, "any minute the SP may pick me up. I have no love for Rethrick, but I don't want to scuttle it. That's why you've got to help me. I'm going to turn the information over to you, to hold, while I bargain with Rethrick. Otherwise I'll have to hold it myself. And if I have it on me — "

He glanced at her. Kelly was staring at the floor, her face tense. Set.

"Well? What do you say? Will you help me, or shall I take the chance the SP won't pick me up with the material? Data enough to destroy Rethrick. Well? Which will it be? Do you want to see Rethrick destroyed? What's your answer?"

The two of them crouched, looking across the fields at the hill beyond. The hill rose up, naked and brown, burned clean of vegetation. Nothing grew on its sides. Halfway up a long steel fence twisted, topped with charged barbed wire. On the other side a guard walked slowly, a tiny figure patrolling with a rifle and helmet.

At the top of the hill lay an enormous concrete block, a towering structure without windows or doors. Mounted guns caught the early morning sunlight, glinting in a row along the roof of the building.

"So that's the Plant," Kelly said softly.

"That's it. It would take an army to get up there, up that hill and over the fence. Unless they were allowed in." Jennings got to his feet, helping Kelly up. They walked back along the path, through the trees, to where Kelly had parked the cruiser.

"Do you really think your green cloth band will get you in?" Kelly said, sliding behind the wheel.

"According to the people in the town, a truckload of laborers will be brought in to the Plant sometime this morning. The truck is unloaded at the entrance and the men examined. If everything's in order they're let inside the grounds, past the fence. For construction work, manual labor. At the end of the day they're let out again and driven back to town."

"Will that get you close enough?"

"I'll be on the other side of the fence, at least."

"How will you get to the time scoop? That must be inside the building, some place."

Jennings brought out a small code key. "This will get me in. I hope. I assume it will."

Kelly took the key, examining it. "So that's one of your trinkets. We should have taken a better look inside your little cloth bag."

"We?"

"The Company. I saw several little bags of trinkets pass out, through my hands. Rethrick never said anything."

"Probably the Company assumed no one would ever want to get back inside again." Jennings took the code key from her. "Now, do you know what you're supposed to do?"

"I'm supposed to stay here with the cruiser until you get back. You're to give me the material. Then I'm to carry it back to New York and wait for you to contact me."

"That's right." Jennings studied the distant road, leading through the trees to the Plant gate. "I better get down there. The truck may be along any time."

"What if they decide to count the number of workers?"

"I'll have to take the chance. But I'm not worried. I'm sure *he* foresaw everything."

Kelly smiled. "You and your friend, your helpful friend. I hope *he* left you enough things to get you out again, after you have the photographs."

"Do you?"

"Why not?" Kelly said easily. "I always liked you. You know that. You knew when you came to me."

Jennings stepped out of the cruiser. He had on overalls and workshoes, and a gray sweatshirt. "I'll see you later. If everything goes all right. I think it will." He patted his pocket. "With my charms here, my good-luck charms."

He went off through the trees, walking swiftly.

The trees led to the very edge of the road. He stayed with them, not coming out into the open. The Plant guards were certainly scanning the hillside. They had burned it clean, so that anyone trying to creep up to the fence would be spotted at once. And he had seen infrared searchlights.

Jennings crouched low, resting against his heels, watching the road. A few yards up the road was a roadblock, just ahead of the gate. He examined his watch. Ten thirty. He might have a wait, a long wait. He tried to relax.

It was after eleven when the great truck came down the road, rumbling and wheezing.

Jennings came to life. He took out the strip of green cloth and fastened it around his arm. The truck came closer. He could see its load now. The back was full of workmen, men in jeans and workshirts, bounced and jolted as the truck moved along. Sure enough, each had an arm band like his own, a swathe of green around his upper arm. So far so good.

The truck came slowly to a halt, stopping at the roadblock. The men got down slowly onto the road, sending up a cloud of dust into the hot midday sun. They slapped the dust from their jeans, some of them lighting cigarettes. Two guards came leisurely from behind the roadblock. Jennings tensed. In a moment it would be time. The guards moved among the men, examining them, their arm bands, their faces, looking at the identification tabs of a few.

The roadblock slid back. The gate opened. The guards returned to their positions.

Jennings slid forward, slithering through the brush, toward the road. The men were stamping out their cigarettes, climbing back up into the truck. The truck was gunning its motor, the driver releasing the brakes. Jennings dropped onto the road, behind the truck. A rattle of leaves and dirt showered after him. Where he had landed, the view of the guards was cut off by the truck. Jennings held his breath. He ran toward the back of the truck.

The men stared at him curiously as he pulled himself up among them, his chest rising and falling. Their faces were weathered, gray and lined. Men of the soil. Jennings took his place between two burly farmers as the truck started up. They did not seem to notice him. He had rubbed dirt into his skin, and let his beard grow for a day. A quick glance he didn't look much different from the others. But if anyone made a count —

The truck passed through the gate, into the grounds. The gate slid shut behind. Now they were going up, up the steep side of the hill, the truck rattling and swaying from side to side. The vast concrete structure loomed nearer. Were they going to enter it? Jennings watched, fascinated. A thin high door was sliding back, revealing a dark interior. A row of artificial lights gleamed.

The truck stopped. The workmen began to get down again. Some mechanics came around them.

"What's this crew for?" one of them asked.

"Digging. Inside." Another jerked a thumb. "They're digging again. Send them inside."

Jennings's heart thudded. He was going inside! He felt at his neck. There, inside the gray sweater, a flatplate camera hung like a bib around his neck. He could scarcely feel it, even knowing it was there. Maybe this would be less difficult than he had thought.

The workmen pushed through the door on foot, Jennings with them. They were in an immense workroom, long benches with half-completed machinery, booms and cranes, and the constant roar of work. The door closed after them, cutting them off from outside. He was in the Plant. But where was the time scoop, and the mirror?

"This way," a foreman said. The workmen plodded over to the right. A freight lift rose to meet them from the bowels of the building. "You're going down below. How many of you have experience with drills?"

A few hands went up.

"You can show the others. We are moving earth with drills and eaters. Any of you work eaters?"

No hands. Jennings glanced at the worktables. Had he worked here, not so long ago? A sudden chill went through him. Suppose he were recognized? Maybe he had worked with these very mechanics.

"Come on," the foreman said impatiently. "Hurry up."

Jennings got into the freight lift with the others. A moment later they began to descend, down the black tube. Down, down, into the lower levels of the Plant. Rethrick Construction was *big*, a lot bigger than it looked above ground. A lot bigger than he had imagined. Floors, underground levels, flashing past one after the other.

The elevator stopped. The doors opened. He was looking down a long corridor. The floor was thick with stone dust. The air was moist. Around him, the workmen began to crowd out. Suddenly Jennings stiffened, pulling back.

At the end of the corridor before a steel door, was Earl Rethrick. Talking to a group of technicians.

"All out," the foreman said. "Let's go."

Jennings left the elevator, keeping behind the others. Rethrick! His heart beat dully. If Rethrick saw him he was finished. He felt in his pockets. He had a miniature Boris gun, but it wouldn't be much use if he was discovered. Once Rethrick saw him it would be all over.

"Down this way." The foreman led them toward what seemed to be an underground railway, to one side of the corridor. The men were getting into metal cars along a track. Jennings watched Rethrick. He saw him gesture angrily, his voice coming faintly down the hall. Suddenly Rethrick turned. He held up his hand and the great steel door behind him opened.

Jennings's heart almost stopped beating.

There, beyond the steel door, was the time scoop. He recognized it at once. The mirror. The long metal rods, ending in claws. Like Berkowsky's theoretical model — only this was real.

Rethrick went into the room, the technicians following behind him. Men were working at the scoop, standing all around it. Part of the shield was off. They were digging into the works. Jennings stared, hanging back.

"Say you — " the foreman said, coming toward him. The steel door shut. The view was cut off. Rethrick, the scoop, the technicians, were gone.

"Sorry," Jennings murmured.

"You know you're not supposed to be curious around here." The foreman was studying him intently. "I don't remember you. Let me see your tab."

"My tab?"

"Your identification tab." The foreman turned away. "Bill, bring me the board." He looked Jennings up and down. "I'm going to check you from the board, mister. I've never seen you in the crew before. Stay here." A man was coming from a side door with a check board in his hands.

It was now or never.

Jennings sprinted, down the corridor, toward the great steel door. Behind there was a startled shout, the foreman and his helper. Jennings whipped out the code key, praying fervently as he ran. He came up to the door, holding out the key. With the other hand he brought out the Boris gun. Beyond the door was the time scoop. A few photographs, some schematics snatched up, and then, if he could get out —

The door did not move. Sweat leaped out on his face. He knocked the key against the door. Why didn't it open? Surely — He began to shake, panic rising up in him. Down the corridor people were coming, racing after him. Open —

But the door did not open. The key he held in his hand was the wrong key.

He was defeated. The door and the key did not match. Either *he* had been wrong, or the key was to be used someplace else. But where? Jennings looked frantically around. Where? Where could he go?

To one side a door was half open, a regular bolt-lock door. He crossed the corridor, pushing it open. He was in a storeroom of some sort. He slammed the door, throwing the bolt. He could hear them outside, confused, calling for guards. Soon armed guards would be along. Jennings held the Boris gun tightly, gazing around. Was he trapped? Was there a second way out?

He ran through the room, pushing among bales and boxes, towering stacks of silent cartons, end on end. At the rear was an emergency hatch. He opened it immediately. An impulse came to throw the code key away. What good had it been? But surely *he* had known what he was doing. *He* had already seen all this. Like God, it had already happened for *him*. Predetermined. *He* could not err. Or could he?

A chill went through him. Maybe the future was variable. Maybe this had been the right key, once. But not any more!

There were sounds behind him. They were melting the storeroom door. Jennings scrambled through the emergency hatch, into a low concrete passage, damp and ill lit. He ran quickly along it, turning corners. It was like a sewer. Other passages ran into it, from all sides.

He stopped. Which way? Where could he hide? The mouth of a major vent pipe gaped above his head. He caught hold and pulled himself up. Grimly, he eased his body onto it. They'd ignore a pipe, go on past. He crawled cautiously down the pipe. Warm air blew into his face. Why such a big vent? It implied an unusual chamber at the other end. He came to a metal grill and stopped.

And gasped.

He was looking into the great room, the room he had glimpsed beyond the steel door. Only now he was at the other end. There was the time scoop. And far down, beyond the scoop, was Rethrick, conferring at an active vidscreen. An alarm was sounding, whining shrilly, echoing everywhere. Technicians were running in all directions. Guards in uniform poured in and out of doors.

The scoop. Jennings examined the grill. It was slotted in place. He moved it laterally and it fell into his hands. No one was watching. He slid cautiously out, into the room, the Boris gun ready. He was fairly hidden behind the scoop, and the technicians and guards were all the way down at the other end of the room, where he had first seen them.

And there it was, all around him, the schematics, the mirror, papers, data, blueprints. He flicked his camera on. Against his chest the camera vibrated, film moving through it. He snatched up a handful of schematics. Perhaps *he* had used these very diagrams, a few weeks before!

He stuffed his pockets with papers. The film came to an end. But he was finished. He squeezed back into the vent, pushing through the mouth and down the tube. The sewerlike corridor was still empty, but there was an insistent drumming sound, the noise of voices and footsteps. So many passages — They were looking for him in a maze of escape corridors.

Jennings ran swiftly. He ran on and on, without regard to direction, trying to keep along the main corridor. On all sides passages flocked off, one after another, countless passages. He was dropping down, lower and lower. Running downhill.

Suddenly he stopped, gasping. The sound behind him had died away for a moment. But there was a new sound, ahead. He went along slowly. The corridor twisted, turning to the right. He advanced slowly, the Boris gun ready.

Two guards were standing a little way ahead, lounging and talking together. Beyond them was a heavy code door. And behind him the sound of voices were coming again, growing louder. They had found the same passage he had taken. They were on the way.

Jennings stepped out, the Boris gun raised. "Put up your hands. Let go of your guns."

The guards gawked at him. Kids, boys with cropped blond hair and shiny uniforms. They moved back, pale and scared.

"The guns. Let them fall."

The two rifles clattered down. Jennings smiled. Boys. Probably this was their first encounter with trouble. Their leather boots shone, brightly polished.

"Open the door," Jennings said. "I want through."

They stared at him. Behind, the noise grew.

"Open it." He became impatient. "Come on." He waved the pistol. "Open it, damn it! Do you want me to — "

"We — we can't."

"What?"

"We can't. It's a code door. We don't have the key. Honest, mister. They don't let us have the key." They were frightened. Jennings felt fear himself now. Behind him the drumming was louder. He was trapped, caught.

Or was he?

Suddenly he laughed. He walked quickly up to the door. "Faith," he murmured, raising his hand. "That's something you should never lose."

"What — what's that?"

"Faith in yourself. Self-confidence."

The door slid back as he held the code key against it. Blinding sunlight streamed in, making him blink. He held the gun steady. He was outside, at the gate. Three guards gaped in amazement at the gun. He was at the gate — and beyond lay the woods.

"Get out of the way." Jennings fired at the metal bars of the gate. The metal burst into flame, melting, a cloud of fire rising.

"Stop him!" From behind, men came pouring, guards, out of the corridor.

Jennings leaped through the smoking gate. The metal tore at him, searing him. He ran through the smoke, rolling and falling. He got to his feet and scurried on, into the trees.

He was outside. *He* had not let him down. The key had worked, all right. He had tried it first on the wrong door.

On and on he ran, sobbing for breath, pushing through the trees. Behind him the Plant and the voices fell away. He had the papers. And he was free.

He found Kelly and gave her the film and everything he had managed to stuff into his pockets. Then he changed back to his regular clothes. Kelly drove him to the edge of Stuartsville and left him off. Jennings watched the cruiser rise up into the air, heading toward New York. Then he went into town and boarded the Intercity rocket.

On the flight he slept, surrounded by dozing businessmen. When he awoke the rocket was settling down, landing at the huge New York spaceport. Jennings got off, mixing with the flow of people. Now that he was back there was the danger of being picked up by the SP again. Two security officers in their green uniforms watched him impassively as he took a taxi at the field station. The taxi swept him into downtown traffic. Jennings wiped his brow. That was close. Now, to find Kelly.

He ate dinner at a small restaurant, sitting in the back away from the windows. When he emerged the sun was beginning to set. He walked slowly along the sidewalk, deep in thought.

So far so good. He had got the papers and film, and he had got away. The trinkets had worked every step along the way. Without them he would have been helpless. He felt in his pocket. Two left. The serrated half poker chip, and the parcel receipt. He took the receipt out, examining it in the fading evening light.

Suddenly he noticed something. The date on it was today's date. He had caught up with the slip.

He put it away, going on. What did it mean? What was it for? He shrugged. He would know, in time. And the half poker chip. What the hell was it for? No way to tell. In any case, he was certain to get through. *He* had got him by, up to now. Surely there wasn't much left.

He came to Kelly's apartment house and stopped, looking up. Her light was on. She was back; her fast little cruiser had beaten the Intercity rocket. He entered the elevator and rose to her floor.

"Hello," he said, when she opened the door.

"You're all right?"

"Sure. Can I come in?"

He went inside. Kelly closed the door behind him. "I'm glad to see you. The city's swarming with SP men. Almost every block. And the patrols — "

"I know. I saw a couple at the spaceport." Jennings sat down on the couch. "It's good to be back, though."

"I was afraid they might stop all the Intercity flights and check through the passengers."

"They have no reason to assume I'd be coming into the city."

"I didn't think of that." Kelly sat down across from him. "Now, what comes next? Now that you have got away with the material, what are you going to do?"

"Next I meet Rethrick and spring the news on him. The news that the person who escaped from the Plant was myself. He knows that someone got away, but he doesn't know who it was. Undoubtedly, he assumes it was an SP man."

"Couldn't he use the time mirror to find out?"

A shadow crossed Jennings' face. "That's so. I didn't think of that." He rubbed his jaw, frowning. "In any case, I have the material. Or, you have the material."

Kelly nodded.

"All right. We'll go ahead with our plans. Tomorrow we'll see Rethrick. We'll see him here, in New York. Can you get him down to the Office? Will he come if you send for him?"

"Yes. We have a code. If I ask him to come, he'll come."

"Fine. I'll meet him there. When he realizes that we have the picture and schematics he'll have to agree to my demands. He'll have to let me into Rethrick Construction, on my own terms. It's either that, or face the possibility of having the material turned over to the Security Police."

"And once you're in? Once Rethrick agrees to your demands?"

"I saw enough at the Plant to convince me that Rethrick is far bigger than I had realized. How big, I don't know. No wonder *he* was so interested!"

"You're going to demand equal control of the Company?"

Jennings nodded.

"You would never be satisfied to go back as a mechanic, would you? The way you were before."

"No. To get booted out again?" Jennings smiled. "Anyhow, I know *he* intended better things than that. *He* laid careful plans. The trinkets. He must have planned everything long in advance. No, I'm not going back as a mechanic. I saw a lot there, level after level of machines and men. They're doing something. And I want to be in on it."

Kelly was silent.

"See?" Jennings said.

"I see."

He left the apartment, hurrying along the dark street. He had stayed there too long. If the SP found the two of them together it would be all up with Rethrick Construction. He could take no chances, with the end almost in sight.

He looked at his watch. It was past midnight. He would meet Rethrick this morning, and present him with the proposition. His spirits rose as he walked. He would be safe. More than safe. Rethrick Construction was aiming at something far larger than mere industrial power. What he had seen had convinced him that a revolution was brewing. Down in the many levels below the ground, down under the fortress of concrete, guarded by guns and armed men, Rethrick was planning a war. Machines were being turned out. The time scoop and the mirror were hard at work, watching, dipping, extracting.

No wonder *he* had worked out such careful plans. *He* had seen all this and understood, begun to ponder. The problem of the mind cleaning. His memory would be gone when he was released. Destruction of all the plans.

Destruction? There was the alternate clause in the contract. Others had seen it, used it. But not the way *he* intended!

He was after much more than anyone who had come before. *He* was the first to understand, to plan. The seven trinkets were a bridge to something beyond anything that —

At the end of the block an SP cruiser pulled up to the curb. Its doors slid open.

Jennings stopped, his heart constricting. The night patrol, roaming through the city. It was after eleven, after curfew. He looked quickly around. Everything was dark. The stores and houses were shut up tight, locked for the night. Silent apartment houses, buildings. Even the bars were dark.

He looked back the way he had come. Behind him, a second SP cruiser had stopped. Two SP officers had stepped out onto the curb. They had seen him. They were coming toward him. He stood frozen, looking up and down the street.

Across from him was the entrance of a swank hotel, its neon sign glimmering. He began to walk toward it, his heels echoing against the pavement.

"Stop!" one of the SP men called. "Come back here. What are you doing out? What's your — "

Jennings went up the stairs, into the hotel. He crossed the lobby. The clerk was staring at him. No one else was around. The lobby was deserted. His heart sank. He didn't have a chance. He began to run aimlessly, past the desk, along a carpeted hall. Maybe it led out some back way. Behind him, the SP men had already entered the lobby.

Jennings turned a corner. Two men stepped out, blocking his way.

"Where are you going?"

He stopped, wary. "Let me by." He reached into his coat for the Boris gun. At once the men moved.

"Get him."

His arms were pinned to his sides. Professional hoods. Past them he could see light. Light and sound. Some kind of activity. People.

"All right," one of the hoods said. They dragged him back along the corridor, toward the lobby. Jennings struggled futilely. He had entered a blind alley. Hoods, a joint. The city was dotted with them, hidden in the darkness. The swank hotel a front. They would toss him out, into the hands of the SP.

Some people came along the halls, a man and a woman. Older people. Well dressed. They gazed curiously at Jennings, suspended between the two men.

Suddenly Jennings understood. A wave of relief hit him, blinding him. "Wait," he said thickly. "My pocket."

"Come on."

"Wait. Look. My right pocket. Look for yourselves."

He relaxed, waiting. The hood on his right reached, dipping cautiously into the pocket. Jennings smiled. It was over. *He* had seen even this. There was no possibility of failure. This solved one problem: where to stay until it was time to meet Rethrick. He could stay here.

The hood brought out the half poker chip, examining the serrated edges. "Just a second." From his own coat he took a matching chip, fitting on a gold chain. He touched the edges together.

"All right?" Jennings said.

"Sure." They let him go. He brushed off his coat automatically. "Sure, mister. Sorry. Say, you should have — "

"Take me in the back," Jennings said, wiping his face. "Some people are looking for me. I don't particularly want them to find me."

"Sure." They led him back, into the gambling rooms. The half chip had turned what might have been a disaster into an asset. A gambling and girl joint. One of the few institutions the Police left alone. He was safe. No question of that. Only one thing remained. The struggle with Rethrick!

Rethrick's face was hard. He gazed at Jennings, swallowing rapidly.

"No," he said. "I didn't know it was you. We thought it was the SP."

There was silence. Kelly sat at the chair by her desk, her legs crossed, a cigarette between her fingers. Jennings leaned against the door, his arms folded.

"Why didn't you use the mirror?" he said.

Rethrick's face flickered. "The mirror? You did a good job, my friend. We *tried* to use the mirror."

"Tried?"

"Before you finished your term with us you changed a few leads inside the mirror. When we tried to operate it nothing happened. I left the plant half an hour ago. They were still working on it."

"I did that before I finished my two years?"

"Apparently you had worked out your plans in detail. You know that with the mirror we would have no trouble tracking you down. You're a good mechanic, Jennings. The best we ever had. We'd like to have you back, sometime. Working for us again. There's not one of us that can operate the mirror the way you could. And right now, we can't use it at all."

Jennings smiled. "I had no idea *he* did anything like that. I underestimated him. *His* protection was even — "

"Who are you talking about?"

"Myself. During the two years. I use the objective. It's easier."

"Well, Jennings. So the two of you worked out an elaborate plan to steal our schematics. Why? What's the purpose? You haven't turned them over to the Police."

"No."

"Then I can assume it's blackmail."

"That's right."

"What for? What do you want?" Rethrick seemed to have aged. He slumped, his eyes small and glassy, rubbing his chin nervously. "You went to a lot of trouble to get us into this position. I'm curious why. While you were working for us you laid the groundwork. Now you've completed it, in spite of our precautions."

"Precautions?"

"Erasing your mind. Concealing the Plant."

"Tell him," Kelly said. "Tell him why you did it."

Jennings took a deep breath. "Rethrick, I did it to get back in. Back to the Company. That's the only reason. No other."

Rethrick stared at him. "To get back into the Company? You can come back in. I told you that." His voice was thin and sharp, edged with strain. "What's the matter with you? You can come back in. For as long as you want to stay."

"As a mechanic."

"Yes. As a mechanic. We employ many — "

"I don't want to come back as a mechanic. I'm not interested in working for you. Listen, Rethrick. The SP picked me up as soon as I left this Office. If it hadn't been for *him* I'd be dead."

"They picked you up?"

"They wanted to know what Rethrick Construction does. They wanted me to tell them."

Rethrick nodded. "That's bad. We didn't know that."

"No, Rethrick. I'm not coming in as an employee you can toss out any time it pleases you. I'm coming in with you, not for you."

"With me?" Rethrick stared at him. Slowly a film settled over his face, an ugly hard film. "I don't understand what you mean."

"You and I are going to run Rethrick Construction together. That'll be the way, from now on. And no one will be burning my memory out, for their own safety."

"That's what you want?"

"Yes."

"And if we don't cut you in?"

"Then the schematics and films go to the SP. It's as simple as that. But I don't want to. I don't want to destroy the Company. I want to get into the Company! I want to be safe. You don't know what it's like, being out there, with no place to go. An individual has no place to turn to, anymore. No one to help him. He's caught between two ruthless forces, a pawn between political and economic powers. And I'm tired of being a pawn."

For a long time Rethrick said nothing. He stared down at the floor, his face dull and blank. At last he looked up. "I know it's that way. That's something I've known for a long time. Longer than you have. I'm a lot older than you. I've seen it come, grow that way, year after year. That's why Rethrick Construction exists. Someday, it'll be all different. Someday, when we have the scoop and the mirror finished. When the weapons are finished."

Jennings said nothing.

"I know very well how it is! I'm an old man. I've been working a long time. When they told me someone had got out of the Plant with schematics, I thought the end had come. We already knew you had damaged the mirror. We knew there was a connection, but we had parts figured wrong.

"We thought, of course, that Security had planted you with us, to find out what we were doing. Then, when you realized you couldn't carry out your information, you damaged the mirror. With the mirror damaged, SP could go ahead and — "

He stopped, rubbing his cheek.

"Go on," Jennings said.

"So you did this alone … Blackmail. To get into the Company. You don't know what the Company is for, Jennings! How dare you try to come in! We've been working and building for a long time. You'd wreck us, to save your hide. You'd destroy us, just to save yourself."

"I'm not wrecking you. I can be a lot of help."

"I run the Company alone. It's my Company. I made it, put it together. It's mine."

Jennings laughed. "And what happens when you die? Or is the revolution going to come in your own lifetime?"

Rethrick's head jerked up.

"You'll die, and there won't be anyone to go on. You know I'm a good mechanic. You said so yourself. You're a fool, Rethrick. You want to manage it all yourself. Do everything, decide everything. But you'll die, someday. And then what will happen?"

There was silence.

"You better let me in — for the Company's good, as well as my own. I can do a lot for you. When you're gone the Company will survive in my hands. And maybe the revolution will work."

"You should be glad you're alive at all! If we hadn't allowed you to take your trinkets out with you — "

"What else could you do? How could you let men service your mirror, see their own futures, and not let them lift a finger to help themselves. It's easy to see why you were forced to insert the alternate-payment clause. You had no choice."

"You don't even know what we are doing. Why we exist."

"I have a good idea. After all, I worked for you two years."

Time passed. Rethrick moistened his lips again and again, rubbing his cheek. Perspiration stood out on his forehead. At last he looked up.

"No," he said. "It's no deal. No one will ever run the Company but me. If I die, it dies with me. It's my property."

Jennings became instantly alert. "Then the papers go to the Police."

Rethrick said nothing, but a peculiar expression moved across his face, an expression that gave Jennings a sudden chill.

"Kelly," Jennings said. "Do you have the papers with you?"

Kelly stirred, standing up. She put out her cigarette, her face pale. "No."

"Where are they? Where did you put them?"

"Sorry," Kelly said softly. "I'm not going to tell you."

He stared at her. "What?"

"I'm sorry," Kelly said again. Her voice was small and faint. "They're safe. The SP won't ever get them. But neither will you. When it's convenient, I'll turn them back to my father."

"Your father!"

"Kelly is my daughter," Rethrick said. "That was one thing you didn't count on, Jennings. *He* didn't count on it, either. No one knew that but the two of us. I wanted to keep all positions of trust in the family. I see now that it was a good idea. But it had to be kept secret. If the SP had guessed they would have picked her up at once. Her life wouldn't have been safe."

Jennings let his breath out slowly. "I see."

"It seemed like a good idea to go along with you," Kelly said. "Otherwise you'd have done it alone, anyhow. And you would have had the papers on you. As you said, if the SP caught you with the papers it would be the end of us. So I went along with you. As soon as you gave me the papers I put them in a good safe place." She smiled a little. "No one will find them but me. I'm sorry."

"Jennings, you can come in with us," Rethrick said. "You can work for us forever, if you want. You can have anything you want. Anything except — "

"Except that no one runs the Company but you."

"That's right. Jennings, the Company is old. Older than I am. I didn't bring it into existence. It was — you might say, *willed* to me. I took the burden on. The job of managing it, making it grow, moving it toward the day. The day of revolution, as you put it.

"My grandfather founded the Company, back in the twentieth century. The Company has always been in the family. And it will always be. Someday, when Kelly marries, there'll be an heir to carry it on after me. So that's taken care of. The Company was founded up in Maine, in a small New England town. My grandfather was a little old New Englander, frugal, honest, passionately independent. He had a little repair business of some sort, a little tool and fix-it place. And plenty of knack.

"When he saw government and big business closing in on everyone, he went underground. Rethrick Construction disappeared from the map. It took government quite a while to organize Maine, longer than most places. When the rest of the world had been divided up between international cartels and world-states, there was New England, still alive. Still free. And my grandfather and Rethrick Construction.

"He brought in a few men, mechanics, doctors, lawyers, little once-a-week newspapermen from the Middle West. The Company grew. Weapons appeared, weapons and knowledge. The time scoop and mirror! The Plant was built, secretly, at great cost, over a long period of time. The Plant is big. Big and deep. It goes down many more levels than you saw. *He* saw them, your alter ego. There's a lot of power there. Power, and men who've disappeared, purged all over the world, in fact. We got them first, the best of them.

"Someday, Jennings, we're going to break out. You see, conditions like this can't go on. People can't live this way, tossed back and forth by political and economic powers. Masses of people shoved this way and that according to the needs of this government or that cartel. There's going to be resistance, someday. A strong, desperate resistance. Not by big people, powerful people, but by little people. Bus drivers. Grocers. Vidscreen operators. Waiters. And that's where the Company comes in.

"We're going to provide them with the help they'll need, the tools, weapons, the knowledge. We're going to 'sell' them our services. They'll be able to hire us. And they'll need someone they can hire. They'll have a lot lined up against them. A lot of wealth and power."

There was silence.

"Do you see?" Kelly said. "That's why you mustn't interfere. It's Dad's Company. It's always been that way. That's the way Maine people are. It's part of the family. The Company belongs to the family. It's ours."

"Come in with us," Rethrick said. "As a mechanic. I'm sorry, but that's our limited outlook showing through. Maybe it's narrow, but we've always done things this way."

Jennings said nothing. He walked slowly across the office, his hands in his pockets. After a time he raised the blind and stared out at the street, far below.

Down below, like a tiny black bug, a Security cruiser moved along, drifting silently with the traffic that flowed up and down the street. It joined a second cruiser, already parked. Four SP men were standing by it in their green uniforms, and even as he watched some more could be seen coming from across the street. He let the blind down.

"It's a hard decision to make," he said.

"If you go out there they'll get you," Rethrick said. "They're out there all the time. You haven't got a chance."

"Please — " Kelly said, looking up at him.

Suddenly Jennings smiled. "So you won't tell me where the papers are. Where you put them."

Kelly shook her head.

"Wait." Jennings reached into his pocket. He brought out a small piece of paper. He unfolded it slowly, scanning it. "By any chance did you deposit it with the Dunne National Bank, about three o'clock yesterday afternoon? For safekeeping in their storage vaults?"

Kelly gasped. She grabbed her handbag, unsnapping it. Jennings put the slip of paper, the parcel receipt, back in his pocket. "So *he* saw even that," he murmured. "The last of the trinkets. I wondered what it was for."

Kelly groped frantically in her purse, her face wild. She brought out a slip of paper, waving it.

"You're wrong! Here it is! It's still here." She relaxed a little. "I don't know what *you* have, but this is — "

In the air above them something moved. A dark space formed, a circle. The space stirred. Kelly and Rethrick stared up, frozen.

From the dark circle a claw appeared, a metal claw, joined to a shimmering rod. The claw dropped, swinging in a wide arc. The claw swept the paper from Kelly's fingers. It hesitated for a second. Then it drew itself up again, disappearing with the paper, into the circle of black. Then, silently, the claw and the rod and the circle blinked out. There was nothing. Nothing at all.

"Where — where did it go?" Kelly whispered. "The paper. What was that?"

Jennings patted his pocket. "It's safe. It's safe, right here. I wondered when *he* would show up. I was beginning to worry."

Rethrick and his daughter stood, shocked into silence.

"Don't look so unhappy," Jennings said. He folded his arms. "The paper's safe — and the Company's safe. When the time comes it'll be there, strong and very glad to help out the revolution. We'll see to that, all of us, you, me and your daughter."

He glanced at Kelly, his eyes twinkling. "All three of us. And maybe by that time there'll be even *more* members to the family!"

THE GREAT C

HE WAS NOT TOLD the questions until just before it was time to leave. Walter Kent drew him aside from the others. Putting his hands on Meredith's shoulders, he looked intently into his face.

"Remember that no one has ever come back. If you come back you'll be the first. The first in fifty years."

Tim Meredith nodded, nervous and embarrassed, but grateful for Kent's words. After all, Kent was the Tribe Leader, an impressive old man with iron-gray hair and beard. There was a patch over his right eye, and he carried two knives at his belt, instead of the usual one. And it was said he had knowledge of letters.

"The trip itself takes not much over a day. We're giving you a pistol. There are bullets, but no one knows how many of them are good. You have your food?"

Meredith fumbled in his pack. He brought out a metal can with a key attached. "This should be enough," he said, turning the can over.

"And water?"

Meredith rattled his canteen.

"Good." Kent studied the young man. Meredith was dressed in leather boots, a hide coat, and leggings. His head was protected by a rusty metal helmet. Around his neck binoculars hung from a rawhide cord. Kent touched the heavy gloves that covered Meredith's hands. "That's the last pair of those," he said. "We won't see anything like them again."

"Shall I leave them behind?"

"We'll hope they — and you — come back." Kent took him by the arm and moved even farther away, so that no one would hear. The rest of the tribe, the men and women and children, stood silently together at the lip of the Shelter, watching. The Shelter was concrete, reinforced by poles that had been cut from time to time. Once, in a remote past, a network of leaves and branches had been suspended over the lip, but that had all rotted away as the wires corroded and broke. Anyhow, there was nothing in the sky these days to notice a small circle of concrete, the entrance to the vast underground chambers in which the tribe lived.

"Now," Kent said. "The three questions." He leaned close to Meredith. "You have a good memory?"

"Yes," Meredith said.

"How many books have you committed to memory?"

"I've only had six books read to me," Meredith murmured. "But I know them all."

"That's enough. All right, listen. We've been a whole year deciding on these questions. Unfortunately we can ask only three, so we've chosen carefully." And, so saying, he whispered the questions into Meredith's ear.

There was silence afterward. Meredith thought over the questions, turning them around in his mind. "Do you think the Great C will be able to answer them?" he said at last.

"I don't know. They're difficult questions."

Meredith nodded. "They are. Let's pray."

Kent slapped him on the shoulder. "All right, then. You're ready to go. If everything goes right, you'll be back here in two days. We'll be watching for you. Good luck, boy."

"Thanks," Meredith said. He walked slowly back to the others. Bill Gustavson handed him the pistol without a word, his eyes gleaming with emotion.

"A compass," John Page said, stepping away from his woman. He handed a small military compass to Meredith. His woman, a young brunette captured from a neighboring tribe, smiled encouragingly at him.

"Tim!"

Meredith turned. Anne Fry was running toward him. He reached out, taking hold of her hands. "I'll be all right," he said. "Don't worry."

"Tim." She looked up at him wildly. "Tim, you be careful. Will you?"

"Of course." He grinned, running his hand awkwardly through her thick short hair. "I'll come back." But in his heart there was a coldness, a block of hardening ice. The chill of death. He pulled suddenly away from her. "Goodbye," he said to all of them.

The tribe turned and walked away. He was alone. There was nothing to do but go. He ran over the three questions once more. Why had they picked him? But someone had to go and ask. He moved toward the edge of the clearing.

"Good-bye," Kent shouted, standing with his sons.

Meredith waved. A moment later he plunged into the forest, his hand on his knife, the compass clutched tightly to him.

* * *

He walked steadily, swinging the knife from side to side, cutting creepers and branches that got in his way. Occasionally huge insects scurried in the grass ahead of him. Once he saw a purple beetle, almost as large as his fist. Had there been such things before the Smash? Probably not. One of the books he had learned was about lifeforms in the world, before the Smash. He could not remember anything about large insects. Animals were kept in herds and killed regularly, he recalled. No one hunted or trapped.

That night he camped on a slab of concrete, the foundation of a building that no longer existed. Twice he awoke, hearing things moving nearby, but nothing approached him, and when the sun appeared again he was unharmed. He opened his ration tin and ate from it. Then he gathered up his things and went on. Toward the middle of the day the counter at his waist began to tick ominously. He stopped, breathing deeply and considering.

He was getting near the ruins, all right. From now on he could expect radiation pools continually. He patted the counter. It was a good thing to have. Presently he advanced a short distance, walking carefully. The ticking died; he had passed the pool. He went up a slope, cutting his way through the creepers. A horde of butterflies rose up in his face and he slashed at them. He came to the top and stood, raising the binoculars to his eyes.

Far off, there was a splash of black in the center of the endless expanse of green. A burned-out place. A great swathe of ruined land, fused metal and concrete. He caught his breath. This was the ruins; he was getting close. For the first time in his life he was actually seeing the remains of a city, the pillars and rubble that had once been buildings and streets.

A wild thought leaped through his mind. He could hide, not go on! He could lie in the bushes and wait. Then, when everyone thought he was dead, when the tribe scouts had gone back, he could slip north, past them, beyond and away.

North. There was another tribe there, a large tribe. With them he would be safe. There was no way they could find him, and anyhow, the northern tribe had bombs and bacteriaspheres. If he could get to them —

No. He took a deep shuddering breath. It was wrong. He had been *sent* on this trip. Each year a youth went, as he was going now, with three carefully-planned questions. Difficult questions. Questions that no man knew answers for. He ran the questions over in his mind. Would the Great C be able to answer them? All three of them? It was said the Great C knew everything. For a century it had answered questions, within its vast ruined house. If he did not go, if no youth were sent — He shuddered. It would make a second Smash, like the one before. It had done it once; it could do it again. He had no choice but to go on.

Meredith lowered his binoculars. He set off, down the side of the slope. A rat ran by him, a huge gray rat. He drew his knife quickly, but the rat went on. Rats — they were bad. They carried the germs.

Half an hour after his counter clicked again, this time with wild frenzy. He retreated. A pit of ruins yawned ahead, a bomb crater, not yet overgrown. It would be better to go around it. He circled off to one side, moving slowly, warily. Once the counter clicked, but that was all. A fast burst, like bullets flying. Then silence. He was safe.

Later in the day he ate more of his rations and sipped water from the canteen. It would not be long. Before nightfall he would be there. He would go down the ruined streets, toward the sprawling mass of stone and columns that was *its* house. He would mount the steps. It had been described to him many times. Each stone was carefully listed on the map back at the Shelter. He knew by heart the street that led there, to the house. He knew how the great doors lay on their faces, broken and split. He knew how the dark, empty corridors would look inside. He would pass into the vast chamber, the dark room of bats and spiders and echoing sounds. And there it would be. The Great C. Waiting silently, waiting to hear the questions. Three — just three. It would hear them. Then it would ponder, consider. Inside, it would whirr and flash. Parts, rods, switches and coils would move. Relays would open and shut.

Would it know the answers?

He went on. Far ahead, beyond miles of tangled forest land, the outline of the ruins grew.

The sun was beginning to set as he climbed the side of a hill of boulders and looked down at what had once been a city. He took his belt-light and snapped it on. The light dimmed and wavered; the little cells inside were almost gone. But he could see the ruined streets and heaps of rubble. The remains of a city in which his grandfather had lived.

He climbed down the boulders and dropped with a thud onto the street. His counter clicked angrily, but he ignored it. There was no other entrance. This was the only way. On the other side a wall of slag cut off everything. He walked slowly, breathing deeply. In the twilight gloom a few birds perched on the stones, and once in a while a lizard slithered off, disappearing into a crack. There was life here, of a sort. Birds and lizards that had adapted themselves to crawling among the bones and remains of buildings. But nothing else came this way, no tribes, no large animals. Most life, even the wild dogs, stayed away from this kind of place. And he could see why.

On he went, flashing his feeble light from side to side. He skirted a gaping hole, part of an underground shelter. Ruined guns stuck up starkly on each side of him, their barrels bent and warped. He had never fired a gun, himself. Their tribe had very few metal weapons. They depended mostly on what they could make, spears and darts. Bows and arrows. Stone clubs.

A colossus rose up before him. The remains of an enormous building. He flashed his light up, but the beam did not carry far enough for him to make it out. Was this the house? No. It was farther. He went on, stepping over what had once been a street barricade, slats of metal, bags of spilled sand, barbed wire.

A moment later he came to it.

He stopped, his hands on his hips, staring up the concrete steps at the black cavity that was the door. He was there. In a moment there would be no turning back. If he went on now, he would be committed. He would have made his decision as soon as his boots touched the steps. It was only a short distance beyond the gaping door, down a winding corridor, in the center of the building.

For a long time Meredith stood, deep in thought, rubbing his black beard. What should he do? Should he run, turn and go back the way he had come? He could shoot enough animals with his gun to stay alive. Then north —

No. They were counting on him to ask the three questions. If he did not, then someone else would have to come later on. There was no turning back. The decision had already been made. It had been made when he had been chosen. Now it was far too late.

He started up the rubbled steps, flashing his light ahead. At the entrance he stopped. Above him were some words, cut in the concrete. He knew a few letters, himself. Could he make these out? Slowly, he spelled: FEDERAL RESEARCH STATION 7 SHOW PERMIT ON DEMAND

The words meant nothing to him. Except, perhaps, the word "federal." He had heard it before, but he could not place it. He shrugged. It did not matter. He went on.

It took only a few minutes to negotiate the corridors. Once, he turned right by mistake and found himself in a sagging courtyard, littered with stones and wiring, overgrown with dark, sticky weeds. But after that he went correctly, touching the wall with his hand to keep from making a wrong turn. Occasionally his counter ticked, but he ignored it. At last a rush of dry, fetid air blew up in his face and the concrete wall beside him abruptly ended. He was there. He flashed his light around him. Ahead was an aperture, an archway. This was it. He looked up. More words, this time on a metal plate bolted to the concrete.

DIVISION OF COMPUTATION
ONLY AUTHORIZED PERSONNEL ADMITTED
ALL OTHERS KEEP OUT

He smiled. Words, signs. Letters. All gone, all forgotten. He went on, passing through the arch. More air blew around him, rushing past him. A startled bat flapped past. By the ring of his boots he knew that the chamber was huge, larger than he had imagined. He stumbled over something and stopped quickly, flashing his light.

At first he could not make out what they were. The chamber was filled with things, rows of things, upright, crumbling, hundreds of them. He stood, frowning and puzzling. What were they? Idols? Statues? Then he understood. They were things to sit on. Rows of chairs, rotting away, breaking into bits. He kicked at one and it fell into a heap, dust rising in a cloud, dispersing into the darkness. He laughed out loud.

"Who is there?" a voice came.

He froze. His mouth opened, but no sound came. Sweat rose on his skin, tiny drops of icy sweat. He swallowed, rubbing his lips with stiff fingers.

"Who is there?" the voice came again, a metallic voice, hard and penetrating, without warmth to it. An emotionless voice. A voice of steel and brass. Relays and switches.

The Great C!

He was afraid, more afraid than ever in his life. His body was shaking terribly. Awkwardly, he moved down the aisle, past the ruined seats, flashing his light ahead.

A bank of lights glimmered, far ahead, above him. There was a whirr. The Great C was coming to life, aware of him, rousing itself from its lethargy. More lights winked into life, more sounds of switches and relays.

"Who are you?" it said.

"I — I've come with questions." Meredith stumbled forward, toward the bank of lights. He struck a metal rail and reeled back, trying to regain his balance. "Three questions. I must ask you."

There was silence.

"Yes," the Great C said finally. "It is time for the questions again. You have prepared them for me?"

"Yes. They are very difficult. I don't think that you will find them easy. Maybe you won't be able to answer them. We — "

"I will answer. I have always answered. Come up closer."

Meredith moved down the aisle, avoiding the rail.

"Yes, I will know. You think they will be difficult. You people have no conception of the questions put to me in times past. Before the Smash I answered questions that you could not even conceive. I answered questions that took days of calculating. It would have taken men months to find the same answers on their own."

Meredith began to pluck up some courage. "Is it true," he said, "that men came from all over the world to ask you questions?"

"Yes. Scientists from everywhere asked me things, and I answered them. There was nothing I didn't know."

"How — how did you come into existence?"

"Is that one of your three questions?"

"No." Meredith shook his head quickly. "No, of course not."

"Come nearer," the Great C said. "I can't make your form out. You are from the tribe just beyond the city?"

"Yes."

"How many are there of you?"

"Several hundred."

"You're growing."

"There are more children all the time." Meredith swelled a little, with pride. "I, myself, have had children by eight women."

"Marvelous," the Great C said, but Meredith could not tell how it meant it. There was a moment of silence.

"I have a gun," Meredith said. "A pistol."

"Do you?"

He lifted it. "I've never fired a pistol before. We have bullets, but I don't know if they still work."

"What is your name?" the Great C said.

"Meredith. Tim Meredith."

"You are a young man, of course."

"Yes. Why?"

"I can see you fairly well," the Great C said, ignoring his question. "Part of my equipment was destroyed in the Smash but I can still see a little. Originally, I scanned mathematical questions visually. It saved time. I see you are wearing a helmet and binoculars. And army boots. Where did you get them? Your tribe does not make such things, does it?"

"No. They were found in underground lockers."

"Military equipment left over from the Smash," the Great C said. "United Nations equipment, by the color."

"Is it true that — that you could make a second Smash come? Like the first? Could you really do it again?"

"Of course! I could do it any time. Right now."

"How?" Meredith asked cautiously. "Tell me how."

"The same way as before," the Great C said vaguely. "I did it before — as your tribe well knows."

"Our legends tell us that all the world was put to the fire. Made suddenly terrible by — by atoms. And that you invented atoms, delivered them to the world. Brought them down from above. But we do not know *how* it was done."

"I will never tell you. It is too terrible for you ever to know. It is better forgotten."

"Certainly, if you say so," Meredith murmured. "Man has always listened to you. Come and asked and listened."

The Great C was silent. "You know," it said presently, "I have existed a long time. I remember life before the Smash. I could tell you many things about it. Life was much different then. You wear a beard and hunt animals in the woods. Before the Smash there were no woods. Only cities and farms. And men were clean-shaven. Many of them wore white clothing, then. They were scientists. They were very fine. I was constructed by scientists."

"What happened to them?"

"They left," the Great C said vaguely. "Do you recognize the name, Einstein? Albert Einstein?"

"No."

"He was the greatest scientist. Are you sure you don't know the name?" The Great C sounded disappointed. "I answered questions even *he* could not have answered. There were other Computers, then, but none so grand as I."

Meredith nodded.

"What is your first question?" the Great C said. "Give it to me and I will answer it."

Sudden fear gripped Meredith, surging over him. His knees shook. "The first question?" He murmured. "Let me see. I must consider."

"Have you forgotten?"

"No. I must arrange them in order." He moistened his lips, stroking his black beard nervously. "Let me think. I'll give you the easiest one first. However, even *it* is very difficult. The Leader of the Tribe — "

"Ask."

Meredith nodded. He glanced up, swallowing. When he spoke his voice was dry and husky. "The first question. Where — where does — "

"Louder," the Great C said.

Meredith took a deep breath. "Where does the rain come from?" he said. There was silence.

"Do you know?" he said, waiting tensely. Rows of lights moved above him. The Great C was meditating, considering. It whirred, a low, throbbing sound. "Do you know the answer?"

"Rain comes originally from the earth, mostly from the oceans," the Great C said. "It rises into the air by a process of evaporation. The agent of the process is the heat of the sun. The moisture of the oceans ascends in the form of minute particles. These particles, when they are high enough, enter a colder band of air. At this point, condensation occurs. The moisture collects into great clouds. When a sufficient amount is collected the water descends again in drops. You call the drops rain."

Meredith rubbed his chin numbly, nodding. "I see." He nodded again. "That is the way it occurs?"

"Yes."

"You're sure?"

"Of course. What is the second question? That was not very hard. You have no conception of the knowledge and information that lies stored within me. Once, I answered questions the greatest minds of the world could not make out. At least, not as fast as I. What's the next question?"

"This is much more difficult." Meredith smiled weakly. The Great C had answered the question about rain, but surely it could not know the answer to this question. "Tell me," he said slowly. "Tell me if you can: What keeps the sun moving through the sky? Why doesn't it stop? Why doesn't it fall to the ground?"

The Great C gave a funny whirr, almost a laugh. "You will be astonished at the answer. The sun does not move. At least, what you see as motion is not motion at all. What you see is the motion of the earth as it revolves around the sun. Since you are on the earth it seems as if you were standing still and the sun were moving. That is not so. All the nine planets, including the earth, revolve about the sun in regular elliptical orbits. They have been doing so for millions of years. Does that answer your question?

Meredith's heart constricted. He began to tremble violently. At last he managed to pull himself together. "I can hardly believe it. Are you telling the truth?"

"For me there is only truth," the Great C said. "It is impossible for me to lie. What is the third question?"

"Wait," Meredith said thickly. "Let me think a moment." He moved away. "I must consider."

"Why?"

"Wait." Meredith stepped back. He squatted down on the floor, staring dully ahead. It was not possible. The Great C had answered the first questions without trouble! But how could it know such things? How could anyone know things about the sun? About the sky? The Great C was imprisoned in its house. How could it know that the sun did not move? His mind reeled. How could it know about something it had not seen? Books, perhaps. He shook his head, trying to clear it. Perhaps, before the Smash, someone had read books on it. He scowled, setting his lips. Probably that was it. He stood up slowly.

"Are you ready now?" the Great C said. "Ask."

"You can't possibly answer this. No living creature could know. Here is the question. How did the world begin?" Meredith smiled. "You could not know. You did not exist before the world. Therefore, it is impossible that you could know."

"There are several theories," the Great C said calmly. "The most satisfactory is the nebular hypothesis. According to this, a gradually shrinking — "

Meredith listened, stunned, only half hearing the words. Could it be? Could the Great C really know how the world had been formed? He drew himself together, trying to catch the words.

" ... There are several ways to verify this theory, giving it credence over the others. Of the others, the most popular, although in disrepute of late, is the theory that a second star once approached our own, causing a violent — "

On and on the Great C went, warming up to its subject. Clearly, it enjoyed the question. Clearly, this was the type of question that had been asked of it in the dim past, before the Smash. All three questions, questions the Tribe had worked on for an entire year, had been easily answered. It did not seem possible. He was stunned.

The Great C finished. "Well?" it said. "Are you satisfied? You can see that I know the answers. Did you really imagine that I would not be able to answer?"

Meredith said nothing. He was dazed, terrified with shock and fear. Sweat ran down his face, into his beard. He opened his mouth, but no words came.

"And now," the Great C said, "since I have been able to answer the questions, please step forward."

Meredith moved forward stiffly, gazing ahead as if in a trance. Around him light appeared, flickering into life, illuminating the room. For the first time he saw the Great C. For the first time the darkness lifted.

The Great C lay on its raised dais, an immense cube of dull, corroded metal. Part of the roof above it had been broken open, and blocks of concrete had dented its right side. Metal tubes and parts lay scattered around on the dais, broken and twisted elements that had been severed by the falling roof.

Once, the Great C had been shiny. Now the cube was dirty and stained. Water had dripped through the broken roof, rain and dirt washed down the walls. Birds had flown down and perched on it, leaving feathers and filth behind. In the original destruction, most of the connecting wires had been cut, the wiring from the cube to the control panel.

And with the metal and wire remnants scattered and heaped around the dais were something else. Littering the dais in a circle before the Great C were piles of bones. Bones and parts of clothing, metal belt buckles, pins, a helmet, some knives, a ration tin.

Remains of the fifty youths who had come before, each with his three questions to ask. Each hoping, praying, that the Great C would not know the answers.

"Step up," the Great C said.

Meredith stepped up on the dais. Ahead of him a short metal ladder led to the top of the cube. He mounted the ladder without comprehension, his mind blank and dazed, moving like a machine. A portion of the metal surface of the cube grated, sliding back.

Meredith stared down. He was looking into a swirling vat of liquid. A vat within the bowels of the cube, in the very depths of the Great C. He hesitated, struggling suddenly, pulling back.

"Jump," the Great C said.

For a long moment Meredith stood on the edge, staring down into the vat, paralyzed with fear and horror. His head rang, his vision danced and blurred. The room began to tilt, spinning slowly around him. He was swaying, reeling back and forth.

"Jump," the Great C said.

He jumped.

A moment later the metal surface slid back into place. The surface of the cube was again unbroken.

Inside, in the depths of the machinery, the vat of hydrochloric acid swirled and eddied, plucking at the body lying inert within it. Presently the body began to dissolve, the component elements absorbed by pipes and ducts, flowing quickly to every part of the Great C. At last motion ceased. The vast cube became silent.

One by one the lights flickered out. The room was dark again.

The last act of absorption was the opening of a narrow slot in the front of the Great C. Something gray was expelled, ejected. Bones, and a metal helmet. They dropped into the piles before the cube, joining the refuse from the fifty who had come before. Then the last light went off and the machinery became silent. The Great C began its wait for the next year.

After the third day, Kent knew that the youth would not return. He came back to the Shelter with the Tribe scouts, his face dark, scowling and saying nothing.

"Another gone," Page said. "I was so damn sure it wouldn't be able to answer those three! A whole year's work gone."

"Will we always have to sacrifice to it?" Bill Gustavson asked. "Will this go on forever, year after year?"

"Some day, we'll find a question it can't answer," Kent said. "Then it'll let us alone. If we can stump it, then we won't have to feed it any more. If only we can find the right question!"

Anne Fry came toward him, her face white. "Walter?" she said.

"Yes?"

"Has it always been — been kept alive this way? Has it always depended on one of us to keep it going? I can't believe human beings were supposed to be used to keep a machine alive."

Kent shook his head. "Before the Smash it must have used some kind of artificial fuel. Then something happened. Maybe its fuel ducts were damaged or broken, and it changed its ways. I suppose it had to. It was like us, in that respect. We *all* changed our ways. There was a time when human beings didn't hunt and trap animals. And there was a time when the Great C didn't trap human beings."

"Why — why did it make the Smash, Walter?"

"To show it was stronger than we."

"Was it always so strong? Stronger than man?"

"No. They say that, once, there was no Great C. That man himself brought it to life, to tell him things. But gradually it grew stronger, until at last it brought down the atoms — and with the atoms, the Smash. Now it lives off us. Its power has made us slaves. It became too strong."

"But some day, the time will come when it won't know the answer," Page said.

"Then it will have to release us," Kent said, "according to tradition. It will have to stop using us for food."

Page clenched his fists, staring back across the forest. "Some day that time will come. Some day we'll find a question too hard for it!"

"Let's get started," Gustavson said grimly. "The sooner we begin preparing for next year, the better!"

OUT IN THE GARDEN

"THAT'S WHERE SHE IS," Robert Nye said. "As a matter of fact, she's always out there. Even when the weather's bad. Even in the rain."

"I see," his friend Lindquist said, nodding. The two of them pushed open the back door and stepped out onto the porch. The air was warm and fresh. They both stopped, taking a deep breath. Lindquist looked around. "Very nice-looking garden. It's really a garden, isn't it?" He shook his head. "I can understand her, now. Look at it!"

"Come along," Nye said, going down the steps onto the path. "She's probably sitting on the other side of the tree. There's an old seat in the form of a circle, like you used to see in the old days. She's probably sitting with Sir Francis."

"Sir Francis? Who's that?" Lindquist came along, hurrying behind him.

"Sir Francis is her pet duck. A big white duck." They turned down the path, past the lilac bushes, crowded over their great wooden frames. Rows of tulips in full bloom stretched out on both sides. A rose trellis stretched up the side of a small greenhouse. Lindquist stared in pleasure. Rose bushes, lilacs, endless shrubs and flowers. A wall of wisteria. A massive willow tree.

And sitting at the foot of the tree, gazing down at a white duck in the grass beside her, was Peggy.

Lindquist stood rooted to the spot, fascinated by Mrs. Nye's beauty. Peggy Nye was small, with soft dark hair and great warm eyes, eyes filled with a gentle, tolerant sadness. She was buttoned up in a little blue coat and suit, with sandals on her feet and flowers in her hair. Roses.

"Sweetheart," Nye said to her, "look who's here. You remember Tom Lindquist, don't you?"

Peggy looked up quickly. "Tommy Lindquist!" she exclaimed. "How are you? How nice it is to see you."

"Thanks." Lindquist shuffled a little in pleasure. "How have you been, Peg? I see you have a friend."

"A friend?"

"Sir Francis. That's his name, isn't it?"

Peggy laughed. "Oh, Sir Francis." She reached down and smoothed the duck's feathers. Sir Francis went on searching out spiders from the grass. "Yes, he's a very good friend of mine. But won't you sit down? How long are you staying?"

"He won't be here very long," her husband said. "He's driving through to New York on some kind of business."

"That's right," Lindquist said. "Say, you certainly have a wonderful garden here, Peggy. I remember you always wanted a nice garden, with lots of birds and flowers."

"It is lovely," Peggy said. "We're out here all the time."

"We?"

"Sir Francis and myself."

"They spend a lot of time together," Robert Nye said. "Cigarette?" He held out his pack to Lindquist. "No?" Nye lit one for himself. "Personally, I can't see anything in ducks, but I never was much on flowers and nature."

"Robert stays indoors and works on his articles," Peggy said. "Sit down, Tommy." She picked up the duck and put him on her lap. "Sit here, beside us."

"Oh, no," Lindquist said. "This is fine."

He became silent, looking down at Peggy and all the flowers, the grass, the silent duck. A faint breeze moved through the rows of iris behind the tree, purple and white iris. No one spoke. The garden was very cool and quiet. Lindquist sighed.

"What is it?" Peggy said.

"You know, all this reminds me of a poem." Lindquist rubbed his forehead. "Something by Yeats, I think."

"Yes, the garden is like that," Peggy said. "Very much like poetry."

Lindquist concentrated. "I know!" he said, laughing. "It's you and Sir Francis, of course. You and Sir Francis sitting there. 'Leda and the Swan'."

Peggy frowned. "Do I — "

"The swan was Zeus," Lindquist said. "Zeus took the shape of a swan to get near Leda while she was bathing. He — uh — made love to her in the shape of a swan. Helen of Troy was born — because of that, you see. The daughter of Zeus and Leda. How does it go ... 'A sudden blow: the great wings beating still above the staggering girl' — "

He stopped. Peggy was staring up at him, her face blazing. Suddenly she leaped up, pushing the duck from her path. She was trembling with anger.

"What is it?" Robert said. "What's wrong?"

"How dare you!" Peggy said to Lindquist. She turned and walked off quickly.

Robert ran after her, catching hold of her arm. "But what's the matter? What's wrong? That's just poetry!"

She pulled away. "Let me go."

He had never seen her so angry. Her face had become like ivory, her eyes like two stones. "But Peg—"

She looked up at him. "Robert," she said, "I *am* going to have a baby."

"What!"

She nodded. "I was going to tell you tonight. *He* knows." Her lips curled. "He knows. That's why he said it. Robert, make him leave! Please make him go!"

Nye nodded mechanically. "Sure, Peg. Sure. But—it's true? Really true? You're really going to have a baby?" He put his arms around her. "But that's wonderful! Sweetheart, that's marvelous. I never heard anything so marvelous. My golly! For heaven's sake. It's the most marvelous thing I ever heard."

He led her back toward the seat, his arm around her. Suddenly his foot struck something soft, something that leaped and hissed in rage. Sir Francis waddled away, half-flying, his beak snapping in fury.

"Tom!" Robert shouted. "Listen to this. Listen to something. Can I tell him, Peg? Is it all right?"

Sir Francis hissed furiously after him, but in the excitement no one noticed him, not at all.

It was a boy, and they named him Stephen. Robert Nye drove slowly home from the hospital, deep in thought. Now that he actually had a son his thoughts returned to that day in the garden, that afternoon Tom Lindquist had stopped by. Stopped by and quoted the line of Yeats that had made Peg so angry. There had been an air of cold hostility between himself and Sir Francis, after that. He had never been able to look at Sir Francis quite the same again.

Robert parked the car in front of the house and walked up the stone steps. Actually, he and Sir Francis had never gotten along, not since the first day they had brought him back from the country. It was Peg's idea from the beginning. She had seen the sign by the farmhouse —

Robert paused at the porch steps. How angry she had been at poor Lindquist. Of course, it was a tactless line to quote, but still... He pondered, frowning. How stupid it all was! He and Peg had been married three years. There was no doubt that she loved him, that she was faithful to him. True, they did not have much in common. Peg loved to sit out in the garden, reading or meditating, or feeding the birds. Or playing with Sir Francis.

Robert went around the side of the house, into the back yard, into the garden. Of course she loved him! She loved him and she was loyal to him. It was absurd to think that she might even consider — That Sir Francis might be —

He stopped. Sir Francis was at the far end of the garden, pulling up a worm. As he watched, the white duck gulped down the worm and went on, looking for insects in the grass, bugs and spiders. Suddenly the duck stopped, warily.

Robert crossed the garden. When Peg came back from the hospital she would be busy with little Stephen. This was the best time, all right. She would have her hands full. Sir Francis would be forgotten. With the baby and all —

"Come here," Robert said. He snatched up the duck. "That's the last worm for you from this garden."

Sir Francis squawked furiously, struggling to get away, pecking frantically. Robert carried him inside the house. He got a suitcase from the closet and put the duck into it. He snapped the lock closed and then wiped his face. What now? The farm? It was only a half hour's drive into the country. But could he find it again?

He could try. He took the suitcase out to the car and dropped it into the back seat. All the way, Sir Francis quacked loudly, first in rage, then later (as they drove along the highway) with growing misery and despair.

Robert said nothing.

Peggy said little about Sir Francis, once she understood that he was gone for good. She seemed to accept his absence, although she stayed unusually quiet for a week or so. But gradually she brightened up again, laughing and playing with little Stephen, taking him out in the sun to hold on her lap, running her fingers through his soft hair.

"It's just like *down*," Peggy said once. Robert nodded, jarred a little. Was it? More like corn silk, it seemed to him, but he said nothing.

Stephen grew, a healthy, happy baby, warmed by the sun, held in tender, loving arms hour after hour in the quiet garden, under the willow tree. After a few years he had grown into a sweet child, a child with large, dark eyes who played pretty much to himself, away from the other children, sometimes in the garden, sometimes in his room upstairs.

Stephen loved flowers. When the gardener was planting, Stephen went along with him, watching with great seriousness each handful of seeds as they went into the ground, or the poor little bits of plants wrapped in their moss, lowered gently into the warm soil.

He did not talk much. Sometimes Robert stopped his work and watched from the living room window, his hands in his pockets, smoking and studying the silent child playing by himself among the shrubs and grass. By the time he was five, Stephen was beginning to follow the stories in the great flat books that Peggy brought home to him. The two of them sat together in the garden, looking at the pictures, tracing the stories.

Robert watched them from the window, moody and silent. He was left out, deserted. How he hated to be on the outside of things! He had wanted a son for so long —

Suddenly doubt assailed him. Again he found himself thinking about Sir Francis and what Tom had said. Angrily, he pushed the thought aside. But the boy was so far from him! Wasn't there any way he could get across to him? Robert pondered.

One warm fall morning Robert went outdoors and stood by the back porch, breathing the air and looking around him. Peggy had gone to the store to shop and have her hair set. She would not be home for a long time.

Stephen was sitting by himself, at the little low table they had given him for his birthday, coloring pictures with his crayons. He was intent on his work, his small face lined with concentration. Robert walked toward him slowly, across the wet grass.

Stephen looked up, putting down his crayons. He smiled shyly, friendlily, watching the man coming toward him. Robert approached the table and stopped, smiling down, a little uncertain and ill at ease.

"What is it?" Stephen said.

"Do you mind if I join you?"

"No."

Robert rubbed his jaw. "Say, what is it you're doing?" he asked presently.

"Doing?"

"With the crayons."

"I'm drawing." Stephen held his picture up. It showed a great yellow shape, like a lemon. Stephen and he studied it together.

"What is it?" Robert said. "Still life?"

"It's the sun." Stephen put the picture back down and resumed his work. Robert watched him. How skillfully he worked! Now he was sketching in something green. Trees, probably. Maybe someday he would be a great painter. Like Grant Wood. Or Norman Rockwell. Pride stirred inside him.

"That looks good," he said.

"Thank you."

"Do you want to be a painter when you grow up? I used to do some drawing, myself. I did cartooning for the school newspaper. And I designed the emblem for our frat."

There was silence. Did Stephen get his ability from him? He watched the boy, studying his face. He did not look much like him; not at all. Again doubt filled his mind. Could it really be that — But Peg would never —

"Robert?" the boy said suddenly.

"Yes?"

"Who was Sir Francis?"

Robert staggered. "What? What do you mean! Why do you ask that?"

"I just wondered."

"What do you know about him? Where did you hear the name?"

Stephen went on working for a while. "I don't know. I think mother mentioned him. Who is he?"

"He's dead," Robert said. "He's been dead for some time. Your mother told you about him?"

"Perhaps it was you," Stephen said. "Somebody mentioned him."

"It wasn't me!"

"Then," Stephen said thoughtfully, "perhaps I dreamed about him. I think perhaps he came to be in a dream and spoke to me. That was it. I saw him in a dream."

"What did he look like?" Robert said, licking his lip nervously, unhappily.

"Like this," Stephen said. He held the picture up, the picture of the sun.

"How do you mean? Yellow?"

"No, he was white. Like the sun is, at noon. A terribly big white shape in the sky."

"In the sky?"

"He was flying across the sky. Like the sun at noon. All ablaze. In the dream, I mean."

Robert's face twisted, torn by misery and uncertainty. Had she told the child about him? Had she painted a picture for him, an idealized picture? The Duck God. The Great Duck in the Sky, descending all ablaze. Then perhaps it *was* so. Perhaps he was not really the boy's father. Perhaps — It was too much to bear.

"Well, I won't bother you any more." Robert said. He turned away, toward the house.

"Robert?" Stephen said.

"Yes?" He turned quickly.

"Robert, what are you going to do?"

Robert hesitated. "How do you mean, Stephen?"

The boy looked up from his work. His small face was calm and expressionless. "Are you going inside the house?"

"Yes. Why?"

"Robert, in a few minutes I'm going to do something secret. No one knows about it. Not even mother." Stephen hesitated, slyly studying the man's face. "Would — would you want to do it with me?"

"What is it?"

"I'm going to have a party in the garden here. A secret party. For myself alone."

"You want me to come?"

The boy nodded.

Wild happiness filled up Robert. "You want me to come to your party? It's a secret party? I won't tell anyone. Not even your mother! Of course I'll come." He rubbed his hands together, smiling in a flood of relief. "I'd be glad to come. Do you want me to bring something? Cookies? Cake? Milk? What do you want me to bring?"

"No." Stephen shook his head. "Go inside and wash your hands and I'll make the party ready." He stood up, putting the crayons away in the box. "But you can't tell anyone about it."

"I won't tell anyone," Robert said. "I'll go wash my hands. Thanks, Stephen. Thanks a lot. I'll be right back."

He hurried toward the house, his heart thumping with happiness. Maybe the boy was his after all! A secret party, a private, secret party. And not even Peg knew about it. It was his boy, all right! There was no doubt of that. From now on he would spend time with Stephen whenever Peg left the house. Tell him stories. How he was in North Africa during the war. Stephen would be interested in that. How he had seen Field Marshal Montgomery, once. And the German pistol he had picked up. And his photographs.

Robert went inside the house. Peg never let him do that, tell stories to the boy. But he would, by golly! He went to the sink and washed his hands. He grinned. It was his kid, all right.

There was a sound. Peg came into the kitchen with her arms full of groceries. She set them on the table with a sigh. "Hello, Robert," she said. "What are you doing?"

His heart sank. "Home?" he murmured. "So soon? I thought you were going to get your hair fixed."

Peggy smiled, small and pretty in her green dress and hat and high heeled shoes. "I have to go back. I just wanted to bring the groceries home first."

"Then you're leaving again?"

She nodded. "Why? You look so excited. Is something going on? What is it?"

"Nothing," Robert said. He dried his hands. "Nothing at all." He grinned foolishly.

"I'll see you later today," Peggy said. She went back into the living room. "Have a good time while I'm gone. Don't let Stephen stay in the garden too long."

"No. No, I won't." Robert waited, listening until he heard the sound of the front door closing. Then he hurried back out onto the porch and down the steps, into the garden. He hurried through the flowers.

Stephen had cleared off the little low table. The crayons and paper were gone, and in their place were two bowls, each on a plate. A chair was pulled up for him. Stephen watched him come across the grass and toward the table.

"What took you so long?" Stephen said impatiently. "I've already started." He went on eating avidly, his eyes gleaming. "I couldn't wait."

"That's all right," Robert said. "I'm glad you went ahead." He sat down on the little chair eagerly. "Is it good? What is it? Something extra nice?"

Stephen nodded, his mouth full. He went on, helping himself rapidly from his bowl with his hands. Robert looked down at his own plate, grinning.

His grin died. Sickened misery filled his heart. He opened his mouth, but no words came. He pushed his chair back, standing up.

"I don't think I want any," he murmured. He turned away. "I think maybe I'll go back in."

"Why?" Stephen said, surprised, stopping a moment.

"I — never cared for worms and spiders," Robert said. He went slowly back, into the house again.

THE KING OF THE ELVES

IT WAS RAINING and getting dark. Sheets of water blew along the row of pumps at the edge of the filling station; the tree across the highway bent against the wind.

Shadrach Jones stood just inside the doorway of the little building, leaning against an oil drum. The door was open and gusts of rain blew in onto the wood floor. It was late; the sun had set, and the air was turning cold. Shadrach reached into his coat and brought out a cigar. He bit the end off it and lit it carefully, turning away from the door. In the gloom, the cigar burst into life, warm and glowing. Shadrach took a deep draw. He buttoned his coat around him and stepped out onto the pavement.

"Darn," he said. "What a night!" Rain buffeted him, wind blew at him. He looked up and down the highway, squinting. There were no cars in sight. He shook his head, locked up the gasoline pumps.

He went back into the building and pulled the door shut behind him. He opened the cash register and counted the money he'd taken in during the day. It was not much.

Not much, but enough for one old man. Enough to buy him tobacco and firewood and magazines, so that he could be comfortable as he waited for the occasional cars to come by. Not very many cars came along the highway any more. The highway had begun to fall into disrepair; there were many cracks in its dry, rough surface, and most cars preferred to take the big state highway that ran beyond the hills. There was nothing in Derryville to attract them, to make them turn toward it. Derryville was a small town, too small to bring in any of the major industries, too small to be very important to anyone. Sometimes hours went by without —

329

Shadrach tensed. His fingers closed over the money. From outside came a sound, the melodic ring of the signal wire stretched along the pavement.

Dinggg!

Shadrach dropped the money into the till and pushed the drawer closed. He stood up slowly and walked toward the door, listening. At the door, he snapped off the light and waited in the darkness, staring out.

He could see no car there. The rain was pouring down, swirling with the wind; clouds of mist moved along the road. And something was standing beside the pumps.

He opened the door and stepped out. At first, his eyes could make nothing out. Then the old man swallowed uneasily.

Two tiny figures stood in the rain, holding a kind of platform between them. Once, they might have been gaily dressed in bright garments, but now their clothes hung limp and sodden, dripping in the rain. They glanced half-heartedly at Shadrach. Water streaked their tiny faces, great drops of water. Their robes blew about them with the wind, lashing and swirling.

On the platform, something stirred. A small head turned wearily, peering at Shadrach. In the dim light, a rain-streaked helmet glinted dully.

"Who are you?" Shadrach said.

The figure on the platform raised itself up. "I'm the King of the Elves and I'm wet."

Shadrach stared in astonishment.

"That's right," one of the bearers said. "We're all wet."

A small group of Elves came straggling up, gathering around their king. They huddled together forlornly, silently.

"The King of the Elves," Shadrach repeated. "Well, I'll be darned."

Could it be true? They were very small, all right, and their dripping clothes were strange and oddly colored.

But *Elves?*

"I'll be darned. Well, whatever you are, you shouldn't be out on a night like this."

"Of course not," the king murmured. "No fault of our own. No fault ... " His voice trailed off into a choking cough. The Elf soldiers peered anxiously at the platform.

"Maybe you better bring him inside," Shadrach said. "My place is up the road. He shouldn't be out in the rain."

"Do you think we like being out on a night like this?" one of the bearers muttered. "Which way is it? Direct us."

Shadrach pointed up the road. "Over there. Just follow me. I'll get a fire going."

He went down the road, feeling his way onto the first of the flat stone steps that he and Phineas Judd had laid during the summer. At the top of the steps, he looked back. The platform was coming slowly along, swaying a little from side to side. Behind it, the Elf soldiers picked their way, a tiny column of silent dripping creatures, unhappy and cold.

"I'll get the fire started," Shadrach said. He hurried them into the house.

Wearily, the Elf King lay back against the pillow. After sipping hot chocolate, he had relaxed and his heavy breathing sounded suspiciously like a snore. Shadrach shifted in discomfort.

"I'm sorry," the Elf King said suddenly, opening his eyes. He rubbed his forehead. "I must have drifted off. Where was I?"

"You should retire, Your Majesty," one of the soldiers said sleepily. "It is late and these are hard times."

"True," the Elf King said, nodding. "Very true." He looked up at the towering figure of Shadrach, standing before the fireplace, a glass of beer in his hand. "Mortal, we thank you for your hospitality. Normally, we do not impose on human beings."

"It's those Trolls," another of the soldiers said, curled up on a cushion of the couch.

"Right," another soldier agreed. He sat up, groping for his sword. "Those reeking Trolls, digging and croaking — "

"You see," the Elf King went on," as our party was crossing from the Great Low Steps toward the Castle, where it lies in the hollow of the Towering Mountains — "

"You mean Sugar Ridge," Shadrach supplied helpfully.

"The Towering Mountains. Slowly we made our way. A rain storm came up. We became confused. All at once a group of Trolls appeared, crashing through the underbrush. We left the woods and sought safety on the Endless Path — "

"The highway. Route Twenty."

"So that is why we're here." The Elf King paused a moment. "Harder and harder it rained. The wind blew around us, cold and bitter. For an endless time we toiled along. We had no idea where we were going or what would become of us."

The Elf King looked up at Shadrach. "We knew only this: Behind us, the Trolls were coming, creeping through the woods, marching through the rain, crushing everything before them."

He put his hand to his mouth and coughed, bending forward. All the Elves waited anxiously until he was done. He straightened up.

"It was kind of you to allow us to come inside. We will not trouble you for long. It is not the custom of the Elves — "

Again he coughed, covering his face with his hand. The Elves drew toward him apprehensively. At last the king stirred. He sighed.

"What's the matter?" Shadrach asked. He went over and took the cup of chocolate from the fragile hand. The Elf King lay back, his eyes shut.

"He has to rest," one of the soldiers said. "Where's your room? The sleeping room."

"Upstairs," Shadrach said. "I'll show you where."

Late that night, Shadrach sat by himself in the dark, deserted living room, deep in meditation. The Elves were asleep above him, upstairs in the bedroom, the Elf King in the bed, the others curled up together on the rug.

The house was silent. Outside, the rain poured down endlessly, blowing against the house. Shadrach could hear the tree branches slapping in the wind. He clasped and unclasped his hands. What a strange business it was — all these Elves, with their old, sick king, their piping voices. How anxious and peevish they were!

But pathetic, too; so small and wet, with water dripping down from them, and all their gay robes limp and soggy.

The Trolls — what were they like? Unpleasant and not very clean. Something about digging, breaking and pushing through the woods ...

Suddenly, Shadrach laughed in embarrassment. What was the matter with him, believing all this? He put his cigar out angrily, his ears red. What was going on? What kind of joke was this?

Elves? Shadrach grunted in indignation. Elves in Derryville? In the middle of Colorado? Maybe there were Elves in Europe. Maybe in Ireland. He had heard of that. But here? Upstairs in his own house, sleeping in his own bed?

"I've heard just about enough of this," he said. "I'm not an idiot, you know."

He turned toward the stairs, feeling for the banister in the gloom. He began to climb.

Above him, a light went on abruptly. A door opened.

Two Elves came slowly out onto the landing. They looked down at him. Shadrach halted halfway up the stairs. Something on their faces made him stop.

"What's the matter?" he asked hesitantly.

They did not answer. The house was turning cold, cold and dark, with the chill of the rain outside and the chill of the unknown inside.

"What is it?" he said again. "What's the matter?"

"The King is dead," one of the Elves said. "He died a few moments ago."

Shadrach stared up, wide-eyed. "He did? But — "

"He was very cold and very tired." The Elves turned away, going back into the room, slowly and quietly shutting the door.

Shadrach stood, his fingers on the banister, hard, lean fingers, strong and thin.

He nodded his head blankly.

"I see," he said to the closed door. "He's dead."

*   *   *

The Elf soldiers stood around him in a solemn circle. The living room was bright with sunlight, the cold white glare of early morning.

"But wait," Shadrach said. He plucked at his necktie. "I have to get to the filling station. Can't you talk to me when I come home?"

The faces of the Elf soldiers were serious and concerned.

"Listen," one of them said. "Please hear us out. It is very important to us."

Shadrach looked past them. Through the window he saw the highway, steaming in the heat of day, and down a little way was the gas station, glittering brightly. And even as he watched, a car came up to it and honked thinly, impatiently. When nobody came out of the station, the car drove off again down the road.

"We beg you," a soldier said.

Shadrach looked down at the ring around him, the anxious faces, scored with concern and trouble. Strangely, he had always thought of Elves as care-free beings, flitting without worry or sense —

"Go ahead," he said. "I'm listening." He went over to the big chair and sat down. The Elves came up around him. They conversed among themselves for a moment, whispering, murmuring distantly. Then they turned toward Shadrach.

The old man waited, his arms folded.

"We cannot be without a king," one of the soldiers said. "We could not survive. Not these days."

"The Trolls," another added. "They multiply very fast. They are terrible beasts. They're heavy and ponderous, crude, bad-smelling — "

"The odor of them is awful. They come up from the dark wet places, under the earth, where the blind, groping plants feed in silence, far below the surface, far from the sun."

"Well, you ought to elect a king, then," Shadrach suggested. "I don't see any problem there."

"We do not elect the King of the Elves," a soldier said. "The old king must name his successor."

"Oh," Shadrach replied. "Well, there's nothing wrong with that method."

"As our old king lay dying, a few distant words came forth from his lips," a soldier said. "We bent closer, frightened and unhappy, listening."

"Important, all right," agreed Shadrach. "Not something you'd want to miss."

"He spoke the name of him who will lead us."

"Good. You caught it, then. Well, where's the difficulty?"

"The name he spoke was — was your name."

Shadrach stared. *"Mine?"*

"The dying king said: 'Make him, the towering mortal, your king. Many things will come if he leads the Elves into battle against the Trolls. I see the rising once again of the Elf Empire, as it was in the old days, as it was before — "

"Me!" Shadrach leaped up. "Me? King of the Elves?"

Shadrach walked about the room, his hands in his pockets. "Me, Shadrach Jones, King of the Elves." He grinned a little. "I sure never thought of it before."

He went to the mirror over the fireplace and studied himself. He saw his thin, graying hair, his bright eyes, dark skin, his big Adam's apple.

"King of the Elves," he said. "King of the Elves. Wait till Phineas Judd hears about this. Wait till I tell him!"

Phineas Judd would certainly be surprised!

Above the filling station, the sun shown, high in the clear blue sky.

Phineas Judd sat playing with the accelerator of his old Ford truck. The motor raced and slowed. Phineas reached over and turned the ignition key off, then rolled the window all the way down.

"What did you say?" he asked. He took off his glasses and began to polish them, steel rims between slender, deft fingers that were patient from years of practice. He restored his glasses to his nose and smoothed what remained of his hair into place.

"What was it, Shadrach?" he said. "Let's hear that again."

"I'm King of the Elves," Shadrach repeated. He changed position, bringing his other foot up on the running board. "Who would have thought it? Me, Shadrach Jones, King of the Elves."

Phineas gazed at him. "How long have you been — King of the Elves, Shadrach?"

"Since the night before last."

"I see. The night before last." Phineas nodded. "I see. And what, may I ask, occurred the night before last?"

"The Elves came to my house. When the old king died, he told them that — "

A truck came rumbling up and the driver leaped out. "Water!" he said. "Where the hell is the hose?"

Shadrach turned reluctantly. "I'll get it." He turned back to Phineas. "Maybe I can talk to you tonight when you come back from town. I want to tell you the rest. It's very interesting."

"Sure," Phineas said, starting up his little truck. "Sure, Shadrach. I'm very interested to hear."

He drove off down the road.

Later in the day, Dan Green ran his flivver up to the filling station.

"Hey, Shadrach," he called. "Come over here! I want to ask you something."

Shadrach came out of the little house, holding a waste-rag in his hand.

"What is it?"

"Come here." Dan leaned out the window, a wide grin on his face, splitting his face from ear to ear. "Let me ask you something, will you?"

"Sure."

"Is it true? Are you really the King of the Elves?"

Shadrach flushed a little. "I guess I am," he admitted, looking away. "That's what I am, all right."

Dan's grin faded. "Hey, you trying to kid me? What's the gag?"

Shadrach became angry. "What do you mean? Sure, I'm the King of the Elves. And anyone who says I'm not — "

"All right, Shadrach," Dan said, starting up the flivver quickly. "Don't get mad. I was just wondering."

Shadrach looked very strange.

"All right," Dan said. "You don't hear me arguing, do you?"

By the end of the day, everyone around knew about Shadrach and how he had suddenly become the King of the Elves. Pop Richey, who ran the Lucky Store in Derryville, claimed Shadrach was doing it to drum up trade for the filling station.

"He's a smart old fellow," Pop said. "Not very many cars go along there any more. He knows what he's doing."

"I don't know," Dan Green disagreed. "You should hear him, I think he really believes it."

"King of the Elves?" They all began to laugh. "Wonder what he'll say next."

Phineas Judd pondered. "I've known Shadrach for years. I can't figure it out." He frowned, his face wrinkled and disapproving. "I don't like it."

Dan looked at him. "Then you think he believes it?"

"Sure," Phineas said. "Maybe I'm wrong, but I really think he does."

"But how could he believe it?" Pop asked. "Shadrach is no fool. He's been in business for a long time. He must be getting something out of it, the way I see it. But what, if it isn't to build up the filling station?"

"Why, don't you know what he's getting?" Dan said, grinning. His gold tooth shone.

"What?" Pop demanded.

"He's got a whole kingdom to himself, that's what — to do with like he wants. How would you like that, Pop? Wouldn't you like to be King of the Elves and not have to run this old store any more?"

"There isn't anything wrong with my store," Pop said. "I ain't ashamed to run it. Better than being a clothing salesman."

Dan flushed. "Nothing wrong with that, either." He looked at Phineas. "Isn't that right? Nothing wrong with selling clothes, is there, Phineas?"

Phineas was staring down at the floor. He glanced up. "What? What was that?"

"What you thinking about?" Pop wanted to know. "You look worried."

"I'm worried about Shadrach," Phineas said. "He's getting old. Sitting out there by himself all the time, in the cold weather, with the rain water running over the floor — it blows something awful in the winter, along the highway — "

"Then you *do* think he believes it?" Dan persisted. "You *don't* think he's getting something out of it?"

Phineas shook his head absently and did not answer.

The laughter died down. They all looked at one another.

That night, as Shadrach was locking up the filling station, a small figure came toward him from the darkness.

"Hey!" Shadrach called out. "Who are you?"

An Elf soldier came into the light, blinking. He was dressed in a little gray robe, buckled at the waist with a band of silver. On his feet were little leather boots. He carried a short sword at his side.

"I have a serious message for you," the Elf said. "Now, where did I put it?"

He searched his robe while Shadrach waited. The Elf brought out a tiny scroll and unfastened it, breaking the wax expertly. He handed it to Shadrach.

"What's it say?" Shadrach asked. He bent over, his eyes close to the vellum. "I don't have my glasses with me. Can't quite make out these little letters."

"The Trolls are moving. They've heard that the old king is dead, and they're rising, in all the hills and valleys around. They will try to break the Elf Kingdom into fragments, scatter the Elves — "

"I see," Shadrach said. "Before your new king can really get started."

"That's right." The Elf soldier nodded. "This is a crucial moment for the Elves. For centuries, our existence has been precarious. There are so many Trolls, and Elves are very frail and often take sick — "

"Well, what should I do? Are there any suggestions?"

"You're supposed to meet with us under the Great Oak tonight. We'll take you into the Elf Kingdom, and you and your staff will plan and map the defense of the Kingdom."

"What?" Shadrach looked uncomfortable. "But I haven't eaten dinner. And my gas station — tomorrow is Saturday, and a lot of cars — "

"But you are King of the Elves," the soldier said.

Shadrach put his hand to his chin and rubbed it slowly.

"That's right," he replied. "I am, ain't I?"

The Elf soldier bowed.

"I wish I'd known this sort of thing was going to happen," Shadrach said. "I didn't suppose being King of the Elves — "

He broke off, hoping for an interruption. The Elf soldier watched him calmly, without expression.

"Maybe you ought to have someone else as your king," Shadrach decided. "I don't know very much about war and things like that, fighting and all that sort of business." He paused, shrugged his shoulders. "It's nothing I've ever mixed in. They don't have wars here in Colorado. I mean they don't have wars between human beings."

Still the Elf soldier remained silent.

"Why was I picked?" Shadrach went on helplessly, twisting his hands. "I don't know anything about it. What made him go and pick me? Why didn't he pick somebody else?"

"He trusted you," the Elf said. "You brought him inside your house, out of the rain. He knew that you expected nothing for it, that there was nothing you wanted. He had known few who gave and asked nothing back."

"Oh." Shadrach thought it over. At last he looked up. "But what about my gas station? And my house? And what will they say, Dan Green and Pop down at the store — "

The Elf soldier moved away, out of the light. "I have to go. It's getting late, and at night the Trolls come out. I don't want to be too far away from the others."

"Sure," Shadrach said.

"The Trolls are afraid of nothing, now that the old king is dead. They forage everywhere. No one is safe."

"Where did you say the meeting is to be? And what time?"

"At the Great Oak. When the moon sets tonight, just as it leaves the sky."

"I'll be there, I guess," Shadrach said. "I suppose you're right. The King of the Elves can't afford to let his kingdom down when it needs him most."

He looked around, but the Elf soldier was already gone.

Shadrach walked up the highway, his mind full of doubts and wonderings. When he came to the first of the flat stone steps, he stopped.

"And the old oak tree is on Phineas's farm! What'll Phineas say?"

But he was the Elf King and the Trolls were moving in the hills. Shadrach stood listening to the rustle of the wind as it moved through the trees beyond the highway, and along the far slopes and hills.

Trolls? Were there really Trolls there, rising up, bold and confident in the darkness of the night, afraid of nothing, afraid of no one?

And this business of being Elf King . . .

Shadrach went on up the steps, his lips pressed tight. When he reached the top of the stone steps, the last rays of sunlight had already faded. It was night.

Phineas Judd stared out the window. He swore and shook his head. Then he went quickly to the door and ran out onto the porch. In the cold moonlight a dim figure was walking slowly across the lower field, coming toward the house along the cow trail.

"Shadrach!" Phineas cried. "What's wrong? What are you doing out this time of night?"

Shadrach stopped and put his fists stubbornly on his hips.

"You go back home," Phineas said. "What's got into you?"

"I'm sorry, Phineas," Shadrach answered. "I'm sorry I have to go over your land. But I have to meet somebody at the old oak tree."

"At this time of night?"

Shadrach bowed his head.

"What's the matter with you, Shadrach? Who in the world you going to meet in the middle of the night on my farm?"

"I have to meet with the Elves. We're going to plan out the war with the Trolls."

"Well, I'll be damned," Phineas Judd said. He went back inside the house and slammed the door. For a long time he stood thinking. Then he went back out on the porch again. "What did you say you were doing? You don't have to tell me, of course, but I just — "

"I have to meet the Elves at the old oak tree. We must have a general council of war against the Trolls."

"Yes, indeed. The Trolls. Have to watch for the Trolls all the time."

"Trolls are everywhere," Shadrach stated, nodding his head. "I never realized it before. You can't forget them or ignore them. They never forget you. They're always planning, watching you — "

Phineas gaped at him, speechless.

"Oh, by the way," Shadrach said. "I may be gone for some time. It depends on how long this business is going to take. I haven't had much experience in fighting Trolls, so I'm not sure. But I wonder if you'd mind looking after the gas station for me, about twice a day, maybe once in the morning and once at night, to make sure no one's broken in or anything like that."

"You're going away?" Phineas came quickly down the stairs. "What's all this about Trolls? Why are you going?"

Shadrach patiently repeated what he had said.

"But what for?"

"Because I'm the Elf King. I have to lead them."

There was silence. "I see," Phineas said, at last. "That's right, you *did* mention it before, didn't you? But, Shadrach, why don't you come inside for a while and you can tell me about the Trolls and drink some coffee and — "

"Coffee?" Shadrach looked up at the pale moon above him, the moon and the bleak sky. The world was still and dead and the night was very cold and the moon would not be setting for some time.

Shadrach shivered.

"It's a cold night," Phineas urged. "Too cold to be out. Come on in — "

"I guess I have a little time," Shadrach admitted. "A cup of coffee wouldn't do any harm. But I can't stay very long ... "

*   *   *

Shadrach stretched his legs out and sighed. "This coffee sure tastes good, Phineas."

Phineas sipped a little and put his cup down. The living room was quiet and warm. It was a very neat little living room with solemn pictures on the walls, gray uninteresting pictures that minded their own business. In the corner was a small reed organ with sheet music carefully arranged on top of it.

Shadrach noticed the organ and smiled. "You still play, Phineas?"

"Not much any more. The bellows don't work right. One of them won't come back up."

"I suppose I could fix it sometime. If I'm around, I mean."

"That would be fine," Phineas said. "I was thinking of asking you."

"Remember how you used to play 'Vilia' and Dan Green came up with that lady who worked for Pop during the summer? The one who wanted to open a pottery shop?"

"I sure do," Phineas said.

Presently, Shadrach set down his coffee cup and shifted in his chair.

"You want more coffee?" Phineas asked quickly. He stood up. "A little more?"

"Maybe a little. But I have to be going pretty soon."

"It's a bad night to be outside."

Shadrach looked through the window. It was darker; the moon had almost gone down. The fields were stark. Shadrach shivered. "I wouldn't disagree with you," he said.

Phineas turned eagerly. "Look, Shadrach. You go on home where it's warm. You can come out and fight Trolls some other night. There'll always be Trolls. You said so yourself. Plenty of time to do that later, when the weather's better. When it's not so cold."

Shadrach rubbed his forehead wearily. "You know, it all seems like some sort of a crazy dream. When did I start talking about Elves and Trolls? When did it all begin?" His voice trailed off. "Thank you for the coffee." He got slowly to his feet. "It warmed me up a lot. And I appreciated the talk. Like old times, you and me sitting here the way we used to."

"Are you going?" Phineas hesitated. *"Home?"*

"I think I better. It's late."

Phineas got quickly to his feet. He led Shadrach to the door, one arm around his shoulder.

"All right, Shadrach, you go on home. Take a good hot bath before you go to bed. It'll fix you up. And maybe just a little snort of brandy to warm the blood."

Phineas opened the front door and they went slowly down the porch steps, onto the cold, dark ground.

"Yes, I guess I'll be going," Shadrach said. "Good night — "

"You go on home." Phineas patted him on the arm. "You run along home and take a good hot bath. And then go straight to bed."

"That's a good idea. Thank you, Phineas. I appreciate your kindness." Shadrach looked down at Phineas's hand on his arm. He had not been that close to Phineas for years.

Shadrach contemplated the hand. He wrinkled his brow, puzzled.

Phineas's hand was huge and rough and his arms were short. His fingers were blunt; his nails broken and cracked. Almost black, or so it seemed in the moonlight.

Shadrach looked up at Phineas. "Strange," he murmured.

"What's strange, Shadrach?"

In the moonlight, Phineas's face seemed oddly heavy and brutal. Shadrach had never noticed before how the jaw bulged, what a great protruding jaw it was. The skin was yellow and coarse, like parchment. Behind the glasses, the eyes were like two stones, cold and lifeless. The ears were immense, the hair stringy and matted.

Odd that he never noticed before. But he had never seen Phineas in the moonlight.

Shadrach stepped away, studying his old friend. From a few feet off, Phineas Judd seemed unusually short and squat. His legs were slightly bowed. His feet were enormous. And there was something else —

"What is it?" Phineas demanded, beginning to grow suspicious. "Is there something wrong?"

Something was completely wrong. And he had never noticed it, not in all the years they had been friends. All around Phineas Judd was an odor, a faint, pungent stench of rot, of decaying flesh, damp and moldy.

Shadrach glanced slowly about him. "Something wrong?" he echoed. "No, I wouldn't say that."

By the side of the house was an old rain barrel, half fallen apart. Shadrach walked over to it.

"No, Phineas. I wouldn't say there's something wrong."

"What are you doing?"

"Me?" Shadrach took hold of one of the barrel staves and pulled it loose. He walked back to Phineas, carrying the barrel stave carefully. "I'm King of the Elves. Who — or what — are you?"

Phineas roared and attacked with his great murderous shovel hands.

Shadrach smashed him over the head with the barrel stave. Phineas bellowed with rage and pain.

At the shattering sound, there was a clatter and from underneath the house came a furious horde of bounding, leaping creatures, dark bent-over things, their bodies heavy and squat, their feet and heads immense. Shadrach took one look at the flood of dark creatures pouring out from Phineas's basement. He knew what they were.

"Help!" Shadrach shouted. "Trolls! Help!"

The trolls were all around him, grabbing hold of him, tugging at him, climbing up him, pummeling his face and body.

Shadrach fell to with the barrel stave, swung again and again, kicking Trolls with his feet, whacking them with the barrel stave. There seemed to be hundreds of them. More and more poured out from under Phineas's house, a surging black tide of pot-shaped creatures, their great eyes and teeth gleaming in the moonlight.

"Help!" Shadrach cried again, more feebly now. He was getting winded. His heart labored painfully. A Troll bit his wrist, clinging to his arm. Shadrach flung it away, pulling loose from the horde clutching his trouser legs, the barrel stave rising and falling.

One of the Trolls caught hold of the stave. A whole group of them helped, wrenching furiously, trying to pull it away. Shadrach hung on desperately. Trolls were all over him, on his shoulders, clinging to his coat, riding his arms, his legs, pulling his hair —

He heard a high-pitched clarion call from a long way off, the sound of some distant golden trumpet, echoing in the hills.

The Trolls suddenly stopped attacking. One of them dropped off Shadrach's neck. Another let go of his arm.

The call came again, this time more loudly.

"Elves!" a Troll rasped. He turned and moved toward the sound, grinding his teeth and spitting with fury.

"Elves!"

The Trolls swarmed forward, a growing wave of gnashing teeth and nails, pushing furiously toward the Elf columns. The Elves broke formation and joined battle, shouting with wild joy in their shrill, piping voices. The tide of Trolls rushed against them, Troll against Elf, shovel nails against golden sword, biting jaw against dagger.

"Kill the Elves!"

"Death to the Trolls!"

"Onward!"

"Forward!"

Shadrach fought desperately with the Trolls that were still clinging to him. He was exhausted, panting and gasping for breath. Blindly, he whacked on and on, kicking and jumping, throwing Trolls away from him, through the air and across the ground.

How long the battle raged, Shadrach never knew. He was lost in a sea of dark bodies, round and evil-smelling, clinging to him, tearing, biting, fastened to his nose and hair and fingers. He fought silently, grimly.

All around him, the Elf legions clashed with the Troll horde, little groups of struggling warriors on all sides.

Suddenly Shadrach stopped fighting. He raised his head, looking uncertainly around him. Nothing moved. Everything was silent. The fighting had ceased.

A few Trolls still clung to his arms and legs. Shadrach whacked one with the barrel stave. It howled and dropped to the ground. He staggered back, struggling with the last Troll, who hung tenaciously to his arm.

"Now you!" Shadrach gasped. He pried the Troll loose and flung it into the air. The Troll fell to the ground and scuttled off into the night.

There was nothing more. No Troll moved anywhere. All was silent across the bleak moon-swept fields.

Shadrach sank down on a stone. His chest rose and fell painfully. Red specks swam before his eyes. Weakly, he got out his pocket handkerchief and wiped his neck and face. He closed his eyes, shaking his head from side to side.

When he opened his eyes again, the Elves were coming toward him, gathering their legion together again. The Elves were disheveled and bruised. Their golden armor was gashed and torn. Their helmets were bent or missing. Most of their scarlet plumes were gone. Those that still remained were drooping and broken.

But the battle was over. The war was won. The Troll hordes had been put to flight.

Shadrach got slowly to his feet. The Elf warriors stood around him in a circle, gazing up at him with silent respect. One of them helped steady him as he put his handkerchief away in his pocket.

"Thank you," Shadrach murmured. "Thank you very much."

"The Trolls have been defeated," an Elf stated, still awed by what had happened.

Shadrach gazed around at the Elves. There were many of them, more than he had ever seen before. All the Elves had turned out for the battle. They were grim-faced, stern with the seriousness of the moment, weary from the terrible struggle.

"Yes, they're gone, all right," Shadrach said. He was beginning to get his breath. "That was a close call. I'm glad you fellows came when you did. I was just about finished, fighting them all by myself."

"All alone, the King of the Elves held off the entire Troll army," an Elf announced shrilly.

"Eh?" Shadrach said, taken aback. Then he smiled. "That's true, I *did* fight them alone for a while. I *did* hold off the Trolls all by myself. The whole darn Troll army."

"There is more," an Elf said.

Shadrach blinked. "More?"

"Look over here, O King, mightiest of all the Elves. This way. To the right."

The Elves led Shadrach over.

"What is it?" Shadrach murmured, seeing nothing at first. He gazed down, trying to pierce the darkness. "Could we have a torch over here?"

Some Elves brought little pine torches.

There, on the frozen ground, lay Phineas Judd, on his back. His eyes were blank and staring, his mouth half open. He did not move. His body was cold and stiff.

"He is dead," an Elf said solemnly.

Shadrach gulped in sudden alarm. Cold sweat stood out abruptly on his forehead. "My gosh! My old friend! What have I done?"

"You have slain the Great Troll."

Shadrach paused.

"I *what?*"

"You have slain the Great Troll, leader of all the Trolls."

"This has never happened before," another Elf exclaimed excitedly. "The Great Troll has lived for centuries. Nobody imagined he could die. This is our most historic moment."

All the Elves gazed down at the silent form with awe, awe mixed with more than a little fear.

"Oh, go on!" Shadrach said. "That's just Phineas Judd."

But as he spoke, a chill moved up his spine. He remembered what he had seen a little while before, as he stood close by Phineas, as the dying moonlight crossed his old friend's face.

"Look." One of the Elves bent over and unfastened Phineas's blue-serge vest. He pushed the coat and vest aside. "See?"

Shadrach bent down to look.

He gasped.

Underneath Phineas Judd's blue-serge vest was a suit of mail, an encrusted mesh of ancient, rusting iron, fastened tightly around the squat body. On the mail stood an engraved insignia, dark and time-worn, embedded with dirt and rust. A moldering half-obliterated emblem. The emblem of a crossed owl leg and toadstool.

The emblem of the Great Troll.

"Golly," Shadrach said. "And *I* killed him."

For a long time he gazed silently down. Then, slowly, realization began to grow in him. He straightened up, a smile forming on his face.

"What is it, O King?" an Elf piped.

"I just thought of something," Shadrach said. "I just realized that — that since the Great Troll is dead and the Troll army has been put to flight — "

He broke off. All the Elves were waiting.

"I thought maybe I — that is, maybe if you don't need me any more — "

The Elves listened respectfully. "What is it, Mighty King? Go on."

"I thought maybe now I could go back to the filling station and not be king any more." Shadrach glanced hopefully around at them. "Do you think so? With the war over and all. With him dead. What do you say?"

For a time, the Elves were silent. They gazed unhappily down at the ground. None of them said anything. At last they began moving away, collecting their banners and pennants.

"Yes, you may go back," an Elf said quietly. "The war is over. The Trolls have been defeated. You may return to your filling station, if that is what you want."

A flood of relief swept over Shadrach. He straightened up, grinning from ear to ear. "Thanks! That's fine. That's really fine. That's the best news I've heard in my life."

He moved away from the Elves, rubbing his hands together and blowing on them.

"Thanks an awful lot." He grinned around at the silent Elves. "Well, I guess I'll be running along, then. It's late. Late and cold. It's been a hard night. I'll — I'll see you around."

The Elves nodded silently.

"Fine. Well, good night." Shadrach turned and started along the path. He stopped for a moment, waving back at the Elves. "It was quite a battle, wasn't it? We really licked them." He hurried on along the path. Once again he stopped, looking back and waving. "Sure glad I could help out. Well, good night!"

One or two on the Elves waved, but none of them said anything.

Shadrach Jones walked slowly toward his place. He could see it from the rise, the highway that few cars traveled, the filling station falling to ruin, the house that might not last as long as himself, and not enough money coming in to repair them or buy a better location.

He turned around and went back.

The Elves were still gathered there in the silence of the night. They had not moved away.

"I was hoping you hadn't gone," Shadrach said, relieved.

"And we were hoping you would not leave," said a soldier.

Shadrach kicked a stone. It bounced through the tight silence and stopped. The Elves were still watching him.

"Leave?" Shadrach asked. "And me King of the Elves?"

"Then you will remain our king?" an Elf cried.

"It's a hard thing for a man of my age to change. To stop selling gasoline and suddenly be a king. It scared me for a while. But it doesn't any more."

"You will? You *will*?"

"Sure," said Shadrach Jones.

The little circle of Elf torches closed in joyously. In their light, he saw a platform like the one that had carried the old King of the Elves. But this one was much larger, big enough to hold a man, and dozens of the soldiers waited with proud shoulders under the shafts.

A soldier gave him a happy bow. "For you, Sire."

Shadrach climbed aboard. It was less comfortable than walking, but he knew this was how they wanted to take him to the Kingdom of the Elves.

COLONY

MAJOR LAWRENCE HALL bent over the binocular microscope, correcting the fine adjustment.

"Interesting," he murmured.

"Isn't it? Three weeks on this planet and we've yet to find a harmful life form." Lieutenant Friendly sat down on the edge of the lab table, avoiding the culture bowls. "What kind of place is this? No disease germs, no lice, no flies, no rats, no — "

"No whiskey or red-light districts." Hall straightened up. "Quite a place. I was sure this brew would show something along the lines of Terra's *eberthella typhi*. Or the Martian sand rot corkscrew."

"But the whole planet's harmless. You know, I'm wondering whether this is the Garden of Eden our ancestors fell out of."

"Were pushed out of."

Hall wandered over to the window of the lab and contemplated the scene beyond. He had to admit it was an attractive sight. Rolling forests and hills, green slopes alive with flowers and endless vines; waterfalls and hanging moss; fruit trees, acres of flowers, lakes. Every effort had been made to preserve intact the surface of Planet Blue — as it had been designated by the original scout ship, six months earlier.

Hall sighed. "Quite a place. I wouldn't mind coming back here again some time."

"Makes Terra seen a little bare." Friendly took out his cigarettes, then put them away again. "You know, the place has a funny effect on me. I don't smoke any more. Guess that's because of the way it looks. It's so — so damn pure. Unsullied. I can't smoke or throw papers around. I can't bring myself to be a picnicker."

"The picnickers'll be along soon enough," Hall said. He went back to the microscope. "I'll try a few more cultures. Maybe I'll find a lethal germ yet."

"Keep trying." Lieutenant Friendly hopped off the table. "I'll see you later and find out if you've had any luck. There's a big conference going on in Room One. They're almost ready to give the go-ahead to the E.A. for the first load of colonists to be sent out."

"Picnickers!"

Friendly grinned. "Afraid so."

The door closed after him. His bootsteps echoed down the corridor. Hall was alone in the lab.

He sat for a time in thought. Presently he bent down and removed the slide from the stage of the microscope, selected a new one and held it up to the light to read the marking. The lab was warm and quiet. Sunlight streamed through the windows and across the floor. The trees outside moved a little in the wind. He began to feel sleepy.

"Yes, the picnickers," he grumbled. He adjusted the new slide into position. "And all of them ready to come in and cut down the trees, tear up the flowers, spit in the lakes, burn up the grass. With not even the common-cold virus around to — "

He stopped, his voice choked off —

Choked off because the two eyepieces of the microscope had twisted suddenly around his windpipe and were trying to strangle him. Hall tore at them, but they dug relentlessly into his throat, steel prongs closing like the claws of a trap.

Throwing the microscope onto the floor, he leaped up. The microscope crawled quickly toward him, hooking around his leg. He kicked it loose with his other foot, and drew his blast pistol.

The microscope scuttled away, rolling on its coarse adjustments. Hall fired. It disappeared in a cloud of metallic particles.

"Good God!" Hall sat down weakly, mopping his face. "What the — ?" He massaged his throat. "What the hell!"

The council room was packed solid. Every officer of the Planet Blue unit was there. Commander Stella Morrison tapped on the big control map with the end of a slim plastic pointer.

"This long flat area is ideal for the actual city. It's close to water, and weather conditions vary sufficiently to give the settlers something to talk about. There are large deposits of various minerals. The colonists can set up their own factories. They won't have to do any importing. Over here is the biggest forest on the planet. If they have any sense, they'll leave it. But if they want to make newspapers out of it, that's not our concern."

She looked around the room at the silent men.

"Let's be realistic. Some of you have been thinking we shouldn't send the okay to the Emigration Authority, but keep the planet our own selves, to come back to. I'd like that as much as any of the rest of you, but we'd just get into a lot of trouble. It's not *our* planet. We're here to do a certain job. When the job is done, we move along. And it is almost done. So let's forget it. The only thing left to do is flash the go-ahead signal and then begin packing our things."

"Has the lab report come in on bacteria?" Vice-Commander Wood asked.

"We're taking special care to look out for them, of course. But the last I heard nothing had been found. I think we can go ahead and contact the E.A. Have them send a ship to take us off and bring in the first load of settlers. There's no reason why — " She stopped.

A murmur was swelling through the room. Heads turned toward the door.

Commander Morrison frowned. "Major Hall, may I remind you that when the council is in session no one is permitted to interrupt!"

Hall swayed back and forth, supporting himself by holding on to the door knob. He gazed vacantly around the council room. Finally his glassy eyes picked out Lieutenant Friendly, sitting halfway across the room.

"Come here," he said hoarsely.

"Me?" Friendly sank farther down in his chair.

"Major, what is the meaning of this?" Vice-Commander Wood cut in angrily. "Are you drunk or are — ?" He saw the blast gun in Hall's hand. "Is something wrong, Major?"

Alarmed, Lieutenant Friendly got up and grabbed Hall's shoulder. "What is it? What's the matter?"

"Come to the lab."

"Did you find something?" The Lieutenant studied his friend's rigid face. "What is it?"

"Come on." Hall started down the corridor, Friendly following. Hall pushed the laboratory door open and stepped inside slowly.

"What it is?" Friendly repeated.

"My microscope."

"Your microscope? What about it?" Friendly squeezed past him into the lab. "I don't see it."

"It's gone."

"Gone? Gone where?"

"I blasted it."

"You blasted it?" Friendly looked at the other man. "I don't get it. Why?"

Hall's mouth opened and closed, but no sound came out.

"Are you all right?" Friendly asked in concern. Then he bent down and lifted a black plastic box from a shelf under the table. "Say, is this a gag?"

He removed Hall's microscope from the box. "What do you mean, you blasted it? Here it is, in its regular place. Now, tell me what's going on? You saw something on a slide? Some kind of bacteria? Lethal? Toxic?"

Hall approached the microscope slowly. It was his all right. There was the nick just above the fine adjustment. And one of the stage clips was slightly bent. He touched it with his finger.

Five minutes ago this microscope had tried to kill him. And he knew he had blasted it out of existence.

"You sure you don't need a psych test?" Friendly asked anxiously. "You look post-trauma to me, or worse."

"Maybe you're right," Hall muttered.

The robot psyche tester whirred, integrating and gestalting. At last its color-code lights changed from red to green.

"Well?" Hall demanded.

"Severe disturbance. Instability ratio up above ten."

"That's over danger?"

"Yes. Eight is danger. Ten is unusual, especially for a person of your index. You usually show about a four."

Hall nodded wearily. "I know."

"If you could give me more data — "

Hall set his jaw. "I can't tell you any more."

"It's illegal to hold back information during a psyche test," the machine said peevishly. "If you do that you deliberately distort my findings."

Hall rose. "I can't tell you any more. But you do record a high degree of unbalance for me?"

"There's a high degree of psychic disorganization. But what it means, or why it exists, I can't say."

"Thanks." Hall clicked the tester off. He went back to his own quarters. His head whirled. Was he out of his mind? But he had fired the blast gun at *something*. Afterward, he had tasted the atmosphere in the lab, and there were metallic particles in suspension, especially near the place he had fired his blast gun at the microscope.

But how could a thing like that be? A microscope coming to life, trying to kill him!

Anyhow, Friendly had pulled it out of its box, whole and sound. But how had it got back in the box?

He stripped off his uniform and entered the shower. While he ran warm water over his body he meditated. The robot psyche tester had showed his mind was severely disturbed, but that could have been the result, rather than the cause, of the experience. He had started to tell Friendly about it but he had stopped. How could he expect anyone to believe a story like that?

He shut off the water and reached out for one of the towels on the rack.

The towel wrapped around his wrist, yanking him against the wall. Rough cloth pressed over his mouth and nose. He fought wildly, pulling away. All at once the towel let go. He fell, sliding to the floor, his head striking the wall. Stars shot around him; then violent pain.

Sitting in a pool of warm water, Hall looked up at the towel rack. The towel was motionless now, like the others with it. Three towels in a row, all exactly alike, all unmoving. Had he dreamed it?

He got shakily to his feet, rubbing his head. Carefully avoiding the towel rack, he edged out of the shower and into his room. He pulled a new towel from the dispenser in a gingerly manner. It seemed normal. He dried himself and began to put his clothes on.

His belt got him around the waist and tried to crush him. It was strong — it had reinforced metal links to hold his leggings and his gun. He and the belt rolled silently on the floor, struggling for control. The belt was like a furious metal snake, whipping and lashing at him. At last he managed to get his hand around his blaster.

At once the belt let go. He blasted it out of existence and then threw himself down in a chair, gasping for breath.

The arms of the chair closed around him. But this time the blaster was ready. He had to fire six times before the chair fell limp and he was able to get up again.

He stood half dressed in the middle of the room, his chest rising and falling.

"It isn't possible," he whispered. "I must be out of my mind."

Finally he got his leggings and boots on. He went outside into the empty corridor. Entering the lift, he ascended to the top floor.

Commander Morrison looked up from her desk as Hall stepped through the robot clearing screen. It pinged.

"You're armed," the Commander said accusingly.

Hall looked down at the blaster in his hand. He put it down on the desk. "Sorry."

"What do you want? What's the matter with you? I have a report from the testing machine. It says you've hit a ratio of ten within the last twenty-four hour period." She studied him intently. "We've known each other for a long time, Lawrence. What's happening to you?"

Hall took a deep breath. "Stella, earlier today, my microscope tried to strangle me."

Her blue eyes widened. "What!"

"Then, when I was getting out of the shower, a bath towel tried to smother me. I got by it, but while I was dressing, my belt — " He stopped. The Commander had got to her feet.

"Guards!" she called.

"Wait, Stella." Hall moved toward her. "Listen to me. This is serious. There's nothing wrong. Four times things have tried to kill me. Ordinary objects suddenly turned lethal. Maybe it's what we've been looking for. Maybe this is — "

"Your microscope tried to killed you?"

"It came alive. Its stem got me around the windpipe."

There was a long silence. "Did anyone see this happen besides you?"

"No."

"What did you do?"

"I blasted it."

"Are there any remains?"

"No," Hall admitted reluctantly. "As a matter of fact, the microscope seems to be all right, again. The way it was before. Back in its box."

"I see." The Commander nodded to the two guards who had answered her call. "Take Major Hall down to Captain Taylor and have him confined until he can be sent back to Terra for examination."

She watched calmly as the two guards took hold of Hall's arms with magnetic grapples.

"Sorry, Major," she said. "Unless you can prove any of your story, we've got to assume it's a psychotic projection on your part. And the planet isn't well enough policed for us to allow a psychotic to run loose. You could do a lot of damage."

The guards moved him toward the door. Hall went unprotestingly. His head rang, rang and echoed. Maybe she was right. Maybe he was out of his mind.

They came to Captain Taylor's offices. One of the guards rang the buzzer.

"Who is it?" the robot door demanded shrilly.

"Commander Morrison orders this man put under the Captain's care."

There was a hesitant pause, then: "The Captain is busy."

"This is an emergency."

The robot's relays clicked while it made up its mind. "The Commander sent you?"

"Yes. Open up."

"You may enter," the robot conceded finally. It drew its locks back, releasing the door.

The guard pushed the door open. And stopped.

On the floor lay Captain Taylor, his face blue, his eyes gaping. Only his head and feet was visible. A red-and-white scatter rug was wrapped around him, squeezing, straining tighter and tighter.

Hall dropped to the floor and pulled at the rug. "Hurry!" he barked. "Grab it!"

The three of them pulled together. The rug resisted.

"Help," Taylor cried weakly.

"We're trying!" They tugged frantically. At last the rug came away in their hands. It flopped off rapidly toward the open door. One of the guards blasted it.

Hall ran to the vidscreen and shakily dialed the Commander's emergency number.

Her face appeared on the screen.

"See!" he gasped.

She stared past him to Taylor lying on the floor, the two guards kneeling beside him, their blasters still out.

"What — what happened?"

"A rug attacked him." Hall grinned without amusement. "Now who's crazy?"

"We'll send a guard unit down." She blinked. "Right away. But how — "

"Tell them to have their blasters ready. And better make that a general alarm to *everyone*."

Hall placed four items on Commander Morrison's desk: a microscope, a towel, a metal belt, and a small red-and-white rug.

She edged away nervously. "Major, are you sure — ?"

"They're all right, *now*. That's the strangest part. This towel. A few hours ago it tried to kill me. I got away by blasting it to particles. But here it is, back again. The way it always was. Harmless.

Captain Taylor fingered the red-and-white rug warily. "That's my rug. I brought it from Terra. My wife gave it to me. I — I trusted it completely."

They all looked at each other.

"We blasted the rug, too," Hall pointed out.

There was silence.

"Then what was it that attacked me?" Captain Taylor asked. "If it wasn't this rug?"

"It looked like this rug," Hall said slowly. "And what attacked me looked like this towel."

Commander Morrison held up the towel to the light. "It's just an ordinary towel! It couldn't have attacked you."

"Of course not," Hall agreed. "We've put these objects through all the tests we can think of. They're just what they're supposed to be, all elements unchanged. Perfectly stable non-organic objects. It's impossible that *any* of these could have come to life and attacked us."

"But something did." Taylor said. "Something attacked me. And it if wasn't this rug, what was it?"

Lieutenant Dodds felt around on the dresser for his gloves. He was in a hurry. The whole unit had been called to emergency assembly.

"Where did I — ?" he murmured. "What the hell!"

For on the bed were *two* pair of identical gloves, side by side.

Dodds frowned, scratching his head. How could it be? He owned only one pair. The others must be somebody else's. Bob Wesley had been in the night before, playing cards. Maybe he had left them.

The vidscreen flashed again. "All personnel, report at once. All personnel, report at once. Emergency assembly of all personnel."

"All right!" Dodds said impatiently. He grabbed up one of the pairs of gloves, sliding them onto his hands.

As soon as they were in place, the gloves carried his hands down to his waist. They clamped his fingers over the butt of his gun, lifting it from the holster.

"I'll be damned," Dodds said. The gloves brought the blast gun up, pointing it at his chest.

The fingers squeezed. There was a roar. Half of Dodd's chest dissolved. What was left of him fell slowly to the floor, the mouth still open in amazement.

Corporal Tenner hurried across the ground toward the main building as soon as he heard the wail of the emergency alarm.

At the entrance to the building he stopped to take off his metal-cleated boots. Then he frowned. By the door were two safety mats instead of one.

Well, it didn't matter. They were both the same. He stepped onto one of the mats and waited. The surface of the mat sent a flow of high-frequency current through his feet and legs, killing any spores or seeds that might have clung to him while he was outside.

He passed on into the building.

A moment later Lieutenant Fulton hurried up to the door. He yanked off his hiking boots and stepped onto the first mat he saw.

The mat folded over his feet.

"Hey," Fulton cried. "Let go!"

He tried to pull his feet loose, but the mat refused to let go. Fulton became scared. He drew his gun, but he didn't care to fire at his own feet.

"Help!" he shouted.

Two soldiers came running up. "What's the matter, Lieutenant?"

"Get this damn thing off me."

The soldiers began to laugh.

"It's no joke," Fulton said, his face suddenly white. "It's breaking my feet! It's — "

He began to scream. The soldiers grabbed frantically at the mat. Fulton fell, rolling and twisting, still screaming. At last the soldiers managed to get a corner of the mat loose from his feet.

Fulton's feet were gone. Nothing but limp bone remained, already half dissolved.

"Now we know," Hall said grimly. "It's a form of organic life."

Commander Morrison turned to Corporal Tenner. "You saw two mats when you came into the building?"

"Yes, Commander. Two. I stepped on — on one of them. And came in."

"You were lucky. You stepped on the right one."

"We've got to be careful," Hall said. "We've got to watch for duplicates. Apparently *it*, whatever it is, imitates objects it finds. Like a chameleon. Camouflage."

"Two," Stella Morrison murmured, looking at the two vases of flowers, one at each end of her desk. "It's going to be hard to tell. Two towels, two vases, two chairs. There may be whole rows of things that are all right. All multiples legitimate except one."

"That's the trouble. I didn't notice anything unusual in the lab. There's nothing odd about another microscope. It blended right in."

The Commander drew away from the identical vases of flowers. "How about those? Maybe one is — whatever they are."

"There's two of a lot of things. Natural pairs. Two boots. Clothing. Furniture. I didn't notice that extra chair in my room. Equipment. It'll be impossible to be sure. And sometimes — "

The vidscreen lit. Vice-Commander Wood's features formed. "Stella, another casualty."

"Who is it this time?"

"An officer dissolved. All but a few buttons and his blast pistol — Lieutenant Dodds."

"That makes three," Commander Morrison said.

"If it's organic, there ought to be some way we can destroy it," Hall muttered. "We've already blasted a few, apparently killed them. They *can* be hurt! But we don't know how many more there are. We've destroyed five or six. Maybe it's an infinitely divisible substance. Some kind of protoplasm."

"And meanwhile — ?"

"Meanwhile we're all at its mercy. Or *their* mercy. It's our lethal life form, all right. That explains why we found everything else harmless. Nothing could compete with a form like this. We have mimic forms of our own, of course. Insects, plants. And there's the twisty slug on Venus. But nothing that goes this far."

"It can be killed, though. You said so yourself. That means we have a chance."

"If it can be found." Hall looked around the room. Two walking capes hung by the door. Had there been *two* a moment before?

He rubbed his forehead wearily. "We've got to try to find some sort of poison or corrosive agent, something that'll destroy them wholesale. We can't just sit and wait for them to attack us. We need something we can spray. That's the way we got the twisty slugs."

The Commander gazed past him, rigid.

He turned to follow her gaze. "What is it?"

"I never noticed two briefcases in the corner over there. There was only one before — I think." She shook her head in bewilderment. "How are we going to know? This business is getting me down."

"You need a good stiff drink."

She brightened. "That's an idea. But — "

"But what?"

"I don't want to touch anything. There's no way to tell." She fingered the blast gun at her waist. "I keep wanting to use it, on everything."

"Panic reaction. Still, we are being picked off, one by one."

Captain Unger got the emergency call over his headphones. He stopped work at once, gathered the specimens he had collected in his arms, and hurried back toward the bucket.

It was parked closer than he remembered. He stopped, puzzled. There it was, the bright little cone-shaped car with its treads firmly planted in the soft soil, its door open.

Unger hurried up to it, carrying his specimens carefully. He opened the storage hatch in the back and lowered his armload. Then he went around to the front and slid in behind the controls.

He turned the switch. But the motor did not come on. That was strange. While he was trying to figure it out, he noticed something that gave him a start.

A few hundred feet away, among the trees, was a second bucket, just like the one he was in. And that *was* where he remembered having parked his car. Of course, he was in the bucket. Somebody else had come looking for specimens, and this bucket belonged to them.

Unger started to get out again.

The door closed around him. The seat folded up over his head. The dashboard became plastic and oozed. He gasped — he was suffocating. He struggled to get out, flailing and twisting. There was a wetness all around him, a bubbling, flowing wetness, warm like flesh.

"Glub." His head was covered. His body was covered. The bucket was turning to liquid. He tried to pull his hands free but they would not come.

And then the pain began. He was being dissolved. All at once he realized what the liquid was.

Acid. Digestive acid. He was in a stomach.

"Don't look!" Gail Thomas cried.

"Why not?" Corporal Hendricks swam toward her, grinning. "Why can't I look?"

"Because I'm going to get out."

The sun shone down on the lake. It glittered and danced on the water. All around huge moss-covered trees rose up, great silent columns among the flowering vines and bushes.

Gail climbed up on the bank, shaking water from her, throwing her hair back out of her eyes. The woods were silent. There was no sound except the lapping of the waves. They were a long way from the unit camp.

"When can I look?" Hendricks demanded, swimming around in a circle, his eyes shut.

"Soon." Gail made her way into the trees, until she came to the place where she had left her uniform. She could feel the warm sun glowing against her bare shoulders and arms. Sitting down in the grass, she picked up her tunic and leggings.

She brushed the leaves and bits of tree bark from her tunic and began to pull it over her head.

In the water, Corporal Hendricks waited patiently, continuing in his circle. Time passed. There was no sound. He opened his eyes. Gail was nowhere in sight.

"Gail?" he called.

It was very quiet.

"Gail!"

No answer.

Corporal Hendricks swam rapidly to the bank. He pulled himself out of the water. One leap carried him to his own uniform, neatly piled at the edge of the lake. He grabbed up his blaster.

"*Gail!*"

The woods were silent. There was no sound. He stood, looking around him, frowning. Gradually, a cold fear began to numb him, in spite of the warm sun.

"*Gail!* GAIL!"

And still there was only silence.

Commander Morrison was worried. "We've got to act," she said. "We can't wait. Ten lives lost already from thirty encounters. One-third is too high a percentage."

Hall looked up from his work. "Anyhow, now we know what we're up against. It's a form of protoplasm, with infinite versatility." He lifted the spray tank. "I think this will give us an idea of how many exist."

"What's that?"

"A compound of arsenic and hydrogen in gas form. Arsine."

"What are you going to do with it?"

Hall locked his helmet into place. His voice came through the Commander's earphones. "I'm going to release this throughout the lab. I think there are a lot of them in here, more than anywhere else."

"Why here?"

"This is where all samples and specimens were originally brought, where the first one of them was encountered. I think they came in with the samples, or as the samples, and then infiltrated through the rest of the buildings."

The Commander locked her own helmet into place. Her four guards did the same. "Arsine is fatal to human beings, isn't it?"

Hall nodded. "We'll have to be careful. We can use it in here for a limited test, but that's about all."

He adjusted the flow of his oxygen inside his helmet.

"What's your test supposed to prove?" she wanted to know.

"If it shows anything at all, it should give us an idea of how extensively they've infiltrated. We'll know better what we're up against. This may be more serious than we realize."

"How do you mean?" she asked, fixing her own oxygen flow.

"There are a hundred people in this unit on Planet Blue. As it stands now, the worst that can happen is that they'll get all of us, one by one. But that's nothing. Units of a hundred are lost every day of the week. It's a risk whoever is first to land on a planet must take. In the final analysis, it's relatively unimportant."

"Compared to what?"

"If they *are* infinitely divisible, then we're going to have to think twice about leaving here. It would be better to stay and get picked off one by one than to run the risk of carrying any of them back to the system."

She looked at him. "Is that what you're trying to find out — whether they're infinitely divisible?"

"I'm trying to find out what we're up against. Maybe there are only a few of them. Or maybe they're everywhere." He waved a hand around the laboratory. "Maybe half the things in this room are not what we think they are ... It's bad when they attack us. It would be worse if they didn't."

"Worse?" The Commander was puzzled.

"Their mimicry is perfect. Of inorganic objects, at least. I looked through one of them, Stella, when it was imitating my microscope. It enlarged, adjusted, reflected, just like a regular microscope. It's a form of mimicry that surpasses anything we've ever imagined. It carries down below the surface, into the actual elements of the object imitated."

"You mean one of them could slip back to Terra along with us? In the form of clothing or a piece of lab equipment?" She shuddered.

"We assume they're some sort of protoplasm. Such malleability suggests a simple original form — and that suggests binary fission. If that's so, then there may be no limits to their ability to reproduce. The dissolving properties make me think of the simple unicellular protozoa."

"Do you think they're intelligent?"

"I don't know. I hope not." Hall lifted the spray. "In any case, this should tell us their extent. And, to some degree, corroborate my notion that they're basic enough to reproduce by simple division — the worse thing possible, from our standpoint.

"Here goes," Hall said.

He held the spray tightly against him, depressed the trigger, aimed the nozzle slowly around the lab. The commander and the four guards stood silently behind him. Nothing moved. The sun shone in through the windows, reflecting from the culture dishes and equipment.

After a moment he let the trigger up again.

"I didn't see anything," Commander Morrison said. "Are you sure you did anything?"

"Arsine is colorless. But don't loosen your helmet. It's fatal. And don't move."

They stood waiting.

For a time nothing happened. Then —

"Good God!" Commander Morrison exclaimed.

At the far end of the lab a slide cabinet wavered suddenly. It oozed, buckling and pitching. It lost its shape completely — a homogeneous jellylike mass perched on top of the table. Abruptly, it flowed down the side of the table on to the floor, wobbling as it went.

"Over there!"

A bunsen burner melted and flowed along beside it. All around the room objects were in motion. A great glass retort folded up into itself and settled down into a blob. A rack of test tubes, a shelf of chemicals ...

"Look out!" Hall cried, stepping back.

A huge bell jar dropped with a soggy splash in front of him. It was a single large cell, all right. He could dimly make out the nucleus, the cell wall, the hard vacuoles suspended in the cytoplasm.

Pipettes, tongs, a mortar, all were flowing now. Half the equipment in the room was in motion. They had imitated almost everything there was to imitate. For every microscope there was a mimic. For every tube and jar and bottle and flask ...

One of the guards had his blaster out. Hall knocked it down. "Don't fire! Arsine is inflammable. Let's get out of here. We know what we wanted to know."

They pushed the laboratory door open quickly and made their way out into the corridor. Hall slammed the door behind them, bolting it tightly.

"Is it bad, then?" Commander Morrison asked.

"We haven't got a chance. The arsine disturbed them; enough of it might even kill them. But we haven't got that much arsine. And, if we could flood the planet, we wouldn't be able to use our blasters."

"Suppose we left the planet."

"We can't take the chance of carrying them back to the system."

"If we stay here we'll be absorbed, dissolved, one by one," the Commander protested.

"We could have arsine brought in. Or some other poison that might destroy them. But it would destroy most of the life on the planet along with them. There wouldn't be much left."

"Then we'll have to destroy all life forms! If there's no other way of doing it we've got to burn the planet clean. Even if there wouldn't be a thing left but a dead world."

They looked at each other.

"I'm going to call the System Monitor," Commander Morrison said. "I'm going to get the unit off here, out of danger — all that are left, at least. That poor girl by the lake ... " She shuddered. "After everyone's out of here, we can work out the best way of cleaning up this planet."

"You'll run the risk of carrying one of them back to Terra?"

"Can they imitate us? Can they imitate living creatures? Higher life forms?"

Hall considered. "Apparently not. They seem to be limited to inorganic objects."

The Commander smiled grimly. "Then we'll go back without any inorganic material."

"But our clothes! They can imitate belts, gloves, boots — "

"We're not taking our clothes. We're going back without anything. And I mean without anything *at all.*"

Hall's lips twitched. "I see." He pondered. "It might work. Can you persuade the personnel to — to leave all their things behind? Everything they own?"

"If it means their lives, I can *order* them to do it."

"Then it might be our one chance of getting away."

The nearest cruiser large enough to remove the remaining members of the unit was two hours' distance away. It was moving Terraside again.

Commander Morrison looked up from the vidscreen. "They want to know what's wrong here."

"Let me talk." Hall seated himself before the screen. The heavy features and gold braid of a Terran cruiser captain regarded him. "This is Major Lawrence Hall, from the Research Division of this unit."

"Captain Daniel Davis." Captain Davis studied him without expression. "You're having some kind of trouble, Major?"

Hall licked his lips. "I'd rather not explain until we're aboard, if you don't mind."

"Why not?"

"Captain, you're going to think we're crazy enough as it is. We'll discuss everything fully once we're aboard." He hesitated. "We're going to board your ship naked."

The Captain raised an eyebrow. "Naked?"

"That's right."

"I see." Obviously he didn't.

"When will you get here?"

"In about two hours, I'd say."

"It's now 13:00 by our schedule. You'll be here by 15:00?"

"At approximately that time," the Captain agreed.

"We'll be waiting for you. Don't let any of your men out. Open one lock for us. We'll board without any equipment. Just ourselves, nothing else. As soon as we're aboard, remove the ship at once."

Stella Morrison leaned toward the screen. "Captain, would it be possible — for your men to — ?"

"We'll land by robot control," he assured her. "None of my men will be on deck. No one will see you."

"Thank you," she murmured.

"Not at all." Captain Davis saluted. "We'll see you in about two hours then, Commander."

"Let's get everyone out onto the field," Commander Morrison said. "They should remove their clothes here, I think, so there won't be any objects on the field to come in contact with the ship."

Hall looked at her face. "Isn't it worth it to save our lives?"

Lieutenant Friendly bit his lips. "I won't do it. I'll stay here."

"You have to come."

"But, Major — "

Hall looked at his watch. "It's 14:50. The ship will be here any minute. Get your clothes off and get out on the landing field."

"Can't I take anything at *all*?"

"Nothing. Not even your blaster ... They'll give us clothes inside the ship. Come on! Your life depends on this. Everyone else is doing it."

Friendly tugged at his shirt reluctantly. "Well, I guess I'm acting silly."

The vidscreen clicked. A robot voice announced shrilly: "Everyone out of the buildings at once! Everyone out of the buildings and on the field without delay! Everyone out of the buildings at once! Everyone — "

"So soon?" Hall ran to the window and lifted the metal blind. "I didn't hear it land."

Parked in the center of the landing field was a long gray cruiser, its hull pitted and dented from meteoric strikes. It lay motionless. There was no sign of life about it.

A crowd of naked people was already moving hesitantly across the field toward it, blinking in the bright sunlight.

"It's here!" Hall started tearing off his shirt. "Let's go!"

"Wait for me!"

"Then hurry." Hall finished undressing. Both men hurried out into the corridor. Unclothed guards raced past them. They padded down the corridors through the long unit building, to the door. They ran downstairs, out onto the field. Warm sunlight beat down on them from the sky overhead. From all the unit buildings, naked men and women were pouring silently toward the ship.

"What a sight!" an officer said. "We'll never be able to live it down."

"But you'll live, at least," another said.

"Lawrence!"

Hall half turned.

"Please don't look around. Keep on going. I'll walk behind you."

"How does it feel, Stella?" Hall asked.

"Unusual."

"Is it worth it?"

"I suppose so."

"Do you think anyone will believe us?"

"I doubt it," she said. "I'm beginning to wonder myself."

"Anyhow, we'll get back alive."

"I guess so."

Hall looked up at the ramp being lowered from the ship in front of them. The first people were already beginning to scamper up the metal incline, into the ship, through the circular lock.

"Lawrence — "

There was a peculiar tremor in the Commander's voice. "Lawrence, I'm — "

"You're what?"

"I'm scared."

"Scared!" He stopped. "Why?"

"I don't know," she quavered.

People pushed against them from all sides. "Forget it. Carry-over from your early childhood." He put his foot on the bottom of the ramp. "Up we go."

"I want to go back!" There was panic in her voice. "I — "

Hall laughed. "It's too late now, Stella." He mounted the ramp, holding on to the rail. Around him, on all sides, men and women were pushing forward, carrying them up. They came to the lock. "Here we are."

The man ahead of him disappeared.

Hall went inside after him, into the dark interior of the ship, into the silent blackness before him. The Commander followed.

At exactly 15:00 Captain Daniel Davis landed his ship in the center of the field. Relays slid the entrance lock open with a bang. Davis and the other officers of the ship sat waiting in the control cabin, around the big control table.

"Well," Captain Davis said, after a while. "Where are they?"

The officers became uneasy. "Maybe something's wrong."

"Maybe the whole damn thing's a joke?"

They waited and waited.

But no one came.

PRIZE SHIP

GENERAL THOMAS GROVES gazed glumly up at the battle maps on the wall. The thin black line, the iron ring around Ganymede, was still there. He waited a moment, vaguely hoping, but the line did not go away. At last he turned and made his way out of the chart wing, past the rows of desks.

At the door Major Siller stopped him. "What's wrong, sir? No change in the war?"

"No change."

"What'll we do?"

"Come to terms. Their terms. We can't let it drag on another month. Everybody knows that. *They* know that."

"Licked by a little outfit like Ganymede."

"If only we had more time. But we don't. The ships must be out in deep-space again, right away. If we have to capitulate to get them out, then let's do it. Ganymede!" He spat. "If we could only break them. But by that time — "

"By that time the colonies won't exist."

"We have to get our cradles back in our own hands," Groves said grimly. "Even if it takes capitulation to do it."

"No other way will do?"

"You find another way." Groves pushed past Siller, out into corridor. "And if you find it, let me know."

The war had been going on for two Terran months, with no sign of a break. The System Senate's difficult position came from the fact that Ganymede was the jump-off point between the System and its precarious network of colonies at Proxima Centauri. All ships leaving the System for deep-space were launched from the immense space cradles on Ganymede. There were no other cradles. Ganymede had been agreed on as the jump-off point, and the cradles had been constructed there.

The Ganymedeans became rich, hauling freight and supplies in their tubby little ships. Over a period of time more and more Gany ships took to the sky, freighters and cruisers and patrol ships.

One day this odd fleet landed among the space cradles, killed and imprisoned the Terran and Martian guards, and proclaimed that Ganymede and the cradles were their property. If the Senate wanted to use the cradles they paid, and paid plenty. Twenty per cent of all freighted goods turned over to the Gany Emperor, left on the moon. And full Senate representation.

If the Senate fleet tried to take back the cradles by force the cradles would be destroyed. The Ganymedeans had already mined them with H-bombs. The Gany fleet surrounded the moon, a little ring of hard steel. If the Senate fleet tried to break through, seize the moon, it would be the end of the cradles. What could the System do?

And at Proxima, the colonies were starving.

"You're certain we can't launch ships into deep-space from regular fields," a Martian Senator asked.

"Only Class-One ships have any chance to reach the colonies," Commander James Carmichel said wearily. "A Class-One ship is ten times the size of a regular intra-system ship. A Class-One ship needs a cradle miles deep. Miles wide. You can't launch a ship that size from a meadow."

There was silence. The great Senate chambers were full, crowded to capacity with representatives from all the nine planets.

"The Proxima colonies won't last another twenty days," Doctor Basset testified. "That means we must get a ship on the way sometime next week. Otherwise, when we do get there we won't find anyone alive."

"When will the new Luna cradles be ready?"

"A month," Carmichel answered.

"No sooner?"

"No."

"Then apparently we'll have to accept Ganymede's terms." The Senate Leader snorted with disgust. "Nine planets and one wretched little moon! How dare they want equal voice with the System members!"

"We could break their ring," Carmichel said, "but they'll destroy the cradles without hesitation if we do."

"If only we could get supplies to the colonies without using space cradles," a Plutonian Senator said.

"That would mean without using Class-One ships."

"And nothing else will reach Proxima?"

"Nothing that we know of."

A Saturnian Senator arose. "Commander, what kind of ships does Ganymede use? They're different from your own?"

"Yes. But no one knows anything about them."

"How are they launched?"

Carmichel shrugged. "The usual way. From fields."

"Do you think — "

"I don't think they're deep-space ships. We're beginning to grasp at straws. There simply is no ship large enough to cross deep-space that doesn't require a space cradle. That's the fact we must accept."

The Senate Leader stirred. "A motion is already before the Senate that we accept the proposal of the Ganymedeans and conclude the war. Shall we take the vote, or are there any more questions?"

No one blinked his light.

"Then we'll begin. Mercury. What is the vote of the First Planet?"

"Mercury votes to accept the enemy's terms."

"Venus. What does Venus vote?"

"Venus votes — "

"*Wait!*" Commander Carmichel stood up suddenly. The Senate Leader raised his hand.

"What is it? The Senate is voting."

Carmichel gazed down intently at a foil strip that had been shot to him across the chamber, from the chart wing. "I don't know how important this is, but I think perhaps the Senate should know about it before it votes."

"What is it?"

"I have a message from the first line. A Martian raider has surprised and captured a Gany Research Station, on an asteroid between Mars and Jupiter. A large quantity of Gany equipment has been taken intact." Carmichel looked around the hall. "Including a Gany ship, a new ship, undergoing tests at the Station. The Gany staff was destroyed, but the prize ship is undamaged. The raider is bringing it here so it can be examined by our experts."

A murmur broke through the chamber.

"I put forth a motion that we withhold our decision until the Ganymedean ship has been examined," a Uranian Senator shouted. "Something might come of this!"

"The Ganymedeans have put a lot of energy into designing ships," Carmichel murmured to the Senate Leader. "Their ships are strange. Quite different from ours. Maybe. ... "

"What is the vote on this motion?" the Senate Leader asked. "Shall we wait until this ship can be examined?"

"Let's wait!" voices cried. "Wait! Let's see."

Carmichel rubbed his paw thoughtfully. "It's worth a try. But if nothing comes of this we'll have to go ahead and capitulate." He folded up the foil strip. "Anyhow, it's worth looking into. A Gany ship. I wonder. ... "

Doctor Earl Basset's face was red with exitement.

"Let me by." He pushed through the row of uniformed officers. "Please let me by." Two shiny Lieutenants stepped out of his way and he saw, for the first time, the great globe of steel and rexenoid that was the captured Ganymedean ship.

"Look at it," Major Siller whispered. "Nothing at all like our own ships. What makes it run?"

"No drive jets," Commander Carmichel said. "Only landing jets to set her down. What makes her go?"

The Ganymedean globe rested quietly in the center of the Terran Experimental laboratory, rising up from the circle of men like a great bubble. It was a beautiful ship, glimmering with an even metallic fire, shimmering and radiating a cold light.

"It gives you a strange feeling," General Groves said. Suddenly he caught his breath. "You don't suppose this — this could be a gravity drive ship? The Ganys were supposed to be experimenting with gravity."

"What's that?" Basset said.

"A gravity drive ship would reach its destination without time lapse. The velocity of gravity is infinite. Can't be measured. If this globe is — "

"Nonsense," Carmichel said. "Einstein showed gravity isn't a force but a warpage, a space warpage."

"But couldn't a ship be built using — "

"Gentlemen!" The Senate Leader came quickly into the laboratory, surrounded by his guards. "Is this the ship? This globe?" The officers pulled back and the Senate Leader went gingerly up to the great gleaming side. He touched it.

"It's undamaged," Siller said. "They're translating the control markings so we can use it."

"So this is the Ganymedean ship. Will it help us?"

"We don't know yet," Carmichel said.

"Here come the think-men," Groves said. The hatch of the globe had opened, and two men in white lab uniforms were stepping carefully down, carrying a semantibox.

"What are the results?" the Senate Leader asked.

"We've made the translations. A Terran crew could operate the ship now. All the controls are marked."

"We should make a study of the engines before we try the ship out," Doctor Basset said. "What do we know about it? We don't know what makes it run, or what fuel it uses."

"How long will such a study take?" the Leader asked.

"Several days, at least," Carmichel said.

"That long?"

"There's no telling what we'll run into. We may find a radically new type of drive and fuel. It might even take several weeks to finish the analysis."

The Senate Leader pondered.

"Sir," Carmichel said, "I think we should go ahead and have a test run. We can easily raise a volunteer crew."

"A trial run could begin at once," Groves said. "But we might have to wait weeks for the drive analysis."

"You believe a complete crew would volunteer?"

Carmichel rubbed his hands together. "Don't worry about that. Four men would do it. Three, outside of me."

"Two," General Groves said. "Count me in."

"How about me, sir?" Major Siller asked hopefully.

Doctor Basset pushed up nervously. "Is it all right for a civilian to volunteer? I'm curious as hell about this."

The Senate Leader smiled. "Why not? If you can be of use, go along. So the crew is already here."

The four men grinned at each other.

"Well?" Groves said. "What are we waiting for? Let's get her started!"

The linguist traced a meter reading with his finger. "You can see the Gany markings. Next to each we've put the Terran equivalent. There's one hitch, though. We know the Gany word for, say, five. *Zahf.* So where we find *zahf* we mark a five for you. See this dial? Where the arrow's at *nesi?* At zero. See how it's marked?"

100	liw
50	ka
5	zahf
0	nesi
5	zahf
50	ka
100	liw

Carmichel nodded. "So?"

"This is the problem. We don't know what the units refer to. Five, but five what? Fifty, but fifty what? Presumably velocity. Or is it distance? Since no study has been made of the workings of this ship — "

"You can't interpret?"

"How?" The linguist tapped a switch. "Obviously, this throws the drive on. *Mel* — start. You close the switch and it indicates *io* — stop. But how you guide the ship is a different matter. We can't tell you what the meter is for."

Groves touched a wheel. "Doesn't this guide her?"

"It governs the brake rockets, the landing jets. As for the central drive we don't know what it is or how you control it, once you're started. Semantics won't help you. Only experience. We can translate numbers only into numbers."

Groves and Carmichel looked at each other.

"Well?" Groves said. "We may find ourselves lost in space. Or falling into the sun. I saw a ship spiral into the sun, once. Faster and faster, down and down — "

"We're a long way from the sun. And we'll point her out, toward Pluto. We'll get control eventually. You don't want to unvolunteer, do you?"

"Of course not."

"How about the rest of you?" Carmichel said, to Basset and Siller. "You're still coming along?"

"Certainly." Basset was stepping cautiously into his spacesuit. "We're coming."

"Make sure you seal your helmet completely." Carmichel helped him fasten his leggings. "Your shoes, next."

"Commander," Groves said, "they're finishing on the vidscreen. I wanted it installed so we could establish contact. We might need some help getting back."

"Good idea." Carmichel went over, examining the leads from the screen. "Self-contained power unit?"

"For safety's sake. Independent from the ship."

Carmichel sat down before the vidscreen, clicking it on. The local monitor appeared. "Get me the Garrison Station on Mars. Commander Vecchi."

The call locked through. Carmichel began to lace his boots and leggings while he waited. He was lowering his helmet into place when the screen glowed into life. Vecchi's dark features formed, lean-jawed above his scarlet uniform.

"Greetings, Commander Carmichel," he murmured. He glanced curiously at Carmichel's suit. "You are going on a trip, Commander?"

"We may visit you. We're about to take the captured Gany ship up. If everything goes right I hope to set her down at your field, sometime later today."

"We'll have the field cleared and ready for you."

"Better have emergency equipment on hand. We're still unsure of the controls."

"I wish you luck." Vecchi's eyes flickered. "I can see the interior of your ship. What drive is it?"

"We don't know yet. That's the problem."

"I hope you will be able to land, Commander."

"Thanks. So do we." Carmichel broke the connection. Groves and Siller were already dressed. They were helping Basset tighten the screw locks of his earphones.

"We're ready," Groves said. He looked through the port. Outside a circle of officers watched silently.

"Say good-bye," Siller said to Basset. "This may be our last minute on Terra."

"Is there really much danger?"

Groves sat down beside Carmichel at the control board. "Ready?" His voice came to Carmichel through his phones.

"Ready." Carmichel reached out his gloved hand, toward the switch marked *mel*. "Here we go. Hold on tight!"

He grasped the switch firmly and pulled.

They were falling through space.

"Help!" Doctor Basset shouted. He slid across the up-ended floor, crashing against a table. Carmichel and Groves hung on grimly, trying to keep their places at the board.

The globe was spinning and dropping, settling lower and lower through a heavy sheet of rain. Below them, visible through the port, was a vast rolling ocean, an endless expanse of blue water, as far as the eye could see. Siller stared down at it, on his hands and knees, sliding with the globe.

"Commander, where — where should we be?"

"Someplace off Mars. But this can't be Mars!"

Groves flipped the brake rocket switches, one after another. The globe shuddered as the rockets came on, bursting into life around them.

"Easy does it," Carmichel said, craning his neck to see through the port. "Ocean? What the hell — "

The globe leveled off, shooting rapidly above the water, parallel to the surface. Siller got slowly to his feet, hanging onto the railing. He helped Basset up. "Okay, Doc?"

"Thanks." Basset wobbled. His glasses had come off inside his helmet. "Where are we? On Mars already?"

"We're there," Groves said, "but it isn't Mars."

"But I thought we were going to Mars."

"So did the rest of us." Groves decreased the speed of the globe cautiously. "You can see this isn't Mars."

"Then what is it?"

"I don't know. We'll find out, though. Commander, watch the starboard jet. It's overbalancing. Your switch."

Carmichel adjusted. "Where do you think we are? I don't understand it. Are we still on Terra? Or Venus?"

Groves flicked the vidscreen on. "I'll soon find out if we're on Terra." He raised the all-wave control. The screen remained blank. Nothing formed.

"We're not on Terra."

"We're not anywhere in the System." Groves spun the dial. "No response."

"Try the frequency of the big Mars Sender."

Groves adjusted the dial. At the spot where the Mars Sender should have come in there was — nothing. The four men gaped foolishly at the screen. All their lives they had received the familiar sanguine faces of Martian announcers on that wave. Twenty-four hours a day. The most powerful sender in the System. Mars Sender reached all the nine planets, and even out into deep-space. And it was always on the air.

"Lord," Basset said. "We're out of the System."

"We're not in the System," Groves said. "Notice the horizontal curve — This is a small planet we're on. Maybe a moon. But it's no planet or moon I've ever seen before. Not in the System, and not the Proxima area either."

Carmichel stood up. "The units must be big multiples, all right. We're out of the System, perhaps all the way around the galaxy." He peered out the port at the rolling water.

"I don't see any stars," Basset said.

"Later on we can get a star reading. When we're on the other side, away from the sun."

"Ocean," Siller murmured. "Miles of it. And a good temperature." He removed his helmet cautiously. "Maybe we won't need these after all."

"Better leave them on until we can make an atmosphere check," Groves said. "Isn't there a check tube on this bubble?"

"I don't see any," Carmichel said.

"Well, it doesn't matter. If we — "

"Sir!" Siller exclaimed. "Land."

They ran to the port. Land was rising into view, on the horizon of the planet. A long low strip of land, a coastline. They could see green; the land was fertile.

"I'll turn her a little right," Groves said, sitting down at the board. He adjusted the controls. "How's that?"

"Heading right toward it," Carmichel sat down beside him. "Well, at least we won't drown. I wonder where we are. How will we know? What if the star map can't be equated? We can take a spectroscopic analysis, try to find a known star — "

"We're almost there," Basset said nervously. "You better slow us down, General. We'll crash."

"I'm doing the best I can. Any mountains or peaks?"

"No. It seems quiet flat. Like a plain."

The globe dropped lower and lower, slowing down. Green scenery whipped past below them. Far off a row of meager hills came finally into view. The globe was barely skimming, now, as the two pilots fought to bring it to a stop.

"Easy, easy," Groves murmured. "Too fast."

All the brakes were firing. The globe was a bedlam of noise, knocked back and forth as the jets fired. Gradually it lost velocity, until it was almost hanging in the sky. Then it sank, like a toy balloon, settling slowly down to the green plain below.

"Cut the rockets!"

The pilots snapped their switches. Abruptly all sound ceased. They looked at each other.

"Any moment ... " Carmichel murmured.

Plop!

"We're down," Basset said. "We're down."

They unscrewed the hatch cautiously, their helmets tightly in place. Siller held a Boris gun ready, as Groves and Carmichel swung the heavy rexenoid disc back. A blast of warm air rolled into the globe, swelling around them.

"See anything?" Basset said.

"Nothing. Level fields. Some kind of planet." The General stepped down onto the ground. "Tiny plants! Thousands of them. I don't know what kind."

The other men stepped out, their boots sinking into the moist soil. They looked around them.

"Which way?" Siller said. "Toward those hills?"

"Might as well. What a flat planet!" Carmichel strode off, leaving deep tracks behind him. The others followed.

"Harmless looking place," Basset said. He picked a handful of the little plants. "What are they? Some kind of weed." He stuffed them into the pocket of his spacesuit.

"*Stop.*" Siller froze, rigid, his gun raised.

"What is it?"

"Something moved. Through that patch of shrubbery over there."

They waited. Everything was quiet around them. A faint breeze eddied through the surface of green. The sky overhead was a clear, warm blue, with a few faint clouds.

"What did it look like?" Basset said.

"Some insect. Wait." Siller crossed to the patch of plants. He kicked at them. All at once a tiny creature rushed out, scuttling away. Siller fired. The bolt from the Boris gun ignited the ground, a roar of white fire. When the cloud dissipated there was nothing but a seared pit.

"Sorry." Siller lowered the gun shakily.

"It's all right. Better to shoot first, on a strange planet." Groves and Carmichel went on ahead, up a low rise.

"Wait for me," Basset called. He fell behind the others. "I have something in my boot."

"You can catch up." The three went on, leaving the Doctor alone. He sat down on the moist ground, grumbling. He began to unlace his boot slowly, carefully.

Around him the air was warm. He sighed, relaxing. After a moment he removed his helmet and adjusted his glasses. Smells of plants and flowers were heavy in the air. He took a deep breath, letting it out again slowly. Then he put his helmet back on and finished lacing up his boot.

A tiny man, not six inches high, appeared from a clump of weeds and shot an arrow at him.

Basset stared down. The arrow, a minute splinter of wood, was sticking in the sleeve of his spacesuit. He opened and closed his mouth but no sounds came.

A second arrow glanced off the transparent shield of his helmet. Then a third and a fourth. The tiny man had been joined by companions, one of them on a tiny horse.

"Mother of Heaven!" Basset said.

"What's the matter?" General Groves' voice came in his earphones. "Are you all right, Doctor?"

"Sir, a tiny man just fired an arrow at me."

"Really?"

"There's — there's a whole bunch of them, now."

"Are you out of your mind?"

"No!" Basset scrambled to his feet. A volley of arrows rose up, sticking into his suit, glancing off his helmet. The shrill voices of the tiny men came to his ears, an excited, penetrating sound. "General, please come back here!"

Groves and Siller appeared at the top of the ridge. "Basset, you must be out of — "

They stopped, transfixed. Siller raised the Boris gun, but Groves pushed the muzzle down. "Impossible." He advanced, staring down at the ground. An arrow pinged against his helmet. "Little men. With bows and arrows."

Suddenly the little men turned and fled. They raced off, some on foot, some on horseback, back through the weeds and out the other side.

"There they go," Siller said. "Should we follow them? See where they live?"

"It isn't possible." Groves shook his head. "No planet has yielded tiny human beings like this. So *small!*"

Commander Carmichel strode down the ridge to them. "Did I really see it? You men saw it, too? Tiny figures, racing away?"

Groves pulled an arrow from his suit. "We saw. And felt." He held the arrow close to the plate of his helmet, examining it. "Look — the tip glitters. Metal tipped."

"Did you notice their costumes?" Basset said. "In a storybook I once read. Robin Hood. Little caps, boots."

"A story. . . . " Groves rubbed his jaw, a strange look suddenly glinting in his eyes. "A book."

"What, sir?" Siller said.

"Nothing." Groves came suddenly to life, moving away. "Let's follow them. I want to see their city."

He increased his pace, walking with great strides after the tiny men, who had not got very far off, yet.

"Come on," Siller said. "Before they get away." He and Carmichel and Basset followed behind Groves, catching up with him. The four of them kept pace with the tiny men, who were hurrying away as fast as they could. After a time one of the tiny men stopped, throwing himself down on the ground. The others hesitated, looking back.

"He's tired out," Siller said. "He can't make it."

Shrill squeaks rose. He was being urged on.

"Give him a hand," Basset said. He bent down, picking the tiny figure up. He held him carefully between his gloved fingers, turning him around and around.

"Ouch!" He set him down quickly.

"What is it?" Groves came over.

"He stung me." Basset massaged his thumb.

"Stung you?"

"Stabbed, I mean. With his sword."

"You'll be all right." Groves went on, after the tiny figures.

"Sir," Siller said to Carmichel, "this certainly makes the Ganymede problem seem remote."

"It's a long way off."

"I wonder what their city will be like," Groves said.

"I think I know," Basset said.

"You know? How?"

Basset did not answer. He seemed to be deep in thought, watching the figures on the ground intently.

"Come on," he said. "Let's not lose them."

They stood together, none of them speaking. Ahead, down a long slope, lay a miniature city. The tiny figures had fled into it, across a drawbridge. Now the bridge was rising, lifted by almost invisible threads. Even as they watched, the bridge snapped shut.

"Well, Doc?" Siller said. "This what you expected?"

Basset nodded. "Exactly."

The city was walled, built of gray stone. It was surrounded by a little moat. Countless spires rose up, a conglomeration of peaks and gables, tops of buildings. There was furious activity going on inside the city. A cacophony of shrill sounds from countless throats drifted across the moat to the four men, growing louder each moment. At the walls of the city figures appeared, soldiers in armor, peering across the moat at them.

Suddenly the drawbridge quivered. It began to slide down, descending into position. There was a pause. Then —

"Look!" Groves exclaimed. "Here they come."

Siller raised his gun. "My Lord! Look at them!"

A horde of armed men on horseback clattered across the drawbridge, spilling out onto the ground beyond. They came straight toward the four spacesuited men, the sun sparkling against their shields and spears. There were hundreds of them, decked with streamers and banners and pennants of all colors and sizes. An impressive sight, on a small scale.

"Get ready," Carmichel said. "They mean business. Watch your legs." He tightened the bolts of his helmet.

The first wave of horsemen reached Groves, who was standing a little ahead of the others. A ring of warriors surrounded him, little glittering armored and plumed figures, hacking furiously at his ankles with miniature swords.

"Cut it out!" Groves howled, leaping back. "Stop!"

"They're going to give us trouble," Carmichel said.

Siller began to giggle nervously, as arrows flew around him. "Shall I give it to them, sir? One blast from the Boris gun and — "

"No! Don't fire — that's an order." Groves moved back as a phalanx of horses rushed toward him, spears lowered. He swung his leg, spilling them over with his heavy boot. A frantic mass of men and horses struggled to right themselves.

"Back," Basset said. "Those damn archers."

Countless men on foot were rushing from the city with long bows and quivers strapped to their backs. A chaos of shrill sound filled the air.

"He's right," Carmichel said. His leggings had been hacked clean through by determined knights who had dismounted and were swinging again and again, trying to chop him down. "If we're not going to fire we better retreat. They're tough."

Clouds of arrows rained down on them.

"They know how to shoot," Groves admitted. "These men are trained soldiers."

"Watch out," Siller said "They're trying to get between us. Pick us off one by one." He moved toward Carmichel nervously. "Let's get out of here."

"Hear them?" Carmichel said. "They're mad. They don't like us."

The four men retreated, backing away. Gradually the tiny figures stopped following, pausing to reorganize their lines.

"It's lucky for us we have our suits on," Groves said. "This isn't funny anymore."

Siller bent down and pulled up a clump of weeds. He tossed the clump at the line of knights. They scattered.

"Let's go," Basset said. "Let's leave."

"Leave?"

"Let's get out of here." Basset was pale. "I can't believe it. Must be some kind of hypnosis. Some kind of control of our minds. It can't be real."

Siller caught his arm. "Are you all right? What's the matter?"

Basset's face was contorted strangely. "I can't accept it," he muttered thickly. "Shakes the whole fabric of the universe. All basic beliefs."

"Why? What do you mean?"

Groves put his hand on Basset's shoulder. "Take it easy, Doctor."

"But General — "

"I know what you're thinking. But it can't be. There must be some rational explanation. There has to be."

"A fairy tale," Basset muttered. "A story."

"Coincidence. The story was a social satire, nothing more. A social satire, a work of fiction. It just seems like this place. The resemblance is only — "

"What are you two talking about?" Carmichel said.

"This place." Bassett pulled away. "We've got to get out of here. We're caught in a mind web of some sort."

"What's he talking about?" Carmichel looked from Basset to Groves. "Do you know where we are?"

"We can't be there," Basset said.

"*Where?*"

"He made it up. A fairy tale. A child's tale."

"No, a social satire, to be exact," Groves said.

"What are they talking about, sir?" Siller said to Commander Carmichel. "Do you know?"

Carmichel grunted. A slow light dawned in his face. "What?"

"Do you know where we are, sir?"

"Let's get back to the globe," Carmichel said.

Groves paced nervously. He stopped by the port, looking out intently, peering into the distance.

"More coming?" Basset said.

"Lots more."

"What are they doing out there *now?*"

"Still working on their tower."

The little people were erecting a tower, a scaffolding up the side of the globe. Hundreds of them were working together, knights, archers, even women and boys. Horses and oxen pulling tiny carts were drawing supplies from the city. A shrill hubbub penetrated the rexenoid hull of the globe, filtering to the four men inside.

"Well?" Carmichel said. "What'll we do? Go back?"

"I've had enough," Groves said. "All I want now is to go back to Terra."

"Where are we?" Siller demanded, for the tenth time. "Doc, you know. Tell me, damn it! All three of you know. Why won't you say?"

"Because we want to keep our sanity," Basset said, his teeth clenched. "That's why."

"I'd sure like to know," Siller murmured. "If we went over in the corner would you tell me?"

Basset shook his head. "Don't bother me, Major."

"It just can't be," Groves said. "How *could* it be?"

"And if we leave, we'll never know. We'll never be sure. It'll haunt us all our lives. Were we really — *here?* Does this place really exist? And is this place really — "

"There was a second place," Carmichel said abruptly.

"A second place?"

"In the story. A place where the people were big."

Basset nodded. "Yes. It was called — What?"

"Brobdingnag."

"Brobdingnag. Maybe it exists, too."

"Then you really think this is — "

"Doesn't it fit his description?" Basset waved toward the port. "Isn't that what he described? Everything small, tiny soldiers, little walled cities, oxen, horses, knights, kings, pennants. Drawbridge. Moat. And their damn towers. Always building towers — and shooting arrows."

"Doc," Siller said. "Whose description?"

No answer.

"Could — could you whisper it to me?"

"I don't see how it can be," Carmichel said flatly. "I remember the book, of course. I read it when I was a child, as we all did. Later on I realized it was a satire of the manners of the times. But good Lord, it's either one or the other! Not a real place!"

"Maybe he had a sixth sense. Maybe he really was there. Here. In a vision. Maybe he had a vision. They say that he was supposed to have been psychotic, toward the end."

"Brobdingnag. The other place." Carmichel pondered. "If this exists, maybe that exists. It might tell us ... We might know, for sure. Some sort of verification."

"Yes, our theory. Hypothesis. We predict that it should exist, too. Its existence would be a kind of proof."

"The L theory, which predicts the existence of B."

"We've got to be sure," Basset said. "If we go back without being sure, we'll always wonder. When we're fighting the Ganymedeans we'll stop suddenly and wonder — was I really there? Does it really exist? All these years we thought it was just a story. But now — "

Groves walked over to the control board and sat down. He studied the dials intently. Carmichel sat down beside him.

"See this, Groves said, touching the big central meter with his finger. "The reading is up to *liw*, 100. Remember where it was when we started?"

"Of course. At *nesi*. At zero. Why?"

"*Nesi* is neutral position. Our starting position, back on Terra. We've gone the limit one way. Carmichel, Basset is right. We've got to find out. We can't go back to Terra without knowing if this really is .... *You know.*"

"You want to throw it back all the way? Not stop at zero? Go on to the other end? To the other *lim?*"

Groves nodded.

"All right." The Commander let his breath out slowly. "I agree with you. I want to know, too. I have to know."

"Doctor Basset." Groves brought the Doctor over to the board. "We're not going back to Terra, not yet. The two of us want to go on."

"On?" Basset's face twitched. "You mean on beyond? To the other side?"

They nodded. There was silence. Outside the globe the pounding and ringing had ceased. The tower had almost reached the level of the port.

"We must know," Groves said.

"I'm for it," Basset said.

"Good," Carmichel said.

"I wish one of you would tell me what it is you're talking about," Siller said plaintively. "Can't you tell me?"

"Then here goes." Groves took hold of the switch. He held it for a moment, sitting silently. "Are we ready?"

"Ready," Basset said.

Groves threw the switch, all the way down.

Shapes, enormous and confused.

The globe floundered, trying to right itself. Again they were falling, sliding about. The globe was lost in a sea of vague misty forms, immense dim figures that moved on all sides of them, beyond the port.

Basset stared out, his jaws slack. "What — "

Faster and faster the globe fell. Everything was diffused, unformed. Shapes like shadows drifted and flowed outside, shapes so huge that their outlines were lost.

"Sir!" Siller muttered. "Commander! Hurry! Look!"

Carmichel made his way to the port.

They were in a world of giants. A towering figure walked past them, a torso so large that they could see only a portion of it. There were other shapes, but so vast and dim they could not be identified. All around the globe was a roaring, a deep undercurrent of sound like the waves of a monstrous ocean. An echoing sound, a booming that tossed and bounced the globe around and around.

Groves looked up at Basset and Carmichel.

"Then it's true," Basset said.

"This confirms it."

"I can't believe it," Carmichel said. "But this is the proof we asked for. Here it is — out there."

Outside the globe something was coming closer, coming ponderously toward them. Siller gave a sudden shout, moving back from the port. He grabbed up the Boris gun, his face ashen.

"Groves!" Basset cried. "Throw it to neutral! Quick! We've got to get away."

Carmichel pushed Siller's gun down. He grinned fixedly at him. "Sorry. This time it's too small."

A hand was reached toward them, a hand so large that it blotted out the light. Fingers, skin with gaping pores, nails, great tufts of hair. The globe shuddered as the hand closed around them from all sides.

"General! Quick!"

Then it was gone. The pressure ceased, winking out. Beyond the port was — nothing. The dials were in motion again, the pointer rising up toward *nesi*. Toward neutral. Toward Terra.

Basset breathed a sigh of relief. He removed his helmet and mopped his forehead.

"We got away," Groves said. "Just in time."

"A hand," Siller said. "Reaching for us. A big hand. Where were we? Tell me!"

Carmichel sat down beside Groves. They looked silently at each other.

Carmichel grunted. "We mustn't tell anyone. No one. They wouldn't believe us, and anyhow, it would be very damaging if they did. A society can't learn something like this. Too much would totter."

"He must have seen it in a vision. Then he wrote it up as a children's story. He knew he could never put it down as fact."

"Something like that. So it really exists. Both exist. And perhaps others. Wonderland, Oz, Pellucidar, Erewhon, all the fantasies, dreams — "

Groves put his hand on the Commander's arm. "Take it easy. We'll simply tell them the ship didn't work. As far as they're concerned we didn't go anywhere. Right?"

"Right." Already, the vidscreen was sputtering, coming to life. An image was forming. "Right. We won't say anything. Just the four of us will know." He glanced at Siller. "Just the three of us, I mean."

On the vidscreen the image of the Senate Leader was fully formed. "Commander Carmichel! Are you safe? Were you able to land? Mars sent us no report. Is your crew all right?"

Basset peered out the port. "We're hanging about a mile up from the city. Terra City. Dropping slowly down. The sky is full of ships. We don't need help, do we?"

"No," Carmichel said. He began to fire the brake rocket slowly, easing the ship down.

"Someday, when the war is over," Basset said, "I want to ask the Ganymedeans about this. I'd like to find out the whole story."

"Maybe you'll get your chance," Groves said, suddenly sobered. "That's right. Ganymede! Our chance to win the war certainly fizzled."

"The Senate Leader is going to be disappointed," Carmichel said grimly. "You may get your wish very soon, Doctor. The war will probably be over shortly, now that we're back — empty handed."

The slender yellow Ganymedean moved slowly into the room, his robes slithering across the floor after him. He stopped, bowing.

Commander Carmichel nodded stiffly.

"I was told to come here," the Ganymedean lisped softly. "They tell me that some of our property is in this laboratory."

"That's right."

"If there are no objections, we would like to — "

"Go ahead and take it."

"Good. I am glad to see there is no animosity on your part. Now that we are all friends again, I hope that we can work together in harmony, on an equal basis of — "

Carmichel turned abruptly away, walking toward the door. "Your property is this way. Come along."

The Ganymedean followed him into the central lab building. There, resting silently in the center of the vast room, was the globe.

Groves came over. "I see they've come for it."

"Here it is," Carmichel said to the Ganymedean. "Your spaceship. Take it."

"Our time ship, you mean."

Groves and Carmichel jerked. "Your *what?*"

The Ganymedean smiled quietly. "Our time ship." He indicated the globe. "There it is. May I begin moving it onto our transport?"

"Get Basset," Carmichel said. "Quick!"

Groves hurried from the room. A moment later he returned with Doctor Basset.

"Doctor, this Gany is after his property." Carmichel took a deep breath. "His — his time machine."

Basset leaped. "His *what?* His time machine?" His face twitched. Suddenly he backed away. "This? A time machine? Not what we — Not — "

Groves calmed himself with an effort. He addressed the Ganymedean as casually as he could, standing to one side, a little dismayed. "May we ask you a couple of questions before you take your — your time ship?"

"Of course. I will answer as best I can."

"This globe. It — it goes through time? Not space? It's a time machine? Goes into the past? Into the future?"

"That is correct."

"I see. And *nesi* on the dial, that's the present."

"Yes."

"The upward reading is the past?"

"Yes."

"The downward reading is the future, then. One more thing. Just one more. A person going back into the past would find that because of the expansion of the universe — "

The Ganymedean reacted. A smile crossed his face, a subtle, knowing smile. "Then you have tried out the ship?"

Groves nodded.

"You went into the past and found everything much smaller? Reduced in size?"

"That's right — because the universe is expanding! And the future. Everything increased in size. Expanded."

"Yes." The Ganymedean's smile broadened. "It is a shock, is it not? You are astonished to find your world reduced in size, populated by minute beings. But size, of course, is relative. As you discover when you go into the future."

"So that's it." Groves let out his breath. "Well, that's all. You can have your ship."

"Time travel," the Ganymedean said regretfully, "is not a successful undertaking. The past is too small, the future too expanded. We considered this ship a failure."

The Gany touched the globe with his feeler.

"We could not imagine why you wanted it. It was even suggested that you stole the ship to use — " the Gany smiled — "to use to reach your colonies in deep-space. But that would have been *too* amusing. We could not really believe that."

No one said anything.

The Gany made a whistling signal. A work crew came filing in and began to load the globe onto an enormous flat truck.

"So that's it," Groves muttered. "It was Terra all the time. And those people, they were our ancestors."

"About fifteenth century," Basset said. "Or so I'd say by their costumes. Middle Ages."

They looked at each other.

Suddenly Carmichel laughed. "And we thought it was — We thought we were at — "

"I knew it was only a child's story," Basset said.

"A social satire," Groves corrected him.

Silently they watched the Ganymedeans trundle their globe out of the building, onto the waiting cargo ship.

NANNY

"WHEN I LOOK BACK," Mary Fields said, "I marvel that we ever could have grown up without a Nanny to take care of us."

There was no doubt that Nanny had changed the whole life of the Fields' house since she had come. From the time the children opened their eyes in the morning to their last sleepy nod at night, Nanny was in there with them, watching them, hovering about them, seeing that all their wants were taken care of.

Mr. Fields knew, when he went to the office, that his kids were safe, perfectly safe. And Mary was relieved of a countless procession of chores and worries. She did not have to wake the children up, dress them, see that they were washed, ate their meals, or anything else. She did not even have to take them to school. And after school, if they did not come right home, she did not have to pace back and forth in anxiety, worried that something had happened to them.

Not that Nanny spoiled them, of course. When they demanded something absurd or harmful (a whole storeful of candy, or a policeman's motorcycle) Nanny's will was like iron. Like a good shepherd she knew when to refuse the flock its wishes.

Both children loved her. Once, when Nanny had to be sent to the repair shop, they cried and cried without stopping. Neither their mother nor their father could console them. But at last Nanny was back again, and everything was all right. And just in time! Mrs. Fields was exhausted.

"Lord," she said, throwing herself down. "What would we do without her?"

Mr. Fields looked up. "Without who?"

"Without Nanny."

"Heaven only knows," Mr. Fields said.

After Nanny had aroused the children from sleep — by emitting a soft, musical whirr a few feet from their heads — she made certain that they were dressed and down at the breakfast table promptly, with faces clean and dispositions unclouded. If they were cross Nanny allowed them the pleasure of riding downstairs on her back.

Coveted pleasure! Almost like a roller coaster, with Bobby and Jean hanging on for dear life and Nanny flowing down step by step in the funny rolling way she had.

Nanny did not prepare breakfast, of course. That was all done by the kitchen. But she remained to see that the children ate properly and then, when breakfast was over, she supervised their preparations for school. And after they had got their books together and were all brushed and neat, her most important job: seeing that they were safe on the busy streets.

There were many hazards in the city, quite enough to keep Nanny watchful. The swift rocket cruisers that swept along, carrying businessmen to work. The time a bully had tried to hurt Bobby. One quick push from Nanny's starboard grapple and away he went, howling for all he was worth. And the time a drunk started talking to Jean, with heaven knows *what* in mind. Nanny tipped him into the gutter with one nudge of her powerful metal side.

Sometimes the children would linger in front of a store. Nanny would have to prod them gently, urging them on. Or if (as sometimes happened) the children were late to school, Nanny would put them on her back and fairly speed along the sidewalk, her treads buzzing and flapping at a great rate.

After school Nanny was with them constantly, supervising their play, watching over them, protecting them, and at last, when it began to get dark and late, dragging them away from their games and turned in the direction of home.

Sure enough, just as dinner was being set on the table, there was Nanny, herding Bobby and Jean in through the front door, clicking and whirring admonishingly at them. Just in time for dinner! A quick run to the bathroom to wash their faces and hands.

And at night —

Mrs. Fields was silent, frowning just a little. At night... "Tom?" she said.

Her husband looked up from his paper. "What?"

"I've been meaning to talk to you about something. It's very odd, something I don't understand. Of course, I don't know anything about mechanical things. But Tom, at night when we're all sleep and the house is quiet, Nanny — "

There was a sound.

"Mommy!" Jean and Bobby came scampering into the living room, their faces flushed with pleasure. "Mommy, we raced Nanny all the way home, and we won!"

"We won," Bobby said. "We beat her."

"We ran a lot faster than she did," Jean said.

"Where is Nanny, children?" Mrs. Fields asked.

"She's coming. Hello, Daddy."

"Hello, kids," Tom Fields said. He cocked his head to one side, listening. From the front porch came an odd scraping sound, an unusual whirr and scrape. He smiled.

"That's Nanny," Bobby said.

And into the room came Nanny.

Mr. Fields watched her. She had always intrigued him. The only sound in the room was her metal treads, scraping against the hardwood floor, a peculiar rhythmic sound. Nanny came to a halt in front of him, stopping a few feet away. Two unwinking photocell eyes appraised him, eyes on flexible wire stalks. The stalks moved speculatively, weaving slightly. Then they withdrew.

Nanny was built in the shape of a sphere, a large metal sphere, flattened on the bottom. Her surface had been sprayed with a dull green enamel, which had become chipped and gouged through wear. There was not much visible in addition to the eye stalks. The treads could not be seen. On each side of the hull was the outline of a door. From these the magnetic grapples came, when they were needed. The front of the hull came to a point, and there the metal was reinforced. The extra plates welded both fore and aft made her look almost like a weapon of war. A tank of some kind. Or a ship, a rounded metal ship that had come up on land. Or like an insect. A sowbug, as they are called.

"Come on!" Bobby shouted.

Abruptly Nanny moved, spinning slightly as her treads gripped the floor and turned her around. One of her side doors opened. A long metal rod shot out. Playfully, Nanny caught Bobby's arm with her grapple and drew him to her. She perched him on her back. Bobby's leg straddled the metal hull. He kicked with his heels excitedly, jumping up and down.

"Race you around the block!" Jean shouted.

"Giddup!" Bobby cried. Nanny moved away, out of the room with him. A great round bug of whirring metal and relays, clicking photocells and tubes. Jean ran beside her.

There was silence. The parents were alone again.

"Isn't she amazing?" Mrs. Fields said. "Of course, robots are a common sight these days. Certainly more so than a few years ago. You see them everywhere you go, behind counters in stores, driving buses, digging ditches — "

"But Nanny is different," Tom Fields murmured.

"She's — she's not like a machine. She's like a person. A living person. But after all, she's much more complex than any other kind. She has to be. They say she's even more intricate than the kitchen."

"We certainly paid enough for her," Tom said.

"Yes," Mary Fields murmured. "She's very much like a living creature." There was a strange note in her voice. "Very much so."

"She sure takes care of the kids," Tom said, returning to his newspaper.

"But I'm worried." Mary put her coffee cup down, frowning. They were eating dinner. It was late. The two children had been sent up to bed. Mary touched her mouth with her napkin. "Tom, I'm worried. I wish you'd listen to me."

Tom Fields blinked. "Worried? What about?"

"About her. About Nanny."

"Why?"

"I — I don't know."

"You mean we're going to have to repair her again? We just got through fixing her. What is it this time? If those kids didn't get her to — "

"It's not that."

"What, then?"

For a long time his wife did not answer. Abruptly she got up from the table and walked across the room to the stairs. She peered up, staring into the darkness. Tom watched her, puzzled.

"What's the matter?"

"I want to be sure she can't hear us."

"She? Nanny?"

Mary came toward him. "Tom, I woke up last night again. Because of the sounds. I heard them again, the same sounds, the sounds I heard before. And you told me it didn't mean anything!"

Tom gestured. "It doesn't. What does it mean?"

"I don't know. That's what worries me. But after we're all asleep she comes downstairs. She leaves their room. She slips down the stairs as quietly as she can, as soon as she's sure we're all asleep."

"But why?"

"I don't know! Last night I heard her going down, slithering down the stairs, quiet as a mouse. I heard her moving around down here. And then — "

"Then what?"

"Tom, then I heard her go out the back door. Out, outside the house. She went into the back yard. That was all I heard for a while."

Tom rubbed his jaw. "Go on."

"I listened. I sat up in bed. You were asleep, of course. Sound asleep. No use trying to wake you. I got up and went to the window. I lifted the shade and looked out. She was out there, out in the back yard."

"What was she doing?"

"I don't know." Mary Fields's face was lined with worry. "I don't know! What in the world *would* a Nanny be doing outside at night, in the back yard?"

It was dark. Terribly dark. But the infrared filter clicked into place, and the darkness vanished. The metal shape moved forward, easing through the kitchen, its treads half-retracted for greatest quiet. It came to the back door and halted, listening.

There was no sound. The house was still. They were all asleep upstairs. Sound asleep.

The Nanny pushed, and the back door opened. It moved out onto the porch, letting the door close gently behind it. The night air was thin and cold. And full of smells, all the strange, tingling smells of the night, when spring has begun to change into summer, when the ground is still moist and the hot July sun has not had a chance to kill all the little growing things.

The Nanny went down the steps, onto the cement path. Then it moved cautiously onto the lawn, the wet blades of grass slapping its sides. After a time it stopped, rising up on its back treads. Its front part jutted up into the air. Its eye stalks stretched, rigid and taut, waving very slightly. Then it settled back down and continued its motion forward.

It was just going around the peach tree, coming back toward the house, when the noise came.

It stopped instantly, alert. Its side doors fell away and its grapples ran out their full lengths, lithe and wary. On the other side of the board fence, beyond the row of shasta daisies, something had stirred. The Nanny peered, clicking filters rapidly. Only a few faint stars winked in the sky overhead. But it saw, and that was enough.

On the other side of the fence a second Nanny was moving, making its way softly through the flowers, coming toward the fence. It was trying to make as little noise as possible. Both Nannies stopped, suddenly unmoving, regarding each other — the green Nanny waiting in its own yard, the blue prowler that had been coming toward the fence.

The blue prowler was a larger Nanny, built to manage two young boys. Its sides were dented and warped from use, but its grapples were still strong and powerful. In addition to the usual reinforced plates across its nose there was a gouge of tough steel, a jutting jaw that was already sliding into position, ready and able.

Mecho-Products, its manufacturer, had lavished attention on this jaw-construction. It was their trademark, their unique feature. Their ads, their brochures, stressed the massive frontal scoop mounted on all their models. And there was an optional assist: a cutting edge, power-driven, that at extra cost could easily be installed in their "Luxury-line" models.

This blue Nanny was so equipped.

Moving cautiously ahead, the blue Nanny reached the fence. It stopped and carefully inspected the boards. They were thin and rotted, put up a long time ago. It pushed its hard head against the wood. The fence gave, splintering and ripping. At once the green Nanny rose on its back treads, its grapples leaping out. A fierce joy filled it, a bursting excitement. The wild frenzy of battle.

The two closed, rolling silently on the ground, their grapples locked. Neither made any noise, the blue Mecho-Products Nanny nor the smaller, lighter, pale-green Service Industries, Inc., Nanny. On and on they fought, hugged tightly together, the great jaw trying to push underneath, into the soft treads. And the green Nanny trying to hook its metal point into the eyes that gleamed fitfully against its side. The green Nanny had the disadvantage of being a medium-priced model; it was outclassed and outweighed. But it fought grimly, furiously.

On and on they struggled, rolling in the wet soil. Without sound of any kind. Performing the wrathful, ultimate task for which each had been designed.

"I can't imagine," Mary Fields murmured, shaking her head. "I just don't know."

"Do you suppose some animal did it?" Tom conjectured. "Are there any big dogs in the neighborhood?"

"No. There was a big red Irish setter, but they moved away, to the country. That was Mr. Petty's dog."

The two of them watched, troubled and disturbed. Nanny lay at rest by the bathroom door, watching Bobby to make sure he brushed his teeth. The green hull was twisted and bent. One eye had been shattered, the glass knocked out, splintered. One grapple no longer retracted completely; it hung forlornly out of its little door, dragging uselessly.

"I just don't understand," Mary repeated. "I'll call the repair place and see what they say. Tom, it must have happened sometime during the night. While we were asleep. The noises I heard — "

"Shhh," Tom muttered warningly. Nanny was coming toward them, away from the bathroom. Clicking and whirring raggedly, she passed them, a limping green tub of metal that emitted an unrhythmic, grating sound. Tom and Mary Fields unhappily watched her as she lumbered slowly into the living room.

"I wonder," Mary murmured.

"Wonder what?"

"I wonder if this will happen again." She glanced up suddenly at her husband, eyes full of worry. "You know how the children love her ... and they need her so. They just wouldn't be safe without her. Would they?"

"Maybe it won't happen again," Tom said soothingly. "Maybe it was an accident." But he didn't believe it; he knew better. What had happened was no accident.

From the garage he backed his surface cruiser, maneuvered it until its loading entrance was locked against the rear door of the house. It took only a moment to load the sagging, dented Nanny inside; within ten minutes he was on his way across town to the repair and maintenance department of Service Industries, Inc.

The serviceman, in grease-stained white overalls, met him at the entrance. "Troubles?" he asked wearily; behind him, in the depths of the block-long building, stood rows of battered Nannies, in various stages of disassembly. "What seems to be the matter this time?"

Tom said nothing. He ordered the Nanny out of the cruiser and waited while the serviceman examined it for himself.

Shaking his head, the serviceman crawled to his feet and wiped grease from his hands. "That's going to run into money," he said. "The whole neural transmission's out."

His throat dry, Tom demanded: "Ever see anything like this before? It didn't break; you know that. It was demolished."

"Sure," the serviceman agreed tonelessly. "It pretty much got taken down a peg. On the basis of those missing chunks—" He indicated the dented anterior hull-sections. "I'd guess it was one of Mecho's new jaw-models."

Tom Fields's blood stopped moving in his veins. "Then this isn't new to you," he said softly, his chest constricting. "This goes on all the time."

"Well, Mecho just put out that jaw-model. It's not half bad ... costs about twice what this model ran. Of course," the serviceman added thoughtfully, "we have an equivalent. We can match their best, and for less money."

Keeping his voice as calm as possible, Tom said: "I want this one fixed. I'm not getting another."

"I'll do what I can. But it won't be the same as it was. The damage goes pretty deep. I'd advise you to trade it in—you can get damn near what you paid. With the new models coming out in a month or so, the salesmen are eager as hell to—"

"Let me get this straight." Shakily, Tom Fields lit up a cigarette. "You people really don't want to fix these, do you? You want to sell brand-new ones, when these break down." He eyed the repairman intently. "Break down, or are *knocked* down."

The repairman shrugged. "It seems like a waste of time to fix it up. It's going to get finished off, anyhow, soon." He kicked the misshapen green hull with his boot. "This model is around three years old. Mister, it's obsolete."

"Fix it up," Tom grated. He was beginning to see the whole picture; his self-control was about to snap. "I'm not getting a new one! I want this one fixed!"

"Sure," the serviceman said, resigned. He began making out a work-order sheet. "We'll do our best. But don't expect miracles."

While Tom Fields was jerkily signing his name to the sheet, two more damaged Nannies were brought into the repair building.

"When can I get it back?" he demanded.

"It'll take a couple of days," the mechanic said, nodding toward the rows of semi-repaired Nannies behind him. "As you can see," he added leisurely, "we're pretty well full-up."

"I'll wait," Tom said tautly. "Even if it takes a month."

"Let's go to the park!" Jean cried.

So they went to the park.

It was a lovely day, with the sun shining down hotly and the grass and flowers blowing in the wind. The two children strolled along the gravel path, breathing the warm-scented air, taking deep breaths and holding the presence of roses and hydrangeas and orange blossoms inside them as long as possible. They passed through a swaying grove of dark, rich cedars. The ground was soft with mold underfoot, the velvet, moist fur of a living world beneath their feet. Beyond the cedars, where the sun returned and the blue sky flashed back into being, a great green lawn stretched out.

Behind them Nanny came, trudging slowly, her treads clicking noisily. The dragging grapple had been repaired, and a new optic unit had been installed in place of the damaged one. But the smooth coordination of the old days was lacking; and the clean-cut lines of her hull had not been restored. Occasionally she halted, and the two children halted, too, waiting impatiently for her to catch up with them.

"What's the matter, Nanny?" Bobby asked her.

"Something's wrong with her," Jean complained. "She's been all funny since last Wednesday. Real slow and funny. And she was gone, for a while."

"She was in the repair shop," Bobby announced. "I guess she got sort of tired. She's old, Daddy says. I heard him and Mommy talking."

A little sadly they continued on, with Nanny painfully following. Now they had come to benches placed here and there on the lawn, with people languidly dozing in the sun. On the grass lay a young man, a newspaper over his face, his coat rolled up under his head. They crossed carefully around him, so as not to step on him.

"There's the lake!" Jean shouted, her spirits returning.

The great field of grass sloped gradually down, lower and lower. At the far end, the lowest end, lay a path, a gravel trail, and beyond that, a blue lake. The two children scampered excitedly, filled with anticipation. They hurried faster and faster down the carefully-graded slope, Nanny struggling miserably to keep up with them.

"The lake!"

"Last one there's a dead Martian stinko-bug!"

Breathlessly, they rushed across the path, onto the tiny strip of green bank against which the water lapped. Bobby threw himself down on his hands and knees, laughing and panting and peering down into the water. Jean settled down beside him, smoothing her dress tidily into place. Deep in the cloudy-blue water some tadpoles and minnows moved, minute artificial fish too small to catch.

At one end of the lake some children were floating boats with flapping white sails. At a bench a fat man sat laboriously reading a book, a pipe jammed in his mouth. A young man and woman strolled along the edge of the lake together, arm in arm, intent on each other, oblivious of the world around them.

"I wish we had a boat," Bobby said wistfully.

Grinding and clashing, Nanny managed to make her way across the path and up to them. She stopped, settling down, retracting her treads. She did not stir. One eye, the good eye, reflected the sunlight. The other had not been synchronized; it gaped with futile emptiness. She had managed to shift most of her weight on her less-damaged side, but her motion was bad and uneven, and slow. There was a smell about her, an odor of burning oil and friction.

Jean studied her. Faintly she patted the bent green side sympathetically. "Poor Nanny! What did you do, Nanny? What happened to you? Were you in a wreck?"

"Let's push Nanny in," Bobby said lazily. "And see if she can swim. Can a Nanny swim?"

Jean said no, because she was too heavy. She would sink to the bottom and they would never see her again.

"Then we won't push her in," Bobby agreed.

For a time there was silence. Overhead a few birds fluttered past, plump specks streaking swiftly across the sky. A small boy on a bicycle came riding hesitantly along the gravel path, his front wheel wobbling.

"I wish I had a bicycle," Bobby murmured.

The boy careened on past. Across the lake the fat man stood up and knocked his pipe against the bench. He closed his book and sauntered off along the path, wiping his perspiring forehead with a vast red handkerchief.

"What happens to Nannies when they get old?" Bobby asked wonderingly. "What do they do? Where do they go?"

"They go to heaven." Jean lovingly thumped the green dented hull with her hand. "Just like everybody else."

"Are Nannies born? Were there always Nannies?" Bobby had begun to conjecture on ultimate cosmic mysteries. "Maybe there was a time before there were Nannies. I wonder what the world was like in the days before Nannies lived."

"Of course there were always Nannies," Jean said impatiently. "If there weren't, where did they come from?"

Bobby couldn't answer that. He meditated for a time, but presently he became sleepy ... he was really too young to solve such problems. His eyelids became heavy and he yawned. Both he and Jean lay on the warm grass by the edge of the lake, watching the sky and the clouds, listening to the wind moving through the grove of cedar trees. Beside them the battered green Nanny rested and recuperated her meager strength.

A little girl came slowly across the field of grass, a pretty child in a blue dress with a bright ribbon in her long dark hair. She was coming toward the lake.

"Look," Jean said. "There's Phyllis Casworthy. She has an *orange* Nanny."

They watched, interested. "Who ever heard of an orange Nanny?" Bobby said, disgusted. The girl and her Nanny crossed the path a short distance down, and reached the edge of the lake. She and her orange Nanny halted, gazing around at the water and the white sails of toy boats, the mechanical fish.

"Her Nanny is bigger than ours," Jean observed.

"That's true," Bobby admitted. He thumped the green side loyally. "But ours is nicer. Isn't she?"

Their Nanny did not move. Surprised, he turned to look. The green Nanny stood rigid, taut. Its better eye stalk was far out, staring at the orange Nanny fixedly, unwinkingly.

"What's the matter?" Bobby asked uncomfortably.

"Nanny, what's the matter?" Jean echoed.

The green Nanny whirred, as its gears meshed. Its treads dropped and locked into place with a sharp metallic snap. Slowly its doors retracted and its grapples slithered out.

"Nanny, what are you doing?" Jean scrambled nervously to her feet. Bobby leaped up, too.

"Nanny! What's going on?"

"Let's go." Jean said, frightened. "Let's go home."

"Come on, Nanny," Bobby ordered. "We're going home, now."

The green Nanny moved away from them; it was totally unaware of their existence. Down the lake-side the other Nanny, the great orange Nanny, detached itself from the little girl and began to flow.

"Nanny, you come back!" the little girl's voice came, shrill and apprehensive.

Jean and Bobby rushed up the sloping lawn, away from the lake. "She'll come!" Bobby said. "Nanny! Please come!"

But the Nanny did not come.

The orange Nanny neared. It was huge, much more immense than the blue Mecho jaw-model that had come into the back yard that night. That one now lay scattered in pieces on the far side of the fence, hull ripped open, its parts strewn everywhere.

This Nanny was the largest the green Nanny had ever seen. The green Nanny moved awkwardly to meet it, raising its grapples and preparing its internal shields. But the orange Nanny was unbending a square arm of metal, mounted on a long cable. The metal arm whipped out, rising high in the air. It began to whirl in a circle, gathering ominous velocity, faster and faster.

The green Nanny hesitated. It retreated, moving uncertainly away from the swinging mace of metal. And as it rested warily, unhappily, trying to make up its mind, the other leaped.

"Nanny!" Jean screamed.

"Nanny! Nanny!"

The two metal bodies rolled furiously in the grass, fighting and struggling desperately. Again and again the metal mace came, bashing wildly into the green side. The warm sun shone benignly down on them. The surface of the lake eddied gently in the wind.

"Nanny!" Bobby screamed, helplessly jumping up and down.

But there was no response from the frenzied, twisting mass of crashing orange and green.

"What are you going to do?" Mary Fields asked, tight-lipped and pale.

"You stay here." Tom grabbed up his coat and threw it on; he yanked his hat down from the closet shelf and strode toward the front door.

"Where are you going?"

"Is the cruiser out front?" Tom pulled open the front door and made his way out onto the porch. The two children, miserable and trembling, watched him fearfully.

"Yes," Mary murmured, "it's out front. But where — "

Tom turned abruptly to the children. "You're sure she's — *dead*?"

Bobby nodded. His face was streaked with grimy tears. "Pieces ... all over the lawn."

Tom nodded grimly. "I'll be right back. And don't worry at all. You three stay here."

He strode down the front steps, down the walk, to the parked cruiser. A moment later they heard him drive furiously away.

He had to go to several agencies before he found what he wanted. Service Industries had nothing he could use; he was through with them. It was at Allied Domestic that he saw exactly what he was looking for, displayed in their luxurious, well-lighted window. They were just closing, but the clerk let him inside when he saw the expression on his face.

"I'll take it," Tom said, reaching into his coat for his checkbook.

"Which one, sir?" the clerk faltered.

"The big one. The big black one in the window. With the four arms and the ram in front."

The clerk beamed, his face aglow with pleasure. "Yes sir!" he cried, whipping out his order pad. "The Imperator Deluxe, with power-beam focus. Did you want the optional high-velocity grapple-lock and the remote-control feedback? At moderate cost, we can equip her with a visual report screen; you can follow the situation from the comfort of your own living room."

"The situation?" Tom said thickly.

"As she goes into action." The clerk began writing rapidly. "And I mean *action* — this model warms up and closes in on its adversary within fifteen seconds of the time it's activated. You can't find faster reaction in any single-unit models, ours or anybody else's. Six months ago, they said fifteen seconds closing was a pipe dream." The clerk laughed excitedly. "But science goes on."

A strange cold numbness settled over Tom Fields. "Listen," he said hoarsely. Grabbing the clerk by the lapel he yanked him closer. The order pad fluttered away; the clerk gulped with surprise and fright. "Listen to me," Tom grated, "you're building these things bigger all the time — *aren't you?* Every year, new models, new weapons. You and all the other companies — building them with improved equipment to destroy each other."

"Oh," the clerk squeaked indignantly. "Allied Domestic's models are *never* destroyed. Banged up a little now and then, perhaps, but you show me one of our models that's been put out of commission." With dignity, he retrieved his order pad and smoothed down his coat. "No, sir," he said emphatically, "our models survive. Why, I saw a seven-year-old Allied running around, an old Model 3-S. Dented a bit, perhaps, but plenty of fire left. I'd like to see one of those cheap Protecto-Corp. models try to tangle with *that.*"

Controlling himself with an effort, Tom asked: "But why? What's it all for? What's the purpose in this — competition between them?"

The clerk hesitated. Uncertainly, he began again with his order pad. "Yes, sir," he said. "Competition; you put your finger right on it. Successful competition, to be exact. Allied Domestic doesn't meet competition — it *demolishes* it."

It took a second for Tom Fields to react. Then understanding came. "I see," he said. "In other words, every year these things are obsolete. No good, not large enough. Not powerful enough. And if they're not replaced, if I don't get a new one, a more advanced model — "

"Your present Nanny was, ah, the loser?" The clerk smiled knowingly. "Your present model was, perhaps, slightly anachronistic? It failed to meet present-day standards of competition? It, ah, failed to come out at the end of the day?"

"It never came home," Tom said thickly.

"Yes, it was demolished ... I fully understand. Very common. You see, sir, you don't have a choice. It's nobody's fault, sir. Don't blame us; don't blame Allied Domestic."

"But," Tom said harshly, "when one is destroyed, that means you sell another one. That means a sale for you. Money in the cash register."

"True. But we all have to meet contemporary standards of excellence. We can't let ourselves fall behind ... as you saw, sir, if you don't mind my saying so, you saw the unfortunate consequences of falling behind."

"Yes," Tom agreed, in an almost inaudible voice. "They told me not to have her repaired. They said I should replace her."

The clerk's confident, smugly-beaming face seemed to expand. Like a miniature sun, it glowed happily, exaltedly. "But now you're all set up, sir. With this model you're right up there in the front. Your worries are over, Mr. ... " He halted expectantly. "Your name, sir? To whom shall I make out this purchase order?"

Bobby and Jean watched with fascination as the delivery men lugged the enormous crate into the living room. Grunting and sweating, they set it down and straightened gratefully up.

"All right," Tom said crisply. "Thanks."

"Not at all, mister." The delivery men stalked out, noisily closing the door after them.

"Daddy, what is it?" Jean whispered. The two children came cautiously around the crate, wide-eyed and awed.

"You'll see in a minute."

"Tom, it's past their bedtime," Mary protested. "Can't they look at it tomorrow?"

"I want them to look at it *now*." Tom disappeared downstairs into the basement and returned with a screwdriver. Kneeling on the floor beside the crate he began rapidly unscrewing the bolts that held it together. "They can go to bed a little late, for once."

He removed the boards, one by one, working expertly and calmly. At last the final board was gone, propped up against the wall with the others. He unclipped the book of instructions and the 90-day warranty and handed them to Mary. "Hold onto these."

"It's a Nanny!" Bobby cried.

"It's a huge, huge Nanny!"

In the crate the great black shape lay quietly, like an enormous metal tortoise, encased in a coating of grease. Carefully checked, oiled, and fully guaranteed. Tom nodded. "That's right. It's a Nanny, a new Nanny. To take the place of the old one."

"For *us*?"

"Yes." Tom sat down in a nearby chair and lit a cigarette. "Tomorrow morning we'll turn her on and warm her up. See how she runs."

The children's eyes were like saucers. Neither of them could breathe or speak.

"But this time," Mary said, "you must stay away from the park. Don't take her near the park. You hear?"

"No," Tom contradicted. "They can go in the park."

Mary glanced uncertainly at him. "But that orange thing might — "

Tom smiled grimly. "It's fine with me if they go into the park." He leaned toward Bobby and Jean. "You kids go into the park anytime you want. And don't be afraid of anything. Of anything or anyone. Remember that."

He kicked the end of the massive crate with his toe.

"There isn't anything in the world you have to be afraid of. Not anymore."

Bobby and Jean nodded, still gazing fixedly into the crate.

"All right, Daddy," Jean breathed.

"Boy, look at her!" Bobby whispered. "Just look at her! I can hardly wait till tomorrow!"

Mrs. Andrew Casworthy greeted her husband on the front steps of their attractive three-story house, wringing her hands anxiously.

"What's the matter?" Casworthy grunted, taking off his hat. With his pocket handkerchief he wiped sweat from his florid face. "Lord, it was hot today. What's wrong? What is it?"

"Andrew, I'm afraid — "

"What the hell happened?"

"Phyllis came home from the park today without her Nanny. She was bent and scratched yesterday when Phyllis brought her home, and Phyllis is so upset I can't make out — "

"*Without her Nanny?*"

"She came home alone. By herself. All alone."

Slow rage suffused the man's heavy features. "What happened?"

"Something in the park, like yesterday. Something attacked her Nanny. Destroyed her! I can't get the story exactly straight, but something black, something huge and black . . . it must have been another Nanny."

Casworthy's jaw slowly jutted out. His thickset face turned ugly dark red, a deep unwholesome flush that rose ominously and settled in place. Abruptly, he turned on his heel.

"Where are you going?" his wife fluttered nervously.

The paunchy, red-faced man stalked rapidly down the walk toward his sleek surface cruiser, already reaching for the door handle.

"I'm going to shop for another Nanny," he muttered. "The best damn Nanny I can get. Even if have to go to a hundred stores. I want the best — and the biggest."

"But, dear," his wife began, hurrying apprehensively after him, "can we really afford it?" Wringing her hands together anxiously, she raced on: "I mean, wouldn't it be better to wait? Until you've had time to think it over, perhaps. Maybe later on, when you're a little more — calm."

But Andrew Casworthy wasn't listening. Already the surface cruiser boiled with quick, eager life, ready to leap forward. "Nobody's going to get ahead of me," he said grimly, his heavy lips twitching. "I'll show them, all of them. Even if I have to get a new size designed. Even if I have to get one of those manufacturers to turn out a new model for me!"

And, oddly, he knew one of them would.

NOTES

All notes in italics are by Philip K. Dick. The year when the note was written appears in parentheses following the note. Most of these notes were written as story notes for the collections THE BEST OF PHILIP K. DICK (published 1977) and THE GOLDEN MAN (published 1980). A few were written at the request of editors publishing or reprinting a PKD story in a book or magazine. The first entry below is from an introduction written for the collection THE PRESERVING MACHINE.

When there is a date following the name of a story, it is the date the manuscript of that story was first received by Dick's agent, per the records of the Scott Meredith Literary Agency. Absence of a date means no record is available. (Dick began working with the agency in mid-1952.) The name of a magazine followed by a month and year indicates the first published appearance of a story. An alternate name following a story indicates Dick's original name for the story, as shown in the agency records.

These five volumes include all of Philip K. Dick's short fiction, with the exception of short novels later published as or included in novels, childhood writings, and unpublished writings for which manuscripts have not been found. The stories are arranged as closely as possible in chronological order of composition; research for this chronology was done by Gregg Rickman and Paul Williams.

* * *

The difference between a short story and a novel comes to this: a short story may deal with murder; a novel deals with the murderer, and his actions stem from a psyche which, if the writer knows his craft, he has previously presented. The difference, therefore, between a novel and a short story is not length; for example, William Styron's The Long March *is now published as a "short novel" whereas originally in* Discovery *it was published as a "long story." This means that if you read it in* Discovery *you are reading a story, but if you pick up the paperback version you are reading a novel. So much for that.*

There is one restriction in a novel not found in short stories: the requirement that the protagonist be liked enough or familiar enough to the reader so that, whatever the protagonist does, the readers would also do, under the same circumstances... or, in the case of escapist fiction, would like to do. In a story it is not necessary to create such a reader identification character because (one) there is not enough room for such background material in a short story and (two) since the emphasis is on the deed, not the doer, it really does not matter — within reasonable limits, of course — who in a story commits the murder. In a story, you learn about the characters from what they do; in a novel it is the other way around: you have your characters and then they do something idiosyncratic, emanating from their unique natures. So it can be said that events in a novel are unique — not found in other writings; but the same events occur over and over again in stories, until, at last, a sort of code language is built up between the reader and the author. I am not sure that this is bad by any means.

Further, a novel — in particular the sf novel — creates an entire world, with countless petty details — petty, perhaps, to the characters in the novel, but vital for the reader to know, since out of these manifold details his comprehension of the entire fictional world is obtained. In a story, on the other hand, you are in a future world when soap operas come at you from every wall in the room... as Ray Bradbury once described. That one fact alone catapults the story out of mainstream fiction and into sf.

What an sf story really requires is the initial premise *which cuts it off entirely from our present world. This break must be made in the reading of, and the writing of, all good fiction... a made-up world must be presented. But there is much more pressure on an sf writer, for the break is far greater than in, say,* Paul's Case *or* Big Blonde *— two varieties of mainstream fiction which will always be with us.*

It is in sf stories that sf action occurs; it is in sf novels that worlds occur. The stories in this collection are a series of events. Crisis is the key to story-writing, a sort of brinkmanship in which the author mires his characters in happenings so sticky as to seem impossible of solution. And then he gets them out... usually. He can *get them out; that's what matters. But in a novel the actions are so deeply rooted in the personality of the main character that to extricate him the author would have to go back and rewrite his character. This need not happen in a story, especially a short one (such long, long stories as Thomas Mann's* Death in Venice *are, like the Styron piece, really short novels). The implication of all this makes clear why some sf writers can write stories but not novels, or novels but not stories. It is because* anything can happen in a story; the author merely tailors his character to the event. So, in terms of actions and events, the story is far less restrictive to the author than is a novel. As a writer builds up a novel-length piece it slowly begins to imprison him, to take away his freedom; his own characters are taking over and doing what they want to do — not what he would like them to do. This is on one hand the strength of the novel and on the other, its weakness.* (1968)

STABILITY written 1947 or earlier [previously unpublished].

ROOG written 11/51. *Fantasy & Science Fiction*, Feb 1953. [First sale.]

The first thing you do when you sell your first story is phone up your best friend and tell him. Whereupon he hangs up on you, which puzzles you until you realize that he is trying to sell stories, too, and hasn't managed to do it. That sobers you, that reaction. But then when your wife comes home you tell her, and she doesn't hang up on you; she is very pleased and excited. At the time I sold Roog *to Anthony Boucher at* Fantasy and Science Fiction *I was managing a record store part time and writing part time. If anyone asked me what I did I always said "I'm a writer." This was in Berkeley, in 1951. Everybody was a writer. No one had ever sold anything. In fact most of the people I knew believed it to be crass and undignified to submit a story to a magazine; you wrote it, read it aloud to your friends, and finally it was forgotten. That was Berkeley in those days.*

Another problem for me in getting everyone to be awed was that my story was not a literary story in a little magazine, but an sf story. Sf was not read by people in Berkeley in those days (except for a small group of fans who were very strange; they looked like animated vegetables). "But what about your serious writing?" people said to me. I was under the impression that Roog *was quite a serious story. It tells of fear; it tells of loyalty; it tells of obscure menace and a good creature who cannot convey knowledge of that menace to those he loves. What could be more serious a theme than this? What people really meant by "serious" was "important." Sf was, by definition, not important. I cringed over the weeks following my sale of* Roog *as I realized the serious Codes of Behavior I had broken by selling my story, and an sf story at that.*

To make matters worse, I now had begun to nurse the delusion that I might be able to make a living as a writer. The fantasy in my head was that I could quit my job at the record store, buy a better typewriter, and write all the time, and still make the payments on my house. As soon as you start thinking that they come for you and haul you away. It's for your own good. When you are discharged later on as cured you no longer have that fantasy. You go back to work at the record store (or the supermarket or polishing shoes). See, the thing is, being a writer is — well, it's like the time I asked a friend of mine what field he was going into when he got out of college and he said, "I'm going to be a pirate." He was dead serious.

The fact that Roog *sold was due to Tony Boucher outlining to me how the original version should be changed. Without his help I'd still be in the record business. I mean that very seriously. At that time Tony ran a little writing class, working out of the living room of his home in Berkeley. He'd read our stories aloud and we'd see — not just that they were awful — but how they could be cured. Tony saw no point in simply making it clear that what you had written was no good; he assisted you in transmuting the thing into art. Tony knew what made up good writing. He charged you (get this) one dollar a week for this. One dollar! If ever there was a good man in this world it was Anthony Boucher. We really loved him. We used to get together once a week and play poker. Poker, opera and writing were all equally important to Tony. I miss him very much. Back in 1974 I dreamed one night that I had passed across into the next world, and it was Tony who was waiting for me to show up there. Tears fill my eyes when I think of that dream. There he was, but transformed into Tony the Tiger, like in that breakfast cereal ad. In the dream he was filled with delight and so was I. But it was a dream; Tony Boucher is gone. But I am still a writer, because of him. Whenever I sit down to start a novel or a story a bit of the memory of that man returns to me. I guess he taught me to write out of love, not out of ambition. It's a good lesson for all activities in this world.*

This little story, Roog, *is about an actual dog — like Tony, gone now. The dog's actual name was Snooper and he believed as much in his work as I did in mine. His work (apparently) was to see that no one stole the food from the owner's garbage can. Snooper was laboring under the delusion that his owners considered the garbage valuable. Every day they'd carry out paper sacks of delicious food and carefully deposit them in a strong metal*

*container, placing the lid down firmly. At the end of the week the garbage can was full —
whereupon the worst assortment of evil entities in the Sol System drove up in a huge truck
and stole the food. Snooper knew which day of the week this happened on; it was always on
Friday. So about five A.M. on Friday, Snooper would emit his first bark. My wife and I
figured that was about the time the garbagemen's alarm clocks were going off. Snooper knew
when they left their houses. He could hear them. He was the only one who knew; everybody
else ignored what was afoot. Snooper must have thought he inhabited a planet of lunatics.
His owners, and everyone else in Berkeley, could hear the garbagemen coming, but no one
did anything. His barking drove me out of my mind every week, but I was more fascinated
by Snooper's logic than I was annoyed by his frantic efforts to rouse us. I asked myself, What
must the world look like to that dog? Obviously he doesn't see as we see. He has developed a
complete system of beliefs, a worldview totally different from ours, but logical given the
evidence he is basing it on.*

*So here, in a primitive form, is the basis of much of my twenty-seven years of profes-
sional writing: the attempt to get into another person's head, or another creature's head, and
see out from his eyes or its eyes, and the more different that person is from the rest of us the
better. You start with the sentient entity and work outward, inferring its world. Obviously,
you can't ever really know what its world is like, but, I think, you can make some pretty
good guesses. I began to develop the idea that each creature lives in a world somewhat
different from all the other creatures and their worlds. I still think this is true. To Snooper,
garbagemen were sinister and horrible. I think he literally saw them differently than we
humans did.*

*This notion about each creature viewing the world differently from all other creatures
— not everyone would agree with me. Tony Boucher was very anxious to have a particular
major anthologizer (whom we will call J.M.) read* Roog *to see if she might use it. Her
reaction astounded me. "Garbagemen do not look like that," she wrote me. "They do not
have pencil-thin necks and heads that wobble. They do not eat people." I think she listed
something like twelve errors in the story all having to do with how I represented the garbagemen. I wrote back, explaining that, yes, she was right, but to a dog — well, all right, the dog
was wrong. Admittedly. The dog was a little crazy on the subject. We're not just dealing with
a dog and a dog's view of garbagemen, but a crazy dog — who has been driven crazy by these
weekly raids on the garbage can. The dog has reached a point of desperation. I wanted to
convey that. In fact that was the whole point of the story; the dog had run out of options and
was demented by this weekly event. And the Roogs knew it. They enjoyed it. They taunted
the dog. They pandered to his lunacy.*

*Ms. J.M. rejected the story from her anthology, but Tony printed it, and it's still in
print; in fact it's in a high school text book, now. I spoke to a high school class who had been
assigned the story, and all of the kids understood it. Interestingly, it was a blind student who
seemed to grasp the story best. He knew from the beginning what the word* Roog *meant. He
felt the dog's despair, the dog's frustrated fury and the bitter sense of defeat over and over
again. Maybe somewhere between 1951 and 1971 we all grew up to dangers and transfor-
mations of the ordinary which we had never recognized before. I don't know. But anyhow,*
Roog, *my first sale, is biographical; I watched the dog suffer, and I understood a little (not
much, maybe, but a little) of what was destroying him, and I wanted to speak for him.
That's the whole of it right there. Snooper couldn't talk. I could. In fact I could write it
down, and someone could publish it and many people could read it. Writing fiction has to do*

with this: becoming the voice for those without voices, if you see what I mean. It's not your own voice, you the author; it is all those other voices which normally go unheard.
The dog Snooper is dead, but the dog in the story, Boris, is alive. Tony Boucher is dead, and one day I will be, and, alas, so will you. But when I was with that high school class and we were discussing Roog, *in 1971, exactly twenty years after I sold the story originally — Snooper's barking and his anguish, his noble efforts, were still alive, which he deserved. My story is my gift to an animal, to a creature who neither sees nor hears, now, who no longer barks. But goddam it, he was doing the right thing. Even if Ms. J.M. didn't understand.* (written 1978)
I love this story, and I doubt if I write any better today than I did in 1951, when I wrote it; I just write longer. (1976)

THE LITTLE MOVEMENT *Fantasy & Science Fiction*, Nov 1952.

BEYOND LIES THE WUB *Planet Stories*, July 1952.
My first published story, in the most lurid of all pulp magazines on the stands at the time, Planet Stories. *As I carried four copies into the record store where I worked, a customer gazed at me and them, with dismay, and said, "Phil, you read* that *kind of stuff?" I had to admit I not only read it, I wrote it.*

THE GUN *Planet Stories*, Sept 1952.

THE SKULL *If*, Sept 1952.

THE DEFENDERS *Galaxy*, Jan 1953. [Parts of this story were adapted for the novel THE PENULTIMATE TRUTH.]

MR. SPACESHIP *Imagination*, Jan 1953.

PIPER IN THE WOODS *Imagination*, Feb 1953.

THE INFINITES *Planet Stories*, May 1953.

THE PRESERVING MACHINE *Fantasy & Science Fiction*, June 1953.

EXPENDABLE ("He Who Waits") *Fantasy & Science Fiction*, July 1953.
I loved to write short fantasy stories in my early days — for Anthony Boucher — of which this is my favorite. I got the idea when a fly buzzed by my head one day and I imagined (paranoia indeed!) that it was laughing at me. (1976)

THE VARIABLE MAN *Space Science Fiction* (British), July 1953.

THE INDEFATIGABLE FROG *Fantastic Story Magazine*, July 1953.

THE CRYSTAL CRYPT *Planet Stories*, Jan 1954.

THE SHORT HAPPY LIFE OF THE BROWN OXFORD *Fantasy & Science Fiction*, Jan 1954.

THE BUILDER 7/23/52. *Amazing*, Dec 1953-Jan 1954.

MEDDLER 7/24/52. *Future*, Oct 1954.

Within the beautiful lurks the ugly; you can see in this rather crude story the germ of my whole theme that nothing is what it seems. This story should be read as a trial run on my part; I was just beginning to grasp that obvious form and latent form are not the same thing. As Heraclitus said in fragment 54: "Latent structure is master of obvious structure," and out of this comes the later more sophisticated Platonic dualism between the phenomenal world and the real but invisible realm of forms lying behind it. I may be reading too much into this simple-minded early story, but at least I was beginning to see in a dim way what I later saw so clearly; in fragment 123, Heraclitus said, "The nature of things is in the habit of concealing itself," and therein lies it all. (1978)

PAYCHECK 7/31/52. *Imagination*, June 1953.

How much is a key to a bus locker worth? One day it's worth 25 cents, the next day thousands of dollars. In this story, I got to thinking that there are times in our lives when having a dime to make a phone call spells the difference between life and death. Keys, small change, maybe a theater ticket — how about a parking receipt for a Jaguar? All I had to do was link this idea up with time travel to see how the small and useless, under the wise eyes of a time traveler, might signify a great deal more. He would know when that dime might save your life. And, back in the past again, he might prefer that dime to any amount of money, no matter how large. (1976)

THE GREAT C 7/31/52. *Cosmos Science Fiction and Fantasy*, Sept 1953. [Parts of this story were adapted for the novel DEUS IRAE.]

OUT IN THE GARDEN 7/31/52. *Fantasy Fiction*, Aug 1953.

THE KING OF THE ELVES ("Shadrach Jones and the Elves") 8/4/52. *Beyond Fantasy Fiction*, Sept 1953.

This story, of course, is fantasy, not sf. Originally it had a downbeat ending on it, but Horace Gold, the editor who bought it, carefully explained to me that prophecy always came true; if it didn't ipso facto it wasn't prophecy. I guess, then, there can be no such thing as a false prophet; "false prophet" is an oxymoron. (1978)

COLONY 8/11/52. *Galaxy*, June 1953.

The ultimate in paranoia is not when everyone is against you but when everything is against you. Instead of "My boss is plotting against me," it would be "My boss's phone is plotting against me." Objects sometimes seem to possess a will of their own anyhow, to the normal mind; they don't do what they're supposed to do, they get in the way, they show an unnatural resistance to change. In this story I tried to figure out a situation which would rationally explain the dire plotting of objects against humans, without reference to any deranged state on the part of the humans. I guess you'd have to go to another planet. The ending on this story is the ultimate victory of a plotting object over innocent people. (1976)

PRIZE SHIP ("Globe From Ganymede") 8/14/52. *Thrilling Wonder Stories*, Winter 1954.

NANNY 8/26/52. *Startling Stories*, Spring 1955.

Citadel Twilight Books Ordering Information

If you like this book, you'll love the books in the Citadel Twilight series. Part science fiction, part mystery, part fantasy, the stories in the Citadel Twilight Series draw you into a world with a mysterious twist, a sense of otherness that eludes description.

Ask for these titles at your bookstore. Or to order direct from the publisher call 1-800-447-BOOK (MasterCard or Visa) or send a check or money order for the books purchased (plus $4.00 shipping and handling for the first book ordered and 75¢ for each additional book) to Citadel Twilight, 120 Enterprise Avenue, Dept. 1153, Secaucus, NJ 07094.

Third Edition

Pharmacy Calculations

for technicians

Don A. Ballington, MS

Midlands Technical College
Columbia, South Carolina

Tova Wiegand Green

Ivy Tech Community College of Indiana Northeast
Fort Wayne, Indiana

EMCParadigm
PUBLISHING

Senior Editor	Christine Hurney
Editorial Assistants	Susan Capecchi, Cheryl Drivdahl
Copy Editor	Pat Lewis
Cover and Text Designer	Leslie Anderson
Desktop Production	Parkwood Composition
Proofreader	Laura Nelson
Indexer	Terry Casey

Publishing Management Team

Bob Cassel, Publisher; Jeanne Allison, Senior Acquisitions Editor; Janice Johnson, Vice President of Marketing; Shelley Clubb, Electronic Design and Production Manager

---

Text and Encore CD ISBN 0-7638-2219-1
Product Number 01658
Text-only ISBN 0-7638-2220-5
Text-only Product Number 04658

Care has been taken to verify the accuracy of information presented in this book. The authors, editors, and publisher, however, cannot accept responsibility for errors or omissions or for consequences from application of the information in this book and make no warranty, expressed or implied, with respect to its content.

Some of the product names used in this book have been used for identification purposes only and may be trademarks or registered trademarks of their respective manufacturers.

Printed in the United States of America.

10 9 8 7 6 5 4 3 2 1

Contributors

Reneé Acosta, RPh, MS
Austin Community College
Austin, Texas

Cheryl Aiken, BS Pharm, PharmD, RPh
Brattleboro Retreat
Brattleboro, Vermont
Vermont Technical College
Randolph Center, Vermont

Nora Chan, PharmD
City College of San Francisco
San Francisco, California

Sharon Dalrymple
North Harris Community College
Houston, Texas

Jeff Gricar, MEd, CPhT
Houston Community College
Houston, Texas

Jane Krause, MS, RPh
Purdue University
West Lafayette, Indiana

Nancy Lim, PhD, RPh, CPhT
North Harris College
Houston, Texas

Courtney McCash
Draughons Junior College
Clarksville, Tennessee

Wilfred Opakunle, PhD
ACT College
Arlington, Virginia

Phil Rushing, BS Pharm
Community Care College
Tulsa, Oklahoma

Bobbi Steelman, CPhT
Draughons Junior College
Bowling Green, Kentucky

Mary Ann Stuhan, RPh
Cuyahoga Community College
Cleveland, Ohio

Judy Weisbard, MPA, CPhT
Chaffey Community College
Rancho Cucamonga, California

Marsha Lynn Wilson
Clarian Health Education Center
Indianapolis, Indiana

Contents

v

Preface

Pharmacy Calculations for Technicians, Third Edition teaches the essential mathematics concepts and skills used on the job by the pharmacy technician. Basic skills in mathematics are required for understanding, calculating, and preparing drug doses, and this comprehensive new edition offers expanded coverage of basic skill reviews on fractions and percents. This text provides intensive practice in pharmacy math calculations, conversions, measurements, and applications of equations, including calculations required for realistic dose and solution preparations. The text also teaches business terms and business math skills essential to pharmacy practice, as well as calculations to determine inventory and purchasing needs, profit margins, and inventory control. The concepts taught in the text are reinforced by the new Encore multimedia CD.

Features of the Third Edition

Features of the third edition include these:
- A new, interactive, multimedia CD presents matching exercises, a glossary, and practice tests to reinforce the learning of pharmacy calculations.
- Key terms with margin definitions and a glossary have been added to the textbook to reinforce the learning of pharmacy terminology.
- More practice problems have been added to the textbook, including intrachapter problem sets designed to reinforce chapter content. Answers showing detailed work for all problem sets are provided on the Internet Resource Center, allowing students to self-check their calculations. When appropriate, both ratio-proportion and dimensional analysis methods of solving problems are used.
- New end-of-chapter Practice Tests provide an opportunity for applying skills learned in the chapter, and they can be used for graded homework assignments. These Practice Tests parallel Chapter Tests provided for the instructor to use as possible assessment tools.

- The coverage of the calculations skills needed by pharmacy technicians working in both hospital and community pharmacy settings has been expanded, including material on alligations, aliquots, and parenterals.
- A new chapter focuses on developing the literacy skills needed to read prescription orders, read drug labels, and provide directions for patients.
- Safety is emphasized with Safety Note sidebars throughout the text to reinforce safe practice.
- A new compounding appendix offers additional problems, including calculations related to total parenteral nutrition and dose safety ranges.

How This Text Is Organized

Each chapter begins with learning objectives to help focus student study. New to this edition, chapter terms are boldfaced within the text and are highlighted with margin definitions. Safety Note sidebars throughout the text reinforce ways the pharmacy technician can play an active role in preventing medication errors, and Remember sidebars reinforce previously learned material. This workbook-style text includes new intrachapter Problem Sets that reinforce the examples demonstrated within each section of the chapter; corresponding self-check answer keys, showing the work needed to complete the calculations, is provided for student reference on this book's Internet Resource Center (IRC). End-of-chapter Practice Tests are also new to this edition. Answer keys showing work are provided for the instructor's reference only, so these Practice Tests become an excellent homework assignment or course evaluation tool. In addition, the Practice Tests parallel the Chapter Tests, provided to instructors for student assessment.

Resources for the Student

In addition to the textbook, students have access to valuable resources to help them master the skills needed to perform pharmacy calculations safely and accurately.

Encore CD The Encore CD included with each textbook is an exciting new feature of the third edition of *Pharmacy Calculations for Technicians*. The Encore CD includes interactive review questions that students can use to test their knowledge of concepts presented in the book. There are two levels of tests—book and chapter. Each level functions in two different modes: in the Review mode, the student receives immediate feedback on each test item and a report of his or her total score; in the reportable Practice Test mode, the results are e-mailed to both the student and the instructor.

The Encore CD also provides Tech Check interactive matching activities that require students to manipulate concepts from the chapter content. The Encore CD includes chapter-specific glossaries, as well as a complete glossary and image bank with key illustrations from all the textbooks in the pharmacy technician series published by EMC Corporation.

Internet Resource Center The Internet Resource Center for this title at www.emcp.com provides additional resources, including answer keys showing work for all the intrachapter Problem Sets, chapter study notes, PowerPoint slide shows, and interactive flash cards for learning the generic and brand names of the top-prescribed drugs.

Resources for the Instructor

Pharmacy Calculations for Technicians, Third Edition is supported by several tools to help instructors plan their course and assess student learning.

Instructor's Guide In addition to suggested course syllabus information, the Instructor's Guide that accompanies *Pharmacy Calculations, Third Edition* includes answers, showing work, for all Practice Tests and appendix exercises. These keys show both ratio-proportion and dimensional analysis methods for problem solving when appropriate. The Instructor's Guide also provides teaching hints for each chapter, Chapter Tests that parallel the end-of-chapter Practice Tests, and two versions of a 75-question, multiple-choice final exam.

Internet Resource Center All the resources from the print Instructor's Guide are available in electronic format on a password-protected section of the Internet Resource Center for this title at www.emcp.com. In addition, the site provides PowerPoint slide shows to enhance class presentations.

ExamView Computerized Test Generator A full-featured computerized test generator on CD offers instructors a wide variety of options for generating both print and online tests. The testbank provides fifty questions for each chapter. Instructors can create custom tests using questions from the testbank, can edit existing questions, or can add questions of their own design.

WebCT and Blackboard WebCT and Blackboard Web course management systems are available to support this product. Each system comes preloaded with course information, chapter outlines, and quizzes.

Resources in the Pharmacy Technician Series

In addition to *Pharmacy Calculations for Technicians, Third Edition*, EMC Corporation publishes several other titles designed specifically for the pharmacy technician curriculum.
- *Pharmacology for Technicians, Third Edition:* includes an Encore CD with every textbook, a workbook, the Internet Resource Center, and for the instructor, a guide, PowerPoint presentations, a testbank, and Web course management systems
- *Pharmacy Practice for Technicians, Third Edition:* includes an Encore CD with every textbook, a workbook, the Internet Resource Center, and, for the instructor, a guide, PowerPoint presentations, a testbank, and Web course management systems
- *Pharmacy Technician Certification Exam Review:* includes two practice exams with answer feedback, study tips, and an Encore CD with over 1900 exam questions is also available.

About the Authors

Don A. Ballington, MS, is the program coordinator of the pharmacy technician training program at Midlands Technical College, in Columbia, South Carolina. He has served as president of the Pharmacy Technician Educators Council and in 2005 received the council's Educator of the Year award, has conducted site visits for pharmacy technician accreditation, and has helped develop the ASHP model curriculum.

He has also been a consulting editor for the *Journal of Pharmacy Technology*. Over the course of his career at Midlands Technical College, he has developed a set of high-quality training materials for pharmacy technicians. These materials have been made available in three national textbooks: *Pharmacology for Technicians, Pharmacy Calculations for Technicians,* and *Pharmacy Practice for Technicians*. All are now available in third editions.

Tova Wiegand Green is the program chair for the medical assisting program and coordinator for the pharmacy technician program at Ivy Tech Community College of Indiana Northeast, in Fort Wayne, Indiana. She has coordinated and taught the statewide pharmacy technician program that is delivered on a two-way video hybrid system in Indiana. In addition, she has served as a consultant for the Indiana Higher Education Technology Services on issues related to teaching on a hybrid, two-way video system, including teaching math skills through distance education. In addition, she has worked as a pharmacy intern for Kroger pharmacies in Indiana.

Acknowledgments

The authors and editorial staff would like to offer a special thank-you to Mary Ann Stuhan for her writing of Chapter 3, Sharon Dalrymple for her contributions that resulted in Appendix B, Courtney McCash for her excellent work in writing assessment material to support this title, and Reneé Acosta for her extensive review of the answer keys. We appreciate your contributions. In addition, we would like to thank Cheryl Aiken for her work writing review and practice test questions for the Encore CD included with this textbook.

The authors and editorial staff invite your feedback on the text and its supplements. Please reach us by clicking the "Contact us" button at www.emcp.com.

Understanding Subdivisions of Numbers, Number Systems, Estimating, and Accuracy

Chapter **1**

Objectives

- Understand fractions and be able to compare them, express them as decimals, and find common denominators.

- Manipulate fractions by adding, subtracting, multiplying, and dividing them.

- Interpret Roman and Arabic numbers and convert values between the two systems.

- Read scientific notation and convert large and small numbers to scientific notation.

- Determine the value of a decimal and accurately round off decimal values.

- Estimate drug doses in order to check the accuracy of final calculations.

- Perform calculations while retaining accuracy and the correct number of significant figures.

1.1 FRACTIONS

fraction
a portion of a whole that is represented as a ratio

When something is divided into parts, each part is considered a **fraction** of the whole. For example, a pie might be divided into eight slices, each one of which is a fraction, or ⅛, of the whole pie. The pie is still whole but has been divided into eight slices. Each slice is a selection—an eighth—of the whole pie, or 1 (the piece of pie) over 8 (the number of slices in the whole pie). In the fraction ⅜, the selection is for 3 of the 8 slices (see Figure 1.1).

Just as we talked about dividing a pie into parts, we can speak of dividing a tablet into parts, a common procedure for both pharmacist and patient. So if we start with a 1000 mg tablet,

$$\frac{1}{2} \text{ tablet} = 500 \text{ mg} \qquad \frac{1}{4} \text{ tablet} = 250 \text{ mg}$$

Figure 1.1

Fractions of the Whole Pie

A whole pie

3 slices = ³/8 of the whole pie

1 slice = ¹/8 of the whole pie

numerator
the number on the
upper part of a fraction

denominator
the number on the
bottom part of a
fraction

Fractions are common (½, ⅔, etc.) or decimal (0.5, 0.66, etc.—decimals are discussed in detail in a later section). A common fraction is composed of the **numerator** (top number) and the **denominator** (bottom number). The numerator represents the portion (1 piece in the case of the pie), and the denominator represents the whole (8 pieces of pie).

$$\text{numerator} \;\rightarrow\; \frac{1}{8} \;\leftarrow\; \text{denominator}$$

A fraction with the same numerator and denominator has a value equivalent to 1.

$$\frac{8}{8} = \frac{5}{5} = \frac{3}{3} = \frac{10}{10} = \frac{15}{15} = 1$$

proper fraction
a fraction with a value
of less than 1 (the
numerator's value is
smaller than the
denominator's value)

improper fraction
a fraction with a value
greater than 1 (the
numerator's value is
larger than the
denominator's value)

A fraction with a value of less than 1 (numerator smaller than denominator) is called a **proper fraction.**

$$\frac{1}{4}, \frac{2}{3}, \frac{7}{8}, \frac{9}{10}$$

A fraction with a value greater than 1 (numerator greater than denominator) is called an **improper fraction.**

$$\frac{6}{5} \; \frac{7}{5} \; \frac{9}{6} \; \frac{15}{8}$$

mixed number
a whole number and a
fraction

A **mixed number** is a whole number and a fraction and can be converted to an improper fraction by multiplying the whole number by the denominator and adding the numerator.

$$5\frac{1}{2} = \frac{(5 \times 2) + 1}{2} = \frac{11}{2}$$

complex fraction
a fraction in which
both the numerator
and the denominator
are fractions

A fraction in which both the numerator and the denominator are fractions is called a **complex fraction.**

$$\frac{¼}{⅛}$$

Comparing Fraction Size

When comparing fractions that have the same numerator, the fraction with the smaller denominator will have the larger value.

$$\frac{1}{10} > \frac{1}{25}$$

Remember
The symbol >
means "is greater
than," and <
means "is less
than."

If two fractions have the same denominator, the fraction with the larger numerator will have the larger value.

$$\frac{3}{6} > \frac{2}{6}$$

Expressing Fractions as Decimals

As the section on decimals later in the chapter will explain, in decimal fractions the denominator is not written but is represented by the location of the number in relation to the decimal point. For now, it is sufficient to know that any fraction may be expressed in decimal form by dividing the numerator by the denominator.

$$\frac{1}{2} = 1 \div 2 = 0.5$$

$$\frac{7}{10} = 7 \div 10 = 0.7$$

Adding and Subtracting Fractions

<table>
<tr><td>common denominator
a number into which
each of the unlike
denominators of two
or more fractions can
be divided evenly</td></tr>
</table>

When adding or subtracting fractions with unlike denominators, it is necessary to create a **common denominator,** a number into which each of the unlike denominators can be divided evenly. Think of it as making both fractions into the same kind of "pie." Creating a common denominator requires transforming each fraction by multiplying it by a form of 1 that represents one entire "pie."

Multiplying a number by 1 does not change the value of the number ($5 \times 1 = 5$). Therefore, if you multiply a fraction by a fraction that equals 1 (such as ⅗), you do not change the value of the fraction. It is this mathematical rule that allows for the conversions in the following examples.

Example 1.1.1　　**Find the sum of ½ + ⅗.**

The lowest number that can be divided evenly by both 2 and 5 is 10. A quick way to determine a possible common denominator is to multiply the two denominators together ($5 \times 2 = 10$). Thus, tenths will be the common denominator for the two fractions, and each fraction must be converted to tenths.

To convert ½ to tenths, multiply ½ by ⅗ (one "pie" of fifths), which equals ⁵⁄₁₀.

$$\frac{1}{2} = \frac{1}{2} \times \frac{5}{5} = \frac{5}{10}$$

To convert ⅗ to tenths, multiply ⅗ by ½ (one "pie" of halves), which equals ⁶⁄₁₀.

$$\frac{3}{5} = \frac{3}{5} \times \frac{2}{2} = \frac{6}{10}$$

Then add ⁵⁄₁₀ + ⁶⁄₁₀, which equals ¹¹⁄₁₀ or 1 and ¹⁄₁₀ (1¹⁄₁₀).

$$\frac{5}{10} + \frac{6}{10} = \frac{11}{10} = 1\frac{1}{10}$$

Example 1.1.2   **Find the sum of ¼ + ³⁄₇.**

The common denominator is 28, since $4 \times 7 = 28$.

$$\frac{1}{4} = \frac{1}{4} \times \frac{7}{7} = \frac{7}{28} \qquad \frac{3}{7} = \frac{3}{7} \times \frac{4}{4} = \frac{12}{28}$$

$$\frac{7}{28} + \frac{12}{28} = \frac{19}{28}$$

$$\frac{1}{4} + \frac{3}{7} = \frac{19}{28}$$

Sometimes, especially when there are three or more fractions, multiplying the denominators is not the best method to use to find a common denominator. In that case, follow the basic guidelines given in Table 1.1.

After two fractions have been converted to a common denominator and added together, it may be necessary to reduce the fraction. This requires canceling. To understand why this works, remember that multiplying a fraction by 1 will not change its value.

$$\frac{a}{b} \times 1 = \frac{a}{b}$$

Table 1.1   General Guidelines for Finding a Common Denominator

1. Examine each denominator in the given fractions for its divisors, or factors.

$$\frac{1}{15} = \frac{1}{3 \times 5} \qquad \frac{5}{6} = \frac{5}{2 \times 3} \qquad \frac{11}{36} = \frac{11}{2 \times 2 \times 3 \times 3}$$

2. See what factors any of the denominators have in common.

$$\frac{1}{15} = \frac{1}{3 \times 5} \text{ has a 3 in its denominator, and } \frac{5}{6} = \frac{5}{2 \times 3} \text{ and}$$

$$\frac{11}{36} = \frac{11}{2 \times 2 \times 3 \times 3} \text{ both have 2 and 3 in their denominators.}$$

3. Form a common denominator by multiplying all the factors that occur in all of the denominators. If a factor occurs more than once, use it the largest number of times it occurs in any denominator.

$$\text{Common denominator} = 5 \times 2 \times 2 \times 3 \times 3$$
$$= 5 \times 4 \times 9$$
$$= 180$$

Note: The product of all of the original denominators is $15 \times 6 \times 36 = 3240$.

Rewrite 1 as $\frac{c}{c}$.

$$\frac{a}{b} = \frac{a}{b} \times 1 = \frac{a}{b} \times \frac{c}{c} = \frac{ac}{bc}$$

Reversing the above steps illustrates the process of canceling.

$$\frac{ac}{bc} = \frac{a}{b} \times \frac{c}{c} = \frac{a}{b}$$

Once the largest number possible has been canceled out of the numerator and denominator, the fraction is said to be in its lowest terms.

Example 1.1.3   **Simplify the fraction $\frac{3}{27}$.**

$$\frac{3 \div 3}{27 \div 3} = \frac{1}{9}$$

When subtracting fractions that have the same denominator, subtract the numerators and place the number over the common denominator. It may be necessary to reduce the answer fraction to its lowest terms.

Example 1.1.4   **Perform the following subtraction.**

$$\frac{5}{6} - \frac{3}{6}$$

Since these fractions already have the common denominator 6, subtract the numerators.

$$\frac{5}{6} - \frac{3}{6} = \frac{2}{6}$$

Simplify: $\frac{2}{6} = \frac{1}{3}$.

Example 1.1.5   **Simplify the following subtraction.**

$$3\frac{3}{4} - \frac{2}{4}$$

Change the mixed fraction to an improper fraction.

$$3\frac{3}{4} = \frac{15}{4}$$

Replace the mixed fraction with the improper fraction in the subtraction, and confirm that the denominators are the same.

$$3\frac{3}{4} - \frac{2}{4} = \frac{15}{4} - \frac{2}{4} \qquad \text{(Both denominators are 4.)}$$

Solve the problem by subtracting the numerators.

$$\frac{15}{4} - \frac{2}{4} = \frac{13}{4}$$

Change the improper fraction to a mixed fraction.

$$\frac{13}{4} = 3\frac{1}{4}$$

When subtracting fractions that have different denominators, find the lowest common denominator, convert to equivalent fractions, subtract the numerators, and place the number over the denominator. It may be necessary to reduce the answer fraction to its lowest terms.

Example 1.1.6 **Perform the following calculation.**

$$\frac{3}{4} - \frac{2}{3}$$

The lowest common denominator is 12, so to convert to equivalent fractions, ¾ must be multiplied by ⅓ and ⅔ by ¼, giving

$$\frac{3}{4} = \frac{9}{12} \qquad \frac{2}{3} = \frac{8}{12}$$

Replace the original fractions and subtract the numerators.

$$\frac{9}{12} - \frac{8}{12} = \frac{1}{12}$$

Example 1.1.7 **Subtract the two given fractions.**

$$2\frac{1}{2} - \frac{6}{3}$$

Change the mixed number to a fraction.

$$2\frac{1}{2} = \frac{(2 \times 2) + 1}{2} = \frac{5}{2}$$

Replace the mixed fraction with the improper fraction.

$$2\frac{1}{2} - \frac{6}{3} = \frac{5}{2} - \frac{6}{3}$$

The lowest common denominator is 6; convert to equivalent fractions.

$$\frac{5}{2} \times \frac{3}{3} = \frac{15}{6} \qquad \frac{6}{3} \times \frac{2}{2} = \frac{12}{6}$$

Rewrite the original problem and subtract the numerators.

$$\frac{15}{6} - \frac{12}{6} = \frac{3}{6}$$

Simplify the answer.

$$\frac{3}{6} = \frac{1}{2}$$

So $2\frac{1}{2} - \frac{5}{3} = \frac{1}{2}$.

Multiplying Fractions

The basic step in multiplying fractions is to multiply numerators by numerators and denominators by denominators. Another way to state this rule is the following: multiply all numbers above the line; then multiply all numbers below the line. Finally, cancel if possible and reduce to lowest terms.

$$\frac{1}{8} \times \frac{1}{2} = \frac{1 \times 1}{8 \times 2} = \frac{1}{16}$$

$$\frac{1}{8} \times \frac{1}{2} \times \frac{2}{3} = \frac{1 \times 1 \times 2}{8 \times 2 \times 3} = \frac{2}{48} = \frac{1}{24}$$

$$5 \times \frac{3}{4} = \frac{5}{1} \times \frac{3}{4} = \frac{15}{4} = 3\frac{3}{4}$$

Table 1.2 provides general guidelines for multiplying fractions.

Dividing Fractions

To divide by a fraction, multiply by its reciprocal (invert it, or turn it over), and then reduce if necessary.

$$\frac{10}{\frac{1}{4}} = \frac{10 \times 4}{1} = \frac{40}{1} = 40$$

$$\frac{1}{\frac{1}{3}} = \frac{1 \times 3}{1} = \frac{3}{1} = 3$$

$$\frac{6}{8} \div \frac{2}{3} = \frac{6}{8} \times \frac{3}{2} = \frac{18}{16} = \frac{9}{8} = 1\frac{1}{8}$$

Table 1.2 Guidelines for Multiplying Fractions

1. Multiplying the numerator by a number increases the value of a fraction.

$$\frac{1}{4} \times \frac{2}{1} = \frac{1 \times 2}{4 \times 1} = \frac{2}{4} = \frac{1}{2}$$

2. Multiplying the denominator by a number decreases the value of a fraction.

$$\frac{1}{4} \times \frac{1}{2} = \frac{1 \times 1}{4 \times 2} = \frac{1}{8}$$

3. The value of a fraction is not altered by multiplying or dividing both the numerator and the denominator by the same number.

$$\frac{1}{4} \times \frac{4}{4} = \frac{1 \times 4}{4 \times 4} = \frac{4}{16} = \frac{1}{4}$$

4. Dividing the denominator by a number is the same as multiplying the numerator by that number.

$$\frac{3}{^{20}\!/_{5}} = \frac{3}{4} \qquad \frac{3 \times 5}{20} = \frac{15}{20} = \frac{3}{4}$$

5. Dividing the numerator by a number is the same as multiplying the denominator by that number.

$$\frac{^{6}\!/_{3}}{4} = \frac{2}{4} = \frac{1}{2} \qquad \frac{6}{4 \times 3} = \frac{6}{12} = \frac{1}{2}$$

Problem Set 1.1

✓ *Self-check your problem set work at* www.emcp.com.

Circle the fraction with the highest value.

1. $\dfrac{1}{2}$ $\dfrac{1}{3}$ $\dfrac{1}{4}$

2. $\dfrac{3}{10}$ $\dfrac{3}{12}$ $\dfrac{3}{8}$

Circle the fraction with the lowest value.

3. $\dfrac{3}{1}$ $\dfrac{4}{1}$ $\dfrac{2}{1}$

4. $\dfrac{2}{6}$ $\dfrac{3}{6}$ $\dfrac{4}{6}$

5. $\dfrac{1}{10}$ $\dfrac{1}{8}$ $\dfrac{1}{6}$

Complete the following operations.

6. $\dfrac{5}{6} + \dfrac{7}{10} + \dfrac{2}{5} =$

7. $\dfrac{21}{32} + \dfrac{1}{12} + \dfrac{31}{48} =$

Reduce the following fractions to their lowest form.

8. $\dfrac{25}{100}$

9. $\dfrac{67}{10}$

10. $\dfrac{11}{5}$

11. $\dfrac{27}{30}$

12. $\dfrac{12}{30}$

13. $\dfrac{\frac{1}{2}}{6}$

Express the following fractions in decimal form.

14. $\dfrac{1}{5}$

15. $\dfrac{1}{20}$

16. $4\dfrac{2}{4}$

17. $\dfrac{30}{100}$

18. $\dfrac{1}{200}$

19. $\dfrac{1}{500}$

20. $1\dfrac{8}{10}$

21. $\dfrac{1}{25}$

22. $\dfrac{1}{125}$

Applications

23. You are to measure ¼ grain of medication into unit dose oral containers. Your bulk container has 375 grains. How many containers will be prepared?

Table sugar is needed for making simple syrup. One formula calls for ½ lb to make enough syrup, a second formula requires ⅘ lb, a third formula needs ¼ lb, and the last formula requires 2½ lb. You need to make one batch of all four formulas.

24. How many bags should you buy if the sugar is packaged in 2 lb bags?

25. How many bags must be purchased if the sugar is packaged in 5 lb bags?

1.2 NUMBER SYSTEMS

Two types of numbers are used in pharmaceutical calculations: Roman and Arabic. The Arabic system is more commonly used in healthcare, although the Roman system is used on a limited basis.

Roman Numerals

The Roman numbering system (numerals) can be traced back to ancient Rome. This system uses letters to represent quantities or amounts, whereas the Arabic system uses numbers, fractions (such as ⅜), and decimals. **Roman numerals** are expressed in either lowercase letters (particularly in calculations) or as capital letters. The most frequently used numerals are the uppercase I, V, and X, which represent 1, 5, and 10, respectively. In writing prescriptions, however, the lowercase letter i is often used to represent the number one, ii to represent two, and so on; and to prevent errors in interpretation, a line is drawn above the symbol, with the dot above the line (for example: ī, īī, īīī). The symbol for ½, if placed after a Roman numeral, is $\overline{ss}$ (for example: 5½ is v$\overline{ss}$). Roman numerals are used to record amount or quantity but have little use in calculations.

Numbers in the Roman system are represented by using combinations of eight letters, most often in capital letters. Table 1.3 lists the common units and their values in the Roman system.

Roman numerals
a numbering system that uses alphabetic symbols to indicate a quantity; uses the letters I, V, and X to represent 1, 5, and 10, respectively

Table 1.3 Comparison of Roman and Arabic Numerals

Roman		Arabic	Roman		Arabic
s̄s	=	½	L or l	=	50
I or i or ĩ	=	1	C or c	=	100
V or v	=	5	D or d	=	500
X or x	=	10	M or m	=	1000

Table 1.4 Guidelines for Interpreting Roman Numerals

1. When a numeral is repeated or a smaller numeral follows a larger one, the values are added together.

   ĩĩ or II = 1 + 1 = 2   VII = 5 + 2 = 7
   LVII = 50 + 5 + 1 + 1 = 57   XXI = 10 + 10 + 1 = 21
   CXIII = 100 + 10 + 1 + 1 + 1 = 113   LXV = 50 + 10 + 5 = 65

2. When a smaller numeral comes before a larger numeral, subtract the smaller value.

   IV = 5 − 1 = 4   IX = 10 − 1 = 9
   CD = 500 − 100 = 400

3. Numerals are never repeated more than three times in sequence.

   III = 3   XXX = 30
   IV = 4   XL = 40

4. When a smaller numeral comes between two larger numerals, subtract the smaller numeral from the numeral following.

   XIX = 10 + (10 − 1) = 19   XIV = 10 + (5 − 1) = 14

Roman numerals may be grouped together to express different quantities. To interpret these numbers, addition and subtraction must be used, as specified in the guidelines shown in Table 1.4.

The Arabic Number System

place value
the location of a numeral in a string of numbers that describes the numeral's relationship to the decimal point

Arabic numbers
a numbering system that uses numeric symbols to indicate a quantity, fractions, and decimals; uses the numerals 0, 1, 2, 3, 4, 5, 6, 7, 8, 9

The Arabic system is also called the decimal system. Ten figures are used: 0, 1, 2, 3, 4, 5, 6, 7, 8, 9. The decimal point serves as the anchor. Each place to the left of the decimal point signals a tenfold increase, and each place to the right signals a tenfold decrease. Figure 1.2 illustrates the relative value of each unit. Memorize the **place values,** which describe each numeral's relationship to the decimal point, for future reference.

In expressions using **Arabic numbers,** the whole numbers are to the left of the decimal point while the fractions are on the right. The positions for the numbers to the right of the decimal point are called decimal places. Table 1.5 provides guidelines for interpreting Arabic numbers.

Figure 1.2

Decimal Units and Values

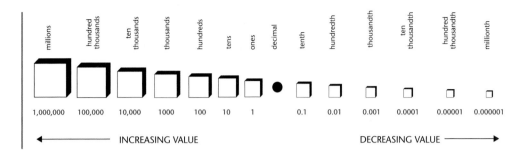

millions	hundred thousands	ten thousands	thousands	hundreds	tens	ones	decimal	tenth	hundredth	thousandth	ten thousandth	hundred thousandth	millionth
1,000,000	100,000	10,000	1000	100	10	1		0.1	0.01	0.001	0.0001	0.00001	0.000001

◄——— INCREASING VALUE   DECREASING VALUE ———►

Table 1.5   Guidelines for Interpreting Arabic Numbers

1. The value of a decimal equal to 1 or more depends on the size of the whole numbers. The higher the value of the whole numbers, the higher the overall value.

   8.2 > 6.2
   20.1 > 14.6
   3.08 > 2.39

2. If the decimal fraction does not have a whole number preceding the decimal point, a zero is used in front of the decimal point. This is called a leading zero. The fraction with the highest tenth will have the highest value.

   0.4 > 0.3
   2.41 > 2.39

3. When the tenths are identical, a number with a decimal fraction that is higher in hundredths will have a higher value.

   0.17 > 0.15
   0.35 > 0.30
   10.66 > 10.64

4. Look at the tenths first. If these are identical, the hundredths will determine the value unless they are also identical. Then the value will be determined by the thousandths.

   0.125 > 0.124

5. The total value of a number is therefore the sum of the different parts, depending on their position.

467.43 represents	400.00	=	four hundreds
	+60.00	=	six tens
	+ 7.00	=	seven ones
	+ 0.40	=	four tenths
	+ 0.03	=	three hundredths

Scientific Notation

scientific notation
a method used to write numbers that have a very large or very small numerical value; uses "× 10" with an exponent

Scientific notation is a method used to write numbers that have a very large or very small numerical value. Because of space issues as well as readability, it is not practical to write out numbers that have a large number of zeros, such as 5.2 trillion or very small numbers such as 0.00000025. Numbers such as these are written as a group of significant figures multiplied by 10 with an exponent. The number in the exponent indicates how many places the decimal has been moved, and the value of the exponent (positive or negative) indicates the direction the decimal was moved. A positive exponent indicates a number greater than 1, and a negative exponent indicates a number smaller than 1. Table 1.6 shows examples of values written in Arabic numbers and in scientific notation.

Table 1.6   Scientific Notation Equivalences

Arabic Number	Scientific Notation	Decimal Place Movement
6500	6.5×10^3	3 places to the left
120,000	1.2×10^5	5 places to the left
921,000,000	9.21×10^8	8 places to the left
4,800,000,000,000	4.8×10^{12}	12 places to the left
0.109	1.09×10^{-1}	1 place to the right
0.000587	5.87×10^{-4}	4 places to the right
0.00000026	2.6×10^{-7}	7 places to the right
0.000000000049	4.9×10^{-11}	11 places to the right

Problem Set 1.2 _____

✓ *Self-check your problem set work at* www.emcp.com.

Give the equivalent Arabic numeral for each of the following Roman numerals.

1. X

2. V

3. DCXXIV

4. MML

5. XLVIII

Give the equivalent Roman numeral for each of the following Arabic numerals.

6. 17

7. 67

8. 1995

In each group of numbers, circle the highest value.

9. 3.1   1.7   4.1

10. 0.5   0.56   0.6

In each group of numbers, circle the lowest value.

11. 2.02   2.12   2.1

12. 0.16   0.167   0.017

Using the following number, list the quantity of each numeral in the named places.

92,375.046

13. tenth place

14. thousandth place

15. hundreds place

State the place value of the underlined digit.

16. 18,<u>2</u>40.6

17. 7.2<u>3</u>91

18. 621.50<u>8</u>

19. <u>0</u>.98

20. 40. <u>0</u>23

Write the following numbers without using scientific notation.

21. 6.8×10^4

22. 1.87×10^6

23. 1.03×10^7

24. 8.4×10^{-4}

25. 7.68×10^{-3}

26. 6.239×10^{-5}

Write the following numbers using scientific notation.

27. 0.00000000329

28. 390,000,000,000

29. 0.0038

30. 52,000,000,000,000,000

31. 3,779,000

32. 0.000000000202

Applications

33. A patient is to take "VII $\overline{ss}$ tablets three times daily." How many tablets must be dispensed for a 7 days' supply?

34. Using the prescription below, answer the following questions.

ASA gr X

Sig: ĭ po daily
Disp: C

   a. What is the strength of the tablet?

   b. What is the daily dose?

   c. What is the quantity to be dispensed?

35. Using the prescription below, answer the following questions.

Drug XYZ gr $\overline{ss}$

Sig: gr ii QAM
Disp: C

Note: QAM (or qam or q am) means "every morning."

   a. What is the dosage strength of the drug XYZ?

   b. How many grains are ordered each day?

   c. How many tablets will be needed for 7 days?

   d. How long will C tablets last the patient?

36. Using the prescription below, answer the following questions.

Erythromycin 250 mg

ĭ qid with food
XXVIII

Note: qid (or QID) means "four times a day."

   a. How many tablets will be dispensed?

   b. How many days will the prescription last?

37. Using the prescription below, answer the following questions.

Glucotrol Tablet 5 mg

ĭĭ q am
ĭ with lunch
ĭĭ 8 pm
30 days' supply

   a. How many tablets are taken each day?

   b. How many tablets will be dispensed?

   c. How long would C tablets last?

1.3 DECIMALS

A fraction in which the denominator is 10 or some multiple of 10 is a decimal fraction or, more simply, a **decimal.** In decimal fractions, the denominator is not written but is represented by the location of the number in relation to the decimal point. (Refer to the section on the Arabic number system.) The decimal point represents the center. Numbers written to the right of the decimal point are decimal fractions with a denominator of 10 or a multiple of 10 and so have a value of less than 1. Numbers written to the left of the decimal point have a value of 1 or greater (whole numbers).

An understanding of decimals is *crucial* to pharmacy calculations because most medication orders are written in metric, which uses decimals. Remember, numbers to the left of the decimal point are whole numbers; numbers to the right of the decimal point are decimal fractions (parts of a whole).

Reading and Writing Decimals

A decimal is read by first reading the whole number, if there is one, to the left of the decimal point, then the decimal point (say "and" or "point"), and then the decimal fraction, to the right of the decimal point.

A decimal is written as a whole number or a zero, then the decimal point (indicating the value of the number to the right of the decimal), and then the fractional portion. The values to the right of the decimal point are multiples of one-tenth: tenths, hundredths, thousandths, ten thousandths, and so on. Figure 1.3 illustrates this relationship in terms of medication.

To further emphasize the value of the calculation when there is no whole number, a zero should be placed to the left of the decimal point. This zero is called a **leading zero.** Using a leading zero will help prevent errors by ensuring a correct reading of the value.

Adding and Subtracting Decimals

When adding or subtracting decimals, place the numbers in columns so that the decimal points are aligned directly under each other. Add or subtract from the far-right column to the left column.

$$
\begin{array}{r} 20.4 \\ +21.8 \\ \hline 42.2 \end{array}
\qquad
\begin{array}{r} 11.2 \\ 13.6 \\ +16.0 \\ \hline 40.8 \end{array}
\qquad
\begin{array}{r} 15.36 \\ -\ 3.80 \\ \hline 11.56 \end{array}
$$

Figure 1.3
Decimal Places

| whole | 0.5 tenths (1 place to the right) | 0.05 hundredths (2 places to the right) | 0.005 thousandths (3 places to the right) | 0.0005 ten thousandths (4 places to the right) |

Multiplying Decimals

Multiply the two decimals as whole numbers. Add the total number of decimal places that are in the two numbers being multiplied (count from right to left), count that number of places from right to left in the answer, and insert a decimal point.

$$
\begin{array}{r}
1.23 \\
\times \quad 2.3 \\
\hline
369 \\
+ \quad 2460 \\
\hline
2.829
\end{array}
$$

(A zero is added to align the columns. Note that no value is added to the number.)

Dividing Decimals

To divide decimal numbers, change both the divisor (the number doing the dividing; the denominator) and the dividend (the number being divided; the numerator) to whole numbers by moving their decimal points the same number of places to the right. If the divisor and the dividend have a different number of digits after the decimal point, choose the one that has more digits and move its decimal point a sufficient number of places to make it a whole number. Then move the decimal point in the other number the same number of places, adding a zero at the end if necessary. In the first example, the divisor has more digits after the decimal point, so move its decimal point three places to the right to make it a whole number. Then move the decimal point in the dividend the same number of places, adding a zero at the end. In the second example, the dividend has more digits after the decimal point, so move its decimal point three places to the right to make it a whole number. Then move the decimal point in the divisor three places to the right also.

$$1.45 \div 3.625 = 0.4 \qquad 1.617 \div 2.31 = 0.7$$

$$\frac{1.45}{3.625} = \frac{1450}{3625} = 0.4 \qquad \frac{1.617}{2.31} = \frac{161.7}{2310} = 0.7$$

Rounding Decimals

accuracy
the correctness of a number in its representation of a given value

Rounding numbers is essential for daily use of mathematical operations. The purpose of rounding is to keep the number we are working with to a manageable size. It is important to recognize, however, that rounding will affect the **accuracy** to which a medication can be determined. In some cases, it may be appropriate to calculate a dose to the nearest whole milliliter and, in other cases, to round to the nearest tenth or hundredth of a milliliter. And depending on the drug and strength prescribed, it may not be possible to accurately measure a very small quantity such as a hundredth of a milliliter.

When numbers with decimals are used to calculate a volumetric dose, a number with multiple digits beyond the decimal often results. It is not practical to retain all of these numbers, as a dose cannot be accurately measured beyond the hundredth or thousandth place for most medications. Most commonly, the dose is rounded to the nearest tenth. It is common practice to round the weight of a dose at the hundredth or thousandth place, or as accurate as the particular measuring device (or medication) will permit.

To round off an answer to the nearest tenth, carry the division out two places, to the hundredth place. If the number in the hundredth place is 5 or greater, add 1 to the tenth place number. If the number in the hundredth place is less than 5, round the number down by omitting the digit in the hundredth place.

5.65 becomes 5.7

4.24 becomes 4.2

The same procedure may be used when rounding to the nearest hundredth place or thousandth place.

3.8421 = 3.84	(hundredth)
41.2674 = 41.27	(hundredth)
0.3928 = 0.393	(thousandth)
4.1111 = 4.111	(thousandth)

As mentioned earlier, when rounding numbers used in pharmacy calculations, it is common to round off to the nearest tenth. However, there are times when a dose is very small and rounding to the nearest hundredth or thousandth may be more appropriate.

The exact dose calculated is 0.08752 g
Rounded to nearest tenth: 0.1 g
Rounded to nearest hundredth: 0.09 g
Rounded to nearest thousandth: 0.088 g

When a number that has been rounded to the tenth place is multiplied or divided by a number that was rounded to the hundredth or thousandth place, the resultant answer must be rounded back to the tenth place. The reason is that the answer can only be accurate to the place to which the highest rounding was made in the original numbers.

Example 1.3.1 **Round off the answer of the following equation to the appropriate decimal. Note that 7.1 is a rounded figure.**

$$3.46 \times 7.1 = 24.566$$

The answer must be rounded back to the tenth place.

Answer = 24.6

Example 1.3.2 **Round off the answer of the following equation to the appropriate decimal. Note that 1.349 is a rounded figure.**

$$0.3563 \times 1.349 = 0.4806487$$

The answer must be rounded to the thousandth place.

Answer = 0.481

trailing zero
a zero that appears at the end of a decimal string and is not needed except when considered significant

In most cases, a zero occurring at the end of a string of digits is not written. This zero is called a **trailing zero.** The exception to this occurs when rounding results in a zero as the last place value. When the last digit resulting from rounding is a zero, this zero should be written because it is considered significant to that particular problem or dosage. In such cases, the amount can be measured out to an exact zero as the place value.

Example 1.3.3   **Round 9.98 to the nearest tenth.**

Answer = 10.0

Example 1.3.4   **Round 0.599 to the nearest hundredth.**

Answer = 0.60

Problem Set 1.3

✓ *Self-check your problem set work at* www.emcp.com.

Write the following decimals.

1. seven hundred eighty-four and thirty-six hundredths

2. nine tenths

Add the following decimals.

3. $0.34 + 1.54 =$

4. $1.39 + 1.339 =$

Subtract the following decimals.

5. $15.36 - 0.987 =$

6. $3.09875 - 0.00045 =$

7. $12.901 - 0.903 =$

Multiply the following decimals and round to the hundredth place.

8. $21.62 \times 21.62 =$

9. $0.9 \times 500 =$

Divide the following decimals and round to the thousandth place.

10. $12 \div 6.5 =$

11. $0.8 \div 0.6 =$

Round the following to the nearest hundredth.

12. 3.872

13. 0.138

14. 0.076

Round the following to the nearest thousandth.

15. 0.1961

16. 0.0488

Multiply the following and round to the appropriate place.

17. $6.7 \times 5.21 =$

18. $0.45 \times 3.1 =$

19. Using the prescription below, answer the following.

Alprazolam 0.25 mg

Sig: 3 tabs po QID
Disp: 100 tablets

Note: QID means "four times a day."

a. How many milligrams is the patient taking with each dose?

b. How many milligrams is the patient taking each day?

c. How many tablets will the patient need for 14 days?

d. Is the prescription written for enough tablets to last the patient until the next office visit in two weeks?

e. The pharmacy plans to charge $7.59 plus the cost of the medication. The available products include:

alprazolam 0.25 mg #100/$14.95
alprazolam 0.5 mg #100/$17.46
alprazolam 1 mg #100/$23.87

Select the appropriate product and calculate the price for the patient. Based on the prescription provided, the pharmacy can only dispense 100 tablets.

20. The physician changes the prescription at the patient's next visit. The prescription is shown below.

Alprazolam 0.25 mg

Sig: 4 tabs po QID
Disp: 175 tablets

The available products include:

alprazolam 0.25 mg #100/$14.95
alprazolam 0.5 mg #100/$17.46
alprazolam 1 mg #100/$23.87

a. How many milligrams at each dose is this?

b. How much would #125 alprazolam 0.5 mg tablets cost the pharmacy?

c. How much would #50 alprazolam 1 mg tablets cost the pharmacy?

d. How many days would #50 alprazolam 1 mg tablets taken QID last?

21. Sterile water comes in bottles of 1 L (= 1000 mL). You will need to pour out 120 mL bottles for each patient.
    a. How many 120 mL bottles will you get from a 1 L bottle?

b. How much will be left over?

22. How many milliliters total will need to be dispensed for the following prescription?

Augmentin 125 mg/5 mL susp

8.5 mL bid days 1–2
5.75 mL bid days 3–7

Note: bid means "twice a day."

23. Round the following to the nearest whole dollar.
    a. $46.92

b. 12 @ $1.26

c. $7.37 divided by 2

24. Calculate the following dollar amounts and round to the nearest cent.
    a. $5.84 × 12 =

b. $0.415 × 269 =

25. Calculate the following test scores to the nearest tenth of a percent.
    a. 34 of 38 questions correct

b. 51 of 60 questions correct

c. 83 of 90 questions correct

1.4 ESTIMATES

Estimating an answer prior to calculating the solution is a simple way of checking to see whether the answer we arrive at is reasonable. Estimating can be used in both simple mathematical equations and more complicated algebraic equations.

There are no set mathematical rules for estimating. Most commonly, estimating is performed by rounding to the nearest whole unit that makes sense for the numbers involved. This may be the ones place, tens place, hundreds place, or even larger. A very common estimate that is used daily is rounding to the nearest whole dollar while shopping.

Estimating Sums

sum
the result of adding two or more numbers together

A **sum** is the result of adding two or more numbers together. When estimating sums, it is common to round the numbers to be added to the nearest ten or hundred or thousand first and then add these rounded numbers. When this is done, the values in the ones place and lower are often ignored. The following calculations compare an actual mathematical computation with a corresponding estimate.

Actual	$73.8 + 42.03 + 18.3 + 87.32$	$= 221.45$
Estimate	$70 + 40 + 20 + 90$	$= 220$
Actual	$623 + 1493 + 1631 + 794 + 86$	$= 4627$
Estimate	$600 + 1500 + 1600 + 800 + 100$	$= 4600$
Actual	$6425 + 2652 + 2328 + 4490$	$= 15{,}895$
Estimate	$6000 + 3000 + 2000 + 5000$	$= 16{,}000$

Safety Note

Estimated values can be used to double-check doses but cannot be relied on for accuracy.

Another common method of estimating sums is to stack the numbers by aligning them on their decimal points; add the numbers in the far-left column using their place value (6428 would be 6000 because the 6 is in the thousands place, for example); and then add one-half of the place value of the far-left column for each number with a value in the second-from-the-left column. It is important to remember that the sum arrived at is an estimate only and cannot be relied on as an accurate dose. An outline of this method appears in Table 1.7, and the following examples demonstrate the steps.

Table 1.7 Steps for Estimating Sums

Step 1. Stack the numbers whose sum is to be estimated so that their decimal points are aligned.

Step 2. Add the numbers in the far-left column using their column place value. For example, if the first number is 735, use 700 as that number's value.

Step 3. Multiply one-half of the place value of the far-left column by the total number of numbers that have place values in the second-from-the-left column.

Step 4. Add the totals determined in Steps 2 and 3 to estimate the sum.

Example 1.4.1   **Estimate the sum of 73.80, 42.05, 18.30, and 87.32.**

Step 1. Stack these four numbers so that their decimal points are aligned.

$$73.80$$
$$42.05$$
$$18.30$$
$$87.32$$

Step 2. Add the numbers in the far-left column using their place value, in this case, the tens column.

$$70 + 40 + 10 + 80 = 200$$

Step 3. Multiply one-half of the place value of the far-left column by the total number of numbers that have place values in the second-from-the-left column in the original problem.

(10 far-left column value ÷ 2) × 4 numbers = 20

Step 4. Add the totals determined in Steps 2 and 3 to determine the estimate.

$$200 + 20 = 220$$

Compare this number to the actual sum of the original numbers, which is 221.47.

Example 1.4.2   **Estimate the sum of 623, 1493, 1631, 794, and 86.**

Step 1. Stack these five numbers so that their decimal points are aligned.

$$623$$
$$1493$$
$$1631$$
$$794$$
$$86$$

Step 2. Add the numbers in the far-left column using their place value, in this case, the thousands column.

$$1000 + 1000 = 2000$$

Step 3. Multiply one-half of the place value of the far-left column by the total number of numbers that have place values in the second-from-the-left column in the original problem.

(1000 far-left column value ÷ 2) × 4 numbers = 2000

Note that because 86 does not have a hundreds place value, the number 4, not 5, is used in this step.

Step 4. Add the totals determined in Steps 2 and 3 to determine the estimate.

$$2000 + 2000 = 4000$$

Compare the estimate with the actual sum of the original numbers, which is 4627.

Example 1.4.3   **Estimate the sum of 6425, 2652, 2328, and 4490.**

Step 1. 6425
2652
2328
4490

Step 2. 6000 + 2000 + 2000 + 4000 = 14,000

Step 3. (1000 far-left column value ÷ 2) × 4 numbers = 2000

Step 4. 14,000 + 2000 = 16,000

Compare the estimate with the actual sum of the numbers, which is 15,895.

Estimating Products and Quotients

product
the result of multiplying one number by another

quotient
the result of dividing one number by another

A **product** is the result of multiplying two numbers together. A **quotient** is the result of dividing one number by another number. When estimating products or quotients, it is common to round each of the original numbers to the nearest whole number. The rounded numbers can be quickly multiplied or divided, and the appropriate number of zeros can be added to the answer.

Example 1.4.4   **Estimate the product of 325 × 618.**

Round the two numbers and multiply them.

$$3 \times 6 = 18$$

Add four zeros to this answer to account for the four places of "25" and "18" in the original problem.

$$180,000$$

Compare the estimate to the actual product, which is 200,850.

Example 1.4.5   **Estimate the product of 843 × 41.**

Round the two numbers and multiply them.

$$8 \times 4 = 32$$

Add three zeros for the "43" and "1."

$$32,000$$

Compare the estimate to the actual product, which is 34,563.

Example 1.4.6   **Estimate the product of 843 × 56.**

Round the two numbers, and multiply them. Note that 56 is rounded up to 6, not down to 5.

$$8 \times 6 = 48$$

Add 3 zeros for the "43" and "6."

$$48,000$$

Compare the estimate to the actual product, which is 47,208.

Example 1.4.7   **Estimate the quotient of 5355 ÷ 4.79.**

Round the two numbers and divide them.

$$5 \div 5 = 1$$

Add three zeros for the "355." Do not add zeros for the numbers to the right of the decimal place in 4.79.

$$1000$$

Compare the estimate to the actual product, which is 1117.95.

Example 1.4.8   **Estimate the product of 14.3 × 0.19.**

Round the two numbers.

14.3 is rounded to 14
0.19 is rounded to 0.2

To avoid the decimal in the estimate operation, simplify 0.2 to 2. The decimal point will be inserted after we have multiplied the two rounded numbers.

$$14 \times 2 = 28$$

We ignored one decimal place in order to perform the estimating process quickly, so now we must account for the decimal. To do this, move the decimal point the same number of places that we ignored, in this case, one place. Thus, 28 becomes 2.8.

Compare the estimate to the actual product, which is 2.717.

In other cases, it may make sense to round to a near factor of 10 or 100 or even larger.

Actual	$18.79 × 6 = $112.74
Estimate	$20.00 × 6 = $120.00
Actual	$424.00 × 2 = $848.00
Estimate	$420.00 × 2 = $840.00

| Actual | $4326 \div 3.78 = 1144.44$ |
| Estimate | $4000 \div 4 \quad = 1000$ |

| Actual | $820 \div 42 = 19.52$ |
| Estimate | $800 \div 40 = 20$ |

Estimating a Drug Dose

Estimating a drug dose before calculating the actual dose is helpful because the estimate can be used to double-check the accuracy of the calculated actual dose. If the amounts do not match, then the answer should be checked carefully. When estimating a drug dose, the first step is to determine if the dose is going to be more or less than the unit dose or available drug strength. Continue estimating the dose by rounding the given dose to simplify the problem and dividing this rounded dose by the available drug strength.

Example 1.4.9   **An order for 12.5 mg of a drug needs to be filled using a 5 mg tablet. Estimate the number of tablets needed for this dose.**

The requested solution has 5 mg of drug for each tablet. Since the order is for 12.5 mg of drug, the dose to be measured out will be larger than 1 tablet.

Simplify the estimation by rounding 12.5 mg down to 10 mg. This will make it easier to use the available dose to determine the value of the requested dose.

10 mg (requested amount) $\div$ 5 mg/tablet (available amount) = 2 tablets

Therefore, the estimate indicates that the dose will be at least 2 tablets.

The actual calculated dose of 2.5 tablets can then be checked by comparing it with the estimate. If an actual dose of 0.25 tablet or 25 tablets was calculated instead, then a quick comparison with the estimated dose of 2 tablets would immediately indicate that the actual dose was calculated incorrectly.

In addition to drug doses, the volume to be dispensed and the size of the container needed can be useful estimates when preparing a drug for dispensing.

Example 1.4.10   **The pharmacy receives an order for a 10-day supply of liquid antibiotic to be taken in a dose of 8.5 mL of medication three times a day. The pharmacy has 100 mL, 200 mL, and 300 mL bottles of this antibiotic in stock. Which size bottle of antibiotic should be dispensed?**

Begin by simplifying the problem by rounding the dose of 8.5 mL/dose to 10 mL/dose. It is important to round up to make sure the patient has enough drug.

Using this rounded value, calculate the amount of drug needed per day by multiplying the estimated dose by the number of doses each day.

10 mL/dose $\times$ 3 doses/day = 30 mL/day

In other words, the patient will need about 30 mL of drug a day.

Since the patient needs to take this drug for 10 days, multiply the amount of drug per day by the number of days of therapy.

30 mL/day $\times$ 10 days = 300 mL

Therefore, the patient will need about 300 mL of the medication.
The actual amount needed is 255 mL, but the 300 mL bottle is the correct choice to fill this prescription.

Problem Set 1.4

✓ *Self-check your problem set work at* www.emcp.com.

Using the stack-up process described in Table 1.7, estimate the sum to the nearest ten place and then calculate the actual value.

1. 231 + 718 + 357 + 609 =

2. 176 + 34 + 49 + 16 =

3. 12.38 + 6.26 + 18.95 + 16.52 =

4. 93.7 + 16 + 48.7 + 12.02 =

5. 0.95 + 6.96 + 0.49 + 12.42 =

Use rounding to estimate the dollar amounts to the nearest whole dollar, and then calculate the actual value.

6. $12.53 − $6.15 =

7. $6.28 + $1.99 + $3.98 =

8. $40 − $34.81 =

9. $100 − $18.29 =

10. $100 − $17.52 − $31.90 =

Estimate the products by rounding the two numbers and then multiplying them. Also calculate the actual value.

11. 6.8 × 7656 =

12. 4.02 × 350.07 =

13. 598.4 × 0.015 =

14. 4569 × 0.0972 =

15. 6183 × 18 =

16. 1253 × 9.1 =

Estimate the quotients by rounding the two numbers and then dividing them. Also calculate the actual value.

17. 185 ÷ 18 =

18. 18,015 ÷ 56 =

19. 584.0 ÷ 8 =

20. 844.23 ÷ 4.4 =

21. 123 ÷ 14 =

Applications

Round and estimate to find the following.

22. An employee of the pharmacy is being sent to the grocery store to buy the following items. Estimate how much petty cash he will need.

Food dye	$1.89
Sugar, 2@	$4.25
Baking soda	$0.79
Cherry flavoring	$2.39
1 gallon bleach	$1.97
Distilled water, 4@	$0.89

23. Estimate how much sterile water for injection (SWFI) you will need for the following reconstitutions: 3.2 mL, 7.6 mL, 1.6 mL, and 4.1 mL. Choose the appropriate vial from the available vials (15 mL SWFI, 30 mL SWFI, and 50 mL SWFI).

24. A patient is receiving the following fluids: IV fluids, 1723 mL; juice, 150 mL; coffee, 126 mL. Estimate the patient's intake to the nearest 10 mL.

25. The following is a patient's parenteral fluid intake for the first twenty-four hours of admittance: 780 mL NS, 3 × 50 mL piggybacks, 250 mL NS, 3 × 1000 mL NS. Estimate the total to the nearest 100 mL amount.

1.5 SIGNIFICANT FIGURES AND MEASUREMENT ACCURACY

significant figures
the figures in a numeral that are known values and have not been rounded or estimated in the process of mathematical calculation, plus the digit in the lowest place value, which is approximate

lowest known place value
the last digit on the right of a written numeral

Rounding and estimating have been discussed as a practical way of using numbers to calculate and measure a dose. In the process, one should not lose sight of the mathematical principle that each numerical value has a certain number of **significant figures.** These significant figures consist of those that are known to be accurate plus the digit in the lowest place value, which is approximate.

The **lowest known place value** is the last digit on the right of a written numeral. This lowest known value is approximate due to many sources of error including the limitation of the instrument used to measure, operator error, temperature variation, and the need to round at a certain point to make the number practical for calculations.

Significant figures are digits that have a practical meaning or value. A leading zero that marks the place of the decimal is not significant as it only marks the place value of the numbers that follow the decimal. Counting of significant figures begins at the first nonzero digit. Table 1.8 provides a short list of "rules" to follow when counting significant figures. Table 1.9 shows several numbers and indicates how many significant figures they have.

In certain cases, when the accuracy of the measurement is known, the trailing zero to the right of the apparent last significant figure may also be considered significant. For example, if the device used to measure a substance is accurate to the nearest tenth, the tenth place may be considered significant even if the last digit is a zero. The zero may be retained to indicate the accuracy of the number. For example,

1.0 has 2 significant figures

Larger numbers have significant figures based on their accuracy to the nearest factor of 10. If a very large amount of a substance is measured, at some point the person doing the measuring must "estimate" the closest amount represented by the device being used. As a result, the last digit recorded cannot be considered to be accurate and is thus not significant. For example, if 2788 is considered accurate from 2780 to 2790, it has only 3 significant figures. Similarly, if 8,341,274 is considered accurate from 8,341,270 to 8,341,280, it has only 6 significant figures.

When the degree of accuracy is known to a certain place value, the significant figures are counted only to that place value. Knowing the level of accuracy is important when considering the weighing capacity and sensitivity of a scale or balance in the pharmacy.

Table 1.8   Rules for Counting Significant Figures

Rule 1. Begin counting at the first nonzero digit.

Rule 2. Continue counting to the right until you reach the place value that is last (or rounded).

Rule 3. Zeros that are located between digits are significant and should be counted.

Rule 4. Do not count zeros that are placed to the left of the first digit. They only mark the place of the decimal.

Rule 5. One or more final zeros may or may not be significant depending on the accuracy to which the number is held.

Table 1.9 Counting Significant Figures

Number	Number of Significant Figures	Rule Applied
1.8	2	1, 2
18.3	3	1, 2
183	3	1, 2
1.832	4	1, 2
1832	4	1, 2
0.183	3	1, 2
0.108	3	1, 2, 3, 4
0.0108	3	1, 2, 3, 4
0.01	1	1, 2, 4
0.8	1	1, 2, 4
8	1	1, 2

Example 1.5.1 **An item is weighed on a balance with a degree of accuracy to the nearest tenth when measuring milliliters. The balance indicates that an item weighs 1.459 mg. How many significant figures does this weight have? What would the rounded value be?**

Because the accuracy of the scale can be relied on only to the tenth place, the number of significant figures is 2. The "59" is not considered significant due to the sensitivity of the scale being used.

The weight would be rounded to 1.5 mg.

Significant figures are also used to describe the relative accuracy of a given number or value. For practical purposes, a number may be considered accurate to within two figures and up to five figures. More significant digits indicate a greater accuracy of known values. A number that is accurate to within two figures has a practical 5% error from the actual measurement. Table 1.10 demonstrates these accuracy translations.

In studying mathematics, numbers may be considered accurate for an infinite number of figures. In the study of pharmacy, however, for practical purposes a range of two to five figures is common.

Numbers greater than 100 have significant figures based on the relative accuracy of the measurement. If a number over 100 is accurate to the nearest 10, the first two digits are considered significant, and the last zero is considered an estimate and thus

Table 1.10 Accuracy Ranges

Accuracy Level	Example
Two-figure accuracy is within 5%.	100 mg is in the range of 95 mg to 105 mg
Three-figure accuracy is within 0.5%.	100 mg is in the range of 99.5 mg to 100.5 mg
Four-figure accuracy is within 0.05%.	100 mg is in the range of 99.95 mg to 100.05 mg
Five-figure accuracy is within 0.005%.	100 mg is in the range of 99.995 mg to 100.005 mg

not significant. This is also true for numbers that are accurate to the nearest 100 or 1000. For example, if the following numbers are accurate to the nearest 10, they will have the indicated number of significant figures.

200 has 2 significant figures
1800 has 3 significant figures
30,000 has 4 significant figures

Similarly, if the following numbers are accurate to the nearest 100, they will have the indicated number of significant figures.

200 has 1 significant figure
1800 has 2 significant figures
30,000 has 3 significant figures

Just as with rounding, when performing calculations with numbers that have a different number of significant figures or have been rounded to different place values, the answer must be rounded to the place value of the least number of decimals.

Example 1.5.2 **Determine the product of 6.5 mg × 4.18 using the appropriate number of accurate and significant figures.**

Note the number of significant figures and the level of accuracy for each number: 6.5 has two significant figures and is accurate to the tenth place, whereas 4.18 has three significant figures and is accurate to the hundredth place.
  Now, determine the product of the two numbers.

$$6.5 \times 4.18 = 27.17$$

Because 6.5 is accurate only to the tenth place, the answer is only accurate to the tenth place. Therefore, 27.17 needs to be rounded to the tenth place. The answer, 27.2, has three significant figures.

Example 1.5.3 **Determine the product of 12.59 × 1572 using the appropriate number of accurate and significant figures.**

Note the number of significant figures and the accuracy of the numbers. Both factors have 4 significant figures. The number 12.59 is accurate to the hundredth place, but 1572 is accurate only to the ones place.
  Now, determine the product of the two numbers.

$$12.59 \times 1572 = 19,791.48$$

The accuracy of the product is considered only to the ones place. Therefore, the answer must be rounded to that place, and the acceptable answer is 19,791.

✓ *Self-check your problem set work at* www.emcp.com.

Identify the number of significant figures in the following amounts. Assume that all final zeros are not significant.

1. 15.4324 grains

2. 1500 mL

3. 0.21 mg

4. $1.07

5. 100,000 mcg

6. 507.2 mg

7. 1.0 kg

8. 0.001 mg

9. 21,204.075 mcg

10. 100 mL

Round the following numbers to three significant figures.

11. 42.75

12. 100.19

13. 0.04268

14. 18.426

15. 0.003918

Round the following to two decimal places and state how many significant figures each has.

16. 0.3479

17. 0.056921

18. 1.9947

19. 0.00986

20. 1.0277

Calculate the following and retain the correct number of decimal places in the calculation.

21. $0.67 \times 95.2 =$

22. $1.26 \times 24 =$

23. $325 \times 0.5 =$

Applications

24. You are to prepare capsules that contain 0.125 g of a drug. You have four partial containers of medication, which weigh 3.2 g, 1.784 g, 2.46 g, and 5.87 g. Assume you have weighed each of the four containers with the same scale, and the accuracy is known to the hundredth gram.
   a. Which amount will need to be rounded?

   b. Which amount is not as accurate as it should be?

   c. What is the amount of the medication that will be left over after making the 0.125 g capsules?

25. A unit dose of an oral medication requires 21.65 mg. You are to prepare 45 doses.
   a. How many milligrams will you need?

   b. How many significant figures does this amount have?

Practice Test

Circle the fraction with the highest value.

1. $\frac{4}{8}$ $\frac{3}{8}$ $\frac{2}{8}$

Express the following fractions in decimal form. Round to the nearest thousandth or zero.

2. $\frac{1}{5}$

3. $\frac{7}{8}$

Give the equivalent Arabic numeral for each of the following Roman numerals.

4. XXXIX

5. CCXVI

Give the equivalent Roman numeral for each of the following Arabic numerals.

6. 1200

7. 473

Write the following numbers without using scientific notation.

8. 9.1×10^8

9. 7.2×10^2

10. 2.538×10^{-5}

11. 2.01×10^{-4}

Write the following numbers using scientific notation.

12. 375,940,000,000

13. 0.000000109

14. 1,800,000

15. 920

In each group of numbers, circle the highest value.

16. 0.31   0.61   0.91

17. 0.33   0.3   0.31

State the place value of the underlined digit.

18. 1.$\underline{3}$6

19. 56.7$\underline{8}$

20. 0.23$\underline{1}$

Write the following decimals.

21. one thousand ninety and six tenths

22. twelve and nine thousand six hundred forty-sevenths

Add the following decimals.

23. $12.2 + 19.7 + 16.57 =$

24. $3.89 + 0.257 + 9.023 =$

Multiply the following decimals.

25. $6.08 \times 3.24 =$

26. $10.728 \times 4.23 =$

Calculate the following, retaining the correct number of decimal places.

27. $15.432 \times 3 =$

28. $208 \times 62.1 =$

Round the following to the nearest tenth.

29. 6.52

30. 83.97

Round the following to the nearest thousandth.

31. 643.7308

32. 4.2619

Multiply the following and round to the appropriate place.

33. $8.23 \times 0.23 =$

34. $0.8015 \times 0.9921 =$

Calculate the following test scores to the nearest tenth of a percent.

35. 34 of 38 questions correct

36. 51 of 60 questions correct

Applications

37. A prescription is to be filled for a patient who needs to take 11 mL of medication two times daily. She needs a 7 days' supply. You have amber ovals (bottles) in three sizes: 120 mL, 240 mL, and 360 mL. Estimate the total volume needed and choose the appropriate container size.

38. The following list indicates the value of various drugs that were destroyed: $41.71, $11.50, $8.93, $10.50, $3.29, $14.34, $68.20. Estimate the total dollar amount to be documented for the loss.

Using Ratios, Percents, and Proportions

Objectives

- Understand the use of ratios and proportions in the pharmacy.
- Solve pharmacy calculations by using ratios and proportions.
- Calculate percentage of error and evaluate measurements using percentage of error.

2.1 NUMERICAL RATIOS

ratio
a numerical representation of the relationship between two parts of the whole or between one part and the whole

A **ratio** is a numerical representation of the relationship between two parts of the whole or of the relationship of one part to the whole. Ratios are written with a colon (:) between the numbers, which may be read as "per," "of," "to," or "in." The ratio 1:2 could mean that the second part has twice the value (e.g., size, number, weight, volume) of the first part, or it could mean that one part is something within a total of two parts. Ratios may also be written as fractions, and it is the ratio in fraction form that is most useful to the pharmacy technician.

1:2	is read as	1 part to 2 parts	and may also be written as $\frac{1}{2}$
3:4	is read as	3 parts to 4 parts	and may also be written as $\frac{3}{4}$
1:20	is read as	1 part to 20 parts	and may also be written as $\frac{1}{20}$
1:10	is read as	1 part to 10 parts	and may also be written as $\frac{1}{10}$

In the above ratios, you may use the words *per, in,* or *of* in place of *to* when reading the ratio. Any unit of description may be substituted for the word *part* or *parts.* For example, we say there are 250 mg per tablet. Other common unit labels include capsule, bottle, gram, milligram, microgram, and liter.

A ratio can be any numerical relation we wish it to be. With medications, we commonly use a ratio to express the weight or strength of a drug per dose or volumetric measurement. Ratios are commonly used to express concentrations of a drug in solution. For example, a 1:100 concentration of a drug means that there is 1 part of the drug in 100 parts of the solution (1 g per 100 mL). It is also common to reverse the order of the values written in a ratio.

250 mg:1 tablet	or	1 tablet:250 mg
1 g:100 mL	or	100 mL:1 g
500 mg:20 mL	or	20 mL:500 mg

The ratio may be manipulated by multiplying or dividing both parts of the ratio by the same factor. We use this application when calculating the volume of a medication to be given or, in some cases, the amount of drug per volume of drug given. See the drug label below when reviewing the following examples.

Example 2.1.1   **How much aminophylline was ordered if two ampules were administered and each ampule contains 500 mg/20 mL?**

For 2 ampules we multiply both parts of the ratio by 2.

$$\frac{500 \text{ mg} \times 2}{20 \text{ mL} \times 2} = \frac{1000 \text{ mg}}{40 \text{ mL}}$$

So, 1000 mg were given.

Example 2.1.2   **How much aminophylline was ordered if half an ampule was administered and each ampule contains 500 mg/20 mL?**

For half of an ampule, we divide both parts of the ratio by 2.

$$\frac{500 \text{ mg} \div 2}{20 \text{ mL} \div 2} = \frac{250 \text{ mg}}{10 \text{ mL}}$$

So, 250 mg were given.

Some medications are ordered in concentrations that are expressed in a ratio. Typically, these medications are available in a very small percentage (less than 1%). The dose form (such as a cream, solution, or liquid mixture) will influence the ratio. The following examples use a 1:10,000 ratio.

1 g active ingredient:10,000 g product for a solid such as a cream
1 g active ingredient:10,000 mL solution for a solution
1 mL active ingredient:10,000 mL mixture for a liquid

Example 2.1.3 **A 1:100 solution has 1 g active ingredient in 100 mL. How much active ingredient is present in 300 mL of this solution?**

Set up a ratio and solve for *x*. In this problem, *x* equals the active ingredient.

$$\frac{x \text{ g}}{300 \text{ mL}} = \frac{1 \text{ g}}{100 \text{ mL}}$$

$$\frac{(300 \text{ mL}) \, x \text{ g}}{300 \text{ mL}} = \frac{(300 \text{ mL}) \, 1 \text{ g}}{100 \text{ mL}}$$

$$x \text{ g} = 3 \text{ g}$$

Therefore, there is 3 g of active ingredient in 300 mL of this solution.

Problem Set 2.1 _____

✓ *Self-check your problem set work at* www.emcp.com.

Express the following ratios as fractions and reduce to the lowest terms.

1. 3:7

2. 8:6

3. 3:4

4. 4:6

5. 1:7

Reduce the following fractions to the lowest terms and express each as a ratio.

6. $\frac{2}{3}$

7. $\frac{6}{8}$

8. $\frac{5}{10}$

9. $\frac{1}{9}$

10. $\frac{1}{10,000}$

Applications

State the ratio for the following doses.

11. 500 mg tablet of metformin

12. 5 mL dose of albuterol containing 2 mg

13. 5 mL dose of amoxicillin containing 250 mg

Use the ratios calculated in the preceding problems to calculate how much drug is in the following doses. Write a sentence explaining how you calculated each answer.

14. ½ tablet of metformin 500 mg

15. 10 mL of albuterol syrup, 2 mg in 5 mL

16. 15 mL of amoxicillin syrup, 250 mg in 5 mL

Fill in the blanks.

17. A 10:1000 solution contains _____ g of active ingredient and _____ mL of product, and 100 mL of that solution contains _____ g.

18. A 1:100 solution contains _____ g of active ingredient and _____ mL of product, and 500 mL of that solution contains _____ g.

19. A 1:250 solution contains _____ g of active ingredient and _____ mL of product, and 1000 mL of that solution contains _____ g.

20. A 1:100 solution contains _____ g of active ingredient and _____ mL of product, and 50 mL of that solution contains _____ g.

2.2 PERCENTS

percent
the number of parts per 100; can be written as a fraction, a decimal, or a ratio

Percent expresses the number of parts compared to a total of 100 parts. Percent means, literally, "per 100" (from the Latin) or hundredths and is the same as a fraction in which the denominator is 100. Percent is represented by the symbol %. A percent can be written as a fraction, a decimal, or a ratio. For example:

30% means there are 30 parts in a total of 100 parts.

$$30:100, \frac{30}{100}, \text{ or } 0.30$$

If a test has 100 questions and you receive a score of 89%, you got 89 of the 100 questions correct.

$$89:100, \frac{89}{100}, \text{ or } 0.89$$

Safety Note
The higher the percentage of a dissolved substance, the greater the strength.

Percent strengths are often used to describe intravenous solutions and topically applied drugs. The higher the percentage of dissolved substances (in a solute or a topical drug), the greater the strength. For example:

A 1% solution contains 1 g of drug per 100 mL of fluid, which may be expressed as 1:100, $\frac{1}{100}$, or 0.01.

A 1% hydrocortisone cream contains 1 g of hydrocortisone per 100 g of cream, which may be expressed as 1:100, $\frac{1}{100}$, or 0.01.

By multiplying the first number in the ratio (the solute) while keeping the second number unchanged, we can increase the strength. Conversely, by dividing the first number in the ratio while keeping the second number unchanged, we can decrease the strength.

Example 2.2.1   **A 5% solution contains 5 g of solute per 100 mL of solution. If the patient is to receive a 10% solution, how many grams of solute will the solution have to contain?**

$$\frac{5 \text{ g} \times 2}{100 \text{ mL}} = \frac{10 \text{ g}}{100 \text{ mL}} = 10\% \text{ solution}$$

Thus, a 10% solution contains 10 g of solute per 100 mL of solution.

Example 2.2.2   **A 2% solution contains 2 g of solute per 100 mL of solution. If the patient is to receive a 1% solution, how many grams of solute will the solution have to contain?**

$$\frac{2 \text{ g} \div 2}{100 \text{ mL}} = \frac{1 \text{ g}}{100 \text{ mL}} = 1\% \text{ solution}$$

Thus, a 1% solution contains 1 g of solute per 100 mL of solution.

When working in the pharmacy, the technician will need to know how to convert between ratios, percents, and decimals. The values in Table 2.1 are equivalent to each other. They are simply expressed in different ways.

Converting a Ratio to a Percent

To express a ratio as a percent, designate the first number of the ratio as the numerator and the second number as the denominator. Multiply the fraction by 100% (which does not change the value), and simplify as needed.

$$5{:}1 = \frac{5}{1} \times 100\% = 5 \times 100\% = 500\%$$

$$1{:}5 = \frac{1}{5} \times 100\% = \frac{100\%}{5} = 20\%$$

$$1{:}2 = \frac{1}{2} \times 100\% = \frac{100\%}{2} = 50\%$$

Table 2.1   **Equivalent Values**

Percent	Fraction	Decimal	Ratio
45%	$\dfrac{45}{100}$	0.45	45:100
0.5%	$\dfrac{0.5}{100}$	0.005	0.5:100

Example 2.2.3

A 1:1000 solution has been ordered. You have a 1% solution, a 0.5% solution, and a 0.1% solution in stock. Will one of these work to fill the order?

$$1:1000 = \frac{1}{1000} \times 100\% = \frac{100\%}{1000} = 0.1\%$$

The 0.1% solution is the same concentration as the ordered 1:1000 solution.

Converting a Percent to a Ratio

To convert a percent to a ratio, first change it to a fraction by dividing it by 100 and then reduce the fraction to its lowest terms. Express this as a ratio by making the numerator the first number of the ratio and the denominator the second number.

$$2\% = 2 \div 100 = \frac{2}{100} = \frac{1}{50} = 1:50$$

$$10\% = 10 \div 100 = \frac{10}{100} = \frac{1}{10} = 1:10$$

$$75\% = 75 \div 100 = \frac{75}{100} = \frac{3}{4} = 3:4$$

$$\frac{1}{2}\% = \frac{1}{2} \div 100 = \frac{\frac{1}{2}}{100} = \frac{1}{2} \times \frac{1}{100} = \frac{1}{200} = 1:200$$

Example 2.2.4

A 0.02% solution has been ordered. You have a 1:1000 solution, a 1:5000 solution, and a 1:10,000 solution in stock. Will one of these work to fill the order?

$$0.02\% = \frac{0.02}{100} = 0.0002 = 0.02:100$$

Simplify the ratio by dividing both sides of the ratio by 0.02.

$$0.02 \div 0.02 = 1$$
$$100 \div 0.02 = 5000$$

The percent 0.02% is represented by the ratio 1:5000. The supply of 1:5000 solution may be used to fill this order.

Converting a Percent to a Decimal

Remember

Multiplying or dividing by 100% does not change the value because 100% = 1.

To convert a percent to a decimal, divide by 100% or insert a decimal point two places to the left of the last number, inserting zeros if necessary, and drop the percent symbol. To change a decimal to a percent, multiply by 100% or move the decimal point two places to the right and write in the percent symbol. (Just as multiplying or dividing a number by 1 does not change the value of the number, multiplying or dividing a number by 100% does not change the value of the number.)

Percent to Decimal

4% = 0.04	4 ÷ 100% = 0.04
15% = 0.15	15 ÷ 100% = 0.15
200% = 2.0	200 ÷ 100% = 2.0

Decimal to Percent

0.25 = 25%	0.25 × 100% = 25%
1.35 = 135%	1.35 × 100% = 135%
0.015 = 1.5%	0.015 × 100% = 1.5%

Problem Set 2.2

✓ Self-check your problem set work at www.emcp.com.

Express the following fractions as percents.

1. $\dfrac{6}{7}$

2. $\dfrac{5}{12}$

3. $\dfrac{1}{4}$

4. $\dfrac{2}{3}$

5. $\dfrac{0.5}{10}$

Express the following ratios as percents.

6. 2:3

7. 1.5:4.65

8. 1:250

9. 1:10,000

10. 1:6

Convert the following percents to fractions.

11. 50%   12. 2%

Convert the following percents to decimals.

13. 6%   15. 126%

14. 12.5%

Calculate the following, rounding off to the nearest hundredth when necessary.

16. 5% of 20   19. 110% of 70

17. 20% of 60   20. 0.2% of 50

18. 19% of 63

Fill in the missing values in the following table.

	Percent	Fraction	Ratio	Decimal
21.	33%	$\dfrac{1}{3}$		
22.	2.5%		1:40	
23.		$\dfrac{1}{2}$		0.5
24.			1:100	0.01
25.	90%			0.90
26.	67%			0.67
27.		$\dfrac{1}{500}$	1:500	
28.	0.45%			0.0045
29.	5%		1:20	
30.	20%	$\dfrac{1}{5}$		

Applications

Choose the appropriate solution from the available stock.

31. A 1:10,000 solution has been ordered. You have a 0.05% solution, a 0.01% solution, and a 1% solution in stock. Which will you choose?

32. A 1:20 solution has been ordered. You have a 5% solution, a 10% solution, and a 20% solution in stock. Which will you choose?

33. A 1:25 solution has been ordered. You have a 0.4% solution, a 0.05% solution, and a 4% solution in stock. Which will you choose?

34. A 1:800 solution has been ordered. You have a 0.01% solution, a 0.125% solution, and a 1.25% solution in stock. Which will you choose?

35. A 1:10 solution has been ordered. You have a 0.09% solution, a 0.01% solution, and a 10% solution in stock. Which will you choose?

2.3 PROPORTIONS

> **proportion**
> an expression of equality between two ratios

A **proportion** is an expression of equality between two ratios. It is notated by a double colon (::) or an equal sign between the two ratios.

$$3{:}4 = 15{:}20 \quad \text{or} \quad 3{:}4 :: 15{:}20 \quad \text{or} \quad \frac{3}{4} = \frac{15}{20}$$

In a proportion, the first and fourth, or outside, numbers are called the extremes. The second and third, or inside, numbers are called the means.

$$3{:}4 \quad = \quad 15{:}20$$

—means—

— extremes —

The product of the means must always equal the product of the extremes in a proportion. You can check for the correctness of the proportion by using this formula.

Given a proportion

$$a{:}b = c{:}d$$

the product of means = the product of extremes

or

$$b \times c = a \times d$$

Example 2.3.1   **Confirm that the proportion 3:4 equals the proportion 15:20.**

$$3{:}4 = 15{:}20$$
$$4 \times 15 = 3 \times 20$$
$$60 = 60$$

The **ratio-proportion method** is one of the most frequently used methods for calculating drug doses in the pharmacy. We can use this method any time one ratio is complete and the other one has a missing component. In other words, if we know three of the four values in a proportion, we can solve for the missing value. When setting up ratios in the proportion, it is important that the numbers remain in the correct ratio and that the numbers have the correct units of measurement in both the numerator and the denominator. Table 2.2 lists the rules for using the ratio-proportion method. Table 2.3 lists the steps for solving for an unknown quantity, which we usually label x.

Example 2.3.2

A drug is available as 250 mg/5 mL. How many milliliters represent a dose of 375 mg?

In this case, set the ordered dose ratio equal to the pharmacy stocked drug ratio. In setting up a proportion, the ratios on the two sides of the equal sign may be flipped over as long as *both* ratios are reversed.

prescription order ratio = pharmacy shelf ratio

$$\frac{x \text{ mL}}{375 \text{ mg}} = \frac{5 \text{ mL}}{250 \text{ mg}}$$

Be sure to check that the unit of measurement in the numerators is the same (both are milliliters) and that the unit of measurement in the denominators is the same (both are milligrams). Then, multiply both sides by 375 mg to cancel the milligram unit and isolate the unknown.

$$\frac{(375 \text{ mg}) \, x \text{ mL}}{375 \text{ mg}} = \frac{(375 \text{ mg}) \, 5 \text{ mL}}{250 \text{ mg}}$$

$$x \text{ mL} = \frac{1875 \text{ mL}}{250}$$

Simplify the fraction by dividing 1875 by 250.

$$x \text{ mL} = 7.5 \text{ mL}$$

Check that the product of the means equals the product of the extremes.

7.5 mL:375 mg = 5 mL:250 mg

$$375 \times 5 = 7.5 \times 250$$

$$1875 = 1875$$

Table 2.2   Rules for Using the Ratio-Proportion Method

- Three of the four amounts must be known.

- The numerators must have the same unit of measurement.

- The denominators must have the same unit of measurement.

Table 2.3   Steps for Solving for *x* in the Ratio-Proportion Method

Step 1. Create the proportion by placing the ratios in fraction form so that the *x* is in the upper-left corner.

Step 2. Check that the unit of measurement in the numerators is the same and the unit of measurement in the denominators is the same.

Step 3. Solve for *x* by multiplying both sides of the proportion by the denominator of the ratio containing the unknown, and cancel.

Step 4. Check your answer by seeing if the product of the means equals the product of the extremes.

Example 2.3.3   The label shown below is the stock your pharmacy has available of tobramycin sulfate. How many milliliters will need to be dispensed to the patient if the prescription is for 150 mg?

$$\frac{x \text{ mL}}{150 \text{ mg}} = \frac{6 \text{ mL}}{60 \text{ mg}}$$

$$\frac{(\cancel{150 \text{ mg}}) \; x \text{ mL}}{\cancel{150 \text{ mg}}} = \frac{(\cancel{150 \text{ mg}}) \; 6 \text{ mL}}{60 \; \cancel{\text{mg}}}$$

$$x \text{ mL} = \frac{900 \text{ mL}}{60}$$

$$x \text{ mL} = 15 \text{ mL}$$

Check that the product of the means equals the product of the extremes.

$$15 \text{ mL} : 150 \text{ mg} = 6 \text{ mL} : 60 \text{ mg}$$
$$150 \times 6 = 15 \times 60$$
$$900 = 900$$

Example 2.3.4

The label shown below is the stock available at your pharmacy. How many milligrams of diazepam will need to be dispensed to the patient if the prescription is for 4 mL?

$$\frac{x \text{ mg}}{4 \text{ mL}} = \frac{5 \text{ mg}}{1 \text{ mL}}$$

$$\frac{(4 \text{ mL}) \, x \text{ mg}}{4 \text{ mL}} = \frac{(4 \text{ mL}) \, 5 \text{ mg}}{1 \text{ mL}}$$

$$x \text{ mg} = 20 \text{ mg}$$

Check that the product of the means equals the product of the extremes.

$$20 \text{ mg:4 mL} = 5 \text{ mg:1 mL}$$
$$4 \times 5 = 20 \times 1$$
$$20 = 20$$

Remember

When setting up a proportion to solve a conversion, the units in the numerators must match, and the units in the denominators must match.

conversion factor
an equivalency equal to 1 that can be used when converting units of measure using the ratio-proportion method

In addition to being useful for calculating drug doses in the pharmacy, the ratio-proportion method can be used for converting between units of measure. To solve a conversion problem, put the unknown and the specific value that is to be converted on the left side of the proportion. On the right side of the proportion, put the conversion factor. The **conversion factor** is an equivalency equal to 1. For example, since 1 g = 1000 mg, an example of a conversion factor is 1 g/1000 mg or 1000 mg/1 g. Additional conversion factors are presented in Appendix C.

Example 2.3.5

How many milligrams are equivalent to 3 g?

Begin the solution by setting up a ratio and solving for *x*, using the conversion factor 1000 mg = 1 g.

$$x \text{ mg:3 g} = 1000 \text{ mg:1 g}$$

$$\frac{x \text{ mg}}{3 \text{ g}} = \frac{1000 \text{ mg}}{1 \text{ g}}$$

The unit of measurement in the numerators is the same (both are milligrams), and the unit of measurement in the denominators is the same (both are grams). Then, multiply both sides by 3 g to cancel the grams and isolate the unknown.

$$\frac{(3 \text{ g}) \, x \text{ mg}}{3 \text{ g}} = \frac{(3 \text{ g}) \, 1000 \text{ mg}}{1 \text{ g}}$$

$$x \text{ mg} = \frac{3000 \text{ mg}}{1} = 3000 \text{ mg}$$

Check that the product of the means equals the product of the extremes.

$$3000 \text{ mg}:3 \text{ g} = 1000 \text{ mg}:1 \text{ g}$$
$$3 \times 1000 = 3000 \times 1$$
$$3000 = 3000$$

Example 2.3.6   **Change 44 lb to kilograms. Your conversion chart in Appendix C states that 1 kg 5 2.2 lb.**

$$\frac{x \text{ kg}}{44 \text{ lb}} = \frac{1 \text{ kg}}{2.2 \text{ lb}}$$

$$\frac{(44 \text{ lb}) \, x \text{ kg}}{44 \text{ lb}} = \frac{(44 \text{ lb}) \, 1 \text{ kg}}{2.2 \text{ lb}}$$

$$x \text{ kg} = \frac{44 \text{ kg}}{2.2}$$

$$x \text{ kg} = 20 \text{ kg}$$

Make sure the product of the means equals the product of the extremes.

$$20 \text{ kg}:44 \text{ lb} = 1 \text{ kg}:2.2 \text{ lb}$$
$$44 = 44$$

The ratio-proportion method can also be used to solve many types of percentage problems. When setting up the ratios, remember that a percentage may be written in fraction form, with the percent value over 100. For example, 95% is equivalent to $^{95}/_{100}$.

Example 2.3.7   **A patient needs to take 75% of a recommended dose before it may be discontinued. The recommended dose is 650 mg. How much must the patient take before it is discontinued?**

Write the percentage (75%) as a fraction ($^{75}/_{100}$) and solve for x.

$$\frac{x \text{ mg}}{650 \text{ mg}} = \frac{75 \text{ mg}}{100 \text{ mg}}$$

$$\frac{(650 \text{ mg}) \, x \text{ mg}}{650 \text{ mg}} = \frac{(650 \text{ mg}) \, 75 \text{ mg}}{100 \text{ mg}}$$

$$x \text{ mg} = 487.5 \text{ mg}$$

Example 2.3.8   **A patient has taken 85% of a recommended dose. If the amount taken is 320 mg, what was the recommended dose?**

Another way of phrasing this question is "320 mg is 85% of what?"

$$\frac{x \text{ mg}}{320 \text{ mg}} = \frac{100 \text{ mg}}{85 \text{ mg}}$$

$$\frac{(320 \text{ mg}) \, x \text{ mg}}{320 \text{ mg}} = \frac{(320 \text{ mg}) \, 100 \text{ mg}}{85 \text{ mg}}$$

$$x \text{ mg} = 376.47 \text{ mg}$$

Problem Set 2.3 _____

✓ *Self-check your problem set work at* www.emcp.com.

Solve for *x* for each of the following ratios. Round your answers to the nearest hundredth when necessary.

1. $\frac{x}{10} = \frac{20}{40}$

2. $\frac{x}{0.6} = \frac{0.8}{6.12}$

3. $\frac{x}{9} = \frac{5}{10}$

4. $\frac{x}{1} = \frac{0.5}{5}$

5. $\frac{x}{50} = \frac{0.4}{125}$

6. $\frac{13}{15} = \frac{5}{x}$

7. $\frac{x}{68} = \frac{72}{90}$

8. $\frac{14}{3} = \frac{x}{52}$

9. $\frac{x}{27} = \frac{49}{51}$

10. $\frac{13}{x} = \frac{52}{64}$

11. $\frac{14}{23} = \frac{27}{x}$

12. $\frac{31}{13} = \frac{51}{x}$

13. $\frac{47}{9} = \frac{x}{15}$

14. $\frac{9}{26} = \frac{x}{31}$

15. $\frac{37}{x} = \frac{11}{23}$

Set up proportions and solve for *x* to answer the following questions. Round your answers to the hundredth place.

16. 72 is what percent of 254?

17. 90% of what number is 44?

18. 44% of what number is 100?

19. 28% of what number is 34?

20. 24.5 is what percent of 45?

Change the following weights using the conversion factor 1 g = 1000 mg.

21. 100 mg = _____ g

22. 247 mg = _____ g

23. 1420 mg = _____ g

24. 495 mg = _____ g

25. 3781 mg = _____ g

26. 0.349 g = _____ mg

27. 1.5 g = _____ mg

28. 0.083 g = _____ mg

29. 0.01 g = _____ mg

30. 2.1 g = _____ mg

Change the following weights using the conversion factor 1 kg = 2.2 lb. Round your answer to the tenth place.

31. 6.3 lb = _____ kg

32. 15 lb = _____ kg

33. 97 lb = _____ kg

34. 115 lb = _____ kg

35. 186 lb = _____ kg

36. 7.5 kg = _____ lb

37. 3.6 kg = _____ lb

38. 79.2 kg = _____ lb

39. 90 kg = _____ lb

40. 0.5 kg = _____ lb

Applications

Set up a proportion using x as the unknown and solve the following. Explain in your own words how you set up your proportion.

41. A drug is available as 500 mg/10 mL. The order calls for 100 mg. How many milliliters will you prepare?

42. Maxicillin is available as a 125 mg tablet. How many tablets are needed to give a dose of 375 mg?

43. Soakamycin is available as a concentration of 20 mg/mL. How many milliliters are needed to prepare a foot soak that contains 300 mg?

44. You are going to buy some folders to file your orders. After checking around, you find that the most cost-effective price is $7.40 per box of 100 folders. You have $15 to spend. How many folders can you buy? (The boxes may not be broken.)

45. The patient is to get an intramuscular injection of 10,000 units of Musclesporin. You have a bottle containing 250,000 units per 15 mL. How many milliliters must be prepared to administer this dose?

46. A dose of 240 mg is ordered. The drug is available as 120 mg tablets. How many tablets are needed to provide the ordered dose?

47. A dose of 250 mg is ordered. The drug is available as a 125 mg/10 mL solution. How many milliliters are needed to provide the ordered dose?

48. A dose of 300 mg is ordered. The drug is available as a 500 mg/10 mL solution. How many milliliters are needed to provide the ordered dose?

49. A dose of 500 mg is ordered. The drug is available as a 125 mg tablet. How many whole tablets are needed to provide the ordered dose?

50. A dose of 30 mg is ordered. The drug is available as a 20 mg/mL solution. How many milliliters are needed to provide the ordered dose?

51. The order calls for 5 mL. How many milligrams is this?

52. The order calls for 80 mg. How many milliliters is this?

53. The order calls for 50 mg. How many milliliters is this?

Use the following drug label to determine the dose needed for questions 51–55.

Each contains **2 mL**

FUROSEMIDE
INJECTION, USP

20 mg/2 mL
(10 mg/mL)
FOR INTRAMUSCULAR OR
SLOW INTRAVENOUS USE

Each mL contains furosemide 10 mg and sodium chloride 7.5 mg in Water for injection. pH adjusted to 8.0–9.3 with sodium hydroxide; hydrochloric acid used, if needed.
PROTECT FROM LIGHT: Store in this box until ready to use.
Do not use if solution is discolored.
Store at controlled room temperature 15°–30° C (59°–86°F).
USUAL DOSE: See package insert for complete prescribing information.
Caution: Federal law prohibits dispensing without prescription.
To open ampuls, ignore color line; break at constriction.

54. The order calls for 12.5 mg. How many milliliters is this?

55. The order calls for 3.5 mL. How many milligrams is this?

2.4 PERCENTAGE OF ERROR

Percentages are used in a variety of ways when preparing medication doses. In the compounding pharmacy, percentages are used in determining the possible percentage of error and the least weighable quantity of a substance for safe preparation. Percentages are also used when doing the business of the pharmacy, such as calculating the percentage of sales, percentage of discount, and percentage of markup. These applications will be covered in Chapter 9.

When weighing a solid or measuring a liquid ingredient in the pharmacy, a certain amount of error is expected. Not all graduated cylinders used in the pharmacy are equally accurate, although they are usually much more accurate than the measuring devices found in patients' homes. Similarly, pharmacy balances, though generally very accurate when compared to other small scales, may exhibit slight variations. Therefore, it is important to know the margin of error that a particular balance or graduated cylinder has.

When weighing any substance, the balance will appear to have weighed correctly. A very small sample, however, may have an unacceptable margin of error. Pharmacy balances are generally marked with their degree of accuracy. This degree of accurateness has been determined by comparing quantities weighed on the balance with the weights obtained from another balance whose accuracy is known. This determination of accuracy is performed in the factory and normally is not done in the pharmacy.

percentage of error
the percentage by which a measurement is inaccurate

If a substance was weighed or measured incorrectly, and we have something that will allow us to more accurately measure the amount in question, we can determine the **percentage of error** by using the following formula:

$$\frac{\text{amount of error}}{\text{quantity desired}} \times 100 = \text{percentage of error}$$

In this equation, the amount of error is the difference between the actual amount and the weighed or measured amount, or

$$\text{actual amount} - \text{measured amount} = \text{amount of error}$$

The percentage of error is considered to be a range both above and below the target measurement, and whether the result is over or under (positive or negative) the target is inconsequential.

Example 2.4.1

You are to dispense 120 mL of a liquid. The original measurement is 120 mL. When you double-check the amount, using a more accurate graduated cylinder, the actual amount is 126 mL. What is the percentage of error of the first measurement?

Determine the difference in the two measurements in order to determine the amount of error.

$$126 \text{ mL} - 120 \text{ mL} = 6 \text{ mL}$$

Use the percentage of error equation to determine the percentage of error of the measurement.

$$\frac{\text{amount of error}}{\text{quantity desired}} \times 100 = \frac{6 \text{ mL}}{120 \text{ mL}} \times 100 = 5\%$$

The percentage of error is 5%.

Example 2.4.2   **You are to dispense 30 g of a powder. The original measurement is 30 g. When you double-check the amount, using a more accurate balance, the actual amount is 31.8 g. What is the percentage of error of the first measurement?**

Determine the difference in the two amounts in order to determine the amount of error.

$$31.8 \text{ g} - 30 \text{ g} = 1.8 \text{ g}$$

Use the percentage of error equation to determine the percentage of error of the measurement.

$$\frac{\text{amount of error}}{\text{quantity desired}} \times 100 = \frac{1.8 \text{ g}}{30 \text{ g}} \times 100 = 6\%$$

The percentage of error is 6%.

Example 2.4.3   **You are to dispense 453 mg of a powder. The original measurement is 453 mg. When you double-check the amount, using a more accurate balance, the actual amount is 438 mg. What is the percentage of error of the first measurement?**

Determine the difference in the two measurements in order to determine the amount of error.

$$453 \text{ mg} - 438 \text{ mg} = 15 \text{ mg}$$

Use the percentage of error equation to determine the percentage of error of the measurement.

$$\frac{\text{amount of error}}{\text{quantity desired}} \times 100 = \frac{15 \text{ mg}}{453 \text{ mg}} \times 100 = 3.3\%$$

Example 2.4.4   **You are to weigh 60 g of a cream base for a topical compound. Your error range is 3%. What will be the least amount and the largest amount acceptable?**

Multiply the percentage (in decimal form) by the target weight.

$$60 \text{ g} \times 0.03 = 1.8 \text{ g}$$

Determine the range.

$$60 \text{ g} - 1.8 \text{ g} = 58.2 \text{ g} \qquad 60 \text{ g} + 1.8 \text{ g} = 61.8 \text{ g}$$

Therefore, the acceptable range is 58.2 g to 61.8 g.

Example 2.4.5   **You are preparing an order by measuring 800 mL from a 1 L normal saline IV bag. When you check the volume of the fluid in a graduated cylinder, the amount measured is actually 820 mL. You have an acceptable range of 2%. What is the percentage of error in this measurement? Did you meet your target?**

Determine the difference in the two measurements in order to determine the amount of error.

$$820 \text{ mL} - 800 \text{ mL} = 20 \text{ mL}$$

Use the percentage of error equation to determine the percentage of error of the measurement.

$$\frac{\text{amount of error}}{\text{quantity desired}} \times 100 = \frac{20 \text{ mL}}{800 \text{ mL}} \times 100 = 2.5\%$$

Because 2.5% is larger than the acceptable percentage of error, the target range was not met.

Problem Set 2.4 _____

✓ *Self-check your problem set work at* www.emcp.com.

Calculate the percentage of error for the following measurements. Assume that the measured amount is equal to the quantity desired.

1. The measured weight was 185 mg, but the actual weight is 189 mg.

2. The measured weight was 500 mg, but the actual weight is 476 mg.

3. The measured weight was 1200 mg, but the actual weight is 1507 mg.

4. The measured weight was 15 mg, but the actual weight is 12.5 mg.

5. The measured weight was 400 mcg, but the actual weight is 415 mcg.

6. The measured volume was 5 mL, but the actual volume is 6.3 mL.

7. The measured volume was 15 mL, but the actual volume is 13 mL.

8. The measured volume was 15 mL, but the actual volume is 20 mL.

9. The measured volume was 1.5 L, but the actual volume is 1.45 L.

10. The measured volume was 700 mL, but the actual volume is 726 mL.

Determine the percentage of error for the following measurements, and identify those within a percentage of error of 3%.

11. The measured volume was 3 mL, but the actual volume is 2.6 mL.

12. The measured volume was 12.5 mL, but the actual volume is 12.1 mL.

13. The measured volume was 1.8 mL, but the actual volume is 1.5 mL.

14. The measured volume was 3.2 mL, but the actual volume is 3.29 mL.

Determine the percentage of error for the following measurements, and identify those within a percentage of error of 6%.

15. The measured weight was 150 mg, but the actual weight is 149 mg.

16. The measured weight was 200 mg, but the actual weight is 192 mg.

17. The measured weight was 30 mg, but the actual weight is 31.5 mg.

18. The measured weight was 454 mg, but the actual weight is 450 mg.

State the acceptable range of error for each of the following.

19. The desired volume is 200 mL, and the percentage of error is 0.5%.

20. The desired volume is 10.3 mL, and the percentage of error is 0.75%.

21. The desired volume is 830 mL, and the percentage of error is 2%.

22. The desired weight is 18 g, and the percentage of error is 0.15%.

23. The desired weight is 750 mg, and the percentage of error is 0.4%.

Applications

24. If a generic drug manufacturer meets a bioavailability comparison to within 20% and a drug normally has a bioavailability of 100 mg, what is the range of accuracy?

25. A new brand of vitamins claims to have bioavailability within 12% of a national brand of vitamin C. The national brand has 500 mg of vitamin C per tablet. What is the range of vitamin C contained in the tablet?

Practice Test

State the ratio for the following doses.

1. 10 mg tablet of glipizide

2. 5 mL dose of azithromycin containing 250 mg

3. 5 mL dose of diphenhydramine containing 12.5 mg

4. A 1:10 solution contains _____ g of active ingredient and _____ mL of product, and 1000 mL of that solution contains _____ g.

5. A 1:100 solution contains _____ g of active ingredient and _____ mL of product, and 250 mL of that solution contains _____ g.

Convert the following percent to fractions.

6. 12.5%

7. 66.67%

Convert the following percents to decimals.

8. 0.5%

9. 93%

Choose the appropriate solution from the available stock.

10. A 1:5 solution has been ordered. You have a 5% solution, a 10% solution, and a 20% solution in stock. Which solution will you choose?

11. A 1:250 solution has been ordered. You have a 0.4% solution, a 0.05% solution, and a 4% solution in stock. Which solution will you choose?

Convert the following using the ratio 1 g:1000 mg

12. 120 mg = _____ g

13. 1800 mg = _____ g

14. A dose of 50 mg is ordered. The drug is available as a 1 mg tablet. How many whole tablets are needed to provide the ordered dose?

15. A dose of 30 mg is ordered. The drug is available as a 20 mg/mL solution. How many milliliters are needed to provide the ordered dose?

Determine the percentage of error for the following measurements. Round to the hundredth place when needed.

16. The measured weight was 325 mg, but the actual weight was 343 mg.

17. The measured weight was 850 mg, but the actual weight was 790 mg.

18. The measured volume was 480 mL, but the actual volume was 473 mL.

19. The measured volume was 125 mL, but the actual volume was 119 mL.
    a. What is the actual percentage of error?

    b. Is the percentage of error within the 3% range?

20. The measured volume was 50 mL, but the actual volume was 57 mL.
    a. What is the actual percentage of error?

    b. Is the percentage of error within the 3% range?

21. State the acceptable range of error if the desired volume is 467 mL and the percentage of error is 1%.

22. State the acceptable range of error if the desired weight is 30 g and the percentage of error is 0.25%.

Developing Literacy Skills

Mary Ann Stuhan, RPh

Objectives

- Identify the elements of a complete prescription order.
- Apply calculation operations in handling prescription orders.
- Recognize the elements of a medication label.
- Apply calculation operations to information on medication labels.

3.1 ELEMENTS OF THE PRESCRIPTION ORDER

prescription
an order for medication for a patient that is written by a physician or a qualified licensed practitioner to be filled by a pharmacist

A **prescription** is an order for a medication or mixture of medications written (or otherwise recorded and/or transmitted) by a practitioner to be filled by a pharmacist. The pharmacy technician will need to interpret the prescription to determine which calculations will be necessary to fill this order correctly and appropriately. Although the legal requirements for information necessary on a prescription are regulated by state law and vary from one state to another, the following elements will appear on every prescription: patient information, prescriber information, and drug designation. Figure 3.1 illustrates the parts of a prescription written for a community pharmacy, and Figure 3.2 illustrates the parts of a prescription written for a hospital pharmacy.

Patient Information

Every prescription order must have enough information to uniquely identify the patient for whom the order was written. This will always include the patient's full name (first and last). Most states also require outpatient prescriptions to include the patient's address (street, city, state). In addition, it is good practice to include the patient's age or date of birth on every prescription, and some states and most insurers require this information.

Prescriptions for inpatients, often referred to as "orders," usually substitute the patient's hospital identification number and room number for the address and are often written on a form prestamped with the patient's admission date, the admitting physician's name, and the patient's date of birth in addition to the patient's name and hospital number. Hospital medication order forms frequently require a notation of the patient's allergy information as well.

Figure 3.1

Elements of a Prescription for a Community Pharmacy

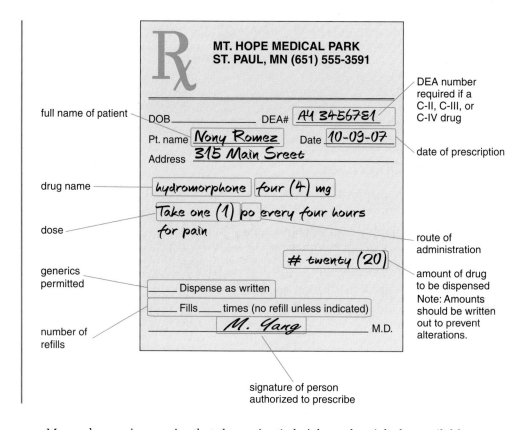

full name of patient

DOB_____ DEA# *A4 3456781*

Pt. name *Nony Romez* Date *10-09-07*

Address *315 Main Sreet*

drug name → *hydromorphone* *four (4) mg*

dose → *Take one (1) po every four hours for pain*

 # twenty (20)

generics permitted

_____ Dispense as written

_____ Fills_____ times (no refill unless indicated)

number of refills

M. Yang M.D.

MT. HOPE MEDICAL PARK
ST. PAUL, MN (651) 555-3591

DEA number required if a C-II, C-III, or C-IV drug

date of prescription

route of administration

amount of drug to be dispensed
Note: Amounts should be written out to prevent alterations.

signature of person authorized to prescribe

Many pharmacies require that the patient's height and weight be available, either on the prescription itself or in the patient's file. (Hospital order forms, as well as outpatient prescription forms, frequently have blanks where the height and weight are to be written.) If height and weight are included, it is important to know the units in which they were determined. Patient weights may be measured as either kilograms (kg) or pounds (# or lb); heights are generally measured as centimeters (cm) or inches (sometimes abbreviated as ″ or in). These are quite different from one another: a 100 kg patient is more than twice the size of a 100 lb patient; a 76 cm patient is most likely a child under three years of age, while a 76″ patient is a very tall adult! (Conversions of height and weight units are covered in Chapters 4 and 5.)

Prescriber Information

In most states, outpatient prescription orders must include the name, authority (medical doctor, doctor of osteopathy, etc.), and address of the prescribing practitioner. Frequently, the prescriber's telephone number is noted. Prescriptions for controlled substances must also bear a registration code known as the **DEA number.** DEA numbers are issued by the Drug Enforcement Administration (DEA), an agency of the federal government, and signify the authority of the holder to prescribe or handle controlled substances. They are *always* formatted to begin with two letters, which are followed by seven digits. The last of the seven digits is a "checksum" digit, calculated by following the steps in Table 3.1.

The first two letters of the DEA number provide information about the prescriber. The first letter usually (but not always) designates the type or authority of the holder. For example, A or B is used for primary-level practitioners such as physicians and dentists, and M is used to indicate mid-level practitioners such as nurse midwives and advanced practice nurses. The second letter in the DEA number is the first letter of the prescriber's last name. So, the first two letters of the DEA

DEA number
a number issued by the Drug Enforcement Administration (DEA) to signify the authority of the holder to prescribe or handle controlled substances; made up of two letters followed by seven digits, the last of which is a checksum digit used to check the validity of the DEA number

Figure 3.2

**Elements of a
Hospital
Medication
Order**

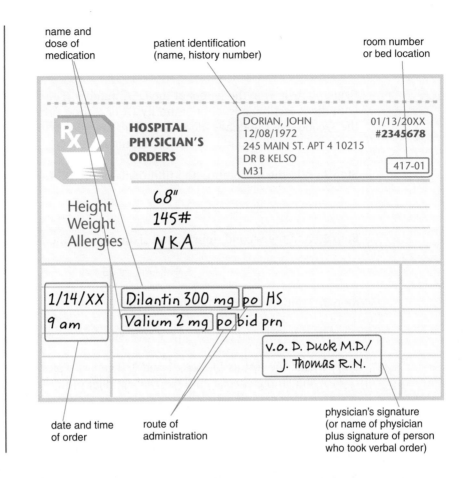

name and
dose of
medication

patient identification
(name, history number)

room number
or bed location

**HOSPITAL
PHYSICIAN'S
ORDERS**

DORIAN, JOHN   01/13/20XX
12/08/1972   **#2345678**
245 MAIN ST. APT 4 10215
DR B KELSO
M31   417-01

Height   68"
Weight   145#
Allergies   NKA

1/14/XX | Dilantin 300 mg | po | HS
9 am | Valium 2 mg | po | bid prn

v.o. D. Duck M.D./
J. Thomas R.N.

date and time
of order

route of
administration

physician's signature
(or name of physician
plus signature of person
who took verbal order)

number for Dr. Mary Smith might be AS or BS, while the first two letters for nurse practitioner David Jones might be MJ.

DEA numbers are carefully regulated, and a DEA number that does not have a correct checksum digit (as determined by the steps in Table 3.1) is considered to be invalid. The checksum digit gives pharmacists and pharmacy technicians one way to check whether a DEA number was falsified. Note that passing the checksum test does not necessarily mean that a DEA number is valid. Many unethical or criminally minded people know the formula and are able to compose DEA numbers that *look* valid but were not issued by the government authority. If a pharmacy technician discovers an invalid DEA number or suspects a problem with the authenticity of a prescription, he or she should notify a pharmacist immediately.

The following examples demonstrate how the steps in Table 3.1 can be used to check for false DEA numbers.

Safety Note

The checksum digit calculation is a necessary but not sufficient condition for the validity of a DEA number.

Table 3.1   DEA Checksum Formula

Step 1. Add the first, third, and fifth digits of the DEA number.

Step 2. Add the second, fourth, and sixth digits of the DEA number.

Step 3. Double the sum obtained in Step 2 (i.e., multiply it by 2).

Step 4. Add the results of Steps 1 and 3. The last digit of this sum should match the checksum digit, the last digit of the DEA number.

Example 3.1.1

A patient brings a prescription for methylphenidate tablets to the pharmacy, signed by Dr. Johnson and bearing a DEA number of BJ 2345678. Is this DEA number valid?

Begin by reviewing the letters of the DEA number. The first letter is consistent with the prescriber's level of authority (A or B for a primary practitioner), and the second letter matches the last name of the physician (J).
 Now, check the validity of the checksum digit.

Step 1. Add the first, third, and fifth digits of the DEA number.

$$2 + 4 + 6 = 12$$

Step 2. Add the second, fourth, and sixth digits of the DEA number.

$$3 + 5 + 7 = 15$$

Step 3. Multiply the sum obtained in Step 2 by 2.

$$15 \times 2 = 30$$

Step 4. Add the results of Steps 1 and 3. The last digit of this sum should match the checksum digit, the last digit of the DEA number.

$$12 + 30 = 42$$

Because the checksum digit is 8, not 2, this DEA number is invalid.

Example 3.1.2

A patient brings a prescription for oxycodone to the pharmacy, signed by nurse-midwife Ann Johnson and bearing a DEA number of MJ 3456781. (In the state where the prescription is received, advanced practice nurses are authorized to prescribe narcotic analgesics.) Is this DEA number valid?

Begin by reviewing the letters of the DEA number. The first letter is consistent with the prescriber's level of authority (M for a nurse practitioner), and the second letter matches the last name of the prescriber (J).
 Now, check the validity of the checksum digit.

Step 1. Add the first, third, and fifth digits of the DEA number.

$$3 + 5 + 7 = 15$$

Step 2. Add the second, fourth, and sixth digits of the DEA number.

$$4 + 6 + 8 = 18$$

Step 3. Multiply the sum obtained in Step 2 by 2.

$$18 \times 2 = 36$$

Step 4. Add the results of Steps 1 and 3. The last digit of this sum should match the checksum digit, the last digit of the DEA number.

$$15 + 36 = 51$$

Because the checksum digit is 1, this DEA number meets the criteria for a valid registration.

Inpatient prescriptions are most often written or transcribed on the premises where the patient is located and where the medication will be administered; such prescriptions may be ordered only by practitioners with privileges within that institution. Physician addresses and DEA numbers are generally not required on the actual medication orders because the institutional pharmacy that will fill the orders usually has this information on file for each authorized practitioner.

Drug Designation

A prescription order must always designate the medication that is intended for the patient. Sometimes, the drug will be identified by its **generic name,** the name by which it was approved by the Food and Drug Administration (FDA) as a unique chemical product safe and effective for use in its approved indication. The generic name of a drug is the same, regardless of the company that manufactures it or the dose form or packaging in which it is supplied. At other times, a physician will specify a brand name drug. The **brand name** is a registered trademark of the manufacturer and may indicate the dose form or packaging of the drug as well. State law and (in the case of inpatients) institutional policy govern the extent to which generic products can be substituted for brand name drugs. In some cases, the pharmacy can automatically substitute an equivalent product with the same generic name (but a different brand name) for cost savings or convenience. In other situations, the pharmacy must supply the exact brand prescribed, unless the pharmacist has discussed a substitution with the prescriber.

Figure 3.3 identifies the standard parts of a drug label for Cleocin Phosphate. As shown in this example, the label of a brand name drug will indicate both the trade and generic names. Medications with a given name (brand or generic) are frequently available in a variety of strengths, doses, or dose forms, and information about the particular strength, dose and dose form is also clearly stated on the drug label. Digoxin, for instance, is available as a generic product and as several branded preparations. It is

Figure 3.3

Parts of a Drug Label

(a) Brand name, (b) Generic name, (c) Dose form, (d) Strength per unit, (e) Package size, (f) Manufacturer, (g) National Drug Code, (h) Special storage and handling requirements

Figure 3.4

Comparison of Dose Forms

(a) 25 mg/5 mL liquid, (b) 25 mg capsules, (c) 50 mg capsules

available as a tablet in two different strengths (0.125 mg and 0.25 mg), a capsule in three strengths (0.05 mg, 0.1 mg, and 0.2 mg), an elixir of 0.05 mg/mL, and injections of 0.1 mg/mL and 0.25 mg/mL. Many other drugs present a similar array of choices (brand names, dose forms, strengths or concentrations), and the proper product to select must be made clear in the prescription order. Figure 3.4 shows labels for the same drug in different dose forms. Note how the labels use color to help distinguish the unique information.

It is important to correctly match a prescription order with the appropriate medication available in the pharmacy. The following example demonstrates this procedure.

Example 3.1.3
The pharmacy receives an order for "EpiPen 1 mg/mL," and epinephrine 1:10,000, 1:2000, and 1:1000 injections are available in stock. Which one matches the order?

EpiPen is a brand name for an epinephrine injection. As discussed in Chapter 2, the available drug concentrations are 1:10,000, or 1 g/10,000 mL; 1:2000, or 1 g/2000 mL; and 1:1000, or 1 g/1000 mL.

Convert the strength of 1 mg/mL into a concentration ratio. Begin by setting up a ratio and solving for x, using the conversion factor 1000 mg = 1 g.

$$\frac{x \text{ mL}}{1000 \text{ mg}} = \frac{1 \text{ mL}}{1 \text{ mg}}$$

$$\frac{(\cancel{1000 \text{ mg}}) \, x \text{ mL}}{\cancel{1000 \text{ mg}}} = \frac{(1000 \, \cancel{\text{mg}}) \, 1 \text{ mL}}{1 \, \cancel{\text{mg}}}$$

$$x \text{ mL} = 1000 \text{ mL}$$

Therefore x mL/1000 mg = 1000 mL/1000 mg, and 1000 mL/1000 mg = 1000 mL/1 g = 1 g/1000 mL, or a ratio of 1:1000. Thus, the 1:1000 injection should be chosen to fill this order.

Quantity to Dispense

Every outpatient prescription order must indicate to the pharmacist what quantity to dispense. Sometimes, the indication is straightforward, as in Figure 3.1, where the physician has written the number of tablets to dispense next to "#" (used as a number sign). This number is often written as a Roman numeral or spelled out ("twenty" for #20) to hinder alteration. At other times, the physician will indicate the number of doses the patient is to take, or the number of days the therapy is to last, and the pharmacy staff will calculate the quantity to dispense from the information on the prescription.

Example 3.1.4

A prescription for antacid reads "Take one ounce three times a day" and instructs the pharmacy to dispense a five-day supply. What volume is to be dispensed?

The patient takes one ounce three times a day, so first determine the number of ounces taken in one day. Note that the units cancel out, as shown below.

$$1 \text{ oz/dose} \times 3 \text{ doses/day} = 3 \text{ oz/day}$$

You can determine the amount to dispense by multiplying the daily dose by the number of days.

$$3 \text{ oz/day} \times 5 \text{ days} = 15 \text{ oz}$$

Example 3.1.5

A prescription for hydromorphone 4 mg tablets reads "Take one every four hours" and instructs the pharmacy to dispense a one-week supply. How many tablets are to be dispensed?

The patient takes one tablet every 4 hours and there are 24 hours in a day. You can determine the number of tablets the patient will need in a single 24-hour period (a day) by setting up a ratio.

$$\frac{x \text{ tablets}}{24 \text{ hours}} = \frac{1 \text{ tablet}}{4 \text{ hours}}$$

$$\frac{(24 \text{ hours}) \ x \text{ tablets}}{24 \text{ hours}} = \frac{(24 \text{ hours}) \ 1 \text{ tablet}}{4 \text{ hours}}$$

$$x \text{ tablets} = 6 \text{ tablets}$$

A week is 7 days, so the pharmacist will dispense the following number of tablets.

$$6 \text{ tablets/day} \times 7 \text{ days/week} = 42 \text{ tablets/week}$$

Which of the following DEA numbers meet the standard validity test?

1. DEA number JC 2169870 for Dr. James Collins

2. DEA number MG 3081659 for nurse-midwife Laura Green

3. DEA number BH 9998070 for Dr. Margaret Hall

4. DEA number AL 6230618 for Dr. George Lewis

5. DEA number AD 7638224 for Dr. Daniel Lopez

6. DEA number BP 4412209 for Dr. Sarah Parker

7. DEA number AP 3051492 for Dr. Donna Perez

8. DEA number MW 2864228 for clinical nurse specialist Thomas Wright

Choose a drug product to fill the following orders.

9. acetic acid 1:400 irrigation
   a. glacial acetic acid

   b. 0.25% acetic acid

   c. 25% acetic acid

   d. 4% acetic acid

10. isoproterenol 5 mg/mL solution
    a. isoproterenol 5% solution

    b. isoproterenol 0.05% solution

    c. isoproterenol 1:200 solution

    d. isoproterenol 1:2 solution

How much medication should be dispensed for the following prescriptions?

11.

Ibuprofen 400 mg tablet #XX

take one four times daily with food

12.

Amoxicillin capsule 500 mg

take one capsule three times daily for 10 days

13.

Prednisone 5 mg tablet

take four tablets twice daily for two days,
then three tablets twice daily for two days,
then four tablets once daily for two days,
then three tablets once daily for two days,
then two tablets once daily for two days,
then one tablet daily for two days

14.

Milk of Magnesia

take one ounce every night at bedtime for one week

15.

Phenytoin 100 mg capsule #CL

take three capsules every morning

3.2 PRESCRIPTION DIRECTIONS

A very important part of each prescription is the *signa* **(sig),** a term that comes from the Latin for "write." It consists of the prescriber's instructions for proper use of the medication and usually includes the following information.

Dose: how much medication the patient will take at each administration. It is generally expressed as a number of units (e.g., tablets, capsules), an amount of drug (e.g., weight in milligrams or grains), or a volume of medication (e.g., ounces, teaspoonfuls).

Route of administration: how the drug is to be administered. Routes of administration include oral (by mouth), injection (into veins, into muscles, under the skin), rectal, or topical (to the eye, ear, skin, or mucous membranes), among others.

Dosing schedule: how often the drug is to be taken and, in some cases, how long therapy is to be continued.

Abbreviations

Healthcare professionals have developed their own shorthand for many aspects of patient care, and it is reflected in the abbreviations used in prescription directions. Many of the abbreviations used in prescriptions are derived from the initials of Latin or Greek phrases. Others come from medical terminology in English, and some even combine terms from multiple languages. Table 3.2 lists some of the most common abbreviations used on prescriptions.

Table 3.2 Common Prescription Abbreviations

Abbreviation	Translation	Abbreviation	Translation
ac	before meals	NKA	no known allergy
bid	twice a day	NKDA	no known drug allergy
c̄	with	npo	nothing by mouth
cap	capsule	pc	after meals
DAW	dispense as written	po	by mouth
D/C	discontinue	prn	as needed
g	gram	q	every
gr	grain	qh	every hour
gtt	drop	q2h	every 2 hours
hs	at bedtime	qid	four times a day
IM	intramuscular	qs	a sufficient quantity
IV	intravenous	stat	immediately
L	liter	tab	tablet
mcg	microgram	tid	three times daily
mEq	milliequivalent	ud	as directed
mL	milliliter	wk	week

Note: Some prescribers may write abbreviations using capital letters or periods. However, periods should not be used with metric units or medical abbreviations as they can be a source of medication errors.

signa (sig)
from the Latin for "write"; the instructions for proper use of the medication included on each prescription, including the dose, route of administration, and dosing schedule

dose
on a prescription, the indication of how much medication the patient will take at each administration

route of administration
on a prescription, the indication of how the medication is to be given

dosing schedule
on a prescription, the indication of how often the drug is to be taken

When abbreviations are standardized (to have only one meaning) and are clearly written or printed, they are useful because they save space and time. Abbreviations can cause problems, however, if they are misinterpreted. Sometimes, this occurs when the same set of letters can have two different meanings. For example, the abbreviation "IVP" means "IV Push" or "administer by injection into the vein from a syringe" when used on a hospital prescription order for an intravenous medication. In another context, however, "IVP" designates "intravenous pyeologram," an X-ray examination of the kidneys, bladder, and urinary tract.

Abbreviations are also problematic when they are not typed or written clearly. The abbreviation "q 6pm," for example, means "every evening at 6 P.M.," but if written hastily or printed on a fax machine low in toner, it may appear to say "q6h," meaning every six hours. The abbreviation "qhs" means "nightly at bedtime," but could be misread as "qhr," meaning "every hour." Some abbreviations are so error-prone that the Joint Commission on Accreditation of Healthcare Organizations (JCAHO) has declared that they are absolutely unacceptable for use in accredited institutions. These are listed in Table 3.3.

Directions for Patients

Because most patients are not familiar with the abbreviations and shorthand used on prescriptions, directions must be "translated" from the sig and "written" on the label placed on the dispensing packaging. Sometimes, descriptive terms are added if appropriate. For example, a prescription for a fentanyl transdermal patch may have the sig "i q 3d." The pharmacy label on the patient's package, however, will read "Apply one patch every 72 hours." Similarly, a prescription for hydrochlorothiazide 25 mg tablets may bear a sig of "12.5 mg po qam," but the patient's label must read "Take one-half tablet by mouth every morning." It is important that directions for patients be set forth in clear and unambiguous terms on the label, even if the doctor and the pharmacist explain verbally in great detail how the medication is to be used. It is easy for patients to misunderstand or forget what they were told days or weeks earlier, and having the label available for instructions at every dose is necessary for safe medication use.

Table 3.3   Unacceptable Abbreviations Formerly in Common Use

Unapproved Abbreviation	Intended Meaning	Misinterpretation	Correct Form to Use
µg	microgram	milligram	microgram or mcg
qd	every day	four times a day	every day
qod	every other day	daily or four times a day	every other day
U	unit	number 0 or 4	units
MgSO4	magnesium sulfate	morphine sulfate	magnesium sulfate
MSO4	morphine sulfate	magnesium sulfate	morphine sulfate

Note: Additional error-prone abbreviations are listed at www.ismp.org.

What is missing from these prescriptions?

36.

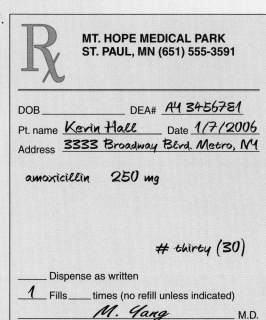

MT. HOPE MEDICAL PARK
ST. PAUL, MN (651) 555-3591

DOB _____ DEA# AY 3456781
Pt. name Kimberly Evans Date 1/6/2006
Address 2888 Main St. Townville, OH

ibuprofen   600 mg tab

Sig: i q6h prn pain

_____ Dispense as written

_____ Fills _____ times (no refill unless indicated)

            M. Yang   M.D.

37.

MT. HOPE MEDICAL PARK
ST. PAUL, MN (651) 555-3591

DOB _____ DEA# AY 3456781
Pt. name Kevin Hall   Date 1/7/2006
Address 3333 Broadway Blvd. Metro, NY

amoxicillin   250 mg

        # thirty (30)

_____ Dispense as written

__1__ Fills _____ times (no refill unless indicated)

            M. Yang   M.D.

Calculate the quantity and write out directions for the patient for each of the following prescriptions.

38.

Clonidine Transdermal System

30 day supply
i q 3 days

39.

Ampicillin 250 mg cap

500 mg po tid × 10 days

40.

Tobradex 5 mL

i gtt left eye bid × 7 days

Answer the following questions.

41. What is a dosing schedule?

42. What are four routes of administration?

43. What are two examples of error-prone abbreviations?

44. What are the intended meanings of the abbreviations you gave in question 43?

45. Why are the abbreviations you gave in question 43 prone to error, and how might they be mistakenly interpreted?

Applying Metric Measurements and Calculating Doses

Objectives

- Identify the basic units and prefixes of the metric system.
- Convert units within the metric system by moving the decimal place, using the ratio-proportion method, and using the dimensional analysis method.
- Calculate drug doses using the ratio-proportion and dimensional analysis methods.
- Calculate doses based on weight and body surface area (BSA).
- Calculate a pediatric dose using the patient's weight or age and the appropriate adult dose.

4.1 BASIC METRIC UNITS

Chapter 1 presented a brief overview of the decimal number system. Because of its accuracy, the decimal system is used in pharmacy measurements: based on subdivisions and multiples of 10, the **metric system** uses decimals to indicate tenths, hundredths, and thousandths.

Identifying Metric Units of Measure

metric system
a measurement system based on subdivisions and multiples of 10; made up of three basic units: meter, gram, and liter

meter
the metric system's basic unit for measuring length

gram
the metric system's basic unit for measuring weight

liter
the metric system's basic unit for measuring volume

The metric system's three basic units are the meter, the gram, and the liter (see Table 4.1). The **meter,** the unit for measuring length, has limited use in the pharmacy; consequently, we discuss its properties only in comparison to common measures used in daily life. The **gram,** the unit for measuring weight, is used in the pharmacy for measuring the amount of medication in solid form and for indicating the amount of solid medication in a solution. The gram is the weight of one cubic centimeter of water at 4° C. The **liter** is the unit used for measuring the volume of liquid medications and liquids for solutions. One liter is equal to 1000 milliliters, and one milliliter is equal to one cubic centimeter.

Table 4.1 Metric Units of Measure

Metric Unit	Measurement
meter (m)	length
gram (g)	weight
liter (L)	volume

Using Metric Prefixes and Abbreviations

The set of prefixes shown in Table 4.2 are used to designate multiples of the basic metric units. The three prefixes most widely used in pharmaceutical calculations are kilo-, milli-, and micro-. The abbreviations shown in Table 4.3 are commonly used for metric measurements.

It is important to memorize the basic metric units along with their prefixes. All units in the metric system use the same prefixes. An example is the gram: the larger unit is the kilogram while two of the smaller units are the milligram and microgram.

Parts of a unit are written as a decimal fraction. For example, two and a half milligrams is written as 2.5 mg. A zero is used if there is no whole number preceding the decimal point. For example, one-half liter is written as 0.5 L, and one-quarter gram is 0.25 g. These place-saving zeros help prevent medication errors.

When writing dose strengths, unnecessary zeros after the decimal point are generally left off to reduce the chance of misreading the value. For example, 0.25 mL, 5 L, and 15.6 mL should not be written as 0.250 mL, 5.0 L, and 15.60 mL.

> *Safety Note*
>
> For a decimal value less than 1, use a leading zero to prevent errors.

Table 4.2 Metric System Prefixes

Prefix	Value
nano (n)	1/1,000,000,000 (one-billionth of the basic unit, or 0.000000001)
micro (mc)	1/1,000,000 (one-millionth of the basic unit, or 0.000001)
milli (m)	1/1000 (one-thousandth of the basic unit, or 0.001)
centi (c)	1/100 (one-hundredth of the basic unit, or 0.01)
deci (d)	1/10 (one-tenth of the basic unit, or 0.1)
kilo (k)	1000 (one thousand times the basic unit)

Table 4.3 Metric Abbreviations

Weight	Volume	Length
kilogram = kg	kiloliter = kL	kilometer = km
gram = g	liter = L	meter = m
milligram = mg	milliliter = mL = cc = cubic centimeter	millimeter = mm
microgram = mcg	microliter = mcL	micrometer = mcm, μm

Problem Set 4.1 _____

✓ *Self-check your problem set work at* www.emcp.com.

State the abbreviation for each of the following metric units.

1. microgram

2. milligram

3. liter

4. gram

5. kilogram

6. meter

7. centimeter

8. milliliter

9. cubic centimeter

10. deciliter

Write the following numbers using an Arabic number with a decimal value and the appropriate abbreviation.

11. six-tenths of a gram

12. fifty kilograms

13. four-tenths of a milligram

14. four-hundredths of a liter

15. four and two-tenths of a gram

16. five-thousandths of a gram

17. six-hundredths of a gram

18. two and six-tenths liters

19. three-hundredths of a liter

20. two-hundredths of a milliliter

Applications

21. The Taro Pharmaceutical Company has donated a container labeled 5 kg of bulk Maxicillin granules. The standard dose is 375 mg. How many single dose units can be obtained from the container?

22. The pharmacy receives the following prescription.

 Levothyroxine Tablets 0.05 mg

ii bid daily until gone
#30

a. How many days will the dispensed medication last?

b. How many milligrams will the patient take over the course of one month (30 days)?

23. If the total daily dose of a drug is 0.9 g and it is given tid, what is the amount of each dose in grams?

24. A patient is to receive 1.2 g of cimetidine per day in four divided doses.
a. How many grams will be in each dose?

b. If the available dose forms are shown in the following labels, which will be chosen?

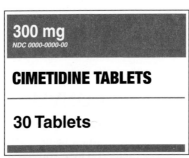

300 mg
NDC 0000-0000-00

CIMETIDINE TABLETS

30 Tablets

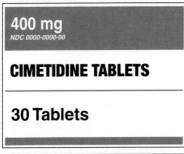

400 mg
NDC 0000-0000-00

CIMETIDINE TABLETS

30 Tablets

800 mg
NDC 0000-0000-00

CIMETIDINE TABLETS

30 Tablets

25. The following prescription for potassium permanganate has been brought into the compounding pharmacy.

1. Weigh out 1 g of potassium permanganate.
2. Add to a 1 L bottle of sterile water for irrigation. (Be sure to wear gloves, as this chemical stains.)
3. Replace cap on bottle and swirl to dissolve potassium permanganate.

The solution expires 30 days after mixing.

a. What is the percentage of potassium permanganate in this solution?

b. If today is August 1, 2007, what expiration date will you place on the bottle?

4.2 CONVERSIONS WITHIN THE METRIC SYSTEM

This section will present three ways to convert units within the metric system: moving the decimal, using the ratio-proportion method, and using the dimensional analysis method. Once you learn the three methods of conversion, you should select the method you are most comfortable with and stick to that method when making conversions. Before calculating a needed dose, you should be confident that the number you are working with is accurate and that the correct conversion has been made.

Moving the Decimal Point

To change the metric units of a number to smaller or larger units, you can multiply or divide by an appropriate multiple of 1000, as determined from Table 4.4. For instance, to convert 5 grams to milligrams, multiply by 1000 to get 5000 milligrams. (Move the decimal point three places to the right.) Multiplying 17 liters by 1,000,000 yields 17,000,000 microliters. (Move the decimal point six places to the right.) Conversely, changing to a larger unit requires division. So, to convert 25 meters to kilometers, divide by 1000 to get 0.025 kilometers. (Move the decimal point three places to the left.) Similarly, 3 microliters divided by 1000 yields 0.003 milliliters, and 22 milliliters divided by 1000 yields 0.022 liters. In each case, move the decimal point three places to the left.

The key to understanding the relationships in the metric system is to remember that the decimal point must be moved three places when converting from one unit to the next.

$$1 \text{ kg} = 1000 \text{ g}$$
$$1 \text{ g} = 1000 \text{ mg}$$
$$1 \text{ mg} = 1000 \text{ mcg}$$
$$1 \text{ L} = 1000 \text{ mL}$$

Table 4.4 **Metric Unit Comparison**

0.001 kg = 1 g = 1000 mg = 1,000,000 mcg

0.001 kL = 1 L = 1000 mL = 1,000,000 mcL

0.001 km = 1 m = 1000 mm = 1,000,000 mcm

When converting from a smaller to a larger unit of measure, move the decimal point three places to the left.

$$4500 \text{ mL} = 4.5 \text{ L}$$
$$1287 \text{ mg} = 1.287 \text{ g}$$
$$480 \text{ mL} = 0.48 \text{ L}$$

When converting from a larger to a smaller unit of measure, move the decimal point three places to the right.

$$0.954 \text{ g} = 954 \text{ mg}$$
$$1.5 \text{ g} = 1500 \text{ mg}$$
$$0.238 \text{ g} = 238 \text{ mg}$$
$$0.621 \text{ mg} = 621 \text{ mcg}$$

Using the Ratio-Proportion Method

If you have difficulty remembering which way to move the decimal point when converting between units of measure in the metric system, the ratio-proportion method introduced in Chapter 2 is an effective alternative. This method is a "fool-proof" way to convert metric units. Set up the conversion by placing the unknown and the value to be converted on one side of the equation and the conversion factor (the ratio of the desired unit to the given unit) on the other side.

Remember

When setting up proportions, units in the numerators must match, and units in the denominators must match.

When setting up proportions to solve for a variable, remember that the units in the numerators must match and so must the units in the denominators. Checking to make sure the units match prior to completing the calculation will ensure accuracy in the conversion. The next examples will each demonstrate a conversion by moving the decimal point, followed by the same conversion using the ratio-proportion method.

Example 4.2.1

Change 2300 mg to grams.

One method is to divide by 1000 by moving the decimal point three places to the left.

$$2300 \text{ mg} = 2.3 \text{ g}$$

Another method is to use a proportion to solve for the unknown.

$$\frac{x \text{ g}}{2300 \text{ mg}} = \frac{1 \text{ g}}{1000 \text{ mg}}$$

$$\frac{(2300 \text{ mg}) \, x \text{ g}}{2300 \text{ mg}} = \frac{(2300 \text{ mg}) \, 1 \text{ g}}{1000 \text{ mg}}$$

$$x \text{ g} = \frac{2300 \text{ g}}{1000}$$

$$x \text{ g} = 2.3 \text{ g}$$

Example 4.2.2 **Change 3.2 mg to micrograms.**

We can multiply by 1000 by moving the decimal point three places to the right.

$$3.2 \text{ mg} = 3200 \text{ mcg}$$

Alternatively, we can use a proportion.

$$\frac{x \text{ mcg}}{3.2 \text{ mg}} = \frac{1000 \text{ mcg}}{1 \text{ mg}}$$

$$\frac{(3.2 \text{ mg}) \, x \text{ mcg}}{3.2 \text{ mg}} = \frac{(3.2 \text{ mg}) \, 1000 \text{ mcg}}{1 \text{ mg}}$$

$$x \text{ mcg} = (3.2) \, 1000 \text{ mcg}$$

$$x \text{ mcg} = 3200 \text{ mcg}$$

Example 4.2.3 **Change 3.785 L to milliliters.**

Multiply by 1000 by moving the decimal point three places to the right.

$$3.785 \text{ L} = 3785 \text{ mL}$$

Or, alternatively,

$$\frac{x \text{ mL}}{3.785 \text{ L}} = \frac{1000 \text{ mL}}{1 \text{ L}}$$

$$\frac{(3.785 \text{ L}) \, x \text{ mL}}{3.785 \text{ L}} = \frac{(3.785 \text{ L}) \, 1000 \text{ mL}}{1 \text{ L}}$$

$$x \text{ mL} = (3.785) \, 1000 \text{ mL}$$

$$x \text{ mL} = 3785 \text{ mL}$$

Example 4.2.4   **Change 454 g to kilograms.**

Divide by 1000 by moving the decimal point three places to the left.

$$454 \text{ g} = 0.454 \text{ kg}$$

Or set up a proportion.

$$\frac{x \text{ kg}}{454 \text{ g}} = \frac{1 \text{ kg}}{1000 \text{ g}}$$

$$\frac{(454 \text{ g}) \, x \text{ kg}}{454 \text{ g}} = \frac{(454 \text{ g}) \, 1 \text{ kg}}{1000 \text{ g}}$$

$$x \text{ kg} = \frac{454 \text{ kg}}{1000}$$

$$x \text{ kg} = 0.454 \text{ kg}$$

Using the Dimensional Analysis Method

dimensional analysis method
a conversion method in which the given number and unit are multiplied by the ratio of the desired unit to the given unit, which is equivalent to 1

The **dimensional analysis method** is based on the principle that multiplying a number by 1 does not change its value. In this method, the given number and unit are multiplied by the ratio of the desired unit to the given unit, which is equivalent to 1. The unit in the denominator will match the given unit, so the units will cancel each other out and the unit remaining in the numerator will be the unit to which we are converting.

Example 4.2.5   **Convert 486 mg to grams.**

$$486 \text{ mg} \times \frac{1 \text{ g}}{1000 \text{ mg}} = 0.486 \text{ g}$$

Example 4.2.6   **Convert 4.5 L to milliliters.**

$$4.5 \text{ L} \times \frac{1000 \text{ mL}}{1 \text{ L}} = 4500 \text{ mL}$$

Example 4.2.7   **Convert 240 mL to liters.**

$$240 \text{ mL} \times \frac{1 \text{ L}}{1000 \text{ mL}} = 0.24 \text{ L}$$

Example 4.2.8   **Convert 0.725 mg to micrograms.**

$$0.725 \text{ mg} \times \frac{1000 \text{ mcg}}{1 \text{ mg}} = 725 \text{ mcg}$$

Remember
If 1 g = 1000 mg, then

$$\frac{1 \text{g}}{1000 \text{ mg}} = 1$$

Multiplying a number by 1 does not change its value.

✓ *Self-check your problem set work at* www.emcp.com.

In the following problems, retain all significant figures and do not round the answers.

Convert the following units within the metric system by using the ratio-proportion method.

1. 1964 mcg = _____ mg

2. 418 mg = _____ g

3. 651 mg = _____ mcg

4. 0.84 mg = _____ mcg

5. 0.012 g = _____ mcg

6. 9,213,406 mcg = _____ g

7. 284 mg = _____ g

8. 9382.5 mcg = _____ mg

9. 12,321 mcg = _____ g

10. 184 g = _____ kg

Convert the following units within the metric system by using the dimensional analysis method.

11. 52 mL = _____ L

12. 2.06 g = _____ mg

13. 16 mg = _____ mcg

14. 256 mg = _____ g

15. 2,703,000 mcg = _____ g

16. 6.9 L = _____ mL

17. 62.5 mg = _____ g

18. 15 kg = _____ g

19. 2,785,000 mcg = _____ g

20. 8.234 mg = _____ mcg

Convert the following using the method you prefer. Show all work.

21. 2 kg = _____ mg

22. 21 L = _____ mL

23. 576 mL = _____ L

24. 823 kg = _____ mg

25. 27 mcg = _____ mg

26. 5000 mcg = _____ mg

27. 20 mcg = _____ mg

28. 4.624 mg = _____ mcg

29. 3.19 g = _____ mg

30. 8736 mcg = _____ mg

31. 830 mL = _____ L

32. 0.94 L = _____ mL

33. 1.84 g = _____ mg

34. 560 mg = _____ g

35. 1200 mcg = _____ mg

36. 125 mcg = _____ mg

37. 0.275 mg = _____ mcg

38. 480 mL = _____ L

39. 239 mg = _____ g

40. 1500 mg = _____ g

41. The following prescription has come into the pharmacy.

**Clarithromycin Granules
125 mg/5 mL**

2 teaspoonsful bid c̄ food
or fluid for 7 days

a. How many milliliters will the patient take daily?

b. How many milliliters should be dispensed for the patient?

c. How many grams will the patient take daily?

42. A patient is to take 1.5 g of amoxicillin prior to a dental procedure. The capsules available are shown in the following label. How many capsules will be dispensed to this patient?

NDC 0000-0000-00

100 capsules

**Amoxicillin
Capsules, USP
250 mg**

R_x only

43. A dose of an antacid is 15 mL. How many doses can be prepared from a 480 mL container?

4.3 PROBLEM SOLVING IN THE PHARMACY

Many pharmacy calculations require problem solving. When faced with a "story problem" or other problem where the calculation needed is not absolutely clear, it is important to begin by asking the question, "What am I looking for?" In dose calculations, this is usually a weight, expressed in milligrams, or a volume, expressed in milliliters.

Using the Ratio-Proportion Method to Solve Story Problems

In Chapter 2, you learned some basic calculations using the ratio-proportion method and applied that same method to converting between units of measure in the metric system. Now you will use ratios and proportions mathematically to compare the active ingredients in a carrier vehicle to other active ingredients in their vehicles. A vehicle is an inert medium, such as a syrup, in which a drug is administered.

Remember

When setting up proportions, units in the numerators must match, and units in the denominators must match.

$$\frac{\text{active ingredient (desired)}}{\text{vehicle (desired)}} = \frac{\text{active ingredient (on hand)}}{\text{vehicle (on hand)}}$$

Keep in mind that the ratios on the two sides of the equation may be reversed, but the same units must appear in both numerators and the same units must appear in both denominators.

The steps outlined in Table 4.5 can be used as a basis for solving story problems or dose calculations using the ratio-proportion method. Usually, the following equation will be used to solve a story problem.

$$\frac{\text{desired amount of drug}}{\text{prescriber's order}} = \text{ratio of pharmacy stock}$$

Table 4.5 Steps for Using Ratio-Proportion Method for Solving Story Problems

Step 1. Read through the entire problem and identify what the question is asking for. This becomes the variable *x*, labeled with the unit you are looking for such as *x* mg or *x* mL.

Step 2. Identify the prescriber's order. Circle the dose ordered by the physician.

Step 3. Identify the appropriate stock available in the pharmacy. The on-hand amount is nearly always a ratio such as 1 mg/tablet or 125 mg/5 mL. Underline this information. This information is sometimes found on the labels of the drugs used in the pharmacy.

Step 4. Identify extraneous information. It is often helpful to draw a single pencil line through any information you identify as not needed. This prevents you from using that information in your setup.

Step 5. Estimate what your answer should be. Compare the ordered dose to what is on hand. Will the dose be larger or smaller than the dose unit given?

Step 6. Use the ratio-proportion method to solve for *x*. When using the ratio-proportion method to solve your problem, place the physician-ordered dose on the left side of the proportion and the pharmacy on-hand ratio on the right side.

Step 7. Round your answer to the appropriate number of significant figures. Weights are typically rounded to the nearest whole milligram, and volumes are typically rounded to the nearest tenth of a milliliter.

Example 4.3.1

A physician has ordered 370 mg of a drug, and you have a 10 mL vial of solution containing 250 mg/3 mL on hand. How many milliliters will you measure out?

Step 1. Identify the question being asked. We need to find out how many milliliters, so *x* mL is the unknown.

Step 2. Identify the prescribed amount and circle it. In this problem, the physician has ordered 370 mg.

Step 3. Identify the product available in the pharmacy and underline it. In this problem, the pharmacy has 250 mg/3 mL of the drug.

Step 4. Identify extraneous information and draw a line through it. In this problem, it is not important to know that the drug comes in a 10 mL vial.

Step 5. Estimate the answer. The ordered dose of 370 mg is larger than the dose strength of 250 mg, so the dose volume should be more than 3 mL.

Step 6. Use the ratio-proportion method to solve for *x*.

$$\frac{\text{desired amount of drug}}{\text{prescriber's order}} = \text{ratio of pharmacy stock}$$

$$\frac{x \text{ mL}}{370 \text{ mg}} = \frac{3 \text{ mL}}{250 \text{ mg}}$$

$$x \text{ mL} = 4.44 \text{ mL}$$

Step 7. Since this is a liquid and volumes are typically rounded to the nearest tenth of a milliliter, round to 4.4 mL.

Example 4.3.2   **A physician has ordered 100 mg of amoxicillin to be given to a child three times a day for 10 days. Amoxicillin is available in a 150 mL bottle with a dose strength of 125 mg/5 mL. How many milliliters will the child need at each dose?**

Step 1. Identify the question being asked. We need to find out how many milliliters, so x mL is the unknown.

Step 2. Identify the prescribed amount and circle it. In this problem, the physician has ordered 100 mg.

Step 3. Identify the product available in the pharmacy and underline it. In this problem, the pharmacy has 125 mg/5 mL of amoxicillin.

Step 4. Identify extraneous information and draw a line through it. In this problem, it is not important to know "three times a day for 10 days" and that the size of the amoxicillin bottle is 150 mL.

Step 5. Estimate the answer. The ordered dose of 100 mg is less than the dose strength of 125 mg, so the dose volume should be less than 5 mL.

Step 6. Use the ratio-proportion method to solve for x.

$$\frac{\text{desired amount of drug}}{\text{prescriber's order}} = \text{ratio of pharmacy stock}$$

$$\frac{x \text{ mL}}{100 \text{ mg}} = \frac{5 \text{ mL}}{125 \text{ mg}}$$

$$x \text{ mL} = 4 \text{ mL}$$

Step 7. No rounding is needed because the answer for this liquid measure does not extend beyond a tenth of a milliliter.

Some medications are ordered by a certain volume rather than by milligrams or weight. For example, a cough syrup may be ordered as 10 mL every four hours, so it will be necessary to calculate how much of the active ingredient is in 10 mL. The steps presented in Table 4.5 can also be used to solve this type of problem. In this case, however, the unknown will be the amount of the active ingredient instead of the overall volume.

Example 4.3.3   **A physician has ordered 10 mL of amoxicillin to be given to a child three times daily for 7 days. Amoxicillin is available in a 150 mL bottle with a dose strength of 250 mg/5 mL. How many milligrams will the child get at each dose?**

Step 1. The unknown is x mg.

Step 2. The prescribed amount is 10 mL amoxicillin.

Step 3. The pharmacy has 250 mg/5 mL of amoxicillin.

Step 4. The extraneous information includes "three times daily for 7 days" and that the size of the amoxicillin bottle is 150 mL.

Step 5. The answer will be more than 250 mg because 10 mL is larger than 5 mL.

Step 6.

$$\frac{x \text{ mg}}{10 \text{ mL}} = \frac{250 \text{ mg}}{5 \text{ mL}}$$

$$x \text{ mg} = 500 \text{ mg}$$

Step 7. No rounding is needed because the answer for this weight does not have a decimal point and the significant figures are correct.

Example 4.3.4 **A physician has ordered cefaclor 375 mg/5 mL oral suspension. A 100 mL bottle is prepared and is labeled to administer 7.5 mL twice daily for 5 days. How many milligrams is the patient receiving at each dose?**

Step 1. The unknown is x mg.
Step 2. The prescribed amount is 7.5 mL cefaclor.
Step 3. The pharmacy has 375 mg/5 mL of cefaclor.
Step 4. The extraneous information includes "twice daily for 5 days" and that the size of the cefaclor bottle is 100 mL.
Step 5. The answer will be more than 375 mg because 7.5 mL is larger than 5 mL.
Step 6.

$$\frac{x \text{ mg}}{7.5 \text{ mL}} = \frac{375 \text{ mg}}{5 \text{ mL}}$$

$$x \text{ mg} = 562.5 \text{ mg}$$

Step 7. The answer of 562.5 mg is rounded to the nearest whole milligram, or 563 mg.

Using Dimensional Analysis to Calculate a Drug Dose

Just as the dimensional analysis method was used in converting metric units earlier in this chapter, it can now be used to solve drug dose problems by "converting" a dose from milligram to tablets, or milligrams to milliliters. This is accomplished by multiplying the dose ordered by the ratio of the on-hand supply. As in the metric conversions practiced earlier in the chapter, the ratio is set up so that the units of the given dose and the units in the denominator will cancel out. When the dimensional analysis method is used to solve drug dose problems, the steps shown in Table 4.5 can still be used to analyze the information. The only difference is in the setup in Step 6.

The dimensional analysis method tends to be used most frequently for simple dose calculations such as the number of tablets. For example, if a doctor has prescribed 100 mg of a drug and you have 50 mg tablets of that drug on hand, you can quickly determine that the patient will need two 50 mg tablets for the prescribed 100 mg dose. Although you may be able to do the calculations in the following exercises in your head, it is important to work through the steps to be sure you understand them.

Example 4.3.5   **A physician has ordered a 25 mg dose of hydrochlorothiazide. You have a 100-count bottle of 50 mg tablets. What will you prepare to fill the order?**

Step 1. The unknown is x tablets.
Step 2. The prescribed amount is 25 mg.
Step 3. The pharmacy has 50 mg tablets.
Step 4. The extraneous information includes "100-count bottle."
Step 5. The answer will be less than 1 tablet, as the requested dose is less than the amount of milligrams in 1 tablet.
Step 6.

$$25 \text{ mg} \times \frac{1 \text{ tablet}}{50 \text{ mg}} = 0.5 \text{ tablet}$$

Step 7. No rounding is required.

Example 4.3.6   **A physician has ordered a 750 mg dose of amoxicillin. You have 150 mL of a 250 mg/5 mL suspension. What will you prepare to fill the order?**

Step 1. The unknown is x mL.
Step 2. The prescribed amount is 750 mg amoxicillin.
Step 3. The pharmacy has 250 mg/5 mL.
Step 4. The extraneous information includes the 150 mL suspension.
Step 5. The answer will be approximately three times larger than the unit given.
Step 6.

$$750 \text{ mg} \times \frac{5 \text{ mL}}{250 \text{ mg}} = 15 \text{ mL}$$

Step 7. No rounding is required.

Problem Set 4.3 _____

✓ *Self-check your problem set work at* www.emcp.com.

Calculate the following doses using the ratio-proportion method.

1. A patient has a prescription order for 30 mg of a drug. The pharmacy has a partial container of 7.5 mg tablets. How many tablets will the patient need?

2. A prescription order is written for 20 mg of medication. The pharmacy has on hand a 10 mL vial of 25 mg/2 mL solution. How many milliliters will be prepared for this patient?

3. A patient is to get 125 mg of carbamazepine suspension. The label at right shows the drug that the pharmacy has in stock. How many milliliters will be prepared for this patient?

> **NDC 0000-0000-00**
>
> **CARBAMAZEPINE USP**
>
> **Suspension**
> **100 mg/5 mL**
>
> **450 mL**
>
> *Dispense in tight, light-resistant container.*
>
> R_x only

4. A patient is to receive 4 mg of haloperidol. The pharmacy has on hand a 1 mL vial of 5 mg/1 mL solution. How many milliliters are needed to fill this prescription?

5. A loading dose of 1750 mg is needed. The pharmacy has on hand a 500-count bottle of 250 mg capsules. How many capsules will be needed to fill this prescription?

6. A patient is to receive an 18 mg dose of hydroxyzine pamoate. The pharmacy has the following medication available. How many milliliters will be prepared for this patient?

NDC 0000-0000-00

HYDROXYZINE PAMOATE

25 mg/5 mL

oral suspension

473 mL (1 pt)

R_x only

7. A patient is to receive 400 mg of erythromycin estolate three times daily. The available drug is shown in the following label. How many milliliters will be prepared for the morning dose?

NDC 0000-0000-00

100 mL

ERYTHROMYCIN ESTOLATE

oral suspension USP

250 mg per 5 mL

R_x only

8. The following order is received by the pharmacy.

R_x

Cloxacillin
275 mg po tid

Zantac (ranitidine hydrochloride)
75 mg bid

Carafate (sucralfate)
500 mg tid ac and hs

a. Cloxacillin is available as 125 mg/5 mL. How many milliliters of medication would you draw up in each oral syringe for the patient?

b. Zantac is available as 25 mg/mL. How many milliliters will you prepare per dose?

c. Carafate is available as 1 g tablets. How many tablets will be needed for one day?

9. A total regimen of therapy calls for 10 mg of a medication to be given to a patient over several days. In the pharmacy, a solution is available with 40 mcg/mL. How many milliliters must be dispensed to complete the regimen?

10. A patient was given 2 mL of the drug shown in the label below. How many milligrams were given to the patient?

NDC 0000-0000-00
20 mL Multiple Dose Vial   Sterile
For use in preparation of large volume parenterals

Gentamicin
SULFATE INJECTION, USP

40 mg/mL
20 mL = 80 mg

For Parenteral Administration Caution: Federal law prohibits dispensing without prescription

NDC 0000-0000-00
20 mL Multiple Dose Vial

ATROPINE
SULFATE INJECTION, USP

400 mcg/mL

(0.4 mg/mL)
FOR SC, IM, OR IV USE

11. A patient receives 1 mg of atropine, shown in the label above. How many milliliters is this?

12. A patient receives 1.2 mL of the atropine solution shown in the label. How many micrograms is this?

13. A 0.63 mL dose of medication is to be given. The pharmacy stock solution contains 80 mg/15 mL. How many micrograms are in the dose?

14. A capsule contains 35 mg of an active ingredient. How many capsules would you need to accumulate 1.05 kg of ingredient?

15. A total regimen of a drug calls for 880 mg to be given. If two doses provide 80 mg, how many doses will have to be given?

16. You have 560 mL of a solution that contains 1600 mg. How many micrograms are in 4 mL of solution? (Round your answer to the nearest tenth.)

17. A total regimen of therapy calls for 10 mg of a medication to be given to a patient over several days. In the pharmacy, a solution is available with 40 mcg/mL. How many milliliters must be dispensed to complete the regimen?

18. A patient is to receive 2000 units of heparin. Heparin is available as 5000 units/mL. How many milliliters do you prepare?

Calculate the following doses using the dimensional analysis method.

19. The pharmacy has received a prescription for 375 mg of Depakene to be taken three times daily, and the medication shown in the following label is to be used to fill the order. How many milliliters will the patient need to take at each dose?

© 2005 Abbott Laboratories, used by permission.

20. A pediatric patient is to take 30 mcg of digoxin each morning, and the medication shown in the label to the right is to be used to fill the order. How many milliliters will the patient take with each dose?

21. A pediatric patient is to take 1.1 mL of digoxin each morning, and the medication shown in the label for question 20 is to be used to fill the order. How many micrograms will the patient take with each dose?

22. A pediatric patient is to take 0.5 mL of furosemide oral solution, and the medication shown in the label to the right is to be used to fill the order. How many milligrams will the child take with each dose?

23. A pediatric patient is to take 0.8 mL of furosemide oral solution, and the medication shown in the label for question 22 is to be used to fill the order. How many milligrams will the child take with each dose?

24. A pediatric patient is to take 6.5 mg of furosemide oral solution, and the medication shown in the label for question 22 is to be used to fill the order. How many milliliters will the child take with each dose?

25. A patient is to take 3 mg of albuterol syrup three times daily as needed, and the medication shown in the following label is to be used to fill the order. How many milliliters should be taken at each dose?

26. A patient is to receive 50 mg of meperidine intramuscularly every 4 to 6 hours as needed, and the medication shown in the label to the right is to be used to fill the order. How many milliliters will the patient need for one dose?

27. A patient is to receive 300 mg of erythromycin estolate two times daily, and the medication shown in the following label is to be used to fill the order. How many milliliters will the patient need to take each day?

NDC 0000-0000-00

100 mL

ERYTHROMYCIN ESTOLATE

oral suspension USP

250 mg per 5 mL

R~x~ only

28. A patient is to receive 225 mg of carbamazepine suspension, and the medication shown in the following label is to be used to fill the order. How many milliliters will be prepared for this patient?

NDC 0000-0000-00

CARBAMAZEPINE USP

Suspension 100 mg/5 mL

450 mL

Dispense in tight, light-resistant container

R~x~ only

29. The following order has been received by the pharmacy.

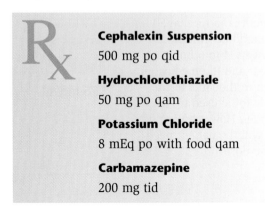

R~x~

Cephalexin Suspension
500 mg po qid

Hydrochlorothiazide
50 mg po qam

Potassium Chloride
8 mEq po with food qam

Carbamazepine
200 mg tid

a. Cephalexin is available in a 200 mL bottle of 250 mg/5 mL suspension. How many milliliters will the patient need for the first day?

b. Hydrochlorothiazide is available from the pharmacy in a 1000-count bottle of 25 mg tablets. How many tablets will be needed for the first day of hospitalization?

c. Potassium chloride is available as a 20 mEq/15 mL sugar-free solution. It contains 5% alcohol. How many milliliters will be measured out for the patient's morning dose?

d. The pharmacy has a 450 mL bottle of 100 mg/5 mL carbamazepine solution. How many milliliters will be prepared for this patient for the first day?

30. A pediatric patient is to receive 20 mg of diphenhydramine elixir, 12.5 mg/5 mL. How many milliliters will be administered?

31. A patient is to take 150 mg of nortriptyline. The pharmacy has on hand 25 mg, 50 mg, and 75 mg capsules.
   a. Select the product that will result in the patient taking the fewest number of capsules daily.

   b. How many capsules will need to be dispensed for a one-week supply?

32. A patient is to take 100 mg of Biaxin, and the following label shows the drug available in the pharmacy. How many milliliters should be given per dose?

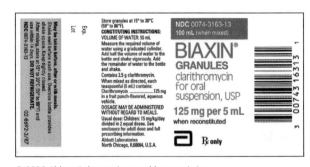

© 2005 Abbott Laboratories, used by permission.

33. A patient takes ¾ tsp of clarithromycin, and the label shown on the previous page is the drug available in the pharmacy. How many milligrams are in this dose?

34. A patient is taking 3 mg of albuterol syrup, 2 mg/5 mL. How many milliliters are in this dose?

35. A patient takes 1½ tsp of albuterol syrup, 2 mg/5 mL. How many milligrams of medication are in this dose?

4.4 CUSTOMIZED DOSES

Most manufacturers offer dose ranges as prescribing guidelines. In some cases, the suggested dose may be based on the patient's weight or the patient's weight and height. Calculations to customize patient-specific doses are important in the pharmacy.

Calculating Doses Based on Weight

The patient's weight may be especially important when calculating a parenteral, pediatric, or geriatric dose of a medication. It is also important for medications that have a low margin of safety. In these cases, manufacturers will offer prescribing guidelines for a medication based upon a therapeutic amount or range per unit of body weight. The most common is milligram of a medication per kilogram of body weight.

Example 4.4.1

A patient weighs 60 kg, and she is to receive a medication of 15 mg/kg. What will her dose be? If the medication is available in a 300 mg capsule, how many will be dispensed?

This problem has two parts. The first part asks for the dose, and the second part asks for the number of capsules to be dispensed. We can solve both parts of this problem using either the ratio-proportion method or the dimensional analysis method.

Part I. Determine the dose.
Solution 1: Using the ratio-proportion method,

$$\frac{x \text{ mg}}{60 \text{ kg}} = \frac{15 \text{ mg}}{1 \text{ kg}}$$

$$\frac{(60 \text{ kg}) \, x \text{ mg}}{60 \text{ kg}} = \frac{(60 \text{ kg}) \, 15 \text{ mg}}{1 \text{ kg}}$$

$$x \text{ mg} = (60) \, 15 \text{ mg}$$

$$x \text{ mg} = 900 \text{ mg}$$

Solution 2: Using the dimensional analysis method,

$$60 \text{ kg} \times \frac{15 \text{ mg}}{1 \text{ kg}} = 900 \text{ mg}$$

Part II. Determine the number of capsules to be dispensed.
Solution 1: Using the ratio-proportion method,

$$\frac{x \text{ capsules}}{900 \text{ mg}} = \frac{1 \text{ capsule}}{300 \text{ mg}}$$

$$\frac{(900 \text{ mg}) \; x \text{ capsules}}{900 \text{ mg}} = \frac{(900 \text{ mg}) \; 1 \text{ capsule}}{300 \text{ mg}}$$

$$x \text{ capsules} = \frac{900 \text{ capsules}}{300}$$

$$x \text{ capsules} = 3 \text{ capsules}$$

Solution 2: Using the dimensional analysis method,

$$900 \text{ mg} \times \frac{1 \text{ capsule}}{300 \text{ mg}} = 3 \text{ capsules}$$

Example 4.4.2   **A patient weighs 74 kg, and he is to receive a medication of 0.4 mg/kg. What will his dose be? If the medication is available in a 15 mg/10 mL solution, how many milliliters of medication will the patient receive in a dose?**

This problem has two parts. The first part asks for the dose, and the second part asks for the amount of milliliters to be dispensed. We can solve both parts of this problem using either the ratio-proportion method or the dimensional analysis method.

Part I. Determine the dose.
Solution 1: Using the ratio-proportion method,

$$\frac{x \text{ mg}}{74 \text{ kg}} = \frac{0.4 \text{ mg}}{1 \text{ kg}}$$

$$\frac{(74 \text{ kg}) \; x \text{ mg}}{74 \text{ kg}} = \frac{(74 \text{ kg}) \; 0.4 \text{ mg}}{1 \text{ kg}}$$

$$x \text{ mg} = (74) \; 0.4 \text{ mg}$$

$$x \text{ mg} = 29.6 \text{ mg}$$

Solution 2: Using the dimensional analysis method,

$$74 \text{ kg} \times \frac{0.4 \text{ mg}}{1 \text{ kg}} = 29.6 \text{ mg}$$

Part II. Determine the number of milliliters to be dispensed.

Solution 1: Using the ratio-proportion method,

$$\frac{x \text{ mL}}{29.6 \text{ mg}} = \frac{10 \text{ mL}}{15 \text{ mg}}$$

$$\frac{(29.6 \text{ mg}) \, x \text{ mL}}{29.6 \text{ mg}} = \frac{(29.6 \text{ mg}) \, 10 \text{ mL}}{15 \text{ mg}}$$

$$x \text{ mL} = \frac{296 \text{ mL}}{15}$$

$$x \text{ mL} = 19.733 \text{ mL, rounded to } 19.7 \text{ mL}$$

Solution 2: Using the dimensional analysis method,

$$29.6 \text{ mg} \times \frac{10 \text{ mL}}{15 \text{ mg}} = 19.733 \text{ mL, rounded to } 19.7 \text{ mL}$$

> **body surface area (BSA)**
> a measurement related to a patient's weight and height, expressed in meters squared (m^2), and used to calculate patient-specific doses of medications

Calculating Doses Based on Body Surface Area (BSA)

Body surface area (BSA) is a measurement that is based on weight and height variables and expressed as meters squared (m^2). BSA is usually estimated using a nomogram. Table 4.6 outlines the steps for using a nomogram, and Figures 4.1 and 4.2 are nomograms used for estimating BSA for children and adults. Some medications such as chemotherapy drugs require BSA to calculate a patient-specific dose.

Example 4.4.3

**A patient is to receive a medication with the dose based on 50 mg/m².
If the patient has a BSA of 0.90 m², what will the dose be? If the medication is available only in 15 mg tablets, how many will be dispensed?**

Part I. Since the dose is to be based on 50 mg/m², multiply by the number of square meters of the BSA, in this case 0.90.

$$0.90 \text{ m}^2 \times \frac{50 \text{ mg}}{\text{m}^2} = 45 \text{ mg}$$

Part II.

$$45 \text{ mg} \times \frac{1 \text{ tablet}}{15 \text{ mg}} = 3 \text{ tablets}$$

Table 4.6 Steps for Reading a Nomogram for Estimating BSA

Step 1. Mark the patient's height on the left column.

Step 2. Mark the patient's weight on the right column.

Step 3. Draw a line or place a straight-edge ruler on the two marks.

Step 4. Read the BSA by noting where the straight edge crosses the center column. When the straight edge crosses between two numbers, the BSA should be estimated to the nearest one-half unit.

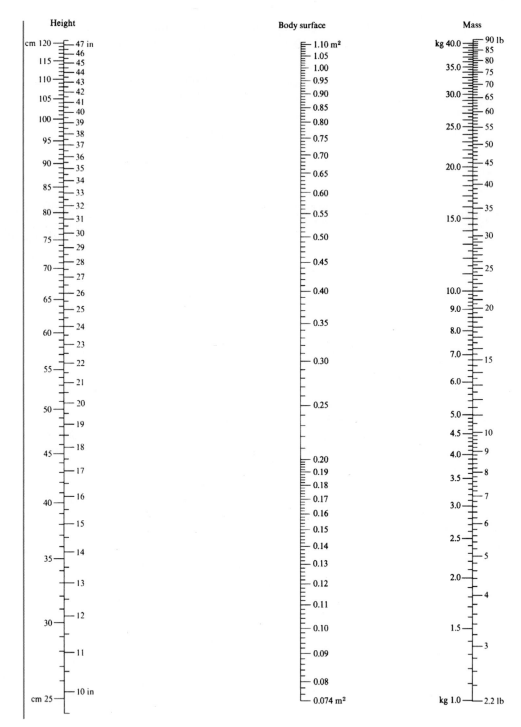

Figure 4.1

Nomogram for Estimating Body Surface Area of Children

Height

cm 120	47 in
115	46
	45
110	44
	43
105	42
	41
100	40
	39
95	38
	37
90	36
	35
85	34
	33
80	32
	31
75	30
	29
70	28
	27
65	26
	25
60	24
	23
55	22
	21
50	20
	19
45	18
	17
40	16
	15
35	14
	13
30	12
	11
cm 25	10 in

Body surface

1.10 m²
1.05
1.00
0.95
0.90
0.85
0.80
0.75
0.70
0.65
0.60
0.55
0.50
0.45
0.40
0.35
0.30
0.25
0.20
0.19
0.18
0.17
0.16
0.15
0.14
0.13
0.12
0.11
0.10
0.09
0.08
0.074 m²

Mass

kg 40.0	90 lb
	85
35.0	80
	75
	70
30.0	65
	60
25.0	55
	50
20.0	45
	40
	35
15.0	
	30
	25
10.0	
9.0	20
8.0	
7.0	15
6.0	
5.0	
4.5	10
4.0	9
3.5	8
3.0	7
	6
2.5	
	5
2.0	
	4
1.5	
	3
kg 1.0	2.2 lb

Reprinted with permission....to come.

Figure 4.2

Nomogram for Estimating Body Surface Area of Adults

Reprinted with permission....to come.

Example 4.4.4   **A patient with a BSA of 1.30 m² is to receive a medication with the dose based on 0.80 mg/m². The prescription is to be divided into three equal doses. How much will each dose be? If the medication is available only as 50 mcg tablets, how many will be dispensed?**

Part I.   Multiply the number of mg/m² by the number of m², which is the BSA.

$$1.30 \; \cancel{m^2} \times \frac{0.80 \; mg}{\cancel{m^2}} = 1.04 \; mg$$

$$1.04 \; mg \div 3 \; doses = 0.35 \; mg$$

Part II.   First convert the dose in milligrams to micrograms, the units of the tablets, by using the equivalency 1 mg = 1000 mcg.

$$0.35 \; mg \times \frac{1000 \; mcg}{1 \; mg} = 350 \; mcg$$

Therefore, a dose is 350 mcg. Since the tablets are 50 mcg each,

$$350 \; mcg \times \frac{1 \; tablet}{50 \; mcg} = 7 \; tablets$$

Calculating Pediatric Doses

If a manufacturer does not suggest an exact pediatric dose for a medication, such as a dose based on body weight or BSA, an appropriate dose may be calculated using the normal adult dose and one of several formulas. **Young's Rule** bases the suggested dose on a child's age in years, and **Clark's Rule** bases the suggested dose on a child's weight. Both formulas include the usual adult dose, but because the manufacturer often provides this as a range (such as 20–30 mg), the physician or pharmacist must determine the "usual dose" for purposes of the formula. Many medications have a wide dose range, and the patient's response and adverse reactions can vary widely, even in adults. For this reason, many physicians prefer to prescribe to children only those medications that have a known suggested pediatric dose. Consequently, Young's and Clark's formulas are used infrequently. A more common method for determining pediatric doses, using dosing tables, will be presented in Chapter 5.

> **Young's Rule**
> a formula used to determine an appropriate pediatric dose by using the child's age in years and the normal adult dose; [age in years/(age in years + 12 years)] × adult dose = pediatric dose
>
> **Clark's Rule**
> a formula used to determine an appropriate pediatric dose by using the child's weight in pounds and the normal adult dose; weight in lb/150 lb × adult dose = pediatric dose

Young's Rule

$$\frac{age \; (in \; years)}{age + 12 \; years} \times adult \; dose = pediatric \; dose$$

Clark's Rule

$$\frac{weight \; (in \; lb)}{150 \; lb} \times adult \; dose = pediatric \; dose$$

Example 4.4.5   A 6-year-old child needs a dose of a medication that has a suggested adult dose of 500 mg. Using Young's Rule, what is the appropriate pediatric dose?

$$\frac{6 \text{ years}}{6 \text{ years} + 12 \text{ years}} \times 500 \text{ mg} = 166.67 \text{ mg}$$

Example 4.4.6   An 80 lb child needs a dose of a medication that has a suggested adult dose of 250 mg. Using Clark's Rule, what is the appropriate pediatric dose?

$$\frac{80 \text{ lb}}{150 \text{ lb}} \times 250 \text{ mg} = 133.33 \text{ mg}$$

Example 4.4.7   Calculate the dose of acetaminophen for a 5-year-old child who weighs 44 lb (20 kg). The normal adult dose is 650 mg every 4 to 6 hours as needed. Determine the child's dose based on Young's Rule and Clark's Rule.

Young's Rule: $\dfrac{5 \text{ years}}{5 \text{ years} + 12 \text{ years}} \times 650 \text{ mg} = 191.18 \text{ mg}$

Clark's Rule: $\dfrac{44 \text{ lb}}{150 \text{ lb}} \times 650 \text{ mg} = 190.67 \text{ mg}$

Example 4.4.8   The manufacturer in Example 4.4.7 recommends a dose range of 10–15 mg/kg for a child age 4–5 years. What is the dose range for the five-year-old child who weighs 20 kg?

$$20 \text{ kg} \times 10 \text{ mg/kg} = 200 \text{ mg}$$
$$20 \text{ kg} \times 15 \text{ mg/kg} = 300 \text{ mg}$$

Thus, the manufacturer's suggested dose range for this child is 200–300 mg. This is a little more than the dose determined by the formulas in Example 4.4.7. For this medication, in fact, the manufacturer specifically recommends a dose of 240 mg per dose for a child between the ages of 4 and 5 years.

*Problem Set 4.4*_____

✓ *Self-check your problem set work at* www.emcp.com.

Use the nomogram to determine the following BSA values. (Round to the hundredth place.)

1. Child of normal height and weight: 28 inches, 20 lb

2. Child of normal height and weight: 34 inches, 32 lb

3. Child of normal height and weight: 48 inches, 51 lb (Approximate your answer.)

4. Child of normal height and weight: 95 cm, 21 kg

5. Young adult of normal height and weight: 141 cm, 42.5 kg

6. Adult: 60 inches, 78 kg

7. Adult: 66 inches, 64 kg

8. Adult: 71 inches, 76 kg

9. Adult: 58 inches, 57 kg

10. Adult: 200 cm, 80 kg

Calculate the following weight-based doses based on the provided recommended dose. (Round to the hundredth place.)

11. Cortisone is dosed at 0.5 mg/kg per day. If the patient weighs 56 kg, what is the dose?

12. A postsurgical patient is to receive 125 mg/kg per day of cephalosporin divided into six doses daily. What will each dose be for a patient weighing 87 kg?

13. A premature infant is to receive 4 mL/kg of a medication. If the infant weighs 1.4 kg, how much medication will be administered?

14. A drug is to be given at a dose of 0.625 mg/kg.
    a. If a patient weighs 80 kg, what is the proper dose?

    b. The dose determined above is to be divided and given three times over the course of 24 hours. What is the size of each dose, to the nearest hundredth?

15. A newborn weighs 6 kg and is to be given medication at 5 mg/kg per day in two divided doses. How much will each dose be?

16. A patient weighs 68.64 kg and is to be dosed at 125 mg/kg per day. How many milligrams is this?

17. A child weighs 10 kg and is to be dosed at 10 mg/kg per day. The medication should be administered in equal doses every 12 hours. How many milligrams are in each dose?

Calculate the following BSA-based doses based on the provided recommended dose.

18. A patient is to receive medication with the dose based on 25 mg/m^2 per day, divided into two equal doses. This patient has a BSA of 1.1 m^2. How much will each dose be?

19. A patient is to receive medication with the dose based on 0.75 mg/m^2. This patient has a BSA of 0.67 m^2. How much of the medication will you prepare? (Round to the nearest hundredth.)

20. The medication order for a patient says that the dose is to be based on 100 mg/m^2. If this patient has a BSA of 0.85 m^2, how much will be prepared?

21. A child is to receive acyclovir at 250 mg/m^2. The child's BSA is 0.71 m^2. What will the dose be?

22. Methotrexate is to be given at 3.3 mg/m^2. The patient has a BSA of 0.83 m^2. What will the dose be?

Determine if the following doses are safe according to the manufacturer's recommended doses.

23. A pediatric patient weighs 40 lb and is 43 inches in height. The manufacturer of vincristine has a recommended dose of 2 mg/m^2. The physician has ordered 1.9 mg of vincristine. Is the physician's order safe according to the recommended dose?

24. A pediatric patient weighs 27 lb and is 30 inches in height. The manufacturer of methotrexate has a recommended dose of 3.3 mg/m^2. The physician has ordered 2.5 mg of methotrexate. Is the physician's order safe according to the recommended dose?

25. A pediatric patient weighs 23 lb and is 32 inches in height. The manufacturer of acyclovir has a recommended dose of 250 mg/m^2 every 8 hours. The physician has ordered 200 mg acyclovir tid. Is the physician's order safe according to the recommended dose?

26. A patient weighs 40.9 kg and is 58 inches in height. The manufacturer of erythromycin has a recommended dose of 50 mg/kg per day. The physician has ordered 300 mg erythromycin tid. Is the physician's order safe according to the recommended dose?

Calculate dose ranges for the following and determine if the prescribed dose is in the recommended safe range.

27. A pediatric patient weighs 36.4 kg and is 48 inches in height. The manufacturer of cefazolin has a recommended dose of 50 to 100 mg/kg per day. The physician has prescribed 250 mg tid.
   a. What is the recommended minimum dose per day?

   b. What is the recommended maximum dose per day?

   c. Is this physician's dose within the recommended safe range?

   d. If the product is available as a 500 mg/ 50 mL solution, how many milliliters will be prepared for one prescribed dose?

28. A pediatric patient weighs 5.45 kg and has a length of 21 inches. The manufacturer of amoxicillin has a recommended dose of 20 to 40 mg/kg per day. The physician has ordered 125 mg tid.
   a. What is the recommended minimum dose per day?

   b. What is the recommended maximum dose per day?

   c. Is the physician's dose within the recommended range?

   d. If the product is available as a 125 mg/ 5 mL suspension, how many milliliters will be prepared for one prescribed dose?

29. A pediatric patient weighs 11.8 kg and is 31 inches in height. The physician has ordered acetaminophen with codeine, and safe dosing of acetaminophen with codeine is based on the amount of codeine. The manufacturer of codeine has a recommended dose of 0.5 to 1 mg/kg per dose. The physician has ordered 10 mL of 12 mg codeine/5 mL oral elixir.
   a. What is the recommended minimum dose per dose?

   b. What is the recommended maximum dose per dose?

   c. How many milligrams of codeine are in the 10 mL of oral elixir?

   d. Is this dose within the recommended safe range?

30. A pediatric patient weighs 9.32 kg and is 28 inches in length. The manufacturer of ibuprofen has a recommended dose of 5 to 10 mg/kg every 6 to 8 hours. The physician has ordered 125 mg q8h.
    a. What is the recommended minimum dose per day?

    b. What is the recommended maximum dose per day?

    c. Is the physician's dose within the recommended range?

    d. If the product is available as a 100 mg/ 5 mL suspension, how many milliliters will be prepared for one prescribed dose?

31. A patient weighs 50 kg and is 65 inches in height. The manufacturer of cephalexin has a recommended dose of 25 to 50 mg/kg per day in 2 or 4 equal doses. The physician has ordered 500 mg bid.
    a. What is the recommended minimum dose per day?

    b. What is the recommended maximum dose per day?

    c. Is the physician's dose within the recommended range?

    d. If the product is available as a 250 mg/ 5 mL suspension, how many milliliters will be prepared for one prescribed dose?

32. A pediatric patient weighs 28.6 kg and is 50 inches in height. The manufacturer of acetaminophen has a recommended dose of 10 to 15 mg/kg per day. The physician has ordered 325 mg/day.
    a. What is the recommended minimum dose per day?

    b. What is the recommended maximum dose per day?

    c. Is the physician's dose within the recommended range?

    d. If the product is available as a 160 mg/ 5 mL suspension, how many milliliters will be prepared for one dose?

33. An 8-year-old child weighs 68 lb (30.9 kg) and is to take acyclovir with a normal adult dose of 600 mg.
    a. Using Young's Rule, what is the appropriate pediatric dose?

    b. Using Clark's Rule, what is the appropriate pediatric dose?

Practice Test

Convert the following units within the metric system.

1. 1821 mcg = _____ mg

2. 6864 mg = _____ g

3. 34.5 mg = _____ mcg

4. 186 g = _____ kg

Calculate the following.

5. A patient is to take 2.25 g of amoxicillin prior to a dental procedure. The capsules available are 250 mg per capsule. How many capsules will be dispensed to this patient?

6. A dose of an antacid is 30 mL. How many doses can be prepared from a 360 mL bottle?

7. A patient has a prescription order for 15 mg of a drug. The pharmacy has a partial container of 2.5 mg tablets. How many tablets will the patient need?

8. A patient is to receive 4 mg of haloperidol. The pharmacy has on hand a 1 mL vial of 5 mg/mL solution. How many milliliters are needed to fill this prescription?

9. A total regimen of therapy calls for 70 mg of a medication to be given to a patient over several days. In the pharmacy, a solution is available with 100 mcg/mL. How many milliliters must be dispensed to complete the regimen?

NDC 0000-0000-00
20 mL Multiple Dose Vial

ATROPINE
SULFATE INJECTION, USP

400 mcg/mL

(0.4 mg/mL)
FOR SC, IM, OR IV USE

10. A patient receives 1.2 mg of atropine, shown in the label above. How many milliliters is this?

11. A patient receives 2.8 mL of the atropine solution shown in the label above. How many micrograms is this?

12. A total regimen of a drug calls for 720 mg to be given. If two doses equal 80 mg, how many doses will have to be given?

13. You have 480 mL of a solution that contains 8 g. How many micrograms are in 4 mL of solution? (Round your answer to the nearest tens place.)

14. A patient is to receive 7000 units of heparin. Heparin is available as 5000 units/mL. How many milliliters do you prepare?

15. A pediatric patient is to take 45 mcg of digoxin each morning. The pediatric elixir is available in a 60 mL dropper bottle with the concentration 0.05 mg/mL. How many milliliters will the patient take with each dose?

Calculate the following weight-based BSA doses based on the provided recommended dose. (Use the nomograms in Figures 4.1 and 4.2 to determine the BSA values when necessary.)

16. Medication is dosed at 8 mg/kg divided into three equal doses daily. The adult patient is 67 inches in height and weighs 63 kg. How many milligrams will be given at each dose?

17. The medication order is dosed at 0.5 mg/m^2 per day. The pediatric patient is 34 inches in height and weighs 32 lb. What is the recommended dose for this patient?

18. A newborn weighs 3.86 kg and is to be given medication at 5 mg/kg per day divided into two doses. How much will each dose be?

19. A patient weighs 73 kg and is 67 inches in height. He is to be dosed at 125 mg/m^2 per day. How many milligrams is this?

20. A pediatric patient weighs 21.8 kg and is 52 inches in height. The manufacturer of acetaminophen has a recommended dose of 10 to 15/kg per day. The physician has ordered 325 mg.
    a. What is the minimum dose per day?

    b. What is the maximum dose per day?

    c. Is the physician's dose within the recommended safe range?

    d. If the product is available as a 160 mg/ 5 mL suspension, how many milliliters will be prepared for one prescribed dose?

21. A 12-year-old child weighs 80 lb (36.36 kg) and is to take zidovudine with a normal adult dose of 600 mg.
    a. Using Young's Rule, what is the appropriate pediatric dose?

    b. Using Clark's Rule, what is the appropriate pediatric dose?

Using Household Measure in Pharmacy Calculations

Chapter **5**

Objectives

- Identify units of household measure and convert between them.
- Solve medication problems by using household measure and the metric system.
- Convert body weight between kilograms and pounds.
- Determine pediatric doses using dosing tables.
- Calculate the amount of medication to be dispensed.
- Calculate temperature conversions between Celsius and Fahrenheit.

5.1 HOUSEHOLD MEASURE

household measure
a system of measure used in homes, particularly in kitchens, in the United States; units of measure for volume include teaspoonful, tablespoonful, cup, pint, quart, and gallon; units for weight are pound and ounce

Household measure is a system of measure used in homes, particularly in kitchens, in the United States. The units of household measure for volume include teaspoonful, tablespoonful, cup, pint, quart, and gallon. The units of household measure for weight are pounds and ounces. Table 5.1 lists the household measure equivalents and their abbreviations. The apothecary and avoirdupois measurements will be presented in Chapter 10.

Measuring volume using the household measure is less accurate than using other systems because the measuring utensils can vary in size. Nevertheless, household volume measure may be used in community pharmacy practice when dispensing drugs that will be administered in the patient's home because patients may not

Table 5.1 Household Measure Equivalents

Volume		Weight
3 teaspoonsful (tsp)	= 1 tablespoonful (tbsp)	1 pound (lb) = 16 ounces (oz)
2 tablespoonsful (tbsp)	= 1 fluid ounce (fl oz)	
8 fluid ounces (fl oz)	= 1 cup	
2 cups	= 1 pint (pt)	
2 pints (pt)	= 1 quart (qt)	
4 quarts (qt)	= 1 gallon (gal)	

Safety Note

To avoid misreading c for c̄ or 0, do not abbreviate *cup*.

have other measuring devices at home. Labels instructing patients on how to take a medication often use household measure units for this reason.

It is important to note that the fluid ounce is the same in household and in apothecary (pharmacy) volume measure. However, the ounces used to signify weight are different. There are 12 oz in an apothecary pound, while there are 16 oz in a household pound. The household pound is the more commonly used equivalence.

Converting Household Volume Measures

Like all systems, units of household volume measure can be converted to larger or smaller units. The following examples will demonstrate this type of conversion.

Example 5.1.1

How many tablespoonsful are in 2 cups of medication?

Begin the solution by noting the appropriate equivalences indicated in Table 5.1.

$$2 \text{ tbsp} = 1 \text{ fl oz}$$
$$1 \text{ cup} = 8 \text{ fl oz}$$

Using these equivalences, the solution can be determined in two ways.

Solution 1: Using the ratio-proportion method, first determine the number of fluid ounces in 2 cups.

$$\frac{x \text{ fl oz}}{2 \text{ cups}} = \frac{8 \text{ fl oz}}{1 \text{ cup}}$$

$$\frac{(2 \text{ cups}) \; x \text{ fl oz}}{2 \text{ cups}} = \frac{(2 \text{ cups}) \; 8 \text{ fl oz}}{1 \text{ cup}}$$

$$x \text{ fl oz} = 16 \text{ fl oz}$$

Second, determine the number of tablespoonsful in 16 fl oz.

$$\frac{x \text{ tbsp}}{16 \text{ fl oz}} = \frac{2 \text{ tbsp}}{1 \text{ fl oz}}$$

$$\frac{(16 \text{ fl oz}) \; x \text{ tbsp}}{16 \text{ fl oz}} = \frac{(16 \text{ fl oz}) \; 2 \text{ tbsp}}{1 \text{ fl oz}}$$

$$x \text{ tbsp} = 32 \text{ tbsp}$$

Solution 2: Using the dimensional analysis method,

$$2 \text{ cups} \times \frac{8 \text{ fl oz}}{1 \text{ cup}} \times \frac{2 \text{ tbsp}}{1 \text{ fl oz}} = 32 \text{ tbsp}$$

Example 5.1.2   **How many 1 tsp doses are in 3 cups of liquid medication?**

Begin the solution by noting the appropriate equivalences indicated in Table 5.1.

$$3 \text{ tsp} = 1 \text{ tbsp}$$
$$2 \text{ tbsp} = 1 \text{ fl oz}$$
$$8 \text{ fl oz} = 1 \text{ cup}$$

Using these equivalences, the solution can be determined in two ways.

Solution 1: Using the ratio-proportion method, first determine the number of fluid ounces in 3 cups.

$$\frac{x \text{ fl oz}}{3 \text{ cups}} = \frac{8 \text{ fl oz}}{1 \text{ cup}}$$

$$\frac{(3 \text{ cups}) \, x \text{ fl oz}}{3 \text{ cups}} = \frac{(3 \text{ cups}) \, 8 \text{ fl oz}}{1 \text{ cup}}$$

$$x \text{ fl oz} = 24 \text{ fl oz}$$

Second, determine the number of tablespoonsful in 24 fl oz.

$$\frac{x \text{ tbsp}}{24 \text{ fl oz}} = \frac{2 \text{ tbsp}}{1 \text{ fl oz}}$$

$$\frac{(24 \text{ fl oz}) \, x \text{ tbsp}}{24 \text{ fl oz}} = \frac{(24 \text{ fl oz}) \, 2 \text{ tbsp}}{1 \text{ fl oz}}$$

$$x \text{ tbsp} = 48 \text{ tbsp}$$

Third, determine the number of teaspoonsful in 48 tbsp.

$$\frac{x \text{ tsp}}{48 \text{ tbsp}} = \frac{3 \text{ tsp}}{1 \text{ tbsp}}$$

$$\frac{(48 \text{ tbsp}) \, x \text{ tsp}}{48 \text{ tbsp}} = \frac{(48 \text{ tbsp}) \, 3 \text{ tsp}}{1 \text{ tbsp}}$$

$$x \text{ tsp} = 144 \text{ tsp}$$

Solution 2: Using the dimensional analysis method,

$$3 \text{ cups} \times \frac{8 \text{ fl oz}}{1 \text{ cup}} \times \frac{2 \text{ tbsp}}{1 \text{ fl oz}} \times \frac{3 \text{ tsp}}{1 \text{ tbsp}} = 144 \text{ tsp}$$

Example 5.1.3 **How many 1 fl oz doses are in 3 pt of liquid medication?**

Begin the solution by noting the appropriate equivalences indicated in Table 5.1.

$$8 \text{ fl oz} = 1 \text{ cup}$$
$$2 \text{ cups} = 1 \text{ pt}$$
$$2 \text{ pt} = 1 \text{ qt}$$

Using these equivalences, the solution can be determined in two ways.

Solution 1: Using the ratio-proportion method, first determine the number of cups in 3 pt.

$$\frac{x \text{ cup}}{3 \text{ pt}} = \frac{2 \text{ cups}}{1 \text{ pt}}$$

$$x \text{ cup} = 6 \text{ cups}$$

Second, determine the number of fluid ounces in 6 cups.

$$\frac{x \text{ fl oz}}{6 \text{ cups}} = \frac{8 \text{ fl oz}}{1 \text{ cup}}$$

$$x \text{ fl oz} = 48 \text{ fl oz}$$

Solution 2: Using the dimensional analysis method,

$$3 \text{ pt} \times \frac{2 \text{ cups}}{1 \text{ pt}} \times \frac{8 \text{ fl oz}}{1 \text{ cup}} = 48 \text{ fl oz}$$

Example 5.1.4 **How many 1 fl oz doses are in 2 qt of liquid medication?**

Begin the solution by noting the appropriate equivalences indicated in Table 5.1.

$$8 \text{ fl oz} = 1 \text{ cup}$$
$$2 \text{ cups} = 1 \text{ pt}$$
$$2 \text{ pt} = 1 \text{ qt}$$

Using these equivalences, the solution can be determined in two ways.

Solution 1: Using the ratio-proportion method, first determine the number of pints in 2 qt.

$$\frac{x \text{ pt}}{2 \text{ qt}} = \frac{2 \text{ pt}}{1 \text{ qt}}$$

$$x \text{ pt} = 4 \text{ pt}$$

Second, determine the number of cups in 4 pt.

$$\frac{x \text{ cup}}{4 \text{ pt}} = \frac{2 \text{ cups}}{1 \text{ pt}}$$

$$x \text{ cup} = 8 \text{ cups}$$

Third, determine the number of fluid ounces in 8 cups.

$$\frac{x \text{ fl oz}}{8 \text{ cups}} = \frac{8 \text{ fl oz}}{1 \text{ cup}}$$

$$x \text{ fl oz} = 64 \text{ fl oz}$$

Solution 2: Using the dimensional analysis method,

$$2 \text{ qt} \times \frac{2 \text{ pt}}{1 \text{ qt}} \times \frac{2 \text{ cups}}{1 \text{ pt}} \times \frac{8 \text{ fl oz}}{1 \text{ cup}} = 64 \text{ fl oz}$$

Converting between Household Measure and the Metric System

Because of the inaccuracy of the measuring tools used in the household measure, it is often preferable to convert all quantities into the metric system. This may seem like additional work for some problems, but using the metric system will serve you better than relying on the household system, which is declining in use. Prescriptions that are interpreted and entered into a computer as part of the patient's record will need to be converted to the metric system. Typically, such computer programs are set up to accept measurements using milliliters and grams.

Although some references list exact values for conversions between the household measure and the metric system, the equivalents shown in Table 5.2 are generally accepted for use for these conversions in daily pharmacy practice. All of these conversion values should be committed to memory.

Table 5.2 **Household Measure and Metric System Conversion Values**

Volume		Weight	
1 tsp	= 5 mL	1 oz	= 30 g**
1 tbsp	= 15 mL	1 lb	= 454 g**
1 fl oz	= 30 mL*	2.2 lb	= 1 kg
1 cup	= 240 mL		
1 pt	= 480 mL*		
1 qt	= 960 mL		
1 gallon	= 3840 mL		

*There are actually 29.57 mL in 1 fl oz, but 30 mL is usually used. When packaging a pint, companies will typically include 473 mL, rather than the full 480 mL.
**There are actually 28.34952 g in an avoirdupois ounce; however, we often round up to 30 g. It is common practice to use 454 g as the equivalent for a pound (28.35 g × 16 oz/lb = 453.6 g/lb, rounded to 454 g/lb).

The following examples show some typical conversion problems the pharmacy technician must be able to solve.

Example 5.1.5

You are to dispense 300 mL of a liquid preparation. If the dose is 2 tsp, how many doses will the whole preparation contain?

> *Remember*
> 1 tsp = 5 mL

Begin solving this problem by converting to a common unit of measure using the conversion values in Table 5.2.

$$1 \text{ dose} = 2 \text{ tsp} = 2 \times 5 \text{ mL} = 10 \text{ mL}$$

Using these converted measurements, the solution can be determined in two ways.

Solution 1: Using the ratio-proportion method and the metric system,

$$\frac{x \text{ doses}}{300 \text{ mL}} = \frac{1 \text{ dose}}{10 \text{ mL}}$$

$$\frac{(300 \text{ mL}) \, x \text{ doses}}{300 \text{ mL}} = \frac{(300 \text{ mL}) \, 1 \text{ dose}}{10 \text{ mL}}$$

$$x \text{ doses} = 30 \text{ doses}$$

Solution 2: Using the dimensional analysis method,

$$300 \text{ mL} \times \frac{1 \text{ dose}}{10 \text{ mL}} = 30 \text{ doses}$$

Example 5.1.6

A patient is to purchase a 12 fl oz bottle of antacid. The patient is to take 15 mL before each meal and at bedtime. How many doses does the bottle contain?

> *Remember*
> 1 fl oz = 30 mL

Begin solving this problem by converting to a common unit of measure using the conversion values in Table 5.2.

$$1 \text{ fl oz} = 30 \text{ mL, so } 0.5 \text{ fl oz} = 15 \text{ mL, and } 12 \text{ fl oz} = 360 \text{ mL}$$

Using these converted measurements, the solution can be determined in three ways.

Solution 1: Using the ratio-proportion method and the metric system,

$$\frac{x \text{ doses}}{360 \text{ mL}} = \frac{1 \text{ dose}}{15 \text{ mL}}$$

$$x \text{ dose} = 24 \text{ doses}$$

Solution 2: Using the dimension analysis method and the metric system,

$$360 \text{ mL} \times \frac{1 \text{ dose}}{15 \text{ mL}} = 24 \text{ doses}$$

Solution 3: Using the dimensional analysis method and the household system,

$$12 \text{ fl oz} \times \frac{1 \text{ dose}}{0.5 \text{ fl oz}} = 24 \text{ doses}$$

Example 5.1.7 **How many 2 tbsp doses are in 480 mL?**

Using the conversion values in Table 5.2, 1 tbsp = 15 mL. Since 1 dose equals 2 tbsp,

$$1 \text{ dose} = 2 \text{ tbsp} = 2 \times 15 \text{ mL} = 30 \text{ mL}$$

Using these converted measurements, this problem can be solved in two ways.

Solution 1: Using the ratio-proportion method,

$$\frac{x \text{ doses}}{480 \text{ mL}} = \frac{1 \text{ dose}}{30 \text{ mL}}$$

$$x \text{ dose} = 16 \text{ doses}$$

Solution 2: Using the dimensional analysis method,

$$480 \text{ mL} \times \frac{1 \text{ dose}}{30 \text{ mL}} = 16 \text{ doses}$$

Example 5.1.8 **Theophylline elixir contains 80 mg/15 mL. A dose is 2 tbsp. How many milligrams are in 1 dose of the theophylline elixir?**

Using the conversion values in Table 5.2,

$$1 \text{ dose} = 2 \text{ tbsp} = 2 \times 15 \text{ mL} = 30 \text{ mL}$$

This problem can be solved in two ways.

Solution 1: Using the ratio-proportion method,

$$\frac{x \text{ mg}}{30 \text{ mL}} = \frac{80 \text{ mg}}{15 \text{ mL}}$$

$$x \text{ mg} = 160 \text{ mg}$$

Solution 2: Using the dimensional analysis method,

$$30 \text{ mL} \times \frac{80 \text{ mg}}{15 \text{ mL}} = 160 \text{ mg}$$

Like volumes, weights can be converted between household measure and metric measure. The most common conversions are between the household measurements of pounds and ounces and the metric kilograms and grams. These conversions were presented in Table 5.2.

Example 5.1.9

A physician has written a prescription for a 1.5 oz tube of ointment. How many grams is this?

Since 1 oz equals 30 g, this problem can be solved in two ways.

Solution 1: Using the ratio-proportion method,

$$\frac{x \text{ g}}{1.5 \text{ oz}} = \frac{30 \text{ g}}{1 \text{ oz}}$$

$$x \text{ g} = 45 \text{ g}$$

Solution 2: Using the dimensional analysis method,

$$1.5 \text{ oz} \times \frac{30 \text{ g}}{1 \text{ oz}} = 45 \text{ g}$$

Example 5.1.10

You have a 1 lb jar of ointment available. You are instructed to use this stock to fill smaller jars with 20 g of ointment each. How many jars can you fill?

Since 1 lb equals 454 g, this problem can be solved in two ways.

Solution 1: Using the ratio-proportion method,

$$\frac{x \text{ jars}}{454 \text{ g}} = \frac{1 \text{ jar}}{20 \text{ g}}$$

$$x \text{ jar} = 22.7 \text{ jars, or 22 full jars}$$

Solution 2: Using the dimensional analysis method,

$$454 \text{ g} \times \frac{1 \text{ jar}}{20 \text{ g}} = 22.7 \text{ jars, or 22 full jars}$$

In both solutions, there is 0.7 jar of ointment remaining. You can figure out how many grams of ointment are leftover with the following calculation.

$$20 \text{ g/jar} \times 0.7 \text{ jar leftover ointment} = 14 \text{ g leftover ointment}$$

Converting Body Weight

As discussed in the previous chapter, drugs are sometimes dosed based on the weight of the patient. Increasingly, drug manufacturers are providing a recommended dose based on a specific dose in milligrams per kilogram of the patient's weight. Because most drugs are dosed on the basis of kilograms, if a patient's weight is documented in pounds, the weight will have to be converted to kilograms before calculating the appropriate dose.

Example 5.1.11

A patient weighs 134 lb. What is this patient's weight in kilograms?

Remember

2.2 lb = 1 kg

Since 1 kg equals 2.2 lb, this problem can be solved in two ways.

Solution 1: Using the ratio-proportion method,

$$\frac{x \text{ kg}}{134 \text{ lb}} = \frac{1 \text{ kg}}{2.2 \text{ lb}}$$

$$x \text{ kg} = 60.909 \text{ kg, rounded to } 60.9 \text{ kg}$$

Solution 2: Using the dimensional analysis method,

$$134 \text{ lb} \times \frac{1 \text{ kg}}{2.2 \text{ lb}} = 60.909 \text{ kg, rounded to } 60.9 \text{ kg}$$

Example 5.1.12

A patient weighs 76 lb. What is this patient's weight in kilograms?

Since 1 kg equals 2.2 lb, this problem can be solved in two ways.

Solution 1: Using the ratio-proportion method,

$$\frac{x \text{ kg}}{76 \text{ lb}} = \frac{1 \text{ kg}}{2.2 \text{ lb}}$$

$$x \text{ kg} = 34.545 \text{ kg, rounded to } 34.5 \text{ kg}$$

Solution 2: Using the dimensional analysis method,

$$76 \text{ lb} \times \frac{1 \text{ kg}}{2.2 \text{ lb}} = 34.545 \text{ kg, rounded to } 34.5 \text{ kg}$$

Although it is important to understand the conversion using both the ratio-proportion and the dimensional analysis methods, a shorthand method for converting a patient's weight from pounds to kilograms is to divide the amount by 2.2 lb/kg. Similarly, you can convert a patient's weight from kilograms to pounds by multiplying it by 2.2 lb/kg.

Example 5.1.13

A patient weighs 58 kg. What is this patient's weight in pounds?

$$58 \text{ kg} \times 2.2 \text{ lb/kg} = 127.6 \text{ lb}$$

Check this answer by converting the answer from pounds back to kilograms.

$$127.6 \text{ lb} \times 1 \text{ kg/2.2 lb} = 58 \text{ kg}$$

Example 5.1.14

A patient in the neonatal ICU weighs 1250 g. How many pounds is this?

First, convert the grams to kilograms.

$$1250 \text{ g} = 1.25 \text{ kg}$$

Second, convert kilograms to pounds.

$$1.25 \text{ kg} \times 2.2 \text{ lb/kg} = 2.75 \text{ lb}$$

Check the answer by converting the answer from pounds back to kilograms.

$$2.75 \text{ lb} \times 1 \text{ kg/2.2 lb} = 1.25 \text{ kg}$$

Problem Set 5.1 _____

✓ *Self-check your problem set work at* www.emcp.com.

Convert the given volumes within the household measure system.

1. 8 cups = _____ pt

2. 3 pt = _____ fl oz

3. 1 pt = _____ tbsp

4. 3 qt = _____ fl oz

5. 28 tsp = _____ fl oz

6. 1 pt = _____ qt

7. 6 cups = _____ tsp

Convert the given volumes between the household measure and metric systems.

8. 80 mL = _____ tbsp

9. 6 fl oz = _____ mL

10. 90 mL = _____ fl oz

11. 800 mL = _____ pt

12. 53 mL = _____ tsp

13. 35 mL = _____ tsp

14. 10 L = _____ gal

15. 4 tbsp = _____ mL

16. 15 mL = _____ tsp

17. 720 mL = _____ pt

18. 30 tsp = _____ mL

19. 120 mL = _____ fl oz

20. ½ gal = _____ mL

21. 2 L = _____ pt

22. Convert the following commonly used volumes to milliliters.

    a. 3 tbsp = _____ mL

    b. 1 fl oz = _____ mL

    c. 2 fl oz = _____ mL

    d. 3 fl oz = _____ mL

    e. 4 fl oz = _____ mL

    f. 5 fl oz = _____ mL

    g. 6 fl oz = _____ mL

    h. 7 fl oz = _____ mL

    i. 8 fl oz = _____ mL

    j. 12 fl oz = _____ mL

    k. 16 fl oz = _____ mL

Convert the following weights between household measure and the metric system.

23. 2 oz = _____ g

24. 1.5 oz = _____ g

25. 8 oz = _____ g

26. 906 g = _____ lb

27. 30 g = _____ lb

28. 0.8 oz = _____ g

Convert the following patient weights from pounds to kilograms.

29. 3.5 lb

30. 14 lb

31. 42 lb

32. 97 lb

33. 112 lb

34. 165 lb

35. 178 lb

36. 247 lb

Applications

In solving these problems, convert all quantities into the metric system even when the problem could be solved using only the household measure.

37. How many 1 tsp doses are in 2 pt, 6 fl oz?

38. How many 2 tsp doses are in 3 cups?

39. How many 1 tbsp doses are in 12 bottles containing 16 fl oz each?

40. How many 5 mL doses are in a 5 fl oz bottle?

41. How many 3 tsp doses are in 1 pt?

42. A dose of 1.5 fl oz is to be given three times daily. How many milliliters will be given in one day?

43. How many 1½ tsp doses are in an 8 fl oz bottle of cough syrup?

44. How many 1 tsp doses are in an 8 fl oz bottle of cough syrup?

45. A medication has 15 mg/mL. How many milligrams are given each day if the patient takes 1 tbsp tid?

46. A patient uses 1.5 fl oz of medication tid. How many milliliters are needed to give two doses?

47. How many 1 tsp doses are in two bottles containing 400 mL each?

48. If a medication is prescribed as 2 tsp/68 kg/day for an adult patient, how many doses would you get in a 300 mL bottle for a patient who weighs 180 lb?

49. A medication is prescribed as 1 tsp/20 kg/day for a pediatric patient. How many doses will a 4 fl oz bottle provide for a 52 lb patient?

50. A laxative medication is prescribed as 2 tbsp/50 kg. How long will a 12 fl oz bottle last for a patient who weighs 172 lb?

5.2 ORAL DOSES

It is important that pharmacy technicians be able to perform calculations involving oral dosing of medications. Oral medications are prescribed over other dose forms whenever possible and appropriate because oral medications typically are safe and cost-effective. Most prescriptions taken orally come in tablet or capsule form, but liquid forms are also common. Liquid medications are used most commonly by children and by adults with a disease that impairs the swallowing reflex. For all dosing calculations, accuracy of conversions from metric to the household system, dosing amounts, and dispensing amounts need to be checked for safety as well as billing purposes.

Determining Pediatric Doses Using Dosing Tables

Not all drugs that are safe and effective for adult use are appropriate for the pediatric population. In the past, formulas using the child's weight or age were used to reduce the normal adult dose to a smaller amount appropriate for the child patient. Today, prescribers are reluctant to use a medication for a child unless the pharmaceutical

Table 5.3 Acetaminophen Dosing

Age	Dose
0–3 mo	40 mg
4–11 mo	80 mg
1–2 yr	120 mg
2–3 yr	160 mg
4–5 yr	240 mg
6–8 yr	320 mg
9–10 yr	400 mg
11 yr to adult	480 mg
adult	325–650 mg q4–6h or 1000 mg 3–4 times daily
adult maximum	4000 mg daily

manufacturer indicates the proper dose. A manufacturer will provide specific age-and/or weight-related prescribing guidelines for pediatric-appropriate doses of a medication as soon as its safety and effectiveness for the pediatric population have been established. These guidelines are provided in dosing tables as a dose range that is a function of the patient's weight and/or age. When a recommended dose is not provided, often the reason is that the Food and Drug Administration has not approved the particular drug for use in children. The dosing tables are satisfactory for many purposes, but when a more accurate calculation is needed, either the weight-based dosing method or the body surface area (BSA) dosing method, which were discussed in Chapter 4, must be used.

> **dosing table**
> a table providing dose recommendations based on the age and/or the weight of the patient; often used for determining the safe dose for a pediatric patient

A typical **dosing table** includes an age range and/or a weight range with corresponding doses. Dosing tables are used for both oral liquids and solid dose forms, but oral liquids are easier for young patients to take and thus are more common.

Dosing tables often appear on over-the-counter (OTC) packaging for products used for children older than two years of age. For medications used for children under age two, the instruction "Consult your physician" appears. The table for children under age two is available to healthcare providers in pharmacies and physicians' offices. Physicians often instruct parents to purchase OTC medications for small children, so appropriate dosing instructions must be provided for these patients. Dosing may need to be translated from metric units to household measure units. The dosing tables in Tables 5.3, 5.4, and 5.5 will be used to complete the following examples.

Table 5.4 Ibuprofen Dosing

Age	Weight	Dose
6–11 mo	12–17 lb	50 mg
12–23 mo	18–23 lb	75 mg
2–3 yr	24–35 lb	100 mg
4–5 yr	36–47 lb	150 mg
6–8 yr	48–59 lb	200 mg
9–10 yr	60–71 lb	250 mg
11 yr	72–95 lb	300 mg

Table 5.5 Pseudoephedrine Dosing

Age	Dose per Day
<2 yr	4 mg q6h
2–5 yr	15 mg q6h
6–12 yr	30 mg q6h
12 yr to adult	30–60 mg q6h

Example 5.2.1

A 12-month-old child weighing 22 lb is to receive one dose of acetaminophen. According to the dosing information in Table 5.3, what is an appropriate dose?

Since the acetaminophen dosing is by age, not weight, use dosing for one to two years. The appropriate dose would be 120 mg.

Example 5.2.2

A parent wants to give her 15-month-old child who weighs 21 lb an appropriate dose of OTC ibuprofen. The package provides the dosing information in Table 5.4. What is the appropriate dose?

The dose can be determined by either age or weight, and for this child, the dosing would be the same. The appropriate dose would be 75 mg.

Dispensing Liquid Medications

Many oral liquid medications are actually solids, suspended in a liquid. These suspensions are often indicated by the number of milligrams per milliliter. For example, amoxicillin is available as a 125 mg/5 mL oral liquid. In other words, 5 mL of the liquid contains 125 mg of amoxicillin.

Oral liquid medications are most often dosed by teaspoonsful, tablespoonsful, fluid ounces, or now, in the metric system, milliliters. Being able to convert accurately between household measure and the metric measure system is a necessary skill for the pharmacy technician. When calculating volumes of oral medication, it is best to convert everything into the same units. The preferred method is to use the metric system. Patient instructions will usually indicate teaspoonsful if the amount is an even half or full teaspoon. However, the instructions should indicate milliliters if the dose is not easily measured using the household system. An oral syringe, as shown in Figure 5.1 is helpful to patients dosing oral liquids using the metric or household systems.

Usually, an oral liquid medication's written prescription includes a specific volume to be given at each dose, as well as the total volume to be dispensed. It is important to have a working knowledge of the volumes of oral liquid medications that are commonly prescribed. Most frequently, the dosage amount is between 2 mL and 60 mL, or roughly ½ tsp to 2 fl oz. Oral doses are often verified in the pharmacy by means of reference and established protocols.

Figure 5.1

Oral Syringe

This oral syringe is marked with both household and metric units of measure.

Example 5.2.3   **The pharmacy receives a prescription for 100 mg of amoxicillin to be taken three times daily for 10 days. The pharmacy has a 150 mL bottle of 125 mg/5 mL amoxicillin. How many milliliters of the suspension will be dispensed, and what will the patient's dosing instructions on the label say?**

Determine what quantity of suspension contains 100 mg amoxicillin. This can be solved in two ways.

Solution 1: Using the ratio-proportion method,

$$\frac{x \text{ mL}}{100 \text{ mg}} = \frac{5 \text{ mL}}{125 \text{ mg}}$$

$$x \text{ mL} = 4 \text{ mL}$$

Solution 2: Using the dimensional analysis method,

$$100 \text{ mg} \times \frac{5 \text{ mL}}{125 \text{ mg}} = 4 \text{ mL}$$

Using the amount determined for a single dose, determine the total amount of suspension to be dispensed for 10 days.

$$4 \text{ mL} \times 3 \text{ doses/day} \times 10 \text{ days} = 120 \text{ mL}$$

The patient's instructions will say, "Take 4 mL three times daily for 10 days." The patient will need a dosing syringe to dispense the required amount of medication.

Example 5.2.4   **If a 12 fl oz bottle of mouthwash contains 0.75 g of the active ingredient, how many milligrams will be in a 1 tbsp dose?**

Begin the problem by converting all of the household measure units to metric units.

$$12 \text{ fl oz} = 360 \text{ mL}$$
$$1 \text{ tbsp} = 15 \text{ mL}$$

Also, convert 0.75 g to 750 mg.

Using these converted values, this problem can be solved in two ways.

Solution 1: Using the ratio-proportion method,

$$\frac{x \text{ mg}}{15 \text{ mL}} = \frac{750 \text{ mg}}{360 \text{ mL}}$$

$$x \text{ mg} = 31.25 \text{ mg}$$

Solution 2: Using the dimensional analysis method,

$$15 \text{ mL} \times \frac{750 \text{ mg}}{360 \text{ mL}} = 31.25 \text{ mg}$$

Example 5.2.5

The pharmacy receives a prescription for amoxicillin suspension 1 g bid. The pharmacy has a supply of amoxicillin 250 mg/5 mL. How many milliliters are in one dose? What will the patient's dosing instructions on the bottle label say?

First determine how many milligrams are needed for one dose.

$$1 \text{ g} = 1000 \text{ mg}$$

Then determine what quantity of suspension contains 1000 mg.

Solution 1: Using the ratio-proportion method,

$$\frac{x \text{ mL}}{1000 \text{ mg}} = \frac{5 \text{ mL}}{250 \text{ mg}}$$

$$x \text{ mL} = 20 \text{ mL}$$

Solution 2: Using the dimensional analysis method,

$$1000 \text{ mg} \times \frac{5 \text{ mL}}{250 \text{ mg}} = 20 \text{ mL}$$

Translate the amount in milliliters to teaspoonful: 5 mL = 1 tsp, so 20 mL = 4 tsp. The patient's instructions will say, "Take 20 mL (or 4 teaspoonsful) two times daily."

Example 5.2.6

A patient is to take 7 mL of amoxicillin 250 mg/5 mL. How many milligrams are present in one dose?

Solution 1: Using the ratio-proportion method,

$$\frac{x \text{ mg}}{7 \text{ mL}} = \frac{250 \text{ mg}}{5 \text{ mL}}$$

$$x \text{ mg} = 350 \text{ mg}$$

Solution 2: Using the dimensional analysis method,

$$7 \text{ mL} \times \frac{250 \text{ mg}}{5 \text{ mL}} = 350 \text{ mg}$$

Example 5.2.7　　**A patient is taking 4 tsp of diphenhydramine elixir at bedtime. He wishes to take oral tablets instead of the elixir. The 12.5 mg/5 mL elixir comes in a 4 fl oz bottle and is 14% alcohol. The 25 mg tablets come in a 100-count bottle. How many tablets will he need to take to equal the dose in the 4 tsp of elixir?**

Begin by determining the milligrams per dose of the oral liquid using one of the following methods.

Solution 1: Using the ratio-proportion method,

$$\frac{x \text{ mg}}{20 \text{ mL}} = \frac{12.5 \text{ mg}}{5 \text{ mL}}$$

$$x \text{ mg} = 50 \text{ mg}$$

Solution 2: Using the dimensional analysis method,

$$20 \text{ mL} \times \frac{12.5 \text{ mg}}{5 \text{ mL}} = 50 \text{ mg}$$

Now, compare the milligrams to the alternative tablet product.

Solution 1: Using the ratio-proportion method,

$$\frac{x \text{ tablets}}{50 \text{ mg}} = \frac{1 \text{ tablet}}{25 \text{ mg}}$$

$$x \text{ tablet} = 2 \text{ tablets}$$

Solution 2: Using the dimensional analysis method,

$$50 \text{ mg} \times \frac{1 \text{ tablet}}{25 \text{ mg}} = 2 \text{ tablets}$$

Since the patient's dose is 50 mg, and the tablets come in 25 mg, he will need to take two tablets to provide the proper amount of the drug.

Example 5.2.8　　**How many milligrams of medication are in 1 tbsp of medication that contains 50 mg/tsp?**

Convert both volumes to the metric system using the following values from Table 5.2.

$$1 \text{ tbsp} = 15 \text{ mL}$$
$$1 \text{ tsp} = 5 \text{ mL}$$

Using these equivalences, this problem can be solved in two ways.

Solution 1: Using the ratio-proportion method,

$$\frac{x \text{ mg}}{15 \text{ mL}} = \frac{50 \text{ mg}}{5 \text{ mL}}$$

$$x \text{ mg} = 150 \text{ mg}$$

Solution 2: Using the dimensional analysis method,

$$15 \text{ mL} \times \frac{50 \text{ mg}}{5 \text{ mL}} = 150 \text{ mg}$$

Calculating the Amount to Dispense

How long the amount of medication dispensed will last the patient must be determined when the prescription is entered into the patient's computerized record. Pharmacies typically bill liquid medications by the milliliter and solid medications by the unit such as a tablet. Insurance companies require claims for reimbursement for prescription drugs to include the amount of drug dispensed. This amount is calculated by multiplying the amount of drug needed for a single day by the number of days of treatment. Not only is this amount needed for insurance purposes, but the pharmacy also needs to ensure that the patient is receiving enough medication to last for the duration of treatment, whether the medication is in liquid or solid form.

Example 5.2.9

A patient is taking 2 tsp of medication every 8 hours. He has a 6 fl oz bottle of medication. How much medication will the patient take in one day, and how many days will the medication last?

Begin by converting all of the stated volumes to the metric system using the conversion values in Table 5.2.

1 tsp = 5 mL; therefore, 2 tsp/dose = 10 mL/dose
1 fl oz = 30 mL; therefore, 6 fl oz/bottle = 180 mL/bottle

Next, determine how much medication is needed for one day of treatment. The dose is every 8 hours, and there are 24 hours in a day, so

24 hr/day × 1 dose/8 hr = 3 doses/day
3 doses/day × 10 mL/dose = 30 mL/day

Finally, determine the number of days the medication will last.

180 mL/bottle × 1 day/30 mL = 6 days/bottle

Example 5.2.10

A patient is to take 1 tsp of a medication twice daily, and she has a 4 fl oz bottle of medication. How much medication will the patient take in a day, and how many days will the medication last?

Begin by converting all of the stated volumes to the metric system using the conversion values in Table 5.2.

1 tsp = 5 mL; therefore, 1 tsp/dose = 5 mL/dose
1 fl oz = 30 mL; therefore, 4 fl oz/bottle = 120 mL/bottle

Next, determine how much medication is needed for one day.
The dose is taken twice daily, so there are 2 doses/day.

$$2 \text{ doses/day} \times 5 \text{ mL/dose} = 10 \text{ mL/day}$$

Finally, determine the number of days the medication will last.

$$120 \text{ mL/bottle} \times 1 \text{ day/10 mL} = 12 \text{ days/bottle}$$

Example 5.2.11 **A patient has a prescription that says the following: "Take Magic Cough syrup 1–2 tsp every 4–6 hours prn cough. Disp: 8 fl oz." How many days will the cough syrup last?**

Begin by converting all of the stated volumes to the metric system using the conversion values in Table 5.2.

$$1 \text{ tsp} = 5 \text{ mL}; \text{ therefore, } 1\text{–}2 \text{ tsp/dose} = 5\text{–}10 \text{ mL/dose}$$
$$1 \text{ fl oz} = 30 \text{ mL}; \text{ therefore, } 8 \text{ fl oz/bottle} = 240 \text{ mL/bottle}$$

Next, determine how much medication is needed for one day. Assume that the patient will take as much medication as possible as frequently as allowed. This will give the minimum number of days the medication will last.
There are 24 hours in a day, so if the patient takes a dose every 4 hours,

$$24 \text{ hr/day} \times 1 \text{ dose/4 hr} = 6 \text{ doses/day}$$
$$6 \text{ doses/day} \times 10 \text{ mL/dose} = 60 \text{ mL/day}$$

Finally, determine the number of days the medication will last.

$$240 \text{ mL/bottle} \times 1 \text{ day/60 mL} = 4 \text{ days/bottle}$$

Note that the bottle will last longer if the patient takes 1 tsp every six hours.

Some prescriptions do not come with explicit instructions as to how much medication is to be dispensed. The prescription may say, "Take 2 tsp every morning for 10 days." The quantity indicated on the prescription may also say "QS," which means to dispense a "quantity sufficient" to meet the needs of the patient with the instructions given. When the duration of treatment is indicated, the amount of medication needed for a single day and the total amount to be dispensed can be calculated as demonstrated in the following examples.

Example 5.2.12 **A patient comes to the pharmacy with a prescription that does not indicate a quantity. It says, "Amoxicillin 125 mg/5 mL, 1 tsp tid for 10 days." What is the total amount of medication to be dispensed?**

Begin by converting all of the dosage volumes to the metric system using the conversion values in Table 5.2.

$$1 \text{ tsp} = 5 \text{ mL}; \text{ therefore, } 1 \text{ tsp/dose} = 5 \text{ mL/dose}$$

Next, determine how much medication is needed for one day. Because "tid" means three times daily,

$$5 \text{ mL/dose} \times 3 \text{ doses/day} = 15 \text{ mL/day}$$

Finally, determine the amount of medication to dispense.

$$15 \text{ mL/day} \times 10 \text{ days} = 150 \text{ mL}$$

Example 5.2.13   **A patient is to take 2 tsp of a medication four times daily for 5 days. How much will be needed?**

Begin by converting all of the dosage volumes to the metric system using the conversion values in Table 5.2.

$$1 \text{ tsp} = 5 \text{ mL; therefore, } 2 \text{ tsp/dose} = 10 \text{ mL/dose}$$

Next, determine how much medication is needed for one day.

$$10 \text{ mL/dose} \times 4 \text{ doses/day} = 40 \text{ mL/day}$$

Finally, determine the amount of medication to dispense.

$$40 \text{ mL/day} \times 5 \text{ days} = 200 \text{ mL}$$

The same procedure is used when calculating the number of tablets needed to fill a prescription or the number of days a given prescription will last.

Example 5.2.14   **A patient has brought in a prescription for an antidiabetic drug. The prescription says, "Take 2 tablets before breakfast, 1 before lunch and supper, and 1 at bedtime." Determine the quantity needed for a 30-day supply.**

Begin by determining the number of tablets required for one day.

$$2 \text{ before breakfast} + 1 \text{ before lunch} + 1 \text{ before supper} + 1 \text{ at bedtime} = 5$$

The patient will take 5 tablets/day, so a 30-day supply wil be

$$5 \text{ tablets/day} \times 30 \text{ days} = 150 \text{ tablets}$$

Example 5.2.15   **A patient is to take a prescription for prednisone that uses a tapered dosing schedule. Determine the number of 5 mg tablets needed.**

Prednisone 5 mg Oral Tablets

Take 40 mg for 2 days
Take 35 mg for 1 day
Take 30 mg for 2 days
Then decrease by 5 mg each day until gone.

In this problem, the number of tablets taken each day changes, so the most straightforward way to determine the number of tablets needed is to make a list of how many tablets the patient will take each day of treatment.

Day 1: 40 mg/day ÷ 5 mg/tablet = 8 tablets
Day 2: 40 mg/day ÷ 5 mg/tablet = 8 tablets
Day 3: 35 mg/day ÷ 5 mg/tablet = 7 tablets
Day 4: 30 mg/day ÷ 5 mg/tablet = 6 tablets
Day 5: 30 mg/day ÷ 5 mg/tablet = 6 tablets
Day 6: 25 mg/day ÷ 5 mg/tablet = 5 tablets
Day 7: 20 mg/day ÷ 5 mg/tablet = 4 tablets
Day 8: 15 mg/day ÷ 5 mg/tablet = 3 tablets
Day 9: 10 mg/day ÷ 5 mg/tablet = 2 tablets
Day 10: 5 mg/day ÷ 5 mg/tablet = 1 tablet

The sum of the daily totals is 50 tablets for a 10-day regimen.

Problem Set 5.2

✓ *Self-check your problem set work at* www.emcp.com.

Aspirin is typically contraindicated in children. If a child is unable to take acetaminophen or ibuprofen, however, aspirin may be used. Additionally, aspirin is indicated for some conditions in children such as antiplatelet therapy and antirheumatic therapy. Determine the milligram dose of aspirin every four hours for each child in the following questions using the dosing table provided.

Aspirin			
Age (years)	Weight		Dose (mg every 4 hr)
	lb	kg	
2–3	24–35	10.6–15.9	162
4–5	36–47	16–21.4	243
6–8	48–59	21.5–26.8	324
9–10	60–71	26.9–32.3	405
11	72–95	32.4–43.2	486
12–14	$96	$43.3	648

1. 4 years

2. 7 years

3. 10 years

4. 14 years

Levothyroxine is indicated for children with hypothyroidism. Many states require infants to be tested for hypothyroidism shortly after birth so that therapy can begin immediately if needed. In adult patients, the dose is adjusted up or down based on blood titers and clinical signs and symptoms. Newborn patients are more difficult to assess, so a standard dosing table based on kilograms has been developed. Determine the daily dose of levothyroxine for each child in the following questions using the dosing table provided.

Levothyroxine		
Age	Normal range per day (mg)	Daily dose per kg (mg)
0–<6 mo	7.5–30	2.4–6
6–<12 mo	30–45	3.6–4.8
1–5 yr	45–80	3–3.6
6–12 yr	60–90	2.4–3
>12 yr	>90	1.2–1.8

5. 6 lb, newborn

6. 7 lb, 12 oz, newborn

7. 23 lb, 11 months

8. 18 lb, 15 months

Applications

Calculate the following using either the dimensional analysis method or the ratio-proportion method.

9. A patient takes 1 tsp daily of a medication with the concentration 80 mg/15 mL. How many milligrams are in one dose?

10. A patient needs to have 60 mg of medication, and the drug has the concentration 120 mg/5 mL. How many teaspoonsful will the patient take?

11. If there are 24 mg in a teaspoonful of liquid medication, how many grams are in 8 fl oz?

12. How many milligrams are in 4 fl oz of liquid medication with the concentration of 65 mg/tbsp?

13. How many milligrams are in a 2 tsp dose of liquid medication if there are 2.5 g in 2 fl oz?

14. How many milligrams are in a 1 tbsp dose of liquid medication if there are 260 mg in 600 mL?

15. A prescription is received for Drug YXZ to be taken 2 tsp bid. The pharmacy's supply of the drug is 25 mg/tsp. How many grams are needed to prepare 20 fl oz?

16. A prescription is received for Drug YXZ to be taken 1 tbsp qam. The pharmacy's supply of the drug is 30 mg/15 mL. How many milligrams are in a 1 tsp dose?

17. A prescription is received for Drug YXZ to be taken 1 tbsp bid. The pharmacy's supply of the drug is 40 mg/mL. How many grams of medication are needed to prepare 1 pint?

18. A patient is taking ¾ tsp of an antibiotic suspension three times a day.
    a. How long will a 150 mL bottle of antibiotic suspension last this patient?

    b. How many milliliters will be left after 10 days?

19. An antibiotic suspension is available in 80 mL, 150 mL, and 200 mL bottles.
    a. What size bottle of antibiotic suspension will a patient need in order to take 1 tsp twice daily for 14 days?

    b. How much will remain after 14 days?

20. How many days will a 12 fl oz bottle last if a patient takes 1 tbsp tid?

21. A patient is on an alternate-day therapy consisting of 2 tsp of a medication one day and 1 tbsp the next. How long will a 300 mL bottle last?

22. If there are 25 mg in a tablespoonful of liquid medication, how many grams are in 20 fl oz?

23. A patient uses an antacid 1 fl oz tid and hs. How many 12 fl oz bottles will this patient need to last 14 days?

24. A mother of two children with poison ivy needs to know how many 4 fl oz bottles of antihistamine to purchase to last 4 days. One child takes 1 tsp tid and the other takes 2 tsp qid.

25. How many prednisone 5 mg tablets are needed to fill the following prescription?

Prednisone 5 mg

Take 4 tab × 2 days
Take 3 tab × 2 days
Take 1 tab × 1 day

26. How many milliliters of nystatin must be dispensed for the following prescription?

Nystatin Suspension

use 1 mL in each cheek pouch q3h, dispense qs 10 days

27. There are 25 mg in a teaspoonful of medication. You are dispensing 12 fl oz.
    a. How many milligrams will be in the bottle?

    b. If the patient is to get a total of 9 g for a full therapy program, how many refills will be needed?

28. For the prescription below, how many fluid ounces of nystatin must be dispensed?

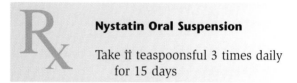

Nystatin Oral Suspension

Take ii teaspoonsful 3 times daily for 15 days

29. A prescription received reads, "Take 2 tbsp of an oral suspension three times daily for 20 days." How many milliliters should be dispensed?

Use the label below to answer the following questions.

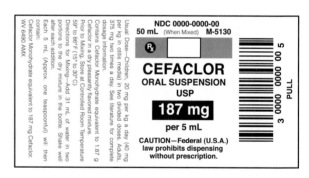

30. How many milligrams are in ¾ tsp?

31. How many milligrams are in 1½ tsp?

32. How many milliliters are needed to provide 125 mg?

33. How many milliliters are needed to provide 500 mg?

34. The following prescription for buttocks cream has been brought into the compounding pharmacy for compounding on January 3, 2007.

Aquaphor
nystatin cream
Desitin ointment
Combine in three equal parts for a total of 180 g. The compound expires in six months.

a. How much of each ingredient will you use?

b. What size of ointment jar (ounces) will you use to store the compound?

c. What expiration date will you put on the compound?

35. The following prescription for absolute (dehydrated) alcohol has been brought into the compounding pharmacy. How many syringes will be sent to the floor?

1. Obtain a 12 fl oz bottle of absolute alcohol from the narcotics cabinet.
2. Filter through a 0.2 micron filter.
3. Send to the floor in 60 mL syringes.

5.3 TEMPERATURE MEASUREMENT

Temperature is a factor in dealing with chemical compounds. Two temperature scales are used to measure temperatures: the **Celsius** system and the **Fahrenheit** system. Both were developed almost 300 years ago.

Understanding Temperature Measurement Systems

Celsius
a thermometric scale in which 100° is the boiling point for water and 0° is the freezing point for water

Daniel Fahrenheit, a German physicist, invented an alcohol thermometer in 1709, a mercury thermometer in 1714, and a temperature scale in 1724. This temperature scale was based on ice water and salt as a low point (0° F) and the human body temperature as the high point (100° F). Fahrenheit used his own body temperature as the standard, but in the years that followed, scientists learned that body temperature varied. Therefore, the Fahrenheit scale was keyed to water for both the low point and the high point. The freezing point of water at sea level was set at 32° F, and the boiling point of water at sea level was set at 212° F.

Fahrenheit
a thermometric scale in which 212° is the boiling point for water and 32° is the freezing point for water

About 1742 Anders Celsius, a Swedish astronomer, developed what became the Celsius or centigrade thermometer. In Celsius measurement, water freezes at 0° C and boils at 100° C.

Converting Celsius and Fahrenheit Temperatures

Both measurement systems are in common use today. Pharmacy personnel must know the two systems and be able to convert back and forth between them. The formulas for converting from one temperature measuring system to another are based on the fact that each Celsius degree equals 1.8 or $\frac{9}{5}$ of each Fahrenheit degree. The conversion formulas are as follows.

Celsius to Fahrenheit: $\quad °F = \left(\frac{9}{5} \times °C\right) + 32$

or

$$°F = (1.8 \times °C) + 32$$

Fahrenheit to Celsius: $°C = \dfrac{5}{9}(°F - 32)$

or

$$°C = \dfrac{°F - 32}{1.8}$$

Example 5.3.1   **Convert 40° C to its equivalent in Fahrenheit.**

$$\left(\dfrac{9}{5} \times 40\right) + 32 = 72 + 32 = 104° \text{ F}$$

or

$$(1.8 \times 40) + 32 = 72 + 32 = 104° \text{ F}$$

Example 5.3.2   **Convert 82° F to its equivalent in Celsius.**

$$\dfrac{5}{9}(82 - 32) = \dfrac{5(50)}{9} = 27.777° \text{ C, rounded to } 27.8° \text{ C}$$

or

$$\dfrac{82 - 32}{1.8} = \dfrac{50}{1.8} = 27.777° \text{ C, rounded to } 27.8° \text{ C}$$

Completing a Temperature Chart

Often medication comes with specific instructions regarding refrigeration. To store medication under "refrigerated" conditions means to store it between 2° C and 5° C (35.6°–41° F). It is very important that temperatures of refrigerators for storing medications be monitored daily.

Most pharmacies have specific charts for recording temperatures of refrigerators and freezers used for storage. See Figure 5.2 and Figure 5.3 for examples of these charts.

Figure 5.2

Refrigerator Temperature Chart (Celsius)

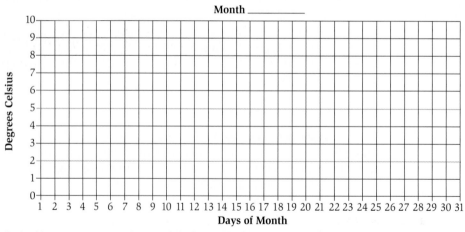

Graph refrigerator temperature on chart once daily. If temperature is less than **2 degrees** or greater than **5 degrees**, check the thermostat setting and correct as necessary. Recheck temperature in one hour, and if temperature is out of stated range, contact maintenance for evaluation and repair. Contact the appropriate area for storage of supplies.

Documentation of Repairs: _____   Documentation of Cleaning: _____

Figure 5.3

Refrigerator Temperature Chart (Fahrenheit)

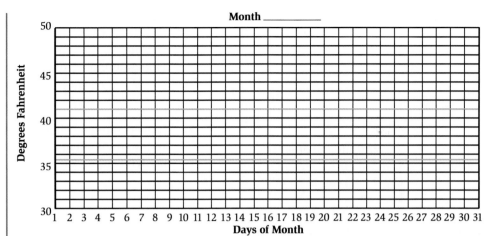

Month _____

Degrees Fahrenheit

50
45
40
35
30

1 2 3 4 5 6 7 8 9 10 11 12 13 14 15 16 17 18 19 20 21 22 23 24 25 26 27 28 29 30 31

Days of Month

Graph refrigerator temperature on chart once daily. If temperature is less than **35.6 degrees** or greater than **41 degrees,** check the thermostat setting and correct as necessary. Recheck temperature in one hour, and if temperature is out of stated range, contact maintenance for evaluation and repair. Contact the appropriate area for storage of supplies.

Documentation of Repairs: _____

Documentation of Cleaning: _____

*Problem Set 5.3*_____

✓ *Self-check your problem set work at* www.emcp.com.

Convert the following Fahrenheit temperatures to Celsius.

1. 0° F

2. 23° F

3. 36° F

4. 40° F

5. 64° F

6. 72° F

7. 98.6° F

8. 100.5° F

9. 102.8° F

10. 105° F

Convert the following Celsius temperatures to Fahrenheit.

11. −15° C

12. 18° C

13. 27° C

14. 31° C

15. 38° C

16. 40° C

17. 49° C

18. 63° C

19. 99.8° C

20. 101.4° C

Applications

21. When making a mixture, you are instructed to heat the mixture to 130° C. You have only a Fahrenheit thermometer. What is the equivalent temperature on the Fahrenheit scale?

22. The following prescription is sent to the hospital pharmacy.

Alteplase in a Syringe

alteplase, 2 mg/mL   50 mg
sterile water for injection   25 mL

1. Reconstitute the alteplase with SWFI.
2. Draw up 5 mL in 10 mL syringes.
3. Label syringes with contents, concentration, and date of preparation.
4. Place syringes in freezer. They should be frozen with the premix piggybacks.

The syringes are stable for six months, or 180 days, −20° C.

a. What is the Fahrenheit temperature at which you should store this product?

b. What expiration date should you put on this compound if today is February 1, 2007?

23. A prescription is sent to the hospital pharmacy requesting a substance to be heated in a 300° F oven for 12–18 hours. At what Celsius temperature does the oven need to be set?

24. Convert the following refrigerator temperatures and log them on the Celsius chart. Note any temperatures out of the safe range.

Date	Degrees F	Degrees C
5/5	36.1	a.
5/6	37.7	b.
5/7	39.0	c.
5/8	35.7	d.
5/9	36.9	e.
5/10	34.9	f.
5/11	36.4	g.
5/12	36.8	h.
5/13	35.5	i.
5/14	38.8	j.

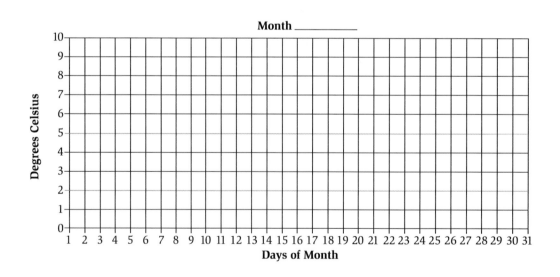

Month _____

Degrees Celsius

Days of Month

25. Convert the following refrigerator temperatures and log them on the Fahrenheit chart. Note any temperatures out of the safe range.

Date	Degrees C	Degrees F
7/12	1.8	a.
7/13	3.1	b.
7/14	2.8	c.
7/15	3.0	d.
7/16	4.5	e.
7/17	3.2	f.
7/18	3.9	g.
7/19	2.5	h.
7/20	4.1	i.
7/21	4.7	j.

Month _____

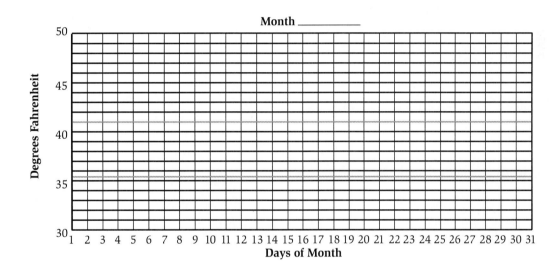

Convert the given volumes within the household measure system.

1. 3 tsp = _____ fl oz

2. 8 fl oz = _____ tsp

Convert the given volumes between the household measure and metric systems.

3. 8 mL = _____ tsp

4. 8 fl oz = _____ mL

Answer the following questions.

5. How many kilograms does a patient weighing 192 lb weigh?

6. How many 5 mL doses are in a 5 fl oz bottle of antibiotic preparation?

7. How many 3 tsp doses are in 500 mL?

Determine the dose of acetaminophen for each of the following children using the dose table provided.

Acetaminophen			
Age	Dose (mg)	Age	Dose (mg)
0–3 mo	40	6–8 yr	320
4–11 mo	80	9–10 yr	400
1–<2 yr	120	11 yr	480
2–3 yr	160	12–14 yr	640
4–5 yr	240	>14 yr	650

8. 22 lb, 11 months

9. 21 lb, 15 months

Calculate the following using either the dimensional analysis or the ratio-proportion method.

10. If there are 125 mg in a teaspoonful of liquid medication, how many grams are in 8 fl oz?

11. If there are 62.5 mg in a teaspoonful of liquid medication, how many milligrams are in a tablespoonful?

12. How many milligrams are in a teaspoonful of liquid medication if there are 75 mg in a tablespoonful?

13. A prescription is received for Drug YXZ to be taken 1 tsp tid. The pharmacy's supply of the drug is 10 mg/200 mL.
    a. How many milligrams are in a 1 tsp dose?

    b. What is a day's dose in milligrams?

14. How long will a 4 fl oz bottle of cough syrup last if the child is using 2.5 mL every 8 hours?

15. How many prednisone 10 mg tablets are needed to fill the following prescription?

 Prednisone 10 mg

Take 80 mg × 2 days
Take 70 mg × 1 day
Take 60 mg × 2 days
Take 50 mg × 1 day
Take 40 mg × 2 days
Take 30 mg × 1 day
Take 20 mg × 2 days
Take 10 mg × 1 day
Take 5 mg × 2 days

Use the label to answer the following questions.

© Eli Lilly and Company. Used with permission.

16. How many milligrams are in ½ tsp?

17. How many milligrams are in ¾ tsp?

18. How many milliliters are needed to provide 40 mg?

19. How many milliliters are needed to provide 5 mg?

20. Convert the following temperatures and log them on the Celsius chart.

Date	Degrees F	Degrees C
6/21	43	a.
6/22	40	b.
6/23	41	c.
6/24	38	d.
6/25	39	e.
6/26	40.5	f.
6/27	37	g.

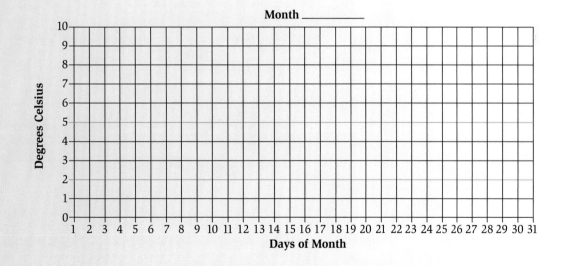

Month _____

Days of Month

Preparing Injectable Medications

Objectives

- Calculate the volume to be measured when given a specific dose.
- Calculate the amount of drug in a given volume.
- Identify drugs that use units as a dose designation.
- Calculate the volume of a substance that has an electrolyte as its primary ingredient.
- Calculate the quantity of units in a given concentration and dose.
- Calculate the volume of insulin to be administered.

6.1 INTRAMUSCULAR AND SUBCUTANEOUS INJECTIONS

injection
a method of administering medications in which a syringe with a shaft or catheter is used to penetrate through the skin or membrane into the tissue below

infusion
the administration of a large volume of liquid medication given parenterally over a long period

parenteral
the administration of medication by injection and not by way of the gastrointestinal system

subcutaneous injection
an injection given into the vascular, fatty layer of tissue under the skin

intramuscular injection
an injection given into the aqueous muscle tissue

intravenous infusion
the injection of fluid into the veins

An **injection** is a method of administering medications in which a syringe with a shaft or catheter is used to penetrate through the skin or membrane into the tissue below. An **infusion** is a type of injection in which a large volume of fluid is administered over a long period through a needle or catheter, usually into a vein. Medications given as injections are considered **parenteral,** which literally means occurring outside the intestines. In other words, the medications do not pass through the gastrointestinal system. There are three types of injections: subcutaneous (SC) injections, intramuscular (IM) injections, and intravenous (IV) infusions. All three types of injections are given by healthcare professionals on a regular basis. A **subcutaneous injection** is given into the vascular, fatty layer of tissue under the layers of skin. Most medications given by this route are quickly absorbed. Patients can self-administer medications such as insulin by this route. An **intramuscular injection** is given into the aqueous muscle tissue. Water-soluble medications are absorbed very rapidly when given intramuscularly, and oil-based medications are absorbed slowly. With proper training, patients can self-administer medications by IM injection, but this route requires more skill and coordination than the SC route and is often more painful as well. An **intravenous infusion** is given into a vein. This route is used when a large amount of fluid must be administered to a patient. Most IV infusions are administered to inpatients, although the trend of home and office administration of IVs is on the rise.

Medications given by injection are often ordered by milligram, and the pharmacy or nursing staff must select and prepare an appropriate concentration of medication from available stock. The amount of medication is calculated using the same methods that were used to calculate liquid oral solutions. In addition to calculating the dose, an estimate should be made so that a syringe with a barrel of the most appropriate size can be selected.

Calculating the Volume of an Injectable Solution

Calculating the volume of medication to be prepared for administration is performed by both the pharmacy staff and the nursing staff who will administer the medications. Some facilities prepare syringes ahead of time for the nursing staff, but others provide the vial and syringe for the nursing staff to draw up just prior to administration. The following examples will demonstrate how to calculate the volume using the ratio-proportion and dimensional analysis methods. When a small volume (less than 20 mL) is to be administered, it is rounded off to the nearest hundredth because the measuring devices can measure to this degree of accuracy. Larger volumes are rounded to the tenth or whole milliliter.

Example 6.1.1   **How many milliliters of the medication shown in the label below must be prepared to provide 12.5 mg of Versed to a patient?**

Solution 1: Using the ratio-proportion method,

$$\frac{x \text{ mL}}{12.5 \text{ mg}} = \frac{1 \text{ mL}}{5 \text{ mg}}$$

$$x \text{ mL} = \frac{(12.5 \text{ mg}) \times 1 \text{ mL}}{5 \text{ mg}} = 2.5 \text{ mL}$$

Solution 2: Using the dimensional analysis method,

$$12.5 \text{ mg} \times \frac{1 \text{ mL}}{5 \text{ mg}} = 2.5 \text{ mL}$$

Example 6.1.2   **How many milliliters of 75 mg/mL Demorol must be prepared to provide 50 mg of meperidine to a patient?**

Solution 1: Using the ratio-proportion method,

$$\frac{x \text{ mL}}{50 \text{ mg}} = \frac{1 \text{ mL}}{75 \text{ mg}}$$

$$x \text{ mL} = \frac{(50 \text{ mg}) \times 1 \text{ mL}}{75 \text{ mg}} = 0.6666 \text{ mL, rounded to } 0.67 \text{ mL}$$

Solution 2: Using the dimensional analysis method,

$$50 \text{ mg} \times \frac{1 \text{ mL}}{75 \text{ mg}} = 0.6666 \text{ mL, rounded to } 0.67 \text{ mL}$$

Example 6.1.3 **How many milliliters of medication must be prepared to provide 35 mg of nitroglycerin if the drug is available as 50 mg/10 mL?**

Solution 1: Using the ratio-proportion method,

$$\frac{x \text{ mL}}{35 \text{ mg}} = \frac{10 \text{ mL}}{50 \text{ mg}}$$

$$x \text{ mL} = \frac{(35 \text{ mg}) \times 10 \text{ mL}}{50 \text{ mg}} = 7 \text{ mL}$$

Solution 2: Using the dimensional analysis method,

$$35 \text{ mg} \times \frac{10 \text{ mL}}{50 \text{ mg}} = 7 \text{ mL}$$

Calculating the Quantity of Drug in an Injectable Solution

The ratio-proportion and dimensional analysis methods can also be used to determine the amount of drug in an injectable solution. The following examples will demonstrate these calculations.

Example 6.1.4 **How many milligrams are in 2 mL of morphine 15 mg/mL?**

Solution 1: Using the ratio-proportion method,

$$\frac{x \text{ mg}}{2 \text{ mL}} = \frac{15 \text{ mg}}{1 \text{ mL}}$$

$$x \text{ mg} = \frac{(2 \text{ mL}) \times 15 \text{ mg}}{1 \text{ mL}} = 30 \text{ mg}$$

Solution 2: Using the dimensional analysis method,

$$2 \text{ mL} \times \frac{15 \text{ mg}}{1 \text{ mL}} = 30 \text{ mg}$$

Example 6.1.5 **How many milligrams are in 0.75 mL of Solu-Medrol 40 mg/1 mL?**

Solution 1: Using the ratio-proportion method,

$$\frac{x \text{ mg}}{0.75 \text{ mL}} = \frac{40 \text{ mg}}{1 \text{ mL}}$$

$$x \text{ mg} = \frac{(0.75 \text{ mL}) \times 40 \text{ mg}}{1 \text{ mL}} = 30 \text{ mg}$$

Solution 2: Using the dimensional analysis method,

$$0.75 \text{ mL} \times \frac{40 \text{ mg}}{1 \text{ mL}} = 30 \text{ mg}$$

Example 6.1.6   **How many milligrams are in 6 mL of furosemide 20 mg/2 mL?**

Solution 1: Using the ratio-proportion method,

$$\frac{x \text{ mg}}{6 \text{ mL}} = \frac{20 \text{ mg}}{2 \text{ mL}}$$

$$x \text{ mg} = \frac{(6 \text{ mL}) \times 20 \text{ mg}}{2 \text{ mL}} = 60 \text{ mg}$$

Solution 2: Using the dimensional analysis method,

$$6 \text{ mL} \times \frac{20 \text{ mg}}{2 \text{ mL}} = 60 \text{ mg}$$

Calculating Ratio Strength

ratio strength
a means of describing the concentration of a liquid medication based on a ratio such as *a* grams:*b* milliliters

The **ratio strength** *a:b* (read as "*a* to *b*") means there are *a* parts of a pure drug in *b* parts of a liquid solution. The units indicated in a ratio strength are *a* grams:*b* milliliters. This is the same unit rule that is used to indicate the percent strength of medications. For example, a 1% solution could be written as 1:100, and the units would be 1 g:100 mL.

Example 6.1.7   **How many grams of a drug are present in 500 mL of a 1:200 solution?**

Solution 1: Using the ratio-proportion method,

$$\frac{x \text{ g}}{500 \text{ mL}} = \frac{1 \text{ g}}{200 \text{ mL}}$$

$$x \text{ g} = \frac{(500 \text{ mL}) \times 1 \text{ g}}{200 \text{ mL}} = 2.5 \text{ g}$$

Solution 2: Using the dimensional analysis method,

$$500 \text{ mL} \times \frac{1 \text{ g}}{200 \text{ mL}} = 2.5 \text{ g}$$

Example 6.1.8   **How many grams of pure drug are in 500 mL of a 1:3000 solution?**

Solution 1: Using the ratio-proportion method,

$$\frac{x \text{ g}}{500 \text{ mL}} = \frac{1 \text{ g}}{3000 \text{ mL}}$$

$$x \text{ g} = \frac{(500 \text{ mL}) \times 1 \text{ g}}{3000 \text{ mL}} = 0.1666 \text{ g, rounded to } 0.17 \text{ g}$$

Solution 2: Using the dimensional analysis method,

$$500 \text{ mL} \times \frac{1 \text{ g}}{3000 \text{ mL}} = 0.1666 \text{ g, rounded to } 0.17 \text{ g}$$

Example 6.1.9 **How many milligrams of pure drug are in 1.5 mL of a 1:1000 solution of epinephrine?**

Solution 1: Using the ratio-proportion method,

$$\frac{x \text{ g}}{1.5 \text{ mL}} = \frac{1 \text{ g}}{1000 \text{ mL}}$$

$$x \text{ g} = \frac{(1.5 \text{ mL}) \times 1 \text{ g}}{1000 \text{ mL}} = 0.0015 \text{ g} = 1.5 \text{ mg}$$

Solution 2: Using the dimensional analysis method,

$$1.5 \text{ mL} \times \frac{1 \text{ g}}{1000 \text{ mL}} = 0.0015 \text{ g} = 1.5 \text{ mg}$$

Example 6.1.10 **How many milliliters are needed to provide 20 mg of a drug if the solution available is 1:500?**

Begin by converting 20 mg to 0.02 g, and then solve for *x*.

Solution 1: Using the ratio-proportion method,

$$\frac{x \text{ mL}}{0.02 \text{ g}} = \frac{500 \text{ mL}}{1 \text{ g}}$$

$$x \text{ mL} = \frac{(0.02 \text{ g}) \times 500 \text{ mL}}{1 \text{ g}} = 10 \text{ mL}$$

Solution 2: Using the dimensional analysis method,

$$0.02 \text{ g} \times \frac{500 \text{ mL}}{1 \text{ g}} = 10 \text{ mL}$$

Problem Set 6.1

✓ *Self-check your problem set work at* www.emcp.com.

Determine the volume to be prepared for an injectable solution. (Round to the hundredth place.)

1. How many milliliters are needed to provide 50 mg of medication if the solution available is 10 mg/2 mL?

2. How many milliliters are needed to provide 80 mg of medication if the solution available is 100 mg/5 mL?

3. How many milliliters are needed to provide 15 mg of medication if the solution available is 10 mg/4 mL?

4. How many milliliters are needed to provide 0.25 mg of medication if the solution available is 1 mg/2 mL?

5. How many milliliters are needed to provide 1.75 mg of medication if the solution available is 1 mg/3 mL?

6. How many milliliters are needed to provide 18 mg of medication if the solution available is 25 mg/mL?

7. How many milliliters are needed to provide 30 mg of medication if the solution available is 25 mg/2 mL?

8. How many milliliters are needed to provide 125 mg of medication if the solution available is 450 mg/20 mL?

9. How many milliliters are needed to provide 3 mg of medication if the solution available is 10 mg/2 mL?

10. How many milliliters are needed to provide 2.5 g of medication if the solution available is 750 mg/4 mL?

Calculate the quantity of drug in an injectable solution.

11. How many milligrams are in 3 mL of a 40 mg/mL solution?

12. How many milligrams are in 2.8 mL of a 5 g/10 mL solution?

13. How many milligrams are in 1.5 mL of a 100 mg/2 mL solution?

14. How many milligrams are in 2.5 mL of a 300 mg/3 mL solution?

15. How many milligrams are in 1.75 mL of a 75 mg/mL solution?

16. How many milligrams are in 1.3 mL of an 80 mg/2 mL solution?

17. How many milligrams are in 0.8 mL of a 250 mg/2 mL solution?

18. How many milligrams are in 0.6 mL of a 100 mg/2 mL solution?

19. How many milligrams are in 3.2 mL of a 250 mg/5 mL solution?

20. How many milligrams are in 0.85 mL of a 4 mg/10 mL solution?

Calculate the amount of drug in a ratio solution.

21. How many milligrams are in 2 mL of a 1:1000 solution?

22. How many micrograms are in 1 mL of a 1:5000 solution?

23. How many micrograms are in 1.5 mL of a 1:10,000 solution?

24. How many micrograms are in 1.4 mL of a 1:2000 solution?

25. How many micrograms are in 2.5 mL of a 1:10,000 solution?

Calculate the volume of solution needed for each requested dose.

26. How many milliliters of 1:1000 solution are needed to provide a 500 mg dose?

27. How many milliliters of 1:10,000 solution are needed to provide a 50 mg dose?

28. How many milliliters of 1:300 solution are needed to provide a 600 mg dose?

29. How many milliliters of 1:500 solution are needed to provide a 250 mg dose?

30. How many milliliters of 1:750 solution are needed to provide a 0.01 g dose?

6.2 OTHER UNITS OF MEASURE

Although most medications are dosed using the units of the metric system such as milligrams or grams, doses of some medications are calculated using other units of measure. Some of these substances are as simple as salts, but others are complicated proteins or hormones such as insulin. Other examples include penicillin V, whose unit is based on the number of bacteria affected, and heparin, whose unit is based on the amount of anti-coagulant property present. Although these substances do have weights, they will be dosed based on their activity, and the weight will often be disregarded.

Calculating Milliequivalents

Many fluids in pharmacy contain dissolved mineral salts known as **electrolytes.** They are so named because they conduct a charge through the solution when connected to electrodes.

Most electrolyte solutions are measured by milliequivalents, which are related to molecular weight. Molecular weights are based on the atomic weight of common elements. The **atomic weight** of an element is the weight of a single atom of that element compared to the weight of a single atom of hydrogen. The **molecular weight** of a compound is the sum of the atomic weights of all atoms in one molecule of the compound. A **millimole (mM)** is the molecular weight expressed as milligrams.

A **milliequivalent (mEq)** is the ratio of the weight of a molecule to its **valence,** or the likely charge or ability to bond with an equally charged molecule.

$$\text{mEq} = \frac{\text{molecular weight}}{\text{valence}}$$

Valence is most familiar as the plus or minus sign next to chemical abbreviations or symbols such as Na^+, Cl^-, or Ca^{++}. The valence of substances used in pharmacy preparations is most commonly plus or minus 1, 2, or 3. Milliequivalents represent both the amount of active substance and the likelihood that the substance, once in the body, will cause a change in the way two compounds are bonded.

Electrolyte solutions and certain drugs, besides being measured by weight at the manufacturer, are also measured in millimoles and milliequivalents. These types of measure are particularly important when working with intravenous solutions. For example, you may be asked to add 28 mEq of sodium chloride to an IV bag. You would then need to calculate the amount of milliliters of sodium chloride solution to add to the IV bag, given an available solution of 4 mEq/mL.

Fortunately, medications commonly used today are standardized, and the calculations needed in the pharmacy will involve determining the volume of a substance that has an electrolyte as its primary ingredient.

electrolytes
substances such as mineral salts that carry an electrical charge when dissolved in a solution

atomic weight
the weight of a single atom of an element compared to the weight of a single atom of hydrogen

molecular weight
the sum of the atomic weights of all atoms in one molecule of a compound

millimole (mM)
molecular weight expressed in milligrams

milliequivalent (mEq)
the ratio of the weight of a molecule to its valence, used to measure the concentration of electrolytes in a volume of solution; also an amount of medication that will provide the patient with a specific amount (equivalent amount) of an electrolyte

valence
the ability of a molecule to bond, as indicated by its positive or negative charge; represented by a plus or minus sign superscript next to an element's chemical symbol

Example 6.2.1

You are requested to add 44 mEq of sodium chloride (NaCl) to an IV bag. Sodium chloride is available as a 4 mEq/mL solution. How many milliliters will you add to the bag?

Solution 1: Using the ratio-proportion method,

$$\frac{x \text{ mL}}{44 \text{ mEq}} = \frac{1 \text{ mL}}{4 \text{ mEq}}$$

$$x \text{ mL} = \frac{(44 \text{ mEq}) \times 1 \text{ mL}}{4 \text{ mEq}} = 11 \text{ mL}$$

Solution 2: Using the dimensional analysis method,

$$44 \text{ mEq} \times \frac{1 \text{ mL}}{4 \text{ mEq}} = 11 \text{ mL}$$

Example 6.2.2   **A patient needs to take a solution of potassium chloride to replace potassium lost due to diuresis. The available solution is shown in the label below. The physician has indicated that the patient needs 15 mEq. How many milliliters will be prepared for the patient?**

Solution 1: Using the ratio-proportion method,

$$\frac{x \text{ mL}}{15 \text{ mEq}} = \frac{15 \text{ mL}}{20 \text{ mEq}}$$

$$x \text{ mL} = \frac{(15 \text{ mEq}) \times 15 \text{ mL}}{20 \text{ mEq}} = 11.25 \text{ mL, rounded to 11 mL}$$

Solution 2: Using the dimensional analysis method,

$$15 \text{ mEq} \times \frac{15 \text{ mL}}{20 \text{ mEq}} = 11.25 \text{ mL, rounded to 11 mL}$$

Example 6.2.3   **You must add 9 mM of an inorganic phosphate to an IV solution and what you have available is 15 mM/5 mL. How many milliliters should you add?**

Solution 1: Using the ratio-proportion method,

$$\frac{x \text{ mL}}{9 \text{ mM}} = \frac{5 \text{ mL}}{15 \text{ mM}}$$

$$x \text{ mL} = \frac{(9 \text{ mM}) \times 5 \text{ mL}}{15 \text{ mM}} = 3 \text{ mL}$$

Solution 2: Using the dimensional analysis method,

$$9 \text{ mM} \times \frac{5 \text{ mL}}{15 \text{ mM}} = 3 \text{ mL}$$

Calculating Units

unit
the amount of activity associated with a medication that has biological impact on a patient

Safety Note
Do not abbreviate international units as IU. Always write out "units."

A number of drugs, including insulin, heparin, corticotropin (ACTH), Factor VIII, penicillin, and some vitamins, are measured in units. A **unit** describes the amount of activity within a unique test system. Drugs that are derived mostly from biological products are expressed in international units, or United States Pharmacopeia (USP) units. Both of these types of units are expressed as "units."

Each drug has a unique biological assay to define its unit of activity. For example, insulin is dosed in units, and the units are based on the amount of glucose that a specific amount of insulin can make available to the cells in a living human being. The degree of activity in this case refers to the insulin's activity. When insulin is prescribed and administered, the dose is based on how much assistance the patient's body will need. Different types and brands of insulin have different weights, but all insulins use a common "unit" of activity. Thus, the weight can be disregarded, and the unit becomes a universal dose for insulin. Insulin syringes are prepared universally and marked according to these standard units. Manufacturers maintain the same concentration of insulin from brand to brand so that the standard insulin syringe will measure out a uniform unit of insulin with a known activity level in the body.

Insulin doses are always calculated in units. Although it is important to know the approximate volume in milliliters, the preparation will most likely involve the use of syringes that are specially marked with units instead of milliliters. Insulin is concentrated as "U-100" insulin, which means that there are 100 units in 1 mL (or 100 units/mL). Insulin syringes are available in the following standard unit sizes:

25 unit
30 unit
50 unit
100 unit

Example 6.2.4

A patient is to receive a bolus (concentrated) dose of heparin. If the dose is 7500 units and you have available 5000 units/mL solution in stock, how many milliliters will the patient receive?

Solution 1: Using the ratio-proportion method,

$$\frac{x \text{ mL}}{7500 \text{ units}} = \frac{1 \text{ mL}}{5000 \text{ units}}$$

$$x \text{ mL} = \frac{(7500 \text{ units}) \times 1 \text{ mL}}{5000 \text{ units}} = 1.5 \text{ mL}$$

Solution 2: Using the dimensional analysis method,

$$7500 \text{ units} \times \frac{1 \text{ mL}}{5000 \text{ units}} = 1.5 \text{ mL}$$

Example 6.2.5   **A patient is to receive 250,000 units of penicillin four times daily for 10 days. You have available a solution of 250,000 units/5 mL. How many milliliters will be dispensed?**

$$\frac{5 \text{ mL}}{\text{dose}} \times \frac{4 \text{ doses}}{\text{day}} = \frac{20 \text{ mL}}{\text{day}}$$

$$\frac{20 \text{ mL}}{\text{day}} \times 10 \text{ days} = 200 \text{ mL}$$

Example 6.2.6   **A patient is to receive 32 units of regular insulin each morning before breakfast. Insulin comes in a 100 units/mL concentration. How many milliliters will the patient receive?**

Solution 1: Using the ratio-proportion method,

$$\frac{x \text{ mL}}{32 \text{ units}} = \frac{1 \text{ mL}}{100 \text{ units}}$$

$$x \text{ mL} = \frac{(32 \text{ units}) \times 1 \text{ mL}}{100 \text{ units}} = 0.32 \text{ mL}$$

Solution 2: Using the dimensional analysis method,

$$32 \text{ units} \times \frac{1 \text{ mL}}{100 \text{ units}} = 0.32 \text{ mL}$$

Example 6.2.7   **A patient is to receive 18 units of regular insulin and 31 units of NPH insulin. Insulin comes in a 100 units/mL concentration. How many milliliters will the patient receive in total?**

Solution 1: Using the ratio-proportion method,

$$\frac{x \text{ mL}}{49 \text{ units}} = \frac{1 \text{ mL}}{100 \text{ units}}$$

$$x \text{ mL} = \frac{(49 \text{ units}) \times 1 \text{ mL}}{100 \text{ units}} = 0.49 \text{ mL}$$

Solution 2: Using the dimensional analysis method,

$$49 \text{ units} \times \frac{1 \text{ mL}}{100 \text{ units}} = 0.49 \text{ mL}$$

✓ *Self-check your problem set work at* www.emcp.com.

Perform the necessary calculations to answer each of the following. (Round to the hundredth place.)

1. An order requires 30 mEq of potassium phosphate. You have a 4.4 mEq/mL solution available. How many milliliters will you put in the IV bag?

2. A 20% potassium chloride solution has a strength of 40 mEq in 15 mL. If you fill an order for 20 mEq, how many milliliters are needed?

3. An order requires 45 mEq of potassium phosphate. You have 4.4 mEq/mL available. How many milliliters will be put in the IV solution?

4. The following order is received by the pharmacy. Sodium chloride is available as 4 mEq/mL. How many milliliters will you add to the bag?

Give 132 mEq of sodium chloride
   in 1000 mL
Infuse at 62 mL/hr

5. A patient needs to take 30 mEq of potassium orally. The solution on hand has 20 mEq/15 mL. How much will be prepared for the patient?

6. A prescription states that a patient must take 32 mEq of potassium. The potassium replacement selected has 8 mEq per tablet. How many tablets will the patient need to take?

7. An order requires 25 mEq of sodium bicarbonate. The solution available contains 7.5% or 8.92 mEq/10 mL. How much will be prepared?

8. An order requires that 18 mEq be added to an IV bag. You have on hand a 20 mL vial of 2 mEq/mL concentrate. How much will be prepared?

9. A patient is to use a sugar- and alcohol-free solution of potassium that contains 40 mEq/15 mL. He is to take 30 mEq daily in two equally divided doses. How many milliliters will each dose be?

10. A prescription has been filled for 15 mL Rum-K with breakfast. Rum-K contains 20 mEq/10 mL. How many milliequivalents is the patient taking with each dose?

11. An order states that you are to add 120 mEq sodium chloride to an IV bag of D_5W. Sodium chloride is available as a 4 mEq/mL concentrate. How many milliliters will you add?

12. A patient is to receive 3500 units heparin, and the following label shows the drug you are to dispense. How many milliliters is this?

LOT/EXP

See package insert for complete product information.
Store at controlled room temperature 20° to 25°C (68° to 77°F) [see USP].
Each mL contains: heparin sodium, 1,000 USP Units. Also, sodium chloride, 9 mg; benzyl alcohol, 9.45 mg added as preservative.
811 317 804
Pharmacia & Upjohn Company
Kalamazoo, MI 49001, USA

NDC 0009-0268-01   10 mL

Heparin Sodium Injection, USP

from beef lung

1,000 Units/mL

For subcutaneous or intravenous use

© Pharmacia Corp. Used with permission.

13. Pen VK (penicillin V–potassium) can be reconstituted to many different concentrations. You are filling an order for 175,000 units and have available a concentration that has already been concentrated to 500,000 units/mL. How many milliliters is the dose?

14. Bicillin CR is given as an intramuscular injection preparation. It comes as 600,000 units/mL, and the dose is 1.5 million units. What is the volume to be administered?

15. A patient needs an injection of heparin. An order for 0.43 mL has been prepared. How many units of heparin are in the dose if it contains 20,000 units/0.8 mL?

16. A physician has ordered 385,000 units of Pen VK (penicillin V–potassium) for a patient. Your stock preparation has 50,000 units/mL. How many milliliters will the dose be?

17. An order calls for 8000 units of heparin in 1000 mL NS. You have a container with 10,000 units/5 mL. How many milliliters will be added to the IV bag?

18. An antibiotic has 750,000 units/mL. The dose is to be 1.5 million units given intramuscularly. How many milliliters will be given?

19. You receive the following prescription, and you have in stock vials of heparin with 10,000 units/5 mL.

    Give 6000 units heparin in
        1000 mL NS
    Infuse 125 mL/hr
    Continue for 24 hours

   a. How many milliliters of heparin will be added to each bag of NS?

   b. What is the total volume of heparin received by the patient?

Calculate the following volumes or amount of units.

20. A patient is using Lantus insulin (100 units/mL) and is to use 8 units. How many milliliters is this?

21. A patient self-administers 0.55 mL of insulin (100 units/mL) every day. How many units is that?

22. A patient is to receive Humulin 70/30 insulin at a dose of 45 units at 8:00 every morning. How many milliliters are to be drawn into the syringe?

23. A patient uses 18 units of insulin each morning and 10 units at 7 P.M. How long will the vial shown in the following label last?

24. A patient uses 20 units of insulin in the morning and 18 units of insulin each evening.
   a. How many units total does the patient use daily?

   b. How many vials (shown in the label) are needed for 30 days?

25. A patient uses 30 units of Regular (R) insulin and 15 of NPH insulin daily. All types of insulin are packaged in 10 mL vials.
   a. If this is given in one injection, what size syringe will be needed? Syringes are available in 25-, 30-, 50-, or 100-unit sizes.

   b. How long will 4 vials (2 of each) of R and NPH last?

26. A patient uses 15 units of Regular (R) and 10 units of Lente (L) each morning. He also uses 15 units of Lente (L) at 5 P.M. with his supper. How many vials of each type of insulin will he need to purchase to last 30 days?

27. A patient uses 18 units of Lantus each morning and 12 units at lunch. How many vials will be needed to last 90 days?

6.3 SOLUTIONS USING POWDERS

powder volume (pv)
the space occupied by dry pharmaceuticals, calculated as the difference between the final volume and the volume of the diluting ingredient, or the diluent volume; the amount of space occupied by lypholized (freeze-dried) medication in a sterile vial, used for reconstitution

In preparing solutions, although the active ingredient is discussed in terms of weight, it also occupies a certain amount of space. With lypholized (freeze-dried) pharmaceuticals in a sterile vial that are used for reconstitution, this space is referred to as **powder volume (pv)**. It is equal to the difference between the final volume (fv) and the volume of the diluting ingredient, or the diluent volume, (dv), as expressed in the following equation:

$$\text{powder volume} = \text{final volume} - \text{diluent volume}$$

or

$$pv = fv - dv$$

Example 6.3.1 **A dry powder antibiotic must be reconstituted for use. The label states that the dry powder occupies 0.5 mL. Using the formula for solving for powder volume, determine the diluent volume (the amount of solvent added). You are given the final volume for three different examples below with the same powder volume.**

Final Volume	Powder Volume
(1) 2 mL	0.5 mL
(2) 5 mL	0.5 mL
(3) 10 mL	0.5 mL

$$dv = fv - pv$$
(1) $dv = 2 \text{ mL} - 0.5 \text{ mL} = 1.5 \text{ mL}$
(2) $dv = 5 \text{ mL} - 0.5 \text{ mL} = 4.5 \text{ mL}$
(3) $dv = 10 \text{ mL} - 0.5 \text{ mL} = 9.5 \text{ mL}$

Example 6.3.2 **You are to reconstitute 1 g of dry powder. The label states that you are to add 9.3 mL of diluent to make a final solution of 100 mg/mL. What is the powder volume?**

Step 1. Calculate the final volume. The strength of the final solution will be 100 mg/mL. Since you start with 1 g = 1000 mg of powder, for a final volume x of the solution, it will have strength 1000 mg/x mL.

Solution 1: Using the ratio-proportion method,

$$\frac{x \text{ mL}}{1000 \text{ mg}} = \frac{1 \text{ mL}}{100 \text{ mg}}$$

$$x \text{ mL} = \frac{(1000 \text{ mg}) \times 1 \text{ mL}}{100 \text{ mg}} = 10 \text{ mL}$$

Solution 2: Using the dimensional analysis method,

$$1000 \text{ mg} \times \frac{1 \text{ mL}}{100 \text{ mg}} = 10 \text{ mL}$$

Step 2. Using the calculated final volume and the given diluent volume, calculate the powder volume.

$$pv = fv - dv$$
$$pv = 10 \text{ mL} - 9.3 \text{ mL} = 0.7 \text{ mL}$$

Example 6.3.3 **A label states that a 5 g quantity of an antibiotic in a bottle should be reconstituted with 8.7 mL saline for injection. The resulting concentration will be 500 mg/mL. What is the powder volume contained in the vial?**

First, convert 500 mg to grams.

$$500 \text{ mg} \times \frac{1 \text{ g}}{1000 \text{ mg}} = 0.5 \text{ g}$$

Second, determine the total number of milliliters that will contain the resultant concentration of 0.5 g/mL.

$$\frac{x \text{ mL}}{5 \text{ g}} = \frac{1 \text{ mL}}{0.5 \text{ g}}$$

$$x \text{ mL} = 10 \text{ mL}$$

Third, subtract the diluent volume from the total volume.

10 mL total volume − 8.7 mL diluent = 1.3 mL powder volume

Problem Set 6.3

✓ *Self-check your problem set work at* www.emcp.com.

Solve the following.

1. You need to make an injectable solution with a final concentration of 375 mg/mL. On hand you have a vial that contains 1.5 g with the instructions to add 3.3 mL. What is the powder volume?

2. The pharmacy must add water to an oral suspension before it can be dispensed to the patient. The dose is to be 250 mg/tsp, and the dry powder is 5 g with a powder volume of 8.6 mL. How much water must you add?

3. An injectable preparation comes packaged as a 1 g vial, and you want a final concentration of 125 mg/2 mL. The vial states that you are to add 14.4 mL diluent. What is the powder volume?

4. The label of a 2 g vial states that you are to add 6.8 mL to get a concentration of 250 mg/mL. What is the powder volume?

5. In question 4, to make a final concentration of 125 mg/mL, how much diluent must you add?

6. The label of a 4 g vial states that you are to add 11.7 mL to get a concentration of 250 mg/mL. What is the powder volume?

7. The label of a 6 g vial says that if you add 12.5 mL of diluent to the vial's contents you will get a concentration of 1 g/2.5 mL. What concentration do you get if you add 2.5 mL?

8. You have added 3.3 mL of diluent to a 1 g vial and now have a final volume of 4 mL. What is the powder volume?

9. How many milliliters of the medication in question 8 do you need for a 100 mg dose?

10. If you add 8.8 mL of diluent to a 2 g vial and get a final concentration of 200 mg/mL, what is the powder volume?

11. A 10 g vial must have 45 mL of diluent added to it. It has a powder volume of 5 mL. How many milligrams will be in each milliliter of the final solution?

12. For an oral suspension, you add 170 mL of fluid and get a final volume of 200 mL. If it contains 8 g of medication, how many milligrams will be in 1 tsp?

13. A 20 g bulk vial label states that if you add 106 mL of diluent, the concentration will be 1 g/6 mL. How much diluent would you add to get a concentration of 1 g/3 mL?

14. You need a concentration of 375 mg/mL. Your vial contains 2 g with instructions to add 3.5 mL of diluent. What is the powder volume?

15. An oral medication requires reconstitution. The dose is 300 mg/tsp. The dry powder is 2.5 g with a volume of 9.6 mL. How much water do you add?

16. A 5 g vial requires that 8.6 mL diluent be added to get a concentration of 250 mg/mL. What is the powder volume?

17. A 10 g vial label says to add 20 mL of diluent to get 1 g per 2.5 mL. What concentration would you get if you added 35 mL?

18. You add 4.3 mL of diluent to a 1 g vial and have a final volume of 5 mL. What is the powder volume?

19. A 5 g vial requires 25 mL to be added. It has a powder volume of 5 mL. How many milligrams are in each milliliter of the final solution?

20. A 20 g vial must have 90 mL of diluent added. It has a powder volume of 10 mL. How many milligrams will be in each milliliter of the final solution?

21. A 3 g vial requires 20 mL of diluent to be added. It has a powder volume of 5 mL. How many milligrams are in each milliliter of the final solution?

22. A pediatric antibiotic requires 67 mL to be added to the bottle for reconstitution. The final volume will be 100 mL. What is the powder volume?

23. If the bottle in question 22 is reconstituted and there are 35 g of active ingredient in the bottle, what will the resulting strength be in milligrams per milliliters?

Solve the following compounding problems.

24. The pharmacy receives the following compound. What is the final concentration in milligrams per milliliters?

Vancomycin Ophthalmic Solution

1. Remove and discard 9 mL of fluid from a commercial tears bottle (15 mL).
2. Add 10 mL SWFI to a vancomycin 500 mg vial. There will be a dry volume of 0.2 mL.
3. Place 10.2 mL of reconstituted vancomycin into "tears" bottle.

25. The pharmacy receives the following compound.

Cephalosporin Intravitreal Ophthalmic Antibiotic Preparation

1. Reconstitute a 1 g vial with 4.4 mL of BSS.
2. Take 1 mL of this and add 9 mL of BSS.
3. Inject 0.1 mL intravitreally.

a. What concentration is the vial of cephalosporin when you reconstitute it in milligrams per milliliters?

b. What milligram dose is the patient receiving?

Practice Test

Determine the volume to be prepared for an injectable solution.

1. How many milliliters are needed to provide 5 mg of medication if the solution available is 10 mg/2 mL?

2. How many milliliters are needed to provide 150 mg of medication if the solution available is 500 mg/5 mL?

3. How many milliliters are needed to provide 0.75 g of medication if the solution available is 1000 mg/3 mL?

4. How many milliliters are needed to provide 0.5 mg of medication if the solution available is 1 mg/mL?

5. How many milliliters are needed to provide 12.5 mg of medication if the solution available is 40 mg/4 mL?

Calculate the quantity of drug in an injectable solution.

6. How many milligrams are in 2.4 mL of a 40 mg/10 mL solution?

7. How many milligrams are in 1.3 mL of a 5 g/20 mL solution?

8. How many milligrams are in 0.9 mL of a 2 mg/mL solution?

9. How many milligrams are in 1.7 mL of a 150 mg/5 mL solution?

10. How many milligrams are in 2.2 mL of a 0.5 g/5 mL solution?

Calculate the quantity of a drug using ratio strength.

11. How many grams are in 600 mL of a 1:200 solution of drug product?

12. How many milligrams are in 5 mL of a 1:5000 solution?

13. How many milligrams are in 0.5 mL of a 1:1000 solution?

14. How many micrograms are in 0.5 mL of a 1:1000 solution?

Perform the necessary calculations to answer the following.

15. How many milliliters would be given to a patient needing 250 mg of drug if the concentration of the medication is 1:250?

16. Prepare the following admixture from your stock solutions of lidocaine 20% and furosemide 10 mg/mL. How much of each drug will be added to the IV bag?

 lidocaine 2.5 g
furosemide 500 mg
1000 mL D$_5$W

17. Potassium chloride comes packaged as 2 mEq/mL in 15 mL vials. How many milliliters would you need to add to this solution? How many milliliters would you need to prepare a full 24-hour supply?

    1000 mL NS with 20 mEq
       potassium chloride
    infuse at 125 mL/hr

18. Fill the order below given the following preparations. How much of each is needed?

    40 g dextrose 5% (5 g/100 mL)
    40 g dextrose 20% (20 g/100 mL)
    sodium chloride 24 mEq
    potassium chloride 10 mEq
    aminophylline 300 mg
    regular insulin 2 units

    a. 40 g dextrose using dextrose 5% (5 g/100 mL)

    b. 40 g drextrose using dextrose 20% (20 g/100 mL)

    c. sodium chloride: 4 mEq/mL

    d. potassium chloride: 2 mEq/mL

    e. aminophylline: 25 mg/mL

    f. insulin: 100 units/mL

19. Pen VK (penicillin V–potassium) can be reconstituted to many different concentrations. You are filling an order for 175,000 units and have available a concentration that has already been reconstituted to 500,000 units/mL. How many milliliters is the dose?

20. Bicillin CR is given as an IM (intramuscular) preparation. It comes as 600,000 units/mL, and the dose is 1.5 million units (1,500,000 units). What is the volume to be administered?

21. A patient is using Lantus insulin (100 units/mL) and is to use 8 units. How many milliliters is that?

22. A patient self-administers 0.55 mL of U-100 insulin (100 units/mL) every day. How many units does that represent?

23. An order requires 30 mEq of potassium phosphate. What you have available is 4.4 mEq/mL of potassium. How many milliliters will you put in the IV bag?

24. In question 23, the phosphate part of the molecule is available as millimoles. If there are 3 mM/mL of phosphate, how many millimoles were dispensed?

25. High-concentration heparin is available as 20,000 units/0.8 mL. How many units are in 0.43 mL?

26. To prepare an arterial line, you must put 5000 units of heparin in 500 mL of normal saline. You have a stock multidose vial that has 10,000 units/10 mL. How many milliliters must be put in the IV bag?

Solve the following problems involving powders that are reconstituted.

27. You need to make an injectable solution with a final concentration of 400 mg/mL. You have a vial that contains 2.5 g with instructions to add 5.5 mL. What is the powder volume?

28. The label of a 10 g vial states that you are to add 187 ml to have a concentration of 500 mg/10 mL. What is the powder volume?

29. The label of a vial states that it contains 1 g in 10 mL. You know that 9.6 mL were added. What is the powder volume?

30. Your bottle of Amoxil (amoxicillin) says to add 39 mL to the bottle to get a solution of 150 mg/tsp. The total amount in the bottle is 2 g. What is the powder volume?

31. A 10 g vial label states that the concentration is 100 mg/mL if you add 87 mL. How much would you need to add to get a concentration of 50 mg/mL?

32. An oral suspension once reconstituted is to have a dose of 250 mg/tsp, and the dry powder is 4 g with a powder volume of 11.3 mL. How much water must you add?

33. An 8 g vial must have 35 mL of diluent added to it. It has a powder volume of 5 mL. How many milligrams will be in each milliliter of the final solution?

34. An oral suspension has a final volume of 300 mL. It contains 12 g of medication and you added 220 mL. How many milligrams will be in each teaspoonful?

35. A 30 g vial must have 76 mL added and has a powder volume of 12.6 mL. How many milligrams per milliliter will be in the final solution?

36. A 1 g vial requires 8.9 mL to be added to have a concentration of 100 mg/mL. What is the powder volume?

Preparing Intravenous Medications

Objectives

- Describe percentage as weight in weight, weight in volume, and volume in volume.
- Calculate the amount of medication in a solution based on a given percentage.
- Calculate the percentage of medication in a given solution.
- Describe the types of IV sets by drops delivered.
- Calculate IV drop rates and flow rates using various sets.
- Estimate and calculate time for IV administration.
- Calculate rates of IV infusion and IV piggyback infusion.

7.1 PERCENTAGE AND RATIO STRENGTH

solution
a mixture of two or more substances

solute
the substance dissolved in the liquid solvent in a solution

solvent
the liquid that dissolves the solute in a solution

weight in weight (w/w)
the number of grams of a drug (solute) in 100 g of the final product (solution)

A **solution** is a mixture of two or more substances. Solutions may exist in any of the three states of matter: gas, liquid, or solid. Solutions can also exist in the following combinations of components:

> two liquids (example: a mixed drink)
> gas in a liquid (example: soda water)
> solid in a liquid (example: salt water)
> solid in a solid (example: grapes in Jello)

In a solution, the substance dissolved in the liquid is called the **solute,** and the liquid is the **solvent.** If both substances are liquids, usually the component representing the greater amount is considered the solvent, and the component representing the smaller amount is the solute. The goal in preparing pharmaceutical solutions is to mix concentrations that result in accurately measured doses.

In general, in comparing two solutions containing the same components, the solution containing the smaller amount of solute is considered dilute. The solution containing the larger amount of solute is considered concentrated. As discussed in Chapter 6, the concentration of one substance dissolved in another substance may be expressed as either a percentage or a ratio strength.

How the concentration of the solute in the solvent is expressed as a percentage depends on which is a solid and/or which is a liquid.

$$\textbf{weight in weight (w/w)} = \frac{\text{number of grams of the drug in}}{100 \text{ g of the final product}}$$

weight in volume (w/v) the number of grams of a drug (solute) in 100 mL of the final product (solution) volume in volume (v/v) the number of milliliters of a drug (solute) in 100 mL of the final product (solution)

$$\text{weight in volume (w/v)} = \frac{\text{number of grams of the drug in}}{\text{100 mL of the final product}}$$

$$\text{volume in volume (v/v)} = \frac{\text{number of milliliters of the drug in}}{\text{100 mL of the final product}}$$

Example 7.1.1   **A 9% solution means there are 9 parts of the drug in 100 parts of the solution. Express this percentage as weight in weight (w/w), weight in volume(w/v), and volume in volume (v/v).**

w/w = 9 g of the drug in 100 g of the final product
w/v = 9 g of the drug in 100 mL of the solution
v/v = 9 mL of the drug in 100 mL of the solution

Example 7.1.2   **Express a 1% hydrocortisone cream as a weight-in-weight percentage.**

A 1% hydrocortisone cream is a compound that contains 1 g of hydrocortisone in each 100 g of 1% hydrocortisone cream.

Example 7.1.3   **Express a 5% solution of dextrose in the form of a weight-in-volume percentage.**

A 5% dextrose solution contains 5 g of dextrose in each 100 mL of D_5W.

Example 7.1.4   **Express 70% rubbing alcohol as a volume-in-volume percentage.**

Seventy percent rubbing alcohol contains 70 mL of pure alcohol in each 100 mL of solution.

The following ratios are important to remember when setting up problems involving percentages.

For w/w problems: $\text{percentage of solution} = \dfrac{\text{g of active ingredient}}{\text{100 g final product}} \times 100\%$

Weight-in-weight problems involve mixing two solids, such as a dry powder and a cream.

For w/v problems: $\text{percentage of solution} = \dfrac{\text{g of active ingredient}}{\text{100 mL solution}} \times 100\%$

Weight-in-volume problems involve adding a solid drug to a liquid, such as a powder dissolved in a syrup.

Remember
NS is the abbreviation for normal saline.

For v/v problems: $\text{percentage of solution} = \dfrac{\text{mL of active ingredient}}{\text{100 mL solution}} \times 100\%$

Volume-in-volume problems involve mixing a pure liquid and another liquid, such as pure alcohol or water.

If the percentage is known, it can be used to find the amount of the active ingredient, as shown in the following example.

Example 7.1.5   **How many grams of dextrose are in a liter of D_5W?**

Note that D_5W means 5% dextrose in water, or a concentration of 5 g/100 mL. Solve this problem by using the ratio-proportion method, but first note that 1 L equals 1000 mL.

$$\frac{x \text{ g}}{1000 \text{ mL}} = \frac{0.05 \text{ g}}{1 \text{ mL}}$$

$$x \text{ g} = 50 \text{ g}$$

The percentage of solid solute in a solution is always calculated in the same manner and is expressed in grams per milliliter. The following formula should be committed to memory.

$$\text{percentage of solution} = \frac{\text{grams of solute}}{\text{milliliters of solution}} \times 100\%$$

The following examples will demonstrate the use of this formula.

Example 7.1.6   **If there are 30 g of dextrose in 500 mL of the solution, what is the percentage of the solution?**

Insert the values into the w/v equation.

$$x\% = \frac{30 \text{ g}}{500 \text{ mL}} \times 100\% = 0.06 \text{ g/mL} \times 100\%$$

$$x\% = 6\%$$

This can also be solved by using the ratio-proportion method.

$$\frac{x \text{ g}}{100 \text{ mL}} = \frac{30 \text{ g}}{500 \text{ mL}}$$

$$x \text{ g} = 6 \text{ g, or } 6\%$$

Example 7.1.7   **If there are 9 g of fat in 240 mL of milk, what is the percentage of the solution?**

Insert the values into the w/v equation.

$$x\% = \frac{9 \text{ g}}{240 \text{ mL}} \times 100\% = 3.75\%$$

This can also be solved by using the ratio-proportion method.

$$\frac{x \text{ g}}{100 \text{ mL}} = \frac{9 \text{ g}}{240 \text{ mL}}$$

$$x \text{ g} = 3.75 \text{ g, or } 3.75\%$$

Example 7.1.8 **If there are 50 g dextrose in a 2 L oral solution, what is the percentage of the solution?**

Convert 2 L to milliliters, and insert the values into the w/v equation.

$$x\% = \frac{50 \text{ g}}{2000 \text{ mL}} \times 100\% = 2.5\%$$

This can also be solved by using the ratio-proportion method.

$$\frac{x \text{ g}}{100 \text{ mL}} = \frac{50 \text{ g}}{2000 \text{ mL}}$$

$$x \text{ g} = 2.5 \text{ g, or } 2.5\%$$

Example 7.1.9 **If there are 875 mg of medication in a 2 tsp dose, what is the percentage of the solution?**

Convert 875 mg to grams, and convert 2 tsp to milliliters (1 tsp = 5 mL). Insert the values into the w/v equation.

$$x\% = \frac{0.875 \text{ g}}{10 \text{ mL}} \times 100\% = 8.75\%$$

This can also be solved by using the ratio-proportion method.

$$\frac{x \text{ g}}{100 \text{ mL}} = \frac{0.875 \text{ g}}{10 \text{ mL}}$$

$$x \text{ g} = 8.75 \text{ g, or } 8.75\%$$

The percentage of solution equation can also be applied to weight-in-weight and volume-in-volume solutions, as shown in the following examples.

Example 7.1.10 **There are 1250 mg of hydrocortisone in 5 oz of ointment. What is the percentage of drug?**

Convert both 1250 mg and 5 oz to grams (1 oz = 30 g). Insert the values into the w/w equation.

$$x\% = \frac{1.25 \text{ g}}{150 \text{ g}} \times 100\% = 0.83\%$$

This can also be solved by using the ratio-proportion method.

$$\frac{x \text{ g}}{100 \text{ g}} = \frac{1.25 \text{ g}}{150 \text{ g}}$$

$$x \text{ g} = 0.83 \text{ g, or } 0.83\%$$

Example 7.1.11　**A 1 pt beverage contains 120 mL of pure alcohol. What is the percentage of alcohol?**

Convert 1 pt to milliliters (1 pt = 480 mL). Insert the values into the v/v equation.

$$x\% = \frac{120 \text{ mL}}{480 \text{ mL}} \times 100\% = 25\%$$

This can also be solved by using the ratio-proportion method.

$$\frac{x \text{ mL}}{100 \text{ mL}} = \frac{120 \text{ mL}}{480 \text{ mL}}$$

$$x \text{ mL} = 25 \text{ mL, or } 25\%$$

INTERNET RESOURCE center

Problem Set 7.1 _____

✓ *Self-check your problem set work at* www.emcp.com.

Express the following as weight-in-weight, weight-in-volume, or volume-in-volume percentages.

1. Express betamethasone dipropionate 0.05% ointment as a weight-in-weight percentage.

2. Express furosemide 10 mg/mL and 11.5% alcohol as a weight-in-volume and a volume-in-volume percentage, respectively.

3. Express ciclopirox 8% topical solution as a weight-in-volume percentage.

Calculate the following.

4. If a patient drinks 8 fl oz of 2% milk, how many grams of fat were consumed?

5. An injection of 1.3 mL lidocaine 2% was given. How many milligrams of lidocaine is this?

6. A dose calls for 2 capsules of 300 mg rifamycin to be given in 1 fl oz of cherry syrup. What is the percentage?

Calculate the percentage of drug in the following drug formulations.

7.

8. oseltamivir 12 mg/mL

9. ibuprofen 100 mg/5 mL

10. morphine sulfate 10 mg/2.5 mL

11. albuterol 2 mg/5 mL

12. budesonide 0.5 mg/2 mL

13.

14. haloperidol decanoate 100 mg/mL

Calculate the amount of drug in milligrams for the following dispensed containers.

15. terconazole 0.8%, 20 g

16. benzoyl peroxide 10%, 30 g cream

17. hydroxypyridinone 0.77%, 45 g

18. ketoconazole 2%, 7 fl oz shampoo

19. permethrin 5%, 60 g cream

20. metronidazole cream 1%, 30 g tube

21. carbamide peroxide 6.5%, 15 mL solution

22. povidone-iodine 7.5%, 4 fl oz cleansing solution

23. lidocaine 1.5%, 10 mL vial

24. ipratropium bromide 0.03%, 30 mL

Calculate the amount of medication in the following doses.

25. You have found a 300 mL bottle of a 7.5% solution on the shelf. If the dose is 1 tsp, how many milligrams are in one dose?

26. How many milligrams are in 1 tbsp of a 0.5% drug product?

27. How many milligrams are in 0.5 mL of a 1:1000 solution?

28. Calculate the percentage of dextrose if 45 g are added to 500 mL of sterile water.

29. How many grams of dextrose are need to make 3500 mL of a 24.5% solution?

30. How many grams are in 600 mL of a 1:200 solution of drug product? What is the percentage of the solution?

31. The following compound is received in the pharmacy. What is the final percentage concentration of tobramycin?

Tobramycin Ophthalmic Solution

1. Obtain a 5 mL bottle of tobramycin ophthalmic solution (3 mg/mL).
2. Add 2 mL of tobramycin injection (40 mg/mL) to the ophthalmic solution.

32. The following compound is received in the pharmacy.

Aminoglycoside: Gentamicin

1. Combine 0.5 mL of gentamicin (4 mg/2 mL) with 0.5 mL BSS.
2. Inject 0.1 mL intravitreally.

a. What is the concentration of the final dilution?

b. What percentage is this concentration?

c. How many milligrams are to be injected?

How many grams of NaCl are in the following volumes of NS (0.9%)?

33. 100 mL

34. 250 mL

35. 500 mL

36. 1000 mL

37. 2225 mL

How many grams of NaCl are in the following volumes of ½NS (0.45%)?

38. 125 mL

39. 250 mL

40. 750 mL

41. 1800 mL

42. 2600 mL

How many grams of dextrose are in the following volumes of D_5W (5%)?

43. 75 mL

44. 385 mL

45. 525 mL

46. 1350 mL

47. 3000 mL

How many grams of dextrose are in the following volumes of $D_{10}W$ (10%)?

48. 100 mL

49. 450 mL

50. 875 mL

51. 1100 mL

52. 2300 mL

7.2 IV FLOW RATES

flow rate
the rate, expressed in milliliters per hour or drops per minute, that medication is flowing through an IV line; also called infusion rate and rate of infusion

The pharmacy staff is responsible for calculating the **flow rate** of a medication to be administered intravenously. This rate is expressed in terms of how many milliliters per hour or drops per minute a patient should receive; it can also be expressed in terms of how much IV fluid should be prepared per shift or per day. The flow rate is often referred to as the infusion rate or rate of infusion.

Physicians typically order the type of IV fluid to be given, any additives required, and the rate at which it should be given as a certain number of milliliters per hour. The nursing staff closely monitors IV fluids to ensure that an appropriate amount of medication is given over the specified time to achieve the intended therapeutic response.

The duration of therapy may be calculated using the following formula.

$$\text{duration of therapy} = \frac{\text{volume of fluid or amount of drug to be infused}}{\text{flow rate}}$$

Safety Note
Round down the duration of therapy to the whole hour.

When calculating the duration of therapy, always round your answer down to the whole hour.

Example 7.2.1

A 1 L IV is running at 125 mL/hr. How often will you send up a new bag?

$$\text{the time the bag will last} = \frac{\text{volume of fluid}}{\text{flow rate}}$$

$$x \text{ hr} = \frac{1000 \text{ mL}}{125 \text{ mL/hr}} = 8 \text{ hr}$$

Using the dimensional analysis method,

$$1 \text{ L} \times 1000 \text{ mL/1 L} \times 1 \text{ hr/125 mL} = 8 \text{ hr}$$

Thus, a new bag will be needed every 8 hours.

Example 7.2.2   **If an IV is running at 150 mL/hr and three 1 L bags are sent to the floor, how long will these bags last?**

$$x \text{ hr} = \text{the time the 3 bags will last}$$

$$x \text{ hr} = \frac{3000 \text{ mL}}{150 \text{ mL/hr}} = 20 \text{ hr}$$

Using the dimensional analysis method,

$$3 \text{ L} \times 1000 \text{ mL}/1 \text{ L} \times 1 \text{ hr}/150 \text{ mL} = 20 \text{ hr}$$

When an order specifies a volume or amount of drug to be given over a specific period of time, the flow rate (expressed in milliliters per hour) can be calculated using the following formula.

$$\text{flow rate} = \frac{\text{volume of fluid or amount of drug to be infused}}{\text{duration of therapy}}$$

The following examples will demonstrate these calculations.

Example 7.2.3   **The following order is sent to the IV room.**

Medication: Solu-Cortef 300 mg
Fluid volume: 300 mL
Time of infusion: 4 hr

What volume of fluid is given per hour, and what amount of drug is given per hour?

Part 1. Determine the volume of fluid given per hour.

$$300 \text{ mL} \div 4 \text{ hr} = 75 \text{ mL/hr}$$

Part 2. Calculate the amount of drug given per hour.

$$300 \text{ mg} \div 4 \text{ hr} = 75 \text{ mg/hr}$$

Example 7.2.4   **The following order is sent to the IV room.**

Medication: cefazolin 500 mg/D_5W
Fluid volume: 50 mL
Time of infusion: ½ hr

What volume of fluid is administered per hour, and what amount of drug is given per hour?

Part 1. Determine the volume of fluid given per hour.

$$50 \text{ mL} \div 0.5 \text{ hr} = 100 \text{ mL/hr}$$

Part 2. Calculate the amount of drug given per hour.

$$500 \text{ mg} \div 0.5 \text{ hr} = 1000 \text{ mg/hr}$$

✓ *Self-check your problem set work at* www.emcp.com.

Answer the following questions.

1. A liter IV bag is running at 50 mL/hr. How long will it last?

2. A liter bag of fluid is hung at 7 P.M. and runs at 100 mL/hr. How long will it last?

3. A 500 mL bag of IV fluid is running at 30 mL/hr. How long will it last?

4. If a patient is given 60 mg of medication in 75 mL over 45 minutes, what is the flow rate in milliliters per hour?

5. A patient receives 20,000 units of heparin in an IV of 100 mL over 45 minutes. What is the flow rate in milliliters per hour?

6. A patient is to receive 2 g of medication in 150 mL over 90 minutes. What is the flow rate in milliliters per hour?

7. The physican has ordered 2800 mL every 24 hours. At what rate should the pump be set in milliliters per hour?

8. A patient is to receive 250 mL over 30 minutes. How many milliliters per hour should the pump be set to?

9. If 500 mL is to be administered over 4 hours, what is the infusion rate in milliliters per hour?

10. If 2000 mL is to be administered over 8 hours, what is the infusion rate in milliliters per hour?

11. A fluid volume of 500 mL is to be given over 2 hours. What is the rate in milliliters per hour?

12. A patient has orders for 500 mL $D_5W\frac{1}{2}NS$ and KVO (keep vein open). The flow rate will be 15 mL/hr. How long will the 500 mL IV bag last if no changes are made in the next 24 hours?

13. A patient is to be given 1 L of $D_5W\frac{1}{2}NS$ + 20 mEq KCl at the rate of 125 mL/hr.
    a. How long will a single bag last the patient?

    b. How many 1 L bags will be needed for this patient for the next 24 hours?

14. A patient is receiving lactated Ringer's at 150 mL/hr. A 1 L bag is started at 7 A.M. from the nursing stock drawer. How many additional bags will the patient need to have to last the rest of this day and until 6 P.M. the following day?

15. A patient is to have three 1 L bags of NS in the next 24 hours. What is the rate in milliliters per hour?

Complete the following table.

#	Rate in mL/hr	Quantity of 1 L bags needed in 24 hr (Round up to nearest 1 L bag)
16.	50 mL/hr	
17.	75 mL/hr	
18.	100 mL/hr	
19.	120 mL/hr	
20.	125 mL/hr	
21.	130 mL/hr	
22.	150 mL/hr	
23.	175 mL/hr	
24.	200 mL/hr	
25.	225 mL/hr	

Interpret the following prescriptions and provide the requested rates.

26. Medication: Solu-Cortef (hydrocortisone) 250 mg
    Fluid volume: 250 mL
    Time of infusion: 4 hr
    How many (a) milliliters per hour? _____

    (b) milligrams per hour? _____

27. Medication: penicillin G 12 million units
    Fluid volume: 500 mL
    Time of infusion: 12 hr
    How many (a) milliliters per hour? _____

    (b) units per hour? _____

28. Medication: 4:1 (4 mg/mL) lidocaine
    Dose: 6 mg/hr
    How many (a) milliliters per hour? _____

    (b) micrograms per hour? _____

29. Medication: Solu-Medrol (methylprednisolone)
    250 mg
    Dose: 20 mg/hr
    Fluid volume: 500 mL
    How many (a) milliliters per hour? _____

    (b) grams per hour? _____

30. Medication: dopamine 40 mg
    Dose: 1 mg/min
    Fluid volume: 500 mL
    How many (a) milliliters per hour? _____

    (b) milligrams per hour? _____

31. Medication: Intropin (dopamine hydrochloride)
    800 mg
    Dose: 12 mcg/kg/min
    Patient weight: 198 lb
    Fluid volume: 500 mL
    How many (a) milliliters per hour? _____

    (b) milligrams per hour? _____

32. Medication: gentamicin 480,000 mcg
    Dose: 4 mcg/kg/min
    Patient weight: 176 lb
    Fluid volume: 750 mL
    How many (a) milliliters per hour? _____

    (b) milligrams per hour? _____

7.3 DROP SETS AND INFUSION RATES

Pharmacy staff and the nursing staff are responsible for calculating the rate of administration for IV fluids in a drops per minute rate (expressed as gtt/min). The nursing staff will use this rate to manually adjust the IV flow at the drop chamber or set the electronic infusion pump at the patient's bedside. The rate in drops per minute can be calculated manually by counting the number of drops of fluid that fall into the drip chamber over a minute. The nurse can then manually adjust the rate up or down by using a clamp on the IV tubing. Most inpatient facilities now utilize electronic infusion pumps to regulate both the volume and the rate of a patient's IV medication. The rate can be adjusted digitally, while the pump uses a clamp to adjust the rate at which the fluid flows through tubing routed through a chamber in the pump. Pumps can be set to give IV fluids in milliliters per hour or drops per minute.

Calculating the flow rate in drops per minute is complicated by the variety of IV sets available. Manufacturers produce calibrated IV tube sets that have different size drops. An IV set is identified by the number of drops it takes to make 1 mL. This calibration is referred to as a **drop set** or a drip set. The most common sets are 10, 15, 20, and 60, meaning 10 gtt/mL, 15 gtt/mL, 20 gtt/mL, and 60 gtt/mL, respectively. The drop sizes for the 10, 15, and 20 calibrations produce macrodrops, and the 60 calibration produces microdrops. The 60 gtt/mL set is called a **mini-drip set.** Figure 7.1 illustrates these different drop sizes. When an IV is started for a patient, the drop set for the IV set tubing will be printed in prominent type on the outside of the IV set package.

The 10 drop and 15 drop sets are commonly used for adult patients, while the 60 drop set is used for pediatric patients or critically ill patients who are being given medications that have a narrow therapeutic window.

drop set
the number of drops an IV set takes to make 1 mL; also called drip set

mini-drip set
a drop set at a rate of 60 gtt/mL

Remember

The abbreviation gtt comes from the Latin word *guttae,* which means "drops."

Figure 7.1

IV Drop Sets

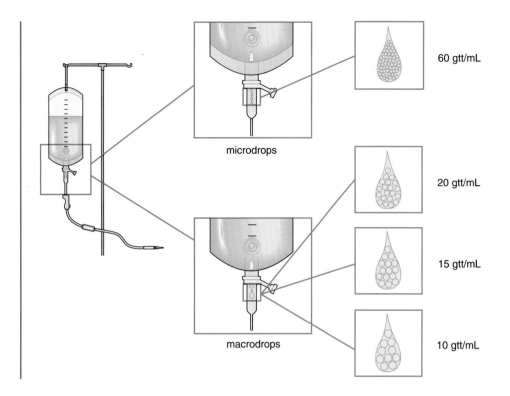

microdrops

60 gtt/mL

20 gtt/mL

15 gtt/mL

macrodrops

10 gtt/mL

To determine the rate in drops per minute at which the IV fluid is to be infused, the volume of fluid, delivery time, and calibration of the administration set must be known. The following formula is used.

$$x \text{ gtt/min} = \frac{(\text{volume of fluid} \div \text{delivery time}) \times (\text{drop rate of administration set used})}{60 \text{ min/hr}}$$

The following examples will demonstrate the use of this formula and will also show how the dimensional analysis method can be used to solve these problems.

Example 7.3.1   **If an IV is running at 60 mL/hr, what is the rate in drops per minute using a 15 drop set?**

Solution 1: Insert the values from the problem statement into the formula to determine the drops per minute. Remember that a 15 drop set runs at a rate of 15 gtt/mL.

$$x \text{ gtt/min} = \frac{(\text{volume of fluid} \div \text{delivery time}) \times (\text{set drop rate})}{60 \text{ min/hr}}$$

$$x \text{ gtt/min} = \frac{(60 \text{ mL} \div 1 \text{ hr}) \times (15 \text{ gtt/mL})}{60 \text{ min/hr}} = 15 \text{ gtt/min}$$

Solution 2: This problem can also be solved using the dimensional analysis method.

$$x \text{ gtt/min} = 60 \text{ mL/hr} \times 15 \text{ gtt/mL} \times 1 \text{ hr/60 min} = 15 \text{ gtt/min}$$

Example 7.3.2   **If 500 mg of a drug is to be administered from a 50 mL minibag over 30 minutes using a 15 drop set, how many drops per minute is that?**

Solution 1: Begin by identifying the amounts to insert into the equation.

> Volume of fluid = 50 mL
> Fluid delivery time = 30 min = 0.5 hr
> Drop rate of administration set = 15 gtt/mL

Insert the values from the problem statement into the formula to determine the drops per minute rate.

$$x \text{ gtt/min} = \frac{(\text{volume of fluid} \div \text{delivery time}) \times (\text{set drop rate})}{60 \text{ min/hr}}$$

$$x \text{ gtt/min} = \frac{(50 \text{ mL} \div 0.5 \text{ hr}) \times (15 \text{ gtt/mL})}{60 \text{ min/hr}} = 25 \text{ gtt/min}$$

Solution 2: This problem can also be solved using the dimensional analysis method.

$$x \text{ gtt/min} = 50 \text{ mL/0.5 hr} \times 15 \text{ gtt/mL} \times 1 \text{ hr/60 min} = 25 \text{ gtt/min}$$

Example 7.3.3   **You are to prepare 750 mg of medication in 75 mL for infusion over 30 minutes, using a 10 drop set. How many drops per minute will that be?**

Solution 1: Begin by identifying the amounts to insert into the equation.

> Volume of fluid = 75 mL
> Fluid delivery time = 30 min = 0.5 hr
> Drop rate of administration set = 10 gtt/mL

Insert the values from the problem statement into the formula to determine the drops per minute rate.

$$x \text{ gtt/min} = \frac{(\text{volume of fluid} \div \text{delivery time}) \times (\text{set drop rate})}{60 \text{ min/hr}}$$

$$x \text{ gtt/min} = \frac{(75 \text{ mL} \div 0.5 \text{ hr}) \times (10 \text{ gtt/mL})}{60 \text{ min/hr}} = 25 \text{ gtt/min}$$

Solution 2: This problem can also be solved using the dimensional analysis method.

$$x \text{ gtt/min} = 75 \text{ mL/0.5 hr} \times 10 \text{ gtt/mL} \times 1 \text{ hr/60 min} = 25 \text{ gtt/min}$$

Other calculations are done in the hospital pharmacy to calculate infusion time, amount of liquid to be delivered in an infusion, and amount of drug to be infused. These problems can be solved by using the dimensional analysis method. The following examples will demonstrate some of these important calculations.

Example 7.3.4 **An IV flow rate is set at 50 gtt/min. Using a 10 drop set, what is the flow rate in milliliters per hour?**

Solution 1: Using the ratio-proportion method, calculate the amount of milliliters in 50 gtt/min.

$$\frac{x \text{ mL}}{50 \text{ gtt/min}} = \frac{1 \text{ mL}}{10 \text{ gtt/min}}$$

$$x \text{ mL} = 5 \text{ mL/min}$$

Then, determine the number of milliliters delivered in 1 hour, which is equal to 60 minutes.

$$\frac{x \text{ mL}}{60 \text{ min}} = \frac{5 \text{ mL}}{1 \text{ min}}$$

$$x \text{ mL} = 300 \text{ mL}$$

Solution 2: This problem can also be solved by using the dimensional analysis method.

$$x \text{ mL/hr} = 1 \text{ mL}/10 \text{ gtt} \times 50 \text{ gtt/min} \times 60 \text{ min/hr} = 300 \text{ mL/hr}$$

Example 7.3.5 **If there is a flow rate of 40 gtt/min using a 15 drop set, how many liters will be delivered over 24 hours?**

Solution 1: Calculate the milliliters given each minute.

$$\frac{40 \text{ gtt}}{\text{min}} \times \frac{1 \text{ mL}}{15 \text{ gtt}} = \frac{2.67 \text{ mL}}{\text{min}}$$

Use this rate to determine how many milliliters will be given in an hour.

$$2.67 \text{ mL} \times 60 \text{ min/hr} = 160.2 \text{ mL/hr}$$

Finally, calculate the number of milliliters in a day.

$$160.2 \text{ mL/hr} \times 24 \text{ hr} = 3844.8 \text{ mL}, \text{ which is converted to } 3.84 \text{ L}$$

Solution 2: This problem can also be calculated using the dimensional analysis method.

$$x \text{ L} = 24 \text{ hr} \times 60 \text{ min/hr} \times 40 \text{ gtt/min} \times 1 \text{ mL}/15 \text{ gtt} \times 1 \text{ L}/1000 \text{ mL} = 3.84 \text{ L}$$

Example 7.3.6 **If a patient is receiving 20 mEq of KCl in 1 L NS and a 10 drop set is used at a rate of 50 gtt/min, how long will the 1 L bag take to infuse?**

Solution 1: Calculate the milliliters given each minute.

$$\frac{50 \text{ gtt}}{\text{min}} \times \frac{1 \text{ mL}}{10 \text{ gtt}} = \frac{5 \text{ mL}}{\text{min}}$$

Use this rate to determine how many milliliters will be given in an hour.

$$5 \text{ mL/min} \times 60 \text{ min/hr} = 300 \text{ mL/hr}$$

Finally, determine how long a 1 L bag will take to infuse at this rate.

$$1000 \text{ mL} \times 1 \text{ hr/300 mL} = 3.33 \text{ hr, or 3 hr}$$

Solution 2: This problem can also be solved using the dimensional analysis method.

$$1 \text{ L} \times 1000 \text{ mL/L} \times 10 \text{ gtt/mL} \times 1 \text{ min/50 gtt} \times 1 \text{ hr/60 min} = 3.33 \text{ hr, or 3 hr}$$

Example 7.3.7   **A patient is getting D$_{10}$W infused at 50 mL/hr using a 10 drop set. What is the drops per minute rate, and how many grams of dextrose is the patient receiving per hour?**

Calculate the drops per minute using dimensional analysis. Note that the drop set is running at a rate of 10 gtt/mL.

$$\frac{1 \text{ hr}}{60 \text{ min}} \times \frac{50 \text{ mL}}{\text{hr}} \times \frac{10 \text{ gtt}}{\text{mL}} = \frac{8.33 \text{ gtt}}{\text{min}}$$

Set up a proportion to determine the grams of dextrose the patient is receiving in an hour from the D$_{10}$W (10 g/100 mL) at a rate of 50 mL/hr.

$$\frac{x \text{ g dextrose}}{50 \text{ mL}} = \frac{10 \text{ g}}{100 \text{ mL}}$$

$$x \text{ g dextrose} = 5 \text{ g}$$

Example 7.3.8   **A physician orders 150 mg of a drug in a 50 mL bag over one hour, using a 15 drop set. How many drops per minute will that be, and how many micrograms of the drug will be in each drop?**

Calculate the drops per minute, using dimensional analysis.

$$x \text{ gtt/min} = 1 \text{ hr/60 min} \times 50 \text{ mL/hr} \times 15 \text{ gtt/mL} = 12.5 \text{ gtt/min}$$

Now, set up a proportion to determine the amount of drug that will be contained in each drop.

$$\frac{x \text{ mg}}{1 \text{ mL}} = \frac{150 \text{ mg}}{50 \text{ mL}}$$

$$x \text{ mg} = 3 \text{ mg/mL}$$

This can be expressed as follows.

$$x \text{ mg} = 3 \text{ mg/15 gtt} = 0.2 \text{ mg/gtt} = 200 \text{ mcg/gtt}$$

The dimensional analysis method can also be used.

$$x \text{ mcg/gtt} = 1 \text{ mL/15 gtt} \times 150 \text{ mg/50 mL} \times 1000 \text{ mcg/mg} = 200 \text{ mcg/gtt}$$

Example 7.3.9   **A patient is getting 16 mEq KCl in 250 mL D$_5$W. A 10 drop set is being used. How many milliequivalents are in each drop?**

Solution 1: Set up a proportion to determine the number of milliequivalents in 1 mL.

$$\frac{x \text{ mEq}}{1 \text{ mL}} = \frac{16 \text{ mEq}}{250 \text{ mL}}$$

$$x \text{ mEq} = 0.064 \text{ mEq/mL}$$

Convert this to milliequivalents in each drop, using the given drop set.

$$0.064 \text{ mEq/mL} \times 1 \text{ mL/10 gtt} = 0.0064 \text{ mEq/gtt}$$

Solution 2: Using the dimensional analysis method,

$$x \text{ mEq/gtt} = 1 \text{ mL/10 gtt} \times 16 \text{ mEq/250 mL} = 0.0064 \text{ mEq/gtt}$$

Problem Set 7.3 _____

✓ *Self-check your problem set work at* www.emcp.com.

Calculate the following.

1. An IV rate is 10 mL/hr. If a 10 drop set is used, what will the rate be in drops per minute?

2. What is the IV flow rate in drops per minute for a child who is receiving 35 mL/hr using a 60 drop set?

3. A patient is to receive 1 g of medication in 100 mL over one hour using a 10 drop set. What is the rate in drops per minute?

4. The nurse will be administering 500 mg of medication in 50 mL over 30 minutes, using a mini-drip set. What is the flow rate in drops per minute?

5. The patient receives 20,000 units of heparin in an IV of 100 mL over 45 minutes. Using a 15 drop set, what is the drops per minute rate?

6. A physician orders 750 mg of a drug in a 100 mL bag over one hour, using a 15 drop set. How many drops per minute will that be?

7. A patient is to be given 1000 mL of LR at 50 mL/hr. What will the drop rate be for a 15 drop set?

8. A patient is to be given 1750 mL at 95 mL/hr. What will the drop rate be if a 15 drop set is used?

9. A physician orders 500 mg of a drug in 50 mL to be given in 30 minutes. If a 10 drop set is used, what will the drop rate be?

10. A patient is to receive 2 g of medication in a liter of NS over 8 hours. If a 15 drop set is used, what will the drop rate be?

11. A patient is to receive 250 mL over 30 minutes using a 15 drop set. How many drops per minute are to be given?

12. A patient is to receive 120 mL/hr. If a 10 drop set is used, what will the drops per minute rate be?

13. If 500 mL is administered at 30 gtt/min using a 10 drop set, what is the flow rate in milliliters per hour?

14. An IV flow rate is set at 45 gtt/min. If a 15 drop set is used, what is the flow rate in milliliters per hour?

15. If 500 mL is administered at 30 gtt/min using a 10 drop set, what is the flow rate in milliliters per hour?

16. The nurse is to administer 750 mL at 30 gtt/min, using a 15 drop set. What is the infusion rate in milliliters per hour?

17. A patient is getting 24 mEq KCl in 500 mL D_5W. A 10 drop set is being used. How many milliequivalents are in each drop?

18. A patient is to be given 1 L of D_5WNS + 1 mEq KCl at the rate of 125 mL/hr.
    a. What will the drops per minute rate be if a 10 drop set is used?

    b. What will the drops per minute rate be if a 15 drop set is used?

c. What will the drops per minute rate be if a 60 drop set is used?

19. A patient is receiving 30 mEq of KCl in 1 L NS, and a 15 drop set is used to deliver 23 gtt/min.
    a. How long will the 1 L bag take to infuse?

    b. How many milliequivalents will the patient be receiving each hour?

20. A patient is getting $D_{10}W$ infused at 50 mL/hr using a 10 drop set.
    a. What is the drops per minute rate?

    b. How many grams of dextrose is the patient receiving per hour?

21. A physician orders 400 mg of a drug in a 100 mL bag over one hour, using a 15 drop set.
    a. How many drops per minute will that be?

    b. How many micrograms will be administered per drop?

7.4 IV PIGGYBACKS

Sometimes, a patient requires only a small amount of fluid for a short period of time. For example, a physician may order that a small volume of fluid and medication be given over a short period of time to improve a clinical outcome. Often drugs are given this way, diluted in IV fluid, in what is called an **IV piggyback (IVPB)**; the drug in solution is administered from a separate IV bag but through the main IV line, interrupting or blending with the first IV. This medication can be given as a onetime dose or intermittently throughout the day. For example, an antibiotic might be given in three doses spread throughout a 24-hour period. The same method used to determine a rate for continual administration of IV fluids can be applied to IVPB solutions. When doing the calculation, it is important to include both the initial volume in an IVPB and the volume that may be added via syringe to the IVPB as an admixture.

> **IV piggyback (IVPB)** a small volume of fluid and medication that is given intravenously in addition to a primary infusion over a short period of time

If the volume of the IVPB is 40 mL or less, typically no changes are made in the flow of the primary IV fluid for adult patients. For amounts greater than 40 mL, however, the flow rate may need to be recalculated to ensure that the patient receives the ordered fluids in the time period specified by the physician. To calculate an adjusted rate in milliliters per hour or drops per minute, the volume remaining in the main IV container is usually checked and then divided by the hours remaining before the next container is to be started.

The following examples demonstrate the basic IVPB calculations.

Chapter 7 • **Preparing Intravenous Medications**

Example 7.4.1   The physician orders 1 g of cefamandole to be infused every 4 hours. It is available as 250 mg/mL. The order indicates that the medication should be given in 100 mL D₅W using a 10 drop set over 45 minutes. What is the rate of infusion?

Step 1. Convert 250 mg to grams, or 0.25 g.
Step 2. Determine how much cefamandole is needed from the vial.

$$\frac{x \text{ mL cefamandole}}{1 \text{ g}} = \frac{1 \text{ mL}}{0.25 \text{ g}}$$

$$x \text{ mL} = 4 \text{ mL}$$

Step 3. Determine the total volume of the fluid to be infused.

$$4 \text{ mL} + 100 \text{ mL} = 104 \text{ mL}$$

Step 4. Determine the infusion rate.

$$x \text{ gtt/min} = \frac{\text{volume of fluid} \times \text{gtt/mL}}{\text{time of infusion}}$$

$$= \frac{104 \text{ mL} \times 10 \text{ gtt/mL}}{45 \text{ min}}$$

$$= 23.1 \text{ gtt/min}$$

Example 7.4.2   The order calls for 20 mg of premixed famotidine to be given in 50 mL IVPB Q12 hours. It is to be administered using a 15 drop set and is to be given over 20 minutes. What is the rate of infusion?

$$x \text{ gtt/min} = \frac{\text{volume of fluid} \times \text{gtt/mL}}{\text{time of infusion}}$$

$$= \frac{50 \text{ mL} \times 15 \text{ gtt/mL}}{20 \text{ min}}$$

$$= 37.5 \text{ gtt/min}$$

Example 7.4.3   The order calls for 1 g of the premixed drug nafcillin to be given in 100 mL IVPB Q6h. Using a 10 drop set, it should be administered over 30 minutes. What is the infusion rate?

$$x \text{ gtt/min} = \frac{100 \text{ mL} \times 10 \text{ gtt/mL}}{30 \text{ min}}$$

$$= 33.3 \text{ gtt/min}$$

Example 7.4.4   A patient weighing 148 lb is to receive tobramycin 2 mg/kg/dose in 50 mL IVPB. A 15 drop set has been ordered, and the drug is to be given over 30 minutes. The following label shows the drug to be used. What is the appropriate infusion rate?

NDC 0000-0000-00
TOBRAMYCIN
Injection, USP equivalent to
40 mg/mL
30 mL multiple dose vial
For IV use. R_x only

Step 1. Convert the patient's weight to kilograms.

148 lb $\times$ 1 kg/2.2 lb = 67.2727 kg, rounded to 67.3 kg

Step 2. Calculate the tobramycin dose by multiplying the patient's weight in kilograms by the amount per kilogram in the order.

67.3 kg $\times$ 2 mg/kg = 134.6 mg

Step 3. Calculate the amount of tobramycin concentrate to be added to the bag.

$$\frac{x \text{ mL}}{134.6 \text{ mg}} = \frac{1 \text{ mL}}{40 \text{ mg}}$$

$$x \text{ mL} = 3.4 \text{ mL}$$

Step 4. Determine the total volume to be infused.

3.4 mL concentrate + 50 mL = 53.4 mL

Step 5. Determine the infusion rate.

$$x \text{ gtt/min} = \frac{53.4 \text{ mL} \times 15 \text{ gtt/mL}}{30 \text{ min}}$$

$$= 26.7 \text{ gtt/min, rounded to 27 gtt/min}$$

INTERNET **RESOURCE** *center*

Problem Set 7.4 _____

✓ *Self-check your problem set work at* www.emcp.com.

Determine the infusion rates in drops per minute for the following orders.

1. Give 50 mL over 15 minutes using a 10 drop set.

2. Give 100 mL over 20 minutes using a 15 drop set.

3. Give 50 mL over 30 minutes using a 15 drop set.

4. Give 60 mL over 30 minutes using a 10 drop set.

5. Give 55 mL over 20 minutes using a 15 drop set.

6. Give 63 mL over 15 minutes using a 15 drop set.

7. Give 58 mL over 15 minutes using a 15 drop set

8. Give 61 mL over 25 minutes using a 10 drop set.

Calculate the following doses in milliliters and then determine the infusion rate.

9. Medication order: ceftriaxone 2 g once daily over 20 min
   Available stock: ceftriaxone 2 g in 50 mL premixed; 15 drop set

10. Medication order: cefotetan 2 g Q12 hours over 30 min
    Available stock: cefotetan 2 g in 50 mL; 10 drop set

11. Medication order: penicillin G 3 million units Q4 hours over 15 min
    Available stock: penicillin G 3 million units in 50 mL premixed; 15 drop set

12. Medication order: acyclovir 10 mg/kg Q8 hours over 20 min; patient weighs 169 lb
    Available stock: acyclovir 50 mg/mL; 50 mL minibag; 15 drop set

13. Medication order: ceftazolin 2 g Q8 hours over 25 min
    Available stock: cefazolin 2 g in 50 mL premixed; 10 drop set

14. Medication order: cefoperazone 2 g once daily over 30 min
    Available: cefoperazone 2 g in 50 mL premixed; 15 drop set

15. Medication order: cefotetan 1 g once daily over 30 min
    Available stock: cefotetan 1 g in 50 mL premixed; 60 drop set

Express the following percentages.

1. Express betaxolol ophthalmic solution 0.25% as a weight-in-volume percentage.

2. Express hexachlorophene 3% emulsion as a weight-in-volume percentage.

Calculate the following.

3. If there are 500 mg in a 1 tsp dose, what percentage is this?

4. If there are 80 g of dextrose in a 1 L IV bag, what is the percentage?

Calculate the percentage of drug in the following drug formulations.

5. valproic acid 250 mg/5 mL

6. potassium chloride 1.48 g per 4 L

Calculate the amount of medication in the following doses.

7. How many grams of sodium chloride are in 3 L of NS?

8. How many milligrams are in 1 tsp of an 8% drug product?

Answer the following questions.

9. An IV fluid is running at 125 mL/hr. How long will a liter last?

10. A 100 mL bag is set to run at 150 mL/hr. If it is started at 7 A.M., when will it run out?

11. If 125 mL is to be given over 15 minutes, what is the rate of infusion in milliliters per minute?

12. A patient is receiving NS at 100 mL/hr. If a 1 L bag is started at 10 A.M. upon admission, what time will it run out?

Interpret the following prescriptions and provide the requested rates.

13. Medication: vancomycin 2 g
    Fluid volume: 250 mL
    Time of infusion: 1 hr, 30 min
    How many (a) milliliters per hour? _____

    (b) milligrams per hour? _____

14. Medication: aminophylline 1 g
    Fluid volume: 500 mL
    Time of infusion: 8 hr
    How many (a) milliliters per hour? _____

    (b) milligrams per hour? _____

15. Medication: nitroprusside 50 mg
    Dose: 5 mcg/kg/min
    Patient weight: 143 lb
    Fluid volume: 250 mL
    How many (a) milliliters per hour? _____

    (b) milligrams per hour? _____

Calculate the following.

16. A child is receiving 20 mL/hr with a mini-drip set. How many drops per minute are administered?

17. An IV is to flow at 60 mL/hr using a 10 drop set. How many drops per minute are administered?

18. A physician orders 750 mg of a drug in a 100 mL bag over 30 minutes. Using a 10 drop set, how many drops per minute is that?

19. If there is a flow rate of 24 gtt/min using a 15 drop set, how many liters will be delivered over 24 hours?

20. If a patient is getting an IV solution at 30 gtt/min and a 10 drop set is used, how long will a 1 L bag of NS last?

Determine the infusion rates in drops per minute for the following orders.

21. Give 105 mL over 30 minutes using a 10 drop set.

22. Give 100 mL over 15 minutes using a 10 drop set.

Calculate the following doses in milliliters and then determine the infusion rate.

23. Medication order: ceftriaxone 2 g once daily over 60 min
Available stock: ceftriaxone 2 g in 50 mL premixed; 60 drop set

24. Medication order: pentamidine 4 mg/kg/dose once daily over 30 min; patient weighs 173 lb
Available stock: pentamidine 300 mg/4 mL; 50 mL minibag; 15 drop set

Using Special Calculations in Compounding

Objectives

- Calculate the amount of drug in a final product that has been diluted.
- Calculate the amount of concentrate and diluent needed to make a desired concentration.
- Calculate the amount of two products needed to prepare a desired concentration.
- Determine the least weighable quantity on a balance with a known accuracy and a given margin of error.
- Recognize when a diluent must be added to an ingredient for weighing and measuring purposes.
- Determine the amount of an aliquot in measuring diluted substances.

8.1 CONCENTRATIONS AND DILUTIONS

concentrate
a highly condensed drug product that is diluted prior to administration

dilution
the product obtained when an inactive ingredient, a diluent, is added to a concentrate

diluent
an inactive substance that is added to a concentrate to make it less concentrated; can be a vehicle or a solvent

Safety Note

An injected dose generally has a volume greater than 0.1 mL and less than 1 mL.

Pharmaceutical preparations come in different strengths to meet the various dosing needs of patients. A **concentrate** is a highly condensed drug product that most often must be diluted for dispensing or administration. A **dilution** is the product obtained when an inactive ingredient, a **diluent,** is added to a concentrate. A diluent, which can be a vehicle or a solvent, is the inactive part of a solution or a mixture and serves to make the resulting solution or mixture less concentrated. A solution results when a solute and solvent mix and the solute is completely dissolved into the solvent.

Medications may be diluted for several reasons. They are sometimes diluted prior to administration to children, infants, and the elderly to meet the dosing requirements of those patients. Medications may also be diluted so that they can be measured more accurately and easily. For example, volumes less than 0.1 mL are usually considered too small to measure accurately. Therefore, the preparation must be diluted further. Many pharmacies have a policy for how much an injection can be diluted. A rule of thumb is that the required dose should have a volume greater than 0.1 mL and less than 1 mL. Accuracy of a weight is dependent on the accuracy of the balance used, as will be discussed later in this chapter.

The following examples will demonstrate the method for solving typical dilution problems. For each, the first step is to use the ratio-proportion method to solve for the volume of the final product by using a ratio of diluted solution to desired concentration. The second step is to determine the amount of diluent simply by subtracting the concentrate from the total volume. Both of these volumes are approximate because they depend on the calibration and accuracy of the measuring devices used.

Typically, the ratio-proportion method is preferred over the dimensional analysis method to solve these problems because it is easier to identify the parts of the equation with the ratio-proportion method.

Although the second step uses subtraction to determine the amount of diluent added, the amount will actually be determined by adding "up to" the desired total quantity. The abbreviation QS for "sufficient quantity" is used to describe the process of adding enough of the last ingredient in a compound to reach the desired volume. It is helpful to calculate the necessary amount beforehand so that an adequate supply of medication is available.

Example 8.1.1

Dexamethasone is available as a 4 mg/mL preparation; an infant is to receive 0.35 mg. Prepare a dilution so that the final concentration is 1 mg/mL. How much diluent will you need if the original product is in a 1 mL vial and you dilute the entire vial?

Step 1. Determine the volume (in milliliters) of the final product. Since the strength of the dexamethasone is 4 mg/mL, a 1 mL vial will contain 4 mg of the active ingredient. Then, for a final volume x of solution, you will have a concentration of $(4/x)$ mg/mL.

Diluted solution   **Desired concentration**

$$\frac{x \text{ mL}}{4 \text{ mg}} = \frac{1 \text{ mL}}{1 \text{ mg}}$$

$$x \text{ mL} = \frac{(4 \text{ mg} \times 1 \text{ mL})}{1 \text{ mg}}$$

$$x \text{ mL} = 4 \text{ mL final product}$$

Step 2. Subtract the volume of the concentrate from the total volume to determine the volume of diluent needed.

4 mL total volume − 1 mL concentrate = 3 mL diluent needed

Therefore, an additional 3 mL of diluent are needed to dilute the original 1 mL of preparation to arrive at a final concentration of 1 mg/mL.

Example 8.1.2

You are instructed to make 1000 mL of a 0.8% w/v solution. You have in stock a concentrate of 95% w/v. How much of the concentrate will you use, and how much diluent will be needed?

Step 1. Determine how many grams there will be in the final product so that you can determine the strength of the solution.

$$\frac{x \text{ g}}{1000 \text{ mL}} = \frac{0.8 \text{ g}}{100 \text{ mL}}$$

$$x \text{ g} = \frac{(1000 \text{ mL}) \times 0.8 \text{ g}}{100 \text{ mL}}$$

$$x \text{ g} = 8 \text{ g in final product}$$

Step 2. Determine how much of the 95% w/v concentrate will be required to provide the desired number of grams.

$$\frac{x \text{ mL}}{8 \text{ g}} = \frac{100 \text{ mL}}{95 \text{ g}}$$

$$x \text{ mL} = \frac{(8 \text{ g}) \times 100 \text{ mL}}{95 \text{ g}}$$

$$x \text{ mL} = 8.42 \text{ mL concentrate}$$

Step 3. Determine how many milliliters of diluent you will need to add to make an 0.8% solution.

1000 mL total volume − 8.42 mL concentrate = 991.58 mL diluent

Example 8.1.3   **You are instructed to make 240 mL of a 0.45% w/v solution. You have a 100% w/v concentrate in stock. How much of the concentrate will you use, and how much diluent will be needed?**

Step 1. Determine the number of grams desired in the final solution.

$$\frac{x \text{ g}}{240 \text{ mL}} = \frac{0.45 \text{ g}}{100 \text{ mL}}$$

$$x \text{ g} = \frac{(240 \text{ mL}) \times 0.45 \text{ g}}{100 \text{ mL}}$$

$$x \text{ g} = 1.08 \text{ g}$$

Step 2. Determine how much of the concentrated solution will be required to provide the desired number of grams.

$$\frac{x \text{ mL}}{1.08 \text{ g}} = \frac{100 \text{ mL}}{100 \text{ g}} = \frac{1 \text{ mL}}{1 \text{ g}}$$

$$x \text{ mL} = 1.08 \text{ mL}$$

Step 3. Determine how many milliliters of diluent will be needed.

240 mL total volume − 1.08 mL concentrate = 238.92 mL diluent

Example 8.1.4   **You are instructed to make 500 mL of a 1:500 w/v solution. You have in stock a concentrate of 80% w/v. How much of the concentrate will you use, and how much diluent will be needed?**

Step 1. Start by determining how many grams should be in the final solution.

$$\frac{x \text{ g}}{500 \text{ mL}} = \frac{1 \text{ g}}{500 \text{ mL}}$$

$$x \text{ g} = 1 \text{ g}$$

Step 2. Determine how many milliliters of the concentrate will be required to provide the desired number of grams.

$$\frac{x \text{ mL}}{1 \text{ g}} = \frac{100 \text{ mL}}{80 \text{ g}}$$

$$x \text{ mL} = 1.25 \text{ mL}$$

Step 3. Now you can determine how many milliliters of diluent will be needed.

500 mL total volume − 1.25 mL concentrate = 498.75 mL diluent

Problem Set 8.1 _____

✓ *Self-check your problem set work at* www.emcp.com.

Calculate the amount of concentrate and diluent for each of the following compounds. Round to the hundredth place for this problem set. Remember that the actual amount measured will be *approximate* due to equipment constraints.

1. Prepare 3 mL of a 10 mg/mL phenobarbital solution from a 65 mg/mL stock solution that comes in a 1 mL vial. How much concentrate and how much diluent are needed to obtain the desired final volume?

2. A drug is supplied as a 40 mg/mL solution in a 50 mL vial. You need to make 10 mL of a 10 mg/mL solution. How much concentrate and diluent will be needed?

3. Folic acid is commonly available as a 5 mg/mL injection. You are to make a preparation that contains 50 mcg/mL in a total volume of 30 mL. How much folic acid and how much diluent must be used?

4. Prepare 10 mL of a 200 mcg/mL folic acid solution by using a 5 mg/mL stock solution. How much folic acid and how much diluent will you need?

5. Prepare 20 mL of a 5 mg/mL tobramycin solution from a 40 mg/mL stock solution. How much tobramycin and how much diluent are needed?

6. Prepare 10 mL of a 50 mg/mL methicillin solution from a stock solution of 250 mg/0.5 mL. How much methicillin and how much diluent are needed?

7. Make 20 mL of a 100 mcg/mL vitamin B_{12} solution from a 1 mg/mL stock solution. How much B_{12} and diluent are needed?

8. Prepare 8 mL of a 5 mg/mL hydrocortisone solution from a 100 mg/2 mL stock solution. How many milliliters of hydrocortisone and diluent are needed?

9. Prepare 15 mL of a 50 mg/mL cefazolin dilution from a stock of 1 g/5 mL. How many milliliters of diluent and stock solution will be needed?

10. Prepare one dose of 0.6 mg gentamicin in 2 mL diluted from a stock solution of 20 mg/mL. How much gentamicin and how much diluent are used?

11. A drug comes packaged as 10 mg/mL. Make a preparation totaling 25 mL of 2 mg/mL concentration. How much drug and how much diluent are used?

12. Nafcillin comes packaged as a powder for constitution at 250 mg/mL. Prepare 20 mL of a 25 mg/mL dilution. How many milligrams of the drug and what volume of diluent are needed?

13. Metoclopramide 5 mg/mL is used to make 10 mL of 0.5 mg/mL solution. What volume of drug and how much diluent are required?

14. Prepare 20 mL of a 50 mg/mL drug dilution from a stock of 2 g/5 mL. How many milliliters of diluent and stock drug solution will be needed?

15. Prepare a 10 mcg/mL solution of a drug with a final volume of 3 mL. How many milliliters of stock drug (50 mcg/mL) will be needed?

16. Prepare 5 mL of a 5 mcg/mL dilution from a stock drug of 50 mcg/mL. How much drug and diluent are needed?

17. You receive an order for 100 mL of a 30% hydrochloric acid solution. You have a 90% solution in stock. How many milliliters of concentrate will you need?

18. A patient needs 10 mL of 4 mcg/mL magnesium sulfate solution. You have 10 mcg/mL on hand.
    a. How much concentrate will you need?

    b. How much diluent?

19. You need 5 mL of heparin 100 units/mL. In stock you have 10,000 units/mL in a 20 mL vial.
    a. How much concentrate will you need?

    b. How much diluent?

20. An order calls for 5 mL of 50 mg/mL Terramycin. On hand you have 200 mg/mL Terramycin.
    a. How much concentrate will you need?

    b. How much diluent?

21. A doctor orders 2 mL of 80 mg/mL tobramycin. The pharmacy stocks 160 mg/mL.
    a. How much concentrate will you need?

    b. How much diluent?

22. An IV of 0.45% sodium chloride 1000 mL needs to be infused. The pharmacy carries only 0.9% sodium chloride 1000 mL.
    a. How much concentrate will you need?

    b. How much diluent?

23. You need 50 mL of 5% dextrose for a patient. You have 70% dextrose 1000 mL on hand.
    a. How much concentrate will you need?

    b. How much diluent?

24. A patient needs 35% dextrose 500 mL. The pharmacy has only 70% dextrose 1000 mL.
    a. How much concentrate will you need?

    b. How much diluent?

25. An IV order calls for 300 mL of Liposyn 10%. The only Liposyn in stock is Liposyn 20%.
    a. How much concentrate will you need?

    b. How much diluent?

8.2 COMPOUND FORMULAS

compounding
the process of using raw ingredients and/or other prepared ingredients to prepare a drug product for a patient

formula
a written document containing the ingredients and instructions needed to prepare a compound

compounded stock solution
a solution that is prepared in a large amount and kept in stock in the pharmacy to be divided for individual prescriptions

Compounding is the process of using raw ingredients and/or other prepared ingredients to prepare a drug product for a patient. This is similar to making a cake from scratch by using ingredients such as butter, sugar, eggs, flour, and baking powder.

A **formula** is a written document prepared by the pharmacist that contains the ingredients and instructions needed to prepare a compound. Some formulas are intended to prepare a single prescription, and others are intended to prepare a **compounded stock solution,** or a large amount to be divided for individual prescription orders later. Commonly used compounds can be made in advance to have on hand as needed.

Some pharmacies routinely prepare compounded products for physicians who prescribe these special preparations on a regular basis.

A pharmacy that prepares these compounds will often have a "recipe" for making a large amount to have on hand for the needs of patients over the coming days or weeks. It is not uncommon to prepare a compound that can be divided and dispensed to as many as twenty patients. Preparing compounds in advance in this way can result in cost savings by reducing the labor needed to make the product and can also save time in providing the compound to the patient. Although the Food and Drug Administration prohibits retail pharmacies from mass manufacturing compounded medications, anticipatory compounding is permitted in small quantities when a particular pharmacy is located near a physician's office that routinely orders a compounded prescription.

Pharmacies store formulas in many ways. They may be maintained as a computerized file system or informally in a card file or binder. Some pharmacies also have different formulas for different prescribers as each prescriber may prefer a slightly different version of a compound.

Safety Note

When enlarging or reducing a formula for compounding, always retain the correct proportion of ingredients from the original formula.

Enlarging or reducing formulas involves taking the recipe for a particular compounded medication and adjusting the amount of the ingredients up or down to meet the needs of the pharmacy's order. This practice is similar to doubling the ingredients in a recipe for cookies in order to make twice as many cookies. It is very important to retain the correct proportion of each ingredient in this process. A cookie made from a doubled batch should have the same ratio of ingredients as a cookie made from a single batch. The same should be true when a formula is doubled in the compounding pharmacy.

Safety Note

Always document calculations before compounding.

Accurate records and documentation of mathematical calculations used in reducing or enlarging a formula are essential. All amounts should be calculated and recorded prior to weighing, measuring, and mixing.

It is always important to make sure that the dispensed compound matches the concentration and the amount ordered. For example, your formula may result in 120 mL of solution and the patient may need only 20 mL. Or the patient may need 60 g of a cream and your formula may be written for 15 g. The following examples will demonstrate the calculations you will need to perform when reducing or enlarging formulas.

Example 8.2.1

You need to prepare 100 mL of an iodine solution for a patient. The pharmacy's formula follows.

R_x

Iodine	30 g
Sodium iodide	25 g
Purified water	QSAD, 1000 mL

The formula indicates the resulting volume is 1000 mL, and your patient needs 100 mL. So, you will need ¹/₁₀ (i.e., 100 mL desired/1000 mL formula) of each amount. Dividing each ingredient amount by 10 will result in the following:

Iodine	30 g ÷ 10	= 3 g
Sodium iodide	25 g ÷ 10	= 2.5 g
Purified water	1000 mL ÷ 10	= 100 mL

Example 8.2.2

You need to prepare 1 lb of coal tar ointment for a patient. Your formula results in 4 oz (120 g) of ointment.

Coal tar	4 g
Salicylic acid	1 g
Triamcinolone 0.1% ung	15 g
Aqua-base ointment	100 g

Since 1 lb = 16 oz, you will need to multiply your formula by 4 to obtain the correct amount of coal tar ointment.

Coal tar	4 g × 4 = 16 g
Salicylic acid	1 g × 4 = 4 g
Triamcinolone 0.1% ung	15 g × 4 = 60 g
Aqua-base ointment	100 g × 4 = 400 g

Example 8.2.3

You need to prepare four syringes for the following order.

Phenol 5% w/v syringes sodium chloride 5 mL

Calculate the amount of phenol needed in each syringe.

$$\frac{x \text{ g}}{5 \text{ mL}} = \frac{5 \text{ g}}{100 \text{ mL}}$$

$$x \text{ g} = 0.25 \text{ g or } 250 \text{ mg/syringe}$$

For four syringes, you will need

$$4 \text{ syringes} \times 250 \text{ mg/syringe} = 1000 \text{ mg phenol}$$

You will also need

$$4 \text{ syringes} \times 5 \text{ mL sodium chloride/syringe} = 20 \text{ mL sodium chloride}$$

Problem Set 8.2 _____

✓ *Self-check your problem set work at* www.emcp.com.

1. Fill the following order by preparing two bags of 500 mL admixture from your stock solutions of lidocaine 20% and furosemide 10 mg/mL. State how much ingredient you add to the two bags.

Lidocaine 2.5 g
Furosemide 500 mg
1000 mL D_5W

2. Fill the following order and prepare enough admixture for a 24-hour time period. How much of each ingredient will you need to bring into the IV room? Potassium chloride comes packaged as 2 mEq/mL in 15 mL vials.

1000 mL NS with 20 mEq
potassium chloride
infuse at 125 mL/hr

3. You are to prepare a 30 g jar of ointment using the following formula. State how much of each ingredient you will need.

Coal tar	4 g
Salicylic acid	1 g
Triamcinolone 1% ung	15 g
Aqua-base ointment	100 g
	yields 120 g

4. Use the following formula to prepare 150 vaginal suppositories. How much of each ingredient will you weigh out?

Progesterone	2.4 g
Polyethylene glycol 3350	30 g
Polyethylene glycol 1000	90 g
	yields 30 vaginal suppositories

5. You need to prepare the following formula for six patients. How much of each of the ingredients will you measure out?

Podophyllum resin	25%
Benzoin tincture	QSAD 20 mL

6. You have a prescription for 12 fl oz of Magic Mixture Number 7, and the pharmacy's formula follows. How much of each ingredient will you measure out?

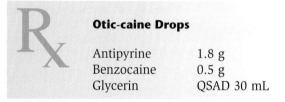

Magic Mixture Number 7

Tetracycline 500 mg capsules	16 capsules
Hydrocortisone suspension	15 mL
Lidocaine oral suspension	30 mL
Mylanta suspension	QSAD 240 mL

7. Prepare four 15 mL dropper bottles of Otic-caine using the following formula. How much of each ingredient will you measure out?

Otic-caine Drops

Antipyrine	1.8 g
Benzocaine	0.5 g
Glycerin	QSAD 30 mL

8. Tetracycline sclerosing solution is used to reduce the size of cysts that form in the kidneys of renal transplant patients. The following formula is used when making tetracycline sclerosing solution. List the ingredients and amounts needed to make a solution containing 2 g of tetracycline.

Tetracycline HCl powder	1 g
Ascorbic acid powder	2.5 g
Sterile saline for injection	10 mL

Instructions
1. Weigh out powders and mix in a nonsterile glass container.
2. Add 10 mL sterile saline and swirl to dissolve.
3. Draw up solution in a 20 mL syringe and push through a 0.22 micron filter.

8.3 ALLIGATIONS

Physicians often prescribe concentrations of medications that are not commercially available, and these prescriptions must be compounded ("added" together) at the pharmacy. When an ordered concentration is not commercially available, either of two methods may be used to fill the prescription in the pharmacy. The first is to use a concentrated stock solution, as in the examples in Section 8.1. This method is used when the amount of concentrate is very small and can be added to the product in a relatively small volume.

The second approach is to combine two different solutions with the same active ingredient in differing strengths. The resulting concentration, which is called an **alligation,** will be greater than the weaker strength, but less than the stronger strength. For example, 1% and 5% hydrocortisone ointments may be combined to provide a 3% ointment. This method is used when the two quantities needed to prepare the desired concentration are both relatively large.

The amount of each solution is calculated by using the **alligation alternate method.** This calculation is used to determine the proportions of given percentages needed to prepare the desired concentration. The alligation alternate method requires changing the percentages to parts of a proportion and then using the proportion to obtain the amounts of the two ingredients. The answer can then be checked by using the following formula.

$$\text{milliliters} \times \text{percent (expressed as a decimal)} = \text{grams}$$

It is important to note that this formula works for any strength of solution.

The following examples will demonstrate the application of the alligation alternate method.

Example 8.3.1

Prepare 250 mL of dextrose 7.5% w/v using dextrose 5% (D$_5$W) w/v and dextrose 50% (D$_{50}$W) w/v. How many milliliters of each will be needed?

Step 1. Set up a box arrangement and at the upper-left corner, write the percent of the highest concentration (50%) as a whole number. At the lower-left corner, write the percent of the lowest concentration (5%) as a whole number, and in the center, write the desired concentration.

alligation
the concentration obtained when two or more solutions of different strengths are combined

alligation alternate method
the mathematical calculation used to determine the amounts of two or more dilutions of differing strengths that will be mixed to prepare a product of a desired strength and quantity

Step 2. Subtract the center number from the upper-left number (note: the smaller from the larger) and put it at the lower-right corner. Now subtract the lower-left number from the center number (again: the smaller from the larger) and put it at the upper-right corner.

50

7.5

5

2.5 mL parts $D_{50}W$

$\dfrac{42.5 \text{ mL parts } D_5W}{45 \quad \text{mL total parts } D_{7.5}W}$

The number 2.5 mL represents the number of parts of the 50% solution that will be needed to make the final 7.5% solution, and the number 42.5 mL represents the number of parts of the 5% solution that will be needed. The sum of these two numbers, 2.5 mL + 42.5 mL = 45 mL, is the total number of parts of the 7.5% solution. In terms of ratios, the ratio of the 5% solution to the 7.5% solution is 42.5:45, and the ratio of the 50% solution to the 7.5% solution is 2.5:45. Much less of the 50% solution is needed to make the 7.5% solution.

Step 3. Calculate the volume needed of each dextrose solution.

50% Dextrose

$$\frac{x \text{ mL of } 50\%}{250 \text{ mL}} = \frac{2.5 \text{ mL parts } D_{50}W}{45 \text{ mL total parts } D_{7.5}W}$$

$$x \text{ mL} = \frac{(250 \text{ mL}) \times 2.5 \text{ mL parts}}{45 \text{ mL total parts } D_{7.5}W}$$

$$x \text{ mL} = 13.8888 \text{ mL } D_{50}W, \text{ rounded to } 13.89 \text{ mL}$$

5% Dextrose

$$\frac{x \text{ mL of } 5\%}{250 \text{ mL}} = \frac{4.25 \text{ mL parts } D_5W}{45 \text{ mL total parts } D_{7.5}W}$$

$$x \text{ mL} = \frac{(250 \text{ mL}) \times 42.5 \text{ mL parts}}{45 \text{ mL total parts } D_{7.5}W}$$

$$x \text{ mL} = 236.11 \text{ mL } D_5W$$

Step 4. Add the volumes of the two solutions together. The sum should equal the required volume of dextrose 7.5%.

$$\begin{array}{r} 236.11 \text{ mL} \\ +13.89 \text{ mL} \\ \hline 250.00 \text{ mL} \end{array}$$

Step 5. Check your answer by calculating the amount of solute (dextrose) in all three solutions. The number of grams of solute should equal the sum of the grams of solutes from the 50% solution and the 5% solution, using the following formula.

$$mL \times \% \text{ (as a decimal)} = g$$

$$250 \text{ mL} \times 0.075 = 18.75 \text{ g}$$
$$13.89 \text{ mL D}_{50}\text{W} \times 0.5 = 6.945 \text{ g}$$
$$236.11 \text{ mL D}_5\text{W} \times 0.05 = 11.805 \text{ g}$$

$$\begin{array}{r} 11.805 \text{ g} \\ +6.945 \text{ g} \\ \hline 18.750 \text{ g} \end{array}$$

The amounts measured to prepare this prescription will be rounded to the nearest milliliter, 14 mL D$_{50}$W and 236 mL D$_5$W.

Example 8.3.2

You are instructed to make 454 g of 3% zinc oxide cream. You have in stock 10% and 1% zinc oxide cream. How much of each percent will you use?

Step 1. We will simplify the step method used in Example 8.3.1 by combining Steps 1 and 2 into a single step and calculating the ratios right at the square, where it is easy to visualize.

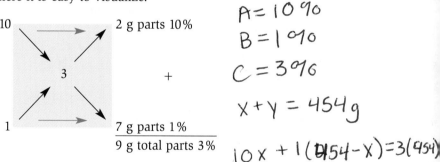

10   2 g parts 10%

3

+

1   7 g parts 1%
9 g total parts 3%

handwritten:
A = 10%
B = 1%
C = 3%
x + y = 454g
10x + 1(454 - x) = 3(454)
10x + 454 - x = 1362
9x + 454 = 1362
   -454   -454
9x = 908
x = 101g
so 101g of 10%
454 - 101 = y
353 g of 1%

Step 2.

10% zinc oxide cream

$$\frac{x \text{ g of 10\%}}{454 \text{ g}} = \frac{2 \text{ g parts 10\%}}{9 \text{ g total parts 3\%}}$$

$$x \text{ g of 10\%} = 101 \text{ g of 10\% zinc oxide cream}$$

1% zinc oxide cream

$$\frac{x \text{ g of 1\%}}{454 \text{ g}} = \frac{7 \text{ g parts 1\%}}{9 \text{ g total parts 3\%}}$$

$$x \text{ g of 1\%} = 353 \text{ g of 1\% zinc oxide cream}$$

Step 3. Check your work.

$$353 \text{ g} + 101 \text{ g} = 454 \text{ g}$$

Example 8.3.3 **You have been instructed to make 30 g of a 6% ointment. You have on hand a 4% and an 8% ointment. How much of each will you use?**

Step 1.

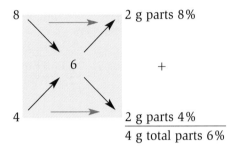

8   2 g parts 8%

6

       +

4   2 g parts 4%

       4 g total parts 6%

Step 2.

8% ointment

$$\frac{x \text{ g of } 8\%}{30 \text{ g}} = \frac{2 \text{ g parts } 8\%}{4 \text{ g total parts } 6\%}$$

$$x \text{ g of } 8\% = 15 \text{ g of } 8\% \text{ ointment}$$

4% ointment

$$\frac{x \text{ g of } 4\%}{30 \text{ g}} = \frac{2 \text{ g parts } 4\%}{4 \text{ g total parts } 6\%}$$

$$x \text{ g of } 4\% = 15 \text{ g of } 4\% \text{ ointment}$$

Step 3. Check your work.

$$15 \text{ g} + 15 \text{ g} = 30 \text{ g}$$

alligation medial method
the mathematical calculation used to find the final concentration created when two or more known quantities of known concentrations are compounded

    On some occasions, you will have to calculate the final concentration or percentage strength of a mixture that is composed of known quantities and percentage strengths of two or more ingredients. The calculation used is called the **alligation medial method.** The resulting percentage is the "middle" or "medial' strength as it is somewhere between the strengths of the ingredients. The following example will demonstrate the alligation medial method calculation.

Example 8.3.4 **You have been asked to prepare a mixture with the following ingredients: 30 g of 1% hydrocortisone cream, 20 g of 0.5% hydrocortisone ointment, and 10 g of Eucerin cream base. What will be the percentage of hydrocortisone in the final mixture?**

Step 1. Determine the amount of active ingredients in each of the items added to the mixture.

Determine the amount of active ingredient in 30 g of 1% hydrocortisone cream.

Solution 1: Using the ratio-proportion method,

$$\frac{x \text{ g}}{30 \text{ g}} = \frac{1 \text{ g}}{100 \text{ g}}$$

$$x \text{ g} = 0.3 \text{ g hydrocortisone}$$

Solution 2: Using the dimensional analysis method,

$$30 \text{ g} \times 1 \text{ g}/100 \text{ g} = 0.3 \text{ g hydrocortisone}$$

Determine the amount of active ingredient in 20 g of 0.5% hydrocortisone ointment.

Solution 1: Using the ratio-proportion method,

$$\frac{x \text{ g}}{20 \text{ g}} = \frac{0.5 \text{ g}}{100 \text{ g}}$$

$$x \text{ g} = 0.1 \text{ g hydrocortisone}$$

Solution 2: Using the dimensional analysis method,

$$20 \text{ g} \times 0.5 \text{ g}/100 \text{ g} = 0.1 \text{ g hydrocortisone}$$

Step 2. Determine the amount of grams in the final mixture.

$$30 \text{ g } 1\% \text{ cream} + 20 \text{ g } 0.5\% \text{ ointment} + 10 \text{ g Eucerin} = 60 \text{ g final mixture}$$

Step 3. Add the active ingredients and divide by the total quantity to determine the final concentration.

$$\frac{0.3 \text{ g} + 0.1 \text{ g}}{60 \text{ g}} \times 100\% = 0.6666\%, \text{ rounded to } 0.7\%$$

Note that the final concentration of 0.7% is between the concentrations of the ingredients. (It is less than 1% and more than 0.5%.)

Problem Set 8.3

✓ *Self-check your problem set work at* www.emcp.com.

Use the alligation alternate method to answer the following problems.

1. Prepare 200 mL of 7.5% dextrose solution using D_5W and $D_{10}W$. How much of each solution will be needed?

2. Prepare 400 mL of D_8W from $D_{20}W$ and sterile water for injection (SWFI). How much of each will be needed? (Note: water is considered to be 0% solution.)

3. Prepare 500 mL of $D_{12.5}W$. You have on hand D_5W, $D_{10}W$, and $D_{20}W$. How much of which two solutions will you need?

4. You must prepare a 250 mL solution of D_6W using SWFI, $D_{10}W$, or $D_{50}W$. How much of which two will you need?

5. Prepare a $D_{7.5}W$ solution beginning with 500 mL of D_5W and adding $D_{50}W$. What will the final volume be, and how much $D_{50}W$ will be used?

6. Prepare 250 mL of 8% dextrose from D_5W and $D_{20}W$. How much of each is needed?

7. Prepare 300 mL of 7.5% dextrose using SWFI and $D_{20}W$. How much of each is needed?

8. Prepare 500 mL of 12.5% dextrose using $D_{10}W$ and $D_{20}W$. How much of each is needed?

9. Prepare 150 mL of 7.5% dextrose from D_5W and $D_{10}W$. How much of each is needed?

10. Prepare 25 mL of 9% dextrose in water. Use D_5W and $D_{20}W$. How much of each fluid is used?

11. The physician has ordered 300 mL of $D_{12.5}W$. You have $D_{10}W$ and $D_{20}W$ available. How much $D_{10}W$ and $D_{20}W$ will you use to prepare 300 mL of $D_{12.5}W$?

300 mL $D_{12.5}W$
KCl 14 mEq

12. Prepare 500 mL of a 15% dextrose solution using D_5W and $D_{50}W$. How much of each solution will be needed?

13. Prepare 100 mL of a 12% dextrose solution using D_5W and $D_{20}W$. How much of each solution will be needed?

14. Prepare 60 g of a 3% cream from a 1% cream and a 10% cream. How many ounces of each cream will you need to weigh out?

15. Prepare 30 g of a 7.5% cream from a 5% and 15% cream. How much of each cream will you need to weigh out?

16. Prepare 1 L of 80% alcohol from 70% and 100%. How much of each do you need to measure out?

17. Prepare 3 L of a 12.5% dextrose solution from D_5W and $D_{50}W$. How much of each solution will be needed?

18. Prepare 100 mL of 5% hydrogen peroxide from a 1.5% and a 30% solution. How much of each solution will be needed?

19. Prepare four 30 g jars of hydrocortisone 3% cream. Use 1% and 5% creams. How much of each cream will be needed?

20. Prepare 2400 g of coal tar ointment 20%. You have on hand coal tar solution and ointment base. How much of each will be needed?

21. Prepare 45 g of 10% zinc oxide using petrolatum and a 20% zinc oxide ointment. How much of each will be needed?

22. Prepare 1 L of 50% alcohol from 70% solution and 15% solution. How much of each solution will be needed?

23. Prepare 1 gallon of a 1:10 solution of bleach using a 2% stable commercial bleach solution and a 100% bleach concentrate. How much of each solution will be needed?

24. Prepare 30 mL of a 1:200 solution by combining a 1:10 and a 1:400 solution. How much of each solution will be needed?

25. Prepare 120 mL of a 1:500 solution by combining a 1:250 and a 1:750 solution. How much of each will be needed?

26. The pharmacy receives the following order, and you have $D_{10}W$ and $D_{20}W$ available.

300 mL $D_{12.5}W$
KCl 14 mEq

a. Calculate the volumes of liquid needed to prepare the order.

b. You will need to prepare three bags of the solution for the next three shifts. How much of each ingredient will you need?

27. The pharmacy receives the following order, and you have the following ingredients to use to fill it: dextrose in 5% and 20%, sodium chloride 4 mEq/mL, potassium chloride 2 mEq/mL, and aminophylline 25 mg/mL.

> 1000 mL dextrose 8%
> Sodium chloride 24 mEq
> Potassium chloride 10 mEq
> Aminophylline 25 mg/mL

a. Calculate the amount of each solution needed to prepare a 1 L bag.

b. After creating the 1 L bag, you are instructed to prepare a second bag, but this one is to be 500 mL. How much of each ingredient will be needed to create the second bag?

Using the alligation medial method, determine the resulting concentration for each of the following compounds.

28. You have mixed equal parts of a 20% and a 5% benzocaine ointment. What is the resulting concentration?

29. You have mixed 20 mL of a 1:400 solution and 30 L of a 1:150 solution. What is the resulting concentration?

30. You have mixed 30 g of 2% cream into 30 g of 8% cream. What is the resulting concentration?

31. You have mixed 100 g of 8% cream into 200 g of 3% cream. What is the resulting concentration?

32. You have mixed 1 L of solution containing 15% alcohol, 500 mL of solution containing 3% alcohol, and 300 mL of solution containing 70% alcohol. What is the resulting concentration?

33. What is the final percentage strength of a mixture made from 30 mL of 1.5% hydrogen peroxide and 10 mL of 30% hydrogen peroxide?

34. What is the percentage strength of a mixture made from 300 mL of 70% alcohol and 200 mL of 95% alcohol?

35. What is the percentage strength of a mixture made from 100 mL each of 50% alcohol, 70% alcohol, and 95% alcohol?

36. What is the percentage strength of a mixture made from 60 g each of 5% coal tar ung and 10% coal tar ung?

37. What is the percentage strength of a mixture made from 20 g of 50% ichthamol, 10 g of 10% ichthamol, and 60 g of 5% ichthamol?

38. What is the percentage strength of a mixture made from 300 mL of witch hazel containing 14% alcohol, 100 mL of 95% alcohol, and 500 mL of distilled water?

39. What is the percentage strength of a mixture made from 60 g of 20% zinc oxide and 120 g of white petrolatum?

40. What is the percentage strength of a mixture containing 20 mL of 2% lidocaine, 10 mL SWFI, and 5 mL sodium bicarbonate?

8.4 LEAST MEASURABLE QUANTITY AND ALIQUOT MEASUREMENTS

At times, you will be handling very small amounts of medications when preparing a compounded prescription in the pharmacy. In these situations, it is essential to know the smallest amount that can be accurately weighed on your balance. The following formula will determine this amount.

$$\frac{100\% \times \text{balance sensitivity}}{\text{permissible \% margin of error}} = \text{least weighable quantity}$$

Example 8.4.1   **A Class A balance has a sensitivity of 6 mg. The order being prepared may have up to a 3% margin of error. What is the smallest amount that can be accurately weighed?**

$$\frac{100\% \times \text{balance sensitivity}}{\text{permissible \% margin of error}} = \frac{100\% \times 6 \text{ mg}}{3\%} = 200 \text{ mg}$$

Example 8.4.2   **A Class A balance has a sensitivity of 6 mg. The order being prepared may have up to a 1% margin of error. What is the smallest amount that can be accurately weighed?**

$$\frac{100\% \times \text{balance sensitivity}}{\text{permissible \% margin of error}} = \frac{100\% \times 6 \text{ mg}}{1\%} = 600 \text{ mg}$$

> **aliquot**
> a measured portion, fraction, or part of an ingredient that is placed into solution or into a mixture of other ingredients to aid in measuring a very small amount

If a very small amount needs to be weighed and the pharmacy balance does not allow for measuring this dose, an aliquot may be used. An **aliquot** is a measured portion, fraction, or part that is placed into solution or into a mixture of other ingredients. The diluted mixture can then be weighed out, and the desired active ingredient can be measured more accurately.

For example, if an order calls for a small amount such as 75 mg and allows for a very small margin of error, we may not be able to accurately weigh out this amount. The least weighable quantity must be calculated. This quantity is what will be measured. Aliquot measuring can be performed using the steps defined in Table 8.1.

Table 8.1   Steps for Weight Aliquot Measuring

Step 1. Calculate the least weighable quantity (LWQ), based on the sensitivity of your balance and the permissible margin of error. This equation has been given in the text above.

Step 2. Determine the amount of the ordered drug that you will actually weigh out. This amount must be equal to or larger than the least weighable quantity. To calculate the amount of drug to weigh out, multiply the amount of drug ordered by a whole number such as 2, 5, 10, or 20, until you have a weighable amount—that is, an amount greater than the least weighable quantity. The whole number you choose is called a *factor*. The factor chosen is arbitrary, but it must result in an amount greater than the least weighable quantity.

Step 3. Determine the amount of diluent (inert ingredient) to add.
  a. First determine the total amount of mixture (drug + diluent) that will be required. The total amount of mixture is calculated by multiplying the amount of drug weighed out (determined in Step 2) by some factor. The factor does not have to be the same as the one that was used in Step 2, but for convenience it often is.

  drug weighed out × factor = total amount of mixture

  b. Calculate the amount of diluent needed by subtracting the amount of the drug weighed out (Step 2) from the total amount of mixture.

  total amount of mixture − drug weighed out = diluent

Step 4. Combine the drug and diluent measured in Steps 2 and 3 and mix them well so that the drug is evenly distributed throughout the mixture.

Step 5. Determine the amount of mixture needed to provide the originally ordered amount by using the ratio-proportion method.

$$\frac{x \text{ mg mixture}}{\text{amount of drug ordered}} = \frac{\text{total amount of mixture}}{\text{amount of drug weighed}}$$

(The total amount of mixture was calculated in Step 3a; the amount of drug weighed out was calculated in Step 2.)

Example 8.4.3 **You receive a prescription for 75 mg of antibiotic in 15 mL of Cherry Syrup USP. A 5% margin of error is allowed, and you are to use a Class A balance with a sensitivity of 6 mg. What amount of aliquot mixture will contain the ordered amount of drug?**

Step 1. Determine the least weighable quantity.

$$\frac{100\% \times \text{balance sensitivity}}{\text{permissible \% margin of error}} = \frac{100\% \times 6 \text{ mg}}{5\%} = 120 \text{ mg}$$

So, at least 120 mg of the active ingredient must be weighed. At least this amount must be weighed for the diluent used as well.

Step 2. Determine the amount to be weighed. Because the amount that is to be weighed out has to be equal to or larger than the least weighable quantity, which in this case is 120 mg, multiply the desired amount by 2.

$$75 \text{ mg} \times 2 = 150 \text{ mg}$$

Step 3. Determine the total amount of mixture that will be required and the amount of inert ingredient.

$$150 \text{ mg active ingredient} \times 2 = 300 \text{ mg total mixture}$$

$$300 \text{ mg total} - 150 \text{ mg active ingredient} = 150 \text{ mg inert ingredient}$$

You will weigh 150 mg of the inert ingredient.

Step 4. Determine the total weight of the drug and diluent by restating the equation from Step 3.

$$150 \text{ mg drug} + 150 \text{ mg inert ingredient} = 300 \text{ mg}$$

Step 5. Determine the amount of mixture needed to provide the originally ordered amount.

$$x \text{ mg mixture} = \frac{(75 \text{ mg drug ordered}) \times (300 \text{ mg mixture})}{150 \text{ mg drug}}$$

$$x \text{ mg mixture} = 150 \text{ mg}$$

So, a 150 mg aliquot will contain 75 mg of the drug, the ordered amount of drug.

Example 8.4.4   **You receive a prescription for 15 mg of antibiotic in 10 mL Cherry Syrup USP. A 3% margin of error is allowed, and you are to use a balance with a sensitivity of 4 mg. What amount of aliquot mixture will contain the ordered amount of drug?**

Step 1. Determine the least weighable quantity.

$$\frac{100\% \times \text{balance sensitivity}}{\text{permissible } \% \text{ margin of error}} = \frac{100\% \times 4 \text{ mg}}{3\%} = 133 \text{ mg}$$

So, at least 133 mg of the active ingredient must be weighed. At least this amount must be weighed for the diluent used as well.

Step 2. Determine the amount to be weighed.

$$15 \text{ mg} \times 10 = 150 \text{ mg}$$

Step 3. Determine the total amount of mixture that will be required and the amount of inert ingredient.

$$150 \text{ mg active ingredient} \times 10 = 1500 \text{ mg total mixture}$$

$$1500 \text{ mg total} - 150 \text{ mg active ingredient} = 1350 \text{ mg inert ingredient}$$

You will weigh 1350 mg of the inert ingredient.

Step 4. Determine the total weight of the drug and diluent.

$$150 \text{ mg drug} + 1350 \text{ mg diluent} = 1500 \text{ mg}$$

Step 5. Determine the amount of mixture needed to provide the originally ordered amount.

$$x \text{ mg mixture} = \frac{(15 \text{ mg drug ordered}) \times (1500 \text{ mg mixture})}{150 \text{ mg drug}}$$

$$x \text{ mg mixture} = 150 \text{ mg}$$

So, a 150 mg aliquot will contain 15 mg of the drug, the ordered amount of drug.

Example 8.4.5 **You receive a prescription for 5 mg of antibiotic in 3 mL of normal saline (NS). A 5% margin of error is allowed, and you are to use a Class A balance with a sensitivity of 4 mg. What amount of aliquot mixture will contain the ordered amount of drug?**

Step 1. Determine the least weighable quantity.

$$\frac{100\% \times \text{balance sensitivity}}{\text{permissible \% margin of error}} = \frac{100\% \times 4 \text{ mg}}{5\%} = 80 \text{ mg}$$

So, at least 80 mg of the active ingredient must be weighed. At least this amount must be weighed for the diluent used as well.

Step 2. Determine the amount to be weighed.

$$5 \text{ mg} \times 20 = 100 \text{ mg}$$

Step 3. Determine the total amount of mixture that will be required and the amount of inert ingredient.

$$100 \text{ mg active ingredient} \times 20 = 2000 \text{ mg total mixture}$$

$$2000 \text{ mg total} - 100 \text{ mg active ingredient} = 1900 \text{ mg inert ingredient}$$

You will weigh 1900 mg of the inert ingredient.

Step 4. Determine the total weight of the drug and diluent.

$$100 \text{ mg drug} + 1900 \text{ mg diluent} = 2000 \text{ mg}$$

Step 5. Determine the amount of mixture needed to provide the originally ordered amount.

$$x \text{ mg mixture} = \frac{(5 \text{ mg drug ordered}) \times (2000 \text{ mg mixture})}{100 \text{ mg drug}}$$

$$x \text{ mg mixture} = 100 \text{ mg}$$

So, a 100 mg aliquot will contain 5 mg of the drug, the ordered amount of drug.

Aliquot measurement can also be used to prepare pharmaceutical preparations that include very small volumes of liquid. In these situations, it is not necessary to determine the least weighable quantity. Instead, you will consider the available syringes in the pharmacy and determine the minimum amount that can be precisely measured. This is typically a volume that will fill at least one-third to one-half of the syringe barrel or can easily be measured in a properly marked graduated cylinder. Volume aliquot measuring can be performed using the steps listed in Table 8.2.

Table 8.2 Steps for Volume Aliquot Measuring

Step 1. Determine the minimum volume that can be measured accurately. This amount will vary because it depends on the size of the syringe or graduated cylinder available.

Step 2. Determine the multiple of the active ingredient that will provide the smallest volume that can be accurately measured.

Step 3. Determine the total volume of the mixture by multiplying the volume of active ingredient by the same multiple (factor) used in Step 2.

Step 4. Determine the amount of diluent needed by subtracting the amount of active ingredient calculated from the mixture total.

Step 5. Determine the amount of mixture needed to provide the originally ordered amount by using the ratio-proportion method.

Example 8.4.6

You receive a prescription for 0.25 mL of a drug. The minimum volume that can be accurately measured in your pharmacy is 1.0 mL. What amount of aliquot mixture will contain the ordered volume of drug?

Safety Note

A trailing zero is appropriate if it is used to communicate the accuracy of a measurement.

Step 1. The minimum volume that can be measured accurately is 1.0 mL. The trailing zero indicates a measurement accuracy to a tenth of a milliliter.

Step 2. Determine the multiple of the active ingredient that will provide the smallest volume that can be accurately measured.

$$0.25 \text{ mL} \times 4 = 1.0 \text{ mL active ingredient}$$

Step 3. Determine the total volume of the mixture.

$$1.0 \text{ mL} \times 4 = 4.0 \text{ mL total mixture}$$

Step 4. Determine the amount of diluent needed.

$$4.0 \text{ mL total} - 1.0 \text{ mL active ingredient} = 3.0 \text{ mL diluent needed}$$

Step 5. Determine the amount of mixture needed to provide the originally ordered amount.

$$\frac{x \text{ mL mixture}}{0.25 \text{ mL drug}} = \frac{4.0 \text{ mL mixture}}{1.0 \text{ mL drug}}$$

$$x \text{ mL mixture} = 1.0 \text{ mL}$$

So, a 1.0 mL aliquot will contain the needed ingredient.

Example 8.4.7 **You receive a prescription for 0.15 mL of a drug. The minimum volume that can be accurately measured in your pharmacy is 0.5 mL. What amount of aliquot mixture will contain the ordered amount of drug?**

Step 1. The minimum volume that can be measured accurately is 0.5 mL. The measurement accuracy is to a tenth of a milliliter.

Step 2. Determine the multiple of the active ingredient that will provide the smallest volume that can be accurately measured.

$$0.15 \text{ mL} \times 4 = 0.6 \text{ mL active ingredient}$$

Step 3. Determine the total volume of the mixture.

$$0.6 \text{ mL} \times 4 = 2.4 \text{ mL total mixture}$$

Step 4. Determine the amount of diluent needed.

$$2.4 \text{ mL total} - 0.6 \text{ mL active ingredient} = 1.8 \text{ mL diluent needed}$$

Step 5. Determine the amount of mixture needed to provide the originally ordered amount.

$$\frac{x \text{ mL mixture}}{0.15 \text{ mL drug}} = \frac{2.4 \text{ mL mixture}}{0.6 \text{ mL drug}}$$

$$x \text{ mL mixture} = 0.6 \text{ mL mixture}$$

So, a 0.6 mL aliquot will contain the needed ingredient.

Problem Set 8.4 _____

✓ *Self-check your problem set work at* www.emcp.com.

Determine the amount of drug, diluent, mixture, and aliquot for each of these aliquot problems using weight. For each problem, first calculate the least weighable quantity; then use the smallest factor possible to calculate the amount of drug to be weighed out. Use the factor given in the problem to calculate the amount of diluent to be added. (***Note:* Sometimes these two factors will be the same; sometimes they will not.**)

1. 20 mg Drug A
   3.5% margin of error allowed
   Torsion balance with a sensitivity of 4 mg
   use the multiple 6 for the diluent

   a. least weighable quantity: _____

   b. amount of drug: _____

   c. amount of mixture: _____

   d. amount of diluent: _____

   e. amount of aliquot: _____

2. 5 mg Drug B
   3% margin of error allowed
   Torsion balance with a sensitivity of 5 mg
   use the multiple 35 for the diluent

   a. least weighable quantity: _____

   b. amount of drug: _____

   c. amount of mixture: _____

   d. amount of diluent: _____

   e. amount of aliquot: _____

3. 12 mg Drug C
    5.5% margin of error allowed
    Torsion balance with a sensitivity of 5 mg
    use the multiple 15 for the diluent

    a. least weighable quantity: _____

    b. amount of drug: _____

    c. amount of mixture: _____

    d. amount of diluent: _____

    e. amount of aliquot: _____

4. 25 mg Drug D
    5% margin of error allowed
    Torsion balance with a sensitivity of 6 mg
    use the multiple 6 for the diluent

    a. least weighable quantity: _____

    b. amount of drug: _____

    c. amount of mixture: _____

    d. amount of diluent: _____

    e. amount of aliquot: _____

5. 6 mg Drug E
    4% margin of error allowed
    Torsion balance with a sensitivity of 6 mg
    use the multiple 25 for the diluent

    a. least weighable quantity: _____

    b. amount of drug: _____

    c. amount of mixture: _____

    d. amount of diluent: _____

    e. amount of aliquot: _____

6. 22.5 mg Drug F
    4% margin of error allowed
    Torsion balance with a sensitivity of 4 mg
    use the multiple 5 for the diluent

    a. least weighable quantity: _____

    b. amount of drug: _____

    c. amount of mixture: _____

    d. amount of diluent: _____

    e. amount of aliquot: _____

7. 17.75 mg Drug G
    5% margin of error allowed
    Torsion balance with a sensitivity of 4 mg
    use the multiple 5 for the diluent

    a. least weighable quantity: _____

    b. amount of drug: _____

    c. amount of mixture: _____

    d. amount of diluent: _____

    e. amount of aliquot: _____

8. 18 mg Drug H
    6% margin of error allowed
    Torsion balance with a sensitivity of 5 mg
    use the multiple 5 for the diluent

    a. least weighable quantity: _____

    b. amount of drug: _____

    c. amount of mixture: _____

    d. amount of diluent: _____

    e. amount of aliquot: _____

9. 30 mg Drug J
    5% margin of error allowed
    Torsion balance with a sensitivity of 5 mg
    use the multiple 4 for the diluent

    a. least weighable quantity: _____

    b. amount of drug: _____

    c. amount of mixture: _____

    d. amount of diluent: _____

    e. amount of aliquot: _____

10. 8.75 mg Drug K
    5% margin of error allowed
    Torsion balance with a sensitivity of 3 mg
    use the multiple 7 for the diluent

    a. least weighable quantity: _____

    b. amount of drug: _____

    c. amount of mixture: _____

    d. amount of diluent: _____

    e. amount of aliquot: _____

Determine the amount of drug, mixture, diluent, and aliquot for each of these aliquot problems using volume. Use the smallest factor (or multiple) possible to calculate the amount of drug to be measured out. Use the factor given in the problem to calculate the amount of diluent to be added. (*Note:* **Sometimes these two factors will be the same; sometimes they will not.**)

11. 0.5 mL Drug L
    1.0 mL is the minimum volume that can be accurately measured
    use the multiple 4 for the diluent

    a. amount of drug: _____

    b. amount of mixture: _____

    c. amount of diluent: _____

    d. amount of aliquot: _____

12. 0.3 mL Drug M
    0.5 mL is the minimum volume that can be accurately measured
    use the multiple 5 for the diluent

    a. amount of drug: _____

    b. amount of mixture: _____

    c. amount of diluent: _____

    d. amount of aliquot: _____

13. 0.75 mL Drug N
    1.0 mL is the minimum volume that can be accurately measured
    use the multiple 5 for the diluent

    a. amount of drug: _____

    b. amount of mixture: _____

    c. amount of diluent: _____

    d. amount of aliquot: _____

14. 0.25 mL Drug O
    1.5 mL is the minimum volume that can be accurately measured
    use the multiple 6 for the diluent

    a. amount of drug: _____

    b. amount of mixture: _____

    c. amount of diluent: _____

    d. amount of aliquot: _____

15. 0.45 mL of Drug P
    1.0 mL is the minimum volume that can be accurately measured
    use the multiple 3 for the diluent

    a. amount of drug: _____

    b. amount of mixture: _____

    c. amount of diluent: _____

    d. amount of aliquot: _____

16. 0.95 mL of Drug Q
    1.5 mL is the minimum volume that can be accurately measured
    use the multiple 2 for the diluent

    a. amount of drug: _____

    b. amount of mixture: _____

    c. amount of diluent: _____

    d. amount of aliquot: _____

17. 0.5 mL of Drug R
    1.0 mL is the minimum volume that can be
    accurately measured
    use the multiple 4 for the diluent

    a. amount of drug: _____

    b. amount of mixture: _____

    c. amount of diluent: _____

    d. amount of aliquot: _____

18. 0.5 mL of Drug S
    1.0 mL is the minimum volume that can be
    accurately measured
    use the multiple 5 for the diluent

    a. amount of drug: _____

    b. amount of mixture: _____

    c. amount of diluent: _____

    d. amount of aliquot: _____

19. 0.85 mL of Drug T
    1.5 mL is the minimum volume that can be
    accurately measured
    use the multiple 2 for the diluent

    a. amount of drug: _____

    b. amount of mixture: _____

    c. amount of diluent: _____

    d. amount of aliquot: _____

20. 0.05 mL of Drug U
    1.0 mL is the minimum volume that can be
    accurately measured
    use the multiple 20 for the diluent

    a. amount of drug: _____

    b. amount of mixture: _____

    c. amount of diluent: _____

    d. amount of aliquot: _____

1. Prepare 8 mL of hydrocortisone solution with a concentration of 5 mg/mL from 100 mg/2 mL stock.
   a. How many milliliters of hydrocortisone are needed?

   b. How many milliliters of diluent are needed?

2. Prepare 5 mL of a 5 mcg/mL solution from a stock solution of 50 mcg/mL.
   a. How much stock solution are needed?

   b. How many milliliters of diluent are needed?

3. An order calls for a total of 500 mL of a 2% solution. You have a 10% soaking solution on hand.
   a. How much concentrate will you need?

   b. How much diluent?

4. A doctor writes a prescription for 280 mL of a 5 mg/mL solution. The pharmacy carries a 20% solution.
   a. How much concentrate will you need?

   b. How much diluent?

5. You need 50 mL of a 10% boric acid solution. The pharmacy carries only 85% boric acid.
   a. How much concentrate will you need?

   b. How much diluent?

6. A doctor orders 1000 mL of 35% dextrose. Your pharmacy carries only 50% dextrose 1000 mL.
   a. How much concentrate will you need?

   b. How much diluent?

7. A hospital pharmacy has 8.5% Aminosyn on hand. The order calls for 500 mL of 2.5% Aminosyn.
   a. How much of the 8.5% will be used to fill the order?

   b. How much diluent?

8. You are to prepare five 60 g jars of ointment using the following formula. How much of each ingredient will you need to create the total amount?

Coal tar	4 g
Salicylic Acid	1 g
Triamcinolone 1% ung	15 g
Aqua-base ointment	100 g

9. You are to prepare 400 mL of 7.5% dextrose solution using D_5W and $D_{10}W$. How much of each solution will be needed?

10. You are to prepare 800 mL of 8% dextrose from D_5W and $D_{20}W$. How much of each is needed?

11. You are to prepare 1000 mL of 7.5% dextrose using SWFI and $D_{20}W$. How much of each is needed?

12. You are to prepare 200 mL of 12.5% dextrose using $D_{10}W$ and $D_{20}W$. How much of each is needed?

13. You are to prepare 500 mL of a 15% dextrose solution using D_5W and $D_{50}W$. How much of each is needed?

14. What fraction of 10% alcohol should be mixed with 70% alcohol to obtain 50% alcohol?

15. A doctor writes an order for a total of 300 mL of 42.5% Liposyn. You have in stock 5% Liposyn and 50% Liposyn. How much of each will you need?

16. You receive an order that calls for 60 g of a 30% ointment. On the shelf you have a 2% and a 50% ointment. How much of each will you use to fill the order?

17. An order calls for 1000 mL of 60% Travasol. On the shelf the pharmacy carries 40% and 70% Travasol. How many milliliters of each will you need to fill the order?

18. An order calls for 30 g of 5% bacitracin ointment. The pharmacy carries only 3% and 10% bacitracin ointment. How many grams of the 3% and 10% ointment will you use to fill the order?

19. What is the percentage strength of a mixture containing 30 mL of 7% iodine and 30 mL of 2% iodine?

20. What is the percentage strength of a mixture containing 30 mL of 70% alcohol, 500 mL of 40% alcohol, and 200 mL of 95% alcohol?

21. A prescription balance with a sensitivity of 6 mg is used to weigh out a substance that is not to have a greater than 5% error. What is the least weighable quantity?

22. Determine the amount of drug, mixture, diluent, and aliquot for the following situation. First, calculate the least weighable quantity, then use the smallest factor possible to calculate the amount of drug to be weighed out. Use the factor given in the problem to calculate the amount of diluent to be added. (These two factors might or might not be the same.)

R_x
    8.5 mg drug XYZ
    5% margin of error allowed
    Torsion balance with a sensitivity of 6 mg
    use the multiple 25 for the diluent

a. Least weighable quantity: _____

b. Amount of drug: _____

c. Amount of mixture: _____

d. Amount of diluent: _____

e. Amount of aliquot: _____

Using Business Math in the Pharmacy

Chapter **9**

Objectives

- Identify and calculate overhead cost.
- Identify net and gross profit.
- Calculate markup and the markup rate.
- Compute discounts.
- Apply average wholesale price to profit calculations.
- Calculate inventory turnover.
- Calculate depreciation.

9.1 CALCULATIONS RELATED TO BUSINESS

All businesses must perform certain accounting operations on a regular basis. Markup, profit, and discounts are calculated every day. Clients are also accustomed to calculating discounts for sales and items on discount. Like any business, the pharmacy must make a **profit;** that is, it must have more receipts than expenses in order to continue to provide customer services. In addition, the technician needs to understand the importance of overhead as it pertains to monthly bills such as rent, taxes, utilities, and inventory supplies kept on hand.

> **profit**
> income minus overhead
>
> **overhead**
> the pharmacy's overall cost of doing business; includes salaries, equipment, operating expenses, and rent

Overhead

The pharmacy's **overhead** is its general cost of doing business. This is the overall cost for the pharmacy, including salaries, equipment, operating expenses, and rent. Profit equals income minus overhead.

Example 9.1.1

Assume that John's Drug Shop has the following annual overhead expenses:

pharmacist's salary	$60,000.00
two technician salaries ($24,500.00 each)	49,000.00
rent	12,000.00
utilities	5,000.00
software maintenance	1,200.00
liability insurance	3,000.00
business insurance	4,000.00
drug purchases	550,000.00
total overhead =	$684,200.00

If a 15% profit is desirable, what amount of income must be received to meet this goal?

Since in this case the profit is to be 15%,

$$\text{overhead} \times 0.15 = \text{profit}$$
$$\$684,200.00 \times 0.15 = \$102,630.00$$

Profit equals incoming receipts minus overhead, so

$$\text{overhead} + \text{profit} = \text{income}$$
$$\$684,200.00 + \$102,630.00 = \$786,830.00$$

When John's Drug Shop has an annual income of $786,830.00, it will be making a 15% profit.

Net Profit

<table>
<tr><td>

net profit
the difference between the selling price and the overall cost of an item

overall cost
for a drug, the sum of the purchase price and the cost to dispense

</td><td>

In pharmacy practice, profit is influenced by the selling prices of drugs. For each drug, the **net profit** (the profit calculated in Example 9.1.1) is the difference between the selling price and the overall cost. The **overall cost** is the sum of the purchase price and the cost to dispense. Cost of dispensing consists of items such as professional handling, which includes processing and recording the prescription, as well as patient consultation.

</td></tr>
</table>

$$\text{purchase price} + \text{cost to dispense} = \text{overall cost}$$

$$\text{selling price} - \text{overall cost} = \text{profit}$$

$$\text{overall cost} \times \text{desired percent profit} = \text{amount of net profit}$$

Example 9.1.2 **Nystatin oral solution costs $20.25/pint. You calculate that it takes $5.10 to dispense the entire contents of one bottle, considering personnel time, pharmacy supplies, shipping, and maintaining the supply. If a 20% profit is the goal for this product, what selling price is required for the pint bottle?**

$$\text{purchase price} + \text{cost to dispense} = \text{overall cost}$$
$$\$20.25 + \$5.10 = \$25.35$$

$$\text{overall cost} \times 0.20 = \text{net profit}$$
$$\$25.35 \times 0.20 = \$5.07$$

$$\text{overall cost} + \text{net profit} = \text{selling price}$$
$$\$25.35 + \$5.07 = \$30.42$$

Gross Profit

<table>
<tr><td>

gross profit
the difference between the selling price and the purchase price; also called *markup*

</td><td>

The difference between the selling price and the purchase price is called **gross profit.** This relation of purchasing and selling does not consider the cost of preparing and dispensing the drug. Thus, the gross profit will always be more than the net profit. Using the example of nystatin oral solution, the gross profit would be $10.17.

</td></tr>
</table>

$$\text{selling price} - \text{purchase price} = \text{gross profit}$$
$$\$30.42 - \$20.25 = \$10.17$$

The **profit margin** is the difference between the cost of doing business (the purchase price, overhead, and preparation) and the selling price or receipts for a product. A negative profit (a loss) occurs when the selling price or receipts for a product is less than the cost of presenting that product for sale.

As just described, like all businesses, pharmacies purchase their products (drugs) at one price and sell them at a higher price. Although pharmacies are subject to governmental laws and regulations regarding the sale of drugs, markup still plays a part in the pricing system.

The markup is computed as

$$\text{selling price} - \text{purchase price} = \text{markup or gross profit}$$

The **markup rate** is computed as

$$\frac{\text{markup}}{\text{cost}} \times 100\% = \text{markup rate}$$

Example 9.1.3 **A 30-day supply of an antidiabetic agent sells for $45.00 and costs the pharmacy $30.00. What is the markup? What is the markup rate?**

The markup is computed as follows:

$$\text{selling price} - \text{purchase price} = \text{markup or gross profit}$$
$$\$45.00 - \$30.00 = \$15.00$$

The markup rate is

$$\frac{\text{markup}}{\text{cost}} \times 100\% = \text{markup rate}$$

$$\frac{\$15.00}{\$30.00} \times 100\% = 50\%$$

Example 9.1.4 **If Zantac 75 in a 12-pack costs the pharmacy $8.35 and the selling price is $10.75, what is the markup? What is the markup rate?**

The markup is

$$\$10.75 - \$8.35 = \$2.40$$

The markup rate is

$$\frac{\text{markup}}{\text{cost}} \times 100\% = \text{markup rate}$$

$$\frac{\$2.40}{\$8.35} \times 100\% = 28.7\%$$

Discount

Sometimes a manufacturer or a supplier offers an item at a lower price to a pharmacy. This reduced price is a **discount.** Similarly, a pharmacy may offer consumers a discount, or a deduction from what is normally charged, as an incentive to purchase an item.

$$\text{purchase price} \times \text{discount rate} = \text{discount}$$

$$\text{purchase price} - \text{discount} = \text{discounted price}$$

Example 9.1.5

Assume the pharmacy purchases five cases of dermatological cream at $100.00 per case. If the account is paid in full within 15 days, the supplier offers a 15% discount on the purchase. What is the total discounted purchase price?

First calculate the full purchase price.

$$\text{quantity of product} \times \text{cost per unit} = \text{total purchase price}$$
$$5 \text{ cases} \times \$100.00 \text{ per case} = \$500.00$$

Next calculate the discount for payment within 15 days.

$$\text{total purchase price} \times \text{discount rate} = \text{discount}$$
$$\$500.00 \times 0.15 = \$75.00$$

Finally, to obtain the discounted price, subtract the discount from the original price.

$$\text{total purchase price} - \text{discount} = \text{discounted purchase price}$$
$$\$500.00 - \$75.00 = \$425.00$$

Example 9.1.6

Jenny's Drug Store offers a 20% discount on a discontinued brand of cough syrup. How much will a $3.45 bottle cost after the discount?

$$\text{purchase price} \times \text{discount rate} = \text{discount}$$
$$\$3.45 \times 0.20 = \$0.69$$

$$\text{purchase price} - \text{discount} = \text{discounted price}$$
$$\$3.45 - \$0.69 = \$2.76$$

The Drugs-R-Us Pharmacy has the following overhead expenses. Use this information to answer questions 1 through 3.

pharmacist(s) salary	$135,000.00
technician(s) salary	52,000.00
rent	23,000.00
utilities	6,000.00
computer maintenance	4,000.00
software subscriptions	2,000.00
liability insurance	4,000.00
business insurance	4,000.00
drug purchases	750,000.00

1. If an 18% profit is desirable, what must the pharmacy's income be in order to meet this goal?

2. If the pharmacy's income is $1,401,489.00, what is its percent profit?

3. If the pharmacy's income is $1,191,692.00, what is its percent profit?

The Key Pharmacy has the following overhead expenses. Use this information to answer questions 4 through 6.

pharmacist salary	$72,000.00
technician salary	52,000.00
rent	13,000.00
utilities	5,500.00
computer maintenance	2,000.00
software subscriptions	1,500.00
liability insurance	4,000.00
business insurance	3,500.00
drug purchases	50,000.00

4. If a 20% profit is desirable, what must the pharmacy's income be in order to meet this goal?

5. If the pharmacy's income is $991,982, what is its percent profit?

6. If the pharmacy's income is $1,248,301, what is its percent profit?

7. The pharmacy calculates that its income for the week was $54,617.53 and that its net profit was $3700.83. The week's drug costs amounted to $47,422.14. What was the overhead for the week?

8. Corner Pharmacy has a weekly overhead of $13,033.06. If this pharmacy is to make a 22% profit, what must its sales of goods and services amount to each week?

Calculate the dollar amount of net profit and the percent profit (markup rate) for the following individual prescription drug items. (Round to whole percents.) The dispensing fee is $4.25 for each prescription.

9. propranolol 10 mg
   Cost: $3.96 per 100 tablets
   Dispense: 50 tablets
   Rx Charge: $8.59

10. amoxicillin 250 mg
    Cost: $8.50 per 500 capsules
    Dispense: 30 capsules
    Rx Charge: $14.80

11. Paxil (paroxetine) 20 mg
    Cost: $118.50 per 100 tablets
    Dispense: 30 tablets
    Rx Charge: $45.50

12. furosemide 40 mg
    Cost: $83.50 per 500 tablets
    Dispense: 100 tablets
    Rx Charge: $23.16

13. levothyroxine 0.1 mg
    Cost: $41.20 per 100 tablets
    Dispense: 90 tablets
    Rx Charge: $41.70

14. cough syrup
    Cost: $37.50 per pint (480 mL)
    Dispense: 8 fl oz bottle
    Rx Charge: $25.34

15. lo-estrogen/progestin oral contraceptive
    Cost: $62.30 per 6 packs of 28
    Dispense: 1 pack of 28
    Rx Charge: $17.90

The pharmacy is selling the following items at a discount this week. Calculate the sale price for each.

16. cough syrup, regular price $5.89 discounted 20%

17. facial tissues, regular price $1.19 discounted 15%

18. hair dye, regular price $7.29 discounted 30%

19. body lotion, regular price $5.69 discounted 15%

20. baby shampoo, regular price $3.89 discounted 25%

21. antacid liquid, regular price $4.26 discounted 30%

22. acetaminophen tablets, regular price $8.69 discounted 50%

23. toothpaste, regular price $2.99 discounted 40%

Calculate the following and state the answer in dollars or percent as indicated.

24. Antiviral ointment costs a pharmacy $12.50 per tube. The standard markup is 30%. What is the total selling price of a box of 12 tubes?

25. Eyedrops with antihistamine are purchased in cases of 36 drop-dispenser bottles. The pharmacy desires a markup of $1.75 per bottle. The purchase price is $111.60 per case. What is the selling price per bottle?

26. Identify the markup and the selling price of an oral antibiotic suspension that costs the pharmacist $15.60 per bottle if the markup rate is 25%.

27. An asthma tablet costs the pharmacy $24.80 for a month's supply, and the selling price is $30.75. Calculate the markup rate.

28. Calculate the gross profit from a medication that costs the pharmacy $520.00 for 1000 tablets and sells for $650.00.

29. The cost of dispensing the medication in question 28 is $2.05 per 100 tablets. Calculate the net profit for selling one tablet.

The pharmacy where you work has received a drug shipment. Calculate the markup and selling price on each item and the total selling cost of all items together.

	Drug	Quantity	Total Purchase Price	Markup Rate	Markup	Selling Price
30.	antibiotic oral solution	1200 mL	$120.50	25%		
31.	foot powder	12 containers	$24.00	15%		
32.	Motrin (ibuprofen)	2000 tablets	$200.00	27%		
33.	Bandaids	10 boxes	$27.50	21%		
34.	antibiotic ointment	18 tubes	$67.50	18%		
35.	birth control pills	24 packs	$840.00	32%		
36.	DiaBeta (glyburide)	600 tablets	$550.00	30%		
37.	**Total**					

9.2 INSURANCE REIMBURSEMENTS FOR PRESCRIPTIONS

pharmacy benefits management (PBM)
a prescription processing service that manages insurance reimbursement for prescriptions to pharmacies

Reimbursement for prescription and pharmacy services is largely controlled by contracts with insurance companies and is often brokered through a large prescription processing service called **pharmacy benefits management (PBM).** Reimbursement may be calculated based on the actual cost of medications, the average wholesale price, or a set contract established for a list of preferred drugs. The amount of money paid by the PBM for a particular prescription is calculated and approved by the PBM's computer or the pharmacy's computer via an online connection. Rarely is this cost calculated by personnel in the pharmacy. Nevertheless, it is helpful to understand the reimbursement process and the methods used to calculate the charges for medication. Patients are very likely to ask questions about charges and reimbursements, so having a basic understanding of the reconciliation process is essential.

Some claims will be reconciled by an individual pharmacy, but others will pass electronically through a PBM or large clearinghouse. These businesses bill the insurance companies under contract and then reimburse the pharmacy periodically for a batch of prescriptions. Reimbursement may be daily, weekly, or monthly. Some large chain pharmacies may even receive a single payment that covers a large number of stores; the individual store does not receive a "check" from the company, but rather an invoice or memo indicating the amount it is being reimbursed. Rejections or denials of prescription drug charges will also come back to the pharmacy in this manner. It is not uncommon to receive an initial online approval for a prescription and then later to receive a rejection or denial of the charges.

When considering profit on an individual prescription, the actual cost of the medication is compared to the amount the pharmacy receives for the dispensed drug. The term *profit* in this situation refers only to the dollar amount of the drug used, and it does not include the cost of materials, labor, or overhead. The amount that is charged over and above the cost of the medication alone is referred to as the **dispensing fee.** The dispensing fee is meant to cover all related costs to filling a prescription, besides the cost of the medication itself, and includes any actual profit gained.

dispensing fee
amount charged over and above the actual cost of the medication; includes profit, cost of materials, cost of labor, and overhead

Average Wholesale Price (AWP) Applications

A pharmacy may potentially receive payment from several different sources. Historically, patients have been responsible for paying for their own medications. More recently, health maintenance organizations and health insurers have become major players in determining the cost of healthcare, including patient medications. The very survival of a pharmacy depends on its ability to contain costs.

average wholesale price (AWP)
the average price that wholesalers charge the pharmacy for a drug; used to determine reimbursement

The **average wholesale price (AWP)** of a drug is an *average* price that wholesalers charge the pharmacy. Usually, third parties reimburse a pharmacy based upon the AWP. Therefore, the pharmacy has an incentive to purchase a drug below its AWP. Drugs are sold below AWP in some situations, such as when volume discounts, set contract prices, or rebates from manufacturers are available.

$$\text{prescription reimbursement} = \text{AWP} \pm \text{percentage} + \text{dispensing fee}$$

Example 9.2.1

A certain tablet comes in a quantity of 60 and has an AWP of $100.00. The pharmacy has an agreement with the supplier to purchase the drug at the AWP minus 15%. The insurer is willing to pay AWP plus 5% plus a $2.00 dispensing fee. A patient on this insurer's plan purchases 30 tablets for $54.50. How much profit does the pharmacy make on this prescription?

First calculate the amount of the discount.

$$\$100.00 \times 0.15 = \$15.00$$

Then calculate the purchase price of the drug.

$$\$100.00 - \$15.00 = \$85.00$$

Therefore, the pharmacy can purchase this drug at $85.00 per 60 tablets. The insurance company will pay the pharmacy AWP + 5%.

$$\$100.00 + (\$100.00 \times 0.05) = \$100.00 + \$5.00$$
$$= \$105.00$$

At that price, the amount the insurance company will pay to fill a prescription for 30 pills is

$$(\$105.00 \div 2) + \$2 \text{ (dispensing fee)} = \$52.50 + \$2.00 = \$54.50$$

Compare this to the pharmacy's cost of 30 tablets.

$$\$85.00 \div 2 = \$42.50$$

Therefore, the pharmacy's profit on 30 tablets is

$$\$54.50 - \$42.50 = \$12.00$$

Example 9.2.2

Two hundred capsules are purchased at AWP minus 20%, where AWP is $125. The insurer allows a charge of AWP plus 3% per 200 capsules. What is the highest charge per capsule allowed by the insurer? What will be the profit per capsule?

The discounted price of 200 capsules is

$$\$125.00 - (\$125.00 \times 0.20) = \$125.00 - \$25.00$$
$$= \$100.00$$

Thus, the cost per capsule to the pharmacy is

$$\$100.00 \div 200 = \$0.50/\text{capsule}$$

The insurance company will pay the pharmacy AWP plus 3% per 200 capsules.

$$\$125.00 + (\$125.00 \times 0.03) = \$125.00 + \$3.75$$
$$= \$128.75$$

Therefore, the pharmacy would be wise to charge

$$\$128.75 \div 200 = \$0.64/\text{capsule}$$

thereby making a profit of

$$\$0.64 - \$0.50 = \$0.14/\text{capsule}$$

Capitation Fee

capitation fee
a form of reimbursement in which the insurer pays the pharmacy a monthly fee to cover all prescriptions needed by a patient during that month

Some insurers use a form of reimbursement in which the pharmacy is paid a monthly fee, called a **capitation fee,** for some patients. The insurer pays the pharmacy the monthly fee whether or not the patients receive prescriptions during that month. The pharmacy in turn must dispense all the patients' prescriptions, even if the cost of the medication and the dispensing fee are more than the monthly fee. When profit is considered in terms of capitation fees, the profit refers only to the cost of the medication, and dispensing fees are not included unless a pharmacy insurance contract or capitation contract specifically states a dispensing fee should be considered.

Example 9.2.3

The Corner Drug Store receives a monthly capitation fee of $250.00 for John Jones. During April, John fills three prescriptions totaling $198.75. How much profit does the capitation fee provide?

In this case the monthly fee exceeds the sum of the prescription costs, yielding a profit for the pharmacy.

$$\$250.00 - \$198.75 = \$51.25$$

Example 9.2.4

Cindy Carver has the same insurance plan as John Jones, with the same capitation fee. During April, Cindy fills four prescriptions at The Corner Drug Store for a total of $301.25. What is the profit margin?

In this case the pharmacy wasn't so fortunate: the total cost of the prescriptions exceeds the monthly fee, which costs the pharmacy money (expressed as a negative number).

$$\$250.00 - \$301.25 = -\$51.25$$

Problem Set 9.2

✓ *Self-check your problem set work at* www.emcp.com.

Calculate the cost to the pharmacy as AWP less 13%.

1. AWP $48.90 per 60 tablets and dispense 20 tablets

2. AWP $84.07 per 100 tablets and dispense 30 tablets

3. AWP $30.25 per 1000 tablets and dispense 100 tablets

Calculate AWP plus 4% plus a $6.25 per prescription dispensing fee.

4. AWP $120.68 per 500 tablets and dispense 30 tablets

5. AWP $39.78 per 100 capsules and dispense 60 capsules

6. AWP $317.50 per 30 tablets and dispense 20 tablets

For the following problems, calculate the requested amounts.

7. AWP $71.35 per 100 tablets and dispense 50 tablets
   a. What is the cost of the medication to the pharmacy if the pharmacy pays AWP less 11.5%?

   b. What is the amount the insurance company will pay for the cost of the medication?

   c. What will be the total amount billed to the insurance company?

   d. What is the profit?

8. AWP $36.35 per metered dose inhaler (MDI) and dispense 2 MDI
   a. What is the cost of the medication to the pharmacy if the pharmacy pays AWP less 11.5%?

   b. What is the amount the insurance company will pay for the cost of the medication?

   c. What will be the total amount billed to the insurance company?

   d. What is the profit?

9. AWP $302.35 per 30 tablets and dispense 10 tablets
   a. What is the cost of the medication to the pharmacy if the pharmacy pays AWP less 11.5%?

   b. What is the amount the insurance company will pay for the cost of the medication?

   c. What will be the total amount billed to the insurance company?

   d. What is the profit?

10. AWP $117.35 per 50 capsules and dispense 6 capsules
    a. What is the cost of the medication to the pharmacy if the pharmacy pays AWP less 11.5%?

   b. What is the amount the insurance company will pay for the cost of the medication?

   c. What will be the total amount billed to the insurance company?

   d. What is the profit?

11. AWP $85.35 per 80 g tube and dispense 15 g jar
    a. What is the cost of the medication to the pharmacy if the pharmacy pays AWP less 11.5%?

   b. What is the amount the insurance company will pay for the cost of the medication?

   c. What will be the total amount billed to the insurance company?

   d. What is the profit?

Calculate the profit for the following.

12. Mountain Health Maintenance pays a capitation fee of $310.00 per month. Six patients on this plan bring in prescriptions during July. The pharmacy's drug costs for the prescriptions (but not the costs of dispensing the drugs) are as follows:

    Patient #1: $15.75, $106.50, $27.80
    Patient #2: $210.00
    Patient #3: $47.50, $105.25, $160.00, $52.60
    Patient #4: $150.00, $210.00, $76.00
    Patient #5: $10.50, $28.00, $62.50
    Patient #6: $210.00, $210.00, $17.00

    a. What is the total capitation?

    b. What is the pharmacy's cost for all of the prescriptions?

    c. Was the pharmacy's gross profit positive or negative?

    d. What was the gross profit?

13. In the preceding question, assume that all drugs were purchased at AWP and that, instead of a capitation fee, the pharmacy was allowed AWP plus 3% and a $2.00 dispensing fee for each drug dispensed.
    a. How much would the pharmacy have received from the insurer?

    b. Is the gross profit more or less than with capitation?

    c. How much more or less?

14. Jackson HMO pays a capitation fee of $275.00 per month to OWL Pharmacy. OWL Pharmacy serves 10 of Jackson's clients. The pharmacy fills prescriptions for five of these clients during the month of June, The pharmacy's costs for these prescriptions are as follows:

    Patient JES: $89.63
    Patient LMS: $126.54 (total cost for 2 prescriptions)
    Patient SMJ: $420.45 (total cost for 5 prescriptions)
    Patient EMJ: $117.50
    Patient BAG: $46.75

    The other five clients did not get any prescriptions during the month of June.
    a. What is the capitation received?

    b. What was the cost to the pharmacy for the above prescriptions?

    c. How much was the pharmacy's loss or gain in serving Jackson HMO's patients?

15. Baker HMO pays a capitation fee of $275.00 per month to OWL Pharmacy. OWL Pharmacy serves 12 of Baker's clients. The pharmacy filled prescriptions for five of these clients during the month of May. The pharmacy's costs for these prescriptions are as follows:

    Patient KGE: $78.26, $75.23, $25.48
    Patient PAD: $128.46, $21.86
    Patient THN: $61.89, $41.20
    Patient WER: $16.50, $5.80, $3.87, $21.67
    Patient REW: $58.24

The other seven clients did not get any prescriptions during the month of May.

    a. What is the capitation received?

    b. What was the cost to the pharmacy for the above prescriptions?

    c. How much was the pharmacy's loss or gain in serving Baker HMO's patients?

16. Blue Care HMO pays a capitation fee of $225.00 per month to Key Pharmacy. Key Pharmacy serves 40 of Blue Care's clients. During the month of May, 12 patients had prescriptions filled at a total cost of $1867.50 plus $60.00 in dispensing costs.
    a. What is the capitation received?

    b. What was the cost to the pharmacy for the above prescriptions (including dispensing costs)?

    c. How much was the pharmacy's loss or gain in serving Blue Care HMO's patients?

17. Insurance-R-Us HMO pays a capitation fee of $210.00 per month to Phicks Pharmacy. Phicks Pharmacy serves 42 of the HMO's clients. During the month of September, 23 patients had 31 prescriptions filled at a total cost to the pharmacy of $2389.00 plus $4.25 per prescription in dispensing costs.
    a. What is the capitation received?

    b. What was the cost to the pharmacy for the above prescriptions (including dispensing costs)?

    c. How much was the pharmacy's loss or gain in serving the HMO's patients?

9.3 INVENTORY APPLICATIONS

inventory
a listing of all items that are available for sale in a business

inventory value
the total value of the drugs and merchandise in stock in the pharmacy on a given day

An **inventory** is a listing of all items that are available for sale in a business. **Inventory value** is defined as the total value of the drugs and merchandise in stock on a given day. Pharmacies must maintain a record of drugs and other supplies and merchandise purchased and sold to know when to reorder and when to adjust inventory levels of each item.

Space must be allocated to maintain inventory. Other considerations include shelving design and refrigeration. Keeping medications on the shelf is a cost to a pharmacy, and a large inventory can hinder cash flow. To minimize the shelf space needed and control costs, a pharmacy should try to manage its inventory so that medications arrive shortly before they are dispensed and sold. Nevertheless, unlike some businesses, a pharmacy may need to keep some very slow-moving drugs in stock as a service to a few customers.

Managing Inventory

Today, most inventory records are computerized. Each time drugs are purchased, the quantity and price are entered into the computer database. As customers buy the drugs, the computer system automatically adjusts the inventory record. Pharmacies usually establish an inventory range for each item, that is, a maximum and a minimum number of units to have on hand. When the inventory drops to the minimum level, the item is purchased to restock the supply. This predetermined order point and the order quantity are based on the historical use of each drug.

Example 9.3.1

The maximum inventory level for ampicillin capsules is 1000 capsules. At the end of the day, the computer prints a list of items to be reordered; the list indicates an inventory level of 75 ampicillin capsules. How many capsules should be ordered to restock the inventory to maximum? If the drug wholesaler supplies ampicillin in bottles of 25, 100, 250, and 500 capsules, how many of each bottle size will fill the order (assuming that you begin with one 500-capsule bottle)?

To replenish the ampicillin inventory to the maximum level (1000), first determine how much the present level differs.

$$1000 \text{ capsules} - 75 \text{ capsules} = 925 \text{ capsules}$$

Then the idea is to purchase the 925 capsules in bottles of 500, 250, 100, and 25. It is good business practice to purchase the smallest possible number of bottles because large-quantity containers are usually a more economical purchase.

$$500 \text{ capsules} + 250 \text{ capsules} + 100 \text{ capsules} + 25 \text{ capsules} = 925 \text{ capsules}$$
  1 bottle   1 bottle   1 bottle   3 bottles

Example 9.3.2   **The inventory of Zantac 150 mg is to be maintained at a minimum of 240 tablets and a maximum of 300 tablets. If 15 tablets are left on the shelf at the end of the day, how many bottles will be ordered to meet the inventory minimum? Zantac 150 mg is commercially available in a 60-tablet bottle.**

First determine the difference between the current inventory and the minimum inventory.

$$240 \text{ tablets} - 15 \text{ tablets} = 225 \text{ tablets}$$

Therefore, it will take at least 225 tablets to bring the inventory up to the minimum level for Zantac 150. But the tablets must be ordered in bottles of 60.

$$225 \text{ tablets} \div 60 \text{ tablets/bottle} = 3.75 \text{ bottles}$$

Rounding up, four bottles must be ordered.

Example 9.3.3   **The inventory of propranolol 10 mg is to be maintained at a minimum of 300 tablets and a maximum of 1500 tablets. If 212 tablets are left on the shelf at the end of the day, how many bottles will you order to meet the inventory minimum? Propranolol is available in 100-tablet, 500-tablet, and 1000-tablet bottles, and you normally order propranolol in a 1000-tablet bottle.**

First determine the minimum number of tablets that need to be ordered.

$$300 \text{ tablets} - 212 \text{ tablets} = 88 \text{ tablets}$$

Although either the 100-tablet or the 500-tablet bottle will work, it is common business practice always to order the same package size. Therefore, even though it significantly surpasses the minimum, you will order one bottle of 1,000 propranolol. The resulting inventory will still be within the acceptable range and will not exceed 1500 tablets.

Example 9.3.4   **You would like to replenish the lip balm that is kept on the pharmacy counter by the cash register, and you need 18 tubes to fill the container. When you look in the wholesale catalog, it states that the lip balm is $10.20/dozen. What do you order?**

You will order 2 dozen—or 24 tubes of lip balm.

Days' Supply

days' supply
a method of inventory management that tries to keep inventory value approximately equal to the cost to the pharmacy of the products sold in a certain number of days; calculated as the value of inventory divided by the average daily cost of products sold

Often today's pharmacies have $75,000.00 to $200,000.00 in inventory sitting on the shelves as drug products. If a large chain has 10 stores in a particular region, the amount of money in goods sitting on the shelf adds up very quickly. Large companies often set goals for lowering the inventory in order to improve cash flow. One method used to set inventory goals for a pharmacy is called **"days' supply,"** which refers to making the value of the inventory approximately equal to the cost to the pharmacy of the products sold in a certain number of days. A common number is in the 25–35 day range. For example, if a pharmacy has a goal of "30 days' supply," its goal is to keep the value of the inventory equal to the total cost to the pharmacy of the products sold in 30 days.

Sometimes, a pharmacy does not know the best number of days to use as a goal in calculating costs. It does know the current inventory value, however, and can easily calculate average daily costs (weekly costs ÷ 7 days). With this information, the pharmacy can determine how many days it will take (what is referred to as "days' supply") for the average daily product costs to equal the value of the inventory. Then the pharmacy can revise the goal as necessary.

$$\text{number of days' supply} = \frac{\text{value of inventory}}{\text{average daily cost of products sold}}$$

Example 9.3.5 **Tom's Pharmacy has a total inventory value of $103,699.00. It had sales last week of $37,546.00, and the cost to the pharmacy of the products sold was $28,837.00. What should the pharmacy's days' supply be in order to keep its inventory value stable?**

Tom's average daily product costs were

$$\$28,837.00 \div 7 \text{ days} = \$4120.00 \text{ (rounded)}$$

Now, according to the above formula, dividing the value of the inventory by the average daily product costs approximately equals the number of days' supply:

$$\text{number of days' supply} = \frac{\$103,699.00}{\$4120.00} = 25$$

Thus, in 25 days, Tom will have sold products approximately equal to the value of his inventory.

Example 9.3.6 **Lisa's Pharmacy has a total inventory value of $176,989.00. Last week it had sales of $45,813.00, and the cost to the pharmacy of the products sold came to $36,592.00. Lisa's goal for the number of days' supply is 29, but she's currently over her goal. How many days' supply is she over, and how much inventory value does this represent?**

The average daily product costs were

$$\$36,592.00 \div 7 \text{ days} = \$5227.00 \text{ (rounded)}$$

At the present time, the number of days' supply for the pharmacy is

$$\frac{\$176,989.00}{\$5227.00} = 34$$

Therefore, it takes 34 days for costs to equal the inventory value. In other words, Lisa is 5 days over.

$$5 \times \$5227.00 = \$26,135.00$$

If Lisa can reduce her inventory by this amount, she will have met her goal of 29 days' supply.

Turnover Rate

If a pharmacy does not maintain computerized inventory, it must perform a physical inventory count at intervals, usually annually or semiannually. The physical inventory value is then used to determine the average inventory as follows.

$$\text{average inventory} = \frac{\text{beginning inventory} + \text{present inventory}}{2}$$

Knowing the average inventory allows a pharmacy to calculate the number of times its inventory was repurchased during a cycle (usually a year).

Dividing total annual purchases of inventory by the average inventory value gives the **turnover rate,** or the number of times the amount of goods in inventory was sold during the year. It is calculated as follows.

$$\text{turnover rate} = \frac{\text{annual purchases of inventory}}{\text{average inventory value}}$$

Knowing this number can help the pharmacist determine if the average inventory level should be increased or decreased, as extra costs may be associated with high or low inventories. Thus, if a pharmacy has an average inventory value of $25,250.00 and annual inventory purchases of $75,000.00, the amount of goods in inventory will turn over 2.97 times, or approximately three times in a year.

$$\text{turnover rate} = \frac{\$75,000.00}{\$25,250.00} = 2.97$$

turnover rate
the number of times the amount of goods in inventory is sold during a year; calculated by dividing total annual purchases of inventory by the average inventory value

Example 9.3.7

A pharmacy does a quarterly inventory count and has an average inventory value of $100,000.00. Annual inventory purchases are $500,000.00. What is the turnover rate?

$$\text{turnover rate} = \frac{\$500,000.00}{\$100,000.00} = 5$$

Depreciation

depreciation
an allowance made to account for the decreasing value of an asset

Depreciation is an allowance made to account for the decreasing value of an asset. Properties owned by the pharmacy are called assets. They are put into two broad categories: current and long-term assets. The assets that can be consumed or converted into cash within one year are current assets, and those that cannot are long-term assets, usually buildings and equipment.

Buildings and equipment lose value due to use, obsolescence, and the passage of time. The straight-line depreciation method of calculating depreciation uses the total cost, the estimated life of the property (in years), and the disposal value in the following formula.

$$\text{annual depreciation} = \frac{\text{total cost} - \text{disposal value}}{\text{estimated life}}$$

Example 9.3.8   **Rafael's Drug Shop buys a compact car for drug deliveries to customers. The cost of the car is $9000.00. Its estimated useful life is five years, and the disposal value is $1200.00. What is the annual depreciation?**

$$\text{annual depreciation} = \frac{\$9000.00 - \$1200.00}{5} = \frac{\$7800.00}{5}$$

$$= \$1560$$

Problem Set 9.3 _____

✓ *Self-check your problem set work at* www.emcp.com.

Calculate the number of packages that need to be re-ordered for each item.

	Drug	Package Size	Minimum # Units	Maximum # Units	Current Inventory	Re-order
1.	tetracycline 250 mg cap	500	120	700	80	
2.	amoxicillin 500 mg cap	500	240	1000	118	
3.	amoxicillin 250 mg cap	500	240	1000	180	
4.	cefaclor 500 mg tab	60	20	120	35	
5.	cefprozil 250 mg tab	100	40	150	28	
6.	cefprozil 500 mg tab	50	20	75	24	
7.	metronidazole 500 mg tab	50	30	120	12	
8.	azithromycin 250 mg cap	30	18	60	36	
9.	doxycylcine 50 mg cap	50	30	150	42	

The current inventory of topical products on the shelf is often checked due to compounding needs, special orders, and poor computer tracking of dispensed partial containers of dermal products. For this reason, re-ordering of topical products must be monitored even with computer-generated orders. The technician has checked the shelf and found the following. Calculate the number of packages that need to be re-ordered for each item.

	Drug	Package Size	Minimum # Units	Maximum # Units	Current Inventory	Re-order
10.	triamcinolone 0.25% cream	15 g	2	4	1	
		80 g	2	4	0	
11.	triamcinolone 0.1% ung	15 g	1	2	1	
		60 g	1	2	1	
		80 g	1	2	0	
12.	triamcinolone 0.1% lotion	60 mL	1	2	1	
13.	fluocinolone 0.025% cream	15 g	1	2	1	
		60 g	1	2	1	
14.	fluocinolone 0.025 ung	60 g	1	2	0 tubes and 1 order waiting	
15.	desoximetasone 0.25% cream	15 g	1	2	0	
		60 g	1	2	0	
		4 oz	1	2	1	
16.	desoximetasone 0.05% gel	15 g	1	1	0 on shelf and 1 order waiting	
		60 g	1	1	0	
17.	halobetasol 0.05% cream	15 g	1	2	1	
		45 g	1	2	1	
18.	fluocinonide 0.05% cream	15 g	1	2	1	
		30 g	2	4	1	
		60 g	2	4	2	
		120 g	1	2	0	
19.	fluocinonide 0.05% gel	15 g	1	1	1	
		30 g	1	3	2	
		60 g	1	3	0	
20.	fluocinonide 0.05% ung	15 g	1	2	1	
		30 g	1	2	1	
		60 g	1	2	1 partial	
		120 g	1	2	1	
21.	fluocinonide 0.05% soln	20 mL	1	1	0	
		60 mL	1	3	1 partial	

Calculate the number of packages that need to be re-ordered for each item.

	Drug	Package Size	Minimum # Units	Maximum # Units	Current Inventory	Re-order
22.	ramipril 5 mg cap	100	120	240	64	
23.	verapamil 120 mg SR	100	80	240	52	
24.	verapamil 240 mg SR	100	120	360	30	
25.	nicardipine 60 mg SR	60	120	240	20	
26.	captopril 50 mg tab	100	150	300	76	
27.	furosemide 40 mg tab	1000	240	1500	134	
28.	doxazosin 2 mg tab	100	80	240	83	
29.	atenolol 50 mg tabs	1000	240	1500	107	
30.	atenolol 100 mg tabs	100	150	300	111	
31.	nifedipine 60 mg tab	300	120	625	12 & 2 Rx for 60 pending	
32.	nifedipine 90 mg tab	100	120	300	63	
33.	lisinopril 5 mg tab	100	90	260	110	
34.	lisinopril 10 mg tab	1000	240	1500	146	
35.	lisinopril 20 mg tab	100	180	250	145	
36.	lisinopril 40 mg tab	100	90	220	152	

37. Review the inventory list below and calculate the necessary purchases to reestablish maximum inventory. Write your answers in the "Purchased" column.

	A　　B	C	D	E	F	G
1	JOHNS DRUG SHOP					
2	Current Drug	Max.	Dispensed	Min.	Current	Purchased
3	Date	Level	Today	Level	Inventory	
4	Eucerin cream, jars	10	1	3	3	
5	Ampicillin caps	4500	500	4000	2400	
6	Eyedrops, bottles	24	4	4	4	
7	Nystatin oral solution	1000 mL	100 mL	200 mL	400 mL	
8	Sterile saline	600 mL	315 mL	100 mL	75 mL	
9						
10						
11						
12						
13						

38. Adam's Pharmacy has a total inventory value of $183,445.00. Last week the pharmacy had sales of $47,293.00, and the cost to the pharmacy for the products sold came to $38,207.00. Adam's goal is to have a days' supply of 28 days.
   a. How many days' supply does Adam have?

   b. How much is he over or under his goal in dollars?

39. Corbin's Pharmacy has a total inventory value of $123,490.00. Last week the pharmacy had sales of $34,829.00, and the cost to the pharmacy for the products sold came to $26,504.00. Corbin's goal is to have a days' supply of 26 days.
   a. How many days' supply does Corbin have?

   b. How much is he over or under his goal in dollars?

40. Karen's Pharmacy has $147,210.00 in inventory. She is currently at her goal of 24 days' supply. What were her approximate sales for last week?

41. Scott's Pharmacy had sales of $51,280.00 last week. What must his daily sales average be this week in order to make $5000.00 more than last week?

42. Bob's Pharmacy has an inventory of $213,840.00. Last week's sales were $63,910.00. What was the percent profit if the cost of last week's sales was $48,891.00?

43. Teri's Pharmacy has an inventory of $164,590.00. Last week's sales, which totaled $58,223.00, brought in a 21% profit. Now Teri's days' supply goal is 31 days.
   a. What was the cost to the pharmacy of the product sold last week?

   b. What is the pharmacy's days' supply?

   c. How much is the value of the days' supply above or below the goal in dollars?

44. Kathy's Pharmacy has an inventory of $184,520.00. Her cost of sales last week was $28,223.00, and she made a 26% profit. Her days' supply goal is 34 days.
   a. What was the amount sold last week?

   b. What is the pharmacy's days' supply?

   c. How much is the value of the days' supply above or below goal in dollars?

45. If a pharmacy's average inventory for the last year was $132,936.00 and the annual cost total was $1,612,000.00, what was the turnover rate?

46. If a pharmacy's average inventory for the last year was $156,200.00 and the annual cost total was $1,768,000.00, what was the turnover rate?

Calculate the turnover rate for the following drugs sold at Adam's Pharmacy.

	Drug	Average Inventory	Annual Purchases	Turnover Rate
47.	metformin 500 mg	$520.00	$20,800.00	
48.	divalproex 250 mg	$178.00	$5760.00	
49.	citalopram 40 mg	$360.00	$7213.00	
50.	raloxifene 60 mg	$320.00	$5060.00	
51.	montelukast chewtab 4 mg	$385.00	$6000.00	

52. John's Drug Shop purchases $52,500.00 of antibiotics annually. The pharmacy does an inventory count twice annually, and its average inventory of antibiotics is $5000.00. What is the pharmacy's turnover rate for antibiotics?

53. The pharmacy has a new cash register system. The system cost $8294.00 and should last six years. Its disposal value is $2138.00. What is the annual depreciation?

54. The hospital pharmacy just purchased two new biological safety hoods at $18,350.00 each. Each should last 12 years if maintained properly. The disposal value is $1567.00 each. What is the annual depreciation?

Practice Test

The OWL Pharmacy has the following overhead expenses.

pharmacist(s) salary	$126,000.00
technician(s) salary	38,000.00
rent	12,000.00
utilities	7,000.00
computer maintenance	1,500.00
software subscriptions	1,500.00
liability insurance	2,500.00
business insurance	3,000.00
drug purchases	425,000.00

1. If a 25% profit is desirable, what must the pharmacy's income be in order to meet this goal?

2. If the pharmacy's income is $1,401,750.00, what is its percent profit?

Calculate the dollar amount of net profit and the percent profit (markup rate) for the following individual prescription drug items. (Round to whole percents.) The dispensing fee is $5.24 for each prescription.

3. Pepcid (famotidine) 40 mg _____
   Cost: $84.30 per 30 tablets
   Dispense: 30 tablets
   Rx Charge: $95.00
   a. net profit

   b. markup rate

Calculate the following and state the answer in dollars or percent as indicated.

4. John's Drug Shop purchases five cases of dermatological cream at $100.00 per case. The invoice specifies a 15% discount if the account is paid in full within 15 days. What is the discounted price?

5. There are 24 tubes of cream per case in question 9. You are to mark each tube up by 20% based on the discounted cost. What will the selling price be per tube?

The pharmacy accountant wants items tabulated as to percent profit. Calculate the markup and percent profit of each of the following items. (Round to whole percents.)

	Item	Cost	Selling Price	Markup	% Profit
6.	amoxicillin	$0.14	$0.28		
7.	nasal spray	$1.45	$2.15		
8.	fungal ointment	$3.25	$4.15		
9.	analgesic tablets	$0.10	$0.15		
10.	contraceptive foam	$1.35	$5.75		

Calculate the cost to the pharmacy as AWP less 12%.

11. AWP $94.45 per 120 g tube and dispense 30 g

12. AWP $12.50 per 1 pint liquid and dispense 120 mL

Calculate AWP plus 3% plus a $5.75 per prescription dispensing fee.

13. AWP $21.35 per 30 g tube and dispense 30 g tube

14. AWP $90.32 per pint liquid and dispense 6 fl oz

Calculate the profit for the following.

15. A prescription is written for a tube of ointment. The AWP is $62.00. Smith's Pharmacy purchases the tube at AWP, and Jones's Pharmacy purchases the tube at AWP minus 10%. The insurer will reimburse at AWP plus 2% plus a $1.50 dispensing fee. How much profit does each pharmacy make?

16. Grant County HMO pays a capitation fee of $195.00 per month to OWL Pharmacy. OWL Pharmacy serves 17 of the HMO's clients. During the month of June, 12 patients had prescriptions filled at a total cost of $867.50 plus $60 in dispensing costs.
    a. What is the capitation received?

    b. What is the cost to the pharmacy for the above prescriptions?

    c. How much was the pharmacy's loss or gain in serving the Grant County HMO patients?

Calculate the number of packages that need to be re-ordered for each item.

	Drug	Package Size	Minimum # Units	Maximum # Units	Current Inventory	Re-order
17.	nicardipine 30 mg SR	60	120	240	18	
18.	captopril 25 mg tab	100	150	300	60	
19.	metoprolol 50 mg tabs	1000	120	1500	83	
20.	metoprolol 100 mg	1000	120	2000	341	

21. Down-the-Street Pharmacy does inventory three times annually, and the average inventory value is $125,825.00. Annual purchases of inventory total $188,737.50. What is the turnover rate?

22. The pharmacy has a van for home deliveries, and its total cost was $18,452.00. Its disposal value is $12,208.00. It has an estimated life of three years. What is the annual depreciation?

23. The pharmacy has some lab equipment that cost $1478.00. Its disposal value is $850.00, and its estimated life is eight years. What is the annual depreciation?

Understanding the Apothecary System

10

Objectives

- Identify symbols and measures of the apothecary system.
- Use the apothecary system to solve medication problems.
- Identify approximately equivalent apothecary and metric units and convert measurements between the two systems.

10.1 APOTHECARY VOLUME AND WEIGHT EQUIVALENCES

apothecary system
literally the system used by an apothecary, a system of measurement used in pharmacy prior to the metric system; units of measure include minims, fluidrams, scruples, grains, ounces, and pounds

Safety Note

Do not confuse ounces and drams in the weight and volume systems. Be sure to use the word *fluid* or the symbol *f* when referring to volume.

Remember

apothecary pound (℔) = 12 oz
household pound (lb) = 16 oz

The **apothecary system,** literally the system used by an apothecary, is one of the oldest systems of measurement. The units of measure in this system are denoted with the special symbols shown in Table 10.1. The apothecary system uses fractions, as opposed to decimals, and because this system is less accurate than the metric system, its use is declining in the United States. Table 10.2 shows the equivalences of the basic measures of volume and weight for the apothecary system. Note that in two instances—the ounce and the dram—the same names are used for measures of both volume and weight. To avoid confusion, always use the word *fluid* when referring to volume measure. Note that whereas in the household system, *fluid ounce* is written as two words, in the apothecary system, *fluidounce* is written as one word, as is *fluidram*. With the equivalents shown in Table 10.2, you can change units to larger or smaller units as demonstrated in the following examples.

Table 10.1 Apothecary Symbols

Volume		Weight	
Unit of Measure	**Symbol**	**Unit of Measure**	**Symbol**
minim	♏	grain	gr
fluidrachm, fluidram	f ʒ	scruple	℈
fluidounce	f ℥	drachm, dram	ʒ
		ounce	℥
		pound	℔ (or #)

Table 10.2 Equivalent Units of Measure within the Apothecary System

Volume		Weight	
60 ♏	= 1 f ʒ	20 gr	= 1 ϶
6 f ʒ	= 1 f ℥ *	3 ϶	= 1 ʒ
16 f ℥	= 1 pt	8 ʒ	= 1 ℥
2 pt	= 1 qt	12 ℥	= 1 ℔ (or #)†
4 qt	= 1 gallon		

*There are actually 8 f ʒ in 1 f ℥ , but pharmacies use 6 f ʒ because convention dictates that 1 f ʒ = 1 tsp = 5 mL.
†The apothecary pound equals 12 ℥ , but the household pound equals 16 oz and is the more commonly used equivalence.

Example 10.1.1 **How many fluidrams are in 3 pt?**

A pint equals 16 f℥; therefore,

$$3 \text{ pt} = 3 \times 16 \text{ f℥} = 48 \text{ f℥}$$

Each fluidounce contains 6 fʒ; therefore,

$$48 \text{ f℥} = 48 \times 6 \text{ fʒ} = 288 \text{ fʒ}$$

In this case, each unit was replaced by its equivalence for the next smallest unit, until the required unit was reached.

Example 10.1.2 **Reduce 7160 ♏ to the smallest possible number of all of the larger units.**

Each fluidram contains 60 ♏. Dividing 7160 by 60 gives 119 with a remainder (r.) of 20; therefore,

$$7160 \text{ ♏} = 119 \text{ fʒ}, 20 \text{ ♏}$$

Note that the remainder is the smaller unit. A fluidounce contains 6 fʒ; since 119 is greater than 6, we can convert 119 fʒ to fluidrams. Dividing 119 by 6 gives 19 r.5; therefore,

$$119 \text{ fʒ} = 19 \text{ f℥}, 5 \text{ fʒ}$$

A pint contains 16 f℥; since 19 is greater than 16, we can convert 19 f℥ to pints. Dividing 19 by 16 gives 1 r.3; therefore,

$$19 \text{ f℥} = 1 \text{ pt}, 3 \text{ f℥}$$

Each quart contains 2 pt, which is greater than the amount we have, so no other units can be replaced. Putting it all together,

$$7160 \text{ ♏} = 1 \text{ pt}, 3 \text{ f℥}, 5 \text{ fʒ}, 20 \text{ ♏}$$

Example 10.1.3

You have 6 ℥ of a dry powder. How many 2 ʒ doses can you make from this?

There are 8 ʒ in an ounce, so

$$6\ ℥ \times \frac{8\ ʒ}{℥} = 48\ ʒ$$

Then determine the number of doses.

$$48\ ʒ \div 2\ ʒ/\text{dose} = 24\ \text{doses}$$

Therefore, 24 doses of 2 ʒ each can be made from 6 ℥ of dry powder.

Example 10.1.4

Reduce 10,000 gr to the smallest possible number of all of the larger units.

A scruple is equal to 20 gr, and 10,000 ÷ 20 = 500, so

$$10,000\ \text{gr} = 500\ ℈$$

A dram is equal to 3 ℈, and 500 ÷ 3 = 166 r.2, so

$$500\ ℈ = 166\ ʒ, 2\ ℈$$

An ounce is equal to 8 ʒ, and 166 ÷ 8 = 20 r.6, so

$$166\ ʒ = 20\ ℥, 6\ ʒ$$

Finally, a pound is equal to 12 ℥, and 20 ÷ 12 = 1 r.8, so

$$20\ ℥ = 1\ ℔, 8\ ℥$$

Putting it all together,

$$10,000\ \text{gr} = 1\ ℔, 8\ ℥, 6\ ʒ, 2\ ℈$$

Example 10.1.5

Convert 68 ʒ to grains.

$$68\ ʒ \times \frac{3\ ℈}{1\ ʒ} = 204\ ℈$$

$$204\ ℈ \times \frac{20\ \text{gr}}{1\ ℈} = 4080\ \text{gr}$$

Example 10.1.6   **Convert 1 ℔ to grains.**

$$1\ ℔ \times \frac{12\ ʒ}{1\ ℔} = 12\ ʒ$$

$$12\ ʒ \times \frac{8\ ʒ}{1\ ʒ} = 96\ ʒ$$

$$96\ ʒ \times \frac{3\ Ƹ}{1\ ʒ} = 288\ Ƹ$$

$$288\ Ƹ \times \frac{20\ gr}{1\ Ƹ} = 5760\ gr$$

Problem Set 10.1 _____

✓ *Self-check your problem set work at* www.emcp.com.

Convert the following.

1. Convert 6 gal to apothecary fluidounces.

2. Convert 1 fʒ, 3 fʒ, 7 ♍ to just minims.

3. Convert 479 fʒ to the smallest possible of all of the larger apothecary units.

4. How many drams are equivalent to 1 ℔, 6 ʒ?

5. Reduce 6000 gr to the smallest number of all of the larger apothecary units.

6. How many fluidrams are equal to 3 qt?

7. Change 10 ʒ, 2 ʒ, 1 Ƹ to grains.

8. Convert 6 pt to fluidrams.

9. Convert 15 ℔ to ounces.

10. Convert 12 fʒ to fluidounces.

10.2 CONVERSIONS BETWEEN THE APOTHECARY AND METRIC SYSTEMS

avoirdupois system
an alternative system of measurement used in pharmacy prior to the metric system

To convert metric measurements to apothecary units and vice versa, you need to know the equivalent measures shown in Table 10.3. This table also provides equivalences in the **avoirdupois system** and the household system. As a general rule, convert all quantities to the metric system as soon as possible in the conversion process to make the conversion as accurate as possible. Metric units are readily comparable from one unit to the next, and unlike the apothecary and household systems, the metric system uses only 10-based conversion factors, which are easier to use in calculations.

Converting Fluidounces

When converting from fluidounces to milliliters in pharmacy calculations, it is common practice to round up; for example, round 29.57 mL up to 30 mL. In this chapter, use 30 mL when converting from fluidounces.

Safety Note

Many manufacturers use 60 mg instead of 65 mg as the equivalent for 1 gr. Read the label to confirm the package contents.

Table 10.3 Apothecary, Avoirdupois, Household, and Metric System Equivalents

	Apothecary	Avoirdupois	Household	Metric
Volume				
	16.23 ℳ			1 mL
	1 f 3		1 tsp	5 mL*
	6 f 3 or 1 f ʒ		6 tsp or 2 tbsp	30 mL (29.57 mL)†
	1 pt		1 pt	480 mL†
	1 qt		1 qt	960 mL
	1 gallon		1 gallon	3840 mL
Weight				
	1 gr			65 mg††
		1 oz		30 g (28.35 g)
			1 oz	30 g
	1 ʒ or 8 ʒ			30 g (31.1 g)
	1 ℔			373.2 g
		1 lb	1 lb	454 g

*There are actually 3.75 mL in 1 f 3 . However, convention dictates that 1 f 3 = 1 tsp = 5 mL.
†There are actually 29.57 mL in 1 f ʒ , but 30 mL is usually used. When packaging a pint, companies will typically include 473 mL, rather than the full 480 mL.
††Many manufacturers use 60 mg instead of 65 mg as the equivalent for 1 gr.

Remember

6 f 3 = 1 f ʒ
8 ʒ = 1 ʒ

Safety Note

The f 3 (or 3) symbol in medication orders is interpreted to mean a teaspoonful.

Remember

16 fl oz = 480 mL
1 fl oz = 30 mL

A special discrepancy to keep in mind is the difference between the true volume of a fluidram and the commonly used volume. Before the household system was created, 1 f 3 = 3.75 mL and 8 f 3 = 1 f ʒ. When the household system was formed, 1 f 3 became synonymous with 1 tsp or 5 mL, thus changing the equivalence to 6 f 3 = 1 f ʒ. Therefore, Table 10.3 states that there are 6 f 3 per 1 f ʒ and 1 f 3 = 5 mL. In this chapter, you will use these conversions.

As Chapter 5 explained, it is common practice to round a household fluid ounce (29.57 mL) up to 30 mL. When measuring this amount, this estimation is often appropriate because the volume differs by such a small amount. When measuring multiple fluid ounces that have been rounded up to 30 mL, however, the discrepancy becomes far more apparent. For example, if asked to measure a pint (16 fl oz), one would measure roughly 480 mL. This becomes problematic because 29.57 mL multiplied by 16 is equal to only 473.12 mL, not 480 mL. Most stock bottles are labeled 473 mL, yet pharmacies bill according to the estimation of 480 mL and measure out fluid ounces in 30 mL increments. For the purposes of this chapter, use the rounded 30 mL and 480 mL values.

Example 10.2.1   **Convert 1 gallon, 12 f ʒ to milliliters.**

Begin solving this problem by noting that according to Table 10.3,

$$1 \text{ gallon} = 3840 \text{ mL}$$

The value of 12 f ʒ can be converted to milliliters in two ways.

Solution 1: Using the ratio-proportion method,

$$\frac{x \text{ mL}}{12 \text{ f} \text{ʒ}} = \frac{30 \text{ mL}}{1 \text{ f} \text{ʒ}}$$

$$x \text{ mL} = 360 \text{ mL}$$

Solution 2: Using the dimensional analysis method,

$$12 \text{ f} \text{ʒ} \times \frac{30 \text{ mL}}{1 \text{ f} \text{ʒ}} = 360 \text{ mL}$$

Add the milliliter equivalent of 1 gallon and 12 fʒ.

$$3840 \text{ mL} + 360 \text{ mL} = 4200 \text{ mL}$$

Example 10.2.2 **Convert 2 pt to milliliters.**

Solution 1: Using the ratio-proportion method,

$$\frac{x \text{ mL}}{2 \text{ pt}} = \frac{480 \text{ mL}}{1 \text{ pt}}$$

$$x \text{ mL} = 960 \text{ mL}$$

Solution 2: Using the dimensional analysis method,

$$2 \text{ pt} \times \frac{480 \text{ mL}}{1 \text{ pt}} = 960 \text{ mL}$$

Example 10.2.3 **Convert 6 fʒ to milliliters.**

Solution 1: Using the ratio-proportion method,

$$\frac{x \text{ mL}}{6 \text{ f} \text{ʒ}} = \frac{30 \text{ mL}}{1 \text{ f} \text{ʒ}}$$

$$x \text{ mL} = 180 \text{ mL}$$

Solution 2: Using the dimensional analysis method,

$$6 \text{ f} \text{ʒ} \times \frac{30 \text{ mL}}{1 \text{ f} \text{ʒ}} = 180 \text{ mL}$$

Example 10.2.4　　**Convert ¾ gallon to milliliters.**

Begin by converting the fraction to a decimal.

$$\text{¾ gallon} = 0.75 \text{ gallon}$$

Solution 1: Using the ratio-proportion method,

$$\frac{x \text{ mL}}{0.75 \text{ gallon}} = \frac{3840 \text{ mL}}{1 \text{ gallon}}$$

$$x \text{ mL} = 2880 \text{ mL}$$

Solution 2: Using the dimensional analysis method,

$$0.75 \text{ gallon} \times \frac{3840 \text{ mL}}{1 \text{ gallon}} = 2880 \text{ mL}$$

Example 10.2.5　　**Convert 8 f℥ to fluidrams.**

First, convert fluidounces to milliliters.
Solution 1: Using the ratio-proportion method,

$$\frac{x \text{ mL}}{8 \text{ f℥}} = \frac{30 \text{ mL}}{1 \text{ f℥}}$$

$$x \text{ mL} = 240 \text{ mL}$$

Solution 2: Using the dimensional analysis method,

$$8 \text{ f℥} \times \frac{30 \text{ mL}}{1 \text{ f℥}} = 240 \text{ mL}$$

Second, convert milliliters to fluidrams.
Solution 1: Using the ratio-proportion method,

$$\frac{x \text{ f}\!\!3}{240 \text{ mL}} = \frac{1 \text{ f}\!\!3}{5 \text{ mL}}$$

$$x \text{ f}\!\!3 = 48 \text{ f}\!\!3$$

Solution 2: Using the dimensional analysis method,

$$240 \text{ mL} \times \frac{1 \text{ f}\!\!3}{5 \text{ mL}} = 48 \text{ f}\!\!3$$

Converting Ounces

Many physicians are accustomed to writing prescription orders in ounces of medication, in both liquid and solid forms. As mentioned earlier, however, the metric system is considered to be a more accurate system and is becoming the system of choice in the United States. Also, many pharmacy computer systems are programmed to accept amounts only in metric units. Therefore, another calculation performed frequently is the conversion of ounces to grams. According to Table 10.3, the apothecary ounce equals 31.1 g, the avoirdupois ounce equals 28.35 g, and the household ounce equals 30 g. In all three cases, it is common practice to round to 30 g.

Remember
Round the value of 1 ounce in all three systems to 30 g.

Example 10.2.6

You have 14 ℥ of a dry chemical. What is the equivalent weight in grams?

Solution 1: Using the ratio-proportion method,

$$\frac{x \text{ g}}{14 \text{ ℥}} = \frac{30 \text{ g}}{1 \text{ ℥}}$$

$$x \text{ g} = 420 \text{ g}$$

Solution 2: Using the dimensional analysis method,

$$14 \text{ ℥} \times \frac{30 \text{ g}}{1 \text{ ℥}} = 420 \text{ g}$$

Example 10.2.7

Convert 23 ℥ to grams.

Solution 1: Using the ratio-proportion method,

$$\frac{x \text{ g}}{23 \text{ ℥}} = \frac{30 \text{ g}}{1 \text{ ℥}}$$

$$x \text{ g} = 690 \text{ g}$$

Solution 2: Using the dimensional analysis method,

$$23 \text{ ℥} \times \frac{30 \text{ g}}{1 \text{ ℥}} = 690 \text{ g}$$

Example 10.2.8

Convert 2 lb (avoirdupois) to grams.

Solution 1: Using the ratio-proportion method,

$$\frac{x \text{ g}}{2 \text{ lb}} = \frac{454 \text{ g}}{1 \text{ lb}}$$

$$x \text{ g} = 908 \text{ g}$$

Solution 2: Using the dimensional analysis method,

$$2 \text{ lb} \times \frac{454 \text{ g}}{1 \text{ lb}} = 908 \text{ g}$$

Converting Grains

A **grain** is the smallest unit of weight in the apothecary system that is used with any frequency in the pharmacy. Even so, this unit of measure is used on only a handful of labels for medications such as nitroglycerin, and the converted dose in milligrams appears on the same label. Nevertheless, you should be aware that the value of a grain can differ. In Table 10.3, the grain is equal to 65 mg, but many other references use 60 mg instead. Most pharmacists use the 65 mg conversion.

Example 10.2.9

How many grams are in 32 gr?

Begin solving this problem by noting the equivalency stated in Table 10.3, and converting the value to grams.

$$1 \text{ gr} = 65 \text{ mg} = 0.065 \text{ g}$$

Solution 1: Using the ratio-proportion method,

$$\frac{x \text{ g}}{32 \text{ gr}} = \frac{0.065 \text{ g}}{1 \text{ gr}}$$

$$x \text{ g} = 2.08 \text{ g}$$

Solution 2: Using the dimensional analysis method,

$$32 \text{ gr} \times \frac{0.065 \text{ g}}{1 \text{ gr}} = 2.08 \text{ g}$$

Example 10.2.10

How many grains are in a 325 mg aspirin tablet?

Solution 1: Using the ratio-proportion method,

$$\frac{x \text{ gr}}{325 \text{ mg}} = \frac{1 \text{ gr}}{65 \text{ mg}}$$

$$x \text{ gr} = 5 \text{ gr}$$

Solution 2: Using the dimensional analysis method,

$$325 \text{ mg} \times \frac{1 \text{ gr}}{65 \text{ mg}} = 5 \text{ gr}$$

A prescription for a 5 gr aspirin tablet may be written as "gr V aspirin."

Problem Set 10.2

✓ *Self-check your problem set work at* www.emcp.com.

Convert the following values to the units indicated.

1. 3 qt = _____ mL

2. 300 mL = _____ f℥

3. 75 mL = _____ f℥

4. 120 mL = _____ f℥

5. 15 mL = _____ f℥

6. 6 pt = _____ mL = _____ f℥

7. 60 mL = _____ f℥ = _____ f℥

8. 180 mL = _____ f℥ = _____ f℥

9. 3 pt = _____ f℥ = _____ mL

10. 8 f℥ = _____ mL = _____ f℥

Convert the following values to milliliters.

11. ½ f℥

12. 1 f℥

13. 2 f℥

14. 3 f℥

15. 4 f℥

16. 5 f℥

17. 6 f℥

18. 7 f℥

19. 8 f℥

20. 9 f℥

21. 10 f℥

22. 11 f℥

23. 12 f℥

24. 13 f℥

25. 14 f℥

26. 15 f℥

27. 16 f℥

28. 1 pt

29. 2 pt

30. 3 pt

Convert the following values to apothecary fluidounces.

31. 240 mL

32. 180 mL

33. 45 mL

34. 90 mL

35. 10 mL

36. 30 mL

37. 360 mL

38. 50 mL

39. 1000 mL

40. 500 mL

41. 960 mL

42. 480 mL

43. 15 mL

44. 60 mL

45. 5 mL

46. 150 mL

47. 120 mL

48. 210 mL

49. 100 mL

50. 200 mL

Calculate the following doses. Round to the hundredth place.

51. A drug is available as 5 gr/f℈, and the order is for 20 mL. How many milligrams will that be?

52. A drug is available as 0.45 g/f℥. The order is for 15 mg. How many milliliters will that be?

53. A medicine is available as 40 mcg/mL, and the order is for 0.4 g. How many fluidrams will that be?

54. You receive an order for ½ gr of medication, and you have on hand tablets of 10 mg, 5 mg, and 2.5 mg strengths. What is the smallest number of tablets you can dispense? What strengths will they be?

55. A drug is available as 1.2 g/f℥. If you prepare a dose of 300 mg, how many fluidrams will you need?

56. You are to prepare a dose of ¹/₅₀ gr. You have available tablets of 650 mcg, 300 mcg, and 150 mcg. What is the least number of tablets you can use (and which tablets) to make up the dose?

57. A medication is packaged as 20 gr/f℥. How many milligrams are in a teaspoonful of this medication?

58. The order requests 600 mg, and the medication is available as 8 gr/f℥. How many milliliters will be needed?

59. You receive an order for 45 gr of medication; you have a concentration of 1 g/tbsp available. How many milliliters will you measure out?

60. A preparation is available as 500 mg/tsp. The pharmacist asks you to measure out 46.296 gr. How many milliliters will you measure out?

61. You have in your pharmacy a dry powder that you are to package in 1 oz packets (avoirdupois). How many grams will you need to make 25 doses of 1 ℥ each?

62. You are to make a gallon of cough preparation that will have 1 gr of active ingredient per teaspoonful. How many grams of active ingredient will you need?

63. You have just finished making a pint of a preparation that has ¹/₁₀ gr/mL. How many milligrams of active ingredient did you use?

64. You have just finished a bulk manufacturing task in which you put 617.28 gr of active ingredient in 4 L of solution. If the usual dose is 1 tbsp, how many milligrams of medication are in each dose?

65. Instructions with a medication call for taking 1 cup (8 f℥) of medication each day. If there is ¹/₅ gr/mL in the medication, how many grams of active ingredient will the patient get daily?

66. A medication order is for 10 gr total. How many 325 mg tablets will you dispense?

67. An order for 3 gr of medication is sent in. You have 5 mg tablets. How many tablets should be dispensed?

68. You prepare a bulk medication of 3 ℔, but you are to dispense in grams. How many grams do you have?

69. You are to prepare 500 mg of a medication that comes in a concentration of 4 gr/f3. How many milliliters will you need?

70. The order received is for 50 gr of medication. The stock solution is 0.75 g/tbsp. How many milliliters should you measure out?

71. A medication is available in a concentration of 44 mg/f3. You are to prepare 132 mg. How many fluidrams is that?

72. You are to make ½ gallon of a medication that will have 2 g of active ingredient per teaspoonful. How many milligrams of active ingredient will you need?

73. You have 2 L of solution with 60 gr of active ingredient. If a dose is 1 tbsp, how many milligrams are in a dose?

74. You are to make suppositories that have 2 gr of the active ingredient in each. If you have 4.16 g of the active ingredient, how many suppositories can be made?

Nitro-stat tablets are available in the following strengths. In milligrams, what are the strengths of the four doses? Round to the tenths place.

75. ¹/₄₀₀ gr

76. ¹/₂₀₀ gr

77. ¹/₁₅₀ gr

78. ¹/₁₀₀ gr

79. If the patient uses his maximum of three tablets in the prescription below, how many milligrams has he used?

Nitro-stat ¹/₁₅₀ gr
Disp: #100
Sig: I tab SL q5 min prn angina
(max 3 tab, then go to hospital,
   if symptoms not relieved)
Store in original container.

Practice Test

Convert the following.

1. 1.5 gallon = _____ pt

2. 1 qt = _____ pt

3. 12 f℥ = _____ f℈

4. 2½ pt = _____ mL

5. 360 mL = _____ f℥

6. 150 mL = _____ f℈

7. 500 mL = _____ f℥

8. 750 mL = _____ f℥

9. 3 pt = _____ mL

10. 150 mL = _____ f℥

11. 20 mL = _____ f℥

12. 2 pt = _____ f℥

13. 40 f℥ = _____ mL

14. 8 f℥ = _____ f℈

Answer the following questions.

15. How many fluidrams are in 3 qt, 1 pt?

16. A drug is available as ½ gr/f℥. If the patient is to receive ¼ gr, how many milliliters will that be?

17. A medication is available as 10 gr/15 mL, and the patient is to receive 30 g. How many fluidounces will you give?

18. A drug is packaged as 36 mg/mL, and you are to give 1.62 g. What volume will that be in fluidounces?

19. How many 0.325 g tablets will you dispense for an order requesting 20 gr?

20. A medication is packaged as 22 mg/f℥, and you are to dispense 132 mg. How many fluidrams will you need?

Additional Practice with Fractions and Percents

Appendix **A**

WORKING WITH FRACTIONS

1. Change each of the mixed numbers in a–j to improper fractions and the improper fractions in k–t to mixed numbers.

a. $3\frac{1}{4}$

b. $5\frac{1}{2}$

c. $6\frac{1}{8}$

d. $5\frac{3}{4}$

e. $6\frac{7}{8}$

f. $8\frac{11}{12}$

g. $9\frac{13}{16}$

h. $12\frac{1}{4}$

i. $13\frac{2}{3}$

j. $14\frac{5}{6}$

k. $\frac{55}{7}$

l. $\frac{75}{8}$

m. $\frac{95}{3}$

n. $\frac{89}{12}$

o. $\frac{125}{9}$

p. $\frac{139}{3}$

q. $\frac{147}{5}$

r. $\frac{269}{6}$

s. $\frac{409}{8}$

t. $\frac{293}{5}$

2. Reduce the following fractions to their lowest terms.

a. $\dfrac{2}{6}$

b. $\dfrac{2}{10}$

c. $\dfrac{4}{10}$

d. $\dfrac{8}{12}$

e. $\dfrac{9}{15}$

f. $\dfrac{8}{18}$

g. $\dfrac{8}{26}$

h. $\dfrac{48}{64}$

i. $\dfrac{52}{76}$

j. $\dfrac{75}{180}$

k. $\dfrac{60}{380}$

l. $\dfrac{85}{120}$

m. $\dfrac{96}{128}$

n. $\dfrac{72}{108}$

o. $\dfrac{75}{195}$

p. $\dfrac{88}{220}$

q. $\dfrac{81}{135}$

r. $\dfrac{156}{252}$

s. $\dfrac{85}{135}$

t. $\dfrac{270}{285}$

3. Add the following fractions.

a. $\dfrac{1}{2} + \dfrac{2}{3} =$

b. $\dfrac{3}{4} + \dfrac{7}{8} =$

c. $\dfrac{1}{3} + \dfrac{2}{7} =$

d. $\dfrac{5}{6} + \dfrac{7}{8} + \dfrac{2}{3} =$

e. $\dfrac{5}{7} + \dfrac{1}{5} + \dfrac{3}{10} =$

f. $\dfrac{1}{4} + \dfrac{7}{12} + \dfrac{1}{2} + \dfrac{7}{8} =$

g. $\dfrac{5}{16} + \dfrac{1}{4} + \dfrac{9}{24} =$

h. $4\dfrac{1}{2} + 2\dfrac{2}{3} =$

i. $9\dfrac{3}{4} + 7\dfrac{7}{8} =$

j. $5\dfrac{7}{8} + 2\dfrac{1}{3} =$

k. $12\dfrac{1}{6} + 13\dfrac{1}{4} =$

l. $8\dfrac{1}{3} + 5\dfrac{5}{6} + 13\dfrac{5}{8} + 19\dfrac{9}{16} =$

4. Subtract the following fractions.

a. $\dfrac{1}{2} - \dfrac{1}{4} =$

b. $\dfrac{3}{4} - \dfrac{1}{8} =$

c. $\dfrac{4}{9} - \dfrac{1}{3} =$

d. $\dfrac{5}{8} - \dfrac{1}{3} =$

e. $\dfrac{5}{12} - \dfrac{1}{8} =$

f. $\dfrac{2}{3} - \dfrac{1}{16} =$

g. $\dfrac{6}{7} - \dfrac{2}{3} =$

h. $\dfrac{11}{16} - \dfrac{5}{12} =$

i. $8\dfrac{3}{4} - 2\dfrac{1}{4} =$

j. $7\dfrac{1}{2} - 2\dfrac{1}{4} =$

k. $15\dfrac{2}{3} - 7\dfrac{1}{8} =$

l. $32\dfrac{3}{5} - 7\dfrac{3}{8} =$

m. $63\dfrac{5}{6} - 17\dfrac{7}{16} =$

n. $13\dfrac{1}{2} - 8\dfrac{3}{4} =$

o. $29\dfrac{1}{3} - 13\dfrac{3}{8} =$

p. $37\dfrac{2}{9} - 21\dfrac{1}{3} =$

q. $41\dfrac{2}{7} - 6\dfrac{9}{10} =$

5. Multiply the following fractions and reduce to lowest terms. Rewrite as a mixed number if necessary.

a. $\dfrac{2}{3} \times \dfrac{5}{12} =$

b. $\dfrac{5}{9} \times \dfrac{4}{8} =$

c. $\dfrac{3}{16} \times \dfrac{4}{5} =$

d. $\dfrac{7}{8} \times \dfrac{2}{3} =$

e. $\dfrac{7}{12} \times 18 =$

f. $\dfrac{5}{9} \times 21 =$

6. Multiply the following mixed numbers.

a. $3\dfrac{1}{2} \times 8\dfrac{1}{4} =$

b. $9\dfrac{3}{8} \times 11\dfrac{5}{6} =$

c. $15\frac{4}{7} \times 6\frac{5}{14} =$

d. $2\frac{1}{2} \times 3\frac{2}{3} \times 2\frac{5}{6} =$

e. $6\frac{1}{8} \times 5\frac{1}{4} \times 3\frac{3}{16} =$

f. $5\frac{2}{3} \times 3\frac{1}{4} \times 8\frac{7}{12} =$

e. $5\frac{1}{2} \div 2 =$

f. $16\frac{5}{9} \div 3 =$

g. $3\frac{1}{2} \div 1\frac{3}{4} =$

h. $15\frac{7}{8} \div 5\frac{9}{16} =$

i. $24\frac{2}{3} \div 5\frac{1}{12} =$

7. A man pays $3000.00 for a microcomputer with an annual maintenance fee that is ⅕ of the purchase price. How much is the annual maintenance fee for this microcomputer?

8. There were 10,240 persons attending a rock concert, and ⅖ of the audience was female. How many girls and women attended the concert?

9. A jigsaw puzzle contains 5240 pieces. Ralph estimates that the puzzle is ⅝ completed. How many pieces have been put in place?

10. Divide the following mixed numbers and fractions.

a. $3\frac{1}{2} \div \frac{3}{4} =$

b. $2\frac{1}{3} \div \frac{5}{6} =$

c. $5\frac{1}{4} \div \frac{3}{8} =$

d. $6\frac{7}{8} \div \frac{5}{16} =$

11. Find the following.

a. $\frac{9}{10}$ of 650

b. $\frac{4}{5}$ of 785

c. $\frac{3}{8}$ of 248

d. $\frac{5}{6}$ of 66

e. $\frac{3}{4}$ of 76

f. $\frac{5}{7}$ of 56

g. $\frac{2}{3}$ of 780

h. $\frac{1}{12}$ of 144

i. $\frac{1}{9}$ of 162

12. An automobile travels 240 miles in 5½ hours. How many miles/hour does the automobile travel?

13. An automobile travels 210⁶⁄₁₀ miles and uses 16²⁄₁₀ gallons of gasoline. What is the mileage in miles/gallon?

14. A student is able to transfer 84¾ credits and 271⅕ quality points into another school. The student's grade point average is the number of quality points divided by the number of credits received. What is the student's grade point average based on the transfer of credits into the new school?

15. An auditorium has 31,437 square feet of seating space. Each seat will take 3½ square feet. How many seats will fill the seating space?

WORKING WITH PERCENTS

1. Convert each of the following percents to a decimal and a reduced fraction. The first problem is completed as an example.

Percent	Decimal Equivalent	Fractional Equivalent
20%	0.2	$\frac{20}{100} = \frac{1}{5}$

a. 30%

b. 5%

c. 8%

d. 7%

e. 15%

2. Compute the amount for each of the following problems, rounding to two decimal places.

a. 52% of $520.00

b. 3% of $1640.00

c. 20% of $1840.00

d. $\frac{1}{2}$% of 3640.00

e. $4\frac{1}{2}$% of $764.00

f. 8% of $514.85

g. 7% of $316.38

h. $17\frac{3}{4}$% of $42.00

3. Last year a musical production was attended by 15,500 persons. This year's attendance was 92% of last year's attendance. How many attended this year?

4. The Monroe City Council voted to impose a 2% tax on personal incomes. If the average income in Monroe is $14,514.00, what is the average tax levied on each taxpayer?

5. Binford Peeples makes $820.00/week. If he receives a raise of 8%, find the amount of (a) his raise and (b) his new salary.

6. Bert Brown and Clara Johnson are partners in a business that has an annual profit of $64,500.00. Mr. Brown receives 47% of the net profit, and Ms. Johnson receives 53%. How much did (a) Mr. Brown and (b) Ms. Johnson receive?

7. Randy Schwartz purchased a condominium for $85,500.00. The depreciation allowance, for tax purposes, is 5% per year. How much is the annual depreciation allowance for the condominium?

8. Roxanne Adams owned a bond worth $2000.00 that paid interest at 8½%/year. How much interest did she earn the first year?

9. The salaries and merit raise indexes for six employees are shown below. Multiply each salary amount by its raise index rate to get the new salary amount.

   a. Salary $1500.00
      Raise Index   108%
      New Salary $ _____

   b. Salary $1450.00
      Raise Index   109%
      New Salary $ _____

   c. Salary $1670.00
      Raise Index   110½%
      New Salary $ _____

   d. Salary $1548.00
      Raise Index   112½%
      New Salary $ _____

   e. Salary $1476.00
      Raise Index   104¾%
      New Salary $ _____

   f. Salary $1950.00
      Raise Index   111%
      New Salary $ _____

10. Dr. Ernest Bishop has a gross earned income of $120,000.00. Of this amount, 42% represents income from patients who paid cash for their medical services, and 58% represents income from patients who charged their medical services. How much of his gross earned income is from (a) cash patients and (b) charge patients?

11. The building owned by Brodnex Jewelry Store has an assessed value of $220,000.00 for property tax purposes. Tax rates are as follows: city, 3.6%; county, 5.3%; and special business, 2.5%. How much tax is owed on the building for (a) city, (b) county, and (c) special business taxes?

12. Bill White owns a house valued at $120,000.00 and furniture worth $25,000.00. The house is insured at 80% of its value, and the furniture at 65% of its value. For how much are (a) the house and (b) the furniture insured? Assuming that the above amounts represent realistic values, (c) how much would Mr. White lose if the house and furniture were completely destroyed by fire?

13. Canty Importers' sales during the first year of operation came to $250,000.00. Second-year sales have been projected to be 125% of first-year sales, while third-year sales have been projected to be 130% of second-year sales. What are the projected sales for (a) the second year and (b) the third year?

14. The Wilson Florist Shop's delivery truck used 2600 liters of gasoline last year. By purchasing a more fuel-efficient truck, the company would realize an estimated 7% savings in gasoline. Assuming this is true, (a) how much gasoline would be saved next year and (b) how much gasoline would be used next year?

15. Connie Gaines gets a monthly salary of $2,400.00. Deductions are made as follows: payroll taxes, 28%; credit union, 8%; and savings account, 12½%. How much is deducted from her check for (a) payroll taxes, (b) credit union, and (c) savings account?

Additional Practice with Compounding

Appendix B

B.1 PEDIATRIC SAFETY

Many patients, especially pediatric patients, require a dose that must be customized according to the weight of the patient. Manufacturers often provide a recommended dose range for use in children based on the child's weight, and the pharmacy technician will usually check prescription orders against the manufacturer's recommended range. Doing this helps the pharmacy and nursing staff to verify that the dose being prescribed and administered is correct and safe. Many facilities have rounding protocols for calculations involving pediatric patients that specify how to round a patient's weight, amounts in milligrams or micrograms, and the volume of fluid to be administered to a pediatric patient. For purposes of Problem Set B.1, patients' weights under 10 lb, expressed either in kilograms or in pounds, should be rounded to the hundredth place; patients' weights of 10 lb or more should be rounded to the tenth place. Medication doses should be rounded to the hundredth place. Devices that measure to a greater degree of accuracy are available for administration of medication to pediatric patients.

Problem Set B.1

1. You receive the following order for a pediatric patient weighing 60 lb. The drug can be given at a range of 15–20 mg/kg/day in 8–12 hour intervals. Is it safe for this child to receive this dose?

   Amikacin 120 mg

   IV Q8H in NS 50 mL

2. You receive the following order for a pediatric patient weighing 47 lb. The drug can be given at a range of 7.5–12 mg/kg/day in 8-hour intervals. Is it safe for this child to receive this dose?

   Tobramycin 60 mg

   IV Q8H IV in 50 mL NS

3. You receive the following order for a 10-day-old patient weighing 3.1 lb. The following chart indicates the dose information for gentamicin. Is it safe for this child to receive this dose?

Gentamicin 15 mg

IV daily

Gentamicin Dose Information

Weight (in kg)	Dose	Interval	Days Old
<1.2	2.5 mg/kg/day	Q24H	No age limit
1.2–2	2.5 mg/kg/day	Q18H	<7
>2	2.5 mg/kg/day	Q12H	<7
>2	2.5 mg/kg/day	Q8H	>7

4. You receive the following order for a 9-day-old patient weighing 2.5 lb. The following chart indicates the dose information for vancomycin. Is it safe for this child to receive this dose?

Vancomycin 8 mg

IV q12h

Vancomycin Dose Information

Weight (in kg)	Dose	Interval	Days Old
<1.2	15 mg/kg/dose	Q24H	No age limit
1.2–2	15 mg/kg/dose	Q18H	<7
1.2–2	15 mg/kg/dose	Q12H	>7
>2	15 mg/kg/dose	Q12H	<7
>2	15 mg/kg/dose	Q8H	>7

B.2 TOTAL PARENTERAL NUTRITION

As a pharmacy technician working in the IV room, you will be asked to apply many of the math skills you have learned. One of the most challenging types of calculations involves Total Parenteral Nutrition (TPN). TPN is used for patients who cannot take in and absorb nutrients through the gastrointestinal tract. Patients who are critically ill for a long period of time may receive TPN. These patients need very precise nutritional replacement due to the fragile state of their metabolic homeostasis.

The main ingredients of TPN include carbohydrates (dextrose), protein components (amino acids), fats (lipids), and sterile water for injection (SWFI). Electrolytes such as potassium, medication, multivitamins (MVI), and trace elements are also included. It is important to remember that stock electrolyte solutions contain more than one electrolyte. For example, potassium always comes paired with another electrolyte (chloride, acetate, or phosphate), and the potassium cannot be separated from its pair (you cannot remove just the potassium from a vial containing 5 mL potassium chloride). Sodium also comes in a pair, as sodium acetate.

Most TPN orders are written for 1 L of solution. Some orders may state a specific volume of an ingredient, but others may state a flow rate and duration that must be used to calculate a volume. When only the duration and flow rate are given, the total volume must be determined prior to calculating the volume of any component.

Pharmacy staff often use a customized grid or table to assist in determining the amounts of individual components in the TPN solution. Figure B.1 shows such a grid, which will be the basis for Example B.1 and Problem Set B.2. The column on the left of the grid lists the individual components typically ordered in a TPN solution. The top row indicates the pharmaceutical products available in the pharmacy to provide the ordered nutrients.

The steps in Table B.1 are used in balancing the quantities of the individual components within the TPN grid. The first four steps in Table B.1 balance the electrolytes—potassium chloride (KCl), potassium acetate, sodium acetate, sodium phosphate (NaPO$_4$)—beginning with KCl. Potassium is the first electrolyte balanced because potassium must remain within a very narrow range in the blood or the heart may be affected. If a member of the pharmacy staff asks the prescriber to change an electrolyte because the electrolyte solutions do not balance, potassium is the one that will rarely change. Example B.1 illustrates the use of the grid in Figure B.1 and the steps in Table B.1.

Figure B.1

TPN Components Grid

TPN Ingredients	Pharmacy Stock								
	potassium chloride (KCl)	potassium acetate	sodium phosphate (NaPO$_4$)	sodium acetate	calcium gluconate	magnesium sulfate	Pepcid	insulin	Total
potassium (K)									
sodium (Na)									
chloride (Cl)									
phosphate (PO$_4$)									
acetate									
calcium (Ca)									
magnesium (Mg)									
multivitamins (MVI)									
trace									
insulin									
Pepcid									

Table B.1 Steps to Balance TPN Components

1. Record the potassium and chloride needed, and indicate the total of each in the far-right column.

2. Record the potassium and acetate needed, and indicate the total of each in the far-right column.

3. Record the sodium and acetate needed, and indicate the total of each in the far-right column.

4. Record the sodium and phosphate needed, and indicate the total of each in the far-right column.

5. Record the calcium, magnesium, and other minerals needed, and indicate the total of each in the far-right column.

6. Check all of the totals in the far-right column to confirm that the amounts match the order.

7. Calculate the volume of each component needed based on the pharmacy's available solutions.

8. Calculate the dextrose, amino acids, fat emulsion, and sterile water for injection as needed to provide the bulk of the volume for the TPN.

Example B.1   **The pharmacy receives the following TPN order.**

R_X

Total TPN volume: 2.5 L

dextrose	23%	PO_4	80 mEq/L
amino acids	11.5 g	acetate	40 mEq/L
K	80 mEq/L	MVI	10 mL/day
Na	100 mEq/L	trace	1 mL/day
Cl	60 mEq/L	Humulin R	73 units/day
Mg	18 mEq/L	Pepcid	60 mg/day
Ca	15 mEq/L		

You have the following stock solutions in the pharmacy.

amino acids	15%	potassium chloride	2 mEq/mL
calcium gluconate	0.48 mEq/mL	potassium phosphate	4.4 mEq/mL
dextrose	70%	sodium acetate	2 mEq/mL
Humulin R insulin	100 units/mL	sodium chloride	4 mEq/mL
lipids	20%	sodium phosphate	4 mEq/mL
magnesium sulfate	4 mEq/mL	sterile water for injection	
Pepcid	10 mg/mL	Zantac	25 mg/mL
potassium acetate	2 mEq/mL		

Balance the quantities of the individual components to determine the ingredients of the final TPN solution.

Step 1. According to the order, we need 80 mEq K. The order also includes 60 mEq Cl, so we can add only 60 mEq KCl. Therefore, we enter 60 mEq in both the potassium box and the chloride box to correspond with 60 mEq KCl. Note that we still need an additional 20 mEq K as the order requires a total of 80 mEq K.

TPN Ingredients	Pharmacy Stock								
	KCl	potassium acetate	NaPO$_4$	sodium acetate	calcium gluconate	magnesium sulfate	Pepcid	insulin	Total
K	60 mEq								60 mEq
Na									
Cl	60 mEq								60 mEq
PO$_4$									
acetate									
Ca									
Mg									
MVI									
trace									
insulin									
Pepcid									

Step 2. The order also requests 40 mEq acetate. Since potassium comes as acetate, we should add 20 mEq in both boxes.

TPN Ingredients	Pharmacy Stock								
	KCl	potassium acetate	NaPO$_4$	sodium acetate	calcium gluconate	magnesium sulfate	Pepcid	insulin	Total
K	60 mEq	20 mEq							80 mEq
Na									
Cl	60 mEq								60 mEq
PO$_4$									
acetate		20 mEq							20 mEq
Ca									
Mg									
MVI									
trace									
insulin									
Pepcid									

Step 3. We cannot use the sodium chloride to fill the order for 100 mEq Na because the ordered amount of chloride has already been included in the TPN solution. However, the pharmacy stock includes sodium acetate, so add 20 mEq to the sodium acetate box.

TPN Ingredients	Pharmacy Stock								
	KCl	potassium acetate	NaPO$_4$	sodium acetate	calcium gluconate	magnesium sulfate	Pepcid	insulin	Total
K	60 mEq	20 mEq							80 mEq
Na				20 mEq					20 mEq
Cl	60 mEq								60 mEq
PO$_4$									
acetate		20 mEq		20 mEq					40 mEq
Ca									
Mg									
MVI									
trace									
insulin									
Pepcid									

Step 4. The order includes a total of 100 mEq Na. In the previous step, we used 20 mEq, so we have 80 mEq left to fill. The order also requests 80 mEq PO_4, so we can add 80 mEq $NaPO_4$ to the chart.

TPN Ingredients	Pharmacy Stock								
	KCl	potassium acetate	$NaPO_4$	sodium acetate	calcium gluconate	magnesium sulfate	Pepcid	insulin	Total
K	60 mEq	20 mEq							80 mEq
Na			80 mEq	20 mEq					100 mEq
Cl	60 mEq								60 mEq
PO_4			80 mEq						80 mEq
acetate		20 mEq		20 mEq					40 mEq
Ca									
Mg									
MVI									
trace									
insulin									
Pepcid									

Step 5. Now add calcium, magnesium, MVI, trace, insulin, and Pepcid to the chart, based on the original order.

TPN Ingredients	Pharmacy Stock								
	KCl	potassium acetate	$NaPO_4$	sodium acetate	calcium gluconate	magnesium sulfate	Pepcid	insulin	Total
K	60 mEq	20 mEq							80 mEq
Na			80 mEq	20 mEq					100 mEq
Cl	60 mEq								60 mEq
PO_4			80 mEq						80 mEq
acetate		20 mEq		20 mEq					40 mEq
Ca					15 mEq				15 mEq
Mg						18 mEq			18 mEq
MVI							10 mL		10 mL
trace							1 mL		1 mL
insulin								73 units	73 units
Pepcid							60 mg		60 mg

Step 6. Check the totals against the original order to confirm that the amounts match.

TPN Ingredients	Total
K	80 mEq
Na	100 mEq
Cl	60 mEq
PO_4	80 mEq
acetate	40 mEq
Ca	15 mEq
Mg	18 mEq
MVI	10 mL
trace	1 mL
insulin	73 units
Pepcid	60 mg

Step 7. Determine how many milliliters of each electrolyte solution are needed to fill the order. According to the order, we need to make a total of 2.5 L of the TPN solution. For each element that is ordered per liter, determine the amount needed for 1 L, and then determine the final volume based on the total order volume of 2.5 L.

KCl: x mL/60 mEq = 1 mL/2 mEq, x mL= 30 mL;
x mL/2.5 L = 30 mL/1 L, x mL= 75 mL
potassium acetate: x mL/20 mEq = 1 mL/2 mEq, x mL = 10 mL;
x mL/2.5 L = 10 mL/1 L, x mL = 25 mL
$NaPO_4$: x mL/80 mEq = 1 mL/4 mEq, x mL = 20 mL;
x mL/2.5 L = 20 mL/1 L, x mL = 50 mL
sodium acetate: x mL/20 mEq = 1 mL/2 mEq, x mL = 10 mL;
x mL/2.5 L = 10 mL/1 L, x mL = 25 mL
calcium gluconate: x mL/15 mEq = 1 mL/0.48 mEq, x mL = 31.25 mL;
x mL/2.5 L = 31.25 mL/1 L, x mL = 78.13 mL
$MgSO_4$: x mL/18 mEq = 1 mL/4 mEq, x mL = 4.5 mL;
x mL/2.5 L = 4.5 mL/1 L, x mL = 11.25 mL

The Pepcid and Humulin R insulin orders are per day, not per liter.

Pepcid: x mL/60 mg = 1 mL/10 mg, x mL = 6 mL
Humulin: x mL/73 units = 1 mL/100 units, x mL = 0.73 mL

The MVI and trace orders were also per day, but the order indicates a specific volume.

MVI: 10 mL
trace: 1 mL

Step 8. Calculate the amounts of dextrose, amino acids, and sterile water for injection that are required. Use an alligation to calculate the amount of dextrose needed for 1 L, and then adjust the amount for the 2.5 L total volume.

70		23 mL parts
	23	
0		47 mL parts
		70 mL total

x mL/1000 mL = 23 mL parts/70 mL total parts; x mL = 328.571 mL, rounded to 328.6 mL
x mL/2.5 L = 328.6 mL/1 L, x mL= 821.5 mL

Calculate the amount of amino acids needed:

x mL/11.5 g = 100 mL/15 g, x mL = 76.6666 mL, rounded to 76.7 mL
x mL/2.5 L = 76.7 mL/1 L, x mL= 191.75 mL, rounded to 191.8 mL

Calculate the amount of sterile water for injection by subtracting the volume of dextrose and amino acids from the total volume.

2500 mL total volume − (821.5 mL dextrose + 191.8 mL amino acids) = 1486.7 mL

Round to the tenth place in solving the following problems.

5. You have received the following TPN order.

R_X

TPN 1.5 L		SO_4	10 mEq
dextrose	35%	Ca	30 mEq
amino acids	7.5%	Mg	10 mEq
K	50 mEq	gluconate	30 mEq
Na	100 mEq	Humulin R	60 units/day
Cl	110 mEq	MVI	10 mL/day
PO_4	40 mEq	trace	1 mL/day

The pharmacy stock consists of the following.

amino acids	15%	potassium chloride	2 mEq/mL
calcium gluconate	0.48 mEq/mL	potassium phosphate	4.4 mEq/mL
dextrose	70%	sodium acetate	2 mEq/mL
Humulin R insulin	100 units/mL	sodium chloride	4 mEq/mL
lipids	20%	sodium phosphate	4 mEq/mL
magnesium sulfate	4 mEq/mL	sterile water for injection	
Pepcid	10 mg/mL	Zantac	25 mg/mL
potassium acetate	2 mEq/mL		

Balance the TPN components.

TPN Ingredients	Pharmacy Stock								
	KCl	NaCl	$NaPO_4$	calcium gluconate	magnesium sulfate	regular insulin	MVI	trace	Total
K									
Na									
Cl									
PO_4									
SO_4									
Ca									
Mg									
gluconate									
regular insulin									
MVI									
trace									

6. You need to run the following TPN order at 42 mL/hr, and you need to make a bag that will contain enough fluid to last for 24 hours.

R_X

dextrose	20%	Ca	12 mEq/L
amino acids	10 g	PO$_4$	30 mEq/L
lipids	5 g	acetate	40 mEq/L
K	40 mEq/L	MVI	10 mL/day
Na	90 mEq/L	trace	1 mL/day
Cl	60 mEq/L	Zantac	100 mg/day
Mg	15 mEq/L		

The pharmacy's stock includes the following.

amino acids	15%	potassium chloride	2 mEq/mL
calcium gluconate	0.48 mEq/mL	potassium phosphate	4.4 mEq/mL
dextrose	70%	sodium acetate	2 mEq/mL
Humulin R insulin	100 units/mL	sodium chloride	4 mEq/mL
lipids	20%	sodium phosphate	4 mEq/mL
magnesium sulfate	4 mEq/mL	sterile water for injection	
Pepcid	10 mg/mL	Zantac	25 mg/mL
potassium acetate	2 mEq/mL		

Balance the TPN components.

TPN Ingredients	KCl	NaCl	NaPO$_4$	sodium acetate	magnesium sulfate	calcium gluconate	MVI	trace	Zantac	Total
K										
Na										
Cl										
Mg										
Ca										
PO$_4$										
acetate										
MVI										
trace										
Zantac										

7. You have a TPN order that needs to be infused at 84 mL/hr. You need to make a bag that will last 24 hours.

$\mathsf{R}_{\!X}$

dextrose	18%	Ca	12 mEq/L
amino acids	9 g	PO_4	40 mEq/L
lipids	10 g	acetate	40 mEq/L
K	60 mEq/L	MVI	10 mL/day
Na	120 mEq/L	trace	1 mL/day
Cl	100 mEq/L	Humulin R	65 units/day
Mg	10 mEq/L	Zantac	150 mg/day

The pharmacy has the following stock ingredients.

amino acids	15%	potassium chloride	2 mEq/mL
calcium gluconate	0.48 mEq/mL	potassium phosphate	4.4 mEq/mL
dextrose	70%	sodium acetate	2 mEq/mL
Humulin R insulin	100 units/mL	sodium chloride	4 mEq/mL
lipids	20%	sodium phosphate	4 mEq/mL
magnesium sulfate	4 mEq/mL	sterile water for injection	
Pepcid	10 mg/mL	Zantac	25 mg/mL
potassium acetate	2 mEq/mL		

Balance the TPN components.

TPN Ingredients	Pharmacy Stock										
	KCl	NaCl	NaPO$_4$	sodium acetate	calcium gluconate	magnesium sulfate	MVI	trace	regular insulin	Zantac	Total
K											
Na											
Cl											
Mg											
Ca											
PO$_4$											
acetate											
MVI											
trace											
insulin											
Zantac											

8. You receive the following TPN order that is to be infused at a rate of 125 mL/hr. You need to make a bag that will last 24 hours.

dextrose	25%	Ca	10 mEq/L
amino acids	12.5 g	PO$_4$	60 mEq/L
lipids	15 g	acetate	30 mEq/L
K	110 mEq/L	MVI	10 mL/day
Na	60 mEq/L	trace	1 mL/day
Cl	80 mEq/L	Pepcid	40 mg/day
Mg	12 mEq/L		

The pharmacy has the following stock ingredients.

amino acids	15%	potassium chloride	2 mEq/mL
calcium gluconate	0.48 mEq/mL	potassium phosphate	4.4 mEq/mL
dextrose	70%	sodium acetate	2 mEq/mL
Humulin R insulin	100 units/mL	sodium chloride	4 mEq/mL
lipids	20%	sodium phosphate	4 mEq/mL
magnesium sulfate	4 mEq/mL	sterile water for injection	
Pepcid	10 mg/mL	Zantac	25 mg/mL
potassium acetate	2 mEq/mL		

Balance the TPN components.

TPN Ingredients	Pharmacy Stock								
	KCl	potassium acetate	NaPO$_4$	magnesium sulfate	calcium gluconate	MVI	trace	Pepcid	Total
K									
Na									
Cl									
Mg									
Ca									
PO$_4$									
acetate									
MVI									
trace									
Pepcid									

9. You receive the following TPN order that is to be infused at a rate of 100 mL/hr. You need a bag that will last 24 hours.

dextrose	22%	Ca	8 mEq/L
amino acids	13 g	PO$_4$	60 mEq/L
lipids	10 g	acetate	40 mEq/L
K	120 mEq/L	MVI	10 mL/day
Na	40 mEq/L	trace	1 mL/day
Cl	60 mEq/L	Humulin R	85 units/day
Mg	10 mEq/L	Pepcid	60 mg/day

The pharmacy has the following stock ingredients.

amino acids	15%	potassium chloride	2 mEq/mL
calcium gluconate	0.48 mEq/mL	potassium phosphate	4.4 mEq/mL
dextrose	70%	sodium acetate	2 mEq/mL
Humulin R insulin	100 units/mL	sodium chloride	4 mEq/mL
lipids	20%	sodium phosphate	4 mEq/mL
magnesium sulfate	4 mEq/mL	sterile water for injection	
Pepcid	10 mg/mL	Zantac	25 mg/mL
potassium acetate	2 mEq/mL		

Balance the TPN components.

| TPN Ingredients | Pharmacy Stock | | | | | | | | | |
	KCl	sodium acetate	KPO$_4$	calcium gluconate	magnesium sulfate	MVI	trace	regular insulin	Pepcid	Total
K										
Na										
Cl										
Mg										
Ca										
PO$_4$										
acetate										
MVI										
trace										
regular insulin										
Pepcid										

B.3 CRITICAL CARE IV MEDICATIONS

Pharmacy technicians may prepare critical care IV medications for cardiac care patients. In addition to accurately mixing medications, IV technicians will need to be able to calculate IV rates in order to determine how long a bag of medication will last. The following problems are examples of these types of calculations. Round to the tenth place.

Problem Set B.3 _____

10. You receive the following order and are directed to mix a 24-hour supply for the CCU. The doctor wants it mixed in 500 mL of dextrose. You have amiodarone 50 mg/mL vials in stock.

Amiodarone 150 mg

IV stat, then 1 mg/min for 6 hours, then 0.5 mg/min for 24 hours (maximum 2.2 g/day)

  a. How many milliliters of amiodarone will you need to add to the bag?

  b. What will the IV rate be in milliliters per hour for the stat dose?

  c. What will the IV rate be in milliliters per hour for the first 6 hours?

  d. What will the IV rate be in milliliters per hour for the remaining 24 hours?

11. The following order for a nitroglycerin drip for a patient weighing 190 lb comes to your pharmacy. You have stock bottles of NTG 25 mg/250 mL in the pharmacy.

NTG 0.6 mcg/kg/min for 10 min

If no improvement, increase by 0.2 mcg/kg/min every 3 to 5 min up to a maximum of 200 mcg/min, until patient improves.

  a. What will the starting IV rate be in milliliters per hour for this patient?

  b. What will the IV rate be in milliliters per hour, if you have to increase the rate three times?

  c. What will the IV rate be in milliliters per hour if the final rate is 2 mcg/kg/min?

  d. Assuming the final rate is used, how long will the bottle last?

12. You receive an order for a dopamine drip for a 160 lb patient. It is to be infused at 3 mcg/kg/min. The rate can be increased by 2 mcg/kg/min every 30 minutes to achieve the desired response. You need to make a bag that contains 250 mg/100 mL. Dopamine comes as 50 mg/mL vials.

    a. How many milliliters of dopamine will you have to add to the bag?

    b. What will the starting IV rate be in milliliters per hour?

    c. If the doctor tells you to increase the rate by 8 mcg/kg/min, what will the new IV rate be in milliliters per hour?

    d. Assuming that the increased rate is used, how many bags will you have to make for a 24-hour supply?

13. A recently ventilated patient who weighs 175 lb receives the following orders.

 vecuronium 0.8 mcg/kg/min
midazolam 0.2 mg/kg/hr

Your hospital has standard bags that you mix for these orders: vecuronium 100 mg in 100 mL NS and midazolam 100 mg in 250 mL of NS. Vecuronium comes as 20 mg/mL vials, and midazolam comes as 5 mg/mL vials.

    a. How many milliliters of vecuronum will you have to add to each bag?

    b. What will the rate be in milliliters per hour for the vecuronium?

    c. How long will the bag of vecuronium last?

    d. How many bags will you have to make a day?

    e. How many milliliters of midazolam will you have to add to each bag?

    f. What will the rate be in milliliters per hour for the midazolam?

    g. How long will the bag of midazolam last?

    h. How many bags will you have to make a day?

B.4 IV EPIDURALS

Another type of IV you may have to prepare is an epidural. These orders are usually written as percents. When making them, it is important to remember the 10% rule: if the total volume you need to add to an IV bag is greater than 10% of the volume of the bag it is being added to, remove the volume of fluid you are adding. For example, if you have to add 250 mL to a 1000 mL bag, you will need to remove 250 mL of fluid from the bag before adding the 250 mL of fluid because 250 mL is greater than 10% of 1000 mL (100 mL). If needed, apply the 10% rule to the problems that follow.

Problem Set B.4

14. You receive the following epidural order.

> R_x
> | morphine | 0.008% |
> | bupivacaine | 0.12% |
> | NS | 250 mL bag |

You have the following stock solutions.

bupivacaine	1%
morphine	10 mg/10 mL vial
NS	250 mL bag

a. What volume of each ingredient will be added to the NS bag?

b. Does the 10% rule apply? If so, how much saline will be removed?

15. You receive the following epidural order.

> R_x
> | bupivacaine | 0.06% |
> | morphine | 0.016% |
> | NS | 250 mL bag |

You have the following stock solutions.

bupivacaine	0.75% solution
morphine sulfate	50 mg/25 mL solution
NS	250 mL bag

a. What volume of each ingredient will be added to the NS bag?

b. Does the 10% rule apply? If so, how much saline will be removed?

B.5 PEDIATRIC PARENTERALS

Other IV calculation problems you may encounter in the pharmacy involve pediatric and newborn dosing. As described in the first section on pediatric safety, you may have to determine if a dose is within a safe range for your patient. Like the pediatric medications discussed earlier, many pediatric and neonatal IV doses are given in chart form. It is important to be able to use a chart to determine if a dose is appropriate for a particular patient.

When determining doses for newborn patients, most hospitals recommend not rounding until the last step in the calculation. This is because many of the medications for these patients have a narrow therapeutic range. If the calculation involves three or four steps, rounding at each step could result in an overdose. Follow this general rule throughout Problem Set B.5 and also follow the instructions on rounding for pediatric patients used in Problem Set B.1.

Problem Set B.5 _____

16. You receive the following order for a 3-day-old patient weighing 2 lb. Using the reference tables provided, is this dose safe?

Loading dose of morphine 0.15 mg IM q2h prn pain, then morphine 0.025 mg/hr IV prn pain for 3 days

17. You receive the following order for a pediatric patient weighing 14 lb. Using the reference tables provided, is this dose safe?

Bolus IV dose of fentanyl 0.01 mg, then IV of 0.3 mg/hr in a 60 mL syringe with a concentration of 1 mg/10 mL

Morphine

Loading Dose			
Route	Dose	Interval	Maximum Dose
IV, IM, subcutaneous	<1 month: 50 mcg–100 mcg/kg/dose ≥1 month: 100 mcg–200 mcg/kg/dose	Q2–4H	15 mg/dose

Maintenance Dose			
Route	Dose	Interval	Maximum Dose
IV infusion	10–40 mcg/kg/hr	continuous infusion	none

Fentanyl

Bolus Loading Dose			
Route	Dose	Interval	Maximum Dose
IV	0.5–2 mcg/kg/single dose	once	none

Maintenance Dose			
Route	Dose	Interval	Maximum Dose
IV infusion	1–4 mcg/kg/hr	continuous infusion	none

B.6 TOPICAL COMPOUNDS

Extemporaneous compounding is a function of the pharmacy because not all drugs are available in every dose form. Therefore, the pharmacy must sometimes create the necessary form based on a prescriber's instructions. Prescribers may indicate exactly how much of each drug is to be mixed to create the required compound in a recipe format, as well as how much should be dispensed to the patient.

Problem Set B.6

18. The following order is received in the pharmacy. Your pharmacy has pure chemicals available. How much of each ingredient will you need to make the compound?

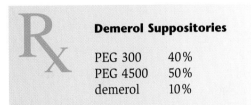

Muscle Rub

methyl salicylate (aq)	5%
menthol	15%
camphor	2%
white petrolatum	10%
vanishing cream QSAD	30 g

19. The following order is received in the pharmacy.

Antioxident Cream

vitamin C	20%
vitamin E	5%
vitamin A	2.5%
glycerin	10%
unibase QSAD	1 oz

You have the following ingredients in stock:

pure vitamin C powder
vitamin E oil, 50%
vitamin A oil, 25%
pure glycerin
unibase

How much of each ingredient will you need to make the cream?

20. You receive the following order in the pharmacy:

Demerol Suppositories

PEG 300	40%
PEG 4500	50%
demerol	10%

Dispense and make 12 suppositories.

Your mold is calibrated so that each suppository weighs 4 g, and demerol is available as 25 mg/mL in 10 mL vials.

a. How much of each ingredient will you need to make the requested number of suppositories?

b. How many milligrams of demerol will be in each suppository?

21. You receive the following order in the pharmacy. You have pure chemicals in stock. How much of each ingredient will you need to make the lip balm?

Medicated Lip Balm

camphor	1%
menthol	1%
glycerin	3%
white wax	8%
white petrolatum QSAD	2 oz

Measures and Conversions

Appendix **C**

Metric	*Volume*	
	1 L = 1000 mL	
	1 mL = 1 cc	
	Weight	
	1 g = 1000 mg	
	1 mg = 1000 mcg	
Household	*Volume*	
	1 gallon = 4 quarts	
	1 qt = 2 pt	
	1 pt = 2 cups = 16 fl oz	
	1 fl oz = 2 tbsp = 6 tsp	
	Weight	
	1 lb = 16 oz	
	Length	
	1 yard = 3 feet	
	1 foot = 12 inches	

Conversions

	Household	Apothecary	Metric
Volume	1 qt = 32 fl oz		0.96 L
	1 pint = 16 fl oz		480 mL *
	1 cup = 8 fl oz		240 mL
	2 tbsp = 1 fl oz	6 f ℨ = 1 f ℥	30 mL *
	1 tbsp	3 f ℨ	15 mL
	1 tsp	1 f ℨ	5 mL †
		1 ♏	0.0625 mL
Weight	2.2 lb		1 kg
	1 lb		454 g
	1 oz	8 ℨ	30 g
Length	1 inch		2.5 cm

* There are actually less than 30 mL in 1 fl oz, but 30 mL is usually used. When packaging a pint, companies will typically include 473 mL, rather than the full 480 mL, thus saving money over time.
† There are actually 3.75 mL in an apothecary f ℨ . However, convention dictates that 1 f ℨ = 5 mL = 1 tsp.

Glossary

A

accuracy the correctness of a number in its representation of a given value

aliquot a measured portion, fraction, or part of an ingredient that is placed into solution or into a mixture of other ingredients to aid in measuring a very small amount

alligation the concentration obtained when solutions of different strengths are combined

alligation alternate method the mathematical calculation used to determine the amounts of two or more dilutions of differing strengths that will be mixed to prepare a product of a desired strength and quantity

alligation medial method the mathematical calculation used to find the final concentration created when two or more known quantities of known concentrations are compounded

apothecary system literally the system used by an apothecary; a system of measurement used in pharmacy prior to the metric system; units of measure include minims, fluidrams, scruples, grains, ounces, and pounds

Arabic numbers a numbering system that uses numeric symbols to indicate a quantity, fractions, and decimals; uses the numerals 0, 1, 2, 3, 4, 5, 6, 7, 8, and 9

atomic weight the weight of a single atom of an element compared to the weight of a single atom of hydrogen

average wholesale price (AWP) the average price that wholesalers charge the pharmacy for a drug; used to determine reimbursement

avoirdupois system an alternative system of measurement used in pharmacy prior to the metric system

B

body surface area (BSA) a measurement related to a patient's weight and height, expressed in meters squared (m^2), and used to calculate patient-specific doses of medications

brand name the name under which the manufacturer markets a drug; a registered trademark of the manufacturer; also known as the trade name

C

capitation fee a form of reimbursement in which the insurer pays the pharmacy a monthly fee to cover all prescriptions needed by a patient during that month

Celsius a thermometric scale in which 100° is the boiling point for water and 0° is the freezing point for water

Clark's Rule a formula used to determine an appropriate pediatric dose by using the child's weight in pounds and the normal adult dose; (weight in lb/150 lb) $\times$ adult dose = pediatric dose

common denominator a number into which each of the unlike denominators of two or more fractions can be divided evenly

complex fraction a fraction in which both the numerator and the denominator are fractions

compounded stock solution a solution that is prepared in a large amount and kept in stock in the pharmacy to be divided for individual prescriptions

compounding the process of using raw ingredients and/or other prepared ingredients to prepare a drug product for a patient

concentrate a highly condensed drug product that is diluted prior to administration

conversion factor an equivalency equal to 1 that can be used when converting units of measure using the ratio-proportion method

D

days' supply a method of inventory management that tries to keep inventory value approximately equal to the cost to the pharmacy of the products sold in a certain number of days; calculated as the value of inventory divided by the average daily cost of products sold

DEA number a number issued by the Drug Enforcement Administration (DEA) to signify the authority of the holder to prescribe or handle controlled substances; made up of two letters followed by seven digits, the last of which is a checksum digit used to check the validity of the DEA number

decimal a fraction value in which the denominator is 10 or a multiple of 10

denominator the number on the bottom part of a fraction

depreciation an allowance made to account for the decreasing value of an asset

diluent an inactive substance that is added to a concentrate to make it less concentrated; can be a vehicle or a solvent

dilution the product obtained when an inactive ingredient, a diluent, is added to a concentrate

dimensional analysis method a conversion method in which the given number and unit are multiplied by the ratio of the desired unit to the given unit, which is equivalent to 1

discount a reduced price

dispensing fee an amount charged over and above the actual cost of the medication; includes profit, cost of materials, cost of labor, and overhead

dose on a prescription, the indication of how much medication the patient will take at each administration

dosing schedule on a prescription, the indication of how often the drug is to be taken

dosing table a table providing dose recommendations based on the age and/or the weight of the patient; often used for determining the safe dose for a pediatric patient

drop set the number of drops an IV set takes to make 1 mL; also called drip set

E

electrolytes substances such as mineral salts that carry an electrical charge when dissolved in a solution

F

Fahrenheit a thermometric scale in which 212° is the boiling point for water and 32° is the freezing point for water

flow rate the rate, expressed in milliliters per hour or drops per minute, that medication is flowing through an IV line; also called infusion rate and rate of infusion

formula a written document containing the ingredients and instructions needed to prepare a compound

fraction a portion of a whole that is represented as a ratio

G

generic name the name under which a drug is approved by the Food and Drug Administration; sometimes denotes a drug that is not protected by a trademark; also referred to as a USAN (United States Adopted Name)

grain the smallest unit of measure in the apothecary system that is used with any frequency in pharmacy

gram the metric system's basic unit for measuring weight

gross profit the difference between the selling price and the purchase price; also called *markup*

H

household measure a system of measure used in homes, particularly in kitchens, in the United States; units of measure for volume include teaspoonful, tablespoonful, cup, pint, quart, and gallon; units for weight are pound and ounce

I

improper fraction a fraction with a value greater than 1 (the numerator's value is larger than the denominator's value)

infusion the administration of a large volume of liquid medication given parenterally over a long period

injection a method of administering medications in which a syringe with a shaft or catheter is used to penetrate through the skin or membrane into the tissue below

intramuscular injection an injection given into the aqueous muscle tissue

intravenous infusion the injection of fluid into the veins

inventory a listing of all items that are available for sale in a business

inventory value the total value of the drugs and merchandise in stock in the pharmacy on a given day

IV piggyback (IVPB) a small volume of fluid and medication that is given intravenously in addition to a primary infusion over a short period of time

L

leading zero a zero that is placed to the left of the decimal point, in the ones place, in a number that is less than zero and is being represented by a decimal value

liter the metric system's basic unit for measuring volume

lowest known place value the last digit on the right of a written numeral

M

markup see *gross profit*

markup rate the markup divided by the cost and multiplied by 100%

meter the metric system's basic unit for measuring length

metric system a measurement system based on subdivisions and multiples of 10; made up of three basic units: meter, gram, and liter

milliequivalent (mEq) the ratio of the weight of a molecule to its valence, used to measure the concentration of electrolytes in a volume of solution; also an amount of medication that will provide the patient with a specific amount (equivalent amount) of an electrolyte

millimole (mM) a molecular weight expressed in milligrams

mini-drip set a drop set at a rate of 60 gtt/mL

mixed number a whole number and a fraction

molecular weight the sum of the atomic weights of all atoms in one molecule of a compound

N

net profit the difference between the selling price and the overall cost of an item

numerator the number on the upper part of a fraction

O

overall cost for a drug, the sum of the purchase price and the cost to dispense

overhead the pharmacy's overall cost of doing business; includes salaries, equipment, operating expenses, and rent

P

parenteral the administration of medication by injection and not by way of the gastrointestinal system

percent the number of parts per 100; can be written as a fraction, a decimal, or a ratio

percentage of error the percentage by which a measurement is inaccurate

pharmacy benefits management (PBM) a prescription processing service that manages insurance reimbursement for prescriptions to pharmacies

place value the location of a numeral in a string of numbers that describes the numeral's relationship to the decimal point

powder volume (pv) the space occupied by dry pharmaceuticals, calculated as the difference between the final volume and the volume of the diluting ingredient, or the diluent volume; the amount of space occupied by lypholized (freeze-dried) medication in a sterile vial, used for reconstitution

prescription an order for medication for a patient that is written by a physician or a qualified licensed practitioner to be filled by a pharmacist

product the result of multiplying one number by another

profit income minus overhead

profit margin the difference between the cost of doing business (the purchase price, overhead, and preparation) and the selling price or receipts for a product

proper fraction a fraction with a value of less than 1 (the numerator's value is smaller than the denominator's value)

proportion an expression of equality between two ratios

Q

quotient the result of dividing one number by another

R

ratio a numerical representation of the relationship between two parts of the whole or between one part and the whole

ratio-proportion method a conversion method based on comparing a complete ratio to a ratio with a missing component

ratio strength a means of describing the concentration of a liquid medication based on a ratio such as *a* grams:*b* milliliters

Roman numerals a numbering system that uses alphabetic symbols to indicate a quantity; uses the letters I, V, and X to represent 1, 5, and 10, respectively

route of administration on a prescription, the indication of how the medication is to be given

S

scientific notation a method used to write numbers that have a very large or very small numerical value; uses "× 10" with an exponent

signa (**sig**) from the Latin for "write"; the instructions for proper use of the medication included on each prescription, including the dose, route of administration, and dosing schedule

significant figures the figures in a numeral that are known values and have not been rounded or estimated in the process of mathematical calculation, plus the digit in the lowest place value, which is approximate

solute the substance dissolved in the liquid solvent in a solution

solution a mixture of two or more substances

solvent the liquid that dissolves the solute in a solution

subcutaneous injection an injection given into the vascular, fatty layer of tissue under the skin

sum the result of adding two or more numbers together

T

trailing zero a zero that appears at the end of a decimal string and is not needed except when considered significant

turnover rate the number of times the amount of goods in inventory is sold during a year; calculated by dividing total annual purchases of inventory by the average inventory value

U

unit the amount of activity associated with a medication that has biological impact on a patient

V

valence the ability of a molecule to bond, as indicated by its positive or negative charge, represented by a plus or minus sign superscript next to an element's chemical symbol

volume in volume (v/v) the number of milliliters of a drug (solute) in 100 mL of the final product (solution)

W

weight in volume (w/v) the number of grams of a drug (solute) in 100 mL of the final product (solution)

weight in weight (w/w) the number of grams of a drug (solute) in 100 g of the final product (solution)

Y

Young's Rule a formula used to determine an appropriate pediatric dose by using the child's age in years and the normal adult dose; [age in years/(age in years + 12 years)] × adult dose = pediatric dose

Index

Product
  defined, 21
  estimating, 21
Profit
  defined, 191
  gross, 192–193
  net, 192
  profit margin, 193
Profit margin, 193
Proper fraction, 2
Proportions, 38–41
  conversion factor, 41
  defined, 38
  extremes, 38
  means, 38
  for metric conversion, 71
  ratio-proportion method, 39–40
  steps for solving for x, 40
  for story problems, 75–76
Pseudoephedrine
  dosing table for, 107

Q

Quantity to dispense on prescription order, 59
Quotients
  defined, 21
  estimating, 21

R

Ratio-proportion method, 39–40
  calculating quantity of drug in injectable solution,
    127–128
  calculating ratio strength, 128–129
  calculating volume of injectable solution, 126–127
  converting between units of measure, 41
  from household to metric system, 99–102
  for metric conversion, 71
  milliequivalents, 131–132
  rules for using, 39
  to solve story problem, 75–76
  solving for x, 40
Ratios, 31–32
  changing percent to ratio, 36
  converting ratio to percent, 35
  defined, 31
  dividing, 32
  equivalent values for, 35
  multiplying, 32
  reading, 31
  uses of, 32
  writing, 31
Ratio strength
  calculating, 128
  for solutions, 143–146
Reimbursement for prescriptions, 197, 199
Roman numerals
  guideline for interpreting, 10
Rounding
  decimals, 15–17
Route of administration
  defined, 61
  prescription directions and, 61

S

Scientific notation, 11–12
Scruple, 213
Signa, 61
Significant figures, 25–27

accuracy and, 26–27
  defined, 25
  rules for counting, 25
Solute, 143
Solutions
  alligations, 173–177
  defined, 143
  percentage, 143–146
  ratio strength, 143–146
  solute, 143
  solvent, 143
  volume in volume, 144–146
  weight in volume, 144–145
  weight in weight, 143–145
Solvent, 143
Story problems
  ratio-proportion method, 75–76
Straight-line depreciation method, 205
Subcutaneous injection, 125
Subtraction
  decimals, 14
  fractions, 3–7
Sum
  defined, 19
  estimating, 19

T

Temperature chart, 118–119
Temperature measurement, 117–119
  Celsius, 117
  converting Celsius and Fahrenheit temperatures, 117–118
  Fahrenheit, 117
  temperature chart, 118–119
Trailing zero, 17
Turnover rate, 205

U

United States Pharmacopeia (USP), 133
Units
  calculating, 133
  defined, 133
  insulin and, 133

V

Valence, 131
Volume
  calculating volume of injectable solution, 126
  powder volume, 136
  volume in volume, 144–146
Volume in volume, 144–146

W

Weight
  customized doses based on, 83
  weight in volume, 144–145
  weight in weight, 143–145
Weight in volume, 144–145
Weight in weight, 143–145

Y

Young's Rule, 88

Z

Zero
  leading, 14
  trailing, 17